THE CYCLE

Phoenix sinks into decay
Haughty dragon yearns to slay.
Lyorn growls and lowers horn
Tiassa dreams and plots are born.
Hawk looks down from lofty flight
Dzur stalks and blends with night.
Issola strikes from courtly bow
Tsalmoth maintains though none knows how.
Vallista rends and then rebuilds
Jhereg feeds on others' kills.
Quiet iorich won't forget
Sly chreotha weaves his net.
Yendi coils and strikes, unseen
Orca circles, hard and lean.
Frightened teckla hides in grass
Jhegaala shifts as moments pass.
Athyra rules minds' interplay
Phoenix rises from ashes gray.

The Adventures of Vlad Taltos

JHEREG
YENDI
TECKLA
TALTOS
PHOENIX
ATHYRA
ORCA
DRAGON
ISSOLA
DZUR

Anthologies
THE BOOK OF JHEREG
THE BOOK OF TALTOS
THE BOOK OF ATHYRA

THE BOOK OF JHEREG

Contains the complete text of
Jhereg, Yendi, and Teckla

Steven Brust

ACE BOOKS, NEW YORK

THE BERKLEY PUBLISHING GROUP
Published by the Penguin Group
Penguin Group (USA) Inc.
375 Hudson Street, New York, New York 10014, USA
Penguin Group (Canada), 90 Eglinton Avenue East, Suite 700, Toronto, Ontario M4P 2Y3, Canada
(a division of Pearson Penguin Canada Inc.) • Penguin Books Ltd., 80 Strand, London WC2R 0RL,
England • Penguin Group Ireland, 25 St. Stephen's Green, Dublin 2, Ireland (a division of Penguin
Books Ltd.) • Penguin Group (Australia), 250 Camberwell Road, Camberwell, Victoria 3124, Australia
(a division of Pearson Australia Group Pty. Ltd.) • Penguin Books India Pvt. Ltd., 11 Community
Centre, Panchsheel Park, New Delhi—110 017, India • Penguin Group (NZ), 67 Apollo Drive,
Rosedale, Auckland 0632, New Zealand (a division of Pearson New Zealand Ltd.) • Penguin Books
(South Africa) (Pty.) Ltd., 24 Sturdee Avenue, Rosebank, Johannesburg 2196, South Africa

Penguin Books Ltd., Registered Offices: 80 Strand, London WC2R 0RL, England

This one's for Liz.
The author (that's me) would like to thank Steven Bond, Reen Brust, the late Lee Pelton,
John Robey, John Stanley, and, especially, Adrian Morgan, who started it all.

This is a work of fiction. Names, characters, places, and incidents either are the product of the author's
imagination or are used fictitiously, and any resemblance to actual persons, living or dead, business
establishments, events, or locales is entirely coincidental. The publisher does not have any control over
and does not assume any responsibility for author or third-party websites or their content.

THE BOOK OF JHEREG

PUBLISHING HISTORY
Ace trade paperback edition / August 1999

Ace trade paperback ISBN: 978-0-441-00615-1

PRINTED IN THE UNITED STATES OF AMERICA

33 32 31 30 29 28 27 26 25 24

Author's Note

One of the questions I'm most often asked is: "In what order would you recommend reading these books?" Unfortunately, I'm just exactly the wrong guy to ask. I made every effort to write them so they could be read in any order. I am aware that, in some measure at least, I have failed (I certainly wouldn't recommend starting with *Teckla*, for example), but the fact that I was trying makes me incapable of giving an answer.

Many people whose opinion I respect believe publication order is best; this volume reflects that belief. For those who want to read the books in chronological order, it would go like this: *Taltos, Yendi, Jhereg, Teckla, Phoenix, Athyra, Orca.*

The choice, I daresay, is yours. In any case, I hope you enjoy them.

Steven Brust
Minneapolis
March 1999

PRONUNCIATION GUIDE

Adrilankha	ah-dri-LAHN-kuh
Adron	Ā-drahn
Aliera	uh-LEER-uh
Athyra	uh-THĪ-ruh
Baritt	BĀR-it
Brust	brŭst
Cawti	KAW-tee
Chreotha	kree-O-thuh
Dragaera	druh-GAR-uh
Drien	DREE-en
Dzur	tser
Iorich	ī-Ō-rich
Issola	î-SŌ-luh
Jhegaala	zhuh-GAH-luh
Jhereg	zhuh-REG
Kiera	KĪ-ruh
Kieron	KĪ-rahn
Kragar	KRAY-gahr
Leareth	LEER-eth
Loiosh	LOI-ōsh
Lyorn	LI-orn
Mario	MAH-ree-ō
Mellar	MEH-lar
Morrolan	muh-RŌL-uhn
Norathar	NŌ-ruh-thahr
Rocza	RAW-tsuh
Serioli	sar-ee-Ō-lee
Taltos	TAHL-tōsh
Teckla	TEH-kluh
Tiassa	tee-AH-suh
Tsalmoth	TSAHL-mōth
Verra	VEE-ruh
Valista	vuhl-ISS-tuh
Yendi	YEN-dee
Zerika	zuh-REE-kuh

JHEREG

Let the winds of jungle's night
Stay the hunter in her flight.

Evening's breath to witch's mind;
Let our fates be intertwined.

Jhereg! Do not pass me by.
Show me where thine egg doth lie.

Prologue

THERE IS A SIMILARITY, if I may be permitted an excursion into tenuous metaphor, between the feel of a chilly breeze and the feel of a knife's blade, as either is laid across the back of the neck. I can call up memories of both, if I work at it. The chilly breeze is invariably going to be the more pleasant memory. For instance . . .

I was eleven years old, and clearing tables in my father's restaurant. It was a quiet evening, with only a couple of tables occupied. A group had just left, and I was walking over to the table they'd used.

The table in the corner was a deuce. One male, one female. Both Dragaeran, of course. For some reason, humans rarely came into our place; perhaps because we were human too, and they didn't want the stigma, or something. My father himself always avoided doing business with other "Easterners."

There were three at the table along the far wall. All of them were male, and Dragaeran. I noted that there was no tip at the table I was clearing, and heard a gasp from behind me.

I turned as one member of the threesome let his head fall into his plate of lyorn leg with red peppers. My father had let me make the sauce for it that time, and, crazily, my first thought was to wonder if I'd built it wrong.

The other two stood up smoothly, seemingly not the least bit worried about their friend. They began moving toward the door, and I realized that they were planning to leave without paying. I looked for my father, but he was in back.

I glanced once more at the table, wondering whether I should try to help the fellow who was choking, or intercept the two who were trying to walk out on their bill.

Then I saw the blood.

The hilt of a dagger was protruding from the throat of the fellow whose face was lying in his plate. It slowly dawned on me what had happened, and I decided that, no, I wasn't going to ask the two gentlemen who were leaving for money.

They didn't run, or even hurry. They walked quickly and quietly past me toward the door. I didn't move. I don't think I was even breathing. I remember suddenly becoming very much aware of my own heartbeat.

One set of footsteps stopped, directly behind me. I remained frozen, while in my mind, I cried out to Verra, the Demon Goddess.

At that moment, something cold and hard touched the back of my neck. I was too frozen to flinch. I would have closed my eyes if I could have. Instead, I stared straight ahead. I wasn't consciously aware of it at the time, but the Dragaeran girl was looking at me, and she started to rise then. I noticed her when her companion reached out a hand to stop her, which she brushed off.

Then I heard a soft, almost silky voice in my ear. "You didn't see a thing," it said. "Got that?" If I had had as much experience then as I do now, I would have known that I was in no real danger—if he'd had any intention of killing me he would have done so already. But I didn't, and so I shook. I felt I should nod, but couldn't manage. The Dragaeran girl was almost up to us now, and I imagine the guy behind me noticed her, because the blade was gone suddenly and I heard retreating footsteps.

I was shaking uncontrollably. The tall Dragaeran girl gently placed her hand on my shoulder. I saw sympathy on her face. It was a look I had never before been given from a Dragaeran, and it was, in its own way, as frightening as the experience I'd just been through. I had an urge to fall forward into her arms, but I didn't let myself. I became aware that she was speaking, softly, gently. "It's all right, they've left. Nothing is going to happen. Just take it easy, you'll be fine . . ."

My father came storming in from the other room.

"Vlad!" he called, "what's going on around here? Why—"

He stopped. He saw the body. I heard him getting sick and I felt ashamed for him. The hand on my shoulder tightened, then. I felt myself stop trembling, and looked at the girl in front of me.

Girl? I really couldn't judge her age at all, but, being Dragaeran, she could be anywhere from a hundred to a thousand years old. Her clothing was black and gray, which I knew meant she was of House Jhereg. Her companion, who was now approaching us, was also a Jhereg. The three who had been at the other table were of the same House. Nothing of any significance there; it was mostly Jhereg, or an occasional Teckla, who came into our restaurant.

Her companion stood behind her.

"Your name is Vlad?" she asked me.

I nodded.

"I'm Kiera," she said. I only nodded again. She smiled once more and turned to her companion. They paid their bill and left. I went back to help clean up after the murdered man—and my father.

"*Kiera*," I thought to myself, "*I won't forget you.*"

When the Phoenix guards arrived some time later, I was in back, and I heard my father telling them that, no, no one had seen what had happened, we'd all been in back. But I never forgot the feel of a knife blade, as it is laid across the back of the neck.

*   *   *

And for another instance . . .

I was sixteen, and walking alone through the jungles west of Adrilankha. The city was somewhat more than a hundred miles away, and it was night. I was enjoying the feeling of solitude, and even the slight fear within my middle as I considered the possibility that I might run into a wild dzur, or a lyorn, or even, Verra preserve me, a dragon.

The ground under my boots alternated between "crunch" and "squish." I didn't make any effort to move quietly; I hoped that the noise I made would frighten off any beast which would otherwise frighten *me* off. The logic of that escapes me now.

I looked up, but there was no break in the overcast that blankets the Dragaeran Empire. My grandfather had told me that there was no such orange-red sky above his Eastern homeland. He'd said that one could see stars at night, and I had seen them through his eyes. He could open his mind to me, and did, often. It was part of his method for teaching witchcraft; a method that brought me, at age sixteen, to the jungles.

The sky lit the jungle enough for me to pick my way. I ignored the scratches on my face and arms from the foliage. Slowly, my stomach settled down from the nausea that had hit when I had done the teleport that brought me here.

There was a good touch of irony there, too, I realized—using a Dragaeran sorcery to bring me to where I could take the next step in learning witchcraft. I hitched the pack on my back, and stepped into a clearing.

This one looked like it might do, I decided. There were heavy grasses for perhaps forty feet in what was, very roughly, a circle. I walked around it, slowly and carefully, my eyes straining to pick out details. All I needed now was to stumble into a chreotha's net.

But it was empty, my clearing. I went to the middle of it and set my pack down. I dug out a small black brazier, a bag of coals, a single black candle, a stick of incense, a dead teckla, and a few dried leaves. The leaves were from the gorynth plant, which is sacred to certain religions back East.

I carefully crumbled the leaves into a coarse powder; then I walked the perimeter of the clearing and sprinkled it before me as I went.

I returned to the middle. I sat there for a time and went through the ritual of relaxing each muscle of my body, until I was almost in a trance. With my body relaxed, my mind had no choice but to follow. When I was ready, I placed the coals in the brazier, slowly, one at a time. I held each one for a moment, feeling its shape and texture, letting the soot rub off on my palms. With witchcraft, everything can be a ritual. Even before the actual enchantment begins, the preparations should be made properly. Of course, one can always just cast one's mind out, concentrating on the desired result, and hope. The odds of success that way aren't very good. Somehow, when done the right way, witchcraft is so much more *satisfying* than sorcery.

When the coals were in the brazier and placed just so, I put the incense among them. Taking the candle, I stared long and hard at the wick, willing it to burn.

I could, certainly, have used a flint, or even sorcery, to start it, but doing it this way helped put me into the proper frame of mind.

I guess the mood of the jungle night was conducive to witchcraft; it was only a few minutes before I saw smoke rising from the candle, followed quickly by a small flame. I was also pleased that I felt no trace of the mental exhaustion that accompanies the completion of a major spell. There had been a time, not so long before, when the lighting of a candle would have left me too weak even for psionic communication.

I'm learning, Grandfather.

I used the candle, then, to start the coals burning, and laid my will upon it to get a good fire going. When it was burning well, I planted the candle in the ground. The scent of the incense, pleasantly sweet, reached my nostrils. I closed my eyes. The circle of crushed gorynth leaves would prevent any stray animals from wandering by and disturbing me. I waited.

After a time—I don't know how long—I opened my eyes again. The coals were glowing softly. The scent of the incense filled the air. The sounds of the jungle did not penetrate past the boundaries of the clearing. I was ready.

I stared deep into the coals and, timing my breathing, I spoke the chant— very slowly, as I had been taught. As I said each word, I *cast* it, sending it out into the jungle as far and as clearly as I could. It was an old spell, my grandfather had said, and had been used in the East for thousands of years, unchanged.

I agonized over each word, each syllable, exploring it, letting my tongue and mouth linger over and taste each of the sounds, and willing my brain to full understanding of each of the thoughts I was sending. As each word left me, it was imprinted on my consciousness and seemed to be a living thing itself.

The last sounds died out very slowly in the jungle night, taking a piece of me with them.

Now, indeed, I felt exhausted. As always when doing a spell of this power, I had to guard myself against falling into a deep trance. I breathed evenly, and deeply. As if sleep-walking, I picked up the dead teckla, and moved it to the edge of the clearing, where I could see it when I was sitting. Then I waited.

I believe it was only a few minutes later that I heard the flapping of wings near me. I opened my eyes and saw a jhereg at the edge of the clearing, near the dead teckla, looking at me.

We watched each other for a while, and then it tentatively moved up and took a small bite from my offering.

It was of average size, if female; a bit large, if male. If my spell had worked, it would be female. Its wing span was about the distance from my shoulder to my wrist, and it was a bit less than that from its snakelike head to the tip of its tail. The forked tongue flicked out over the rodent, tasting each piece before ripping off a small chunk, chewing, and swallowing. It ate very slowly, watching me watching it.

When I saw that it was nearly done, I began to compose my mind for psionic contact, and to hope.

Soon, it came. I felt a small, questing thought within me. I allowed it to grow. It became distinct.

"What is it you want?" I "heard" with surprising clarity.

Now came the real test. If this jhereg had come as a result of my spell, it would be female, with a nest of eggs, and what I was about to suggest wouldn't send it into an attack rage. If it was just a jhereg who was passing by and saw some carrion lying free for the taking, I could be in trouble. I had with me a few herbs which might prevent me from dying of the jhereg's poison—but then, again, they might not.

"Mother," I thought back to it, as clearly as I could, *"I would like one of your eggs."*

It didn't attack me, and I picked up no feeling of puzzlement or outrage at the suggestion. Good. My spell had brought her, and she would be at least receptive to bargaining. I felt excitement growing in me and forced it down. I concentrated on the jhereg before me. This part was almost a ritual in itself, but not quite. It all depended on what the jhereg thought of me.

"What," she asked, *"do you offer it?"*

"I offer it long life," I answered. *"And fresh, red meat without struggle, and I offer it my friendship."*

The animal considered this for a while, then said, *"And what will you ask of it?"*

"I will ask for aid in my endeavors, such as are in its power. I will ask for its wisdom, and I will ask for its friendship."

For a time then, nothing happened. She stood there, above the skeletal remains of the teckla, and watched me. Then she said, *"I approach you."*

The jhereg walked up to me. Its claws were long and sharp, but more useful for running than for fighting. After a full meal, a jhereg will often find that it weighs too much to become airborne and so must run to escape its enemies.

She stood before me and looked closely into my eyes. It was odd to see intelligence in small, beady snake eyes, and to have nearly human-level communication with an animal whose brain was no larger than the first joint of my finger. It seemed, somehow, unnatural—which it was, but I didn't find that out for quite some time.

After a while, the jhereg "spoke" again.

"Wait here," she said. And she turned and spread her batlike wings. She had to run a step or two before taking off, and then I was alone again.

Alone . . .

I wondered what my father would say, if he were alive to say anything. He wouldn't approve, of course. Witchcraft was too "Eastern" for him, and he was too involved in trying to be a Dragaeran.

My father died when I was fourteen. I never knew my mother, but my father would occasionally mutter something about the "witch" he had married. Shortly before his death, he squandered everything he had earned in forty years of running a restaurant in an effort to become even more Dragaeran—he bought a title. Thus we became citizens, and found ourselves linked to the

Imperial Orb. The link allowed us to use sorcery, a practice which my father encouraged. He found a sorceress from the Left Hand of the Jhereg who was willing to teach me, and he forbade me to practice witchcraft. Then he found a swordmaster who agreed to teach me Dragaeran-style swordsmanship. My father forbade me to study Eastern fencing.

But my grandfather was still around. One day I explained to him that, even when I was full-grown, I would be too short and too weak to be effective as a swordsman the way I was being taught, and that sorcery didn't interest me. He never offered a word of criticism about my father, but he began teaching me fencing and witchcraft.

When my father died, he was pleased that I was a skilled enough sorcerer to teleport myself; he didn't know that teleports made me physically ill. He didn't know how often I would use witchcraft to cover up the bruises left by Dragaeran punks, who would catch me alone and let me know what they thought of Easterners with pretensions. And he most certainly never knew that Kiera had been teaching me how to move quietly, how to walk through a crowd as if I weren't there. I would use these skills, too. I'd go out at night with a large stick, and I'd find one of my tormenters alone, and leave him with a few broken bones.

I don't know. Perhaps if I'd worked a little harder at sorcery I'd have been good enough to save my father. I just don't know.

After his death, it was easier to find time to study witchcraft and fencing, despite the added work of running a restaurant. I started to get quite good as a witch. Good enough, in fact, that my grandfather finally said that he couldn't teach me any more, and gave me instructions in how to take the next step on my own. The next step, of course, was . . .

She returned to the clearing, with a flapping of wings. This time she flew right up to me, landing in front of my crossed legs. In her right claw, a small egg was clutched. She extended it.

I forced down my excitement. It had worked! I held out my right hand, after making sure it was steady. The egg dropped into it. I was somewhat startled by its warmth. It was of a size that fit well into my palm. I carefully placed it inside my jerkin, next to my chest.

"*Thank you, mother,*" I thought to her. "*May your life be long, your food plentiful, and your children many.*"

"*And you,*" she said, "*long life and good hunting.*"

"*I am not a hunter,*" I told her.

"*You will be,*" she said. And then she turned from me, spread her wings, and flew out from the clearing.

Twice in the following week I almost crushed the egg that I carried around next to my chest. The first time I got into a fight with a couple of jerks from the House of the Orca; and the second, I started to carry a box of spices against my chest while working in the restaurant.

The incidents shook me up, so I decided to make sure that nothing happened again that would put the egg in danger. To protect myself against the former, I learned diplomacy. And to take care of the latter, I sold the restaurant.

Learning diplomacy was the more difficult task. My natural inclinations didn't run that way at all, and I had to be on my guard all the time. But, eventually, I found that I could be very polite to a Dragaeran who was insulting me. Sometimes I think it was that, more than anything else, which trained me to be successful later on.

Selling the restaurant was more of a relief than anything else. I had been running it on my own since my father died, and doing well enough to make a living, but somehow I never thought of myself as a restaurateur.

However, it did bring me up rather sharply against the problem of what I was going to do for a living—both immediately and for the rest of my life. My grandfather offered me a half-interest in his witchcraft business, but I was well aware that there was hardly enough activity to keep him going alone. I also had an offer from Kiera, who was willing to teach me her profession, but Easterner thieves don't get good prices from Dragaeran fences. Besides, my grandfather didn't approve of stealing.

I sold the place with the problem still unresolved, and lived off the proceeds for a while. I won't tell you what I got for it; I was still young. I moved into new quarters then, too, since the place above the restaurant was going to be taken by the new owner.

Also, I bought a blade. It was a rather light rapier, made to my measurements by a swordsmith of House Jhereg, who overcharged me shamefully. It was just strong enough to be able to counter the attacks of the heavier Dragaeran sword, but light enough to be useful for the ripostes by which an Eastern fencer can surprise a Dragaeran swordsman, who probably doesn't know anything beyond attack-defend-attack.

Future unresolved, I sat back and tended my egg.

About two months after I had sold the restaurant, I was sitting at a card table, doing a little low-stakes gambling at a place that allowed Easterners in. That night I was the only human there, and there were about four tables in action.

I heard raised voices from the table next to me and was about to turn around, when something crashed into my chair. I felt a momentary surge of panic as I almost crushed the egg against the edge of the table, and I stood up. The panic transformed itself to anger, and, without thinking, I picked up my chair and broke it over the head of the guy who'd fallen into me. He dropped like a hawk and lay still. The guy who'd pushed him looked at me as if deciding whether to thank me or attack me. I still had the chair leg in my hand. I raised it, and waited for him to do something. Then a hand gripped my shoulder and I felt a familiar coldness on the back of my neck.

"We don't need fighting in here, punk," said a voice behind my right ear. My adrenalin was up, and I almost turned around to smash the bastard across the face, despite the knife he held against me. But the training I'd been giving myself came to the fore, and I heard myself saying, evenly, "My apologies, good sir. I assure you it won't happen again." I lowered my right arm and dropped the chair leg. There was no point in trying to explain to him what had happened if he hadn't seen it—and even less if he had. When there's a problem, and an Easterner is involved, there is no question about who is at fault. I didn't move.

Presently I felt the knife being taken off of my neck.

"You're right," said the voice. "It won't happen again. Get out of here and don't come back."

I nodded once. I left my money on the table where it was, and walked out without looking back.

I settled down somewhat on my way home. The incident bothered me. I shouldn't have hit the guy at all, I decided. I had let my fear take over, and I reacted without thinking. This would never do.

As I climbed up the stairs to my apartment, my mind returned to the old problem of what I was going to do. I'd left almost a gold Imperial's worth of coins lying on the table, and that was half a week's rent. It seemed that my only talents were witchcraft and beating up Dragaerans. I didn't think that there was much of a market for either.

I opened the door and relaxed on the couch. I took out the egg, to hold it for a while as a means of soothing my nerves—and stopped. There was a small crack in it. It must have happened when I banged against the table, although I'd thought it had escaped harm.

It was then and there, at the age of sixteen, that I learned the meaning of anger. A sheet of white fire flashed through me, as I remembered the face of the Dragaeran who had pushed the other into me, killing my egg. I learned that I was capable of murder. I intended to seek out that bastard, and I was going to kill him. There was no question in my mind that he was a dead man. I stood up and headed for the door, still holding the egg—

—And stopped again.

Something was wrong. I had a feeling, which I couldn't pin down, that was getting through the barrier of my anger. What was it? I looked down at the egg, and suddenly understood in a burst of relief.

Although not consciously aware of it, I had somehow gotten a psionic link to the being inside the egg. I was feeling something through it, on some level, and that meant that my jhereg was still alive.

Anger drained from me as quickly as it had come, leaving me trembling. I went back into the middle of the room and set the egg down on the floor, as softly as I could.

I felt along the link, and identified the emotion I was getting from it: determination. Just raw, blind purpose. I had never been in contact with such singleness of aim. It was startling that a thing that small could produce such high-powered emotion.

I stepped away from it, I suppose from some unreasoning desire to "give it air," and watched. There was an almost inaudible "tap, tap," and the crack widened. Then, suddenly, the egg split apart, and this ugly little reptile was lying amid broken shell fragments. Its wings were tightly drawn up against it, and its eyes were closed. The wings were no larger than my thumb.

It—*It? He*, I suddenly knew. He tried to move; failed. Tried to move again, and got nowhere. I felt that I should be doing something, although I had no idea what. His eyes opened, but didn't seem to focus on anything. His head lay on the floor, then moved—pitifully.

I felt along my link to him, and now felt confusion and a little fear. I tried to send back feelings of warmth, protection, and all that good stuff. Slowly, I walked up and reached for him.

Surprisingly, he must have seen my motion. He obviously didn't connect the movement with the thoughts he was getting from me, however, for I felt a quick burst of fear, and he tried to move away. He failed and I picked him up—gingerly. I got two things for this: my first clear message from him and my first jhereg bite. The bite was too small, and the poison still too weak for it to affect me, but he was certainly in possession of his fangs. The message was amazingly distinct.

"Mamma?" he said.

Right. Mamma. I thought that over for a while, then tried to send a message back.

"No, Daddy," I told him.

"Mamma," he agreed.

He stopped struggling and seemed to settle down in my hand. I realized that he was exhausted and then realized that I was, too. Also, we were both hungry. At that point it hit me—What the hell was I going to feed him? All the time I'd been carrying him, I'd known that he was going to hatch someday, but it had never really sunk in that there was actually going to be a real, live jhereg there.

I carried him into the kitchen and started hunting around. Let's see . . . milk. We'll start with that.

I managed to get out a saucer and pour a little milk into it. I set it down on the counter and set the jhereg down next to it, his head actually in the saucer.

He lapped up a little and didn't seem to be having any trouble, so I scouted around a little more and finally came up with a small piece of hawk wing. I placed it in the saucer; he found it almost at once. He tore a piece off (he had teeth already—good) and began chewing. He chewed it for close to three minutes before swallowing, but when he did, it went down with no trouble. I relaxed.

After that, he seemed more tired than hungry, so I picked him up and carried him over to the couch. I lay down and placed him on my stomach. I dozed off shortly thereafter. We shared pleasant dreams.

The next day, someone came to my door and clapped, around midafternoon. When I opened the door, I recognized the fellow immediately. He was the one who'd been running the game the day before and had told me not to come back—with a knife held against the back of my neck for added emphasis.

I invited him in, being the curious type.

"Thank you," he said. "I am called Nielar."

"Please sit down, my lord. I'm Vlad Taltos. Wine?"

"Thank you, but no. I don't expect to be staying very long."

"As you wish."

I showed him to a seat and sat down on the couch. I picked up my jhereg and held him. Nielar arched his eyebrows, but didn't say anything.

"What can I do for you, then?" I asked.

"It has come to my attention," he said, "that I was, perhaps, in the wrong when I faulted you for the events of yesterday."

What? A Dragaeran apologizing to an Easterner? I wondered if the world was coming to an end. This was, to say the least, unprecedented in my experience. I mean, I was a 16-year-old human, and he was a Dragaeran who was probably close to a thousand.

"It's very kind of you to say so, my lord," I managed.

He brushed it off. "I will also add that I liked the way you handled yourself."

He did? I didn't. What was going on here?

"What I'm getting at," he continued, "is that I could use someone like you, if you have a mind to work for me. I understand that you don't have a job at the moment, and—" He finished with a shrug.

There were several thousand questions I wanted to ask him, starting with, "How did you find out so much about me and why do you care?" But I didn't know how to go about asking them, so I said, "With all respect, my lord, I can't see what kind of things I can do for you."

He shrugged again. "For one thing, preventing the kind of problems we had last night. Also, I need help from time to time collecting debts. That sort of thing. I normally have two people who assist me in running the place, but one of them had an accident last week, so I'm shorthanded just at the moment."

Something about the way he said "accident" struck me as strange, but I didn't take any time out to guess at what he meant.

"Again with all respect, my lord, it doesn't seem to me that an Easterner is going to look very imposing when standing up to a Dragaeran. I don't know that I—"

"I'm convinced that it won't be any problem," he said. "We have a friend in common, and she assured me that you'd be able to handle this kind of thing. As it happened, I owe her a favor or two, and she asked me to consider taking you on."

She? There wasn't any doubt, of course. Kiera was looking out for me again, bless her heart. Suddenly things were a lot clearer.

"Your pay," he continued, "would be four Imperials a week, plus ten percent of any outstanding debts you are sent to collect. Or, actually, half of that, since you'll be working with my other assistant."

Sheesh! Four gold a week? That was already more than I usually made while I was running the restaurant! And the commission, even if it were split with—

"Are you sure that this assistant of yours isn't going to object to working with a hum—an Easterner?"

His eyes narrowed. "That's my problem," he said. "And, as a matter of fact, I've already discussed it with Kragar, and he doesn't mind at all."

I nodded. "I'll have to think it over," I said.

"That's fine. You know where to reach me."

I nodded and showed him to the door, with pleasant words on all sides. I looked down at my jhereg as the door snicked shut. "Well," I asked him, "what do you think?"

The jhereg didn't answer, but then, I hadn't expected him to. I sat down to think and to wonder if the question of my future were being settled, or just put off. Then I put it aside. I had a more important question to settle—what was I going to name my jhereg?

I called him "Loiosh." He called me "Mamma." I trained him. He bit me. Slowly, over the course of the next few months, I developed an immunity to his poison. Even more slowly, over the course of years, I developed a partial immunity to his sense of humor.

As I stumbled into my line of work, Loiosh was able to help me. First a little, then a great deal. After all, who notices another jhereg flying about the city? The jhereg, on the other hand, can notice a great deal.

Slowly, as time went on, I grew in skill, status, friends, and experience.

And, just as his mother had predicted, I became a hunter.

1

*"Success leads to stagnation;
Stagnation leads to failure."*

I SLIPPED THE POISON dart into its slot under the right collar of my cloak, next to the lockpick. It couldn't go in too straight, or it would be hard to get to quickly. It couldn't go in at too much of an angle, or I wouldn't have room left for the garrot. Just so . . . there.

Every two or three days I change weapons. Just in case I have to leave something sticking in, on, or around a body. I don't want the item to have been on my person long enough for a witch to trace it back to me.

This could, I suppose, be called paranoia. There are damn few witches available to the Dragaeran Empire, and witchcraft isn't very highly thought of. It is not likely that a witch would actually be called in to investigate a murder weapon and try to trace it back to the murderer—in fact, so far as I know, it has never been done in the 243 years since the end of the Interregnum. But I believe in caution and attention to detail. That is one reason I'm still around to practice my paranoia.

I reached for a new garrot, let the old one drop into a box on the floor, and began working the wire into a tight coil.

"Do you realize, Vlad," said a voice, "that it's been over a year since anyone has tried to kill you?"

I looked up.

"Do you realize, Kragar," I said, "that if you keep walking in here without my seeing you, I'll probably die of a heart attack one of these days and save them the trouble?"

He chuckled a little.

"No, I mean it, though," he continued. "More than a year. We haven't had any trouble since that punk—What was his name?"

"G'ranthar."

"Right, G'ranthar. Since he tried to start up a business down on Copper Lane, and you quashed it."

"All right," I said, "so things have been quiet. What of it?"

"Nothing, really," he said. "It's just that I can't figure out if it's a good sign or a bad sign."

I studied his 7-foot frame sitting comfortably facing me against the back wall

of my office. Kragar was something of an enigma. He had been with me since
I had joined the business side of House Jhereg and had never shown the least
sign of being unhappy taking orders from an "Easterner." We'd been working
together for several years now and had saved each other's lives often enough
for a certain amount of trust to develop.

"I don't see how it can be a bad sign," I told him, slipping the garrot into
its slot. "I've proven myself. I've run my territory with no trouble, paid off the
right people, and there's only once when I've had even a little trouble with the
Empire. I'm accepted now. Human or not," I added, enjoying the ambiguity
of the phrase. "And remember that I'm known as an assassin more than anything else, so who would want to go out of his way to make trouble for me?"

He looked at me quizzically for a moment. "That's why you keep doing
'work,' isn't it?" he said thoughtfully. "Just to make sure no one forgets what
you can do."

I shrugged. Kragar was being more direct about things than I liked, and it
made me a bit uncomfortable. He sensed this, I guess, and quickly shifted back
to the earlier topic. "I just think that all this peace and quiet means that you
haven't been moving as fast as you could, that's all. I mean, look," he continued, "you've built up, from scratch, a spy ring that's one of the best in the
Jhereg—"

"Not true," I cut in. "I don't really have a spy ring at all. There are a lot of
people who are willing to give me information from time to time, and that's
it. It isn't the same thing."

He brushed it aside. "It amounts to the same thing when we're talking about
information sources. And you have access to Morrolan's network, which *is* a
spy ring in every sense of the word."

"Morrolan," I pointed out, "is not in the Jhereg."

"That's a bonus," he said. "That means you can find out things from people
who wouldn't deal with you directly."

"Well—all right. Go on."

"Okay, so we have damn good free-lance people. And our own enforcers are
competent enough to have anyone worried. I think we ought to be using what
we have, that's all."

"Kragar," I said, fishing out a slim throwing dagger and replacing it in the
lining of my cloak, "would you kindly tell me why it is that I should *want*
someone to be after my hide?"

"I'm not saying that you should," said Kragar. "I'm just wondering if the
fact that no one is means that we're slipping."

I slid a dagger into the sheath on the outside of my right thigh. It was a
paper-thin, short throwing knife, small enough to be unnoticeable even when
I sat down. The slit in my breeches was equally unnoticeable. A good compromise, I felt, between subtlety and speed of access.

"What you're saying is that you're getting bored."

"Well, maybe just a little. But that doesn't make what I said any less true."

I shook my head. "Loiosh, can you believe this guy? He's getting bored, so he wants to get me killed."

My familiar flew over from his windowsill and landed on my shoulder. He started licking my ear.

"Big help you are," I told him.

I turned back to Kragar. "No. If and when something comes up, we'll deal with it. In the meantime, I have no intention of hunting for dragons. Now, if that's all—"

I stopped. At long last, my brain started functioning. Kragar walks into my office, with nothing on his mind except the sudden realization that we should go out and stir up trouble? No, no. Wrong. I know him better than that.

"Okay," I said. "Out with it. What's happened now?"

"Happened?" he asked innocently. "Why should something have happened?"

"I'm an Easterner, remember?" I said sarcastically. "We get feelings about these things."

A smile played lightly around his lips. "Nothing much," he said. "Only a message from the personal secretary to the Demon."

Gulp. "The Demon," as he was called, was one of five members of a loose-knit "council" which, to some degree, controlled the business activities of House Jhereg. The council, a collection of the most powerful people in the House, had never had an official existence until the Interregnum, but they'd been around long before then. They ran things to the extent of settling disputes within the organization and making sure that things didn't get so messy that the Empire had to step in. Since the Interregnum they had been a little more than that—they'd been the group that had put the House back together after the Empire began to function again. Now they existed with clearly defined duties and responsibilities, and everyone who did anything at all in the organization gave part of the profits to them.

The Demon was generally acknowledged to be the number-two man in the organization. The last time I had met with someone that high up was in the middle of a war with another Jhereg, and the council member I'd spoken to had let me know that I'd better find a way to get things settled, or he would. I have no pleasant memories of that meeting.

"What does he want?" I asked.

"He wants to meet with you."

"Oh, crap. Double crap. Dragon dung. Any ideas why?"

"No. He did pick a meeting place in our territory, for whatever that's worth."

"It isn't worth a whole lot," I said. "Which place?"

"The Blue Flame restaurant," said Kragar.

"The Blue Flame, eh? What does that bring to mind?"

"I seem to recall that you 'worked' there twice."

"That's right. It's a real good place for killing someone. High booths, wide aisles, low lighting, and in an area where people like to mind their own business."

"That's the place. He set it up for two hours past noon, tomorrow."

"*After* noon?"

Kragar looked puzzled. "That's right. After noon. That means when most people have eaten lunch, but haven't eaten supper yet. You must have come across the concept before."

I ignored his sarcasm. "You're missing the point," I said, flipping a shuriken into the wall next to his ear.

"Funny, Vlad—"

"Quiet. Now, how do you go about killing an assassin? Especially someone who's careful not to let his movements fall into any pattern?"

"Eh? You set up a meeting with him, just like the Demon is doing."

"Right. And, of course, you do everything you can to make him suspicious, don't you?"

"Uh, maybe *you* do. *I* don't."

"Damn right you don't! You make it sound like a simple business meeting. And that means you arrange to buy the guy a meal. And that means you *don't* arrange it for some time like two hours past noon."

He was quiet for a while, as he tried to follow my somewhat convoluted logic. "Okay," he said at last, "I agree that this is somewhat abnormal. Now, why?"

"I'm not sure. Tell you what; find out everything you can about him, bring it back here, and we'll try to figure it out. It might not mean anything, but . . ."

Kragar smiled and pulled a small notebook from inside his cloak. He began reading. "The Demon," he said. "True name unknown. Young, probably under eight hundred. No one heard of him before the Interregnum. He emerged just after it by personally killing two of the three members of the old council who survived the destruction of the city of Dragaera and the plagues and invasions. He built an organization from what was left, and helped make the House profitable again. As a matter of fact, Vlad," he said, looking up, "it seems that it was his idea to allow Easterners to buy titles in the Jhereg."

"Now that's interesting," I said. "So I have him to thank for my father being able to squander the profits from forty years of work in order to be spat upon as a Jhereg, in addition to being spat upon as an Easterner. I'll have to find some way to thank him for that."

"I might point out," said Kragar, "that if your father hadn't bought that title, you wouldn't have had the chance to join the business end of the House."

"Maybe. But go on."

"There isn't much more to tell. He didn't exactly make it to the top; it would be more accurate to say that he made it somewhere, and then declared the top to be where he was. You have to remember that things were pretty much a mess back then.

"And of course, he was tough enough, and good enough to make it stick. As far as I can tell, he hasn't had any serious threats to his power since he got there. He has a habit of spotting potential challengers while they're still weak, and getting rid of them. In fact—do you remember that fellow, Leonyar, we took out last year?"

I nodded.

"Well, I think that may have come indirectly from the Demon. We'll never know for sure, of course, but as I said: he likes to get rid of potential problems early."

"Yeah. Do you think he could see *me* as a 'potential problem?' "

Kragar thought that over. "I suppose he might, but I don't quite see why. You've been staying out of trouble, and as I said before, you haven't really been moving very fast since the first couple of years. The only time there's been any problem was the business with Laris last year, and I think everyone knows that he forced it on you."

"I hope so. Does the Demon do 'work'?"

Kragar shrugged. "We can't say for sure, but it looks like he does. We know that he used to. As I said, he took out those two council members personally, back when he was getting started."

"Great. So in addition to whatever he could have set up, he might be planning to do the job himself."

"I suppose he could."

"But I still can't figure out—look, Kragar, with someone like the Demon, something like this wouldn't happen by accident, would it?"

"Something like—?"

"Like carefully arranging a meeting in just such a way as to arouse my suspicions."

"No, I don't think he—What is it?"

I guess he caught the look on my face, which must have been simply precious. I shook my head. "That's it, of course."

"What," he asked, "is what?"

"Kragar, arrange for three bodyguards for me, okay?"

"Bodyguards? But—"

"Make them busboys or something. You won't have any trouble; I own half interest in the place. Which, I might add, I'm sure the Demon is aware of."

"Don't you think he'll catch on?"

"Of *course* he'll catch on. That's the point. He knows that I'm going to be nervous about meeting him, so he deliberately set up the meeting with an ir- regularity to make me suspicious, so I'll have an excuse to have protection there. He's going out of his way to say, 'Go ahead and do what you have to, to feel safe, I won't be offended.' "

I shook my head again. I was starting to get dizzy. "I hope I don't ever have to go up against the son-of-a-bitch. He's devious."

"*You're* devious, boss," said Kragar. "I sometimes think you know Dra- gaerans better than other Dragaerans do."

"I do," I said flatly. "And that's because I'm not one."

He nodded. "Okay, three bodyguards. Our own people, or free-lance?"

"Make one of them our own, and hire the other two. There isn't any need to rub his nose in it, in case he recognizes our people."

"Right."

"You know, Kragar," I said thoughtfully, "I'm not real happy about this. He must know me well enough to know that I'd figure out what he was doing, which means this could be a setup after all." I held up my hand as he started to speak. "No, I'm not saying that I think it *is*, just that it could be."

"Well, you could always tell him that you can't make it?"

"Sure. Then, if he isn't planning to kill me now, he'd be sure to after that."

"Probably," admitted Kragar. "But what else can you do?"

"I can bitch a lot and go meet with him. Okay, that's tomorrow. Anything else going on?"

"Yeah," he said. "Some Teckla got mugged the night before last, a couple of blocks from here."

I cursed. "Hurt bad?"

Kragar shook his head. "A fractured jaw and a couple of bruises. Nothing serious, but I thought you'd like to know."

"Right. Thanks. I take it you haven't found the guy who did it?"

"Not yet."

"Well, find him."

"It'll cost."

"Screw the cost. It'll cost more if all our customers get scared away. Find the guy and make an example of him."

Kragar raised an eyebrow.

"No," I said, "not that much of an example. . . . And find a healer for that Teckla—on us. I take it he was a customer?"

"Everyone around here is a customer, one way or another."

"Yeah. So pay for a healer and reimburse him. How much did the guy get, by the way?"

"Almost two Imperials. Which could have been the Dragon Treasury, to hear him tell it."

"I suppose so. Tell you what: Why don't you have the victim come up and see me, and I'll pay him back personally and give him a talk about crime in the streets and how bad I feel, as a fellow citizen, of course, about what happened to him. Then he can go home and tell all his friends what a nice guy Uncle Vlad the Easterner is, and maybe we'll even pull in some new business out of the deal."

"Sheer genius, boss," said Kragar.

I snorted. "Anything else?"

"Nothing important, I guess. I'll go arrange for your protection for tomorrow."

"Fine. And make it good people. As I say, this has me worried."

"Paranoia, boss."

"Yep. Paranoid and proud."

He nodded and left. I wrapped Spellbreaker around my right wrist. The two-foot length of gold chain was the one weapon that I didn't change, since I had no intention of ever leaving it behind me. As its name implied, it broke spells. If I was going to be hit with a magical attack (unlikely, even if this *was* a setup), I'd want it ready. I flexed my arm and tested the weight. Good.

I turned to Loiosh, who was still resting comfortably on my right shoulder. He'd been strangely silent during the conversation.

"What's the matter?" I asked him psionically. *"Bad feelings about the meeting tomorrow?"*

"No, bad feelings about having a Teckla in the office. Can I eat him, boss? Can I? Huh? Huh?"

I laughed and went back to changing weapons with an all-new enthusiasm.

2

"There is no substitute for good manners—except fast reflexes."

THE BLUE FLAME IS on a short street called Copper Lane just off Lower Kieron Road. I arrived fifteen minutes early and carefully selected a seat that put my back to the door. I'd decided that if Loiosh, working along with the people we had planted here, couldn't give me enough warning, the difference it would make if I were facing the door probably wouldn't matter. This way, in case the meeting was legitimate, which I strongly suspected it was, I was showing the Demon that I trusted him and negating any feelings of "disrespect" he might get from seeing that I had brought protection. Loiosh was perched on my left shoulder, watching the door.

I ordered a white wine and waited. I spotted one of my enforcers busing dishes, but couldn't identify either of the free-lancers. Good. If I couldn't spot them, there was a good chance that the Demon couldn't. I sipped my wine slowly, still chucking slightly over the meeting I'd had earlier with the Teckla (what was his name?) who'd been mugged. It had gone well enough, though I had had to work to avoid bursting out laughing from my trusty jhereg familiar's constant psionic appeals of "Aw, c'mon, boss. *Please* can't I eat him?" I have a nasty familiar.

I kept a tight control on the amount of wine I was drinking—the last thing I needed right now was to be slowed down. I flexed my right ankle, feeling the hilt of one of my boot-knives press reassuringly against my calf. I nudged the table an inch or so away from me, since I was sitting in a booth and couldn't position my chair. I noted the locations of the spices on the table, as objects to throw, or things to get in the way. And I waited.

Five minutes after the hour, according to the Imperial Clock, I received a warning from Loiosh. I set my right arm crosswise on the table, so that my hand was hand was two inches away from my left sleeve. That was as close as I wanted to come to holding a weapon. A rather large guard-type appeared in front of my table, nodded to me, and stepped back. A well-dressed Dragaeran in gray and black approached and sat down opposite me.

I waited for him to speak. It was his meeting, so it was up to him to set the tone; also, my mouth was suddenly very dry.

"You are Vladimir Taltos?" he asked, pronouncing my name correctly.

I nodded and took a sip of wine. "You are the Demon?"

He nodded. I offered wine and we drank to each other's health; I wouldn't swear to the sincerity of the toast. My hand was steady as I held the glass. Good.

He sipped his wine delicately, watching me. All of his motions were slow and controlled. I thought I could see where a dagger was hidden up his right sleeve; I noticed a couple of bulges where other weapons might be in his cloak. He probably noticed the same in mine. He was, indeed, young for his position. He looked to be somewhere between eight hundred and a thousand, which is thirty-five or forty to a human. He had those eyes that never seemed capable of opening to more than slits. Like mine, say. Kragar was right; this was an assassin.

"We understand," he said, swirling the wine in his glass, "that you do 'work.' "

I kept the surprise off my face. Was I about to be offered a contract? From the Demon? Why? Perhaps this was just an effort to get me off my guard. I couldn't figure it. If he really wanted me for something, he should have gone through about half a dozen intermediaries.

"I'm afraid not," I told him, measuring my words. "I don't get involved with that kind of thing."

Then, "I have a friend who does."

He looked away for a moment, then nodded. "I see. Could you put me in touch with this 'friend?' "

"He doesn't get out much," I explained. "I can get a message to him, if you like."

He nodded, still not looking at me. "I suppose your 'friend' is an Easterner, too?"

"As a matter of fact, he is. Does it matter?"

"It might. Tell him we'd liked him to work for us, if he's available. I hope he has access to your information sources. I suspect this job will require all of them."

Oh, ho! So that's why he'd come to me! He knew that my ways of obtaining information were good enough that even he would have trouble matching them. I allowed myself a little bit of cautious optimism. This just might be legitimate. On the other hand, I still couldn't see why he'd come personally.

There were several questions I very badly wanted to ask him, such as, "Why me?" and "Why you?" But I couldn't approach them directly. The problem was, he wasn't going to give me any more information until he had a certain amount of commitment from me—and I didn't feel like giving him that commitment until I knew more.

"Suggestions, Loiosh?"

"You could ask him who the target is."

"That's exactly what I don't want to do. That commits me."

"Only if he answers."

"What makes you think he won't answer?"

"*I'm a jhereg, remember?*" he said sarcastically. "*We get feelings about these things.*"

One of Loiosh's great skills is throwing my own lines back at me. The damnable thing about it was that he might be simply telling the truth.

The Demon remained politely silent during the psionic conversation—either because he didn't notice it, or out of courtesy. I suspected the latter.

"Who?" I said aloud.

The Demon turned back to me, then, and looked at me for what seemed to be a long time. Then he turned his face to the side again.

"Someone who's worth sixty-five thousand gold to us," he said.

This time I couldn't keep my expression from showing. Sixty-five thousand! That was . . . let me see . . . over thirty, no *forty* times the standard fee! For that kind of money I could build my wife the castle she'd been talking about! Hell, I could build it twice! I could bloody well retire! I could—

"Who are you after?" I asked again, forcing my voice to stay low and even. "The Empress?"

He smiled a little. "Is your friend interested?" He was no longer pronouncing the quotation marks, I noted.

"Not in taking out the Empress."

"Don't worry. We aren't expecting Mario." As it happened, that was the wrong thing for him to say just then. It started me thinking . . . for the kind of gold he was talking about, he *could* hire Mario. Why wouldn't he?

I thought of one reason right away: The someone who had to be taken out was so big that whoever did the job would have to be eliminated himself, afterwards. They would know better than to try that on Mario; but with me, well, yes. I wasn't so well protected that I couldn't be disposed of by the resources the Demon had at his disposal.

It fit in another way, too: It explained why the Demon had shown up personally. If he was, in fact, planning to have me take a fall after doing the job, he wouldn't care that I knew that he was behind it and wouldn't want a lot of other people in his organization to know. Hiring someone to do something and then killing him when he does it is not strictly honorable—but it's been done.

I pushed the thought aside for the moment. What I wanted was a clear idea of what was going on. I had a suspicion, yes; but I wasn't a Dzur. I needed more than a suspicion to take any action.

So the question remained, who was it that the Demon wanted me to nail for him? Someone big enough that the man who did it had to go too. . . . A high noble? Possible—but why? Who had crossed the Demon?

The Demon was sharp, he was careful, he didn't make many enemies, he was on the council, he—wait! The council? Sure, that had to be it. Either someone on the council was trying to get rid of him, or he finally decided that being number two wasn't enough. If it was the latter, sixty-five thousand wasn't enough. I knew who I'd be going after, and he was as close to untouchable as it is possible to get. In either case, it didn't sound hopeful.

What else could it be? Someone high up in the Demon's organization suddenly deciding to open his mouth to the Empire? Damn unlikely! The Demon wouldn't make the kind of mistakes that led to that. No, it had to be someone on the council. And that, as I'd guessed, would mean that whoever did the job might have a lot of trouble staying alive after: he'd have too much information on the fellow who had given him the job and he'd know too much about internal squabbles on the council.

I started to shake my head, but the Demon held his hand up. "It isn't what you think," he said. "The only reason we aren't trying to get hold of Mario is because there have to be certain conditions attached to the job—conditions that Mario wouldn't accept. Nothing more than that."

I felt a brief flash of anger, but pushed it back down before it showed. What the hell made him think he could stick me with conditions that Mario wouldn't accept? (Sixty-five thousand gold, that's what.) I thought a little longer. The problem was, of course, that the Demon had a reputation for honesty. He wasn't known as the type who'd hire an assassin and then set him up. On the other hand, if they were talking about sixty-five thousand, things were desperate in some fashion already. He could be desperate enough to do a lot of things he otherwise wouldn't do.

The figure sixty-five thousand gold Imperials kept running through my head. However, one other figure kept meeting it: one hundred and fifty gold. That's the average cost of a funeral.

"I think," I told him at last, "that my friend would not be interested in taking out a member of the council."

He nodded in appreciation of the way my mind worked, but said, "You're close. An ex-member of the council."

What? More and more riddles.

"I hadn't realized," I said slowly, "that there was more than one way to leave the council." And, if the guy had taken that way, they certainly didn't need my services.

"Neither had we," he said. "But Mellar found a way."

At last! A name! Mellar, Mellar, let me see . . . right. He was awfully tough. He had a good, solid organization, brains, and, well, enough muscle and resources to get and hold a position on the council. But why had the Demon told me? Was he planning to kill me after all if I turned him down? Or was he taking a chance on being able to convince me?

"What way is that?" I asked, sipping my wine.

"To take nine million gold in council operating funds and disappear."

I almost choked.

By the sacred balls of the Imperial Phoenix! Absconding with Jhereg funds? With *council* funds? My head started hurting.

"When—when did this happen?" I managed.

"Yesterday." He was watching the expression on my face. He nodded grimly. "Nervy bastard, isn't he?"

I nodded back. "You know," I said, "you're going to have one bitch of a time keeping this quiet."

"That's right," he said. "We just aren't going to be able to for very long." For a moment his eyes went cold, and I began to understand how the Demon had gotten his name. "He took everything we had," he said tightly. "We all have our own funds, of course, and we've been using them in the investigation. But on the kind of scale we're working on, we can't keep it up long."

I shook my head. "Once this gets out—"

"He'd better be dead," the Demon finished for me. "Or every two-silverpiece thief in the Empire is going to think he can take us. And one of them will do it, too."

Something else hit me at that point. I realized that, for one thing, I could accept this job quite safely. Once Mellar was dead, it wouldn't matter if word got out what he'd tried. However, if I turned it down, I was suddenly a big risk and, shortly thereafter, I suspected, a small corpse.

Once again, the Demon seemed to guess what I was thinking.

"No," he said flatly. He leaned forward, earnestly. "I assure you that if you turn me down, nothing will happen to you. I know that we can trust you— that's one reason we came to you."

I wondered briefly if he were reading my mind. I decided that he wasn't. An Easterner is not an easy person to mind-probe, and I doubted that he could do it without my being aware of it. And I was *sure* he couldn't do it without Loiosh noticing.

"Of course, if you turn us down and then let something slip . . ."

His voice trailed off. I suppressed a shudder.

I did some more hard thinking. "It would seem to me," I said, "that this has to be done soon."

He nodded. "And that's why we can't get Mario. There's no way we can rush him."

"And you think you can rush my friend?"

He shrugged. "I think we're paying for it."

I had to agree with that. There was, at least, no time limit. But I had never before accepted "work" without the understanding that I had as much time as I needed. How much, I wondered, would it throw me off to have to hurry?

"Do you have *any* idea where he went?"

"We strongly suspect that he headed out East. At least, if I were pulling something like this, that's where I'd go."

I shook my head. "That doesn't make sense. Dragaerans out East are treated about the same as Easterners are treated here—worse, if anything. He'd be considered, if you'll pardon the expression, a demon. He'd stand out like a Morganti weapon in the Imperial Palace."

He smiled. "True enough, but we have the fewest resources there, so it would take a while for word to get back to us. Also, we've had the best sorceresses from the Left Hand looking for him since we found out what happened, and we can't find him."

I shrugged. "He could have put up a block against tracing."

"He definitely has done that."

"Well, then—"

He shook his head. "You have no idea of the kind of power we're pouring into this. We could break down any block he could put up, no matter how long he's been planning it, or who the sorcerer is who put the block up. If he was anywhere within a hundred miles of Adrilankha we'd have broken it by now, or at least found a general area that we couldn't penetrate."

"So, you can guarantee that he isn't within a hundred miles of the city?"

"Right. Now, it's possible that he's in the jungle to the west, in which case we'll probably find him within the next day or two. But I'd guess he'd bolted for the East."

I nodded slowly. "So you came to me, figuring that I can operate out there easier than a Dragaeran."

"That's right. And, of course, we know that you have an extremely formidable information network."

"My information network," I said, "doesn't extend to the East." That was almost true. My sources back in my ancestral homeland were few and far between. Still, there wasn't any reason to let the Demon in on everything I had.

"Well, then," he said, "there's an additional bonus for you. By the time this is over, you'll probably have something where you didn't before."

I smiled at his riposte, and nodded a little.

"And so," I said, "you want my friend to go out to wherever Mellar is hiding and get your gold back?"

"That would be nice," he admitted. "But it's secondary. The main thing is to make sure that no one gets the idea that it's safe to steal from us. Even Kiera, bless her sweet little fingers, hasn't tried *that*. I'll add that I take this whole thing very personally. And I will feel very warmly toward whomever does this particular little job for me."

I sat back, and thought for a long time, then. The Demon was politely silent. Sixty-five thousand gold! And, of course, having the Demon owe me a favor was better than a poke in the eye with a Morganti dagger by all means.

"Morganti?" I asked.

He shrugged. "It has to be permanent, however you want to do it. If you happen to destroy his soul in the process, I won't be upset. But it isn't necessary. Just so that he ends up dead, with no chance of anyone revivifying him."

"Yeah. You say that the Left Hand is working on locating him?"

"Right. The best they've got."

"That can't be helping your security any."

He shrugged. "They know who; they don't know why. As far as they're concerned, it's a personal matter between Mellar and me. You may not realize it, but the Left Hand tends to take less of an interest in what the council is doing than the lowest pimp on the streets. I'm not worried about security from that end. But if this goes on too long, word will get out that I'm looking for Mellar, and someone who notices that the council is having financial trouble will start counting the eggs."

"I suppose. Okay, I suspect that my friend will be willing to take this on.

He's going to need whatever information you have about Mellar as a starting point."

The Demon held his hand out to the side. The bodyguard, who had been standing politely (and safely) out of earshot, placed a rather formidable-looking sheaf of papers in it. The Demon handed these over to me. "It's all there," he said.

"All?"

"As much as we know. I'm afraid it may not be as much as you'd like."

"Okay." I briefly ruffled through the papers. "You've been busy," I remarked.

He smiled.

"If there's anything else I need," I said, "I'll get back to you."

"Fine. It should be obvious, but your friend is going to have all the help he needs on this one."

"In that case, I presume you're going to continue with your searching? You have access to better sorcerers than my friend has; you could keep going on that front."

"I intend to," he said drily. "And I should also mention something else. If we happen to run into him before you do and see an opportunity, we're going to take him ourselves. I mean no disrespect by that, but I think you can understand that this is a rather special situation."

"I can't say I like it," I said, "but I understand." I wasn't at all happy about it, in fact. Sure, my fee would be safe, but things like that can cause complications—and complications scare me.

I shrugged. "I think you can understand, too—and *I* mean no disrespect by *this*—that if some Teckla gets in the way, and my friend thinks the guy's going to bungle it, my friend will have to put him down."

The Demon nodded.

I sighed. Communication was such a fine thing.

I raised my glass. "To friends," I said.

He smiled and raised his. "To friends."

3

"Everyone is a predator."

"WORK" COMES IN THREE variations, each with its own effect, purpose, price—and penalty.

The simplest is not used often, but happens enough to have acquired the term "standard." The idea is that you want to warn an individual away from a certain course of action, or toward another. In this case, for a fee that starts at fifteen hundred gold and goes up from there depending on how hard the target is, an assassin will arrange for the selected individual to become dead. What happens after that doesn't much matter to the killer, but as often as not the body will eventually be found by a friend or relative, who may or may not be willing and able to have the person revivified.

Revivification costs heavily—up to four thousand gold for difficult cases. Even the easiest takes an expert sorcerer to perform, and it is never a sure thing.

In other words, the victim will wake up, if he does, with the knowledge that there is someone out there—and he usually knows who—who doesn't really care if he lives or dies and is willing to expend at least fifteen hundred gold Imperials to prove this.

This is rather chilling knowledge. It happened to me once, when I started pushing into the territory of a fellow who was just the least bit tougher than I was. I got the message, all right. I knew just what he was telling me, without any room for mistakes. "I can take you any time I want, punk, and I'd do it, too, only you aren't worth more than fifteen hundred gold to dispose of."

And it worked. I was returned to life by Sethra Lavode, after Kiera found my body lying in a gutter. I backed off. I've never bothered the guy since, either. Of course, someday . . .

Now you should understand, to begin with, that there are some rather strict laws concerning the circumstances under which one person may legally kill another, and they involve things like "authorized dueling area," "Imperial witnesses," and the like. Assassination just never seems to qualify as a legal taking of a life. This brings us to the biggest single problem with the kind of job I've just mentioned—you have to be sure that the victim doesn't get a look at your face. If he were to be returned to life and he went to the Empire (strictly against Jhereg custom, but . . .), the assassin could find himself arrested for murder.

There would follow an inquisition and the possibility of conviction. A conviction of murder will bring a permanent end to an assassin's career. When the Empire holds an execution, they burn the body to make sure no one gets hold of it to revivify it.

At the other extreme from simply killing someone and leaving his body to be found and, possibly, revivified, is a special kind of murder which is almost never done. To take an example, let us say that an assassin whom you have hired is caught by the Empire and tells them who hired him, in exchange for his worthless soul.

What do you do? You've already marked him as dead—no way the Empire can protect him enough to keep a top-notch assassin out. But that isn't enough; not for someone low enough to talk to the Empire about you. So what do you do? You scrape together, oh, at least six thousand gold, and you arrange to meet with the best assassin you can find—an absolute top-notch professional— and give him the name of the target, and you say, "Morganti."

Unlike any other kind of situation, you will probably have to explain your reasons. Even the coldest, most vicious assassin will find it distasteful to use a weapon that will destroy a person's soul. Chances are he won't do it unless you have a damn good reason why it has to be done that way and no other. There are times, though, when nothing else will do. I've worked that way twice. It was fully justified both times—believe me, it was.

However, just as the Jhereg makes exceptions in the cases where a Morganti weapon is to be used, so does the Empire. They suddenly forget all about their rules against the torture of suspects and forced mind-probes. So there are very real risks here. When they've finished with you, whatever is left is given to a Morganti blade, as a form of poetic justice, I suppose.

There is, however, a happy middle ground between Morganti killings and fatal warnings: the bread and butter of the assassin.

If you want someone to go and you don't want him coming back, and you're connected to the organization (I don't know any assassin stupid enough to "work" for anyone outside the House), you should figure that it will cost you at least three thousand gold. Naturally, it will be higher if the person is especially tough, or hard to get to, or important. The highest I've ever heard of anyone being paid is, well, excuse me, sixty-five thousand gold. Ahem. I expect that Mario Greymist was paid a substantially higher fee for killing the old Phoenix Emperor just before the Interregnum, but I've never heard a figure quoted.

And so, my fledgling assassins, you are asking me how you make sure that a corpse remains properly a corpse, eh? Without using a Morganti weapon, whose problems we've just discussed? I know of three methods and have used all of them, and combinations, during my career.

First, you can make sure that the body isn't found for three full days, after which time the soul will have departed. The most common method for doing this is to pay a moderate fee, usually around three to five hundred gold, to a sorceress from the Left Hand of the Jhereg, who will guarantee that the body is undisturbed for the requisite period. Or, of course, you can arrange to secrete the body yourself—risky, and not at all pleasant to be seen carrying a body around. It causes talk.

The second method, if you aren't so greedy, is to pay these same sorceresses something closer to a thousand, or even fifteen hundred of your newly acquired gold, and they will make sure that, no matter who does what, the body will never be revivified. Or, third, you can make the body unrevivifiable: burn it, chop off the head . . . use your imagination.

For myself, I'll stick with the methods I developed in the course of my first couple of years of working: hours of planning, split-second timing, precise calculations, and a single, sharp, accurate knife.

I haven't bungled one yet.

Kragar was waiting for me when I returned. I filled him in on the conversation and the result. He looked judicious.

"It's too bad," he remarked when I had finished, "that you *don't* have a 'friend' you can unload this one on."

"What do you mean, friend?" I said.

"I—" he looked startled for a minute, then grinned.

"No, you don't," he said. "You took the job; you do it."

"I know, I know. But what did you mean? Don't you think we're up to it?"

"Vlad, this guy is *good*. He was on the *council*. You think you can just walk up to him and put a dagger into his left eye?"

"I never meant to imply that I thought it was going to be easy. So, we have to put a little work into it—"

"A little!"

"All right, a lot. So we put a lot of work into the setup. I told you what I'm getting for it, and you know what your percentage is. What's happened to your innate sense of greed, anyway?"

"I don't need one," he said. "You've got enough for both of us."

I ignored that.

"The first step," I told him, "is locating the guy. Can you come up with some method for figuring out where he might be hiding?"

Kragar looked thoughtful. "Tell you what, Vlad; just for variety this time, *you* do all the setup work, and when you're done, *I'll* take him out. What do you say?"

I gave him the most eloquent look I could manage.

He sighed. "All right, all right. You say he's got sorcery blocked out for tracing?"

"Apparently. And the Demon is using the best there is to look for him that way, in any case."

"Hmmm. Are we working under the assumption that the Demon is right, that he's out East somewhere?"

"Good point." I thought about it. "No. Let's not start out making any assumptions at all. What we *know*, because the Demon guaranteed it, is that

Mellar's nowhere within a hundred-mile radius of Adrilankha. For the moment, let's assume that he could be anywhere outside of that."

"Which includes a few thousand square miles of jungle."

"True."

"You aren't going out of your way to make my life easy, are you?"

I shrugged. Kragar was thoughtfully silent for a while.

"What about witchcraft, Vlad? Do you think you can trace him with that? I would doubt that he thought to protect himself against it, even if he could."

"Witchcraft? Let me think—I don't know. Witchcraft really isn't very good for that sort of thing. I mean, I could probably find him, to the extent of getting an image and a psionic fix, but there isn't any way of going from there to a hard location, or teleport coordinates, or anything really useful. I guess we could use it to make sure he's alive, but I suspect we can safely assume that, anyway."

Kragar nodded, and looked thoughtful. "Well," he said after a time, "if you have any kind of psionic fix at all, maybe you can come up with something Daymar could use to find out where he is. He's good at that kind of thing."

Now there was an idea. Daymar was strange, but psionics were his specialty. If anyone could do it, he could.

"I'm not sure we want to get that many people involved in this," I said. "The Demon wouldn't be real happy about the number of potential leaks we'd have to generate. And Daymar isn't even a Jhereg."

"So don't mention it to the Demon," said Kragar. "The thing is, we have to find him, right? And we know we can trust Daymar, right?"

"Well—"

"Oh, come on, Vlad. If you ask him not to talk about it, he won't. Besides, where else can you get expert help, on that level, without paying a thing for it? Daymar enjoys showing off; he'd do it for free. What can we lose?"

I raised my eyebrow and looked at him.

"There is that," he admitted. "But I think the risk involved in telling Daymar as much as we have to tell him is pretty damn small. Especially when you consider what we're getting for it."

"If he can do it."

"I think he can," said Kragar.

"All right," I said, "I'm sold. Quiet a minute while I figure out what I'm going to need."

I ran through, in my mind, what I was going to have to do to locate Mellar, and what I'd have to do so that Daymar could trace him afterwards. I wished I knew more about how Daymar did things like that, but I could make a reasonable guess. It seemed that it would be a pretty straightforward spell, which really should work if Mellar had no blocks against witchcraft.

I built up a mental list of what I'd need. Nothing out of the ordinary; I already had everything except for one small matter.

"Kragar, put word out on the street that I'd like to arrange to see Kiera. At her convenience, of course."

"Okay. Any preference on where you meet?"

"No, just some—wait!" I interrupted myself, and thought for a minute. In my office, I had witchcraft protections and alarms. I knew these were hard to beat, and I wasn't happy about taking any chances at all of this information leaking out. The Demon would be upset, anyway, if he knew that I was dealing with Kiera. I didn't really like the idea of having one of his people see me talking with her in some public place. On the other hand, Kiera was . . . well, Kiera. Hmmm. Tough question.

Hell with it, I decided. I'd just shock the staff a little. It'd be good for them. "I'd like to meet her here, in my office, if that's all right with her."

Kragar looked startled and seemed about to say something, but changed his mind, I guess, when he realized that I'd just gone over all of the objections myself. "All right," he said. "Now about Daymar. You know what kind of problems we have reaching him; do you want me to figure out a way?"

"No, thanks. I'll take care of it."

"All by yourself? My goodness!"

"No, I'm going to get Loiosh to help. There, feel better?"

He snickered and left. I got up and opened the window. *"Loiosh,"* I thought to my familiar, *"find Daymar."*

"As Your Majesty requests," he answered.

"Feel free to save the sarcasm."

A telepathic giggle is an odd thing to experience. Loiosh flew out the window.

I sat down again and stared off blankly for a while. How many times had I been in this position? Just at the beginning of a job, with no idea of where it was going, or how it would get there. Nothing, really, except an image of how it should end; as always, with a corpse. How many times? It isn't really a rhetorical question. This would be the forty-second assassination I'd done. My first thought was that it was going to be somewhat different than the others, at some level, in some way, to some degree. I have clear memories of each one. The process I go through before I do the job is such that I can't forget any of them—I have to get to know them too well. This would certainly be a problem if I were given to nightmares.

The fourth one? He was the button man who would always order a fine liqueur after dinner and leave half the bottle instead of a tip. The twelfth was a small-time muscle who liked to keep his cash in the largest denominations he could. The nineteenth was a sorcerer who carried a cloth around with him to polish his staff with—which he did constantly. There is always something distinct about them. Sometimes it is something I can use; more often it is just something that sticks out in my memory. When you know someone well enough, he becomes an individual no matter how hard you try to think of him as just a face—or a body.

But if you take it back a level, you once more wind up with the similarities being important. Because when they come to me as names mentioned in a conversation, over a quiet meal, with a purse handed over which will contain somewhere between fifteen hundred and four thousand gold Imperials, they *are* all the same, and I treat them the same: plan the job, do it.

I usually worked backwards: after finding out everything I could about his habits, and following him, tracking him, and timing him for days, sometimes for weeks, I'd decide where I wanted it to happen. That would usually determine the time and often the day as well. Then it was a matter of starting from there and working things so that all of the factors came together then and there. The execution itself was only interesting if I made a mistake somewhere along the line.

Kragar once asked me, when I was feeling particularly mellow, if I enjoyed killing people. I didn't answer, because I didn't know, but it set me to thinking. I'm still not really sure. I know that I enjoy the planning of a job, and setting it in motion so that everything works out. But the actual killing? I don't think I either consciously enjoy it or fail to enjoy it; I just do it.

I leaned back and closed my eyes. The beginning of a job like this is like the beginning of a witchcraft spell. The most important single thing is my frame of mind when I begin. I want to make absolutely sure that I have no preconceived notions about how, or where, or anything. That comes later. I hadn't even begun to study the fellow yet, so I didn't have anything to really go on. The little I did know went rolling around my subconscious, free-associating, letting images and ideas pop up and be casually discarded. Sometimes, when I'm in the middle of planning, I'll get a sudden inspiration, or what appears to be a sudden burst of brilliance. I fancy myself an artist at times like this.

I came out of my reverie slowly, with the feeling that there was something I should be thinking about. I wasn't really fully awake yet, so it took me awhile to become aware of what it was. There was a stray, questing thought fluttering around in my forebrain.

After a while, I realized that it had an external source. I gave it some freedom to grow and take shape enough for me to recognize it, and discovered that someone was trying to get into psionic contact with me. I recognized the sender.

"Ah, Daymar," I thought back. *"Thank you."*

"No problem," came the clear, gentle thought. *"You wanted something?"* Daymar had better mental control, and more power, than anyone I'd ever met. I got the feeling from him that he had to be careful, even in mental contact, lest he burn my mind out accidentally.

"I'd like a favor, Daymar."

"Yes?" He had a way of making his "yes" last about four times as long as it should.

"Nothing right now," I told him. *"But sometime within the next day or so, I expect to need some locating done."*

"Locating? What kind of locating?"

"I expect to have a psionic tag on a fellow I'm interested in finding, and I'll want some way to figure out exactly where he is. Kragar thinks you can do it."

"Is there some reason why I couldn't just trace him now?"

"He has a block up against sorcery tracing spells," I told him. *"I don't think even you can get past them."*

I was damn sure Daymar couldn't get past a block that was holding off the best sorcerers of the Left Hand, but a little judicious flattery never hurt anything.

"Oh," he said. *"Then how do you expect to put a tag on him?"*

"I'm hoping he didn't protect himself against witchcraft. Since witchcraft uses psionic power, we should be able to leave a mark on him that you can find."

"I see. You're going to try to fix him with a witchcraft spell, and then I locate him psionically from the marks left by that. Interesting idea."

"Thank you. Do you think it will work?"

"No."

I sighed. Daymar, I thought to myself, someday I'm going to . . . *"Why not?"* I asked, with some hesitation.

"The marks," he explained, *"won't stay around long enough for me to trace them. If they do, they'll also be strong enough for him to notice, and he'll just wipe them out."*

I sighed again. Never argue with an expert.

"All right," I said, *"do you have any ideas for something that would work?"*

"Yes," he said.

I waited, but he didn't go on. Daymar, I said to myself, some day I'm *definitely* going to . . . *"What is it?"*

"The reverse."

"The reverse?"

He explained. I asked a few questions, and he was able to answer them, more or less.

I began thinking of what kind of spell I'd have to do to get the kind of effect he was talking about. A crystal, I decided, and then I'd start the spell out just like the other one, and then . . . I remembered that Daymar was still in contact with me—which, in turn, brought up another point that I really ought to clarify, given whom I was dealing with.

"Are you willing to do the locating for me?" I asked.

There was a brief pause, then: *"Sure—If I can watch you do the witchcraft spell."*

Why am I not surprised? I sighed to myself once more. *"It's a deal,"* I said. *"How do I get in touch with you? Can I count on finding you at home if I send Loiosh again?"*

He thought about that, then: *"Probably not. I'll open up for contact for a few seconds on the hour, each hour, starting tomorrow morning. Will that do?"*

"That will be fine," I said. *"I'll get in touch with you before I start the spell."*

"Excellent. Until then."

"Until then. And Daymar, thanks."

"My pleasure," he said.

Actually, I reflected, it probably was. But it wouldn't have been politic to say so. The link was broken.

Sometime later, Loiosh returned. I opened the window in answer to his knocking. Why he preferred to knock, rather than just contact me, I don't know. After he was in, I closed it behind him.

"Thanks."

"Sure, boss."

I resumed reading; Loiosh perched on my right shoulder this time, and pretended to be reading along with me. Or, who knows? Maybe he really did learn to read somehow and just never bothered to inform me. I wouldn't put it past him.

The job was under way. I couldn't really go any further until I had some idea of where Mellar was, so I turned my attention to who he was, instead. This kept me occupied until my next visitor arrived, a few hours later.

4

"Inspiration requires preparation."

MY RECEPTIONIST, IN THE two years he'd been with me, had killed three people outside the door of my office.

One was an assassin whose bluff didn't quite work. The other two were perfectly innocent fools who should have known better than to try to bluster their way past him.

He was killed once, himself, delaying another assassin long enough for me to heroically escape out the window. I was very relieved when we were successful in having him revivified. He fulfills the function of bodyguard, recording secretary, buffer, and whatever else either Kragar or I need. He may well be the highest-paid receptionist in the world.

"Uh, boss?"

"Yes?"

"Uh, Kiera is here."

"Oh, good! Send her in."

"That's Kiera the Thief, boss. Are you sure?"

"Quite sure, thank you."

"But—okay. Should I escort her in, and keep an eye—"

"That won't be necessary" (or sufficient, I thought to myself). "Just send her in."

"Okay. Whatever you want."

I put down the papers and stood up as the door opened. A small Dragaeran female form entered the room. I recalled with some amusement that I had thought her tall when we had first met, but then, I was only eleven at the time. And, of course, she was still more than a head taller than I, but by now I was used to the size difference.

She moved with ease and grace, almost reminiscent of Mario. She flowed up to me and greeted me with a kiss that would have made Cawti jealous if she were the jealous type. I gave as good as I got, and pulled up a chair for her.

Kiera had a sharp, rather angular face, with no noticeable House characteristics—the lack of which was typical for a Jhereg.

She allowed me to seat her and made a quick glance around the office. Her eyes clicked from one place to another, making notes of significant items. This wasn't surprising; she'd taught me how to do it. On the other hand, I suspected that she was looking for different things than I would be.

She favored me with a smile.

"Thanks for coming, Kiera," I said, as warmly as I could.

"Glad to," she said softly. "Nice office."

"Thanks. How's business been?"

"Not hurting, Vlad. I haven't had any contract jobs in a while, but I've been doing all right on my own. How about you?"

I shook my head.

"What is it, problems?" she asked, genuinely concerned.

"I went and got greedy again."

"Uh, oh. I know what that means. Somebody offered something too big to pass up, eh? And you couldn't resist, so you're in over your head, right?"

"Something like that."

She slowly shook her head. Loiosh interrupted, then, flapping over to her and landing on her shoulder. She renewed their acquaintance, scratching under his chin. "The last time that happened," she said after a while, "you found yourself fighting an Athyra wizard, right in his own castle, as I recall. That kind of thing isn't healthy, Vlad."

"I know, I know. But remember: I won."

"With help."

"Well . . . yes. One can always use a little help."

"Always," she agreed. "Which, I imagine, brings us to this. It must be something big, or you wouldn't have wanted to meet here."

"Perceptive as always," I said. "Not only big, but nasty. I can't risk anyone catching wind of this. I'm hoping no one saw you come in; I can't risk being seen with you and having certain parties guess that I'm letting you in on what's going on."

"No one saw me come in," she said.

I nodded. I knew her. If she said no one had seen her, I had no reason to doubt it.

"But," she continued, "what are your own people going to say when they find you've been meeting me in your own office? They'll think you've finally gone 'into the jungle,' you know." She was smiling lightly; baiting me. She knew her reputation.

"No problem," I said. "I'll just let it slip that we've been lovers for years."

She laughed. "Now there's an idea, Vlad! We should have thought of that cycles ago!"

This time I laughed. "Then what would *your* friends say? Kiera the Thief, consorting with an Easterner? Tut, tut."

"They won't say anything," she said flatly. "I have a friend who does 'work.' "

"Speaking of which—"

"Right. To business. I take it you want something stolen."

I nodded. "Do you know of a certain Lord Mellar, House Jhereg? I think he's officially a count, or a duke, or some such."

Her eyes widened, slightly. "Going after big game, aren't you, Vlad? You certainly *are* in over your head. I know him, all right. I've helped him out a couple of times."

"Not recently!" I said, with a sudden sinking feeling.

She looked at me quizzically, but didn't ask what I meant. "No, not in the last few months. It wasn't anything big, any of the times. Just sort of an exchange of favors; you know how it goes."

I nodded, quite relieved. "He isn't a friend, or anything, is he?"

She shook her head. "No. We just did a few things for each other. I don't owe him."

"Good. And speaking of owing, by the way . . ." I placed a purse on my desk in front of her. It held five hundred gold Imperials. She didn't touch it yet, of course. "How would you like to have me owe you still another favor?"

"I'm always happy to have you in my debt," she said lightly. "What does he have that you want?"

"Any of a number of things. A piece of clothing would be good. Hair would be excellent. Anything that has a long association with him."

She shook her head once more, in mock sadness. "More of your Eastern witchcraft, Vlad?"

"I'm afraid so," I admitted. "You know how we are, always like to keep our hand in, and all."

"I'll bet." She took the purse and stood up. "Okay, you're on. It shouldn't take more than a day or two."

"No hurry," I lied politely. I stood as she left, and bowed her out.

"How long do you think it will actually take her?" asked Kragar.

"How long have you been sitting there?"

"Not too long."

I shook my head in disgust. "I wouldn't be surprised if we had it tomorrow."

"Not bad," he said. "Did you talk to Daymar?"

"Yes."

"And?"

I explained the outcome of our conversation. He shrugged over the technical details of the witchcraft, but caught the gist of it. He laughed a bit when I explained that Daymar had managed to include himself in the spell.

"Well, do you think it will work?" he asked.

"Daymar thinks it will work; I think it will work."

He seemed satisfied with this answer. "So nothing happens until we hear from Kiera, right?"

"Right."

"Good. I think I'll go catch up on my sleep."

"Wrong."

"What now, Oh Master?"

"You're getting as bad as Loiosh."

"*What's that supposed to mean, boss?*"

"*Shut up, Loiosh.*"

"*Right, boss.*"

I picked up the notes on Mellar that I'd been reading and handed them to Kragar. "Read," I said. "Let me know what you think."

He ruffled through them briefly. "There's a lot here."

"Yeah."

"Look, Vlad, my eyes are sore. How about tomorrow?"

"Read."

He sighed and started reading.

"You know what strikes me, Vlad?" he asked a bit later.

"What?"

"There's been something funny about this guy since he first showed up in the organization."

"What do you mean?"

He paged through the notes quickly and continued. "He moved too fast. He made it from nowhere to the top in just over ten years. That's damned quick. I've never heard of anyone except you moving that quickly, and you have the excuse of being an Easterner.

"I mean, look," he went on. "He starts out protecting a little brothel, right? A muscle. A year later he's running the place; a year after that he has ten more. In eight years he's got a territory bigger than you have now. A year after that, he wipes out Terion and takes his place on the council. And a year after that, he grabs up the council funds and vanishes. It's almost as if he had the whole thing figured out when he started."

"Hmmm. I see what you're saying, but isn't ten years a long time to set up one job?"

"You're thinking like an Easterner again, Vlad. It isn't a long time if you expect to have a two-thousand- or three-thousand-year lifetime."

I nodded and thought over what he'd suggested.

"I can't see it, Kragar," I said finally. "How much gold was it that he got?"

"Nine million," he said, almost reverently.

"Right. Now, that's a lot. That's one hell of a lot. If I ever have a tenth of that in one place at one time I'll retire. But would you throw away a position on the council for it?"

Kragar started to speak, stopped.

I continued, "And that isn't the only way to get nine million gold either. It isn't the best, the fastest, or the easiest. He could have gone free-lance and done a lot better than that over those same ten years. He could have held up the Dragon Treasury, and doubled it at least, and not be taking any more risk than he is with this thing."

Kragar nodded. "That's true. Are you saying that he wasn't after the gold?"

"Not at all. I'm suggesting that he may have developed a sudden need to have a few million and this was the only way to get it in a hurry."

"I don't know, Vlad. Just looking at his whole history, it sure seems like he had this planned out from the start."

"But why, Kragar? No one works his way up to a seat on the council for money. You have to be after power to do something like that—"

"You should know," said Kragar, smirking.

"—and you don't throw away that kind of power unless you have to."

"Maybe he lost interest in it," he said. "Maybe he was just after the thrill of getting to the top, and after he made it, he went after a new thrill."

"If that's true," I remarked, "he's going to get his thrills, and then some. But doesn't that go against your He-Planned-It-All-From-the-Start theory?"

"I suppose it does. I'm beginning to get the feeling that we don't have enough information; all we're doing is guessing."

"True enough. So how about if you start collecting the information, eh?"

"Me? Look, Vlad, my boots are in the shop this week getting new soles. Why don't we hire a flunky and get him to do the legwork for us, okay?"

I told him where he could hire the flunky and what he could have him do.

He sighed. "All right, I'm going. What are you going to be working on?"

I thought for a minute. "A couple of things," I said. "For one, I'm going to try to think up a good reason for someone to suddenly decide to leave the council in such a way as to get the whole Jhereg down on his ass. Also I'm going to check in with Morrolan's spy ring and contact some of our own people. I want to dig up as much information as I can, and it wouldn't hurt to have both of us working on it. After that—I think I'll visit the Lady Aliera."

Kragar was about halfway out the door, but as I finished speaking, he stopped and turned around. "Who?" he asked, incredulous.

"Aliera e'Kieron, House of the Dragon, Morrolan's cous—"

"I know who she is, I just couldn't believe I heard you straight. Why not ask the Empress, while you're at it?"

"I have a few questions about this guy that I want to check out, and they're just the kind of thing she's good at. Why not? We've been friends for quite a while."

"Boss, she's a *Dragon*. They don't *believe* in assassination. They consider it a *crime*. If you go up to her and—"

"Kragar," I interrupted, "I never said that I was going to go up to her and say, 'Aliera, I'm trying to assassinate this guy, how would you like to help set him up?' Give me credit for a little finesse, all right? All we have to do is find some reasonable excuse for her to be interested in Mellar, and she'll be happy to help out."

"A 'reasonable excuse,' eh? Just out of curiosity, do you have any idea how to find an excuse like that?"

"As a matter of fact," I said nastily, "I do. Easiest thing in the world. I just give you the assignment."

"Me? Dammit, Vlad, you've already got me working on background, as well as trying to figure out a nonexistent event to provide an insufficient reason for a vanished Jhereg to do the impossible. I can't—"

"Sure you can. I have confidence in you."

"Go suck yendi eggs. How?"

"You'll think of something."

5

"There are dangers in eyesight too keen."

THE ONLY SIGNIFICANT THING that happened the rest of the day was the arrival of a courier from the Demon, along with a rather impressive escort and several large purses. The full sixty-five thousand Imperials. It was official now; I was committed.

I gave Kragar the purses to put into safekeeping, and went home for the day. My wife, I'm sure, knew that something was up, but didn't ask about it. I had no good reason for not mentioning anything to her, but I didn't.

The next morning I found a small envelope on my desk. I slit it open and several human, or Dragaeran, hairs fell out. There was also a note which read, "From his pillow.—K." I destroyed the note and reached out for psionic contact with my wife.

"Yes, Vlad?"

"Are you busy, sweetheart?"

"Not really. Just practicing a little knife-throwing."

"Hey! I wish you wouldn't do that!"

"Why not?"

"Because you can already beat me seven out of ten times."

"I'm going for eight out of ten. You've been getting uppity lately. What's up? Do you have some 'work' for me?"

"No such luck. Drop on by and I'll tell you about it."

"Right away?"

"As soon as it's convenient."

"Okay. I'll be over shortly."

"Fine. Meet me in the lab."

"Oh," she said, understanding, and the link was broken.

I left word with my receptionist that I wasn't going to be taking any messages for the next two hours and walked down a few flights of stairs. Loiosh rode complacently on my left shoulder, looking around as if he were conducting an inspection. I came to a small room in the basement and unlocked the door.

In this building, locks are next to useless as a means of actually keeping people out of places, but they are effective as a way of saying "Private."

It was a smallish room, with a low table in the exact center and several mounted lamps along the wall. I kindled these. In a corner of the room was a small chest. The middle of the table held a brazier, with a few unburned coals in it. I dumped these out and got more from the chest.

I focused, briefly, on one of the candles and was rewarded by a flame. I used it to light the others, then put out the lamps.

I checked the time and found that I still had a little while before I could contact Daymar. I checked the placement of the candles and watched the flickering shadows for a moment.

Removing a few more items from the chest, including a piece of incense, I set them on the table next to the brazier, placing the incense among the coals. Next, I took a candle and held the flame next to a coal. A moment of concentration, and the fire spread evenly and quickly. The smell of incense began to introduce itself to the various nooks and corners of the room.

Soon Cawti arrived and greeted me with a sunshine smile. She was an Easterner, a small, pretty woman with dzur-black hair and fluid, graceful movements. If she'd been a Dragaeran, she might have been born into the House of the Issola, and taught them all something about "courtliness." And something about "surprise," as well.

Her hands were small, but strong, and could produce knives out of nowhere. Her eyes burned—sometimes with the impish delight of a mischievous child, sometimes with the cold passion of a professional killer, sometimes with the rage of a Dragonlord going into battle.

Cawti was one of the deadliest assassins I had ever met. She and her partner, then a defrocked Dragonlord, had made one of the most sought-after teams of killers in the Jhereg, going under the somewhat melodramatic names of "The Sword and the Dagger." I had deemed it a high honor when an enemy of mine had considered me worth the expense of hiring the team to take me out. I'd been quite surprised when I woke up afterwards and found that they hadn't managed to make it permanent. For that, thank Kragar's alertness, Morrolan's speed and fighting ability, and Aliera's rather exceptional skill in healing and revivification.

Some couples fall in love and end up trying to kill each other. We'd done it the other way around.

Cawti was also a competent witch, though not quite as skilled as I. I explained to her what was going to be needed, then we made small talk.

"*Boss!*"

"*Yes, Loiosh?*"

"*I hate to interrupt—*"

"*Like hell you do.*"

"*But it's time to contact Daymar.*"

"*Already? Okay, thanks.*"

"*Well, I suppose you're welcome.*"

I reached out, thinking of Daymar, concentrating, remembering the "feel" of his mind.

"*Yes?*" he said. He was one of few people whose voice I could actually hear when we were in contact. In the other cases it was because I knew them well enough for my imagination to supply the voice. With Daymar it was simply the strength of the contact.

"Would you mind showing up?" I asked him. *"We'd like to get started on this spell."*

"Fine. Just let me . . . Okay, I've got a fix on you. I'll be right there."

"Give me a minute first, so I can turn off some protections and alarms. I don't want to have forty-eleven things go off when you teleport in."

I ordered our teleport protections taken down for a few seconds. Daymar appeared in front of me—floating, cross-legged, about three feet off the floor. I rolled my eyes; Cawti shook her head sadly. Loiosh hissed. Daymar shrugged, and stretched his legs down; stood up.

"You left off the thunderclap and the lightning flash," I told him.

"Should I try again?"

"Never mind."

Daymar stood roughly seven feet, three inches tall. He had the sharp, well-chiseled features of the House of the Hawk, although they were somewhat gentler, softer, than those of most Hawklords I've met. He was incredibly thin, looking almost transparent. It seemed that his eyes rarely focused, giving him the appearance of looking past whatever he was observing, or at something deep inside it. We had been friends since the time I had almost killed him for mind-probing one of my people. He'd done it out of curiosity, and I think he never understood why I objected.

"So," Daymar asked, "who is this you want located?"

"A Jhereg. With luck, I should have what you wanted for the trace. Will this do?"

I handed him a small crystal I'd taken from the chest. He inspected it carefully, although I'm damned if I know what he was looking for. He nodded and gave it back to me.

"I've seen better," he remarked, "but it will do."

I set it carefully down on the right side of the brazier. I opened the envelope I'd gotten from Kiera and removed about half of the dozen or so strands of hair. These I set on top of the envelope on the left side of the brazier; the others I would save in case I had to try the spell again.

It was interesting, I reflected, how much a witchcraft spell resembles an assassination, as opposed to either of them being similar to sorcery. To use sorcery, all you do is reach out through your link to the Imperial Orb, grab some power, shape it, and throw it. With witchcraft, however, you have to plan carefully and precisely so that you don't end up searching around for some implement you need, right at the moment of using it.

The room began to get smoky with the lingering scent of incense. I took my position in front of the brazier; Cawti automatically stood to my right, and I motioned Daymar to stand at my left, and back. I let my mind drift and linked up mentally with Cawti. It was not necessary for there to be physical contact between us for this to happen, which is one reason why I like to work with her. One of the clear advantages witchcraft enjoys over sorcery is that more than one witch can participate in a single spell. I felt my power diminish and increase at the same time; which is strange to say and even stranger to experience.

I laid a few leaves on the coals, which obliged by making the proper hissing sounds. They were large, broad leaves from the Heaken tree, which only grows out East. They had been prepared by being soaked in purified water for a number of hours, and by diverse enchantments. A large gout of steam-smoke rose up, and Cawti began chanting, low and almost inaudible. As the leaves began to blacken and burn, my left hand found the envelope and the hairs. I rolled them around on my fingertips for a moment. I felt things start to happen—the very first sign of a witchcraft spell starting to have any kind of effect is when certain senses begin to feel sharper. In this case, each hair felt distinct and unique to my fingertips, and I could almost make out tiny details on each one. I dropped them onto the burning leaves, as Cawti's chanting became more intense, and I could almost pick out the words.

At that moment, a sudden rush of power flooded my mind. I felt giddy, and I would certainly have lost my end of the spell if I had actually begun it. A thought came into being, and I heard Daymar's pseudo-voice say, *"Mind if I help?"*

I didn't answer, trying to cope with more psychic energy than I'd ever had at my disposal before. I had a brief urge to answer, "No!" and hurl the energy back at him as hard as I could, but it wouldn't have done more than hurt his feelings. I observed my own anger at this unasked-for-interference as if it were in a stranger.

Any spell, no matter how trivial it really is, involves some degree of danger. After all, what you're really doing is building up a force of energy from your own mind and manipulating it as if it were something external. There have been witches whose minds have been destroyed by mishandling this power. Daymar, of course, couldn't know this. He was just being his usual helpful, meddlesome self.

I gritted my teeth and tried to use my anger to control the forces we had generated, to direct them into the spell. Somewhere, I felt Loiosh fighting to hold onto his control and take up what I couldn't handle. Loiosh and I were so deeply linked that anything that happened to me would happen to him. The link broadened, more and more power flooded through it, and I knew that, between the two of us, we'd either be able to handle it, or our minds would be burned out. I would have been as scared as a teckla if my anger hadn't blocked it—and the rage I felt was sustained, perhaps, by my knowledge of the fear underlying it.

It hung in the balance, and time stretched to both horizons. I heard Cawti, as if from a great distance, chanting steadily, strongly, although she must have felt the backwash of forces as much as I. She was helping, too. I had to direct the energy into the spell, or it would find release some other way. I remember thinking, at that moment, *"Daymar, if you've hurt my familiar's mind, you are one dead Dragaeran."*

Loiosh was straining. I could feel him, right at his limit, trying to absorb power, control it, channel it. This is why witches have familiars. I think he saved me.

I felt control had come, and fought to hang onto it long enough to throw it into the spell. I wanted to rush through the next part, but resisted the temptation. You do *not* rush through any phase of a witchcraft spell.

The hairs were burning; they merged and combined into a part of the steam and smoke and they should still be tied to their owner. I fought to identify exactly which isolated puff of smoke held the essence of those burning hairs and therefore was an unbreakable bond to my target.

I lifted my arms until my hands were at the outermost perimeter of the grayish-white cloud. I felt the fourway pull of energy—me to Daymar to Loiosh to Cawti and back. I let it flow out through my hands, until the smoke stopped rising—the first visible sign that the spell was having an effect. I held it there for an instant and slowly brought my hands closer together. The smoke became more dense in front of me, and I flung the energy I held at and through it. . . .

There is a cry of "charge" and five thousand Dragons come storming at the place the Eastern army is entrenched. . . . Making love to Cawti that first time—the moment of entry, even more than the moment of release; I wonder if she plans to kill me before we're finished, and I don't really care. . . . The Dzur hero, coming alone to Dzur mountain, sees Sethra Lavode stand up before him, Iceflame alive in her hand. . . . A small girl-child with big brown eyes looks at me and smiles. . . . The energy bolt, visible as a black wave, streaks toward me, and I swing Spellbreaker at it, wondering whether it will work. . . . Aliera stands up before the shadow of Kieron the Conqueror, there in the midst of the Halls of Judgment, in the Paths of the Dead, beyond Deathsgate Falls. . . .

And with it all, at that moment, I held in my mind everything I knew about Mellar, and all of my anger at Daymar, and above it all, on top of everything, my desire, my will, my hope. I flung it at the small cloud of steam-smoke rising from the brazier; I reached through it, beyond it, within it, toward the one who was tied to it.

Cawti chanted strongly, with no break in her voice, in words I still couldn't quite make out. Loiosh, within me, part of my being, was searching and hunting. And Daymar, away from us, and yet a part of us too, stood out as a beacon of light, which I grabbed, and shaped, and pushed through.

I felt a response. Slowly, very slowly, an image formed in the smoke. I forced energy into it as it began to grow distinct. I forced myself to ignore the face itself, which was only a distraction at this point. And, with agonizing slowness, I . . . lowered . . . my . . . right . . . hand . . . and . . . began . . . dropping . . . control . . . of . . . the . . . spell. . . .

Piece by minute, fractional piece, Loiosh picked up the threads of control, accepted them, handled them. Exhaustion was my enemy then, and I fought it back. The jhereg had taken the power, and was handling it all, by the green scales of Barlen!

I allowed myself to look at the image for the first time, as my right hand found the small crystal. The face was middle-aged and showed features reminiscent of the House of the Dzur. I carefully raised the crystal to eye level, dropped the last threads of control over the spell, and held my breath.

The image was steady; I had trained Loiosh well. Cawti was no longer chanting. She had done her part and was now just supplying power for the last stage of the spell. I studied the image through the crystal, closing my left eye. It was, of course, distorted, but that didn't matter; the image appeared through it enough to be identified.

A moment of intense concentration; I reached for the energy Cawti and Daymar were offering and burned the face into the container before my eye. My right eye was blinded for a moment, and I felt slightly dizzy as I bore down on it, trying to use up all of the excess power we had built up.

I heard Cawti sigh and relax. I sagged against the back wall, and Loiosh sagged against my neck. I heard Daymar sigh. There was now a milky haze within the crystal. I knew, without trying it, that by an act of will the haze could be cleared and Mellar's face would appear in it. More important, there was now a connection between Mellar, wherever he might be, and the crystal. The chances of his ever detecting this link were so small as to approach nonexistent. I nodded my satisfaction to Cawti, as we stood there for a few minutes catching our collective breath.

After a time, I blew out the candles, and Cawti lit the lamps along the wall. I opened the vent to let the smoke out, along with the smell of the incense, which now seemed cloying and sweet. The room brightened, and I looked around. Daymar had a distant look on his face, and Cawti seemed flushed and tired. I wanted to order wine from someone upstairs, but even the energy required for psionic contact seemed too much.

"Well," I announced to the room in general, "I guess he didn't have any protections against witchcraft."

Daymar said, "That was very interesting, Vlad. Thanks for letting me come along."

I suddenly realized that he had no idea that he'd almost destroyed me with his "help." I tried to think of some way to tell him, but gave up. I'd just remember it in the future, if he was ever around when I did more witchcraft. I held out the crystal to him; he accepted it. He studied it carefully for a few seconds, then nodded slowly.

"Well," I asked, "can you pin down where he is from that?"

"I think so. I'll try, anyway. How soon do you need it?"

"As soon as you can get it to me."

"Okay," he said. Then, casually, "By the way, why are you looking for him, anyway?"

"Why do you want to know?"

"Oh, just curious."

That figured. "I'd rather not say, if you don't mind," I told him.

"Have it your way," he said, miffed. "Going to kill him, eh?"

"Daymar—"

"Sorry. I'll let you know when I've found him. It shouldn't take more than a day or so."

"Good. I'll see you then. Or," I added as an afterthought, "you can just give it to Kragar."

"Fine," he said, nodding, and vanished.

I forced my legs to work and pushed away from the wall. I killed the lamps and helped Cawti out the door; locked it.

"We'd better get some food," I said.

"Sounds good. Then a bath, then about twenty years of sleep."

"I wish I could take the time for the last two, but I'm going to have to get back to work."

"Okay," she said cheerfully, "I'll sleep for you, too."

"Damned helpful of you."

Leaning on each other, we took the stairs, one at a time. I felt Loiosh, still lying against the side of my neck, sleeping.

6

"True heroics must be carefully planned—and strenuously avoided."

CAWTI AND I SHARED a lunch at one of the restaurants that I had an interest in. We ate slowly and allowed our strength to return. The sense of physical exhaustion that accompanies witchcraft is usually very short-lived; the psionic drain is longer. By halfway through the meal I felt comfortable again and well rested. On the other hand, I still felt that it would be something of an effort even to achieve psionic contact. I hoped no one would need to reach me during lunch.

We ate the meal in silence, enjoying each other's company, feeling no need to talk. As we were finishing, Cawti said, "So, you get work, while I stay home and wither away from boredom."

"You don't look withered to me," I said, checking. "And I don't remember your asking me for help with that little matter last month."

"Hmmmmph," she said. "I didn't need any help with that, but this looks like something big. I recognized the target. I hope you're getting a reasonable price for him."

I told her what I was getting for him.

She raised her eyebrows. "Nice! Who wants him?"

I looked around the restaurant, which was almost deserted. I didn't like taking chances, but Cawti deserved an answer. "The whole bloody Jhereg wants him, or will if and when they find out."

"What did he do?" she asked. "He didn't start talking, did he?"

I shuddered. "No, not that, thank Verra. He ran off with nine million gold in council operating funds."

She looked stunned and was silent for a moment, as she realized that I wasn't kidding. "When did this happen?"

"Three days ago, now." I thought for a second, then, "I was approached by the Demon, personally."

"Whew! Battle of the giant jhereg," she said. "Are you sure you aren't getting involved in more than you can handle?"

"No," I answered, cheerfully.

"My husband, the optimist," she remarked. "I suppose you've already accepted."

"That's right. Would I have gone to all of that trouble to locate him if I hadn't?"

"I suppose not. I was just hoping."

Loiosh woke up with a start, looked around, and jumped down from my shoulder. He began working on the remains of my tsalmoth ribs.

"Do you have any idea why you got the job?" she asked, suddenly worried. I could see her mind making the same jumps as mine had.

"Yes, and it makes sense." I explained the Demon's reasoning to her and she seemed satisfied.

"What do you think about subcontracting this one?"

"Nope," I said, "I'm too greedy. If I subcontract it, I won't be able to build you that castle."

She chuckled a little.

"Why?" I continued. "Do you and Norathar want to do it?"

"Not likely," she answered drily. "It sounds too dangerous. And she's retired in any case. Besides," she added, rather nastily, "you couldn't afford us."

I laughed and lifted my glass to her. Loiosh moved over to her plate and began working on it. "I guess you're right," I admitted, "I'll just have to stumble along on my own."

She grinned for a moment, then turned serious. "Actually, Vlad, it is something of an honor to be given a job like this."

I nodded. "I guess it is, to a degree. But the Demon is convinced that Mellar is out East somewhere; he figures that I can operate better than a Dragaeran out there. Since you went into pseudo-retirement, there aren't many humans who do 'work.' "

Cawti looked thoughtful for a moment. "What makes him think that Mellar is in the East?"

I explained his thinking on the matter, and Cawti nodded. "That makes sense, in a way. But, as you yourself said, he'd stand out in the East like a lightning bolt. I can't believe that Mellar is so naive that he'd think the House wouldn't go after him."

I thought this over. "You may be right. I do have a few friends in the East I can check with. In fact, I was planning on trying to get hold of them if Daymar can't find out where he is. I don't really see what else we can do but check out the Demon's theory, at this point."

"There isn't anything, I suppose," she said. "But it makes me a little nervous. Do you have any idea how long Mellar's been planning this move? If there was some way to figure that, it would give us an idea of how hard he's going to be to track down."

"I'm not sure. It seems to me that it doesn't make sense unless it was a sudden, spur of the moment kind of thing, but Kragar has an idea that he's been planning it all along, from the minute he joined the Jhereg, in fact."

"If Kragar is right, he must have something planned for this," she said. "In fact, if it was that long, he should have realized that someone would, or at least, *could* try to trace him using witchcraft. If that were the case, he would have some way to set up a block against it."

"On the other hand," she continued, "if he *did* plan it for that long and somehow couldn't block witchcraft, or didn't think of it, it may mean the Demon underestimated his defenses."

"What do you mean?" I asked.

"Well, don't you think that, in years, you could come up with a sorcery block that even the Left Hand couldn't break down in the time they've had?"

I thought that over for a long time. "He couldn't do it, Cawti. It's always easier to break down a block than it is to set one up. There is no way he could get the resources to put up a strong enough trace-block to keep out the Left Hand. The impression I got was that the Demon had the best there is working on it. I'd defy Sethra Lavode to put up a block that would hold them out for more than a day."

"Then why haven't they found him?" she asked, pointedly.

"Distance. Before they can break down the block, they have to find the right general area. That takes time. Even a standard teleport trace spell can be difficult if the person teleports far enough away. That's why the Demon is figuring the East. Using just standard tracing spells, it could take years to find him, if that's where he went."

"I suppose you're right," she conceded. "But I'm nervous about the thing."

"Me too," I said. "And that isn't all I'm nervous about."

"What else?"

"Time. The Demon wants this done a lot faster than I like to work. What it boils down to is that I have to make sure Mellar is taken out before everyone in the Jhereg finds out what he did. And that could happen any day."

Cawti shook her head. "That's bad, Vlad. Why, by the Demon Goddess, did you accept the job with a time limit? I've never heard of one even being offered that way."

"Neither have I. I took it that way because those were the terms. And it isn't really a time limit, as such, although he implied it could come to that later. It's just that I have to move as fast as I can."

"That's bad enough," she said. "You work fast, you make mistakes. And you can't afford to make a mistake."

I had to agree. "But you understand his position, don't you? If we don't get him, we've just shot the reputation of the Jhereg council. There won't be any way to keep House funds secure, once people get the idea that it can be done. Hell, I just put sixty-five thousand gold into a room in the office and forgot about it. I know it's safe, because there isn't anyone who would dare touch it. But, once this gets started . . ." I shrugged.

"And the other thing," I went on, "is that he told me straight out that if one of his people finds Mellar before I do, they aren't going to wait for me."

"Why should that bother you?" she asked. "You'll still have the payment."

"Sure. That isn't the problem. But think about it: some clod goes up to Mellar to take him out. Who is it going to be? It's not going to be a professional, because the Demon is going to want to say, 'Hey, you, go nail this guy here and now,' and no professional will agree to work that way. So it's going to be some two-silverpiece muscle, or maybe a button-man who thinks he can handle it himself. Then what? Then the guy bungles it, that's what. And I'm left trying to take Mellar out after he's been alerted. Oh, sure, the guy might succeed, but he might not. I don't trust amateurs."

Cawti nodded. "I see the problem. And I'm beginning to understand the reason for the price he's paying."

I stood up, after making sure that Loiosh had finished his meal. "Let's get going. I may as well try to get something done with the rest of the day."

Loiosh found a napkin, carefully rubbed his face in it, and joined us. I didn't pay, of course, since I was a part owner, but I did leave a rather healthy tip.

Out of habit, Cawti stepped out of the door an instant before me and scanned the street. She nodded, and I came out. There had been a time, not too long before, when that had saved my life. Loiosh, after all, can't be *everywhere*. We walked back to the office.

I kissed her goodbye at the door and went up, while she headed back to our apartment. Then I sat down and began going over the day's business. I noted with some satisfaction that Kragar had found the punk who'd mugged the Teckla the other day, at a cost of only four hundred gold or so, and had carried out my instructions. I destroyed the note and picked up a proposal that a new gambling establishment be opened by one of my button-men who wanted to better himself. I felt somewhat sympathetic. I'd gotten started that way, too.

"Don't do it, Vlad."

"Wha—? Kragar, would you cut it out?"

"Give the guy at least another year to prove himself. He's too new for that kind of trust."

"I swear, Kragar, one of these days I'm going to—"

"Daymar reported in."

"What?" I switched modes. "Good!"

Kragar shook his head.

"Not good?" I asked. "He shouldn't have been able to tell this quickly that he couldn't find the guy. Did he change his mind about helping us?"

"No. He found Mellar, all right."

"Excellent. Then what's the problem?"

"You aren't going to like this, Vlad. . . ."

"Come on, Kragar, out with it."

"The Demon was wrong; he didn't go out East after all."

"Really? Then where?"

Kragar slumped in his chair a little bit. He put his head on his hand and shook his head.

"He's at Castle Black," he said.

Slowly, a piece at a time, it sunk in.

"That bastard," I said softly. "That clever, clever bastard."

*   *   *

The Dragaeran memory is long.

The Empire has existed—I don't know—somewhere between two and two-and-a-half *hundred thousand* years. Since the creation of the Imperial Orb, back at the very beginning, each of the Seventeen Houses has kept its records, and the House of the Lyorn has kept records of them all.

At my father's insistence, I knew at least as much about the history of House Jhereg as any Dragaeran born into the House. Jhereg records do, I will admit, tend to be somewhat more scanty than those of other Houses, since anyone with enough pull, or even enough gold, can arrange to have what he wants deleted, or even inserted. Nevertheless, they are worth studying.

About ten thousand years ago, nearly a full turn of the cycle before the Interregnum, the House of the Athyra held the throne and the Orb. At this time, for a reason which is lost to us, a certain Jhereg decided that another Jhereg had to be removed. He hired an assassin, who traced the fellow to the keep of a noble of the House of the Dragon. Now, by Jhereg tradition (with good, solid reasons behind it that I may go into later), the target would have been quite safe if he'd stayed in his own home. No assassin will kill anyone in his house. Of course, no one can stay in his house forever, and if this Jhereg tried to hide that way, he would have found it impossible to leave, either by teleporting or by walking, without being followed. It could be, of course, that he didn't know he'd been marked for extinction—usually one doesn't know until it's too late.

But, for whatever reason, he was in the home of a Dragonlord. The assassin knew that he couldn't put up a trace spell around the home of a neutral party. The person would find out and almost certainly take offense, which wouldn't be good for anyone.

There is, however, no Jhereg custom that says that you have to leave someone alone just because he's over at a friend's house. The assassin waited long enough to be sure that the fellow wasn't planning to leave right away; then he got in past the Dragonlord's defenses and took care of his target.

And then the jaws of Deathsgate swung open.

The Dragons, it seemed, didn't approve of assassins plying their trade on guests. They demanded an apology from House Jhereg and got one. Then they demanded the assassin's head, and instead got the head of their messenger returned to them in a basket.

They were just sending the Dragons a message.

The Dragons got the message and sent back one of their own. Somehow, they found out who had issued the contract. The day after the messenger was returned to them, they raided the home of this fellow. They killed him and his family, and burned down his house. Two days later, the Dragon heir to the throne was found just outside the Imperial Palace with a six-inch spike driven through his head.

Four bars along Lower Kieron Road, all owned by the Jhereg, and all housing some illegal activity upstairs or in back, were raided and burned, and many of the patrons were killed. Every Jhereg in all of them were killed. Morganti weapons were used on several.

The next day, the Warlord of the Empire disappeared. Pieces of her were found over the next few days at the homes of various Dragon nobles.

The House of the Dragon declared that it intended to wipe House Jhereg out of the Cycle. The Dragons said that they fully intended to kill each and every Jhereg in existence.

House Jhereg responded by sending assassins after each Dragon general who commanded more than a thousand troops and then began working its way down.

The e'Kieron line of the Dragons was almost wiped out, and for a while it seemed that the e'Baritt line had been.

Have you heard enough?

All in all, it was a disaster. The "Dragon-Jhereg War" lasted about six months. At the end, when the Athyra Emperor forced a meeting between the surviving Dragon leaders and the Jhereg council and forced a peace treaty down both of their throats, there had been some changes. The best brains, the best generals, and the best warriors in the House of the Dragon were dead, and House Jhereg was damn near out of business.

It is admitted by the Jhereg that they came out pretty much the losers. This should be expected, since they were at the bottom of the cycle, and the Dragons were near the top. But still, the Dragons don't boast of the outcome.

It was fortunate that the Athyra reign was long, and the Phoenix reign even longer after that, or there would have been real trouble having a House of the Dragon strong enough to take the throne and the Orb when their turn came, following the Phoenix. It took the Jhereg the entire time until their turn at the throne, nearly half the cycle away, which worked out to several thousand years, to achieve a stable business.

I summed it up, as I went over the whole affair in my mind. Since that time, no Dragon has given sanctuary to a Jhereg, and no Jhereg has attempted to assassinate anyone in the home of a Dragonlord.

Castle Black was the home of Lord Morrolan e'Drien, of the House of the Dragon.

"How do you think he did it?" asked Kragar.

"How the hell should I know?" I said. "He found some way of tricking Morrolan into it, that's for sure. Morrolan would be the last person on Dragaera to deliberately let his home be used by a Jhereg on the run."

"Do you think Morrolan will kick him out, once he finds out that he's been used?"

"That depends on exactly how Mellar tricked him. But if Morrolan actually invited him there, he'll never agree to allowing him to be harmed, and he won't deny him sanctuary, not unless Mellar sneaked in without an invitation."

Kragar nodded and sat quietly for a while, thinking.

"Well, Vlad," he said at last, "he can't stay there forever."

"No. He can stay there long enough, though. All he has to do is to set up a new identity and figure out a good place to run. We can't keep up a vigilance on him for hundreds of years, and he can afford to wait that long if he has to.

"And what's more," I continued, "we can't even wait more than a few days. Once the information gets out, we've blown it."

"Do you think we can put up a tracer net around Castle Black, so we can at least find him if he leaves?"

I shrugged. "I suspect Morrolan wouldn't mind that. He might even do it himself, if he's as upset about being used this way as I expect him to be. But we still have the time problem."

"I don't suppose," said Kragar slowly, "that, since Morrolan is a friend of yours, he might, just this once . . ."

"I don't even want to ask him. Oh, I will, if we get desperate enough, but I don't think we have much of a chance of his agreeing. He was a Dragonlord long before he was a friend of mine."

"Do you think we might be able to make it look like an accident?"

I thought about that for a long time. "No. For one thing, the Demon wants it known that the Jhereg killed him—that's sort of the point of doing it in the first place. For another, I'm not sure it's possible. Remember: this has to be permanent. By Morrolan's rules, we can kill him as many times as we want, as long as we make sure he can be, and *is*, revivified after. People are killed every day at Castle Black, but he hasn't had one permanent death there since he had the place built. There's no point in having an accident that isn't permanent; and do you have any idea how hard it would be to set up an 'accident' so he's killed unrevivifiably? What am I supposed to do, have him trip and fall on a Morganti dagger?

"And another thing," I went on, "if we were to kill him that way, you can be damn sure that Morrolan would throw everything he had into an investigation. He takes a lot of pride in his record and would probably feel 'dishonored' if someone were to die, even accidentally, at Castle Black."

I shook my head. "It's really a strange place. You know how many duels are fought there every day? And not one of them on any terms other than no cuts to the head, and revivification afterwards. He'd check everything himself, twenty times, if Mellar had an 'accident,' and chances are good that he'd find out what happened."

"All right," said Kragar. "I'm convinced."

"There's one more thing. Just to put this away, or anything like it, I'd better make it clear that I consider Morrolan a friend, and I'm not going to let him get hurt like that if there's any way I can prevent it. I owe him too much."

"You're rambling, boss."

"Shut up, Loiosh. I was done anyway."

Kragar shrugged. "Okay, you've convinced me. So what *can* we do?"

"I don't know yet. Let me think about it. And if you get any more ideas, let me know."

"Oh, I will. Someone has to do your thinking for you. Which reminds me—"

"Yes?"

"One piece of good news out of this whole thing."

"Oh, really? What is it?"

"Well, now we have an excuse to talk to the Lady Aliera. After all, she is Morrolan's cousin, and she is staying with him, last I heard. From what I know about her, by the way, she isn't going to be at all pleased that her cousin is being used by a Jhereg. In fact, she'll probably end up an ally, if we work it right."

I took out a dagger and absently started flipping it as I thought that over. "Not bad," I agreed. "Okay, then I'll make seeing her and Morrolan my first priority."

Kragar shook his head, in mock sorrow. "I don't know, boss. First the witchcraft thing, and now this business with Aliera. I've been coming up with all the ideas around here. I think you're slipping. What the hell would you do without me, anyway?"

"I'd have been dead a long time ago," I said. "Want to make something of it?"

He laughed and got up. "Nope, not a thing. What now?"

"Tell Morrolan that I'm coming to see him."

"When?"

"Right away. And get a sorcerer up here to do a teleport. The way I'm feeling right now, I don't trust my own spells."

Kragar walked out the door, shaking his head sadly. I put my dagger away and held out an arm to Loiosh. He flew over and landed on my shoulder. I stood by the window and looked out over the streets below. It was quiet and only moderately busy. There were few street vendors in this part of town and not really a lot of traffic until nightfall. By then I'd be at Castle Black, some two hundred miles to the Northeast.

Morrolan, I knew, was going to be mighty angry at someone. Unlike a Dzur, however, an angry Dragon is unpredictable.

"*This could get really ugly, boss,*" said Loiosh.

"Yeah," I told him. "*I know.*"

7

"Always speak politely to an enraged Dragon."

My FIRST REACTION, YEARS before, upon hearing about the Castle Black, had been contempt. For one thing, black has been considered the color of sorcery for hundreds of thousands of years on Dragaera, and it takes a bit of gall to name one's home that. Also, of course, is the fact that the Castle floats. It hangs there, about a mile off the ground, looking real impressive from a distance. It was the only floating castle then in existence.

I should mention that there had been many floating castles before the Interregnum. I guess the spell isn't all that difficult, if you care to put enough work into it in the first place. The reason that they are currently out of vogue is the Interregnum itself. One day, over four hundred years ago now, sorcery stopped working . . . just like that. If you look around in the right places in the countryside you will still find broken husks and shattered remnants of what were once floating castles.

Lord Morrolan e'Drien was born during the Interregnum, which he spent mostly in the East, studying witchcraft. This is very rare for a Dragaeran. While the Easterners were using the failure of Dragaeran sorcery to turn the tables and invade *them* for a change, Morrolan was quietly building up skill and power.

Then, when Zerika, of the House of the Phoenix, came strolling out of the Paths of the Dead with the Orb clutched in her greedy little hands, Morrolan was right there, helping her stomp her way to the throne. After that, he was instrumental in driving back the Easterners, and he helped cure the plagues they left behind them as remembrances of their visit.

All this conspired to make him more tolerant of Easterners than is normal for a Dragaeran, particularly a Dragonlord. That is partly how I ended up working for him on a permanent basis, after we almost killed each other the first time we met. Little misunderstandings, and all.

I slowly came to realize that the Lord Morrolan was actually worthy of having a home called Castle Black—not that he would have cared a teckla's squeal what I thought of it in any case. I also came to understand part of the reason behind the name.

You must understand that Dragonlords, particularly when they are young (if you've been paying attention, you'll note that Morrolan was under five hundred), tend to be—how shall I put this—excitable. Morrolan knew quite well that naming his keep what he did was somewhat pretentious, and he also knew that, from time to time, people would mock him for it. When that happened, he would challenge them to duel and then take great delight in killing them.

Lord Morrolan, of the House of the Dragon, was one of damn few nobles who deserved the title. I have seen him show most of the attributes one expects of a noble: courtesy, kindness, honor. I would also say that he is one of the most bloodthirsty bastards I have ever met.

I was welcomed to Castle Black, as always, by Lady Teldra, of the House of the Issola. I don't know what Morrolan paid her for her services as reception committee and welcoming service. Lady Teldra was tall, beautiful, and graceful as a dzur. Her eyes were as soft as an iorich's wing, and her walk was smooth, flowing, and delicate as a court dancer's. She held herself with the relaxed, confident poise of, well, of an issola.

I bowed low to her, and she returned my bow along with a stream of meaningless pleasantries that made me very glad I had come and almost made me forget my mission.

She showed me to the library, where Morrolan was seated, going over some kind of large tome or ledger, making notes as he went.

"Enter," said Morrolan.

I did, and bowed deeply to him; he acknowledged.

"What is it, Vlad?"

"Problems," I told him, as Lady Teldra swished back to her position near the castle entrance. "What else do you think I'd be doing here? You don't think I'd deign to visit you socially, do you?"

He permitted himself a smile and held out his right arm to Loiosh, who flew over to it and accepted some head-scratching. "Of course not," he responded. "That was only an illusion of you at the party the other day."

"Exactly. How clever of you to notice. Is Aliera around?"

"Somewhere. Why?"

"The problem also involves her. And, for that matter, Sethra should be in on it too, if she's available. It would be easier if I could explain to all of you at once."

Morrolan's brows came together for a moment; then he nodded to me. "Okay, Aliera is on her way, and she'll mention it to Sethra."

Aliera arrived almost immediately, and Morrolan and I stood for her. She gave us each a small bow. Morrolan was a bit tall for a Dragaeran. His cousin Aliera, however, was the shortest Dragaeran I have ever known; she could have been mistaken for a tall human. Bothered by this, it was her habit to wear gowns that were too long, and then make up the difference by levitating rather than walking. There have been those who made disparaging remarks about this. Aliera, however, was never one to hold a grudge. She almost always revivified them afterwards.

Both Morrolan and Aliera had something of the typical Dragon facial features—the high cheekbones, rather thin faces and sharp brows of the House; but there was little else in common. Morrolan's hair was as black as mine, whereas Aliera had golden hair—rare in a Dragaeran and almost unheard of in a Dragonlord. Her eyes were normally green, another oddity, but I've seen them change from green to gray, and occasionally to ice blue. When Aliera's eyes turn blue, I'm very, very careful around her.

Sethra arrived just after her. What can I tell you about Sethra Lavode? Those who believe in her say she has lived ten thousand years (some say twenty). Others say she is a myth. Call her life unnatural, feel her undead breath. Color her black for sorcery, color her gray for death.

She smiled at me. We were all friends here. Morrolan carried Blackwand, which slew a thousand at the Wall of Baritt's Tomb. Aliera carried Pathfinder, which they say served a power higher than the Empire. Sethra carried Iceflame, which embodied within it the power of Dzur Mountain. I carried myself rather well, thank you.

We all sat down, making us equals.

"And so, Vlad," said Morrolan, "what's up?"

"My ire," I told him.

His eyebrows arched. "Not at anyone I know, I hope."

"As a matter of fact, at one of your guests."

"Indeed? How dreadfully unfortunate for you both. Which one, if I may ask?"

"Do you know a certain Lord Mellar? Jhereg?"

"Why, yes. It happens that I do."

"Might I inquire as to the circumstances?"

(Giggle.) *"You're starting to sound like him, boss."*

"Shut up, Loiosh."

Morrolan shrugged. "He sent word to me a few weeks ago that he'd acquired a certain book I've been interested in, and made an appointment to bring it by. He arrived with it . . . let me see . . . three days ago now. He has remained as my guest since that time."

"I presume he actually had the book?"

"You presume correctly." Morrolan indicated the tome he'd been reading as I entered. I looked at the cover, which bore a symbol I didn't recognize.

"What is it?" I asked him.

He looked at me for a moment, as if wondering whether I was trustworthy, or perhaps whether he should allow himself to be questioned; then he shrugged.

"Pre-Empire sorcery," he said.

I whistled in appreciation, as well as surprise. I glanced around the room quickly, but none of the others seemed astonished by this revelation. They had probably known all along. I keep finding things out about people, just when I think I know them. "Does the Empress know about this little hobby of yours?" I asked him.

He smiled a little. "Somehow I keep forgetting to mention it to her."

"How unlike you," I remarked.

When he didn't say anything, I asked, "How long have you been studying it?"

"Pre-Empire sorcery? It's been rather an interest of mine for a hundred years or so. In fact, the Empress undoubtedly knows; it isn't all that much of a secret. Naturally, I've never acknowledged it officially, but it's a bit like owning a Morganti blade: if they need an excuse to harass a fellow, they have one. Other than that they won't bother one about it. Unless, of course, one starts using it."

"Or unless one happens to be a Jhereg," I muttered.

"There is that, isn't there?"

I turned back to the main subject. "How did Mellar end up staying here, after he delivered the book?"

Morrolan looked thoughtful. "Would you mind terribly if I asked what this is all about?"

I glanced around the room again and saw that Sethra and Aliera also seemed interested. Aliera was sitting on the couch, an arm thrown casually across it, a wineglass in her other hand (Where had she gotten it?) held so that the light from the large ceiling lamp reflected off it and made pretty patterns on her cheek. She surveyed me coolly from under her eyelids, her head tilted slightly.

Sethra was looking at me steadily, intently. She had chosen a black upholstered chair which blended with her gown, and her pale white, undead skin shone out. I felt a tension in her, as if she had a feeling that something unpleasant was going on. Knowing Sethra, she probably did.

Morrolan sat at the other end of the couch from Aliera—relaxed, and yet looking as if he were posing for a painting. I shook my head.

"I'll tell you if you insist," I said, "but I'd rather find out a little more first, so I have a better idea of what I'm talking about."

"Or how much you feel like telling us?" asked Aliera, sweetly.

I couldn't repress a smile.

"I might point out," said Morrolan, "that if you want our help with anything, you're going to have to give us essentially the whole story."

"I'm aware of that," I said.

Morrolan gathered in the others' opinions with a glance. Aliera shrugged with her wineglass, as if it made no difference in the world to her. Sethra nodded, once.

Morrolan turned back to me. "Very well, then, Vlad. What exactly did you wish to know?"

"How was it that Mellar happened to stay here after delivering the book? You aren't in the habit of inviting Jhereg into your home."

Morrolan permitted himself another smile. "With a few exceptions," he said.

"Some of us are special."

"Shut up, Loiosh."

"Count Mellar," said Morrolan, "contacted me some four days ago. He informed me that he had a volume that he thought I'd want and politely suggested that he drop by and deliver it."

I interrupted. "Didn't it seem a bit odd that he'd hand it over himself, rather than have a flunky deliver it?"

"Yes, it did occur to me as odd. But after all, such a book *is* illegal and I made the assumption that he didn't want anyone to know that he had it. His employees, after all, were Jhereg. How could he trust them?" He paused for a moment, to see if I'd respond to the cut, but I let it go by. "In any case," he continued, "the Count appeared to be a very polite fellow. I did a bit of checking around on him, and found him to be a trustworthy sort, for a Jhereg. After deciding that he probably wouldn't make any trouble, I invited him to dine with me and a few other guests, and he accepted."

I glanced quickly at Aliera and Sethra. Sethra shook her head, indicating that she hadn't been there. Aliera was looking moderately interested. She nodded.

"I remember him," she said. "He was dull."

With that ultimate condemnation, I turned back to Morrolan, who continued. "The dinner went well enough that I felt no compunction about inviting him to the general party. I will admit that a few of my coarser guests, who don't think well of Jhereg, tried to give him trouble in one fashion or another, but he was quite friendly and went out of his way to avoid problems.

"So I gave him an invitation to stay here for seventeen days, if he cared to. I will admit to being somewhat startled when he accepted, but I assumed he wanted a short vacation or something. What else did you wish to know?"

I held up my hand, asking for a moment's grace while I sorted out this new information. Could he . . . ? What were the chances? How sure could Mellar be?

"Do you have any idea," I asked, "how he might have gotten his hands on the book in the first place?"

Morrolan shook his head. "The one stipulation that he had for returning it was that I make no effort to find out how he got it. You see, at one time it held a place in my library. It was, as you would say, 'lifted.' I might add this occurred before I started making improvements in my security system."

I nodded. Unfortunately, it was all fitting in rather well.

"Didn't that make you suspicious?" I asked.

"I assumed that it was a Jhereg who stole it, of course. But, as you should be aware of more than I, there are endless possibilities as to how this fellow could have received it, 'legitimately,' if you will. For example, the fellow who had taken it could have found that he couldn't sell it safely, and Count Mellar might have done him a favor by making sure that I never found out the details of the crime. Jhereg do tend to operate that way, you know."

I knew. "How long ago was this book stolen?"

"How long? Let me think . . . it would be . . . about ten years ago now, I believe."

"Damn," I muttered to myself, "so Kragar was right."

"What is it, Vlad?" asked Aliera. She was genuinely interested, now.

I looked at the three of them. How should I go about this? I had a sudden urge to answer, "Oh, nothing," get up, and see how close I could get to the

door before they stopped me. I didn't really like the idea of having the three
of them fly into a sudden rage—with me being the bearer of bad tidings and
all. Of course, I didn't really think any of them would hurt me, but . . .

I tried to think of an indirect approach and got nowhere.

"Suggestions, Loiosh?"

"Tell 'em straight out, boss. Then teleport."

"I can't teleport fast enough. Serious suggestions, Loiosh?"

Nothing. I had found a way to shut him up. Somehow my joy at this discovery was somewhat dimmed, under the circumstances.

"He's using you, Morrolan," I said, flatly.

" 'Using' me? How, pray tell?"

"Mellar is on the run from the Jhereg. He's staying here for one reason only:
he knows that no Jhereg can touch him while he's a guest in a Dragonlord's
home."

Morrolan's brows came together. I felt a storm brewing over the horizon.
"Are you quite certain of this?" he asked, mildly.

I nodded. "I think," I said slowly, "that if you were to do some checking,
you'd find that it was Mellar himself who took the book, or else hired someone
to take it. It all fits in. Yes, I'm sure."

I glanced over at Aliera. She was staring at Morrolan, with a look of shock
on her face. The cute dilettante who'd been sitting there seconds ago was gone.

"Of all the nerve!" she burst out.

"Oh, he's nervy all right," I told her.

Sethra cut in. "Vlad, how could Mellar have known that he'd be invited to
stay at Castle Black?"

I sighed inwardly. I had hoped that no one would ask me that. "That's no
trick. He must have done a study on Morrolan and found out what he'd have
to do to receive an invitation. I hate to say this, Morrolan, but you are rather
predictable in certain matters."

Morrolan shot me a look of disgust, but, fortunately, was not otherwise
affected. I noticed that Sethra was gently stroking the hilt of Iceflame. I shuddered. Aliera's eyes had turned gray. Morrolan was looking grim. He stood up
and began pacing in front of us. Aliera, Sethra, and I held our peace. After a
couple of trips, he said, "Are you certain he knows that the Jhereg is after
him?"

"He knows."

"And," Morrolan continued, "you are convinced that he would have been
aware of this when he first contacted me?"

"Morrolan, he planned it that way. I'll go even further; according to all the
evidence we have, he's been planning this whole thing for at least ten years."

"I see." He shook his head, slowly. His hand came to rest on the hilt of
Blackwand, and I shuddered again. After a time, he said, "You know how I
feel concerning treatment and safety of my guests, do you not?"

I nodded.

"Then you are no doubt aware that we cannot harm him in any way—at least, not until his seventeen days are up."

I nodded again. "Unless he leaves of his own free will," I put in.

He looked at me, suspiciously.

Aliera spoke, then. "You aren't going to just let him get away with this, are you?" she asked. There was just the hint of an edge to her voice. I suddenly wished that I had Kragar's ability to be unnoticeable.

"For today, my dear cousin, and thirteen more days after, he is perfectly safe here. After that," his voice suddenly turned cold and hard, "he's dead."

"I can't give you the details," I said, "but in thirteen days he will have irreparably damaged the Jhereg."

Morrolan shrugged, and Aliera gave me a brushing-off motion. So what? Who cared about the Jhereg, anyway? But I noticed Sethra nodding, as if she understood.

"And in thirteen days," she put in, "he'll be long gone."

Aliera gave a toss of her head and stood, flinging her cloak to the side and bringing her hand down to Pathfinder's hilt. "Let him try to hide," she said.

"You are missing the point," said Sethra. "I'm not doubting that you and Pathfinder will be able to track him down. What I'm saying is that with all the time he's had, he'll be able to, at least, make it difficult for you. It could take you days to find him if, for example, he goes out East. And in the meantime," her voice took on a cutting edge, "he'll have succeeded in using a Dragon to hide from the Jhereg."

This hit the two of them, and they didn't like it. But there was something else that was bothering me.

"Aliera," I said, "are you *sure* that there isn't anything he could do to prevent you from finding him with Pathfinder? It doesn't make sense that he'd work for this long on such an intricate scheme, only to let you and Morrolan track him down and kill him."

"As you may recall," she said, "I've only had Pathfinder for a few months, and it's hardly common knowledge that I have a Great Weapon at all. It's something that he couldn't have counted on. If I didn't have it, he could have figured on escaping us."

I accepted that. Yes, it was possible. No matter how carefully you plan things, there is always the chance that you could miss something important. This is a risky business we're in.

Aliera turned to Morrolan. "I don't think," she said, "that we should wait the rest of those seventeen days."

Morrolan turned away.

"Here it comes, boss."

"I know, Loiosh. Let's hope Sethra can handle it—and wants to."

"Don't you see," continued Aliera, "that this, this *Jhereg* is trying to make you nothing more than a bodyguard from his own House?"

"I'm quite aware of this, I assure you, Aliera," he answered softly.

"And that doesn't bother you? He's dishonoring the entire House of the Dragon! How *dare* he use a Dragonlord?"

"Ha!" said Morrolan. "How dare he use *me*? But it's rather obvious that he *does* dare, and equally obvious that he's gotten away with it." Morrolan's gaze was fixed on her. He was either challenging her or waiting to see if she would challenge him. Either way, I decided, it didn't much matter.

"He hasn't gotten away with it yet," said Aliera, grimly.

"And what exactly does that mean?" asked Morrolan.

"Just what it sounds like. He hasn't gotten away with anything. He's assuming that, just because he's a guest, he can insult you as much as he wants, and no one will touch him."

"And he is correct," said Morrolan.

"Is he?" asked Aliera. "Is he really? Are you sure?"

"Quite sure," said Morrolan.

Aliera matched stares with him for a while, then she said, "If you choose to ignore the insult to your honor, that's your business. But when an insult is given to the entire House of the Dragon, it's my business, too."

"Nevertheless," said Morrolan, "since the insult was delivered through me, it is my right, and my duty, to avenge it, don't you think?"

Aliera smiled. She sat back, relaxed, the very picture of one who's just had her worries removed. "Oh, good!" she said. "So you'll kill him after all!"

"Why certainly I shall," said Morrolan, showing his teeth, "thirteen days from now."

I glanced at Sethra to see how this was affecting her. She hadn't yet said anything, but the look on her face was far from pleasant. I was hoping that she'd be willing and able to mediate between the two of them if things started to get pushed too far. Looking at her, however, made me wonder if she had any such inclination.

Aliera wasn't smiling any more. Her hand gripped the hilt of Pathfinder, and her knuckles were white. "That," she explained, "is doing nothing. I will not permit a Jhereg to—"

"You will not touch him, Aliera," said Morrolan. "So long as I live, no guest in my house need fear for his life. I don't care who he is, why he's here; so long as I have extended him my welcome, he may consider himself safe.

"I have entertained my own blood enemies at my table, and arranged Morganti duels with them. I have seen the Necromancer speaking quietly to one who had been an enemy of hers for six incarnations. I have seen Sethra," he gestured toward her, "sitting across from a Dzurlord who had sworn to destroy her. I will not allow you, my own cousin, to cast my name in the mud; to make me an oathbreaker. Is that how you would preserve the honor of the House of the Dragon?"

"Oh, speak on, great protector of honor," she said. "Why not go all the way? Put up a poster outside the Jhereg barracks, saying that you are always willing to protect anyone who wants to run from their hired killers?"

He ignored the sarcasm. "And can you explain to me," he said, "how it is that we can defend our honor as a House if each member does not honor even his own words?"

Aliera shook her head and continued in a softer voice. "Don't you see, Morrolan, that there is a difference between the codes of honor, and of practice, that have come down from the traditions of the House of the Dragon, and your own custom? I'm not objecting to your having your little customs; I think it's a fine thing. But it isn't on the same level as the traditions of the House."

He nodded. "I understand that, Aliera," he said. "But it isn't just a 'custom' I'm talking about; it's an oath that I've sworn to make Castle Black a place of refuge. It would be different if we were at, say, Dzur Mountain."

She shook her head. "I just don't understand you. Of course you want to live by your oath, but does that mean that you have to allow yourself, and the House, to be used by it? He isn't just living under your oath, he's abusing it."

"That's true," agreed Morrolan. "But I'm afraid he's correct. There simply isn't any chance of my breaking it, and he realizes that. I'm rather surprised that you can't understand that."

I decided the time was right to intervene. "It seems to me that—"

"Silence, Jhereg," snapped Aliera. "This doesn't concern you."

I reconsidered.

"It isn't that I can't understand it," she went on to Morrolan, "it's just that I think your priorities are wrong."

He shrugged. "I'm sorry you feel that way."

It was the wrong thing to say. Aliera rose, and her eyes, I saw, had turned ice blue. "As it happens," she said, "it wasn't my oath, it was yours. If you were no longer master of Castle Black, we wouldn't have this problem, would we? And I don't recall anything in your oath that prevents a guest from attacking you!"

Morrolan's hand was white where he gripped the hilt of Blackwand. Loiosh dived under my cloak. I would have liked to do the same.

"That's true," said Morrolan, evenly. "Attack anyway."

Sethra spoke for the first time, gently. "Need I point out the guest laws, Aliera?"

She didn't answer. She stood, gripping her blade, and staring hard at Morrolan. It occurred to me then that she didn't want to attack Morrolan at all; she wanted him to attack her. I wasn't surprised at her next statement.

"And guest laws," Aliera said, "apply to all hosts. Even if they claim to be Dragons, but don't have the courage to avenge an insult done to all of us."

It almost worked, but Morrolan stopped himself. His tone matched the color of her eyes: "You may consider it fortunate that I have the rule I do, and that you are as much a guest as this Jhereg, although it is clear that he knows far more than you about the courtesy a guest owes a host."

"Ha!" cried Aliera, drawing Pathfinder.

"Oh, shit," I said.

"All right, Morrolan, then I release you from your oath, as regards me. It doesn't matter anyway, since I'd much rather be a dead dragon than a live teckla!" Pathfinder stood out like a short green rod of light, pulsating gently.

"You don't seem to realize, cousin," he said, "that you don't have power over my oath."

Now Sethra stood up. Thank the Lords of Judgment, she hadn't drawn Iceflame. She calmly stepped between them. "You both lose," she said. "Neither of you has any intention of attacking the other, and you both know it. Aliera wants Morrolan to kill her, which preserves her honor and breaks his oath, so that he may as well go ahead and kill Mellar. Morrolan wants Aliera to kill him, being the one to break guest-laws, so she can then go ahead and kill Mellar herself. I, however, have no intention of allowing either of you to be killed or dishonored, so you may as well forget the provocations."

They stood that way for a moment, then Morrolan allowed the ghost of a smile to pass over his lips. Aliera did the same. Loiosh peeked out from under my cloak, then resumed his position on my right shoulder.

Sethra turned to me. "Vlad," she said, "isn't it true that you are—" she stopped, reconsidered, and tried again, "—that you know the person who is supposed to kill Mellar?"

I rubbed my neck, which I discovered had become rather tense, and said drily, "I expect I could put a hand on him."

"Good. Maybe we should all start trying to think of ways to help out this fellow, instead of ways to goad ourselves into murdering each other."

Morrolan and Aliera both scowled at the idea of helping a Jhereg, then shrugged.

I gave a short prayer of thanks to Verra that I'd thought of asking Sethra to show up.

"How much time is there that the assassin can wait?" asked Sethra.

How the hell did she find out so much? I asked myself, for the millionth time since I'd known her. "Maybe a few days," I said.

"All right, what can we do to help?"

I shrugged. "The only thing I can think of is just what Aliera thought of earlier—tracing him with Pathfinder. The problem is that we need some way of getting him to leave soon enough, without, of course, forcing him to."

Aliera took her seat again, but Morrolan turned and headed for the door. "All things considered," he said, "I don't think it quite proper that I include myself in this. I trust you all," he looked significantly at Aliera, "not to violate my oath, but I don't think it would be right for me to conspire against my own guest. Excuse me." Bowing, he left.

Aliera picked up the threads of the conversation. "You mean, trick him into leaving?"

"Something like that. I don't know, maybe put a spell on him, so he thinks he's safe. Can that be done?"

Sethra looked thoughtful, but Aliera cut in before she could speak. "No, that won't do," she said. "I expect it could be done, but, in the first place, Morrolan would detect it. And, in the second place, we can't use any form of magic against him without violating Morrolan's oath."

"By Adron's Disaster!" I said, "you mean we can't trick him, either?"

"No, no," said Aliera. "We're free to convince him to leave on his own, even if we have to lie to do it. But we can't use magic against him. Morrolan doesn't see any difference between, for instance, using an energy bolt to blast him, or using a mind implant to make him leave."

"Oh, that's just charming," I said. "I don't suppose either of you has any idea of how we're going to accomplish this?"

They both shook their heads.

I stood up. "All right, I'll be heading back to my office. Please keep thinking about it, and let me know if you get anywhere."

They nodded and settled back, deep in discussion. I didn't think much of the chances of their actually coming up with something. I mean, they were both damn good at what they did, but what they did wasn't assassination. On the other hand, I could be surprised. In any case, it was certainly better having them work with me than against me.

I bowed, and left.

8

"There is no such thing as sufficient preparation."

I RETURNED TO MY office and allowed my stomach to recover from the aftereffects of the teleport. After about ten minutes, I contacted my secretary. *"Please ask Kragar to step in here,"* I communicated.

"But, boss—he went in five minutes ago."

I looked up and found him seated in his usual place and looking innocent. *"Never mind."*

I shook my head. "I really wish you'd stop doing that."

"Doing what?"

I sighed. "Kragar, Aliera is willing to help us."

"Good. Do you have a plan yet?"

"No, only the start of one. But Aliera, and, by the way, Sethra Lavode, are trying to come up with the rest of it."

He looked impressed. "Sethra? Not bad. What happened?"

"Nothing—but just barely."

"Eh?"

I gave him a report on what had occurred. "So," I concluded, "now we need to figure out how we're going to get Mellar to leave early."

"Well," he said thoughtfully, "you could ask the Demon."

"Oh, sure. And if he doesn't have any ideas, I'll ask the Empress. And—"

"What's wrong with asking the Demon? Since you're going to be talking to him anyway, why not take the op—"

"I'm going to what?"

"The Demon wants to meet with you, right away. A message came in just before you did."

"What does he want to meet with me about?"

"He didn't say. Maybe he's come across some information."

"Information he could just send over. Dammit, he'd better not be jogging my sword-arm. He knows better than that."

"Sure he does," snorted Kragar. "But what the hell are you going to do about it if he decides to do it anyway?"

"There is that, isn't there?"

He nodded.

"When, and where? No, let me guess, same time and place, right?"

"Half-right. Same place, but noon."

"Noon? But isn't it already—" I stopped, concentrated a moment, and got the time. By the Great Sea of Chaos, it was barely half an hour before noon! That whole conversation had taken less than an hour. Verra!

"That means he's buying me lunch, doesn't it?"

"Right."

"And it also means that we don't really have time to set up something, in case *he's* set up something."

"Right again. You know, Vlad, we'd be within our rights to just refuse to meet with him. You aren't bound by something like this."

"Do you think that's a good idea?"

He thought for a minute, then shook his head.

"Neither do I," I said.

"Well, would you like me to put someone in there as a guest? We could arrange for one or two people—"

"No. He'd pick up on it, and we can't let that happen at this point. It would indicate that we don't trust him. Which we don't, of course, but . . ."

"Yeah, I know."

He shrugged and changed the subject. "About this business with Aliera and Sethra, do you have any ideas on how we're going to convince Mellar to leave Castle Black?"

"Well," I said, "we could invite him to a business meeting."

Kragar chuckled. "Next idea," he said.

"I don't know. That's been the problem from the beginning, hasn't it?"

"Uh-huh."

I shrugged. "Maybe something will come up. By the way, if there's anything more we can do in terms of digging into Mellar's background, let's do it. I'd dearly love to find a weak spot in him just about now."

He nodded. "It would be nice, wouldn't it?"

"Dammit, he came from somewhere. The information we got from the Demon doesn't start until he joined the Jhereg. We don't know a damned thing before then."

"I know, but how are we supposed to dig up more than the Demon could?"

"I don't know . . . Yes! I do! Aliera! That was what I'd wanted her help with in the first place, and then when things got hot over there I never thought about asking her."

"Asking her what?"

"Well, among other things, she specializes in genetic research."

"So?"

"So tell me—what House was Mellar born into?"

"I assume Jhereg. What makes you think differently?"

"I don't, but we have no reason to be sure. If it is Jhereg, there's a chance that Aliera could lead us to his parents, and we could start digging there. If not, that would tell us something worthwhile in itself and might lead us in other directions."

"Okay. I guess that isn't something the Demon would have been able to check out. Are you going to contact her yourself, or do you want me to set up another appointment?"

I thought it over before answering. "You set it up," I decided. "As long as this mess continues, we do everything formally. Make it for this evening, early, if possible. If I'm still alive. Ask her to check him over."

"Okay, I'll take care of it. If you're dead, I'll apologize to her for you."

"Oh, good. That's a great load off my mind."

Once again, I had my back to the door. My right arm was next to my wineglass; I could get a dagger from my left arm-sheath and throw it well enough to hit a moving wine cork from fifteen feet away in less than half a second. Loiosh kept his eyes fixed on the door. I was keenly aware that, if I were, indeed, about to be removed, none of these things would really give me enough of an edge.

My palms, however, were dry. There were three reasons for this: first, I had been in many situations before where I might suddenly have to move at top speed to save my life. Second, I really didn't think it very likely that the Demon was going to take me out. There are simpler ways to do it, and I was pretty sure by this time that everything was legitimate. And third, I continually wiped my hands on the legs of my breeches.

"Here he comes, boss."

"Alone?"

"Two bodyguards, but they're waiting by the door."

The Demon slid smoothly into the seat across from me. "Good afternoon," he said. "How are things coming?"

"They're coming. I recommend the tsalmoth in garlic butter."

"As you say." He signaled over a waiter, who took our orders with enough respect to show that he knew who I, at least, was. The Demon picked out a light *Nyroth* wine to go along with it, showing that he also knew something about eating.

"Things are looking a little more urgent now, Vlad. May I call you Vlad?" he added.

"Tell him, 'no,' boss."

"Of course." I chuckled. "I'll call you 'Demon.'"

He smiled, without showing how bored he must have been at the remark. "As I was saying—things *are* starting to look serious. It seems that a few too many people know already. The best sorceresses in the Left Hand have figured out that someone big is interested in finding Mellar, but there wasn't any way to avoid that. On the other hand, there are a few others who are wondering about some cutbacks we've had to make in our operations. All it's going to take is for someone to start putting the two things together, and then things get unpleasant real fast."

"So, are you—" I stopped, as the soup came. Out of reflex, I passed my left hand over it briefly, but there wasn't any poison, of course. Poison is clumsy and unpredictable, and few Dragaerans knew enough about the metabolism of an Easterner to leave me seriously worried about it.

I continued when the waiter left. "Are you saying you want me to push it a bit?" I held down my annoyance; the last thing this side of Deathgate I wanted just then was for the Demon to get the idea that I was upset.

"As much as you can without risking mistakes. But that wasn't really what I wanted—I know you're moving as fast as you can."

Sure, he did. The soup was flat, I decided.

"We've learned something that may interest you," he continued.

I waited.

"Mellar is holed up in Castle Black."

He looked for a reaction from me, and, when he didn't get one, continued.

"Our sorcerers broke through about two hours ago, and I got in touch with your people right away. So, you can forget checking out East. The reason we couldn't find him for so long was because Castle Black is close to two hundred miles from Adrilankha—but, of course, you know that. You work for Morrolan, right?"

"Work for him? No. I'm on his payroll as a security consultant, nothing more."

He nodded. He worked on his soup for a while, then, "You didn't seem surprised when I told you where he was."

"Thank you very much," I said.

The Demon let me know that he had teeth and raised his glass in salute. Smiling, say the sages, comes from an early form of baring the teeth. While jhereg don't bare their teeth, Jhereg do. "Did you know?" asked the Demon, bluntly.

I nodded.

"I'm impressed," he said. "You move quickly."

I continued to wait, while finishing up my soup. I still didn't know why he was here, but I was quite sure that it wasn't in order to compliment me on my information sources, or to give me information he could have had sent over by a courier.

He picked up his wineglass and looked into it, swirled it around a little, and sipped it. Crazily, he suddenly reminded me of the Necromancer. "Vlad," he said, "I think we may have a possible conflict of interest developing here."

"Indeed?"

"Well, it is known that you are a friend of Morrolan. Now, Morrolan is harboring Mellar. It would seem that our goals, and his goals, might not run along the same paths."

I still didn't say anything. The waiter showed up with the main course, and I checked it, and started in. The Demon pretended not to notice my gesture. I pretended not to notice when he did the same thing.

He continued, after swallowing and making the obligatory murmur of satisfaction. "Things could get very unpleasant for Morrolan."

"I can't imagine how," I said, "unless you plan to start another Dragon-Jhereg war. And Mellar, no matter what he did, can't be worth that much."

Now it was the Demon who said nothing. I got a sinking feeling in the pit of my stomach.

I said slowly, "He *can't* be worth another Dragon-Jhereg war."

He still said nothing.

I shook my head. Would he really go ahead and try to nail Mellar right in Morrolan's castle? Gods! He was saying that he would! He'd bring every Dragon on Dragaera down on our heads. This could be worse than the last one. It was the reign of the Phoenix, which made the Dragons correspondingly higher on the Cycle. The higher a House is, the more fate tends to favor it. I don't know the why or how of that, but it works that way. The Demon knew it, too.

"Why?" I asked him.

"At this point," he said slowly, "I don't think that there is any need to start such a war. I think that it can be worked around, which is why I'm talking to you. But, I will say this: if I'm wrong, and the only options I can see are letting Mellar get away with this or starting another war, I'll start the war. Why? Because if we have a war, things will get bad, yes, very bad, but then it will be over. We know what to expect this time, and we'll be ready for it. Oh, sure, they'll hurt us. Perhaps badly. But we will recover, eventually—in a few thousand years.

"On the other hand, if Mellar gets away with this, there won't be an end to it. Ever. As long as House Jhereg lasts, we'll have to contend with thieves plotting after our funds. We'll be crippled forever."

His eyes became thin lines, and I saw his teeth clench for a moment. "*I* built us up after Adron's Disaster. *I* made a dispirited, broken House into a viable business again. I'm willing to see my work set back a thousand years, or ten thousand years if I have to, but I'm not willing to see us weakened forever."

He sat back. I let his remarks sink in. The worst thing was, he was right. If I were in his position, I would probably find myself making the same decision. I shook my head.

"You're right," I told him. "We have a conflict of interest. If you give me enough time, I'll finish my work. But I'm not going to let you nail someone in Castle Black. I'm sorry, but that's how it is."

He nodded, thoughtfully. "How much time do you need?"

"I don't know. As soon as he leaves Castle Black, I can get him. But I haven't come up with a way to get him to leave yet."

"Will two days do it?"

I thought that over. "Maybe," I said finally. "Probably not."

He nodded and was silent.

I used a piece of only slightly stale bread to get the rest of the garlic butter (I never said it was a good restaurant for *eating* in), and asked him, "What is your idea for avoiding the Dragon-Jhereg war?"

He shook his head, slowly. He wasn't going to give me any more information about that. Instead, he signaled the waiter over and paid him. "I'm sorry," he told me as the waiter walked away. "We'll have to do it without your cooperation. You could have been very helpful." He left the table and walked toward the door.

The waiter, I noticed, was returning with the change. I absently waved him away. That's when it hit me. The Demon would have realized that this outcome was possible, but wanted to give me a chance to save myself. Oh, shit. I felt the waves of panic start up, but forced them down. I wouldn't leave this place, I decided, until help arrived. I started to reach out for contact with Kragar.

The waiter hadn't caught my signal and was still approaching. I started to gesture him away again when Loiosh screamed a warning into my mind. I caught the flicker of motion almost at the same time. I pushed the table away from me and reached for a dagger at the same moment that Loiosh left my shoulder to attack. But I also knew, in that instant, that both of us would be too late. The timing had been perfect, the setup professional. I turned, hoping to at least get the assassin.

There was a gurgling sound as I turned and stood up. Instead of lunging at me, the "waiter" fell against me, then continued on to the floor. There was a large kitchen cleaver in his hand, and the point of a dagger sticking out of his throat.

I looked around the room as the screams started. It took me a while, but I finally located Kragar, seated at a table a few feet from mine. He stood up and walked over to me. I felt myself start trembling, but I didn't allow myself to fall back into my chair until I was sure the Demon had left.

He had. His bodyguards were gone, probably having been out the door before the assassin's body had fallen. Wise, of course. Any of his people left here were dead. Loiosh returned to my shoulder, and I felt him glancing around the room, as if to make any guilty party cower in shame. There would be none of them left now. He'd taken his best shot, and it had almost worked.

I sat down and trembled for a while.

"Thanks, Kragar. Were you there the whole time?"

"Yeah. As a matter of fact, you looked right through me a couple of times. So did the Demon. So did the waiters," he added sourly.

"Kragar, the next time you feel like ignoring my orders, do it."

He gave me his Kragar smile. "Vlad," he said, "never trust anyone who calls himself a demon."

"I'll remember that."

The Imperial guards would be showing up in a few minutes, and there were a few things I had to get done before they arrived. I was still trembling with unused adrenalin as I walked over to the kitchen, through it, and into the back office. The owner, a Dragaeran named Nethrond, was sitting behind his desk. He had been my partner in this place since I'd taken half-ownership of it in exchange for canceling out a rather impressive sum he owed me. I suppose he had no real reason to love me, but still . . .

I walked in, and he looked at me as if he were seeing Death personified.

Which, of course, he was. Kragar was behind me and stopped at the door to make sure no one came in to ask Nethrond to sign for an order of parsley or something.

I noticed he was trembling. Good. I no longer was.

"How much did he pay you, dead man?"

(Gulp) "Pay me? Who—?"

"You know," I said conversationally, "you've been a rotten gambler for as long as I've known you. That's what got you into this in the first place. Now, how much did he pay you?"

"B-b-b-but no one—"

I reached forward suddenly and grabbed his throat with my left hand. I felt my lips drawing up into a classic Jhereg sneer. "You are the only one, besides me, authorized to hire anyone in this place. There was a new waiter here today. I didn't hire him, therefore you did. It happened that he was an assassin. As a waiter, he was even worse than the fools you usually hire to drive customers away. Now, I think his main qualifications as a waiter were the gold Imperials you got for hiring him. I want to know how much."

He tried to shake his head in denial, but I was holding it too tightly. He started to speak the denial, but I squeezed that option shut. He tried to swallow; I relaxed enough to let him. He opened his mouth, closed it again, and then opened it and said, "I don't know what you—"

I discovered, with some surprise, that I had never resheathed the dagger that I'd drawn when first attacked. It was a nice tool; mostly point, and about seven inches long. It fitted well into my right hand, which is moderately rare for a Dragaeran weapon. I used it to poke him in the sternum. A small spot of blood appeared, soaking through the white chef's garment. He gave a small scream and seemed about to pass out. I was strongly reminded of our first conversation, when I'd let him know that I was his new partner and carefully outlined what would happen if the partnership didn't work out. His House was Jhegaala, but he was doing a good Teckla imitation.

He nodded, then, and managed to hand me a purse from next to him. I didn't touch it.

"How much is in it?" I asked.

He gurgled and said, "A th-thousand gold, M-milord."

I laughed shortly. "That isn't even enough to buy me out," I said. "Who approached you? Was it the assassin, the Demon, or a flunky?"

He closed his eyes as if he wanted me to disappear. I'd oblige him momentarily.

"It was the Demon," he said in a whisper.

"Really!" I said. "Well, I'm flattered that he takes such an interest in me."

He started whimpering.

"And he guaranteed that I'd be dead, right?"

He nodded miserably.

"And he guaranteed protection?"

He nodded again.
I shook my head sadly.

I called Kragar in to teleport us back to the office. He glanced at the body,
his face expressionless.
"Shame about that fellow killing himself, isn't it?" he said.
I had to agree.
"Any sign of guards?"
"No. They'll get here eventually, but no one is in any hurry to call them, and
this isn't their favorite neighborhood to patrol."
"Good. Let's get back home."
He started working the teleport. I turned back to the body.
"Never," I told it, "trust anyone who calls himself a demon."
The walls vanished around us.

9

"You can't put it together again unless you've torn it apart first."

OVER THE YEARS, I have developed a ritual that I go through after an attempt has been made to assassinate me. First, I return to my office by the fastest available means. Then I sit at my desk and stare off into space for a little while. After that I get very, very sick. Then I return to my desk and shake for a long time.

Sometime in there, while I'm alone and shaking, Cawti shows up, and she takes me home. If I haven't eaten, she feeds me. If it is practical, she puts me to bed.

This was the fourth time that I had almost had my tale of years snipped at the buttocks. It wasn't possible for me to sleep this time, since Aliera was expecting me. When I had recovered sufficiently to actually move, I went into the back room to do the teleport. I am a good enough sorcerer to do it myself when I have to, although generally I don't bother. This time I didn't feel like calling in anyone else. It wasn't that I didn't trust them. . . . Well, maybe it was.

I took out my enchanted dagger (a cheap, over-the-counter enchanted dagger, but better than plain steel), and began carefully drawing the diagrams and symbols that aren't at all necessary for a teleport, but *do* help settle one's mind down when one is feeling that one's magic might not be all it ought to be.

Cawti kissed me before I left and seemed to hang onto me a bit more than she had to. Or maybe not. I was feeling extraordinarily sensitive, just at the moment.

The teleport worked smoothly and left me in the courtyard. I spun quickly as I arrived, almost losing lunch in the process. No, there wasn't anyone behind me.

I walked toward the great double doors of the castle, looking carefully around. The doors swung open before me, and I had to repress an urge to dive away from them.

"Boss, would you settle down?"

"No."

"No one is going to attack you at Castle Black."

"So what?"

"So what's the point in being so jumpy?"

"It makes me feel better."

"Well, it bothers hell out of me."

"Tough."

"Take it easy, all right? I'll take care of you."

"I'm not doubting you, it's just that I feel like being jumpy, all right?"

"Not really."

"Then lump it."

He was right, however. I resolved to relax just a bit as I nodded to Lady Teldra. She pretended that there was nothing odd in my having her walk in front of me by five paces. I trusted Lady Teldra, of course, but this could be an impostor, after all. Well, it could, couldn't it?

I found myself in front of Aliera's chambers. Lady Teldra bowed to me and left. I clapped, and Aliera called to me to come in. I opened the door, letting it swing fully open, while stepping to the side. Nothing came out at me, so I risked a look inside.

Aliera was sitting by the back of the bed, staring off into space. I noted that, curled up as she was, she could still draw Pathfinder. I scanned the room carefully.

Entering, I moved a chair so my back was against the wall. Aliera's eyes focused on me, and she looked puzzled.

"Is something wrong, Vlad?"

"No."

She looked bemused, then quizzical. "You're quite sure," she said.

I nodded. If I were going to take someone out from that position, I thought, how would I go about it? Let's see. . . .

Aliera raised her hand suddenly, and I recognized the gesture as the casting of a spell.

Loiosh hissed with indignation as I hit the floor rolling, and Spellbreaker snapped out.

I didn't feel any of the tingling that normally accompanies Spellbreaker's intercepting magic aimed at me, however. I lay there, looking at Aliera, who was watching me carefully.

"What's gotten into you, anyway?" asked Aliera.

"What was that spell?"

"I wanted to check your genetic background," she said drily. "I thought I'd look for some latent Teckla genes."

I cracked up. This just broke me up completely. I sat on the floor, my body shaking with laughter, and felt tears stream down my face. Aliera, I'm sure, was trying to figure out whether to join me, or to cure me.

I settled down, finally, feeling much better. I got back into the chair and caught my breath. I wiped the tears from my face, still chuckling. Loiosh flew quickly over to Aliera, licked her right ear, and returned to my shoulder.

"Thanks," I said, "that helped."

"What was the problem, anyway?"

I shook my head, then shrugged. "Someone just tried to kill me," I explained. She looked more puzzled than ever. "So?"

That almost broke me up again, but I contained it, with great effort.

"It's my latent Teckla genes," I said.

"I see."

Gods! What a nightmare! I was pulling out of it, though. I started to think about business again. I had to make sure that Mellar didn't go through what I'd just gone through. "Were you able to do whatever it is you do on Mellar?" I asked.

She nodded.

"Did he detect it?"

"No chance," she said.

"Good. And did you learn anything of interest?"

She looked strange again, just as she had when I first walked in. "Vlad," she asked me, "what made you ask about his genes? I mean, it is a little specialty of mine, but everyone has his little specialties. Why did you happen to ask about this?"

I shrugged. "I haven't been able to learn anything about his background, and I thought you might be able to learn something about his parents that would help. It isn't something that's easily found out, you know. Normally, I don't have any trouble finding everything I need to about a person, but this guy isn't normal."

"I'll agree with you there!" she said fervently.

"What does that mean? You found something?"

She nodded significantly in the direction of the wine cabinet. I rose and fetched a bottle of Ailour dessert wine, and presented it to her. She held it for a moment, did a quick spell to chill it down, and returned it to me. I opened it and poured. She sipped hers.

"I found out something, all right."

"You're sure he didn't detect it?"

"He had no protection spells up, and it's really quite easy to do."

"Good! So, what is it?"

She shook her head. "Gods, but it's weird!"

"What is? Will you tell me already? You're as bad as Loiosh."

"Remember that crack next time you roll over in bed and find a dead teckla on your pillow."

I ignored him. Aliera didn't rise to the bait. She just shook her head in puzzlement. "Vlad," she said slowly, "he has Dragon genes."

I digested that. "You're sure? No possible doubt?"

"None. If I'd wanted to take more time, I could have told you which line of the Dragons. But that isn't all—he's a cross-breed."

"Indeed?" was all I said. Cross-breeds were rare, and almost never accepted by any House except the Jhereg. On the other hand, they had an easier time of it than Easterners, so I wasn't about to get all teary-eyed for the fellow.

She nodded. "He's clearly got three Houses in his genes. Dragon and Dzur on one side, and Jhereg on the other."

"Hmmm. I see. I wasn't aware that you could identify Jhereg genes as such. I'd thought that they were just a mish-mash of all the other Houses."

She smiled. "If you get a mish-mash, as you put it, together for enough generations, it becomes identifiable as something in and of itself."

I shook my head. "This is all beyond me, anyway. I don't even know how you can pick out a gene, much less recognize it as being associated with a particular House."

She shrugged. "It's something like a mind-probe," she said, "except that you aren't looking for the mind. And, of course, you have to go much deeper. That's why it's so hard to detect, in fact. Anyone can tell when his mind is being examined, unless the examiner is an expert, but having your finger mind-probed is a bit trickier to spot."

This image came to mind of the Empress, with the Orb circling her head, holding up a severed finger and saying, "Now talk! What till have you been in?" I chuckled, and missed Aliera's next statement.

"I'm sorry, Aliera, what was that?"

"I said that determining a person's House isn't hard at all if you know what you're looking for. Surely you realize that each animal is different, and—"

"Wait a minute! 'Each animal is different,' sure. But we aren't talking about animals, we're talking about Dragaerans." I repressed a nasty remark at that point, since Aliera didn't seem to be in the right mood for it.

"Oh, come on, Vlad," she answered. "The names of the Houses aren't accidents."

"What do you mean?"

"Okay, for instance, how do you suppose the House of the Dragon got its name?"

"I guess I've always assumed it was because you have characters similar to that of dragons. You're bad-tempered, reptilian, used to getting your own way—"

"Hmmmph! I guess I asked for that, eater of carrion. But you're wrong. Since I'm of the House of the Dragon, it means that if you go back a few hundred thousand generations, you'll find actual dragons in my lineage."

And you're proud of this? I thought, but didn't say. I must have looked as shocked as I felt, though, because she said, "I'd thought you realized this."

"It's the first I've heard of it, I assure you. Do you mean, for example, that Chreothas are descended from actual chreothas?"

She looked puzzled. "Not 'descended' exactly. It's a bit more complicated than that. All Dragaerans are initially of the same stock. But things changed when—How shall I put this? All right: Certain, uh, beings once ruled on Dragaera. They were a race called Jenoine. They used the Dragaeran race (and, I might add, the Easterners) as stock to practice genetic experimentation. When they left, the Dragaerans divided into tribes based on natural kinship, and the Houses were formed from this after the formation of the Empire by Kieron the Conqueror."

She didn't add "my ancestor," but I felt it anyway.

"The experiments they did on Dragaerans involved using some of the wildlife of the area as a gene pool."

I interrupted. "But Dragaerans can't actually crossbreed with these various animals, can they?"

"No."

"Well, then how—"

"We don't really know how they went about it. That's one thing I've been researching myself, and I haven't solved it yet."

"What did these—Jenine?"

"Jen-o-ine."

"Jenoine. What did these Jenoine do to Easterners?"

"We aren't really sure, to tell you the truth. One popular theory is that they bred in psionic ability."

"Hmmm. Fascinating. Aliera, has it ever occurred to you that Dragaerans and Easterners could be of the same stock originally?"

"Don't be absurd," she said sharply. "Dragaerans and Easterners can't interbreed. In fact, there are some theories which claim that Easterners aren't native to Dragaera at all, but were brought in by the Jenoine from somewhere else to use as controls for their tests."

" 'Controls?' "

"Yes. They gave the Easterners psionic abilities equal to, or almost equal to, that of Dragaerans. Then they started messing around with Dragaerans, and sat back to see what the two races would do to each other."

I shuddered. "Do you mean that these Jenoine might still be around, watching us—"

"No," she said flatly. "They're gone. Not all of them are destroyed, but they rarely come to Dragaera anymore—and when they do, they can't dominate us as they did long ago. In fact, Sethra Lavode fought with and destroyed one only a few years ago."

My mind flashed back to my first meeting with Sethra. She had looked a bit worried, and said, "I can't leave Dzur Mountain just now." And later, she had looked exhausted, as if she'd been in a fight. One more old mystery cleared up.

"How were they destroyed? Did the Dragaerans turn on them?"

She shook her head. "They had other interests besides genetics. One of them was the study of Chaos. We'll probably never know exactly what happened, but, in essence, an experiment got out of control, or else an argument came up between some of them, or something, and boom! We have a Great Sea of Amorphia, a few new gods, and no more Jenoine."

So much, I decided, for my history lesson for today. I couldn't deny being interested, however. It wasn't really my history, but it had some kind of fascination for me, nevertheless. "That sounds remarkably like what happened to Adron on a smaller scale, a few years back. You know, the thing that made the Sea of Chaos up north, the Interregnum. . . . Aliera?"

She was looking at me strangely and not saying anything.

A light broke through. "Say!" I said, "That's what pre-Empire sorcery is!

The sorcery of the Jenoine." I stopped long enough to shudder, as I realized the implications. "No wonder the Empire doesn't like people studying it."

Aliera nodded. "To be more precise, pre-Empire sorcery is direct manipulation of raw chaos—bending it to one's will."

I found myself shuddering again. "It sounds rather dangerous."

She shrugged, but didn't say more. Of course, she would see it a little differently. Aliera's father, I had learned, was none other than Adron himself, who had accidentally blown up the old city of Dragaera and created a sea of amorphia on its site.

"I hope," I said, "that Morrolan isn't planning on doing another number like your father did."

"He couldn't."

"Why not? If he's using pre-Empire sorcery . . ."

She grimaced prettily. "I'll correct what I said before. Pre-Empire sorcery is not *exactly* direct manipulation of chaos; it's one step removed. Direct manipulation is something else again—and that's what Adron was doing. He had the ability to use, in fact, the ability to *create* amorphia. If you combine that with the skills of pre-Empire sorcery . . ."

"And Morrolan doesn't have the skill to create amorphia? Poor fellow. How can he live without it?"

Aliera chuckled. "It isn't a skill one can learn. It goes back to genes again. So far as I know, it is only the e'Kieron line of the House of the Dragon that holds the ability—although it is said that Kieron himself never used it."

"I wonder," I said, "how genetic heritage interacts with reincarnation of the soul."

"Oddly," said Aliera e'Kieron.

"Oh. So, anyway, that explains where the Dragaeran Houses come from. I'm surprised that the Jenoine wasted their time breeding an animal like the Jhereg into some Dragaerans," I said.

"That's another one I owe you, boss."

"Shut up, Loiosh."

"Oh," said Aliera, "but they didn't."

"Eh?"

"They played around with jheregs and found a way to put human-level intelligence into a brain the size of a rednut, but they never put any jhereg genes into Dragaerans."

"There, Loiosh. You should feel grateful to the Jenoine, for—"

"Shut up, boss."

"But I thought you said—"

"The Jhereg is the exception. They didn't start out as a tribe the way the others did."

"Then how?"

"Okay, we have to go back to the days when the Empire was first being formed. In fact, we have to go back even further. As far as we know, there were originally about thirty distinct tribes of Dragaerans. We don't know the exact number, since there were no records being kept back then.

"Eventually, many of them died off. Finally, there were sixteen tribes left. Well, fifteen, plus a tribe of the Teckla, which really didn't do much of anything."

"They invented agriculture," I cut in. "That's something."

She brushed it aside. "The tribes were called together, or parts of each tribe, by Kieron the Conqueror and a union of some of the best Shamans of the time, and they got together to drive the Easterners out of some of the better lands."

"For farming," I said.

"Now, in addition to the tribes, there were a lot of outcasts. Many of them came from the tribe of the Dragon—probably because the Dragons had higher standards than the others—" She tossed her head as she said this; I let it go by.

"Anyway," she continued, "there were a lot of outcasts, mostly living in small groups. While the other tribes were coming together under Kieron, a certain ex-Dragon named Dolivar managed to unite most of these independent groups—primarily by killing any of the leaders who didn't agree with the idea.

"So they got together, and, I guess more sarcastically than anything else, they began calling themselves 'the tribe of the Jhereg.' They lived mostly off the other tribes—stealing, looting, and then running off. They even had a few Shamans."

"Why didn't the other tribes get together to wipe them out?" I asked.

She shrugged. "A lot of the tribes wanted to, but Kieron needed scouts and spies for the war against the Easterners, and the Jheregs were obviously the only ones who could manage it properly."

"Why did the Jheregs agree to help?"

"I guess," she remarked drily, "Dolivar decided it was preferable to being wiped out. He met with Kieron before the Great March started, and got an agreement that, if his 'tribe' helped out, they would be included in the Empire when it was over."

"I see. So that's how the Jhereg became part of the Cycle. Interesting."

"Yes. It also ended up killing Kieron."

"What did?"

"The bargain; the strain of forcing the tribes to adhere to the bargain after the fighting was over and the other tribes no longer saw that the Jhereg could be of any value to them. He was eventually killed by a group of Lyorn warriors and Shamans who decided that he was responsible for some of the problems the Jheregs brought to the Empire."

"So," I said, "we owe it all to Kieron the Conqueror, eh?"

"Kieron," she agreed, "and this Jhereg chieftain named Dolivar who forced the deal in the first place, and then forced the others in his tribe to agree to it."

"Why is it, I wonder, that I've never heard of this Jhereg chieftain? I don't know of any House records on him, and you'd think he'd be considered some kind of hero."

"Oh, you can find him if you dig enough. As you know better than I, The Jhereg isn't too concerned with heroes. The Lyorns have records of him."

"Is that how you found out all this?"

She shook her head, "No. I learned a lot of it talking to Sethra. And some I remembered, of course."

"*What!?*"

Aliera nodded. "Sethra was there, as Sethra. I've heard her age given at ten thousand years. Well, that's wrong. It's off by a factor of twenty. She is, quite literally, older than the Empire."

"Aliera, that's impossible! Two hundred thousand years? That's ridiculous!"

"Tell it to Dzur Mountain."

"But . . . and you! How could *you* remember?"

"Don't be a fool, Vlad. Regression, of course. In my case, it's a memory of past lives. Did you think reincarnation was just a myth, or a religious belief, like you Easterners have?"

Her eyes were glowing strangely, as I fought to digest this new information.

"I've seen it through my own eyes—lived it again.

"I was there, Vlad, when Kieron was backed into a corner by an ex-Dragon named Dolivar, who had been Kieron's brother before he shamed himself and the whole tribe. Dolivar was tortured and expelled.

"I share the guilt there, too, as does Sethra. Sethra was supposed to hamstring the yendi, but she missed—deliberately. I saw, but I didn't say anything. Perhaps that makes me responsible for my brother's death, later. I don't know . . ."

"Your brother!" This was too much.

"My brother," she repeated. "We started out as one family. Kieron, Dolivar, and I."

She turned fully toward me, and I felt a rushing in my ears as I listened to her spin tales that I couldn't quite dismiss as mad ravings or myths.

"I," she said, "was a Shaman in that life, and I think I was a good one, too. I was a Shaman, and Kieron was a warrior. He is still there, Vlad, in the Paths of the Dead. I've spoken to him. He recognized me.

"Three of us. The Shaman, the warrior—and the traitor. By the time Dolivar betrayed us, we no longer considered him a brother. He was a Jhereg, down to his soul.

"His soul . . ." she repeated, trailing off.

"Yes," she continued, " 'Odd' is the right way to describe the way heredity of the body interacts with reincarnation of the soul. Kieron was never reincarnated. I have been born into a body descended from the brother of my soul. And you—" she gave me a look that I couldn't interpret, but I suddenly knew what was coming. I wanted to scream at her not to say it, but, throughout the millennia, Aliera has always been just a little faster than me. "—You became an Easterner, brother."

10

"One man's mistake is another man's opportunity."

ONE DAMN THING AFTER another.

I returned to my office and looked at nothing in particular for a while. I needed time, probably days, to get adjusted to this information. Instead, I had about ten minutes.

"Vlad?" said Kragar. "Hey, Vlad!"

I looked up. After a moment, I focused in on Kragar, who was sitting opposite me and looking worried.

"What is it?" I asked him.

"That's what I was wondering."

"Huh?"

"Is something wrong?"

"Yes. No. Hell, Kragar, I don't know."

"It sounds serious," he said.

"It is. My whole world has just been flipped around, and I haven't sorted it out yet."

I leaned toward him, then, and grabbed his jerkin. "Just one thing, old friend: If you value your sanity, never, but *never* have a deep, heart-to-heart talk with Aliera."

"Sounds *really* serious."

"Yeah."

We sat in silence for a moment. Then I said, "Kragar?"

"Yeah, boss?"

I bit my lip. I'd never broached this subject before, but . . .

"How did you feel when you were kicked out of the House of the Dragon?"

"Relieved," he said, with no hesitation. "Why?"

I sighed. "Never mind."

I tried to force the mood and the contemplation from me and almost succeeded. "What's on your mind, Kragar?"

"I was wondering if you found out anything," he said, in all innocence.

Did I find out anything? I asked myself. The question began to reverberate in my head, and I heard myself laughing. I saw Kragar giving me a funny look; worried. I kept laughing. I tried to stop, but couldn't. Ha! Did I learn anything?

Kragar leaned across the desk and slapped me once—hard.

"Hey boss," said Loiosh, *"cut it out."*

I sobered up. *"Easy for you to say,"* I told him. *"You haven't just learned that you once were everything you hate—the very kind of person you despise."*

"So? You haven't just learned that you were supposed to be a blithering idiot, except that some pseudo-god decided to have a little fun with your ancestors," Loiosh barked back.

I realized that he had a point. I turned to Kragar. "I'm all right now. Thanks."

He still looked worried. "Are you sure?"

"No."

He rolled his eyes. "Great. So, if you can avoid having hysterics again, what *did* you learn?"

I almost did have hysterics again, but controlled myself before Kragar could slap me again. What had I learned? Well, I wasn't going to tell him that, or that, uh, or that either. What did that leave? Oh, of course.

"I learned that Mellar is the product of three Houses," I said. I gave him a report on that part of the discussion.

He pondered the information.

"Now that," he said, "is interesting. A Dzur, eh? And a Dragon. Hmmm. Okay, why don't you see what you can dig up about the Dzur side, and I'll work on the Dragons."

"I think it would make more sense to do it the other way around, since I have some connections in the Dragons."

He looked at me closely. "Are you quite sure," he said, "that you want to use those connections just at the moment?"

Oh. I thought about that, and nodded. "Okay, I'll check the Dzur records. What do you think we should look for?"

"I'm not sure," he said. Then he cocked his head for a minute and seemed to be thinking about something, or else he was in psionic contact. I waited.

"Vlad," he said, "do you have any idea what it's like to be a cross-breed?"

"I know it isn't as bad as being an Easterner!"

"Isn't it?"

"What are you getting at? You know damn well what I've had to put up with."

"Oh, sure, Mellar isn't going to have all the problems you have, or had. But suppose he inherited the true spirit of each House. Do you have any idea how frustrating it would be for a Dzur to be denied his place in the lists of heroes of the House, if he was good enough to earn it? Or a Dragon, denied the right to command all the troops he was competent to lead? The only House that would take him is us, and Hell, Vlad, there are even some Jhereg that would make him eat Dragon-dung. Sure, Vlad; you have it worse in fact, but he can't help but feel that he's entitled to better."

"And I'm not?"

"You know what I mean."

"I suppose," I conceded. "I see your point. Where are you going with it?"

Kragar got a puzzled look on his face. "I don't know, exactly, but it's bound to have an effect on his character."

I nodded. "I'll keep that in mind."

"Okay, I'll get started right away."

"Fine. Oh, could you try to get that crystal with Mellar's face in it back from Daymar? I may want to use it."

"Sure. When do you need it?"

"Tomorrow morning will be fine. I'm taking the evening off. I'll start on it tomorrow."

Kragar's eyes were sympathetic, which was rare. "Sure, boss. I'll cover for you here. See you tomorrow."

I ate mechanically and thanked the Lords of Judgment that it was Cawti's night to cook and clean. I didn't think I'd be up to it.

After eating, I rose and went into the living room. I sat down and started trying to sort out some things. I didn't get anywhere. Presently, Cawti came in and sat down next to me. We sat in silence for a while.

I tried to deny what Aliera had told me, or pass it off as a combination of myth, misplaced superstition, and delusion. Unfortunately, it made too much sense for that to work. Why, after all, had Sethra Lavode been so friendly to me, a Jhereg and an Easterner? And Aliera obviously believed all of this, or why had she treated me as almost an equal on occasion?

But, more than that was the undeniable fact that it *felt* true. That was the really frightening thing—somewhere, deep within me, doubtless in my "soul," I knew that what Aliera had said was true.

And that meant—what? That the thing that had driven me into the Jhereg— my hatred of Dragaerans—was in fact a fraud. That my contempt for Dragons wasn't a feeling of superiority for my system of values over theirs, but was in fact a feeling of inadequacy going back, how long? Two hundred thousand years? Two hundred and fifty thousand years? By the multi-jointed fingers of Verra!

I became conscious of Cawti holding my hand. I smiled at her, a bit wanly perhaps.

"Want to talk about it?" she asked, quietly.

That was another good question. I wasn't sure if I wanted to talk about it or not. But I did, haltingly, over the course of about two hours. Cawti was quietly sympathetic, but didn't seem really upset.

"Really, Vlad, what's the difference?"

I started to answer, but she stopped me with a shake of her head. "I know. You've thought that it was being an Easterner that made you what you are, and now you're wondering. But being human is only one aspect, isn't it? The fact that you had an earlier life as a Dragaeran—maybe several, in fact— doesn't change what you've gone through in this life."

"No," I admitted. "I suppose not. But—"

"I know. Tell you what, Vlad. After this is all over and forgotten, maybe a year from now, we'll go talk to Sethra. We'll find out more about what happened and maybe, if you want to, she'll take you back to that time, and you can experience it again. *If* you want to. But in the meantime, forget it. You are who you are, and whatever went into making that is all to the good, as far as I'm concerned."

I squeezed her hand, glad that I'd discussed it with her. I felt a bit more relaxed and started to feel tired. I kissed Cawti's hand. "Thanks for the meal," I said.

She raised her eyebrow. "I'll bet you don't even know what it was," she said.

I thought for a minute. Jhegaala eggs? No, she'd made that yesterday.

"Hey!" I said. "It was *my* night to do the cooking, wasn't it?"

She grinned broadly. "Sure was, comrade. I've tricked you into owing me still another one. Clever, aren't I?"

"Damn," I said.

She shook her head in mock sadness. "That makes it, let me see now, about two hundred and forty-seven favors you owe me."

"But who's counting, right?"

"Right."

I stood up then, still holding her hand. She followed me into the bedroom, where I paid back her favor, or she did me another one, or we did one for each other, depending on exactly how one counts these things.

The servants of Lord Keleth admitted me to his castle with obvious distaste. I ignored them.

"The Duke will see you in his study," said the butler, looking down at me.

He held out his hand for my cloak; I gave him my sword instead. He seemed surprised, but took it. The trick to surviving a fight with a Dzur hero is not to have one. The trick to not having one is to seem as helpless as possible. Dzur heroes are reluctant to fight when the odds aren't against them.

I'd been proud of the scheme that had led me here. It was nothing unusual, of course, but it was good, solid, low-risk, and had a high probability of gain. Most important, it was very—well—*me*. I'd been worried that my encounter with Aliera had dulled my edge, somehow changed me, made me less able to conceive and execute an elegant plan. The execution of this one was still unresolved, but I was no longer worried about the conception.

I was escorted to the study. I noted signs of disrepair along the way: chipping grate on the floor, cracks in the ceiling, places along the wall that had probably once held expensive tapestries.

The butler ushered me into the study. The Duke of Keletharan was old and what passes for "squat" in a Dragaeran, meaning that his shoulders were a bit broader than usual, and you could actually see the muscles in his arms. His face was smooth (Dzurlords don't go in for wrinkles, I guess), and his eyes had that bit of upward slant associated with the House. His eyebrows were remarkably bushy, and he would have had a wispy white beard, if Dragaerans had beards. He was seated in a straight-backed chair with no arms. A broadsword hung at his side, and a wizard's staff was leaning against the desk. He didn't invite me to sit down; I did anyway. It is best to get certain things established at the beginning of a conversation. I saw his lips tighten, but that was all. Good. Score one for our side.

"Well, Jhereg, what is it?" he asked.

"My lord, I hope I didn't disturb you!"

"You did."

"A small matter has come to my attention which requires that I speak with you."

Keleth looked up at the butler, who bowed to us and left. The door snicked shut behind him. Then the Duke allowed himself to look disgusted. "The 'small matter,' no doubt, being four thousand gold Imperials."

I tried to look like I was trying to look apologetic. "Yes, my lord. According to our records, it was due over a month ago. Now, we have tried to be patient, but—"

"Patient, hell!" he snapped. "At the interest rates you charge, I'd think you could stand to hold off a little while with a man who's having a few minor financial troubles."

That was a laugh. As far as I could tell, his troubles were anything but "minor," and it was doubtful that they would end any time in the near future. I decided, however, that it wouldn't be politic to mention this, or to suggest that he wouldn't be having these problems at all if he could control his fondness for s'yang-stones. Instead, I said, "With all respect, my lord, it seems that a month is a reasonable length of time to hold off. And, again with all respect, you knew the interest rates when you came to us for help."

"I came to you for 'help,' as you put it, because—never mind." He had come to us for "help," as I'd put it, because we had made it clear to him that if he didn't, we would make sure that the whole Empire, particularly the House of the Dzur, knew that he couldn't control his urge to gamble, or pay off his debts when he lost. Perhaps having a reputation as a rotten gambler would have been the worst thing about it, to him.

I shrugged. "As you wish," I said. "Nevertheless, I must insist—"

"I tell you I just don't have it," he exploded. "What else can I say? If I had the gold, I'd give it to you. If you keep this up, I swear by the Imperial Phoenix that I'll go to the Empire and let them know about a few untaxed gambling games I'm aware of, and certain untaxed moneylenders."

Here is where it is helpful to know whom you are dealing with. In most such cases, I would have carefully let him know that if he did that, his body would be found within a week, probably behind a lower-class brothel, and looking as if he were killed in a fight with a drunken tavern brawler. I've used this technique before on Dzur heroes, and with good effect. It isn't the idea of being killed which scares them, it is the thought of people thinking that they'd been killed in a tavern brawl by some nameless Teckla.

I knew this would frighten Keleth, but it would also send him into a murderous rage, and the fact that I was "unarmed and helpless" might not stop him. Also, if he didn't kill me on the spot, it would certainly guarantee that he'd carry out his threat of going to the Empire. Clearly, a different approach was called for.

"Oh, come now, Lord Keleth," I said. "What would *that* do to your reputation?"

"No more than it would do to it to have you expose my personal finances anyway, for not paying off your blood money."

Dzur tend to be careless with terms, but I didn't correct him. I gave him my patient-man-trying-to-be-helpful-but-almost-exasperated sigh. "How much time do you need?"

"Another month, maybe two."

I shook my head, sadly. "I'm afraid that's quite impossible. I guess you'll just have to go to the Empire. It means that one or two of our games will have to find new locations, and a certain moneylender will have to take a short vacation, but I assure you that it won't hurt us nearly as much as it will hurt you."

I stood up, bowed low, and turned to leave. He didn't rise to see me out, which I thought was rude, but understandable, under the circumstances. Just before my hand touched the doorknob, I stopped, and turned around. "Unless—"

"Unless what?" he asked, suspiciously.

"Well," I lied, "it just occurred to me that there may be something you could help me out with."

He stared at me, long and hard, trying to guess what kind of game I was playing. I kept my face expressionless. If I'd wanted him to know the rules, I'd have written them out.

"And what is that?" he asked.

"I'm looking for a little information that involves the history of your House. I could find out myself, I suppose, but it would take a little work that I don't feel like doing. It is possible, I'm sure, for you to find out. In fact, you might even know already. If you could help me, I'd appreciate it."

He was still suspicious, but he was beginning to sound eager, too. "And what form," he asked, "will this 'appreciation' take?"

I pretended to think it over. "I think I could arrange for a two-month extension for you. In fact, I'd even go so far as to freeze the interest—if you can find this information for me quickly enough."

He chewed on his lower lip for a while, thinking it over, but I knew I had him. This was too good a chance for him to pass up. I'd planned it that way.

"What is it you want to know?" he said at last.

I reached into an inner pocket of my cloak and removed the small crystal I'd gotten back from Daymar. I concentrated on it, and Mellar's face appeared. I showed it to him.

"This person," I said. "Do you know him, or could you find out who he is, what connection he has with the House of the Dzur, or who his parents were?

Anything you can find out would be helpful. We know that he has some connection with your House. You can see it in his face, if you look closely."

Keleth's face went white as soon as he saw Mellar. I was surprised by the reaction. Keleth knew him. His lips became a thin line and he turned away.

"Who is he?" I asked.

"I'm afraid," said Keleth, "that I can't help you."

The question at that point wasn't "Should I press?" or even, "How much should I press?" It was, rather, "How should I press?" I decided to continue the game I'd started.

I shrugged and put the crystal away. "I'm sorry to hear that," I said. "As you wish. I've no doubt that you have good reasons for not wishing to share your information. Still, it is a shame that your good name must be befouled." I turned away again.

"Wait, I—"

I turned back to him. I was beginning to get dizzy. He seemed to be struggling with himself. I stopped worrying; I could see which side would win.

His face was a mask of twisted rage, as he said, "Damn you, Jhereg! You can't do this to me!"

There was, of course, nothing to say to this blatantly incorrect statement of our positions. I waited patiently.

He sank back into his chair, and covered his face with his hands. "His name," he said at last, "is Leareth. I don't know where he came from, or who his parents are. He appeared twelve years ago and joined our House."

"Joined your House? How can one join the House of the Dzur?" That was startling. I'd thought only the Jhereg allowed one to buy a title.

Lord Keleth looked at me as if he were about to snarl. I suddenly recalled Aliera's contention that the Dzurlords were descended, in part, from actual dzur. I could believe it.

"To join the House of the Dzur," he explained in the most vicious monotone I've ever heard, "you must defeat, in equal combat, seventeen champions chosen by the House." His eyes suddenly turned bleak. "I was the fourteenth. He is the only man I can remember hearing of who has succeeded since the Interregnum."

I shrugged. "So, he became a Dzurlord. I don't see what is so secret about that."

"We later learned," said Keleth, "something of his origins. He was a crossbreed. A mongrel."

"Well, yes," I said slowly, "I can see where that could be a touch annoying, but—"

"And then," he interrupted, "after he'd only been a Dzur for two years, he just gave up all his titles and joined House Jhereg. Can't you see what that means? He made fools of us! A mongrel can defeat the best the House of the Dzur has, and then chooses to throw it all away—" He stopped and shrugged.

I thought it over. This Leareth must be one hell of a swordsman.

"It's funny," I said, "that I've never heard of this incident. I've been investigating this fellow pretty thoroughly."

"It was kept secret by the House," said Keleth. "Leareth promised us that he'd have the whole Empire told of the story if he was killed or if any Dzur attempted to harm him. We'd never be able to live it down."

I felt a sudden desire to laugh out loud, but I controlled it for health reasons. I was starting to like this guy Mellar, or Leareth, or whatever. I mean, for the past twelve years, he'd had the entire House of Heroes by the balls. The two most important things to the House of the Dzur, as to an individual Dzurlord, are honor and reputation. And this Mellar had managed to play one off against the other.

"What happens if someone else kills him?" I asked.

"We have to hope it looks like an accident," he said.

I shook my head, and stood up. "Okay, thanks. You've given me what I needed. You can forget about paying the loan for two months, and the interest. I'll handle the details. And if you ever need my help for something, just let me know. I'm in your debt."

He nodded, still downcast.

I left him and picked up my blade from the servant.

I walked out of the castle, thinking. Mellar was not going to be easy. He had outfought the best warriors in the House of the Dzur, outmaneuvered the best brains in House Jhereg, and caught the House of the Dragon out on a point of honor.

I shook my head sadly. No, this wasn't going to be easy. And then something else hit me. If I did succeed in this, I was going to make a lot of Dzurlords mighty unhappy. If they ever found out who had killed him, they wouldn't wait for evidence, as the Empire would. This didn't exactly make my day, either.

Loiosh gave me an Imperial chewing out for not having brought him along, most of which I ignored. Kragar filled me in on what he'd learned: nothing.

"I found a few servants who used to work in the Dragon records," he said. "They didn't know anything."

"What about some that still do?" I asked.

"They wouldn't talk."

"Hmmmm. Too bad."

"Yeah. I put my Dragon outfit on and found a Lady of the House who was willing to do some looking for me, though."

"But you didn't get anything there, either?"

"Well, I wouldn't say that, exactly."

"Oh? Oh."

"How about you?"

I took great relish in delivering the information I'd gotten, since it was rare that I was able to one-up him on a point like this.

He dutifully noted everything, then said, "You know, Vlad, no one wakes up one morning and discovers that he is good enough to fight his way into the Dzur. He must have worked on that for quite a while."

"That makes sense," I said.

"Okay, that will give me something to work with. I'll start checking it through from that angle."

"Do you think it'll help?"

"Who can say? If he was good enough to get into the Dzur, he's got to have been trained somewhere. I'll see what I can find."

"Okay," I said. "And there's something else that bothers me, by the way."

"Yes?"

"Why?"

Kragar was silent for a moment, then he said, "There are two possibilities I can think of. First, he could have wanted to become part of the House because he felt it his right, and then discovered that it didn't help—that he was treated the same after as before, or that he didn't like it."

"That makes sense. And the other?"

"The other possibility is that there was something he wanted, and he had to be a Dzur to get it. And there was no need to stay in the House after he had it."

That made sense, too, I decided. "What kind of thing could it be?" I asked.

"I don't know," he said. "But if that's what it is, then I think we'd damn well better find out."

Kragar leaned back in his chair for a moment, watching me closely. Probably, still worried about yesterday. I didn't say anything; best to let him discover in his own way that I was all right. I *was* all right, wasn't I? I watched myself for a moment. I *seemed* all right. It was strange.

I shook the mood off. "Okay," I said, "start checking it. Let me know as soon as you have something."

He nodded, then said, "I heard something interesting today."

"Oh, what did you hear?"

"One of my button-men was talking, and I overheard him say that his girl friend thinks something is wrong with the council."

I felt suddenly sick. "Wrong how?"

"She didn't know, but she thought it was something pretty big. And she mentioned Mellar's name."

I knew what that meant, of course. We didn't have much time left. Maybe a day, perhaps two. Three at the most. Then it would be too late. The Demon was certainly hearing rumors by now, too. What would he do? Try to get to Mellar, of course. Me? Would he make another try for me? What about Kragar? Or, for that matter, Cawti? Normally, no one would be interested in them, since it was I who was at the top. But would the Demon be trying for them now, in order to get to me?

"Shit," I said.

He agreed with my sentiments.

"Kragar, do you know who this fellow's girl friend is?"

He nodded. "A sorceress. Left Hand. Competent."

"Good," I said. "Kill her."

He nodded again.

I stood up and took off my cloak. Laying it across my desk, I began removing things from it, and from various places around my person. "Would you mind heading down to the arsenal and picking up the standard assortment for me? I may as well do something useful while we're talking."

He nodded and departed. I found an empty box in the corner and began putting discarded weapons in it.

"Still ready to protect me, Loiosh?"

"Somebody has to, boss."

He flew over from his windowsill and landed on my right shoulder. I scratched him under the chin with my right hand, which brought my wrist up to eye level. Spellbreaker, wrapped tightly around my forearm, gleamed golden in the light. I had hopes of that chain being able to defend me against any magic I might encounter; and the rest of my weapons, if used properly, gave me a chance of taking out anyone using a normal blade. But it all depended on getting sufficient warning.

And, as an assassin, one thing kept revolving around in my head: Given time and skill, anyone can be assassinated. *Anyone.* My great hope, and my great fear, all rolled into one.

I took a dagger out of the box in front of me and checked its edge—Box? I looked up and saw that Kragar had returned.

"Would you mind telling me how you keep doing that?" I asked.

He smiled and shook his head in mock sadness. I looked at him, but learned nothing new. Kragar was about as average a Dragaeran as it is possible to get. He stood just about seven feet tall. His hair was light brown over a thin, angular face over a thin, angular body. His ears were just a bit pointed. No facial hair (which was why I grew a mustache), but other than that it was hard to tell a Dragaeran from a human by looking only at his face.

"How?" I repeated.

He raised his eyebrows. "You really want to know?" he asked.

"Are you really willing to tell me?"

He shrugged. "I don't know, to be honest. It isn't anything I do deliberately. It's just that people don't notice me. That's why I never made it as a Dragonlord. I'd give an order in the middle of a battle and no one would pay any attention. They gave me so much trouble over it that I finally told 'em all to jump off Deathgate Falls."

I nodded and let it pass. The last part, I knew, was a lie. He hadn't left the House of the Dragon on his own; he'd been expelled. I knew it, and he knew I knew it. But that was the story he wanted to give, so I accepted it.

Hell, I had my own scars that I didn't let Kragar scratch at; I could hardly begrudge him the right to keep me away from his.

I looked at the dagger that was still in my hand, made sure of the edge and balance, and slipped it into the upside-down spring-sheath under my left arm.

"I'm thinking," said Kragar, changing the subject, "that you don't want Mellar to know you're involved in this any sooner than you have to."

"Do you think he'll come after me?"

"Probably. He's going to have something of an organization left, even now. Most of it will have scattered, or be in the middle of scattering, but he's bound to have a few personal friends willing to do things for him."

I nodded. "I hadn't planned to advertise it."

"I suppose not. Do you have any thoughts yet on how to approach the problem of getting him to leave Castle Black?"

I added another dagger to the pile of weapons in the "used" box. I picked out a replacement, tested it, and slipped it into the cloak's lining sheath outside of where my left arm would be. I checked the draw and added a little more oil to the blade. I worked it back and forth in the sheath and continued.

"No," I told him, "I don't have the hint of an idea yet, to tell you the truth. I'm still working on it. I don't suppose you have anything?"

"No. That's your job."

"Thanks heaps."

I tested the balance on each of the throwing darts, and filled the quills with my own combination of blood, muscle, and nerve poison. I set them aside to dry, discarded the used ones, and looked at the shuriken.

"My original idea," I said, "was to convince him that we'd stopped looking for him and then maybe set up something attractive-looking in terms of escape. Unfortunately, I don't think I'll be able to do that in three days. Damn, but I hate working under a time limit."

"I'm sure Mellar would be awfully sorry to hear that."

I thought that over for a minute. "Maybe he would, come to think of it. I think I'll ask him."

"What?"

"I'd like to see him myself, talk to him, get a feel for what he's like. I still don't really know enough about him."

"You're nuts! We just agreed that you don't want to go anywhere near him. You'll let him know that you're after him and put him on the alert!"

"Will he figure that out? Think about it. He must know that I'm working for Morrolan. By now, he is aware that Morrolan is onto him, so he's probably expecting a visit from Morrolan's security people. And if he does suspect that I'm after him, so what? Sure, we lose an edge, but he isn't going to leave Castle Black until he's ready to, or until Morrolan kicks him out. So what is he going to do about it?

"He can't kill me at Castle Black for the same reason that I can't kill him there. If he guesses that I'm the one who's going to take him, he'll guess that I'm revealing it to him so that he'll bolt, and he'll just hole up tighter than ever."

"Which," pointed out Kragar, "is exactly what we *don't* want."

I shrugged. "If we're going to get him to leave, we'll have to come up with something weird and tricky enough to force him out no matter how badly he wants to stay. This isn't going to matter one way or the other."

Kragar pondered this for a while, then nodded. "Okay, it sounds workable. Want me to come along?"

"No thanks. Keep things running here, and keep working on Mellar's background. Loiosh will protect me. He promised."

11

*"When the blameless
And the righteous die,
The very gods
For vengeance cry."*

THEY SAY THAT THE banquet hall of Castle Black has never been empty since it was built, over three hundred years ago. They also say that more duels have been fought there than in Kieron Square outside the Imperial Palace.

You teleport in at approximately the center of the courtyard of the Castle Black. The great double doors of the keep open as you approach, and your first sight of the interior of the castle shows you a dimly lit hallway in which Lady Teldra is framed, like the Guardian, that figure that stands motionless atop Deathgate Falls, overlooking the Paths of the Dead, where the real becomes the fanciful—but only by degrees.

Lady Teldra bows to you. She bows exactly the right amount for your House and Rank, and greets you by name whether she knows you or not. She says such words as will make you to feel welcome, whether your mission be of friendship or hostility. Then, if it be your desire, you are escorted up to the banquet hall. You ascend a long, black-marble stairway. The stairs are comfortable if you are human, a bit shallow (hence, elegant) if you are Dragaeran. They are long, winding, sweeping things, these stairs. There are lamps along the wall that highlight paintings from the long, violent, sometimes strangely moving history of the Dragaeran Empire.

Here is one done by the Necromancer (you didn't know she was an artist, did you?), which shows a wounded dragon, reptilian head and neck curled around its young, as its eyes stare through you and pierce your soul. Here is one by a nameless Lyorn showing Kieron the Conqueror debating with the Shamans—with his broadsword. Cute, eh?

At the top, you may look to the right and see the doors of the actual dining hall. But if you turn to the left, you soon come to a large set of double doors, standing open. There is always a guard here, sometimes two. As you look through, the room makes itself felt only a little at a time. First, you notice the picture that fills the entire ceiling; it is a depiction of the Third Seige of Dzur Mountain, done by none other than Katana e'M'archala. Looking at it, and tracing the details from wall to wall, gives you an idea of just how massive the room really is. The walls are done in black marble, thinly veined with silver. The room is dark, but somehow there is never any problem seeing.

Only then do you become aware of people. The place is always packed. The tables around the edges, where food and drink are served, are focal points for an endless migration of humanity, if I may use the word. At the far end there are double doors again, these letting out onto a terrace. At other sides are smaller doors which lead to private rooms where you can bring some innocent fool to tell your life story to, if you so choose, or ask a Dragon general if he really had that last counterattack planned all along.

Aliera uses these rooms often. Morrolan, seldom. Myself, never.

"You know, boss—this place is a friggin' menagerie."

"Very true, my fine jhereg."

"Oh, we're a wit, today; yes, indeed."

I shouldered my way through the crowd, nodding to acquaintances and sneering at enemies as I went. Sethra Lavode spotted me, and we chatted for a few minutes about nothing. I didn't really know how to deal with her any more, so I cut the conversation short. She gave me a warm-despite-the-cold kiss on the cheek; she either knew or suspected, but wasn't talking.

I exchanged pleasant smiles with the Necromancer, who then turned her attention back to the Orca noble she was baiting.

"By the Orb, boss; I swear there are more undead than living in this damn place."

I gave a cold stare to the Sorceress in Green, which she returned. I nodded noncommitally at Sethra the Younger, and took a good look around.

In one corner of the room, the crowd had cleared for a Dzur and a Dragon, who were shouting insults at each other in preparation for carving each other up. One of Morrolan's wizard-guards stood by, casting the spells that would prevent any serious damage to the head, and laying down the Law of the Castle with regard to duels.

I continued searching until I spotted one of Morrolan's security people. I caught his eye, nodded to him, and he nodded back. He slowly drifted toward me. I noted that he did a fair-to-good job of moving through the crowd without disturbing anyone or giving the impression that he was heading anywhere in particular. Good. I made a mental note about him.

"Have you seen Lord Mellar?" I asked him when he reached me.

He nodded. "I've been keeping an eye on him. He should be over in the corner near the wine-tasting."

We continued to smile and nod as we talked—just a chance meeting of casual acquaintances.

"Good. Thanks."

"Should I be ready for trouble?" he asked.

"Always. But not in particular at the moment. Just stay alert."

"Always," he agreed.

"Is Morrolan here at the moment? I haven't seen him."

"Neither have I. I think he's in the library."

"Okay."

I began walking toward the wine-tasting.

I scanned in one direction, Loiosh in the other. He rode on my right shoulder, as if daring anyone to make a remark about his presence. He spotted Mellar first.

"There he is, boss."

"Eh? Where?"

"Against the wall—see?"

"Oh, yes. Thanks."

I approached slowly, sizing him up. He had been hard to spot because there was nothing particularly distinctive about him. He stood just under seven feet tall. His hair was dark brown and somewhat wavy, falling to just above his shoulders. I suppose a Dragaeran would have considered him handsome, but not remarkably so. He had an air about him, like a jhereg. Watchful, quiet, and controlled; very dangerous. I could read "Do Not Mess With Me" signs on him.

He was speaking to a noble of the House of the Hawk that I didn't know, and who was almost certainly unaware that, as he spoke, Mellar was constantly scanning the crowd, perhaps even unconsciously, alert, looking. . . . He spotted me.

We looked at each other for a moment as I approached, and I felt myself come under expert scrutiny. I wondered how many of my weapons and devices he was spotting. A good number, of course. And, naturally, not all of them. I walked up to him.

"Count Mellar," I said. "How do you do? I am Vladimir Taltos."

He nodded to me. I bowed from the neck. The Hawklord turned at the sound of my voice, noted that I was an Easterner, and scowled. He addressed Mellar. "It seems that Morrolan will let anyone in these days."

Mellar shrugged, and smiled a little.

The Hawklord bowed to him then, and turned away. "Perhaps later, my lord."

"Yes. A pleasure meeting you, my lord."

Mellar turned back to me. "Baronet, isn't it?"

I nodded. "I hope I didn't interrupt anything important."

"Not at all."

This was going to be different than my dealing with the Dzurlord, Keleth. Unlike him, Mellar knew all the rules. He'd used my title to let me know that he knew who I was—implying that it might be safe to tell him more. I knew how the game was played as well.

This was a strange conversation in other ways, however. For one thing, it simply isn't my custom to speak to people that I'm going to nail. Before I'm ready, I don't want to go anywhere near them. I have no desire to give the target any idea who I am or what I'm like, even if he doesn't realize that I'm going to become his executioner.

But this was different. I was going to have to get him to set himself up. That meant that I needed to know the bastard better than I'd ever known any other target in my career. And, just to put the honey in the klava, I knew less about him than I did about anyone else I'd ever set out after.

So, I had to find out a few things about him, and he, no doubt, would like to find out a few things about me; or at least what I was doing here. I thought up and rejected a dozen or so opening gambits before I settled on one.

"I understand from Lord Morrolan that you acquired a book he was interested in."

"Yes. Did he tell you what it was?"

"Not in detail. I hope he was satisfied with it."

"He seemed to be."

"Good. It's always nice to help people."

"Isn't it, though?"

"How did you happen to get hold of the volume? I understand that it's quite rare and hard to come by."

He smiled a little. "I'm surprised Morrolan asked," he said, which told me something. Not much perhaps, but it confirmed that he knew that I worked for Morrolan. File that away.

"He didn't," I said. "I was just curious myself."

He nodded, and the smile came on again briefly.

We made small talk for a while longer, each letting the other be the first to commit himself to revealing how much he knew in a gambit to learn what the other knew. I decided, after a while, that he was not going to be first. He was the one with only a little to gain, so—

"I understand Aliera introduced herself to you."

He seemed startled by the turn of the conversation. "Why, yes, she did."

"Quite remarkable, isn't she?"

"Is she? In what way?"

I shrugged. "She's got a good brain, for a Dragonlord."

"I hadn't noticed. She seemed rather vague, to me."

Good! Unless he was a lot sharper than he had any right to be, and a damn good liar (which was possible), he hadn't realized that she'd been casting a spell as she was speaking to him. That gave me a clue as to his level of sorcery—not up to hers.

"Indeed?" I said. "What did you talk about?"

"Oh, nothing, really. Pleasantries."

"Well, that's something, isn't it? How many Dragons do you know who will exchange pleasantries with a Jhereg?"

"Perhaps. On the other hand, of course, she may have been trying to find something out about me."

"What makes you think so?"

"I didn't say I thought so, just that she may have been. I've wondered myself as to her reasons for seeking me out."

"I can imagine. I haven't noticed that Dragons tend toward subtlety, however. Did she seem irritated with you?"

I could see his mind working. How much, he was thinking, should I tell this guy, hoping to pull information out of him? He couldn't risk a lie that I would recognize, or I wouldn't be of any further use to him, and he couldn't really know how much I knew. We were both playing the same game, and either one of us could put the limit on it. How much did he want to know? How badly did he want to know it? How worried was he?

"Not on the surface," he said at last, "but I did get the impression that she might not have liked me. It ruined my whole day, I'm telling you."

I chuckled a little. "Any idea why?"

This time I'd gone too far. I could see him clam up.

"None at all," he said.

Okay, so I'd gotten a little, and he'd gotten a little. Which one of us had gotten more would be determined by which one of us was alive after this was over.

"*Well, Loiosh, did you find out anything?*"

"*More than you did, boss.*"

"*Oh? What in specific?*"

Mental images of two faces appeared to my mind's eye.

"*These two. They were watching you the entire time from a few feet away.*"

"*Oh, really? So he has bodyguards, eh?*"

"*At least two of them. Are you surprised?*"

"*Not really. I'm just surprised that I didn't pick up on them.*"

"*I guess they're pretty good.*"

"*Yeah. Thanks, by the way.*"

"*No problem. It's a good thing that one of us stays awake.*"

I made my way out of the banquet hall and considered my next move. Let's see. I really should check in with Morrolan. First, however, I wanted to talk to one of the security people and arrange for some surveillance on those two bodyguards. I wanted to learn a bit about them before I found myself confronting them on any important issue.

Morrolan's security officer on duty had an office just a few doors down from the Library. I walked in without knocking—the nature of my job putting me a step above this fellow.

The person who looked up at me as I stepped in was called Uliron, and he should have been working the next shift, not this one. "What are you doing here?" I asked. "Where is Fentor?"

He shrugged. "He wanted me to take his shift this time, and he'd take mine. I guess he had some kind of business."

I was bothered by this. "Do you do this often?" I asked.

"Well," he said, looking puzzled, "both you and Morrolan said it was all right for us to switch from time to time, and we logged it last shift."

"But do you do it often?"

"No, not really very often. Does it matter?"

"I don't know. Shut up for a minute; I want to think."

Fentor was a Tsalmoth, and he'd been with Morrolan's security forces for over fifty years. It was hard to imagine him suddenly being on the take, but it is possible to bring pressures down on anyone. Why? What did they want?

The other thing I couldn't figure out was why I had such a strong reaction to the switch. Sure, it was coming at a bad time, but they'd done it before. I almost dismissed it, but I've learned something about my own hunches: the only time they turn out to be meaningful is when I ignore them.

I sat on the edge of the desk and tried to sort it out. There was something significant about this; there had to be. I drew a dagger and started flipping it.

"*What do you make of this, Loiosh?*"

"*I don't make anything of it, boss. Why do you think there's something wrong?*"

"*I don't know. Just that there's a break in routine, right now, when we know that the Demon wants to get at Mellar, and he isn't going to let the fact that Mellar is in Castle Black stop him.*"

"*You think this could be a shot at Mellar?*"

"*Or the setup for it. I don't know. I'm worried.*"

"*But didn't the Demon say that there wouldn't be any need to start a war? He said it could be 'worked around.' *"

"*Yes, he did. I hadn't forgotten that. I just don't see how he can do it—*"

I stopped. At that moment, I saw very clearly how he could do it. That, of course, was why the Demon had tried to get my cooperation and then tried to kill me when I wouldn't give it. Oh, shit.

I didn't want to take the time to run down the hall. I reached out for contact with Morrolan. There was a good chance that I was already too late, of course, but perhaps not. If I could reach him, I would have to try to convince him not to leave Castle Black, under any circumstances. I'd have to . . . I became aware that I wasn't reaching him.

I felt myself slipping into automatic—where my brain takes off on its own, and lets me know what I'm supposed to do next. I concentrated on Aliera, and got contact.

"*Yes, Vlad? What is it?*"

"*Morrolan. I can't reach him, and it's urgent. Can you find him with Pathfinder?*"

"*What's wrong, Vlad?*"

"*If we hurry, we might be able to get him before they make him unrevivifiable.*"

The echo of the thoughts hadn't died out in my head before she was standing next to me, Pathfinder naked in her hand. I heard a gasp from behind me, and remembered Uliron.

"Hold the keep for us," I told him. "And pray."

I sheathed my dagger; I wanted to have both hands free. If I don't know what I'm going to run into, I consider hands to be more versatile than any given weapon. I longed to unwrap Spellbreaker and be holding it ready, but I didn't. I was better off this way.

Aliera was deep in concentration, and I saw Pathfinder begin to emit a soft green glow. This was something I despised—having to sit there, ready to do something, but waiting for someone else to finish before I could. I studied Pathfinder. It shimmered green along its hard, black length. Pathfinder was a short weapon, compared to most swords that Dragaerans use. It was both shorter and heavier than the rapiers I liked to use, but in Aliera's hands it was light and capable. And, of course, it was a Great Weapon.

What is a Great Weapon? That's a good question. I wondered the same thing myself as I watched Aliera concentrating, her eyes narrowed to slits, and her hand steadily holding the pulsating blade.

As far as my knowledge goes, however, there is this: a Morganti weapon, made by one of the small, strange race called Serioli that dwell in the jungles and mountains of Dragaera, is capable of destroying the soul of the person it kills. They are, all of them, strange and frightening things, endowed with a kind of sentience. They come in differing degrees of power, and some are enchanted in other ways.

But there are a few—legend says seventeen—that go beyond "a kind of sentience." These are the Great Weapons. They are, all of them, powerful. They all have enough sentience to actually *decide* whether or not to destroy the soul of the victim. Each has its own abilities, skills, and powers. And each one, it is said, is linked to the soul of the one who bears it. It can, and will, do anything necessary to preserve its bearer, if he is the One chosen for it. And the things those weapons can do . . .

Aliera tugged at my sleeve and nodded when I looked up. There was a twist down in my bowels, the walls vanished, and I felt sick, as usual. We were standing in what appeared to be an unused warehouse. Aliera gave a gasp, and I followed her glance.

Morrolan's body was lying on the floor a few feet from us. There was a dark red spot on his chest. I approached him, feeling sicker than ever. I dropped to my knee next to him and saw that he wasn't breathing.

Aliera sheathed Pathfinder and dropped down beside me. She ran her hands over Morrolan's body once, her face closed with concentration. Then she sat back and shook her head.

"Unrevivifiable?" I asked.

She nodded. Her eyes were cold and gray. Mourning, if there was to be any, would come later.

12

"Tread lightly near thine own traps."

"Is there anything we can do, Aliera?"

"I'm not sure," she said. "Bide." She carefully ran her hands once more over Morrolan's body, while I made a cursory survey of the warehouse. I didn't find anything, but there were several areas that I couldn't see.

"I can't break it," she said at last.

"Break what?"

"The spell preventing revivification."

"Oh."

"However, the sorcerer who put it on could, if it's done soon enough. We'll have to find him quickly."

"Her," I corrected automatically.

She was up in an instant, staring at me. _"You know who did it?"_

"Not exactly," I said. "But I think we're safe in limiting it to the Left Hand of the Jhereg, and most of them are female."

She looked puzzled. "Why would the Jhereg want to kill Morrolan?"

I shook my head. "I'll explain later. Right now, we have to find that sorceress."

"Any suggestions as to how we do this?"

"Pathfinder?"

"Has nothing to work with. I need a psionic image, or at least a face or a name. I've checked around the room, but I'm not able to pick up anything."

"You generally don't with Jhereg. If she's competent, she wouldn't have had to feel any strong emotions in order to do what she did."

She nodded. I began looking around the room, hoping to find some kind of clue. Loiosh was faster, however. He flew around the perimeter and quickly spotted something.

"Over here, boss!"

Aliera and I rushed over there, and almost tripped over another body, lying face down on the floor. I turned it over and saw Fentor's face staring up at me. His throat had been cut by a wide-bladed knife, used skillfully and with precision. The jugular had been neatly slit.

I turned to Aliera, to ask if he was revivifiable, but she was already checking. I stepped back to give her room.

She nodded, once, then laid her left hand on his throat. She held it there for a moment and removed it. The wound was closed, and from where I stood I could only barely make out a faint scar.

She continued checking over his body and turned it over to make sure that there was nothing on his back. She turned it over again and laid both of her hands on his chest. She closed her eyes, and I could see the lines of tension on her face.

Fentor started breathing.

I let the air out of my lungs, realizing that I'd been holding it in.

His eyes fluttered open. Fear, recognition, relief, puzzlement, understanding. I wondered what my own face had looked like, that time Aliera had brought me back to life.

He reached up with his right hand and touched his throat; he shivered. He saw me, but had no reaction that indicated guilt. Good; he hadn't been bought off, at least. I'd have liked to have given him time to recover, but we couldn't afford it. Every second we waited made it that much less likely that we could find the sorceress who had finished off Morrolan. And we had to find her and make her—

I reached out for contact with Kragar. After a long time, or so it seemed, I reached him.

"*What is it, boss?*"

"*Can you get a fix on me?*"

"*It'll take a while. Problems?*"

"*You guessed it. I need a Morganti blade. Don't bother making it untraceable this time, just make it strong.*"

"*Check. Sword, or dagger?*"

"*Dagger, if possible, but a sword will do.*"

"*Okay. And you want it sent to where you are?*"

"*Right. And hurry.*"

"*All right. Leave our link open, so I can trace down it.*"

"*Right.*"

I turned back to Fentor. "What happened? Briefly."

He closed his eyes for a moment, collecting his thoughts.

"I was sitting at the security office, when—"

"No," I interrupted. "We don't have time for the whole thing right now. Just what happened after you got here."

He nodded. "Okay. I showed up, was slugged. When I woke up I was blindfolded. I heard some talking, but I couldn't make out anything anyone said. I tried to reach you, and then Morrolan, but they had some kind of block up. I sat there for about fifteen minutes and tried to get out. Someone touched me on the throat with a knife to let me know I was being watched, so I stopped. I felt someone teleport in, around then, and then someone cut my throat." He winced and turned away. When he turned back, his face was composed again. "That's all I know."

"So we still don't have anything," I said.

"Not necessarily," said Aliera. She turned to Fentor. "You say you heard voices?"

He nodded.

"Were any of them female?"

He squinted for a moment, trying to remember, then nodded.

"Yes. There was definitely a woman there."

She reached forward again and placed her hand on his forehead.

"Now," she instructed, "think about that voice. Concentrate on it. Try to hear it in your mind."

He realized what was going on and looked over at me, his eyes wide. No one, no matter how innocent, enjoys being mind-probed.

"Do it," I said. "Cooperate."

He dropped his head back and closed his eyes.

After about a minute, Aliera opened her eyes and looked up. "I think I've got it," she said. She drew Pathfinder, and Fentor gasped and tried to draw away.

At about that moment, there was a small popping sound, and I heard Kragar's pseudo-voice say, *"Okay, here it is."*

I saw a sheathed dagger at my feet.

"Good work," I told him, and cut the link before he could get around to asking any questions.

I drew the dagger and studied it. The instant it was out of the sheath, I recognized it as Morganti. I felt the blade's sentience ringing within my mind, and I shuddered.

It was a large knife, with a point and an edge. Two edges, in fact, as it was sharpened a few inches along the back. The blade was about sixteen inches long, and had a wicked curve along the back where it was sharpened. A knife-fighter's weapon. The hilt was large, and quite plain. The handle was a trifle uncomfortable in my hand; it had been made for Dragaerans, of course.

I sheathed it, and hung it on my belt, on the left side. It was next to the sword, in front of it, and set up for a cross-body draw. I tested it a few times, to make sure that its placement didn't interfere with getting to my sword. I looked over at Aliera and nodded that I was ready. "Fentor," I said, "when you're feeling strong enough, contact Uliron; he'll arrange to get you back. Consider yourself temporarily suspended from duties."

He managed a nod, as I felt the gut-wrenching twist of a teleport take effect.

Some general pointers on assassination and similar activities: Do not have yourself teleported so that when you arrive at the scene, you are feeling sick to your stomach. Particularly avoid it when you have no idea whatsoever as to where you're going to end up. Failing these, at least make sure that it isn't a crowded tavern at the height of the rush hour, when you don't know exactly where your victim is. If you do, the people around you will have time to react to you before you can begin to move. And, of course, don't do it in a place where your victim is sitting at a table surrounded by sorceresses.

If, for some reason, you have to violate all of the above rules, try to have next to you an enraged Dragonlord with a Great Weapon. Fortunately, I wasn't here to do an assassination. Well, not exactly.

Aliera faced one direction; I faced the other. I spotted them first, but not before I heard a shout and saw several people go into various types of frenzied actions. If this was a typical Jhereg-owned establishment, there could be up to a half-dozen people here who regularly brought body-guards with them. At least some of the bodyguards would recognize me, and hence be aware that an assassin was now among them.

"Duck, boss!"

I dropped to one knee, as I spotted the table, and so avoided a knife that came whistling at my head. I saw someone, female, point her finger at me. Spellbreaker fell into my hand, and I swung it out. It must have intercepted whatever it was that she was trying to do to me; I wasn't blasted, or paralyzed, or . . . whatever.

A problem occurred to me just then: I had recognized the table because there were a lot of people at it that I knew to be with the Left Hand, and because they had reacted to my suddenly showing up. One of them, therefore, must have understood what I was doing there (which was confirmed by Aliera's presence), and acted accordingly. I could safely kill all but her. But which one was it? I couldn't tell by looking at them. By this time, they were all standing up and ready to destroy us. I was paralyzed as surely as if a spell had hit me.

Aliera wasn't, however. She must have asked Pathfinder which one it was as soon as she had seen the table—just a fraction of a second after I did. As it happened, she didn't feel like stopping long enough to let me in on the secret. She jumped past me, Pathfinder arcing wildly. I saw what must have been another spell aimed at me, and I swung Spellbreaker again—caught it.

Aliera had her left hand in front of her. I could see multicolored light striking it. Pathfinder connected with the head of a sorceress with light brown, curly hair, who would have been quite pretty if it weren't for the look on her face and the dent in her forehead.

I shouted over the screams as I rolled along the floor, hoping to present a difficult target. "Dammit, Aliera, which one?"

She cut again, and another fell, her head departing her shoulders and coming to rest next to me. But Aliera had heard me. Her left hand stopped blocking spells and she pointed directly at one of the sorceresses for a moment. It was someone I didn't know. Something seemed to strike Aliera at that moment, but Pathfinder emitted a bright green flash for an instant and she continued with the mayhem.

My left hand found three shuriken, and I flipped them at one of the sorceresses who was trying to do something or other to Aliera.

You know, that's what I hate most about fighting against magic: you never know what they're trying to do to you until it hits. The sorceress knew what hit her, however. Two of the shuriken got past whatever defenses she had. One caught her just below the throat, the other in the middle of her chest. It wouldn't kill her, but she wouldn't be fighting anyone for a while.

I noticed Loiosh, about then, flying into people's faces and forcing them to fend him off, or else heal the poison. I began to work my way toward our target. Grab her, then have Aliera teleport us out and put up trace blocks.

The sorceress beat us to it.

I was on my feet and moving toward her. I was perhaps five steps away when she vanished. At the same moment something hit me. I discovered that I couldn't move. I'd been running and I wasn't especially in balance, so I hit the floor rather hard. I ended up on my back, in a position where I could see Aliera, torn between helping me and trying to trace and follow the vanished sorceress.

"I'm fine!" I lied to her psionically. *"Just get that bitch and stuff her some-where!"*

Aliera promptly vanished, leaving me all alone. Paralyzed. What the hell had I done that for? I asked myself.

At the edge of my line of sight (the paralysis was complete enough that I couldn't even move my eyeballs, which is remarkably frustrating) I saw one of the sorceresses pointing her finger at me. I would, I suppose, have prepared to die if I had known how.

She didn't get a chance to complete the spell, however.

At that moment, a winged shape hit her face from the side, and I heard her scream and she fell out of my line of sight.

"Loiosh, back off and get out of here!"

"Go to Deathsgate, boss."

So where did he think I *was* going?

The sorceress was back in my line of sight, now, and I saw a look of rage on her face. She held out her hand again, but it wasn't pointed at me this time. She tried to follow Loiosh with her hand, but was having problems. I couldn't see the jhereg, but I knew what he must be doing.

I couldn't move to activate Spellbreaker, much less do something meaningful. I could have tried to summon Kragar, but it would all be over before I could even contact him. Witchcraft also just took too damn long.

I would have screamed if I could have. It wasn't so much that they were going to kill me; but, lying there, utterly helpless, while Loiosh was going to be burned to a crisp, I almost exploded with frustration. My mind hammered at the invisible bonds that held me, as I recklessly drew on my link to the Orb for power, but there was not a chance that I could break the bindings. I just wasn't a sorcerer of the same class as they were. If only Aliera were here.

That was a laugh! They wouldn't have been able to bind her like this. If they had the nerve to try, she'd dissolve them all in chaos. . . .

Dissolve them in chaos.

The phrase rang through my mind, and echoed through the warehouse of my memory. "I wonder how genetic heritage interacts with reincarnation of the soul."

"Oddly."

I was Aliera's brother.

The thoughts took no time whatsoever. I knew what I had to do then, although I had no idea how to do it. But at that point I didn't care. Let the whole world blow up. Let the entire planet be dissolved in chaos. The sorceress, who was still within my range of vision, became my whole world for a moment.

I envisioned her dissolving, dissipating, vanishing. All of the sorcerous energy I had summoned and been unable to use, I threw, then, and my rage and frustration guided it.

I have heard, since, that those who were looking on saw a stream of something like formless, colorless fire shoot from me toward the tall sorceress with the finger pointing off into the air, who never saw it coming.

As for me, I suddenly felt myself drained of energy, of hate, of everything. I saw her fall in upon herself and dissolve into a swirling mass of all the colors I could conceive of, and several that I couldn't.

Screams reached my ears. They meant nothing. I found that I could move again when my head suddenly hit the floor, and I realized that it had been up at an angle. I tried to look around, but couldn't raise my head. I think someone yelled, "It's spreading!" which struck me as odd.

"*Boss, get up!*"

"Wha—? Oh. Later, Loiosh."

"*Boss, now! Hurry! It's moving toward you!*"

"What is?"

"*Whatever it was that you threw at her. Hurry, boss! It's almost reached you!*"

That was odd enough that I forced my head up a little bit. He was right. There seemed to be almost a pool of—something—that more or less centered where the sorceress had been standing. Now that was strange, I thought.

Several things occurred to me at once. First, that this must be what happened when something dissolved into amorphia—it spread. Second, that I really should control it. Third, that I had no idea at all of how one went about controlling chaos—it seemed rather a contradiction in terms, if you see my point. Fourth, I became aware that the outermost tendrils were damn close to me. Finally, I realized that I just plain didn't have the strength to move.

And then there was another cry, from off to my side, and I became aware that someone had teleported in. That almost set me off laughing. No, no, I wanted to say. You don't teleport *in* to a situation like this, you teleport *out*.

There was a bright green glow off to my right, and I saw Aliera, striding directly up to the edge of the formless mass that filled that part of the room. Loiosh landed next to me, and began licking my ear.

"*C'mon boss. Get up now!*"

That was out of the question, of course. Much too much work. But I did succeed in holding my head up enough to watch Aliera. That was very interesting, in a hazy, unimportant sort of way. She stopped at the edge of the formless mass and held out Pathfinder with her right hand. Her left hand was raised up, palm out, in a gesture of warding.

And, so help me Verra, it stopped spreading! I thought I was imagining things at first, but no, it had certainly stopped spreading. Then, slowly, it assumed a single, uniform color: green. It was very interesting, watching it change. It started at the edges and then worked in until the entire mass was a sort of emerald shade.

She began gesturing with her left hand, then, and the green mass began to shimmer, and slowly it turned blue. I thought it was very pretty. I looked closely. Was it my imagination, or did the blue mass seem a bit smaller than it had been? I looked around the edges of where it had been and confirmed it. There was nothing there, now. The wooden floor of the restaurant was gone, and it pulled back to reveal the edge of what appeared to be a pit. I looked up, and discovered that part of the ceiling was missing as well.

Gradually, I began to see the blue mass shrinking. It took on the form, slowly, of a circle, or rather a sphere, about ten feet in diameter. Aliera was moving forward, levitating over the hole in the floor. The ten feet became five feet, then a foot, then Aliera's body obscured it completely.

I felt strength returning to me. Loiosh was still next to me, licking my ear. I heaved myself up to a sitting position as Aliera turned and came toward me, appearing to walk over the nothingness below her. When she reached me, she grasped my shoulder and forced me to stand up. I couldn't read the expression on her face. She held out her hand to me when I was stable on my feet again. In her hand was a small, blue crystal. I took it, and felt a warmth from it, pulsating gently. I shuddered.

She spoke for the first time. "A bauble for your wife," she said. "Tell her how you got it if you wish; she'll never believe you, anyway."

I looked around. The room was empty. Hardly surprising. No one with any brains feels like rubbing shoulders with an uncontrolled mass of raw amorphia.

"How—How did you do it?" I asked.

She shook her head.

"Spend fifty or a hundred years studying it," she said. "Then walk into the Great Sea of Chaos and make friends with it—after assuring yourself that you have the e'Kieron genes. After you do all that, maybe, if you absolutely have to, you can risk doing something like what you did."

She stopped for a minute, and said, "That was really incredibly stupid, you know."

I shrugged, not feeling a whole lot like answering just then. I was, however, beginning to feel a bit more like myself. I stretched, and said, "We'd better get going, before the Imperial Guards show up."

Aliera shrugged, made a brushing-off motion, and started to say something when Loiosh suddenly said, *"Guards, boss!"* and I heard the sound of feet tromping. Right on cue.

There were three of them, pulling their grim, official faces, and holding great-swords. Their eyes focused on me, not seeming to notice Aliera at all. I could hardly blame them, of course. They hear about a big mess in a Jhereg-owned bar, come in, and see an Easterner in the colors of House Jhereg. What are they supposed to think?

I had three weapons pointing at me, then. I didn't move. Looking at them, I gave myself even odds of fighting my way out, given that Loiosh was there and these fools generally don't know much about dealing with poison or thrown weapons of any kind. I didn't do anything about it, of course. Even if I'd felt in top shape and there was only one of them, I wouldn't have touched him. You do *not* kill Imperial Guards. Ever. You can bribe them, plead with them, reason with them; you don't fight them. If you do, there are only two possible outcomes: either you lose, in which case you are dead; or you win, in which case you are dead.

But this time, it turned out, I had no reason to worry. I heard Aliera's voice, over my shoulder. "Leave us," she said.

The guard turned his attention to her, seemingly for the first time. He raised his eyebrows, recognizing her for a Dragonlord, and not quite knowing how to take all this. I felt tremendous amounts of sympathy for the fellow.

"Who are you?" he asked, approaching her, but keeping his blade politely out of line.

Aliera flung back her cloak, and placed her hand on the hilt of Pathfinder. They must have sensed what it was immediately, for I saw them all recoil somewhat. And they knew, as I knew, that there was all the difference in the world between an Imperial Guard killed by a Jhereg and a fight between Dragons.

"I," she announced, "am Aliera e'Kieron. This Jhereg is mine. You may go."

He looked nervous for a moment, licked his lips, and turned back to the others. As far as I could tell, they didn't express an opinion one way or the other. He turned back to Aliera and looked at her for a moment. Then he bowed and, without a word, turned and left, his fellows falling in behind. I would be very interested in hearing what they put in their reports, I decided.

Aliera turned back to me. "What hit you?" she asked.

"A complete external binding, as far as I can tell. They didn't get my ears, or for that matter, my heart or lungs, but they got just about everything else."

She nodded. I suddenly remembered what we'd been doing there.

"The sorceress! Did you get her?"

She smiled, nodded, and patted the hilt of Pathfinder.

I shuddered again. "You had to destroy her?"

She shook her head. "You forget, Vlad—this is a Great Weapon. Her body is back in Castle Black, and her soul is here, where we can get at it whenever we want it." She chuckled.

I shuddered still another time. I'm sorry, but some things bother me. "And Morrolan's body?"

"He's at Castle Black, too. The Necromancer is looking after him, seeing if she can find a way to break the spell. It doesn't look hopeful unless we can convince our friend to help."

I nodded. "Okay, then let's get going."

At this point I suddenly remembered that, when those Imperial Guards were here, I'd been carrying a high potency Morganti weapon on my person. If I'd remembered that at the time, I don't know what I would have done, but I'd have been a lot more worried. This was the first time I'd come close to actually getting caught with one, and I was suddenly very happy that Aliera was along.

By the time we returned to Castle Black, my stomach was more than just a little irritated with me. If I'd eaten recently, I would probably have lost the meal. I resolved to be extra kind to my innards the rest of the day.

Morrolan has a tower, high up in his castle. It is the center of much of his power, I'm told. Besides himself, very few people are allowed up there. I'm one, Aliera is another. Still another is the Necromancer. The tower is the center of Morrolan's worship of Verra, the Demon Goddess he serves. And I do mean "serves." He has been known to sacrifice entire villages to her.

The tower is always dark, lit only by a few black candles. There is a single window in it, which does not look down on the courtyard below. If you're lucky, it doesn't look upon anything at all. If you aren't, it will look upon things which may destroy your sanity.

We laid Morrolan's body on the floor beneath the window. On the altar in the center of the room was the sorceress. Her head was propped up, so that she could see the window. This was at my suggestion. I had no intention of actually using the window for anything, but having her see it would help with what we were trying to do.

The Necromancer aided Aliera, who revivified the sorceress. It could, conceivably, have been the other way around, too. There are few who know more about the transfer of souls, and the mysteries of death, than the Necromancer. But it was Aliera's Great Weapon, so she did the necessary spells.

The sorceress's eyes fluttered open, and her face went through the same patterns that Fentor's had, earlier, except that it ended with fear.

This part was my job. I had no desire to give her time to take in her surroundings more than casually, or to orient herself. The fact that she had been picked by whoever had killed Morrolan guaranteed that she was good, which guaranteed that she was tough. I didn't figure to have an easy time of this, by any means.

And so the first thing she saw when she opened her eyes was the window. It was politely empty at the moment, but nonetheless effective. And before she had time to adjust to that, she saw my face. I was standing over her and doing my best to look unfriendly.

"Well," I said, "did you enjoy the experience?"

She didn't answer. I wondered what it was like, having your soul eaten, so I asked her. She still didn't answer.

By this time, she would be cognizant of several things—including the chains that held her tied to the altar and the spells in the room which kept her from using sorcery.

I waited for a moment, to make sure it all sank in properly. "You know," I said conversationally, "Aliera enjoyed killing you that way. She wanted to do it again."

Fear. Controlled.

"I wouldn't let her," I said. "I wanted to do it."

No reaction.

"You okay, boss?"

"Damn! Is it showing that much?"

"Only to me."

"Good. No, I'm not okay, but there isn't anything I can do about it, either."

"Perhaps," I went on to her, "it is a flaw in my character, but I truly enjoy using Morganti weapons on you bitches."

Still nothing.

"That's why we brought you back, you know." As I said it, I drew the dagger Kragar had supplied me with and held it before her eyes. They widened with recognition. She shook her head in denial.

I'd never had to do anything like this before, and I wasn't liking it now. It wasn't as if she'd done something wrong—she'd just accepted a standard contract, much as I would have done. Unfortunately, she'd gotten involved with the wrong people. And, unfortunately, we needed her cooperation because she'd done a good job. I couldn't stop myself from identifying closely with her.

I touched her throat with the back of the blade, above the edge. I felt it fighting me—trying to turn around, to get at the skin, to cut, to drink.

She felt it too.

I held onto control. "However, being an honorable sort, I have to inform you that if you cooperate with us, I won't be allowed to use this on you. A pity, if that were to happen."

Her face showed the gleam of hope she felt, and she hated herself for it. Well, after all, I didn't feel real good about myself just then either, but that's the game.

I grabbed her hair, and lifted her head a bit more. Her eyes landed on Morrolan's figure, lying directly under the window, which still showed only black. "You know what we want," I said. "I, personally, don't give a teckla's squawk if you do it or not. But some others here do. We arrived at a compromise. I have to ask you, just once, to remove the spell you put on. If you don't agree, I can have you. If you do, Morrolan gets to decide what to do with you."

She was openly trembling, now.

To a Jhereg professional, a contract is an almost sacred bond. Most of us would rather lose our souls than break a contract—in the abstract. However, when it comes right down to the moment, well . . . we'd soon see. I'd never been in the kind of situation she was in, and I prayed to Verra that I never would be, feeling very much the hypocrite. I think I would have broken about there, myself. Well, maybe not. It's so hard to say.

"Well, what is it?" I asked, harshly. I saw her face torn with indecision. Sometimes I truly loathe the things I do. Maybe I should have been a thief after all.

I grabbed hold of her dress and raised it up, exposing her legs. I pulled at one knee. Loiosh hissed, right on cue, and I said, aloud, "No! Not until I'm done with her!"

I licked the forefinger of my left hand and wetted down a spot on the inside of her thigh. She was close to tears, now, which meant she was also close to breaking. Well, now or never.

"Too late," I said with relish, and lowered the Morganti blade, slowly and deliberately, toward her thigh. The point touched.

"No! My god, stop! I'll do it!"

I dropped the knife onto the floor and grabbed her head again and supported her shoulders. She was facing Morrolan's body; her own was shaking with sobs. I nodded to Aliera, who dropped the protection spell which had cut off her sorcery. If she'd been faking, she was now in a position to put up a fight. But she knew damn well that she wouldn't be able to win against both Aliera and me, not to mention the Necromancer.

"Then do it now!" I snapped. "Before I change my mind."

She nodded, weakly, still sobbing quietly. I saw her concentrate for a moment.

The Necromancer spoke for the first time. "It is done," she said.

I let the sorceress fall back. I felt sick again.

The Necromancer stepped up to Morrolan's body and began working on it. I didn't watch. The only sounds were the sobbing of the sorceress and, very faintly, our breathing.

After a few minutes, the Necromancer stood up. Her dull, undead eyes looked almost happy for a moment. I looked over at Morrolan, who was breathing now, evenly and deeply. His eyes opened.

Unlike the others, his first reaction was anger. I saw a scowl form on his lips, then confusion. He looked around.

"What happened?" he asked.

"You were set up," I said.

He looked puzzled and shook his head. He held a hand up, and I assisted him to his feet. He looked at all of us, his eyes coming to rest on the sorceress, who was still sobbing quietly.

He looked back and forth at Aliera and me for a moment, then asked, "Who is this one?"

"Left Hand," I explained. "She was retained, I expect, by whoever did the job on you. She was to make sure you couldn't be revivified. She did it, too. But of course, whoever put the spell on can take it off again, and we convinced her to remove it."

He looked thoughtfully at her. "She's pretty good then, eh?"

"Good enough," said Aliera.

"Then," said Morrolan, "I suspect she did more than that. Someone hit me as soon as I arrived at that—place."

"Warehouse," I said.

"That warehouse. Someone succeeded in stripping away all of my defensive spells. Could that have been you, my lady?"

She looked over at him bleakly, but didn't respond.

"It must have been," I said. "Why hire two sorceresses when you only need one?"

He nodded.

I retrieved the dagger from the floor, sheathed it, and handed it to Morrolan. He collects Morganti weapons, and I didn't ever want to see this one again. He looked at it and nodded. The knife disappeared into his cloak.

"Let's get out of here," I said.

We headed for the exit. Aliera caught my eye, and she couldn't quite keep the disgust from her face. I looked away.

"What about *her*?" I asked Morrolan. "We guaranteed her her soul if she'd help us, but made no promises other than that."

He nodded, looked back at her, and drew a plain-steel dagger from his belt.

The rest of us went out the door, none of us really desirous of seeing the end of the affair.

13

"The bite of the yendi can never be fully healed."

MORROLAN HAD CAUGHT UP to us by the time we reached the library, and his dagger was sheathed. I tried to put the whole incident out of mind. I failed, of course.

In fact—and here's a funny thing, if you're in the mood for a laugh—I had done forty-one assassinations at this point, and I had never been bothered by one. I mean, not a bit. But this time, when I actually hadn't even hurt the bitch, it bothered me so much that for weeks afterward I'd wake up seeing her face. It could be that she laid some kind of curse on me, but I doubt it. It's just that, oh, Hell. I don't want to talk about it.

Fentor was in the library when we arrived. When he saw Morrolan, he almost broke down. He rushed up and fell to his knees, casting his head down. I thought I was going to get sick all over again, but Morrolan was more understanding.

"Get up," he said gruffly. "Then sit down and tell us about it."

Fentor nodded and stood. Morrolan guided him to a seat and poured him a glass of wine. He drank it thirstily, failing to appreciate the vintage, while we found seats and poured wine for ourselves. Presently, he was able to speak.

"It was this morning, my lord, that I received a message."

"How?" Morrolan interrupted.

"Psionic."

"All right, proceed."

"He identified himself as a Jhereg and he said he had some information to sell me."

"Indeed? What kind of 'information?' "

"A name, my lord. He said that there was going to be an attempt made on Mellar, one of our guests, and that the assassin didn't care that he was here." Fentor gave an apologetic shrug, as if to apologize for his contact's lack of judgment. "He said the assassin was good enough to beat our security system."

Morrolan looked at me and raised his eyebrow. I was in charge of security, he was saying, in his eloquent way. *Could* it be beaten?

"Anyone can be assassinated," I told Morrolan, drily.

He allowed his lips to smile a bit, nodded, and returned his attention to Fentor.

"Did you really think," Morrolan asked him, "that they were prepared to start another Dragon-Jhereg war?"

I opened my mouth to speak, but thought better of it. Let him finish his tale.

"I was afraid he might," said Fentor. "In any case, I thought it would be a good idea to get the name, just to be safe."

"He was willing to give you the name of the assassin?" I found myself asking.

He nodded. "He said that he was desperate for money, and had come across it, and knew Morrolan would be interested."

"I don't suppose," said Morrolan, "that it occurred to you to bring this information to me before you tried to do anything yourself?"

Fentor was silent for a moment, then he asked, "Would you have done it, my lord?"

"Most assuredly not," said Morrolan. "I would hardly submit to anyone's extortion." He lifted his chin slightly.

(Be still, my beating stomach.)

Fentor nodded. "I assumed that you would have that reaction, my lord. On the other hand, it's my job to make sure nothing happens to your guests, and I thought I'd need any advantage I could get, if there really was an assassin who was going to try for Mellar."

"How much did he want?" I asked.

"Three thousand gold Imperials."

"Cheap," I remarked, "given what he was risking."

"Where did the gold come from?" Morrolan asked.

Fentor shrugged. "I'm not really poor," he said. "And since I was doing it on my own—"

"I suspected as much," said Morrolan. "You will be reimbursed."

Fentor shook his head. "Oh, I still have the gold," he said. "They never took it."

I could have told him that. After all, we were dealing with professionals.

Fentor continued. "I arrived at the teleport coordinates they gave me and was hit as soon as I got there. I was blindfolded and then killed. I had no idea what had happened, or why, until I got up, after Aliera revivified me, and saw—" he choked for a minute, and looked away "—and saw your body, my lord. That was when I arranged to have us teleported back."

I felt a momentary twinge of sympathy for him. We probably should have let him know about Morrolan's corpse a few feet away, but then, I hadn't exactly been in the mood for polite chit-chat, nor had the time for it.

Morrolan nodded sagely as he finished.

"I've temporarily relieved him from duty," I put in.

Morrolan stood up, and went over to him. He looked down on Fentor for a moment, then he said, "All right. I approve of the motivations behind your actions. I understand and sympathize with your reasoning. But there is not to be a repetition of this action in the future. Is this understood?"

"Yes, my lord. And thank you."

Morrolan clapped him on the shoulder. "Very well," he said. "You are restored to duty. Get back to work."

Fentor bowed and left. Morrolan shut the door behind him after seeing him out, sat down, and sipped his wine.

"No doubt," he said, "you are all hoping to hear what happened to me."

"You guessed it," I said.

He shrugged. "I received a message, from the same individual who contacted Fentor, most likely. Fentor, he claimed, was being held. I was *instructed*," he said the word as if it tasted bad, "to withdraw my protection of the Lord Mellar and remove him from my home. They told me that if I didn't, they would kill Fentor. They threatened to use a Morganti blade on him if I made any attempt to rescue him."

"So naturally," I said, "you went charging right in there."

"Naturally," he agreed, ignoring my sarcasm. "I kept him talking long enough to trace where he was, put up my standard protection spells, and teleported in."

"Was Fentor alive then?" I asked.

He nodded. "Yes. While I was trying the trace, I made them put me in contact with him, to verify that he was alive. He was unconscious, but living.

"In any case," he continued, "I arrived. That, uh, lady we just left threw some kind of spell. I assume it was preset. I didn't realize that it was her until just now, of course, but whatever it was removed my protections against physical attack." He shook his head. "I'm forced to admire their timing. You would have appreciated it, Vlad. Before I was really aware of what had happened, something hit me in the back of the head and I saw a knife coming toward me. Most unpleasant. I had no time to counterattack in any way. As they intended, of course."

I nodded. "They knew what they were doing. I should have figured it out sooner."

"How did you catch on at all?" asked Aliera.

"Certain parties had mentioned that they had found a way to kill Mellar without bringing the whole House of the Dragon down on their heads. It took me way too long, but it finally occurred to me that the one way to do that, without getting Mellar to leave Castle Black, would be if Morrolan were to turn up conveniently dead. Then, of course, there wouldn't be a problem, since he'd no longer be Morrolan's guest, as it were."

Morrolan shook his head, sadly.

I continued. "As soon as I found out that Fentor and Uliron had changed shifts, I knew something was up. I figured out what it had to be, contacted Aliera, and, well, you know the rest."

He didn't, of course, but I wasn't really in the mood to tell him how I almost managed to dissolve myself—and half of Adrilankha—in raw chaos.

Morrolan looked at me hard. "And who," he asked, "is this person, who came up with this marvelous scheme?"

I matched his stare, and shook my head. "No," I said. "That information I can't give even you."

He looked at me a moment longer, then shrugged. "Well, my thanks, in any case."

"You know what the real irony is?" I said.

"What?"

"I've been trying to come up with some way to prevent another Dragon-Jhereg war myself, and when one drops right into my lap, I chuck it out."

Morrolan allowed himself a small smile. "I don't really think they'd go that far, do you?" he asked.

I started to nod, stopped. Damn right they'd go that far! And, knowing the Demon, he wouldn't waste a lot of time being about it!

"What's wrong, Vlad?" asked Aliera.

I shook my head and contacted Fentor.

"Yes, my lord?"

"Are you back on duty?"

"Yes, my lord."

"Run a full check on all our secure areas. Now. Make sure nothing's been breached. I want it done an hour ago. Move!"

I held the contact while he gave the necessary orders. If I were going to take out Mellar, how would I get past Morrolan's security system? I ran it through my mind. I'd set the damn thing up myself, however, so of course *I* couldn't see any flaws in it. Ask Kiera? Later, if there was time. If it wasn't already too late.

"Everything checks, my lord."

"Okay. Bide a moment."

Morrolan and Aliera were looking at me, puzzled. I ignored them. Now . . . forget the windows—no one gets in that way. Tunnel? Ha! From a mile in the air? When Morrolan can detect any sorcery done around the castle? No way. A hole in the wall? If they weren't going to use sorcery, which they shouldn't be able to, it would take too long. Doors? The main door had witchcraft, sorcery, and Lady Teldra. Forget that. Rear doors? Servants' entrances? No, we had guards.

Guards. Could the guards have been bribed? It would take, how many? Damn! Only two. How long did he have to set this up? Not more than two days. No, he couldn't find two guards who would take in only two days, without finding one who would talk first. Kill all the ones who said no?

"Fentor, any deaths of guards within the last two days?"

"No, my lord."

Okay, good. No one was bribed. What else? Replace a guard? Oh, shit, *that's* what I'd do.

"Fentor, do we have any new guards working today? People who have been on the payroll less than three days? If not, check for servants. But check for guards first."

That's what I'd do, of course. Take a job as a guard, or a servant, and wait for the perfect moment. All I'd have to do is arrange for the right guard to be busy, or ill, or to need sudden days off, maybe bribe one person, maybe not even have to, if I could get access to the records and slip my name in.

"As a matter of fact, yes. We have someone new outside the banquet hall. The guard who normally has that duty—"

I broke the link. I was already running and half out the door before I heard Morrolan and Aliera shouting after me. The Necromancer, who hadn't said a word the entire time, remained behind. After all, what was another death, more or less, to her?

I charged down to the banquet hall at full tilt. Loiosh, however, was faster. He was flapping his way about ten paces ahead of me when I saw the two guards outside the door. I saw that they recognized me. They bowed slightly and came to alert as I started to get close. I noticed, from fifty feet away, that one of them had a dagger concealed under his uniform, which is very un-Dragonlike. Thank Barlen, we were in time.

Morrolan was close to my heels as I approached. The guard with the concealed dagger locked eyes with me for a moment; then he turned and bolted into the room, Loiosh close behind him. Morrolan and I raced after him. I took out a throwing knife; Morrolan drew Blackwand. I cringed involuntarily from the things that that unsheathed blade did to my mind, but I didn't let it slow me down.

There were shouts from inside the hall, doubtless in response to Morrolan's psionic orders. I ran past the door. For a moment, I couldn't see him, obscured as he was by the crowd. Then I saw Loiosh strike. There was a scream, and I saw a sword flash.

We stopped. Mellar was now in plain view, looking not at all concerned. He favored Morrolan with a look of inquiry. At his very feet was the "guard." The latter's head was a few feet off to the side. A real guard stood over the body, his longsword bare and dripping. He looked up at Morrolan, who nodded to him.

Morrolan and I walked up to the body and removed a dagger from the outstretched hand. He took it and studied it for a moment. He said "good job," to the guard.

The guard shook his head. "Thank the jhereg," he said, looking at Loiosh with an expression of wonder on his face. "If he hadn't slowed him down, I'd never have made it in time."

"Finally, someone who appreciates me."

"Finally, you do a day's work."

"Two dead teckla on your pillow."

We ignored Mellar completely and walked back out of the room.

"All right," snapped Morrolan as we left. "Get this place cleaned up."

Aliera appeared beside us, and we headed back toward the library. Morrolan handed me the dagger. I touched it, and knew at once that it was Morganti. I shuddered and handed it back to him. There were just too damn many of those things floating around, lately.

"You realize what this means, don't you?" he said.

I nodded.

"And you knew this would happen?"

"I guessed it. When the attempt to nail you didn't work, they had to go ahead and get him anyway.

"We've been lucky," I added. "I've been too slow to pick up on most of this. If Mellar had happened to walk by the door any time in the last hour, it would be all over by now."

We entered the library. The Necromancer nodded a greeting to us and gestured with her wineglass, the strange, perpetual half-smile on her face. I've always liked her. Some day I hope to understand her. On the other hand, perhaps I'd better hope not to. As we seated ourselves, I said to Morrolan, "I've been meaning to get around to talking to you since I found out about the bodyguards."

"Bodyguards? Whose? Mellar's?"

"Right. As far as I can tell, he has two of them."

"As far as who can tell, boss?"

"Shut up, Loiosh."

"That is rather interesting," said Morrolan. "He most assuredly had no bodyguards when he arrived."

I shrugged. "So they aren't on your guest list. That makes them fair game, doesn't it?"

He nodded. "It appears that he doesn't especially trust my oath."

Something about that bothered me, but I couldn't quite put my finger on it.

"Possibly," I said. "But it's more likely that he doesn't trust the Jhereg not to start another war, just to get him."

"Well, he's correct in that, is he not, Vlad?"

I nodded, and looked away.

"Whoever this Mellar was in the Jhereg" said Morrolan, "he certainly must have hurt some pretty big people."

"Big enough," I said.

Morrolan shook his head. "I just can't believe that the Jhereg would be that stupid. Both Houses were very nearly destroyed the first time, and the last time—"

" 'Last time?' " I echoed. "It's only happened once, as far as I know."

He seemed surprised. "Didn't you know? But of course, it wouldn't be something the Jhereg would discuss excessively. I wouldn't know myself if Aliera hadn't told me about it."

"Told you what?" My voice sounded faint and hollow in my own ears.

Aliera cut in. "It happened once more. It started the same as before—with a Jhereg killed by an assassin while he was a guest in a Dragonlord's home. The Dragons retaliated, the Jhereg retaliated, and . . ." She shrugged.

"Why haven't I heard of this before?"

"Because things went to Hell after that, and it never got really well recorded. Briefly, the Jhereg who was killed was the friend of the Dragonlord, and he was helping him out on something. Someone found out what he was doing and put a stop to it.

"The Dragons demanded that the assassin be turned over to them, and, this time the Jhereg agreed. I guess House Jhereg felt that he should have known better, and also it may have been a private quarrel on some level. In any case, the assassin escaped from the Dragonlord's home before he was killed. He killed a couple of Dragons on the way out, then he killed a couple of the Jhereg bosses who had turned him in. He was killed himself, later, but by then it was too late to stop anyone."

"Why? If it was just the one individual—"

"This was during the reign of a decadent Phoenix, so nobody was trusting anybody. The Jhereg thought that it was the Dragons who had killed the bosses, and the Dragons thought it was the Jhereg who had arranged the escape."

"And then things went to Hell, you say? Right then?"

She nodded. "The Jhereg killed enough of the right Dragonlords, including some wizards, so that a certain one, who'd been planning a coup, found himself forced to move too soon, and to rely too heavily on magic. And, without his best sorcerers, the spell got out of control, even after the Emperor was dead, and . . ." Her voice trailed off. It started to sink in. I can subtract as well as anyone can, and if the first Dragon-Jhereg war was when it was, then the second one had to be . . . decadent Phoenix . . . Dragon coup . . . went to Hell . . . spell got out of control . . . dead Phoenix Emperor. . . .

"Adron," I said.

She nodded. "My father. The assassin had reasons of his own to hate the Emperor and was working with father to find a way to poison the Emperor when things fell apart. As you know, it was Mario who finally killed the Emperor, when he tried to use the Orb against the Jhereg. Another Phoenix tried to grab the throne, and father had to move too quickly. The next thing you know, we have a sea of amorphia where the city of Dragaera used to be, no Emperor, no Orb, and no Empire. It was close to two hundred years before Zerika turned up with the Orb."

I shook my head. Just too damn many shocks in too damn few days. I couldn't handle it.

"And now," I said, "it's going to start up again."

Morrolan nodded at this. We were all silent for a time, then Morrolan said quietly, "And if that happens, Vlad, which side will you be on?"

I looked away.

"You know," he continued, "that I'd be one of House Jhereg's first targets."

"I know," I said. "I also know that you'd be in the front lines trying to waste the organization. As would Aliera, for that matter. And, by the way, *I'd* be one of the first ones the Dragons went after."

He nodded. "Do you think you could convince the Jhereg to let this one go?"

I shook my head. "I'm not an Issola, Morrolan, and I don't have that sharp a tooth. And, to tell you the truth, I'm not all that sure that I'd do it if I could.

I've heard all the reasons why Mellar has to go, and they're hard to argue with."

"I see. Perhaps you could convince them to wait. As you know, he'll only be staying here a few more days."

"No way, Morrolan. It can't be done."

He nodded. We sat there in silence for a time; then I said, "I don't suppose there is any way, just this once, that you could let us have him? All you have to do is kick him out, you know. I hadn't intended to even ask, but . . ."

Aliera looked up, intent for a moment.

"Sorry, Vlad. No."

Aliera sighed.

"All right," I said. "I didn't really think you would."

We were all quiet again, for a few minutes; then Morrolan spoke once more. "I probably don't have to say this, but I will remind you that if anything, anything at all, happens to him in this house, I'm not going to rest until I find out the cause. I'm not going to hold back, even if it's you.

"And if it *is* you, or any other Jhereg, I will personally declare war on the House, and I'll have the backing of every Dragon in the Empire. We have been friends for a long time, and you have saved my life on more than one occasion, but I will not allow you, or anyone else, to get away with the murder of one of my guests. You understand that, don't you?"

"Morrolan," I said, "if I had intended to do anything like that, I wouldn't have asked you about it, would I? I would have done it already. We've known each other for—how long?—four years? I'm surprised that you know me so little that you'd think I'd abuse your friendship."

He shook his head, sadly. "I never thought you would. I just had to make sure that the matter was stated clearly, and in the open, all right?"

"All right. I guess I had it coming to me for asking you what I did, anyway. I'll be heading off now. I'm going to have to think about this."

He stood as I did. I bowed to him, to Aliera, and to the Necromancer. Aliera bowed back; the Necromancer looked out at me from within her dark eyes, and she smiled. As I turned toward the door, Morrolan gripped my shoulder.

"Vlad, I'm sorry."

I nodded. "Me, too," I said.

14

"Oft 'tis startling to reveal what the murky depths conceal."

CAWTI KNEW ME BETTER than any other being that I'm aware of, with the possible exception of Loiosh. She suppressed any desire she might have had for conversation and allowed me to brood in silence as we ate. She squelched the suggestion that I take her turn at cooking since she'd taken mine, and carefully cooked something bland and uninteresting so that I'd feel no compulsion to compliment her on it. Clever lady, my wife.

Our apartment was a small, second-story number, which had two virtues: it was well-lit and it had a large kitchen. There is one way to tell an apartment owned by a member of the Jhereg from any other kind of apartment: the lack of spells to prevent or detect burglary. Why? Simple. No common thief is going to lighten the apartment of a member of the organization except by mistake. If a mistake like that happens, I will have everything back within two days, guaranteed. Kragar may have to arrange for a few broken bones to do it, but it will get done. The only other kind of burglar there is, is someone like Kiera; someone specifically commissioned to get into my place and get something. If this happens, there just isn't any kind of defense I could put up that would matter a teckla's squawk. Keep Kiera out? Ha!

So we sat, snug and secure, in our little kitchen, and I said, "You know what the problem is?"

"What?"

"Every time I try to think of how to do it, all I can think of is what happens if I don't."

She nodded. "It's still hard for me to believe that the Demon would consciously and deliberately go out and start a Dragon-Jhereg war."

I shook my head. "What choice does he have, really?"

"Well, if you were in his position, would you?"

"That's just the thing," I said. "I think I would. Sure, they'd chew us up and spit us out again, but if Mellar gets away with this, it's slow death for the whole organization. If you get every punk on the street thinking that he can burn the council, one of them is bound to succeed, eventually. And then, even more will try, and it'll just keep getting worse."

It hit me, then, that I was parroting everything the Demon had told me. I shrugged. So what? It was true. If only there were some way to get rid of Mellar without a war—but, of course, there had been a way. The Demon had found one.

Sure, just kill Morrolan, he had thought. That was why he had given me that chance, back at the Blue Flame, to cooperate. Well, he was an honorable sort, after all, I couldn't deny that.

I wondered what his next move would be. He could take another try for me, or Morrolan, or skip it and go straight for Mellar. I guessed that he would try for Mellar, since time was becoming rather critical, with people already starting to talk. How much longer could this be held under our cloaks? Another day? Two, if we were lucky? Cawti was speaking, I realized.

"You're right," she was saying. "He has to be taken out."

"And I can't touch him while he's at Castle Black."

"And the Jhereg isn't about to wait until he leaves."

Not anymore, they wouldn't. How would the attack come this time? No matter, they couldn't set anything up in a day, and Morrolan had tightened his security again. It would wait until tomorrow. It had to. I wasn't good for much of anything today.

"Just as you said," I told her. "Caught between a dragon and a dzur."

"Wait a minute, Vlad! What about a Dzur? Couldn't you maneuver a Dzur hero into taking him out for you? We could try to find one of the younger ones, who doesn't know the story about him, maybe a wizard. You know how easy it is to manipulate Dzur heroes."

I shook my head. "No good, beloved," I said, thinking of Morrolan's speech earlier. "Aside from the chance that Morrolan would figure out what happened, I'm just not willing to do that to him."

"But if he never found out—"

"No. I'd know that I was the one who had caused his oath to be broken. Remember, Mellar isn't just at the home of a Dragonlord, which would be bad enough; Morrolan in particular has made a point of having Castle Black be a kind of sanctuary for anyone and everyone he invites. It means too much to him for me to trifle with it."

"My, my, aren't we the honorable sort today?"

"Shut up, Loiosh. Clean your plate."

"It's your plate."

"Besides," I added to Cawti, "how would you feel if you had taken the job, and the target was holed up with Norathar?"

The mention of her old friend and partner stopped her. "Hmmmm. Norathar would understand," she said after a while.

"Would she?"

"Yes . . . well, no, I suppose not."

"Right. And you wouldn't ask her to, would you?"

She was silent for a while longer, then, "No."

"I didn't think so."

She sighed. "Then I don't see any way out."

"Neither do I. The 'way out,' as you put it, is to convince Mellar to leave

Castle Black of his own free will and then nail him when he does. We can trick him however we want, or set up any kind of fake message, but can't actually attack him, or use any form of magic against him while he's there."

"Wait a minute, Vlad. Morrolan won't let us attack him, or use magic, but if we, say, deliver a note that convinces him to leave, that's okay? Morrolan won't care?"

"Right."

A look of utter confusion passed over her features. "But . . . but that's ridiculous! What difference does it make to Morrolan how we get him out, if we do? What does using magic have to do with it?"

I shook my head. "Have I ever claimed to understand Dragons?"

"But—"

"Oh, I can almost see it, in a way. We can't actually *do* anything to him, is the idea."

"But isn't tricking him 'doing something' to him?"

"Well, yes. Sort of. But it's different, at least to Morrolan. For one thing, it's a matter of free choice. Magic doesn't give the victim a choice; trickery does. I also suspect that part of it is that Morrolan doesn't think we'll be able to do it. And he has a point there. You know Mellar is going to be on his guard against anything like that. I don't really see how we're going to be able to do anything."

"I don't either."

I nodded. "I've got Kragar digging into his background, and we're hoping we'll find some weak spot there, or something we can use. I'll have to admit I'm not real hopeful."

She was silent.

"I wonder," I said a little later, "what Mario would do."

"Mario?" she laughed. "He would hang around him, with no one seeing him, for years if he had to. When Mellar finally left Castle Black, however and whenever, Mario would be there, and take him."

"But the organization can't wait—"

"They'd wait for Mario."

"Remember, I took this on with time constraints."

"Yes," she said softly, "but Mario wouldn't have."

That stung a bit, but I had to admit that it was true, especially since I'd come to the same realization when the Demon had first proposed the job to me.

"In any case," she went on, "there's only one Mario."

I nodded sadly.

"And what," I asked her then, "would you and Norathar have done, if the thing had been given to you?"

She thought about that for a long time, then she said, "I'm not really sure, but remember that Morrolan isn't that close a friend of ours; or at least he wasn't when we were still working. Chances are we'd put some sort of spell on Mellar to get him to leave and make damn sure Morrolan never found out."

That didn't help, either.

"I wonder what Mellar would do? I understand he was a pretty fair assassin himself, on his way up. Maybe we'll invite him over some time and ask him."

Cawti laughed easily. "You'll have to ask him at Castle Black. I understand he isn't getting out much these days."

I idly watched Loiosh nibble at the scraps of our meal. I got up and wandered into the living room. I sat there for a while, thinking and looking at the light brown walls, but nothing came.

I still couldn't shake the nagging feeling that I'd gotten when I'd been talking to Morrolan. I tried to recall the part of the conversation that had triggered it. Something about bodyguards.

"Cawti," I called.

Her voice came back from the kitchen. "Yes, dear?"

"Did you know that Mellar has a couple of bodyguards?"

"No, but I'm not surprised."

"I'm not either. They must be pretty good, too, because they were watching me while I talked to Mellar, and I didn't notice them at all."

"Did you mention them to Morrolan?"

"Yes. He seemed a little surprised."

"I suppose. You know you're free to do them, don't you? Since they obviously sneaked in, they aren't guests."

"That's true," I agreed. "It also proves how good they are. Slipping into Castle Black isn't the work of an amateur, if our protections are half as good as I think they are. Of course, we hadn't increased the guards then, but still . . ."

She finished up her cleaning, and sat down next to me. I rested my head on her shoulder. She moved away from me, then, and patted her lap. I stretched out and crossed my legs. Loiosh flew over and landed on my shoulder, nuzzling me with his head.

There was still something about those bodyguards that seemed funny. I couldn't quite put my finger on it, which was incredibly frustrating. In fact, there was something strange about this whole affair that I couldn't quite see.

"Do you think," said Cawti a little later, "that you might be able to buy off one of the bodyguards?"

"What do you think?" I said. "If you have a whole organization to choose from, don't you think you could find two people in it who were completely trustworthy? Especially if you had an extra nine million gold to pay them with?"

"I guess you're right," she admitted. "On the other hand, there are other kinds of pressures we could bring to bear."

"In two days, Cawti? I don't think so."

She nodded, and gently stroked my forehead. "And," she said, "even if we did, I don't suppose it would really help. If we can't take him anyway, it won't do any good to convince one of the bodyguards to step back at the right time."

Cling! I had it! Not much, perhaps, but I suddenly knew what had been bothering me. I sat up on the couch, startling Loiosh, who hissed his indignation at me.

I leaned over and kissed Cawti, long and hard.

"What was that for?" she asked, a little breathlessly. "Not, you understand, that I mind."

I gripped her hand, and locked eyes, and concentrated, letting her share my thoughts. She seemed a bit startled at first, but quickly settled into it. I brought up the memory of standing at the entranceway, and past it, running, and the sight of the dead assassin with a Morganti dagger in his hand. I played over the whole thing, remembering expressions, glimpses of the room, and things only an assassin would have noticed—as well as things an assassin should have noticed if they'd been there.

"Hey, boss, want to run by the part of me getting the guy one more time?"

"Shut up, Loiosh."

Cawti nodded as it unfolded, and shared it with me. We reached the point where Morrolan handed me the dagger, and I broke out of it.

"There," I said, "does anything strike you as odd?"

She thought it over. "Well, Mellar seemed pretty calm for someone who has almost been killed, and with a Morganti dagger. But other than that . . ."

I brushed it aside. "Chances are, he never realized that it was Morganti. Yes, it was odd, but I don't mean that."

"Then I don't see what you're referring to."

"I'm referring to the strange action of the bodyguards at the assassination attempt."

"But the bodyguards did nothing at the assassination attempt."

"That was the strange action."

She nodded, slowly.

I continued. "If the Dragon guard had been just a little bit slower, Mellar would have been cut down. I can't reconcile that with our conclusion that they are competent. I suppose Mellar might have had time to get a weapon out, or something, but he sure didn't look like it. The bodyguards were just nowhere to be seen. If they're as good as we think they are, they should have been all over the assassin before Morrolan's guard had time to show steel."

"Ahem!"

"Or Loiosh had time to strike," I added.

"They couldn't be that fast."

Cawti looked thoughtful. "Could it be that they just weren't around? That Mellar sent them on some kind of errand?"

"That, my dear, is exactly what I'm thinking. And if so, I'd very much like to find out what it was that they were doing."

She nodded. "Of course," she said, "it could be that they were there, and were good enough to see that Morrolan's guard was going to stop him."

"That is also possible," I said. "But if they're that good, I'm really scared."

"Do you know if they are still with him?"

"Good point," I said. "Just a minute while I check."

I contacted one of Morrolan's people in the banquet hall, asked, and was answered. "They're still around," I said.

"Which means that they weren't bought off by the Demon, or the assassin. Whatever reason they had for their 'strange action,' it was good enough for Mellar."

I nodded. "And that, my dearest love, is a good place to start looking tomorrow. Come on, let's go to bed."

She gave me her wide-eyed-innocent look. "What did you have in mind, my lord?"

"What makes you think I have something in mind?"

"You always do. Are you trying to tell me that you don't have everything planned out?" She walked into the bedroom.

"Nothing," I said, "has been planned out since I started this damned job. We'll just have to improvise."

I gave myself two days to complete the thing. I was aware that I was being unduly optimistic.

I arrived at the office somewhat early the next morning, hoping to spend the day looking for a solid plan, or at least the shade of a direction. I was congratulating myself on having beaten Kragar, who is normally an early riser, when I heard him coughing gently. He was seated opposite me, with his smug little, I've-been-sitting-here-for-ten-minutes-now look.

I gave him a moderate-to-dangerous Jhereg sneer and said, "What did you find out?"

"Well," he said, "why don't we start out with the bad news, before we get to the bad news, the bad news, or the other bad news."

"Damn. You're just full of high spirits today, aren't you?"

He shrugged.

"Okay," I said, "what's the bad news?"

"There have been rumors," he stated.

"Oh, joy. How accurate are they?"

"Not very. No one has quite put together the rumors of something unusual going on with Mellar, and the ones about the Jhereg's having financial trouble."

"Can it wait two days?"

He looked doubtful. "Maybe. Somebody's going to have to start answering questions soon, though. Tomorrow would be better, and today would be better still."

"Let me put it this way: will the day after tomorrow be too late?"

He looked thoughtful. "Probably," he said at last.

I shook my head. "Well, at any rate, it isn't me who's going to have to answer the questions."

"There is that," he agreed. "Oh, and one piece of good news."

"Really? Well, break out the kilinara, by Verra's hair! We'll have a bloody celebration."

"*I'll bring the dead teckla.*"

"Don't drink yourself into a stupor yet. All it is, is that we've gotten that sorceress you wanted."

"The one who was spreading rumors? Already? Good! give the assassin a bonus."

"I already have. He said it was half luck—she just happened to be in the perfect place, and he took her right away."

"Good. You *make* luck like that, though. Remember the guy."

"I will."

"Okay, now for the rest. Did you find out anything about Mellar's background?"

"Plenty," he said, taking out his notebook and flipping it open. "But, so far as I can tell, none of it is going to be of any real help to us."

"Forget about that for now; let's at least try to get some idea of who the hell he really is; then we'll see if that gives us anything to work with."

Kragar nodded, found his place, and began reading. "His mother lived the happy and fulfilling life of a Dragon-Dzur halfbreed. She wound up a whore. His father, it seems, was into a whole lot of different things, but was certainly an assassin. Reasonably competent, too. As far as I can tell, his father died during the fall of the city of Dragaera. We think the same thing happened to his mother. He hid out during the Eastern invasions, and showed up again after Zerika took the throne. He tried to claim kinship with the House of the Dragon and was rejected, of course. He tried the same thing with the House of the Dzur, with the same results."

"Wait a minute," I said, "you mean this was before he fought his way in?"

"Right. Oh, by the way, his real name is Leareth—or rather that was the name he was born with. That was the name he used the first time he joined the Jhereg."

"The first time?"

"Right. It took one hell of a lot of digging to find out, but we did. He was using the name Leareth, of course, and there are no references to anyone of that name in Jhereg records."

"Then how—"

"Lyorn records. It cost us about two thousand gold to do, by the way. And, it turns out, 'someone' had managed to bribe a few Lyorns. A lot of records that should have mentioned him, or his family, weren't there. Part of it was just luck that we ran across something that he'd missed, or couldn't get access to. The rest was clever planning, brilliant execution—"

"Money," I said.

"Right. And I found a young Lyorn lady who couldn't resist my obvious charms."

"I'm surprised she noticed you."

"Ah! They never do, until it's too late, you know."

I was impressed, in any case, both with Kragar, and with Mellar. Bribing Lyorns to get access to records isn't easy, and bribing them to actually alter records is almost unheard of. It would be like bribing an assassin to give you the name of the guy who gave him the contract.

"Actually," Kragar continued, "he didn't officially join House Jhereg then, which was one reason we had so much trouble. He worked for it on a straight free-lance basis."

" 'Worked?' "

"That's right."

"I don't believe this, Kragar! How many assassins are we going to run into? I'm beginning to feel like I'm one of a horde."

"Yeah. It just isn't safe to walk the streets at night, is it?" he smirked.

I gestured toward the wine cabinet. It was a bit early for me, but I felt the need of something to help me keep up with the shocks. "Was he good?" I asked.

"Competent," he agreed, as he poured us each a glass of Baritt's Valley white. "He did only small-time stuff, but never muffed one. It seems that he never took on anything that was worth over three thousand."

"That's enough to make a living," I said.

"I guess so. On the other hand, he also didn't spend very much time at it. He didn't take on 'work' more than once or twice a year, in fact."

"Oh?"

"Yeah. Here's the killer, if you'll excuse the expression: all the time he was working for the Jhereg, he was spending most of his free time studying swordsmanship."

"Really?"

"Really. And, get this, he was studying under Lord Onarr."

I sat up in my chair so suddenly that I almost dumped Loiosh, who complained rather bitterly about the abuse. "Oh, ho!" I said. "So that's how he got so good with the blade that he could beat seventeen Dzur heroes!"

He nodded grimly.

I asked, "Do you have any guesses as to why Onarr was willing to take him on as a student?"

"No guesses—I know exactly. It's a real sweet story, too. Onarr's wife apparently contracted one of the plagues during the Interregnum. Mellar, or I guess he was called Leareth then, found a witch to cure it. As you know, sorcery was inoperable then, and there were damn few Easterner witches willing to work on Dragaerans, and even fewer Dragaerans who knew witchcraft."

"I know all about it," I said shortly.

Kragar stopped and gave me a look.

"My father died of one of the Plagues," I explained. "*After* the Interregnum, when they were pretty much beaten. He didn't know sorcery. I did, but not quite enough. We could have cured him with witchcraft, either myself or my grandfather, but he wouldn't let us. Witchcraft was too 'Eastern,' you see. Dad wanted to be a Dragaeran. That's why he bought a title in the Jhereg and made me study Dragaeran-style swordsmanship and sorcery. And, of course, after dumping all of our money out the window, there wasn't any left to hire a sorcerer. I'd have died of the same plague if my grandfather hadn't cured me."

Kragar spoke softly. "I didn't know that, Vlad."

"Anyway, go on," I said abruptly.

"Well," he continued, "if you haven't guessed it already it was Mellar who had arranged with a witch to give Onarr's wife the plague in the first place. So he comes up, just as she's dying, saves her, and Onarr is very, very grateful. Onarr is so grateful, in fact, that he's willing to teach swordsmanship to a houseless cross-breed. Nice story, isn't it?"

"Interesting. Some elegant moves, there."

"Isn't it interesting? You'll note the timing, I'm sure."

"Yeah. He started this before he tried to join the House of the Dzur the first time, or the House of the Dragon."

"Right. Which means, unless I miss my guess, that he knew exactly what would happen when he tried to claim membership."

I nodded. "That puts a bit of a different light on things, doesn't it? It makes his attempting to join the Dragon and the Dzur not so much confusing, as downright mystifying."

Kragar nodded.

"And another thing," I said. "It would appear that his planning goes back a lot longer than the ten years we were thinking of. It's more like two hundred."

"Longer than that," said Kragar.

"Oh, that's right. He started during the Interregnum, didn't he? Three hundred, then? Maybe four hundred?"

"That's right. Impressive, isn't it?"

I agreed. "So continue."

"Well, he worked with Onarr for close to a hundred years, in secret. Then he fought his way into the House of the Dzur when he felt he was ready, and from there you know the story."

I thought it over a bit, trying to sort it out. It was too early to see if there was anything there that I could use, but I wanted to try to understand him as well as I could.

"Did you ever find any clues about why he wanted to get into the Dzur, the second time, when he fought his way in?"

Kragar shook his head.

"Okay. That's something I'd like to find out. What about sorcery? Has he studied it at all?"

"As far as I can tell, only a little."

"Witchcraft?"

"No way."

"Well, so we have something, anyway, for all the good it will do us."

I sipped my wine, as the information began to sink in, or rather, as much of it as I could handle just then. Studied under Onarr, eh? And fought his way into the Dzur, only to leave and join—or rather, rejoin—the Jhereg, and get to the top, and then lighten the whole council. Why? Just to show that he could do it? Well, he was part Dzur, but I still couldn't quite see it. And that business with Onarr, and all that plotting and scheming. Strange.

"You know, Kragar, if it ever comes down to any kind of straight fight with this guy, I think I'm in trouble."

He snorted. "You have a talent for understatement. He'll carve you into stew."

I shrugged. "On the other hand, remember that I use Eastern-style fencing. That could throw him off a bit, since he's one of you hack-hack-cut types."

"A damn good one!"

"Yeah."

We sat there for a while, in silence, sipping our wine. Then Kragar asked, "What did you find? Anything new?"

I nodded. "Had a busy day yesterday."

"Oh, really? Tell me about it."

So I gave him an account of the day's events, the new information I'd gotten. Loiosh made sure that I got the part about the rescue right. When I told him about the bodyguards, he was impressed and puzzled.

"That doesn't make sense, Vlad," he remarked. "Where would he have sent them?"

"I don't have the vaguest. Although, after what you've just told me, I can see another explanation. I'm afraid I don't like it much, either."

"What's that?"

"It could be that the bodyguards are sorcerers, and that Mellar figures that he can handle any physical attack himself."

"But it didn't look like he was doing anything at all, did it?"

I shook my head. "No, I have to admit it didn't. But maybe he was figuring to beat the guy only if he had to, and was counting on Morrolan's guards to stop him. Which, after all, they did. With help," I amended, quickly.

Kragar shook his head. "Would you count on someone else to be quick enough?"

"Well, no. But then, I'm not the fighter that Mellar is; we already know that."

Kragar looked highly unconvinced. Well, so was I.

"The only thing that really makes sense," he said, "is if you were right originally: he had some mission for them and they happened to be off doing it when the assassin came in for his move."

"Maybe," I said. Then, "Wait a minute, I must be slipping or something. Why don't I check it?"

"What?"

"Just a minute."

I reached out for contact, thinking of that guard who I had talked to in the banquet hall. I'd made a mental note of him, now, what was his name?

"*Who is it?*"

"*This is Lord Taltos,*" I said. (Let us be pretentious.)

"*Yes, my lord. What is it?*"

"*Have you been keeping an eye on those two bodyguards of Mellar's?*"

"*I've been trying, my lord. They're pretty slippery.*"

"*Okay, good. Were you on duty during the assassination attempt last night?*"

"Yes, my lord."

"Were the bodyguards there?"

"No, my lord—wait! I'm not sure. . . . Yes. Yes, they were."

"No possible doubt?"

"No, my lord. I had them marked just before it happened, and they were still there when I found them again just a few seconds afterwards."

"Okay, that's all. Good work."

I broke the link and told Kragar what I'd found out. He shook his head, sadly.

"And another nice theory blown through Deathsgate."

"Yeah."

I just couldn't figure it. Nothing about this business made sense. I couldn't see why he did it, or why his bodyguards seemed so cavalier about the whole thing, or any of it. But nothing happens for no reason. There had to be an explanation somewhere. I took out a dagger and started flipping it.

Kragar grunted. "You know the funny thing, Vlad?"

"What? I'd love to hear something funny just around now."

"Poor Mellar, that's what's funny."

I snorted. " 'Poor Mellar!' What about poor us? He's the one who started this whole thing, and we're going to get ourselves wiped out because of it."

"Sure," said Kragar. "But he's dead anyway, one way or another. He started this thing, and there isn't any way that he's going to survive it. The poor fool came up with this truly gorgeous scheme to steal Jhereg gold and live through it, and he worked on it, as far as we can tell, for a good three hundred years. And, instead of having it work, he's going to die anyway, and take two houses with him."

"Well," I said, "I'm sure he wouldn't cry about taking the two Houses with him—" I stopped. "The poor fool," Kragar had said. But we knew Mellar was no fool. How can you come up with something like this, spend hundreds of years, thousands of Imperials, and then trip up because you didn't realize that the Jhereg would take an action which, even to me, seemed logical and reasonable? That wasn't just foolishness, that was downright stupidity. And there was just no way I was going to start thinking that Mellar was stupid. No, either he knew some way of coming out of this alive, or . . . or . . .

Click, click, click. One by one, things started to fall into place. Click, click, wham! The look on Mellar's face, the actions of the bodyguards, the fighting his way into the House of the Dzur, all of it fit. I found myself filled with awe at the magnificence of Mellar's plan. It was tremendous! I found myself, against my will, filled with admiration.

"What is it, Vlad?"

"What is it, boss?"

I just shook my head. My dagger had stopped in mid-toss, and I was so stunned I didn't even catch it. It hit my foot, and it was only blind luck that the hilt was down. But I expect that even if it had landed point first in my foot, I wouldn't have noticed. It was so damn beautiful! For a while, I almost wondered whether I had the heart to stop it, even if I could think of a way. It was so *perfect*. As far as I could tell, in the hundreds of years of planning and execution, he hadn't made *one* mistake! It was incredible. I was running out of adjectives.

"Damn it, Vlad! Talk! What's going on?"

"You should know," I told him.

"What?"

"You pointed to it first, a couple of times, the other day. Verra! Was it only a day or two ago? It feels like years. . . ."

"What did I point to? Come on, damn you!" Kragar said.

"You're the one who started telling me what it would be like to grow up a cross-breed."

"So?"

"So we still couldn't help thinking of him as a Jhereg."

"Well, he *is* a Jhereg."

I shook my head. "Not genetically, he isn't."

"What does genetics have to do with it?"

"Everything. That's when I should have realized it; when Aliera told me what it really meant to be of a certain House. Don't you see, Kragar? But no, you wouldn't. You're a Jhereg, and you—we—don't look at things that way. But it's true. You *can't* deny your House, if you're a Dragaeran. Look at yourself, Kragar. To save my life, you had to disobey my orders. That isn't a Jhereg thing to do at all—the only time a Jhereg will disobey orders is when he's planning to kill his boss. But a Dragon, Kragar, a Dragon will sometimes find that the only way to fulfill his commander's wishes is to violate his commands, and do what has to be done, and risk a court-martial if he has to.

"That was the Dragon in you that did it, despite your opinion of the Dragons. To a Dragaeran, his House controls everything. The way he lives, his goals, his skills, his strengths, his weaknesses. There is nothing, but *nothing* that has more influence on a Dragaeran than his House. Than the House he was *born* into, no matter how he was raised.

"It's different with humans, perhaps, but . . . I should have seen it. Damn! I should have seen it. A hundred things pointed to it."

"For the love of the Empire, Vlad! What?"

"Kragar," I said, settling down a bit, "think for a minute. This guy isn't just a Jhereg, he's also got the bloodlust of a Dragon, and the heroism of a Dzur."

"So?"

"So check your records, old friend. Remember his father? Why don't you find out more about him? Go ahead, do the research. But I'll tell you right now what you're going to find.

"His father killed someone, another Jhereg, just before the Interregnum. The Jhereg he killed was protected by a Dragonlord; to be exact, by Lord Adron. Mellar's plan *wasn't* concocted to get Jhereg gold and get out alive—the whole point of it was to get himself killed. For more than three hundred years he's been planning things so that he'd be killed, perhaps with a Morganti weapon;

he didn't care. And he'd be killed, and the information he'd planted would come out about the Dzur, and he'd wash their faces with mud. And, at the same time, the two Houses that he hates the most, the Dragons and the Jhereg, would destroy each other. The whole thing was done for revenge, Kragar—revenge for the way a cross-breed is treated and revenge for the death of his father.

"Revenge as courageous as a Dzur, as vicious as a Dragon, and as cunning as a Jhereg. That's what this is all about, Kragar."

Kragar looked like a chreotha who's just found that a dragon has wandered into its net. He went through the same process I had, of every little detail falling into place, and like me, he began to shake his head in wonderment, his face a mask of stony shock. "Oh, shit, boss," was all he said.

I nodded in agreement.

15

"Staring into the dragon's jaw, one quickly learns wisdom."

THE BANQUET HALL OF Castle Black appeared the same as it had the last time. A few different faces, a few of the same faces, many faceless faces. I stood in the doorway for a moment, then stepped inside. I wanted to gather my thoughts a little, and let my stomach finish its recovering act before I began any serious work.

"Can you believe, boss, that Morrolan actually likes it this way?"

"You know Dragons, Loiosh."

Kragar had taken an hour and had verified each of my guesses as regarded Mellar's parentage. It seemed that his father had indeed been the one whose work had set off the second Dragon-Jhereg war, which Kragar had never heard of either. The references to it among the Lyorn records had been scattered, but clear. The thing had happened, and more or less as I'd been told.

Everything fit together very nicely. And I wasn't a bit closer to figuring out what to do about it than I'd been the day before. That was the really annoying thing. All of this information really ought to be food for something besides the satisfaction of solving a puzzle. Oh, sure, it meant that I knew now that certain things wouldn't work, since Mellar had no intention of leaving Castle Black alive, but I hadn't had any idea of what to do before, so that didn't really affect anything. It occurred to me that the more I found out, the more difficult, instead of easier, the thing became. Maybe I should arrange to forget most of this.

There was, I realized then, still one more mystery to solve. It wasn't a big one, or, I expected, a difficult one, but I was somewhat curious about why Mellar had brought bodyguards with him at all, if he didn't intend to try to save his life. Not very important, perhaps, but by now I couldn't afford to overlook anything. This was what had brought me back to the banquet hall: to take a look at them and see if there was anything I could learn, guess, or at least eliminate.

I wandered through the crowd, smiling, nodding, drinking. After about fifteen minutes, I spotted Mellar. I brought up the memory of the two faces that Loiosh had given me and found the two bodyguards, a few feet away.

I moved as close to them as I figured was safe and looked at them. Yes, they were both fighters. They had that way of moving, of standing, that indicated physical power. Both were large men, with big, capable hands, and they were both skilled in observing a crowd without seeming to.

Why were they doing it, though? I was convinced, by now, that they had no intention of stopping an assassin, so they must have some other purpose. A small part of me wanted to just take them both out, here and now, but I had no intention of doing so until I knew what their business was. And, of course, there was no guarantee that I'd succeed.

I was very careful to avoid having them notice my scrutiny, but you can never be sure, of course. I checked them as carefully as I could for concealed weapons, but oddly, I didn't spot any. They both had swords, standard Dragaeran longswords, and they each had a dagger. But I couldn't see anything concealed on any of them.

After five minutes, I turned and started to leave the banquet hall, making my way carefully through the mass of humanity. I had almost reached the door, when Loiosh interrupted my contemplation.

"Boss," he said, *"tough-guy warning, behind you."*

I turned in time to see one of them coming up to me. I waited for him. He stopped about one foot in front of me, which is what I call "intimidation range." I wasn't intimidated. Well, maybe just a little. He didn't waste any time with preliminaries.

"One warning, whiskers," he said. "Don't try it."

"Try what?" I asked innocently, although I felt my heart drop a few inches. I ignored the insult; the last time I'd let the term bother me, I hadn't had any. But the implications of the statement were, let us say, not pleasing.

"Anything," was his answer. He looked at me for a few seconds more, then he turned and walked away.

Damn! So Mellar *did* know I was after him. But why would he want to stop me? Oh, of course, he didn't. He was working under the assumption that I was out for him, and that I had no idea of why he was doing this. That made sense; if I had somehow given myself away, which was certainly possible, then it would be out of character for him to ignore it. He was playing the game to the hilt. (Interesting choice of words there, I noticed.)

This made me feel somewhat better, but not a whole lot. It was a Bad Thing that Mellar knew where the threat was coming from. While the bodyguards wouldn't actually stop a direct attack on Mellar, the fact that they were aware of me seriously cut my chances of getting away with anything tricky—and whatever I came up with now, it was going to have to be something tricky. I felt the first glimmerings of the younger brother to despair stir within me as I left the hall. I forced the feeling down.

Just outside the door, I stopped and got in touch with Aliera. Who knows, I thought, maybe she and Sethra have come up with something. In any case, I felt that I ought to let them know what we'd learned.

"What is it, Vlad?"

"Mind if I come up and see you? I have some information that you probably don't want to hear."

"*I can hardly wait,*" she said. "*I'll be expecting you in my chambers.*"

I walked down the hall to the stairs and met Morrolan, descending. I nodded to him and started to pass by. He motioned to me. I stopped, and he walked up the hall toward the library. I followed dutifully and sat down after he had closed the door behind me. The situation reminded me unpleasantly of a servant being called in for a dressing down for not scrubbing the chamberpots sufficiently.

"Vlad," he said, "perhaps you would care to enlighten me on just exactly what is occurring around here?"

"Eh?"

"Something has happened somewhere that I don't know about. I can feel it. You are preparing to move on Mellar, aren't you?"

By Verra's fingers! Did the whole Empire know?

He began ticking off points. "Aliera is rather upset about this whole matter and doesn't know quite what to do. You were acting the same way, as of yesterday. Today, I am informed that you have been, if I may put it so, snooping around Mellar. I see Aliera and she is just as pleased with life as you can imagine. Then I see you walking up the stairs, I assume to see my cousin, and you appear to know what you're doing all of a sudden. Now, would you mind telling me exactly what it is you two are planning?"

I was silent for a while; then I said, slowly and carefully, "If I'm acting any different today than yesterday, it's because we just solved the mystery—not the problem. I still don't have any idea of what I'm going to do about it. I will say, however, that I have no intention of doing anything that will, in any way, compromise you, your oath, or your House. I believe I stated that yesterday, and I have no reason to change my mind. Is that sufficient?"

"*Go, boss, go!*"

"*Shut up, Loiosh.*"

Morrolan stared at me, long and hard, as if he were trying to read my mind. I flatter myself, however, that even Daymar would have trouble doing that without my noticing. Morrolan, I think, also respects me too much to do so without asking first. And in any case, hawk-eyes should stay on Hawklords, where they belong.

He nodded, once. "All right, then," he said. "We'll say no more about the matter."

"Frankly," I said, "I don't know what is on Aliera's mind. As you guessed, I was heading up to see her when I ran into you. But I don't have anything planned with her—yet. I hope she doesn't have anything planned without me."

He looked grim. "I like that rather less," he said.

I shrugged. "As long as I'm here, tell me: have you checked over those bodyguards?"

"Yes, I took a look at them. What of it?"

"Are they sorcerers?"

He seemed to debate with himself for a moment. Then he nodded. "Yes, both of them. Quite competent, too."

Damn. The good news just kept piling up.

"Okay, then. Is there anything else you wanted?"

"No—yes. I would appreciate it if you would keep an eye on Aliera."

"Spy on Aliera?"

"No!" he said emphatically. "Just, if she tries to do something that she should, perhaps, not do—I think you understand—try to discuss it with her, all right?"

I nodded, as the last piece of the puzzle fell into its place. Of course! That was what Mellar was worried about! He had bodyguards so that he wouldn't be killed by a non-Jhereg. He had, indeed, heard of Pathfinder.

The solving of this last piece of the mystery put me no closer to its solution; no surprise. I took my leave of Morrolan and headed up the stairs to Aliera's chambers. I felt his eyes on my back the whole way.

"What kept you?" asked Aliera.

"Morrolan wanted to have a chat."

I noted that Aliera did, indeed, seem to be in fine spirits today. Her eyes were bright green and shining. She relaxed against the back of her bed, absently stroking a cat that I'd not been introduced to. Loiosh and the cat eyed each other with abstract hunger.

"I see," she said. "What about?"

"He seems to think that you have something in mind. For that matter, so do I. Care to tell me about it?"

She arched her eyebrows and smiled. "Maybe. You go first."

The cat rolled over on its back, demanding that its stomach be attended to. Its long, white fur stood out a little, as it chose to deny that Loiosh existed. Aliera obliged it.

"Hey, boss."

"Yes, Loiosh?"

"Isn't it disgusting how some people cater to the whims of dumb animals?"
I didn't answer.

"For starters, Aliera, the idea we had before won't work."

"Why not?"

It seemed that she wasn't too worried. I was beginning to be.

"A number of reasons," I said. "But the main thing is that Mellar has no intention of leaving here."

I explained our deductions about Mellar's plans and motives. Surprisingly, her first reaction was similar to mine—she shook her head in admiration. Then, slowly, her eyes turned a hard metallic gray. I shuddered.

"I'm not going to let him get away with this, Vlad. You know that, don't you?"

Well, I hadn't actually known, but I'd been afraid of something like it. "What are you going to do?" I asked softly.

She didn't say anything, but her hand came to rest on Pathfinder's hilt.

I kept my voice soft, even, and controlled. "If you do, you are aware that Morrolan will be forced to kill you."

"So what?" she asked, simply.

"Why don't we find a better way?"

"For example?"

"Dammit, I don't know! What do you think I've been racking my brains about for the last few days? If we can find some way to convince him to leave, we can still follow the original idea—you trace him with Pathfinder, and then we take him wherever he ends up. If I just had more time!"

"How much time do you have?"

That was a very good question. If we were very, very lucky, the news wouldn't get out for three more days. But, unfortunately, I couldn't count on being lucky. And, what was worse, neither could the Demon. What would his next effort be like? I asked myself again. And how much of a chance would I have to stop it? I didn't like the answer I got to that last question.

"Today and tomorrow," I told her.

"And what," she asked, "happens then?"

"Deathsgate opens up. The matter is taken out of my hands, my body turns up somewhere, and I miss out on a fine Dragon-Jhereg war. *You* get to see the war. Lucky you."

She gave me a nasty grin. "I might enjoy it," she said.

I smiled back at her. "You might at that."

"However," she admitted, "it wouldn't do the House any good."

I agreed with that, too.

"On the other hand," she said, "if I kill him, there's no problem. The two Houses don't fight, and only the Dzur are hurt, and who cares about them, anyway? Well, maybe we can think of some way to intercept the information about them before it gets out."

"They aren't the problem," I told her. "The problem is that you end up dead, or having to kill Morrolan. I don't consider either possibility to be an ideal outcome."

"I have no intention of killing my cousin," Aliera stated.

"Great. Then you leave him alive, with his reputation dead."

She shrugged. "I am not unconcerned about my cousin's honor," she informed me. "It's just that I'm more concerned with precedence than Morrolan."

"There's another thing, too," I added.

"Oh?"

"To be honest, Aliera, I'm not convinced that you can take Mellar. He's got two experts guarding him, both of them good fighters, and both good sorcerers. I've already told you who trained him as a swordsman, and remember that he was good enough to fight his way into the House of the Dzur. He's determined that only a Jhereg is going to get him, and I'm afraid he may have what it takes to back that up. I'm not at all sure that you'll be able to kill him."

She listened patiently to my monologue, then gave me a cynical smile. "Somehow," she said, "I'll manage."

I decided to change the subject. There was only one other thing I had to try—and that was liable to get me killed. I didn't really feel like doing it, so I asked, "Where is Sethra, by the way?"

"She's returned to Dzur Mountain."

"Eh? Why?"

Aliera studied the floor for a while, then turned her attention back to the cat. "She's getting ready."

"For . . ."

"A war," said Aliera.

Just wonderful. "She thinks it will come to that?"

Aliera nodded. "I didn't tell her what I plan on doing, so she's assuming it's going to happen."

"And she wants to make sure that the Dragons win, eh?"

Aliera gave me a look. "It isn't our custom," she explained, "to fight to lose."

I sighed. Well, now or never, I decided.

"Hey, boss, you don't want to do that."

"You're right. But it's what I'm paid for. Now shut up."

"One final thing, Aliera," I said.

Her eyes narrowed; I guess she picked up something from the tone of my voice. "And that is . . . ?"

"I still work for Morrolan. He pays me, and I therefore owe him a certain amount of loyalty. What you propose doing is in direct violation of his wishes. I won't let you do it."

And, just like that, even as I finished speaking, Pathfinder was in her hand, its point level with my chest. She measured me coolly with her eyes. "Do you think you can stop me, Jhereg?"

I matched her gaze. "Probably not," I admitted. What the Hell? Looking at her, I could see that she was prepared to kill me at once. "If you do, Aliera, Loiosh will kill your cat."

No response. Sheesh! Sometimes I think Aliera has no sense of humor at all.

I looked down the length of the blade. Two feet separated it from my chest—and my soul, which had once been her brother's. I recalled a time, it seemed like ages now, when I had been in a similar position with Morrolan. Then, as now, my thoughts had turned to figuring out which weapon was closest. A poison dart would be a waste of time. My poison works fast, but not *that* fast. I'd have to hit a nerve. Fat chance. I was going to have to go for a kill—anything else wouldn't do. My odds that time had been poor. This time they were worse. At least Morrolan didn't have his weapon out.

I looked back to her eyes. A person's eyes are the first things that let you know when he is about to make a move. I felt the hilt of the dagger up my right sleeve—point out. A sharp, downward motion would be required, and it would be in my hand; an upward motion after that would have it on the way to her throat. From this range, I couldn't miss. From this range, neither could she. I'd probably be dead before she was, and they wouldn't be able to revivify me.

"Just say the word, boss. I'll be at her eyes before—"

"Thanks, but hold, for now."

That last time, Morrolan had changed his mind about killing me because he'd had a use for me, and I'd stopped just short of mortal insult. This time, I felt sure, Aliera would not change her mind—once she decided on a course of action she was as stubborn in pursuing it as I was. After all, I thought bitterly, in an odd sort of way we were related.

I readied myself for action—I would have to get the drop on her to have any chance at all, so there was no point in waiting. It was odd; I realized that everything I'd been doing since I'd spoken to the Demon had been directed either at finding a way to kill Mellar, or risking my life to prevent someone from solving my problem.

I timed my breathing and studied her. Ready, now . . . wait . . . I stopped. What the Hell are you doing, Vlad? Kill Aliera? Be killed by her? What, by the great sea of chaos, would that solve? Sure, Vlad, sure. Good thinking. All we need now is for you to kill a guest of Morrolan's—and the wrong one at that! Sure, all we need now is for Aliera to be dead. That would—

"Wait a minute!" I said. "I've got it!"

"You've got what?" she asked coolly. She wasn't taking any chances on me—she knew what a tricky bastard I was.

"Actually," I said in a more normal tone of voice, "you've got it."

"And what, pray tell, have I got?"

"A Great Weapon," I said.

"Yes, I certainly do," she admitted, not giving an inch.

"A weapon," I continued, "that is irrevocably linked to your soul."

She waited calmly for me to go on, Pathfinder still pointed straight at my heart.

I smiled, and for the first time in days, I actually meant it. "You aren't going to kill Mellar, my friend. *He's* going to kill *you!*"

16

"The adding of a single thread changes the garment."

THERE WAS ABSOLUTELY NO question about it: I was doing too much tele-porting these last few days. I forced myself to take a few minutes to relax at the teleport area for my office building, then went charging up the stairs like a dzur on the hunt. I skimmed past my secretary before he had time to unload mundane business on me and said, "Get Kragar up here. Now."

I stepped into the office and plumped down. Time for some hard thinking. By the time my stomach had settled, the details of the plan were beginning to work themselves out. Timing would have to be precise, but that was nothing new. There were a few things I would have to check on, to make sure they could be done, but these I'd make sure of in advance, and maybe I could find a way around any problems that turned up.

I realized that I was also going to have to depend a lot more on other people than I was at all comfortable with, but life is full of risks.

I started ticking off points, when I realized that Kragar was sitting there, waiting for me to notice him. I sighed. "What's the news today, Kragar?"

"The rumor mill is about to explode—it's leaking from several directions."

"Bad?"

"Bad. We aren't going to be able to keep this under our cloaks for very long; there's too much going on. And the bodies didn't help either."

"Bodies?"

"Yeah. Two bodies turned up this morning. Both sorceresses, Left Hand."

"Oh. Right. One of them would be the one we discussed before."

"Yeah. I don't know who the other one was. My guess is that the Demon found someone else who was spreading too many rumors."

"Could be. Was she killed with a single dagger blow to the heart?"

He looked startled. "Yes, she was. How did you know?"

"And there was a spell on her to prevent revivification, right?"

"Right. Who was she, Vlad?"

"I never learned her name, but she was just what you said, a sorceress from the Left Hand. She was involved in setting up and taking out Morrolan, and he took it personally. I didn't actually know that it would be single shot to the heart, but that's how he was nailed, and he does have a certain sense of poetic justice."

"I see."

"Anything else worth noting?"

He nodded. "Yeah. I wouldn't go outside today, if I were you."

"Oh? What did you hear?"

"It seems that the Demon doesn't like you."

"Oh, wonderful. How did you find this out?"

"We have a few friends in his organization, and they've heard rumors."

"Great. Has he hired anyone?"

"No way of being sure, but it wouldn't surprise me."

"Terrific. Maybe I'll invite him over for a friendly game of 'Spin the Dagger,' and let the whole thing get settled that way."

Kragar snorted.

"Do you think," I asked, "that he'll back off if we finish this Mellar business for him?"

"Maybe. Probably, in fact, if we can do it in time—that is, before the word gets out too far. From what I hear, that isn't too long from now. I guess the council members are starting to feel the bite of digging into their own purses. They aren't going to be able to avoid giving an explanation too much longer."

"That's all right. They aren't going to have to."

He sat up suddenly. "You have something?"

"Yeah. Nothing I'm horribly proud of, but it ought to do the trick—at least part of it."

"What part is that?"

"The hard part."

"What—?"

"Wait a minute."

I stood up and went over to the window. I made an automatic glance down at the street below, then opened the window.

"*Loiosh, see if you can find Daymar. If you do, ask him if he would mind putting in an appearance here.*"

For once, Loiosh didn't make any remarks as he left.

"Okay, Vlad, so what is it?"

"Get a message out that I would very badly like to see Kiera. Then draw off a thousand gold from the treasury, and bring it up here."

"What—?"

"Just do it, okay? I'll explain everything later, after everyone is here."

" 'Everyone?' How many should I figure on?"

"Uh, let me see . . . five. No, six."

"Six? Should I rent a convention hall?"

"Scram."

I settled back to wait and went over the plan again. The rough spot, as I saw it, was whether or not Kiera could pull off the switch. Of course, if anyone could, she could, but it was going to be difficult even for her, I suspected.

There was, to be sure, an even rougher spot, but I tried to avoid thinking about that.

Alarms. "Bing bing," and "Clang," and everything else, both psionic and audible, went off all over the place. I hit the floor rolling and had a dagger ready to throw as my receptionist came bursting in, sword in one hand, dagger in the other. Then I realized what had happened—I saw Daymar floating cross-legged, about three feet off the floor.

I was rather pleased that before he had time to uncross his legs and stand up (or stand down, as the case may be), there were a total of four of my people in the office, weapons drawn and ready.

I stood up, resheathed my dagger, and held my hand up. "False alarm," I explained, "but good job."

Daymar was looking around him with an expression of mild interest on his face. My receptionist was looking unhappy about putting his weapons away. "He broke right through our teleport blocks like they weren't even there! He—"

"I know. But it's all right, never mind."

They stood for a moment, then shrugged and left, casting glances at Daymar, who was now looking bewildered.

"Did you have teleport blocks up?" he said. "I didn't notice any."

"I should have thought to have them turned off. It doesn't matter. Thanks for showing up."

"No problem. What do you need?"

"More help, old friend. Sit down, if you wish." I set an example by picking up my chair and sitting myself down in it. "How are you at illusions?"

He considered this. "Casting them, or breaking them?"

"Casting them. Can you do a good one, quickly?"

"By 'quickly,' I assume you mean fast enough so that no one sees the intermediate stages. Is that right?"

"That, and with little or no warmup time. How are you at it?"

He shrugged. "How is Kiera at stealing?"

"Funny you should bring that up. She should be here—soon, if I'm lucky."

"Oh, really? What's going on, if you don't mind my asking?"

"Hmmm. If it's all right with you, I'd like to wait on the explanations until everyone shows up."

"Oh. Well, that's fine with me. I'll just meditate for a while." And, lifting his legs off the floor, he closed his eyes and began to do so.

At that moment, I heard Loiosh tapping on the window. I opened it. He flew in and landed on my right shoulder. He looked at Daymar, hissed a hiss of puzzlement, and looked away.

I reached out for contact with my wife, found her. *"Honey, could you come over to the office?"*

"Certainly. I don't suppose you have work for me, do you?"

"Not exactly, but the next thing to it."

"Vlad! You've got something!"

"*Yep.*"

"*What is—? No, I suppose you want to wait 'til I'm there, right? I'll be right over.*"

I repeated the process with Aliera, who agreed to teleport in. This time, however, I remembered to drop the protection spells before she arrived.

She looked around. "So this is your office. It looks quite functional."

"Thank you. It's small, but it suits my humble life-style."

"I see."

She noticed Daymar, then, who was still floating some three or four feet off the floor. She rolled her eyes in a gesture that was remarkably like Cawti's. Daymar opened his eyes and stood up.

"Hello, Aliera," he said.

"Hello, Daymar. Mind-probed any teckla, lately?"

"No," he answered with a straight face, "did you have one that you wanted mind-probed?"

"Not at the moment," she said. "Ask me again next Cycle."

"I'll be sure to."

He probably would, too, I reflected, if they were both still around then.

Cawti arrived at that moment, in time to avoid any further clashes between Hawk and Dragon. She greeted Aliera warmly. Aliera gave her a cheery smile, and they went off into a corner to gossip. The two of them had become close friends in recent months, based in part on a mutual friendship with Lady Norathar. Norathar was a Dragon turned Jhereg turned Dragon, who had been Cawti's partner, if you recall. Aliera had been instrumental in returning to Norathar her rightful place as a Dragonlord. Well, so had I, but never mind. That's another story.

It occurred to me, then, that Norathar was another one who would be somewhat caught in the middle by this whole thing. Her two best friends were going to have to try to kill each other, and she had loyalties on both sides. I put it out of my mind. We were here to prevent her from having to make that choice.

Kiera entered shortly, followed by Kragar. He handed me a large purse, which I immediately turned over to Kiera.

"Still another job, Vlad? I ought to teach you the craft. You could save a lot of time and money if you could do it on your own."

"Kiera," I said, "there aren't enough hours in the day for me to learn your art. Besides, my grandfather doesn't approve of stealing. Are you willing to help me out in this? It's in a good cause."

She absently weighed the purse, no doubt able to tell within a few Imperials how much was in it. "It is?" she said. "Oh, well. I guess I'll help you out anyway." She smiled her little smile and looked at the others in the room.

"Oh, yes," I said. "Kiera, this is Aliera e'Kieron—"

"We know each other," interrupted Aliera.

They smiled at each other, and I was surprised to note that the smiles seemed genuine. For a while I'd been afraid that Kiera had once stolen something of Aliera's. Friendships do turn up in the oddest places.

"Okay," I said, "let's get down to business. I think everyone knows everyone, right?"

There was no disagreement.

"Good. Let's get comfortable."

Kragar had, without my mentioning it, made sure that there were six chairs in the room, and had sent out for a good wine and six glasses. These arrived, and he went around the room making sure everyone's was full, before sitting down himself. Daymar disdained the chair, preferring to float. Loiosh assumed his position on my right shoulder.

I began to feel a little nervous about the whole thing. I had gathered in that room a master thief, a high noble of the House of the Hawk, a Dragonlord who traced her lineage back to Kieron himself, and a highly skilled assassin. And Kragar. I was just a bit troubled. Who was I to use these people as if they were common Jhereg to be hired and sent out?

I caught Aliera's eye. She was looking at me steadily and confidently. Cawti, also, was waiting patiently for me to describe how we were going to get out of this.

That's who I was, of course. Cawti's husband, Aliera's friend, and more . . . and the one who knew, possibly, how to handle this situation.

I cleared my throat, took a sip of wine, and organized my thoughts. "My friends," I said, "I would like to thank each of you for coming here, and agreeing to help me out on this. With some of you, it is, of course, in your own best interest, for one reason or another, that this matter be favorably settled. And to you, I would like to add that I am honored that you are trusting me to handle it. To those of you with no direct interest, I am deeply grateful that you are willing to help me at all. I give you my assurance that I won't forget this."

"Get to the point."

"Shut up, Loiosh."

"As to the problem, well, most of you know what it is, to one degree or another. Put simply, a high noble in the Jhereg is under the protection of Lord Morrolan, and it is necessary that he be killed, and not later than tomorrow at that, or," I paused for another sip of wine and for effect, "or events will occur to the severe detriment of some of us."

Aliera snorted at the understatement. Kiera chuckled.

"The important thing to remember is the time limit. For reasons that I would prefer not to go into, we have only today and tomorrow. Today would be much better, but I'm afraid that we're going to have to take today to iron out difficulties, and to practice our parts.

"Now, it is important to some of us," I looked quickly at Aliera, but her face betrayed no emotion, "that nothing be done which would compromise Morrolan's reputation as a host. That is, we can't do anything to this person, Mellar, while he is a guest at Castle Black, nor can we force him to leave by threats or by magic, such as mind-control."

I looked around the room. I still had everyone's attention. "I think I've found a method. Allow me to demonstrate what I have in mind, first, so we can get the hard part down before I go on with the rest of it. Kragar, stand up for a moment, please."

He did so. I came around the desk and drew my rapier. His eyebrows arched, but he said nothing.

"Assume for a moment," I said, "that you have weapons secreted about your person at every conceivable point."

He smiled a little. Assume, Hell!

"Draw your blade," I continued, "and get into a guard position."

He did so, standing full forward, with his blade pointed straight at my eyes, level with his own head. His blade was a lot heavier and somewhat longer than mine, and it formed a straight line from his eyes to mine. His palm was down, his elbow out. There was a certain grace apparent, although I still consider the Eastern *en garde* position to be more elegant.

I stood for a moment, then attacked, simulating the Dragaeran move for a straight head cut. I came at his head, just below the line of his blade, giving me a sharp angle up.

He made the obvious parry, dropping his elbow so that his sword also angled up, even more sharply than mine. Also, the strong of his blade was matched against the weak of mine. This lined him up very well for a cut down at my head; however, before he could take it, I moved in and . . .

I felt something strike my stomach, lightly. I looked down, and saw his left hand there. Had this been a real fight, there would have been a dagger clutched in that hand. Had we been alone, he would probably have used a real dagger and avoided hitting me with it, but he wasn't keen on letting all of these people in on where he kept his extra blades. I resumed a normal position, saluted him, and sheathed my blade.

"Where," I asked, "did you get the dagger from?"

"Left forearm sheath," he said, with no hesitation.

"Good. Is there anywhere else you could have gotten it from that would have worked as well?"

He looked thoughtful for a moment, then he said, "I was assuming a spring-loaded type of forearm sheath, set for left-hand use. If he has it set for a right-hand draw, which is just as common, then I'd expect a simple waist sheath would be the one he'd go for. Either way it would be fast. I can use the fact that the whole left side of your body is undefended, and I can attack with the same motion I draw with. An upper thigh sheath would mean dropping my arm lower than I have to, there isn't any reason to go cross-body, and anything else is worse."

I nodded. "Okay. Cawti, anything to add, or do you agree?"

She thought for a moment, then shook her head. "No, he's right. It would be one of those two."

"Good. Kragar, I want you to secure two Morganti daggers."

He looked surprised for a moment, then shrugged. "Okay. How strong do you want them?"

"Strong enough for anyone to tell that they are Morganti, but not so strong that they are apparent when they're sitting in their sheaths, okay?"

"Okay, I can find a couple like that. And, let me guess, you want one to be the right size for a waist sheath, and the other to be the right size for a forearm sheath."

"You've got it. Let me see for a minute. . . ." I had looked very closely for the weapons Mellar was carrying, but I hadn't been so much concerned with how big they were as where they were. I tried to remember. . . . Where was that little bulge? Ah, yes. And when he had turned from talking to the Hawklord, I had seen how much hilt from the waist sheath? Right. It looked like a standard bone hilt. How long a blade would make it balance right? And how wide? I'd have to guess, but I felt I could come pretty close.

"Waist sheath," I announced. "Overall length, approximately fourteen inches, of which half is blade. Just a fraction over an inch wide at the widest. Forearm sheath: call it nine inches overall. The blade is about five-and-a-half inches long, and about three-quarters of an inch wide near the guard." I stopped. "Any problem?"

He looked uncomfortable. "I don't know, Vlad. I should be able to get them, but I can't count on it. I'll talk to my supplier, and see what he has, but you're being damn precise."

"I know. Do the best you can. Remember, they don't have to be untraceable this time."

"That will help."

"Good."

I turned to Kiera. "Now, the big question. Can you lighten Mellar of a pair of daggers without his noticing, and, more of a problem, without his bodyguard noticing? I'm referring, of course, to the waist and forearm daggers."

She just smiled in answer.

"Okay, now, can you return them again? Can you put them back without his noticing?"

Her brows came together. " 'Return them?' I don't know . . . I think so . . . maybe. I take it you mean substituting two new ones for the ones he has, right?"

I nodded.

"And," I added, "remember that they're going to be Morganti daggers, so they have to stay unnoticeable during the switch."

She brushed it off. "If I can do it at all, the fact that they're Morganti won't make any difference." She took on a vacant expression for a moment, and I noticed her hand twitching, as she mentally went through the motions that would be needed. "The waist dagger," she said finally, "can be done. About the other one . . ." she continued to look thoughtful. "Vlad, do you know if he has a spring-loaded mechanism for the left-hand, or just a reverse right-hand draw setup?"

I thought about it. I brought up my memory of seeing him again, and the bulge that had to be that blade, but I couldn't quite pin it down. "I don't know. I'm sure he has something, I mean, one or the other, but I just can't tell which one. Hmmmm, it just occurred to me, that if he has the reverse draw type, he won't use it for what we're talking about doing, so it really doesn't matter. We can assume—"

"Say, Vlad," said Kragar suddenly. "Remember that he's been trained as a master swordsman. That means he'll figure on fighting sword and dagger. Chances are, he's got the spring mechanism, so he can just twist his wrist and have a blade pop into his left hand."

I nodded.

Kiera said, "Do you have a forearm sheath, Vlad?"

It made me uncomfortable to discuss it, but I realized what she had in mind, and it was a reasonable question. I nodded.

"Spring, or right-hand draw?"

"Right-hand draw," I said.

She stood up. "Those are easier," she said, "but that will make up for the fact that you'll be watching for it. Let's see what I can do . . ." She crossed in front of Cawti and Kragar and stood in front of my desk. She set her wineglass down a few inches from my own. I was holding it loosely, and the cuff was open a little, which should work to her advantage.

I kept my eyes on my arm and her hand where she set the glass down. So far as I could tell, her hand never came closer than three inches from mine.

She walked back to her chair and sat down again.

"How was that?" she asked.

I pulled back my sleeve, and checked the sheath. It held the same dagger it always had.

"Fine," I said, "except for the little matter that—" I stopped. She was smiling that smile of hers that I knew so well. She reached into her cloak, pulled out a dagger, and held it up. I heard a gasp, and saw Kragar staring at it.

He gave a quick twist to his left wrist, and suddenly a knife appeared in his hand. He looked at it, and his mouth dropped open. He held it as if it were a poisonous snake. He closed his mouth again, swallowed, and handed the dagger back to Kiera. She returned Kragar's to him.

"Misdirection," she explained.

"I'm convinced," said Kragar.

"Me, too," I said.

Kiera looked pleased.

I suddenly felt a lot better. This thing might actually work.

"I saw the whole thing, boss."

"Sure you did, Loiosh."

"Good," I said. "Now, Aliera, did you see that stroke I made at Kragar, with a bind following it?"

"Yes."

"Can you make the exact same attack?"

"I suspect so," she answered drily.

"Okay. I'll work on it with you. It's going to have to be perfect."

She nodded.

I turned to Cawti. "You're going to have to do a simple takeout."

"Any particular fashion?"

"Very quick, very quiet, and very unnoticeable. I'll be providing a distraction, which should help somewhat, but we have to be absolutely sure that no one sees you do it, or Mellar will be alerted too soon, and the whole thing blows up."

"Can I kill the guy?"

"No problem. Your target is an uninvited guest, so anything that happens to him is his problem."

"That makes things easier. I don't think I'll have any difficulty."

"Remember, he's a damn good sorcerer, and you aren't going to have much time to check him over."

"So? I eat sorcerers for breakfast."

"You'll have to cook me up one, sometime."

She smiled, slightly. "Does he have any protective spells up at the moment?"

I looked over at Aliera, who had checked the two of them out after I had left her.

"No," she said. "They're both good enough to get defenses up quickly if they have to, but I guess they don't want to call attention to themselves by using spells in Castle Black unless they actually have to."

"You keep referring to 'they,' " said Kiera. "Which one am I going to be taking out?"

"That's just the problem," I said. "We don't know. It will be whichever one is on Mellar's left, and we don't know which one that will be. Does that present a problem?"

She gave me what I call her I-know-something-you-don't-know smile, and made a dagger appear in her right hand. She spun it in the air, caught it, and made it disappear. I held myself answered.

"Daymar," I said, turning to him, "you're going to have to throw an illusion at me. It's going to have to be fast, thorough, and undetectable."

Daymar looked suddenly doubtful. "Undetectable? Morrolan will be able to tell that I'm throwing a spell in his castle no matter how subtle I am."

"Morrolan won't be there, so you don't need to worry about him. It does, however, have to be good enough so that a topnotch sorcerer, who *will* be there, doesn't notice it. Of course, he'll be rather busy at the time."

Daymar thought for a minute. "How long does the illusion have to stay on?"

"About five seconds."

"No problem, then."

"Good. Then that's everything. Now, here's the plan. . . ."

*   *   *

"I like it, Vlad," said Kragar, "up to the teleport. That leaves you in a pretty miserable position, doesn't it? Why don't we go back to the original plan that you worked up with Aliera at that point?"

"You aren't thinking it through," I told him. "We're really pulling an elaborate hoax. It has to happen fast enough for Mellar to act while he's disoriented and confused. In fact, we're going to have to make him panic. Someone like Mellar isn't going to panic easily, and it isn't going to last very long. If we give him time to think it through, he'll realize what happened and just teleport back. We'll be right back where we started."

"Do you think," asked Kragar, "that we can get Morrolan to put up a teleport block around Castle Black so he can't come back there? Or maybe Aliera can do it."

"Aliera isn't going to be in any condition to put up or keep up a teleport block, if you remember. And if Morrolan is there to do it, he'll interfere in the earlier part of the plan, and we won't be able to bring it off at all."

"What about," said Cawti "letting Morrolan in on it from the beginning?"

Aliera answered for me. "He'd never permit me to do what I'm going to do, even if he agreed with the rest—which he wouldn't, by the way."

"Why not?"

"Because he's Morrolan. When this is over, if it works, he'll agree that it was a fine thing to do. But in the meantime, he'll try to stop it if he can."

"What do you mean," Cawti asked, "about his not permitting you to do what you are going to do?"

"Just what I said. Even if he wasn't involved in any other way, he'd at least try to stop that part."

"Why? If you aren't in any danger—"

"I never said," replied Aliera softly, "that I wouldn't be in any danger."

Cawti looked at her sharply. "I don't pretend to understand Great Weapons, but if it isn't safe—"

"Nothing is 'safe.' This is a better chance than I'd get if I did something that forced Morrolan to kill me."

Cawti looked troubled. "But Aliera, your *soul*—"

"So what? I think I have a good chance of surviving, and this leaves Morrolan with his honor intact and the problem solved. The other way, Morrolan and I both end up worse off, with no chance at all for things to work out right. This is our best chance."

Cawti still looked unhappy, but she didn't say anything more on the subject. Kragar said, "What about if Daymar throws a second illusion so I can get in on it?"

"No good," I said. "Who's going to do the teleport then? We can't do it ourselves, remember, because that's using magic against a guest at Castle Black. I'm convinced that it will be one of the two bodyguards who does the teleport, so they can make it untraceable at the same time."

"Even if Mellar asks you to do it?"

I looked at Aliera, who nodded. "Even then," she said. "He has to leave under his own power, or by the hand of one of his own people, or Morrolan will almost certainly take offense."

"Well—I suppose. But there has to be some way that we can get help to you."

I shrugged. "Sure, it could be that they don't get their trace-blocks up fast enough, so you could find me then. And I expect that Aliera will be able to find me with Pathfinder—after she recovers." I carefully didn't add "if she recovers."

"And how long," said Kragar, "will that take?"

"Who can say?" said Aliera. "Nothing like this has ever been done before, so far as I know."

Cawti looked grim. "And there isn't any way we're going to be able to find you ourselves?"

"Well," I said, "it would be nice if you tried. But I'm sure that some kind of block will be put up, and the guy doing it is good. Without having Pathfinder, you'll have to spend quite a while breaking down his spell."

Cawti looked away. "From what I hear, Vlad, you aren't in the same class with him as a fighter."

"I'm aware of that. But I fight Eastern-style, remember? And my intention is to take him before he even knows that I'm not who I'm supposed to be."

"Which reminds me," said Aliera. "If it does come down to a fight, you're going to have to keep him busy the whole time."

"I expect that he'll take care of that," I said drily. "But why?"

"Because if he realizes what has just happened—and the way you spoke of him, he will—he'll just teleport right back to Castle Black if you give him the chance to."

Great. "You're right," I admitted. "He probably will. How long will it take him, do you think?"

"To do the teleport? If I'm right in my assessment, it will take him only two or three seconds."

"So I can't allow him more than two seconds of breathing time during the fight." I shrugged. "That's all right. As I said, I don't expect him to allow *me* any breathing time, if it comes down to a fight. But I'm hoping it won't."

"By the way," said Kragar, "what happens if he turns to you and tells you to teleport him out?"

"I'm hoping he'll ask the other guy—which is a fifty-fifty chance. If he does turn to me, I'll do a dumb and stupid look and pretend that I'm in a state of shock. That should be believable."

Daymar snapped his fingers. "The Necromancer!" he said. "She won't have to trace the teleport; she can use her own ways of getting to you."

"Not without psionic contact," I said. "And chances are that whatever blocks they put up against tracing the teleport will block out general tracing spells as well—and that means that you won't be able to contact me, and I won't be able to contact you."

"Oh," said Daymar.

"Well," I asked the room in general, "can anyone think of any alternatives? Anything I might have missed?"

There was silence.

"I didn't think so," I said. "All right, that's what we've got. Let's get to work."

Kragar left to procure the daggers. The others went off to practice their parts. I went into the weapons closet and found two identical knives. They were long, thin stilettos, with seven inches of blade.

I picked one up and sharpened it carefully, spending over an hour on it. I wouldn't have to coat this one with nonreflective black paint, I decided, since there wasn't going to be much sneaking around involved here after I had it in my hand.

It isn't that I'm not willing to use any weapon I can get at to finish a job; it's just that I feel that I'm better off if I have a blade in mind from the beginning and know it exactly. That is why I picked out two identical weapons. After sharpening the one, I wouldn't touch it again until I left for Castle Black tomorrow. That way, it would have very little, if any, association with me. Since it had so little of my "feel" about it, I could safely leave it right at the scene. This is much safer than being caught later with it on me—since there is no way to disguise the link between murder weapon and victim.

I picked up the duplicate, felt the weight and balance, and held it for a while. I took a few cuts and lunges with the thing in either hand, and then concentrated for a while on using my left hand with it.

I drew my rapier and fenced a little, practicing flipping it at a target on the wall between parry and riposte. In fact, I would never plan on throwing a knife at someone if this were a standard job, but in this case, it might be necessary.

I took out a few pieces of wood, then, and set them against the wall, and plunged the knife into them several times, alternating strokes. I used every type of attack I could think of, each several times.

I was satisfied. It was a good blade. Not very good for cutting, but it was unlikely that the death blow would be a cut. It threw well enough—although not perfectly—and it fit very well into my hand for any kind of stabbing motion that I was likely to make.

I picked out a sheath for it, and, after some thought, secured it to the outside of my left leg, just above the knee. The knife was a bit too long to be concealed effectively, but my cloak would cover it up pretty well, and it was perfectly placed for maximum speed of draw if I were fencing. Well, no; around the back of my neck would have been better for that, but then I'd have it in my hand in somewhat of an overhand position, which wouldn't be as good as an underhanded grip for stabbing in the middle of a bind, for example.

Loiosh watched my preparations in silence for a while, then he said, *"There is one problem with your plan, boss."*

"That being?"

"The 'distraction' part."

"What about it?"

"If I'm busy distracting people, that means I'm not along when you take off."

"I know."

"Well, I don't like it!"

"To be perfectly honest with you, old friend, neither do I."

17

"No matter how subtle the wizard,
a knife between the shoulder blades will
seriously cramp his style."

EVERY CITIZEN OF THE Dragaeran Empire has a permanent link to the Imperial Orb, which circles the head of the Empress with colors that change to reflect the sovereign's mood at the moment.

This one link serves many functions at the same time. Perhaps the most important one, to most people, is that it allows the use of the power from the great sea of amorphia (as distinct from the lesser one that Adron created), which provides the energy for sorcery. To anyone skilled enough, this power can be shaped, molded, and used for just about anything—depending, of course, on the skill of the user.

One of its less important functions, to most people, is that one need only concentrate briefly in the proper way, and one knows precisely what time it is, according to the Imperial Clock.

I have, I will admit, some small skill in sorcery. I mean, I can start a fire with it, or teleport if I have to, or kill someone with it—if he isn't very good, and I get lucky. On the other hand, I only rarely have a use for it. But the Imperial Clock has been a friend that I could count on for years.

Eight hours past noon, every other day (and today was one), Morrolan inspected his guard positions personally. He would go outside of Castle Black, and teleport from tower to tower, speaking with the guards and checking them over. There was rarely, if ever, anything to correct or to criticize, but it was very effective for troop morale. It was also one of relatively few things that Morrolan did with any regularity.

Eight hours past noon, on this day, the day after we had met in my office, Morrolan was inspecting his guard positions, and so was not in the banquet hall of Castle Black.

I was.

Daymar was there as well, standing next to me. Cawti was around somewhere, as was Kiera. Aliera was somewhere outside the hall, waiting.

I tried to be inconspicuous. I didn't drink anything, because I didn't want anyone to notice that my hand was trembling.

I looked around the room for a while and finally spotted Mellar. Kiera was standing about ten feet away from him, to his rear, and looking in my direction. I decided that I must, at least in part, be succeeding in being inconspicuous, since none of my acquaintances had yet seen me. Good. If we could just hold onto that kind of luck for another couple of minutes, it wouldn't matter.

Okay. Relax, hands. Shoulder muscles, loosen up. Stomach, unknot. Neck, ease up. Knees, loose your stiffness—it's time to go.

I nodded to Kiera. She nodded back. I was no longer nervous.

From where I stood, I had a plain view of Kiera as she walked past one of Mellar's bodyguards, reached for a glass of wine past him, and walked away. I never saw her make the transfer. In fact, I wondered whether it had been made at all until Kiera caught my eye and nodded. I looked at her right hand, which was at her side. She had two fingers out, the rest in a fist. Both weapons planted. Good. I let my eyes acknowledge.

Here we go, I said to myself.

I glanced around the room then. This was the one part that I didn't have planned out—because I couldn't know who would be here from one day to the next—or one moment to the next.

Over near a table, about twenty feet away from me, I spotted the Hawklord who had been speaking to Mellar the other day. Perfect! I owed him one. I moved over toward him, planning my part. I observed the contents of the table and fitted it in. I took enough time getting there to give Loiosh his instructions in detail.

"Know your part, Loiosh?"

"Worry about your own lines, boss. I'm just doing what comes naturally."

I leaned on the table, briefly raised my nobility a couple of notches, and said, "I say, hand me a glass of that Kiereth, four thirty-seven, will you?"

For a minute, I was afraid I'd overdone it when he actually started reaching for it, but then he caught himself, and turned to face me fully, his voice and eyes cold.

"I don't fetch for Jhereg," he announced. "Or Easterners."

Good. He was mine, now.

I pretended amusement. "Oh, indeed?" I responded, turning on my best sardonic smile. "Nervous about serving your betters, eh? Well, that's quite all right."

He glared, then, and his hand went to his sword hilt. Then, remembering where he was, I suppose, he let go of it.

"I must ask Morrolan," he said, "why he allows inferiors to share his accommodations."

It occurred to me that I should encourage him to do so, just to see how long he lasted—but I had a part to play. "Do that," I said. "I must admit to being curious as well. Let me know how it is that he justifies your presence here, among gentlefolk."

There were a few people watching us now, wondering whether the Hawk would challenge me, or simply attack. I didn't really care, as it happened.

He felt the crowd watching too. "Do you think," he said, "to claim equality with Dragaerans?"

"At least," I replied, smiling.

He smiled back, having mastered his temper. "What a quaint notion. A Dragaeran would not think to speak to anyone that way unless he was ready to back it up with steel."

I laughed aloud. "Oh, always, anytime," I said.

"Very well. My seconds will call upon you in the morning."

I pretended surprise.

"They will?" I said. "My seconds will call upon you in the alley."

I turned my back on him and walked away.

"*What?*" came the enraged cry behind me. I had taken three steps when I heard the sound of steel being drawn. I continued walking briskly.

"*Now, Loiosh!*"

"*On my way, boss.*"

I felt the jhereg leave my shoulder, as I continued walking smoothly and evenly away from the Hawklord. Now, at this point, was when I was going to need all of the skills Kiera had taught me years before.

I heard a cry behind me, and the shouts of "It bit me!" and "Help!" and "Get a healer!" and "Where's the damn Jhereg?" and "Look, he's dying!"

There would be no eyes on me, I knew, as I walked toward Mellar. His bodyguards, I noted, didn't seem especially alert, although they, of all the crowd, must have recognized the distraction for what it was.

Mellar's face was calm. I was taken with sudden admiration for him. This was what he'd been expecting. He figured to die here and now and was ready for it. His bodyguards knew, and weren't making any effort to stop it. Could I have stood there like that, waiting for, perhaps, a Morganti dagger in my back? Not a chance.

I smiled to myself. He was about to get a surprise, however. I continued toward him, coming around the back. I was aware of the crowd around me as I blended in with it, but no one was aware of me. I had, to all intents and purposes, vanished. The art of the assassin. It would take an exceptional skill to spot me at this point—a skill that was beyond even the two bodyguards, I was sure.

Mellar stood, unmoving, awaiting the touch of a blade. He'd been flirting with a young female Tsalmoth who was playing dumb teckla maiden, while Mellar pretended he believed it. She was looking at him curiously now, because he'd stopped speaking.

And, amazingly, he actually began to smile. His lips curled up into the barest, thinnest smile.

"*Now, Aliera!*"

"*Here I come!*"

May Verra protect thy soul, lady who was my sister. . . .

The smile faded from Mellar's face as a shrill, drunken voice rang out through the room.

"Where is he?" cried Aliera. "Show me the teckla who would dishonor my cousin's name!"

A path cleared in front of Aliera. I got a glimpse of the Necromancer, a shocked look on her face. It is rare to see her shocked. She would probably have done something, but she was just too far away.

Speaking of too far away . . .

"*Loiosh?*"

"*I'm busy, dammit! They won't let me go! I'm trying to get over there, but—*"

"Forget it. Like we discussed. We just can't risk it. Stay where you are."

"*But—*"

"No."

I moved in as Aliera did—she from the front, and I from the back. Of course. *Good luck, boss.*"

I moved into position and noticed a sudden tension in Mellar's back. He must have recognized the naked blade in Aliera's hand as Morganti. I'm sure the whole room was aware of it.

I was in position, so I could hear everything he said. I heard him curse under his breath. "Not her, dammit!" he hissed to his bodyguards. "Stop her."

The two of them moved forward to bar Aliera's path, but she was the quickest. From her upraised left hand, a green scintillating light flashed out. Then I saw something that I'd heard about, but had never actually seen before. The energy she sent at them split; forked into two bolts, which caught the two bodyguards full in the chest. They were flung backwards and fell heavily. If we'd given them time to think, they would certainly have realized that Aliera couldn't be very drunk to throw a spell like that. They were both good enough to block part of the effects and they began to pick themselves up.

And, at that moment, Cawti, my wife, who had once been called "The Dagger of the Jhereg," struck. Silently, swiftly, and with perfect accuracy.

I don't think anyone else in the room would have seen it even if they hadn't all been busy staring at Aliera, who was waving Pathfinder around drunkenly over her head. But one of the two fallen bodyguards, as he tried to pick himself up, tried to cry out, found that he no longer had a larynx to do it with, and fell back.

And then I felt a tingling sensation as Daymar's spell took effect. Daymar threw his second spell just as quickly, and the dead bodyguard became invisible.

I stood up in his place. I matched paces with my "partner," but we saw we couldn't get there in time. I strongly suspect that the other fellow was a great deal more disturbed by this than I was.

Mellar also realized that we would be too late to save him. He now had two choices: he could allow Aliera to kill him, thus dying amid the ruins of three hundred or more years of planning, or he could fight Aliera.

His sword was out in a flash, and he took his guard position as Aliera swayed toward him. He certainly knew by now that he was going to have to kill her, if he could. His mind, I knew, would be working hard now; planning his blow, estimating her timing, and realizing gratefully that he could kill her without making it permanent if he was careful. He had to make sure that she died, but he must avoid any blow to the head.

He fell back a step. "My lady, you're drunk—" he began, but Aliera struck before he could finish. Pathfinder swung in a tight arc, straight for the right side of his head. If he'd been any slower, or the attack had been any more difficult to parry, it would have all been over for Mellar right there. But he made the obvious parry, and Aliera stepped in to bind.

He was too good a swordsman to miss the obvious opening, and he didn't. The back of my mind noted that he did, indeed, have a spring mechanism for his left sleeve dagger.

There was a flash of motion by his left hand, and his dagger caught her in the abdomen.

He must have realized, even before it struck her, that something was wrong. As it hit, I could feel within my mind the sentience that identifies a Morganti weapon.

Aliera screamed. It may or may not have been genuine, but it was one of the most horrendous screams I have ever heard. I shuddered to hear it, and to see the look on her face as the soul-eating blade entered her body. Mellar moved forward and tried vainly to draw it out, but its own power held it in as Aliera slumped to the floor, her screams dying away. The blade came free in Mellar's hand.

There was a moment of silence, and lack of motion. Mellar stared down at the knife. The other bodyguard and I stood next to him, frozen, as everyone else. Realization grew in Mellar that he had just thrown away any claim to protection he could have had from Morrolan. Anyone could kill him now, with no recriminations. He would be feeling his whole plan falling into pieces, and, no doubt, could only think of one thing: escape. Try to get out of this mess and come up with something else.

And, in this moment of weakness, of near panic, the final stroke came, administered by Daymar, to complete his feeling of disorientation and push him over the edge.

Mellar felt the mind-probe hit and cried out. I didn't know at that time whether he was sufficiently disoriented that his mental defenses were down. The mind-probe might have worked, or might have failed, but it worked as far as I was concerned: Mellar turned to me. "Get us out of here!" he yelled. It was unfortunate that he chose to look at me instead of the other bodyguard, but I had known that it could happen.

I didn't look back at him; just stared straight ahead. He saw, no doubt, the stunned and stupefied expression I was wearing. I heard the unmistakable note of panic in his voice, now, as he turned to the other bodyguard. The crowd was beginning to react, and I sincerely hoped that Sethra the Younger or the Necromancer didn't get to him before we were able to get out of here.

"Move!" he said to the other bodyguard. "Get us out!"

At that moment, I think, something must have clicked in him, and he turned back to me, his eyes growing wider still. Either Daymar's spell was fading so I no longer looked like the bodyguard I was imitating, or he noticed a mannerism that I didn't perform right. He was backing away from me as the walls vanished around us.

As best I could, I ignored the nausea that accompanied the teleport and made a fast decision.

If he hadn't realized that something was wrong, if he had happened to turn to the other one first, there would have been no problem. I would have simply killed him and finished off the bodyguard as best I could. Now, however, it was different.

I had time to take out either Mellar, or the other bodyguard, but I couldn't get both before they got in a cut or two at me. Which one should I go for?

The bodyguard would be setting up a teleport block and a spell to prevent tracing, while Mellar had already drawn his blade. Also, Mellar was closer.

However, I had to make sure that Mellar was killed permanently. As I've said, it is no easy thing to kill someone in such a way that he can't be revivified. With him ready and facing me, it wouldn't be as easy as it would have been if I'd had a free shot at the back of his head. What if I took him out, but wasn't able to make it permanent? And then the bodyguard were to nail me? The latter would just teleport again with Mellar's body, and get him brought back at his leisure. If I went for the guard, I could take the time and do a thorough job on Mellar, and not have to worry about Mellar skipping off on me.

What decided me, however, was the fact that the bodyguard was a sorcerer. That gave him a bigger advantage over me in this situation than I liked.

I didn't stop to think about any of this; it just flashed through my mind as I moved.

I threw myself backward, and, as my right hand went for my blade, my left hand found three poison darts. I flipped them toward the bodyguard and mentally recited a short prayer to Verra.

Mellar's first swing, which occurred just about then, missed; I had managed to get just out of range. Gods! He was strong! I was on the ground by then, but I had my rapier out. I rolled to my left and came up . . .

. . . in time to parry, just barely, a cut that would have split my skull open. My arm rang from the blow of his heavier sword, and I heard the welcome sound of a body falling off to my left. The bodyguard was out of it, at least. Thank you, Verra.

At that point I first became aware of my surroundings. We were outside, in a jungle area. That would put us somewhere to the west of Adrilankha, which meant at least three hundred miles from Castle Black. They weren't going to be able to trace the teleport in time to help me, then; not if the sorcerer/bodyguard had been able to get his spell off. I would have to assume that I was on my own.

Mellar struck again. I fell back as fast as I could, hoping like Hell that there was no obstruction behind me. At the best of times, I was nowhere near as good a fighter as Mellar, and at this moment my stomach was churning and it was taking a great deal of effort just to keep my eyes focused on him. On the other hand, an inferior swordsman can hold off a superior swordsman for quite a while, as long as he can keep retreating. I could only hope that he would let up enough to give me a chance to throw my dagger at him, and that I was able to hit him with it—without being nailed at the same time. At that moment, I would have let him get through to me if I could have been sure of doing a complete job on him in exchange. I looked for the chance, in fact.

He, however, had no intention of giving me any such opportunity. Whether he guessed my intentions or not I don't know, but he didn't let up for an instant. He kept hacking at my head and advancing. His left hand found a knife.

I felt a cold shiver run up my spine as I realized that he was now holding the Morganti blade that I had set him up with, one of the two we gave him, to make sure that he used one on Aliera. He noticed it, then, and his eyes widened. For the first time, he smiled. It was a very unpleasant smile to be on the wrong end of. The same could be said for the dagger. Somehow, at that moment, the irony of the whole thing was lost on me.

I kept falling back. The only thing that had kept me alive so far, I knew, was the fact that he wasn't used to a fencer who presented only the side of his body, rather than the full forward of the sword-and-dagger Dragaeran style. He, of course, was fighting full forward, with a dagger up in a position to strike, or parry, or cast spells with.

He wasn't about to cast spells with it, and he didn't need to parry because I hadn't had a chance to attack yet. Not even a simple riposte—and now he had two blades to my one. Also, he was a good enough swordsman that it wouldn't take him long to learn how to deal with my kind of swordplay.

He was quite content, meanwhile, to keep me busy until I ran up against a tree or tripped on a log, as I inevitably would in this jungle. Then it would be all over—he'd come in with the dagger, and my soul would go to feed a sentience in nine inches of cold steel.

He spoke for the first time. "It was all a trick from the beginning, wasn't it?"

I didn't answer, not having the breath.

"I can see it now," he continued. "It might have worked, too, if you were a better swordsman, or if you had nailed me when you had the chance, instead of going for my friend back there."

That's right, you bastard, I thought. Rub it in.

"But as it is," he continued, "they should know the truth by now at Castle Black. If I can figure it out from here, they can certainly figure it out from there, where they have the body and the blade to look at. What's to stop me from just going back there?"

I stopped and tried to bind him, parrying strongly. He took a cut at me with the dagger, however, and I had to jump back. I'd had no chance for an attack.

"It is unfortunate," he went on, "that I can teleport, or it might have worked anyway."

It takes you two or three seconds to teleport, my friend, and I don't intend to give you two or three seconds. Sorry, but I don't psych.

He must have realized that, too, because he stopped talking. I managed to put my left hand on the stiletto I'd selected to destroy him with, and I pulled it out. I cradled it in my hand like a jhereg holds her egg. I thought, very briefly, about trying to flip it at him, but to do that I'd have to turn full forward. If I did that, he'd have me before I could even loose it, and my head would be rolling on the ground.

For a moment, then, I considered that. If I fell to his sword, the dagger couldn't hurt me. It requires a living soul to feed such a blade. My soul would be safe, and, just maybe, I could take him with me.

I threw away the idea and stepped back again. No, he was going to have to do it all himself—that much I'd take from him. I was not about to let him cut me down and leave me here, for the wild jhereg to feed on my corpse, to complete the irony of the situation.

. . . Jhereg? Wild jhereg? I felt a sudden breeze, cool against the back of my neck, reminiscent of the feel of a knife's edge, and of other things.

A memory came back to haunt me, from years ago. This same jungle it was. . . . Could I . . . ?

I was just distracted enough by the thought that I almost missed a parry. I jumped backward, and his deflected sword ripped into my side. I felt the blood start to flow, and it began to hurt. Verra be thanked, my stomach was settling down.

Witchcraft is similar to sorcery in many ways, but uses one's own psionic powers rather than an external energy source. The rituals and incantations were used to force the mind down the right path, and to direct the power. How much were they really necessary?

My mind reached back . . . back . . . back to the time I had summoned the jhereg who was Loiosh's mother from these very jungles. His mother was, quite likely, long dead, but I didn't need her. Could I do it again?

Probably not.

"*Come to me, blood of my House. Join me, hunt with me, find me.*"

I almost stumbled, and was almost killed, but didn't and was not. What the Hell was it? Come on, brain, think!

As my grandfather had taught me long ago, I let my arm, and my wrist, and even my fingers do all the work of keeping me alive. My mind had other things to do, the swordarm would just have to take care of itself.

Something . . . something about . . . wings? No, *winds*, that was it, winds. . . .

"*Let the winds of Jungle's night . . .*"

Something, perhaps the look on Mellar's face, warned me of the tree behind me. Somehow I stepped around it without being spitted.

"*Stay the hunter in her flight.*"

I felt myself weakening. Blood loss, of course. I didn't have time for that.

"*Evening's breath to witch's mind . . .*"

I wondered whether Loiosh would ever speak to me again. I wondered whether anyone would be able to speak to me again.

"Let our fates be intertwined."

Mellar changed tactics, suddenly, and his sword thrust at my chest, instead of chopping at my head. I was forced into a clumsy parry, and he caught me with the tip. Was that a rib cracking, or just a good imitation? I brought up my blade before the dagger could sweep down, and made a leap backward. He followed immediately.

"Jhereg! Do not pass me by!"

As he closed, perhaps just a touch too cockily, I tried a full-extension stop-thrust—Dragaeran swordplay has nothing like it—dropping to one knee and cutting up under his sword-arm. He was as surprised as I that my first offensive move got through, and it gave me time to get back before he countered. He bled a little from high on his right side. It was too much to hope for that this would affect his sword-arm, but it gave me more time.

"Show me where thy soul doth lie!"

My side screamed with pain as I stepped back still further. Each parry caused red flashes before my eyes, and I felt that I was near to blacking out. I felt drained, too. I mean, *drained*. I don't think I had ever put that much into a spell.

I moved back out of the way of another blow that almost slit open my belly. He followed with a cut with the dagger that was almost faster than I could see, but I was moving back, so it missed. I stepped back again, before he could set himself. . . .

What? Was there . . . ? Come on, brain! Mind, relax . . . be receptive . . . listen . . .

"Who?" came the thought to my forebrain.

"One who needs you," I managed, as I almost stumbled. I hung on to my consciousness with everything I had.

"What have you to offer?"

Oh, Demon Goddess! I don't have time for this! I wanted to start crying, to tell them all to just go away.

He caught my blade with the dagger, and the sword swept down; I squirmed to the side, made it.

"Long life, O Jhereg. And fresh, red meat, with no struggle or search. And, sometimes, the chance to kill Dragaerans."

All in all, one Hell of a time to be bargaining.

Mellar did a fillip with his wrist that should have been impossible with that heavy a sword. He connected lightly with the side of my head—as heavily as he could, given what he was doing, and as lightly as it was possible for him to, considering the size of the weapon he had.

But I still didn't black out. I took a chance, then, because I had to, and lunged, cutting down at his forehead. He stepped back and parried with his dagger. I backed up another step before the sword came sweeping down at me again. It occurred to me that, even if the jhereg should choose to respond, it might be too far away to do me any good.

"And what do you ask?"

Mellar was smiling again. He could see that I was going, and all he had to do was wait. He continued pressing the attack.

"For the future, aid in my endeavors, and your friendship, and your wisdom. For the present, save my life!"

Once again, Mellar struck at the side of my head and got through. There was a ringing in my ears, and I felt myself start to fall. I saw him move in, raising the dagger and grinning broadly . . .

. . . and then he was turning, startled, as a winged shape struck at his face. He moved back and took a swipe with his sword; missed.

I dropped my sword and caught myself with my right hand. I heaved myself up from there until I was standing; barely. Mellar took another swing at the jhereg. I transferred the dagger to my right hand, and fell forward, walking being somewhat beyond my powers at that point. My left hand grasped his left arm, his dagger-arm, and swung him around.

He turned, and I saw panic in his eyes, and his dagger began to arc toward my neck. I tried to hold back his right arm, which was swinging forward with the sword, but it slipped from my grasp.

I thrust straight in, then, with everything that was left in me.

The stiletto took him in the left eye, burying itself to the hilt in his brain. He screamed then—a long wail of despair, and he lost interest in removing my head. I saw the light of life go out in his right eye, and I might even have rejoiced if I'd been capable of it.

I was screaming then, as well, as we twisted, toppled, fell. We landed on each other, with me face up, and the only thing still in the air was his lifeless arm, holding a living dagger in a fist that wouldn't let go. I watched it, unable to do anything, as it fell . . . fell . . . fell . . . and hit the ground next to my left ear.

I could feel its frustration, and had a crazy moment of sympathy for any hunter that loses its prey by such a small margin.

A thought, then, came into my mind and set up housekeeping. *"I accept,"* it said.

Just what I need, I remember thinking, another wiseass jhereg.

I didn't quite lose consciousness, although I don't think I was completely conscious, either. I remember lying there, feeling damned helpless, and watching the jhereg take bits out of Mellar's corpse. At some time in there, various animals came up and sniffed me. I think one of them was an Athyra; I'm not sure about the others. Each time, the jhereg looked up from its meal and hissed a warning. They backed off.

Eventually, perhaps half an hour later, I heard a sudden disturbance. The jhereg looked over, hissed, and I looked too. Aliera was there, holding Pathfinder. With her were Cawti and Kragar and Loiosh.

The other jhereg was female. She hissed at Loiosh. With the jhereg, the female is dominant. (With the Jhereg, the matter is still up in the air.)

Cawti rushed up to me with a cry and sat down. She carefully placed my head on her lap and began stroking my forehead. Aliera began inspecting and treating my various wounds. I'd be hard pressed to say which helped more, but it was nice getting all the attention.

Kragar assisted Aliera, after verifying that the two corpses were, indeed, corpses.

Loiosh had found the other jhereg. They were looking at each other.

Aliera said something then, I think it was about Daymar's mind-probe having worked, but I wasn't really listening, so I'm not sure.

Loiosh spread his wings and hissed. The female spread her wings further and hissed louder. They were silent for a while, then exchanged hisses again.

I tried to communicate with Loiosh, but found nothing. At first I thought that it was because my mind was still too exhausted from the spell I'd done, but then I realized that it was because Loiosh was blocking me out. He'd never done that before. I got a sinking feeling.

Suddenly, the two of them rose into the air. I lacked the strength to look up and follow their flight, but I knew what must be happening. Tears blinded me, and desperation gave me a small loan against my future energy holdings. I tried to force my way into his mind, and I sent out my desperate call, trying to pierce the barriers he had erected against me.

"*No! Come back!*" I think I called.

Cawti's face above me began to waver, as my body and mind gave up their fight at last, admitted defeat, and the darkness that had been hovering over and around me finally found entry.

Nevertheless, the contact was as sharp and distinct as it had ever been, sneaking under the gate even as it closed.

"*Look, boss. I've worked for you nonstop for more than five years now. You'd think I could have a few days off for my honeymoon!*"

Epilogue

"Failure leads to maturity; maturity leads to success."

On MY TERMS, THIS time.

The Blue Flame was quiet at this hour, with three waiters, a busboy, a dishwasher, and three customers.

All of them were enforcers who worked for me. All of them, at one time or another, had done 'work.'

This time I faced the door, and my back was against the wall. I had a dagger out, lying openly on the table next to my right hand.

I wished Loiosh was back, but he wasn't necessary this time. I was making the rules, and we were playing with my stones. Somewhere, Cawti and Kragar were watching.

Let him try . . . anything. Anything at all. Sorcery? Ha! No spell would go in this place that didn't have Aliera's approval. Try to bring in an assassin? Maybe, if he wanted to pay for Mario, he could come up with something I'd worry about. Other than that, however, I wasn't about to get upset.

A face appeared in the doorway, followed by another.

The Demon had brought two bodyguards with him. They stopped in the doorway and looked around. Being competent, they saw how things were and spoke to the Demon quietly for a while. I saw him shake his head. Good. He was smart, and he was gutsy. He was going to do it my way because he knew, at this point, that it was the only way it would get done—he was too good a businessman not to realize that it had to get done.

I saw him signal his men to wait by the door, and he came forward alone.

I rose as he reached me, and we sat down at the same moment.

"Lord Taltos," he said.

"Demon," I said.

He looked at the dagger, seemed about to speak, and changed his mind. At this point, he could hardly blame me, after all.

Since I had requested the meeting, I ordered the wine. I chose a rare dessert wine, made by the Serioli. He spoke first while we waited for the wine to arrive.

"I note that your familiar is missing," he said. "I hope he isn't ill."

"He isn't ill," I said. "But thank you for asking."

The wine came. I allowed the Demon to approve it. It's the little touches that make the fine host. I sipped mine and let it flow down my throat. Cool, and sweet, but neither icy nor cloying. That was why I'd chosen it. It had seemed appropriate.

"I was afraid," the Demon continued, "that he'd eaten something that had disagreed with him."

I chuckled. I decided that I'd come to like this guy, if we didn't kill each other first.

"I take it the body has been found," I said.

He nodded. "It's been found. A bit jhereg-eaten, but there isn't any harm in that, certainly."

I agreed with his sentiments.

"And," he went on, "I received your message."

I nodded. "So I see. I have what I claimed to."

"All of it?"

"All of it."

He waited for me to go on. I was enjoying it enough so that I didn't even mind the pain I felt from the events of the day before. One reason that I'd arranged to have the place full of my people was that I didn't want it to get out how much trouble I had walking in. Standing for the Demon had cost me; hiding that fact had cost me even more. Aliera is good, but it still takes time.

"How did you get it?" he asked.

"From his mind."

The Demon arched his eyebrows. "I'm rather surprised," he admitted. "I wouldn't have expected him to be subject to mind-probes."

"I have some good people working for me," I told him. "And, of course, we caught him at a good time."

He nodded and sipped his wine. "I should tell you," he said, "that, as far as I'm concerned, it's all over."

I waited for him to continue. This was what I'd arranged the meeting for, after all.

He took another sip of his wine. "To the best of my knowledge and belief," he said, choosing his words carefully, "no one in the organization has anything against you, means you any harm, or will profit from any harm that comes to you."

That last wasn't true in a literal sense, but we both knew what he meant—and he had his reputation to hold on to. I didn't think he would lie to me about it. I was satisfied.

"Good," I said. "And allow me to say I hold no ill will over anything that happened—or almost happened—before. I believe that I understand what was going on, and there is no cause there for complaint on my part."

He nodded.

"As for the other," I went on, "if you send an escort over to my office, say at the fourth hour past noon, I'll be able to supply them with your goods to return to you."

He nodded his satisfaction at the arrangements. "There are a few other things," he said.

"Such as . . . ?"

He stared off into space for a moment, then turned back to me. "Certain of my friends are exceptionally pleased with the work you did yesterday."

"I beg your pardon?"

He smiled. "I mean, the work your 'friend' did yesterday."

"Yes. Go on."

He shrugged. "Certain of them felt that perhaps a bonus is in order."

"I see. Well, that I'll gladly accept, on my friend's behalf, of course. But, before we go into that, perhaps you will allow me to buy you dinner?"

He smiled. "Why yes, that would be very kind of you."

I called a waiter over. He was, actually, a lousy waiter, but that was all right; I think the Demon understood.

More than our apartment, more than my office, the library at Castle Black has seemed like home base to me.

How many times in the past had Morrolan and I, or Morrolan, myself, and Aliera, or a host of others, sat in this room and said some form of "Thank Verra, it's over"?

"Thank Verra, it's over," said Aliera.

I lay on my back on the lounge chair. As I said, Aliera was good, but it takes time to heal completely. My sides still ached, and my head gave me no end of trouble. Still, in the three days since Mellar had passed from among the living, and the two days since I'd met with the Demon to arrange for nine million gold to be returned (and to insure that no more attempts were going to be made on my life), I had pretty well made the transition back to humanity.

Cawti sat next to me, gently brushing my forehead from time to time. Loiosh had returned and sat perched on my chest, as near to the shoulder as my position allowed. His mate took the other side. I felt quite contented with life, all in all.

Morrolan sat opposite me, staring into his wineglass. His long legs were stretched out in front of him. He looked up. "What are you calling her?" he asked.

"Her name is Rocza," I said. On hearing her name, she leaned down and licked my ear. Cawti scratched her head. Loiosh hissed a jealous warning, whereupon Rocza looked up, hissed back, licked Loiosh under his snakelike chin. He sat back, mollified.

"My, aren't we domestic?" said Morrolan.

I shrugged.

He continued to look at the female jhereg curiously. "Vlad, I know as much about witchcraft as any Easterner, you must admit—"

"Yes, that's true."

"—and I don't see how you can have a second familiar. I had always understood that the relationship between witch and familiar is such that it is impossible for it to occur with more than one animal.

"For that matter," he continued, "I've never heard of making a familiar from any adult animal. Don't you have to acquire the thing as an egg, in order to achieve the proper link?"

Loiosh hissed at Morrolan, who smiled a little and cocked his head.

"I'm calling *you* a 'thing,' that's who," Morrolan said.

Loiosh hissed again and went back to licking Rocza's chin.

"Well, Morrolan," I said, "why don't you find out for yourself? You're a witch, why don't you get a familiar?"

"I already have one," he answered, dryly. He gently stroked the hilt of Blackwand, and I shuddered involuntarily.

"Rocza isn't really my familiar, in any case," I explained. "She's Loiosh's mate."

"But still, she came to you. . . ."

"I called for help and she heard. We were able to strike a bargain similar to the one a witch makes with the mother of his familiar for the egg, but it wasn't exactly the same. I did use the same spell, or a close variant, to achieve initial contact," I admitted. "But that's where the similarity ends. After I got contact, we more or less just spoke. I guess she liked me."

Rocza looked up at me and hissed. I got the feeling that it was intended to be laughter, but I'm not sure. Loiosh broke in at that point. *"Look, boss, no one likes to be spoken of as if he isn't there, okay?"*

"Sorry, chum."

I stretched myself out, enjoying the feeling that there was blood circulating, and all those other good things.

"I can't tell you how happy I was when those two let me know that they weren't going to kill each other, though," I summed up.

"Hmmmmph!" said Aliera. "You sure couldn't tell us then. You were too busy going down for the third time."

"Was it that close?" I asked.

"It was that close."

I shuddered. Cawti stroked my forehead, gently.

"It works both ways, I guess. I was also mightily pleased to see that you made it after all. I didn't tell you before, but I was plenty worried about that whole business," I said.

"*You* were worried!" said Aliera.

"I still don't understand that, Aliera," said Kragar, who, I discovered, had been sitting next to her the entire time. "How is it that you survived the Morganti dagger?"

"Just barely," said Aliera.

He shook his head. "When you first went over it, you said it would work out, but you never said how."

"Why? Do you want to try it? I don't really recommend having your soul eaten as a form of entertainment."

"Just curious . . ."

"Well, basically, it has to do with the nature of Great Weapons. Pathfinder is linked to me, which really means it's linked to my soul. When the dagger threatened to destroy me, Pathfinder acted to preserve me by drawing my soul into itself. When the threat was gone, I was able to return to my body. And, of course, we had the Necromancer standing by, just in case there were problems."

She looked thoughtful for a moment. "It is an interesting perspective from in there," she remarked.

"It is a rather frightening one from out here," put in Morrolan. "I thought we'd lost you."

Aliera smiled at him. "I'm not that easy to get rid of, cousin."

"In any case," I said. "It all worked out."

"Yes," said Morrolan. "I would imagine that you did rather well for yourself out of the affair."

"In more ways than one," I said.

"I suppose," said Morrolan.

I shook my head. "It isn't just the obvious. It seems that certain parties were quite pleased with the return of the gold, in addition to everything else. I've been given responsibility for a somewhat larger area."

"Yeah," said Kragar, "and you didn't even have to ask your friend to kill anyone for it."

I let that pass.

"I should point out, though," said Kragar, "that, in actual fact, you don't have any more responsibility than you did before."

"I don't?"

"Nope. You just make more money. *I'm* the one with more responsibility. Who do you think does all the work, anyway?"

"Loiosh," I answered.

Kragar snorted. Loiosh hissed a laugh.

"You are hereby forgiven, boss."

"Lucky me."

Morrolan was looking puzzled. "Speaking of the gold reminds me of something. How *did* you discover where it was?"

"Daymar took care of it," I told him. "Just before Mellar teleported me out, Daymar did a mind-probe on him. It was the only time he could have had a chance of succeeding, with Mellar completely disoriented. He caught him with his psychic pants down, you might say. Daymar found out where he had hidden the gold and found out about the arrangements he'd made for the information about the Dzur to get out. And, of course, it was the mind-probe itself that finally broke down Mellar and sent him into a panic."

"Oh," said Morrolan, "so you *did* find out about the information he had on the Dzur."

"Yep," I said. "And we suppressed it."

"How did you do that?" asked Morrolan.

I looked over at Kragar, who had actually handled the matter. He smiled a little.

"It wasn't difficult," he said. "Mellar had given it to a friend of his in a sealed envelope. We picked up this friend, brought him to the dock where we'd dumped Mellar's body, and pointed out to him that there was no reason for him to keep the thing anymore. We talked a little, and he ended up agreeing."

Best not to know any more, I decided.

"What I don't understand," Kragar continued, "is *why* you didn't want the information to come out, Vlad. What difference does it make to us?"

"There were a couple of reasons for it," I told him. "For one thing, I made it clear to a few Dzurlords I know that I was doing it. It never hurts to have Dzur heroes owe you favors. And the other reason was that Aliera would have killed me if I hadn't."

Aliera smiled a little, but didn't deny it.

"So, Vlad," said Morrolan, "are you going to retire, now that you are wealthy? You could certainly buy a castle out of town and turn properly decadent if you chose to. I'd be curious. I've never had the pleasure of seeing a decadent Easterner."

I shrugged. "I may buy a castle somewhere, since Cawti's been wanting one, and now we can afford a few luxuries like a higher title in the Jhereg, but I doubt I'll retire."

"Why not?"

"You're rich. Are you retiring?" I asked him.

He snorted. "From what should I retire? I've been professionally decadent for as long as I can remember."

"Well, there is that . . . Say!"

"Yes?"

"How about if we both retire! What do you think about selling Castle Black? I can give you a good price on it."

"Depend on it," he said.

"Oh, well. Just asking."

"Seriously, though, Vlad; have you ever thought about quitting the Jhereg? I mean, you don't really need them anymore, do you?"

"Ha! I've thought about quitting the Jhereg a great deal, but so far I've always managed to be just a little bit quicker than whoever wanted me out."

"Or luckier," said Kragar.

I shrugged. "As for leaving voluntarily, I don't know."

Morrolan looked at me carefully. "You don't actually *enjoy* what you do, do you?"

I didn't answer, not really knowing at the time. I mean, did I? Especially now, when my biggest reason, my hatred for all things Dragaeran, turned out not to have the cause I had thought it did. Or did it?

"You know, Aliera," I said, "I'm still not really sure about this genetic inheritance through the soul. I mean, sure, I felt something for it, but I also lived through what I lived through, and I guess that shaped me more than you'd think. I am what I am, in addition to what I was. Do you understand what I mean?"

Aliera didn't answer; she just looked at me, her face unreadable. An uncomfortable silence settled over the room, as we all sat there with our thoughts. Kragar studied the floor, Cawti caressed my forehead, Morrolan seemed to be looking around for another subject.

He found one, finally, and broke the silence by saying, "There is still a thing that I fail to understand, concerning you and Rocza."

"What is that?" I asked, as relieved as everyone else.

He studied the floor in front of the couch. "Exactly how do you plan on housebreaking her?"

I felt myself going red as the odor reached my nose, and Morrolan wryly called for his servants.

YENDI

*When I was young, I was taught that every citizen
of the Dragaeran Empire was born into one of the
seventeen Great Houses, each named for an animal.
I was taught that humans, or "Easterners," such as
I, were worthless scum. I was taught that the only
choices we had, if we wished to amount to anything, were to swear fealty to some lord and become part of the peasant class in the House of the
Teckla, or, as my father did, buy Orders of Nobility
in the House of the Jhereg.*

*Later, I found a wild jhereg, and trained him, and
set about to leave my mark on Dragaeran society.*

*When I was older, I learned that most of what I
had been taught were lies.*

1

"Stay out of sight, in case they get rude."

KRAGAR SAYS THAT LIFE is like an onion, but he doesn't mean the same thing by it that I do.

He talks about peeling it, and how you can go deeper and deeper, until finally you get to the center and nothing is there. I suppose there's truth in that, but in the years when my father ran a restaurant, I never peeled an onion, I chopped them; Kragar's analogy doesn't do much for me.

When I say that life is like an onion, I mean this: if you don't do anything with it, it goes rotten. So far, that's no different from other vegetables. But when an onion goes bad, it can do it from either the inside, or the outside. So sometimes you get one that looks good, but the core is rotten. Other times, you can see a bad spot on it, but if you cut that out, the rest is fine. Tastes sharp, but that's what you paid for, isn't it?

Dzurlords like to fancy themselves as pantry chefs who go around cutting the rotten parts out of onions. Trouble is, they generally can't tell the good from the bad. Dragon-lords are good at finding bad spots, but when they find one they like to throw out the whole barrelful. A Hawklord will find a bad spot every time. He'll watch you cook the thing, and eat it, and he'll nod sagaciously when you spit it out again. If you ask why he didn't tell you about it, he'll look startled and say, "You didn't ask."

I could go on, but what's the point? In the House Jhereg, we don't care teckla droppings about bad spots. We're just here to sell onions.

But sometimes someone will pay me to remove a bad spot. This had earned me thirty-two hundred gold Imperials that day, and to let the tension drain out I visited the more or less permanent party at the keep of the Lord Morrolan. I was sort of on his staff, as a security consultant, which gave me a standing invitation.

Lady Teldra let me in as I recovered from the teleport and I made my way to the banquet hall. I studied the mass of humanity (I use the term loosely) from the doorway, looking for familiar faces, and soon spotted the tall form of Morrolan himself.

Guests who didn't know me watched as I moved toward him; some made remarks intended for me to overhear. I always attract attention at Morrolan's parties—because I'm the only Jhereg there; because I'm the only "Easterner" (read: "human") there; or because I walk in with my jhereg familiar, Loiosh, riding on my shoulder.

"Nice party," I told Morrolan.

"Where are the trays of dead teckla, then?" said Loiosh psionically.

"Thank you, Vlad. It pleases me that you are here."

Morrolan always talks like that. I think he can't help it.

We wandered over to a table where one of his servants was pouring out small draughts of various wines, commenting on them as he did. I got a glass of red Darloscha and sipped it. Nice and dry, but it would have been better chilled. Dragaerans don't understand wine.

"Good evening, Vlad; Morrolan."

I turned and bowed low to Aliera e'Kieron, Morrolan's cousin and Dragon Heir to the Throne. Morrolan bowed and squeezed her hand. I smiled. "Good evening, Aliera. Any duels, yet?"

"Why yes," she said. "Did you hear?"

"As a matter of fact, no; I was being facetious. You really do have a duel lined up?"

"Yes, for tomorrow. Some teckla of a Dzurlord noticed how I walk and made remarks."

I shook my head and tsked. "What's his name?"

She shrugged. "I don't know. I'll find out tomorrow. Morrolan, have you seen Sethra?"

"No. I assume she is at Dzur Mountain. Perhaps she will show up later. Is it important?"

"Not really. I think I've isolated a new e'Mondaar recessive. It'll wait."

"I am interested," said Morrolan. "Would you be pleased to tell me of it?"

"I'm not sure what it is yet . . ." said Aliera. The two of them walked off. Well, Morrolan walked. Aliera, who was the shortest Dragaeran I've ever met, levitated, her long, silver-blue dress running along the ground to hide the fact. Aliera had golden hair and green eyes—usually. Although she wasn't carrying it now, she also had a sword that was longer than she was. She had taken it from the hand of Kieron the Conquerer, the head of her line, in the Paths of the Dead. There's a story in there, too, but never mind.

Anyway, they walked away, and I drew on my link with the Imperial Orb, did a small sorcery spell, and chilled the wine. I sipped it again. Much better.

"The problem for tonight, Loiosh, is: how am I going to get laid?"

"Boss, sometimes you disgust me."

"Tell me about it."

"Aside from that, if you own four brothels—"

"I've decided I don't like visiting brothels."

"Eh? Why not?"

"You wouldn't understand."

"Try me."

"All right. Put it this way: sex with Dragaerans feels more than half like bestiality, anyway. With whores, it feels like paying the . . . whatever."

"Go on, boss. Finish the sentence. Now I'm curious."

"Oh, shut up."

"What is it about killing someone that makes you so horny, anyway?"

"Got me."

"You need a wife."

"Go to Deathsgate."

"We did that once, remember?"

"Yeah. And I remember how you felt about the giant jhereg there."

"Don't start on that, boss."

"Then shut up about my sex life."

"You brought it up."

There was nothing to say to that, so I let it drop. I sipped my wine again, and felt that peculiar, nagging sensation of there's-something-I-ought-to-be-thinking-about that heralds someone trying to reach me psionically. I quickly found a quiet corner and opened up my mind for contact.

"How's the party, boss?"

"Not bad, Kragar. What's up that can't wait for morning?"

"Your bootblack is here. He's going to be made Issola Heir to the Throne tomorrow, so he's finishing up his calls."

"Funny. What is it really?"

"A question. Did you open up a new gambling joint in Malak Circle?"

"Of course not. You'd have heard about it long ago."

"That's what I thought. Then there's a problem."

"I see. Some punk thinking we won't notice? Or is somebody trying to muscle in?"

"It looks professional, Vlad. He's got protection there."

"How many?"

"Three. And I know one of them. He's done 'work.' "

"Oh."

"What do you think?"

"Kragar, you know how a chamber pot gets when it isn't emptied for a few days?"

"Yeah?"

"And you know how, when you finally do empty it, there's all that stuff stuck on the bottom?"

"Yeah?"

"Well, that stuff on the bottom is how I feel about this."

"Gotcha."

"I'll be right over."

I found Morrolan in a corner with Aliera and a tall Dragaeran who had the facial features of the House of the Athyra and was dressed all in forest green. She looked down at me, figuratively and literally. It's frustrating being both a Jhereg and an Easterner—people sneer at you for both reasons.

"Vlad," said Morrolan, "this is the Sorceress in Green. Sorceress, this is Baronet Vladimir Taltos."

She nodded, almost imperceptibly. I bowed with a deep flourish, dragging the back of my hand over the floor, bringing it up over my head, and saying, "Gentle lady, I am every bit as charmed to meet you as you are to meet me."

She sniffed and looked away.

Aliera's eyes were twinkling.

Morrolan looked troubled, then shrugged.

"Sorceress in Green," I said. "I've never met an Athyra who wasn't a sorcerer, and the green I can see, so I can't say the title tells me—"

"That will be sufficient, Vlad," said Morrolan. "And she isn't—"

"Sorry. I wanted to tell you that something's come up. I'm afraid I'll have to leave." I turned to the Sorceress. "I'm sorry to do this to you, my dear, but try not to let it ruin your evening."

She looked back at me and smiled sweetly. "How would you," she said, "like to be a newt?"

Loiosh hissed.

"I asked you to desist, Vlad," said Morrolan sharply.

I dropped it. "I'll be leaving, then," I said, bowing my head.

"Very well. If there's anything I can do, let me know."

I nodded. Unfortunately for him, I remembered the remark.

Do you know what the single biggest difference between a Dragaeran and an Easterner is? It isn't that they are so much taller and stronger than we are; I'm living proof that size and strength aren't that important. It isn't that they live two or three thousand years compared to our fifty or sixty; in the crowd I hang around with, no one expects to die of old age anyway. It isn't even that they have a natural link with the Imperial Orb that allows them to use sorcery; Easterners (such as my late, unlamented father) can buy titles in the House of the Jhereg, or swear fealty to some noble, move out to the countryside and become a Teckla—thereby becoming citizens and getting the link.

No, the biggest difference that I've found is this: a Dragaeran can teleport without feeling sick to his stomach afterwards.

I arrived in the street outside my office about ready to throw up. I took a few deep breaths and waited while my gut settled down. I had had one of Morrolan's sorcerers do the actual spell. I can do it myself, but I'm not very good; a rough landing makes things even worse.

My offices at this time were on Copper Lane, in back of a small gambling operation, which was in back of a psychedelic herb shop. My offices consisted of three rooms. One was a screening room, where Melestav, my receptionist-bodyguard, sat. To his right was Kragar's office and the files, and behind Melestav was my actual office. Kragar had a small desk and one hard wooden chair—there wasn't room for anything else. The screening room had four chairs that were almost comfortable. My desk was a bit bigger than Kragar's, smaller than Melestav's, and had a well-padded swivel chair facing the door. Next to the door were two comfortable chairs, one of which would be occupied by Kragar when he showed up.

I told Melestav to let Kragar know I was in and sat down at my desk to wait.

"Uh, boss?"

"Oh." I sighed as I realized that, once again, Kragar had sneaked in without my seeing him. He claims that he doesn't do it on purpose—that he's just naturally sneaky.

"What have you found out, Kragar?"

"Nothing I didn't tell you before."

"Okay. Let's go blow some money."

"Both of us?"

"No. You stay out of sight, in case they get rude."

"Okay."

As we went out I ran a hand through my hair. This let me rub my arm against the right side of my cloak, so I could make sure that various pieces of hardware were in place. With my left hand I adjusted the collar, letting me check a few more on that side.

Out on the street, I gave a quick look around, then walked the block and a half up to Malak Circle. Copper Lane is what is called a one-and-a-half-cart street, which makes it wider than many. The buildings are packed tightly together, and most of them have windows only on the upper stories. Malak Circle is a turnaround, with a fountain that hasn't worked as long as I can remember. Copper Lane ends there. Lower Kieron Road enters from the left as you approach from Copper Lane, and leaves again, slightly wider, ahead, and to the right.

"Okay, Kragar," I said, "where—" I stopped. "Kragar?"

"Right in front of you, boss."

"Oh. Where is it?"

"First door to the left of the Fountain Tavern. Inside, up the stairs, and to the right."

"Okay, Stay alert."

"Check."

"Loiosh, try to find a window you can look in. If not, just stay in touch."

"Right, boss." He flew off.

I went in, up a narrow stairway with no handrail, and came to the top. I took a deep breath, checked my weapons once more, and clapped.

The door opened at once. The guy who stood there was dressed in black and gray for House Jhereg, and had a broadsword strapped to his side. He was damn near seven and a half feet tall and broader than is usual for a Dragaeran. He looked down at me and said, "Sorry, Whiskers. Humans only," and shut the door. Dragaerans often seem confused about who the "humans" are.

Being called "Whiskers" didn't bother me—I'd deliberately grown a mustache because Dragaerans can't. But to be shut out of a game that shouldn't even be here without my permission displeased me immensely.

I quickly checked the door and found that it was bound with sorcery. I gave a flick of my right wrist and Spellbreaker, two feet of thin gold chain, came into my hand. I lashed out at the door and felt the spell fail. I put the chain away as the door was flung open again.

The guy's eyes narrowed and he started moving toward me. I smiled at him. "I'd like to speak to the proprietor, if I may."

"I see," he said, "that you're going to need help getting down the stairs." He moved toward me again.

I shook my head. "It's sad that you can't cooperate with a simple request, dead man."

He moved in, and my right sleeve dagger was in my hand. Then I was past him, ducking under his arms. Six inches of steel were buried, at an upward angle, between his fourth and fifth ribs, twisted to notch on the sternum. I stepped into the room as I heard vague moaning and coughing noises from behind me, followed by the sound of a falling body. Contrary to popular myth, the guy would probably remain alive for over an hour. But contrary to another popular myth, he would be in shock and so wouldn't be able to do anything to keep himself alive.

The room was small, with only one window. There were three tables of s'yang stones in action, one with five players, the other two with four. Most of the players seemed to be Teckla, a couple of Jhereg, and there was one Tsalmoth. There were two other Jhereg there, just as Kragar had told me, who seemed to be working for the place. They were both moving at me quickly, one was drawing his sword. Oh me, oh my.

I put a table between myself and one of them, then kicked it over toward him. At that moment, the window broke and Loiosh flew straight at the other. I could forget about that guy for a few minutes, anyway.

The one I'd kicked the table at, scattering coins and stones and customers, stumbled a bit. I drew my rapier and cut his wrist as his arm was flailing around in front of me. He dropped the blade, and I stepped in and kicked him between the legs. He moaned and doubled over. I brought the pommel of my blade down on his head and he dropped.

I moved to the other one. *"Enough, Loiosh. Let him alone, and watch my back."*

"Right, boss."

The guy tried to get his blade out as I approached and Loiosh left him, but mine was already out. I touched his throat with the point and smiled. "I'd like to speak to the manager," I said.

He stopped moving. He looked at me coldly, with no trace of fear in his eyes. "He's not here."

"Tell me who he is and you'll live," I said. "Don't, and you'll die."

He remained silent. I moved the point of my blade up until it was opposite his left eye. The threat was clear: if his brain was destroyed, he wouldn't be in any condition to be revivified. There was still no sign of fear, but he said, "Laris."

"Thank you," I told him. "Lie down on the floor."

He did so. I turned to the customers. "This place is closed," I said. They began heading for the door.

At that moment, there was a woosh of displaced air, and five more Jhereg were in the room, swords drawn. Oops. Without a word being spoken, Loiosh was on my shoulder.

"Kragar, take off."

"Right."

I drew recklessly on my link and tried to teleport, but failed. I sometimes wish teleport blocks could be outlawed. I lunged at one of them, scattered a handful of sharp pointy things with my left hand, and jumped through the already broken window. I heard cursing sounds behind me.

I tried a quick levitation spell, which must have worked a little bit since landing didn't hurt. I kept moving, in case they had sharp pointy things, too. I tried the teleport again, and it worked.

I found myself on my back, right outside the door to the shop containing my offices. I threw up.

I climbed to my feet, dusted off my cloak, and went inside. The proprietor was looking at me curiously.

"There's a mess on the street outside," I told him. "Clean it up."

"Laris, eh boss?" said Kragar a bit later. "One of our next-door neighbors. He controls about ten square blocks. He only has a couple of operations that face our territory, so far."

I put my feet up on my desk. "More than twice as much area as I have," I mused.

"It looked like he was expecting trouble, didn't it?"

I nodded. "So, is he just testing us, or is he really trying to move in on me?"

Kragar shrugged. "Hard to say for sure, but I think he wants to move in."

"Okay," I said, sounding a lot calmer than I felt. "Can we talk him out of it, or is it war?"

"Are we up to a war?"

"Of course not," I snapped. "I've only had my own area for half a year. We should have been expecting something like this. Damn."

He nodded.

I took a deep breath. "Okay, how many enforcers do we have on our payroll?"

"Six, not counting the ones who are permanently assigned to someplace."

"How are our finances?"

"Excellent."

"Then that's something, anyway. Suggestions?"

He looked uncomfortable. "I don't know, Vlad. Would it do any good to talk to him?"

"How should I know? We don't know enough about him."

"So that," he said, "ought to be our first step. Find out everything we can."

"If he gives us time," I said.

Kragar nodded.

"We have another problem, boss."

"What's that, Loiosh?"

"I'll bet you're really *horny, now*."

"Oh, shut up."

2

"I'm going to want protection."

W HEN I ENTERED THE organization, some three years before, I was working for a guy named Nielar as what we call a "muscle." He controlled a small gambling operation on North Garshos Street. He paid his dues to Welok the Blade.

Welok was a sort of mid-level boss. His area went from Potter's Market Street in the north to Millennial in the south, and from Prance in the west to One-Claw in the east.

All of these areas were pretty tentative and, when I went to work for Nielar, the northern edge, along Potter's, was *very* tentative. The first time I "worked," and the third, were to further the Blade's desire to make this border more certain. His northern neighbor was a peaceable kind of guy named Rolaan, who was trying to negotiate with Welok because he wanted Potter's but didn't want a war. Rolaan became more peaceable after he fell from his third-floor office one day. His lieutenant, Feet Charno, was even more peaceable, so the problem was resolved nicely. I've always suspected Feet of arranging Rolaan's death, because otherwise I can't account for Welok's leaving Charno alone, but I never found out for sure.

That was three years ago. About then I stopped working for Nielar, and went to work for the Blade himself. The Blade's boss was Toronnan, who ran things from the docks in the east to the "Little Deathsgate" area in the west, and from the river in the south to Issola Street in the north.

About a year and a half after Rolaan took the trip to Deathsgate Falls, Welok had a dispute with someone in the Left Hand of the Jhereg. I think the someone was working in the same territory as Welok (our interests don't usually overlap), but I don't know exactly what the problem was. One day Welok just vanished, and his spot was filled by one of his lieutenants—a guy named Tagichatn, whose name I still can't pronounce right.

I'd been working as a troubleshooter for the Blade, but this new guy didn't think much of Easterners. My first day, I walked into his office, a little place on Copper Lane between Garshos and Malak Circle. I explained what I'd been doing for Welok, and asked him if he wanted to be called "lord," or "boss," or if I should try to figure out how to say his name. He said, "Call me God-boss," and we were off.

Inside of a week I loathed him. Inside of a month, another ex-lieutenant of Welok's broke away and started running his own territory right in the middle of Tagichatn's. This was Laris.

Two months of "God-boss" was all I could take. Many of us who worked for him noticed that he made no move against Laris. This was taken as a sign of weakness. Eventually, someone either inside or outside of Tagichatn's organization would make use of this. I don't know what would have happened if he hadn't decided to commit suicide—by stabbing himself in the left eye.

He died late one night. That same night I made contact with Kragar, who'd worked with me for Nielar, and off and on for Welok. Recently, Kragar had been working as a bouncer in a tavern on Pier Street. I said, "I just inherited a piece of property. How would you like to help me hold it?"

He said, "Is it dangerous?"

I said, "Damn right it's dangerous."

He said, "No thanks, Vlad."

I said, "You start at fifty gold a week. If we're still around after two weeks, you get seventy-five plus ten percent of what I make."

He said, "One hundred after two weeks, plus fifteen percent of the gross."

"Seventy-five. Fifteen percent of the net."

"Ninety. Fifteen percent of the net before you split with upstairs."

"Seventy-five. Ten percent before I split."

"Done."

The next morning Tagichatn's secretary came in and found Kragar and me set up in the offices. I said, "You can work for me if you want. Say yes, and you get a ten percent raise. Say no, and you walk out of here alive. Say yes and try to cross me, and I'll feed you to the orcas."

He said no. I said, "See you."

Then I went to an enforcer named Melestav who also hated our ex-boss and who I'd worked with a couple of times. I'd heard he did "work," and I knew he was careful. I said, "The boss wants you to be his personal secretary and bodyguard."

"The boss is nuts."

"I'm the boss."

"I'm in."

I got a map of the city and drew a box around where the dead man's territory had been. Then I drew another box inside the first one. For some reason, in this area of Adrilankha bosses tended to mark the areas by half-streets. That is, instead of saying, "I have Dayland and you have Nebbit," they'd say, "I have up to the west side of Dayland, you have from the east side of Dayland." So the box I drew went from halfway down Pier Street, where Laris's territory ended, to Dayland; Dayland to Glendon; Glendon to Undauntra; Undauntra to Solom; Solom to Lower Kieron Road; and Lower Kieron Road to Pier Street.

I had Melestav get in touch with the other lieutenant and the two button-men who'd worked directly for Tagichatn, and had them meet me a block from Toronnan's offices. When they did, I told them to follow me. I didn't explain anything, I just took them to the office. When we got there, I had them wait just outside and I asked to see the boss.

They let me in while the others waited outside. Toronnan had light hair, cut short and neat. He wore doublet and hose, which isn't usual for a working Jhereg, and every stitch of his gray-and-black outfit was in perfect condition. Also, he was short for a Dragaeran, maybe six feet nine inches, and of a small build. All in all, he looked like a Lyorn recordsmith. He'd made his reputation with a battle-axe.

I said, "My lord, I am Vladimir Taltos." I took out the map and pointed to the first box. "With your permission, I am now in charge of this area." I pointed to the smaller box within it. "I think I can handle this much. There are gentlemen waiting outside who, I'm sure, would be happy to divide up the rest any way you see fit. I haven't discussed the matter with them." I bowed.

He looked at me, looked at the map, looked at Loiosh (who had been sitting on my shoulder the entire time), and said, "If you can do it, Whiskers, it's yours."

I thanked him and got out, leaving him to explain matters to the rest of them.

I went back to the office, looked over the books, and discovered that we were almost broke. I had about five hundred personally, which can keep a family eating and living comfortably for maybe a year. What I now controlled were four brothels; two gambling halls; two moneylending operations; and one cleaner, or fence, or dealer-in-stolen-merchandise. There were no button-men. (A funny term, that: sometimes it means *full-time enforcer on the payroll*, and sometimes it means *sublieutenant*. I usually mean the latter.) I did, however, have six enforcers working full-time. I also knew several enforcers who worked free-lance.

I visited each of my businesses and made them the same offer. I put a purse with fifty gold in it on the table and said, "I'm your new boss. This is a bonus, or a good-bye gift. Take your pick. If you take it as a bonus and try to mess with me, make a list of your mourn-singers, because you'll need them."

Now doing this left me with damn little cash. They all stayed, and I held my breath. When Endweek showed up, no one except Nielar, who was now in my territory, came by. I think they were waiting to see what I did. At this point, I didn't have enough money to pay for independent muscle, and I was afraid to use an enforcer (what if he wouldn't do it?), so I walked down to the operation nearest my office, a brothel, and found the manager. Before he could say anything, I pinned the right side of his cloak to the wall with a throwing knife, about knee level. I did the same with his left side. I put a shuriken into the wall next to each ear, close enough to cut. Then Loiosh went after him and raked his claws down the guy's face. I went up and hit him just below his sternum, then kneed him in the face when he doubled over. He began to understand that I wasn't happy.

I said, "You've got one minute, by the Imperial Clock, to put my money in my hand. When you've done that, Kragar is going over your books; then he's going to talk to every tag here and find out how much action you've had. If I am one copper short, you are a dead man."

He left his cloak in the wall and got the money. While he did this, I reached Kragar psionically and had him come down. When I had the purse, we waited for Kragar.

The guy said, "Look, boss, I was on my way over—"

"Shut your face or I'll tear out your windpipe and make you eat it."

He shut. When Kragar arrived I went back to my office. Kragar returned about two hours later, and we found out that the books balanced. He had ten tags working, four men and six women, usually taking five clients a day, at three Imperials per. The tags earned four gold a day. Meals came to about nine silver orbs, or call it half a gold a day. He had an enforcer there full time who was paid eight Imperials a day. Miscellaneous expenses were allotted another Imperial.

Each tag took one day a week off, so the place should be taking in 135 gold a day, on the average. The expenses were 51 a day, so the daily profit should average in the mid-80s. Five days to the week (in the East a week is seven days; I'm not sure why) should give about 425 gold a week, of which the manager keeps 25 percent—a little over a hundred. That meant that I should see 320-some gold every week. I had 328, some silver, and some copper. I was satisfied.

I was even more satisfied when, over the next hour, the rest of them showed up with their various takes for the week. They all said something like, "Sorry, boss, I got delayed."

I responded with something like, "Don't get delayed any more."

By the end of the day, I had collected more than 2,500 Imperials. Of course, I had to pay Kragar, my secretary, and the enforcers with that; but it still left me with more than 2,000, half of which I sent on to Toronnan, half of which I could keep.

I was not at all displeased by this. For an Easterner kid who used to work his ass off running a restaurant that earned eight gold in a good week, a thousand plus wasn't bad. I wondered why I hadn't gotten into this end sooner.

The only other major thing I did for the next few months was buy a small narcotics and psychedelics business to give me a cover for my life-style. I hired a bookkeeper to make everything look good. I also hired a few more enforcers because I wanted to be ready for any possible trouble from my managers or from punks trying to muscle in.

Mostly what I had them do was what I call "hang-around duty." This involves just what it says—hanging around the neighborhood. The reason for doing this was that this neighborhood was very popular with young toughs, mostly of the House of the Orca, who'd wander through and harass people. Most of these kids were broke most of the time, when they weren't mugging the Teckla who made up the majority of the citizenry. They came here because it was close to the docks and because Teckla lived here. "Hang-around" duty meant finding these jerks and booting them the Phoenix out of there.

When I was growing up, and collecting lumps from guys who'd go out "whisker-cutting," most of them were Orcas. Because of this, I gave my enforcers very explicit instructions about what to do to anyone they caught a second time. And, because these instructions were carried out, in less than three weeks my area was one of the safest in Adrilankha after dark. We started spreading rumors, too—you know, the virgin with the bag of gold at midnight—and it got so I almost believed them myself.

By my figuring, the increase in business paid for the extra enforcers in four months.

During that period, I "worked" a few times to increase my cash supply and to show the world that I could still do it. But, as I said, nothing much happened that concerns us now.

And then my good neighbor, Laris, showed me why I hadn't gotten into this end sooner.

The day after I'd tried to break up the game and ended by throwing up on the street, I sent Kragar to find people who worked with or knew Laris. I killed time around the office, throwing knives and swapping jokes with my secretary. ("How many Easterners does it take to sharpen a sword? Four: one to hold the sword and three to move the grindstone.")

Kragar came back just before noon.

"What did you find out?"

He opened a little notebook and scanned through it.

"Laris," he said, "started out as a collector for a moneylender in Dragaera City. He spent thirty or forty years at it, then made some connections and began his own business. While he was collecting he also 'worked' once or twice, as part of the job.

"He stayed a moneylender and made a good living at it for about sixty years, until Adron's Disaster and the Interregnum. He dropped out of sight then, like everyone else, and showed up in Adrilankha about a hundred and fifty years ago selling Jhereg titles to Easterners."

I interrupted. "Could he have been the one—"

"I don't know, Vlad. It occurred to me, too—about your father—but I couldn't find out."

"It doesn't matter. Go on."

"Okay. About fifty years ago he went to work for Welok as an enforcer. It looks like he 'worked' a few more times, then started running a small area directly under Welok, twenty years ago, when Welok took over from K'tang the Hook. When the Blade took the trip—"

"From there I know it."

"Okay. So now what?"

I thought this over. "He hasn't had any real setbacks, has he?"

"No."

"He's also never been in charge of a war."

"That isn't quite true, Vlad. I was told that he pretty much ran the fight against the Hook by himself, which was why Welok turned the area over to him."

"But if he was only an enforcer then—"

"I don't know," said Kragar. "I get the feeling that there was more to it than that, but I'm not sure just what it is."

"Hmmmm. Could he have been running another area during that time? Behind the scenes, or something?"

"Maybe. Or he might have had some kind of club over Welok's head."

"That," I said, "I find hard to believe. The Blade was one tough son-of-a-bitch."

Kragar shrugged. "One story I heard is that Laris offered him the Hook's area, if he could run it. I tried to verify that, but no one else had heard of it."

"Where did *you* hear it?"

"A free-lance enforcer who worked for Laris during the war. A guy named Ishtvan."

"*Ishtvan?* An Easterner?"

"No, just a guy with an Eastern name. Like Mario."

"If he's like Mario, I want him!"

"You know what I mean."

"Yeah. Okay, send a messenger to Laris. Tell him I'd like to get together with him."

"He's going to want to know where."

"Right. Find out if there's a good restaurant that he owns, and make it there. Say, noon tomorrow."

"Check."

"And send a couple of enforcers in here. I'm going to want protection."

"Right."

"Get going."

He got.

"Hey, boss. What's this about 'protection'?"

"What about it?"

"You got me, don'tcha? What'd ya need those other clowns for?"

"Peace of mind. Go to sleep."

One of the enforcers who'd been with me from the time when I took over the area was called N'aal the Healer. He got the name first, the story goes, when he was sent to collect on a late payment from a Chreotha noble. He and his partner went to the guy's flat and clapped at the door. They asked for the money, and the guy snorted and said, "For what?"

N'aal came up with a hammer. "I'm a healer," he said. "I see you got a whole head. I can heal that for you." The Chreotha got the message, and N'aal got the gold. His partner spread the story around and the name stuck.

Anyway, N'aal the Healer walked in about two hours after I'd told Kragar to send the messenger. I inquired as to his business.

"Kragar had me deliver a message," he said.

"Oh. Did you get an answer?"

"Yeah. I saw one of Laris's people and delivered it. Word came back that it was fine with him."

"Good. Now, if Kragar would just show up, I could find out where—"

"I'm right here, boss."

"Eh? Oh. Jerk. Get lost, N'aal."

"Where am I?" he said, as he headed out the door. Kragar flipped it shut with his foot and stretched out.

"Where is it set up for?" I asked him.

"A place called 'The Terrace.' Good place. You won't get out for less than a gold apiece."

"I can stand it," I said.

"They make a mean pepper sausage, boss."

"Now, how would you know that?"

"I hit their garbage dump once in a while."

Ask a stupid question . . .

"Okay," I continued to Kragar, "Did you arrange protection for me?"

He nodded. "Two. Varg and Temek."

"They'll do."

"Also, I'll be there. Just sort of being quiet and hanging around. I doubt he'll even notice me." He smirked.

"Fair enough. Any advice?"

He shook his head. "I'm as new at this as you are."

"Okay. I'll do my best. Any other business?"

"No. Everything's running smooth, as usual."

"May it stay that way," I said, rapping my knuckles on the desk. He looked at me, puzzled.

"An Eastern custom," I explained. "It's supposed to bring good luck."

He still looked puzzled, but didn't say anything.

I took out a dagger and started flipping it.

Varg was of a nastier school than I. He was one of those people who just reek of danger—the kind who would kill you as soon as look at you. He was Kragar's size, which is just a bit short, and had eyes that slanted upward, indicating that there was Dzur blood somewhere in his ancestry. His hair was shorter than most, dark, and worn slicked back. When you spoke with him, he held himself perfectly motionless, making no extraneous gestures of any kind, and he'd stare at you with those narrow, bright blue eyes. His face was without emotion, except when he was beating someone up. Then his face would twist into a Jhereg sneer that was among the best I'd ever seen, and he projected enough hate to make an army of Teckla run the other way.

He had absolutely no sense of humor.

Temek was tall and so thin you could hardly see him if you came at him sideways. He had deep, brown eyes—friendly eyes. He was a weapons master. He could use an axe, a stick, a dagger, a throwing knife, any kind of sword, shuriken, darts, poisons of all types, rope, or even a Verra-be-damned piece of paper. Also, he was a pretty good sorcerer for a Jhereg outside of the Bitch Patrol—the Left Hand. He was the only enforcer I had that I knew, with one hundred percent certainty, had done "work"—because Kragar had given him the job at my orders.

A month before this business with Laris started, a certain Dzurlord had borrowed a large sum from someone who worked for me, and was refusing to pay it back. Now this Dzurlord was what you call "established"; that is, he was considered a hero by the House of the Dzur, and had earned it several times over. He was a wizard (which is like a sorcerer, only more so), and more than just a little bit good with a blade. So he figured that there was nothing we could do if he decided not to pay us. We sent people over to plead with him to be reasonable, but he was rude enough to kill them. This cost me fifteen hundred gold for my half of the revivification on one of them (the moneylender, of course, paid the other half), and five thousand gold to the family of the second, who couldn't be revivified.

Now I did not consider these sums to be trifling. Also, the guy we'd lost had been a friend at one time. All in all, I was irritated. I told Kragar, "I do not want this individual to pollute the world any longer. See that this is attended to."

Kragar told me that he'd hired Temek and paid him thirty-six hundred gold— not unreasonable for a target as formidable as this Dzur was. Well, four days later—four days, mark you, not four weeks—someone stuck a javelin through the back of Lord Hero's head and pinned his face to a wall with it. Also, his left hand was missing.

When the Empire investigated, all they learned was that his hand had been blown off by his own wizard staff exploding, which also accounted for the failure of all his defensive spells. The investigators shrugged and said, "Mario did it." Temek was never even questioned. . . .

So I brought Temek and Varg in the next morning and had them close the door and sit down.

"Gentlemen," I explained, "I am going to a restaurant called 'The Terrace' in a few hours. I am going to have a meal with a certain man and speak to him. There is a chance that he will wish to do me bodily harm. You are to prevent this from happening. Clear?"

"Yes," said Varg.

"No problem, boss," said Temek. "If he tries anything, we'll make pieces out of him."

"Good." This was the kind of talk I liked. "I want an escort there and back, too."

"Yes," said Varg.

"No extra charge," said Temek.

"We leave here fifteen minutes before noon."

"We'll be here," said Temek. He turned to Varg. "Wanna look the place over first?"

"Yes," said Varg.

Temek turned back to me. "If we aren't back on time, boss, my woman lives above Cabron and Sons, and she's got a thing for Easterners."

"That's kind of you," I told him. "Scatter."

He left. Varg dropped his eyes to the floor briefly, which is what he used for a bow, and followed him. When the door had closed, I counted to thirty, slowly, then went past my secretary, and out into the street. I saw their retreating backs.

"Follow them, Loiosh. Make sure they do what they said they were going to."

"Suspicious, aren't you?"

"Not suspicious; paranoid. Go."

He went. I followed his progress for a ways, then went back inside. I sat down in my chair and got out a brace of throwing knives that I keep in my desk. I swiveled left to face the target, and started throwing them.

Thunk. Thunk. Thunk.

3

"This Laris teckla is no teckla."

"*Hey, boss! Let me in.*"

"Coming, Loiosh."

I wandered out of the office, into the shop, and opened the door. Loiosh landed on my shoulder.

"Well?"

"*Just like they said, boss. They went in, and I watched through the doorway. Varg stood and looked around, Temek got a glass of water. That's all. They didn't talk to anyone, and it didn't look like they were in psionic communication.*"

"Okay. Good."

By then I was back in the office. I consulted the Imperial Clock through my link and found that I still had over an hour. It's the waiting that really gets to you in this business.

I leaned back, put my feet up on the desk, and stared at the ceiling. It was made of wooden slats that used to be painted. A preservation spell would have cost about thirty gold, and would have kept the paint fresh for at least twenty years. But "God-boss" hadn't done it. Now the paint, a sick white, was chipping and falling. An Athyra would probably have taken this as a sign. Fortunately I wasn't an Athyra.

Unfortunately, Easterners have always been superstitious fools.

"Boss? Varg and Temek."

"Send them in."

They entered. "Right on time, boss!" said Temek. Varg just looked at me.

"Okay," I said, "let's go."

The three of us left the office, went into the shop. I was heading toward the door when—

"*Hold it a minute, boss.*" I knew that tone of telepathy, so I stopped.

"What is it, Loiosh?"

"*Me first.*"

"Oh? Oh. All right."

I stepped to the side. I was about to tell Varg to open the door when he came up and did it. I noted that. Loiosh flew out.

"*All clear, boss.*"

"*Okay.*"

I nodded. Varg stepped out first, then I, then Temek. We turned left and strolled up Copper Lane. My grandfather, while teaching me Eastern fencing, had warned me against being distracted by shadows. I told him, "Noish-pa, there *are* no shadows near the Empire. The sky is always—"

"I know, Vladimir, I know. Don't be distracted by shadows. Concentrate on the target."

"Yes, Noish-pa."

I don't know why that occurred to me, just then.

We reached Malak Circle and walked around it to the right, then headed up Lower Kieron Road. I was in enemy territory. It looked just like home.

Stipple Road joined Lower Kieron at an angle, coming in from the southwest. Just past this point, on the left, was a low stone building nestled in between a cobbler's shop and an inn. Across the street was a three-story house, divided into six flats.

The low building was set back about forty feet from the street, and there was a terrace with maybe a dozen small tables set up on it. Four of these were occupied. Three of them we ignored, because there were women or kids at them. The fourth, close to the door, had one man, in the black and gray of House Jhereg. He might as well have been wearing a sign saying "ENFORCER."

We noted him and continued. Varg walked inside first. While we waited, Temek glanced around openly, looking like a tourist at the Imperial Palace.

Varg came out and nodded. Loiosh flew in and perched at the back of an unoccupied booth. "*Looks good, boss.*"

I entered, and stopped just past the threshold. I wanted to let my eyes adjust to the dim light. I also wanted to turn and bolt back home. Instead, I took a couple of deep breaths and walked in.

As the inviter, it was up to me to select the table. I found one against the back wall. I sat so I could watch the entire room (I noticed a couple more of Laris's people in the process), while Varg and Temek took a table about fifteen feet away. It had an unobstructed view of mine, yet was politely out of earshot.

At precisely noon, a middle-aged (say around a thousand) Jhereg walked into the room. He was of medium height, average girth. His face was nondescript. He wore a medium-heavy blade at his side and a full cloak. There were none of the telltale signs of the assassin about him. I saw no bulges where weapons were likely to be hidden, his eyes didn't move as an assassin's would, he didn't hold himself with the constant readiness that I, or any other assassin, would recognize. Yet—

Yet he had something else. He was one of those rare people who radiates power. His eyes were steady, but cold. His arms were relaxed at his sides, his cloak thrown back. His hands looked perfectly normal, yet I was aware that I feared them.

I was an assassin, trying to be a boss. Laris had maybe "worked" once or twice, but he *was* a boss. He was made to run Jhereg businesses. He would command loyalty, treat his people well, and suck every copper piece possible from everything he had a hand in. If things had worked out differently I might have gone with Laris instead of Tagichatn, and he and I could have done well together. It was a shame.

He slid in across from me, bowing and smiling warmly. "Baronet Taltos," he said. "Thank you for the invitation. I don't get here often enough; it's a good place."

I nodded. "It's my pleasure, my lord. I've heard it highly spoken of. I'm told it's very well-managed."

He smiled at that, knowing that I knew, and bowed his head to acknowledge the compliment. "I'm told you know something of the restaurant business yourself, Baronet."

"Call me Vlad. Yes, a little bit. My father—"

We were interrupted by the waiter. Laris said, "The pepper sausage is particularly good."

"See, boss, I—"

"Shut up, Loiosh."

"So I've heard." I told the waiter, "Two please," and turned back to Laris. "A red wine, I think, my lord. Per—"

"Laris," he corrected.

"Laris. Perhaps a Kaavren?"

"Excellent."

I nodded to the enforcer—excuse me, the "waiter"—who bowed and left. I gave Laris as warm a smile as I could. "This would be a nice kind of place to run," I told him.

"You think so?" he said.

I nodded. "It's quiet, a good, steady clientele—that's the important thing, you know. To have regular customers. This place has been here a long time, hasn't it?"

"Since before the Interregnum, I'm told."

I nodded as if I'd known it all along. "Now some people," I said, "would want to expand this place—you know, add an extension, or another floor—but why? As it is, it brings in a good living. People like it. I'll bet you that if they expanded it, it would be out of business in five years. But some people don't understand that. That's why I admire the owners of this place."

Laris sat and listened to my monologue with a small smile playing at his lips, nodding occasionally. He understood what I was saying. Around the time I finished, the waiter showed up with the wine. He gave it to me to open; I poured some for Laris to approve. He nodded solemnly. I filled his glass, then mine.

He held the glass up to eye level and looked into it, rotating it by the stem. Khaav'n reds are full wines, so I imagine none of the light penetrated. He lowered the glass and looked at me, leaning forward.

"What can I say, Vlad? Some guy's been working for me for a long time. One of the people who helped me organize the area. A good guy. He comes up to me and says, 'Hey, boss, can I start up a game?'

"What am I supposed to tell him, Vlad? I can't say no to a guy like that, can

I? But if I put him anywhere in my area, I'll be cutting into the business of other people who've been with me a long time. That's not fair to them. So I looked around a bit. You've only got a couple of games going, and there's plenty of business, so I figure, 'Hey, he'll never even notice.'

"I should have checked with you first, I know. I do apologize."

I nodded. I'm not sure what I expected, but this wasn't it. When I told him that expanding into my area would be a mistake, he came back by claiming that he wasn't doing any such thing—that it was just a one-time favor for someone. Should I believe this? And, if so, should I let him get away with it?

"I understand, Laris. But, if you don't mind my asking, what if it happens again?"

He nodded as if he'd been expecting the question. "When my friend explained to me that you had visited the place and seemed very unhappy about it, I realized what I'd done. I was just trying to word an apology to you when I got your invitation. As for the future—well, Vlad, if it comes up, I promise to speak to you about it before I do anything. I'm sure we'll be able to work something out."

I nodded thoughtfully.

"Goatshit, boss."

"Eh? What do you mean?"

"This Laris teckla is no teckla, boss. He knew what he was doing by moving someone into your area."

"Yeah . . ."

At that point our pepper sausages showed up. Laris—and Loiosh—were right; it was very good. They served it with green rice covered with cheese sauce. They had a sprig of parsley on the side, like an Eastern restaurant does, but they had fried it in butter, lemon juice, and some kind of rednut liqueur—a nice effect. The pepper sausage had the meat of lamb, cow, kethna, and, I think, two different kinds of game birds. It also had black pepper, red pepper, white pepper, and Eastern red pepper (which I thought showed extraordinarily good taste). The thing was hot as Verra's tongue and quite good. The cheese sauce over the rice was too subtle to match the sausage, but it killed the flames nicely. The wine should probably have been stronger, too.

We didn't talk while we ate, so I had more time to consider everything. If I let him have this, what if he wanted more? Go after him then? If I didn't let him have the game, could I stand a war? Maybe I should tell him that I'd go for his idea, just to gain time to prepare, and then come after him when he tried to make another move. But wouldn't that give him time to prepare, too? No, he was probably already prepared.

This last was not a comforting thought.

Laris and I pushed our plates away at the same moment. We studied each other. I saw everything that epitomized a Jhereg boss—smart, gutsy, and completely ruthless. He saw an Easterner—short, short-lived, frail, but also an assassin, and everything that implied. If he wasn't at least a little worried about me, he was a fool.

But still . . .

I suddenly realized that, no matter what I decided, Laris had committed himself to taking over my business. My choices were to fight or concede. I had no interest in conceding. That settled part of it.

But it still didn't tell me what to do. If I allowed that one game to operate, it might give me time to prepare. If I shut it down, I would be showing my own people that I couldn't be played with—that I intended to hold what was mine. Which of those was more important?

"I would think," I said slowly, "that I can stand—more wine? Allow me. That I can stand to have your friend in my area. Say ten percent? Of the total income?"

His eyes widened a bit; then he smiled. "Ten percent, eh? I hadn't thought of that solution." His smile broadened and he slapped the table with his free hand. "All right, Vlad. Done!"

I nodded and raised my glass in salute, then sipped from it. "Excellent. If this works out well, there isn't any reason that we couldn't broaden the experiment, eh?"

"Absolutely!"

"Good. I'll expect the money at my office every Endweek in the first two hours after noon. You do know where my office is, don't you?"

He nodded.

"Good. Naturally, I'll trust your bookkeeping."

"Thank you," he said.

I raised my glass. "To a long and mutually profitable partnership."

He raised his. The edges touched, and there was the ringing sound which denotes fine crystal. I wondered which one of us would be dead in a year. I sipped the dry, full wine, savoring it.

I got behind my desk and collapsed into the chair.

"Kragar, get your ass in here."

"Coming, boss."

"Temek."

"Yeah, boss?"

"Find Narvane, Glowbug, and Wyrn and Miraf'n. Get them here five minutes ago."

"I'm gone." He teleported out, just to be flashy.

"Varg, I want two of them as bodyguards. Which?"

"Wyrn and Miraf'n."

"Good. Now where is—oh. Kragar, go talk to the Bitch Patrol. I want a teleport block around this whole building. A good one."

"Both ways?"

"No. Just to keep people out."

"Okay. What's going on?"

"What the hell do you think is going on?"

"Oh. When?"

"We might have until Endweek."

"Two days?"

"Maybe."

"Vlad, what do you do these things for?"

"Go."

He shuffled out.

It wasn't long before Temek returned with Glowbug. I don't know what Glowbug's real name was, but he had bright, shining blue eyes and a love of the long-handled mace. He was really a pleasant, almost jovial guy, but when he started to come at a customer with that mace, his eyes would light up like some Iorich fanatic's and the customer would decide that, yeah, he could probably find the money somewhere.

It occurs to me that I may be giving you the idea that if you borrow money from me and are thirty seconds late in making a payment, you'll have sixty-five toughs climbing into your windows. No. If we worked like that, it would cost more in free-lance or staff muscle than we'd make, especially with all the potential customers who'd be driven away.

Let me give you an example. About a month and a half before this—eight weeks, I think it was—one of my lenders came in and explained that a guy was into him for fifty gold and wouldn't be able to make his payment. The lender wanted to let it slide, but was that okay with me?

"What's he paying?"

"Five and one," he said, meaning five gold a week principal, plus one gold a week until it was paid off.

"First payment?"

"No. He's made four full, and just the interest for three weeks."

"What happened to him?"

"He runs a tailor shop and hab on Solom. He wanted to try a new line, and it took a quick fifty to get an exclusive. The line—"

"I know, hasn't taken off yet. What's his business worth?"

"Maybe three or four big."

"Okay," I told the guy. "Give him six weeks free. Tell him if he can't start doing at least the interest after that, he's got a new partner until we're paid off."

So you see, we aren't all that bad. If somebody is really having trouble and trying to pay, we'll work with him. We want his business again, and we don't make a copper by hurting people. But there are always jokers who think it can't happen to them, or bigmouths who want to show how tough they are, or back-alley lawsmiths who talk about going to the Empire. These people kept me in eating money—and then some—for more than three years.

Narvane, who arrived just a few minutes after Temek and Glowbug, was a specialist. He was one of very few sorcerers who worked for our end of the Jhereg, most Jhereg sorcerers being women and staying with the Left Hand. He was quiet, indrawn, and had vaguely Dragon facial features: thin face and high cheekbones, a long, straight nose and very dark eyes and hair. He was called in when a job required dismantling personal protection spells on someone, or clairvoyance, at which I'd match him up against any Dzur wizard I'd met, and even most Athyras.

Three of them leaned against the wall. Temek had his arms folded while he whistled "Hearing About You" off key and stared at the ceiling; Narvane was staring at the floor with his hands clasped in front of him; Glowbug was looking around, as if checking out how defensible the place was. Varg stood away from the wall, not moving, looking like something midway between a statue and a set bomb.

Kragar showed up as the silence was becoming uncomfortable. He said, "The first hour after noon, tomorrow."

"Okay."

Wyrn and Miraf'n came in together. They were already a team when Welok hired them and had remained a team when they started for me. As far as I knew, neither of them had ever done "work," but they had a very good reputation. Wyrn resembled an Athyra—he had pale blue-gray eyes and always looked like he was on something mind-altering. When he stood, he swayed a bit from side to side like an old tree, his arms hanging limp like drooping branches. His hair was light and shaggy, and he had a way of looking at you, with his head cocked to the side and a dreamy half-smile at the corners of his mouth, that would send chills up and down your spine.

Miraf'n was huge. He was more than eight feet tall, making even Morrolan look short. Unlike most Dragaerans, he had muscles one could actually see. On occasion, he would play stupid and get a big, silly grin on his face, pick up someone he wanted to intimidate, and tell Wyrn, "Betcha I can throw this one farther than I threw the last one. Wanna bet?"

And Wyrn would go, "Put him down, big fella. He was only kidding about testifying against our friend. Weren't you?"

And the guy would agree that yes, it was only a joke, and in poor taste at that, and he was very sorry that he'd bothered the two gentlemen . . .

"Melestav! Come in here a minute, and close the door behind you."

He did, and did. I put my feet up on the desk and scanned the bunch of them.

"Gentlemen," I said, "we're about to get hit. If we're lucky, we have two days to prepare. Starting right now, none of you goes out alone. You're all targets, so get used to it. You'll each be getting orders from me about exactly what you'll be doing, but for now, I just want to let you know that things are starting. You know how it goes—travel in pairs, stay at home as much as you can: the whole deal. And if any of you gets any offers from the other side, I want to hear about it. That isn't just for me, but if you turn them down, you become even more of a target, and I'll want to take that into account. And, by the way, if you don't turn them down, you become much, much more of a target. Remember that—you do not want to fuck with me, gentlemen; I'll destroy you.

"Any questions?"

There was silence for the moment; then Temek said, "What does he have?"

"That's a good question," I said. "Why don't you and Narvane go find out for me?"

"I knew I shouldn't have opened my mouth," he said sadly.

"Oh, yeah," I said. "Another thing—your salaries just doubled. But to pay you, we need to have income. And to have income, we need to keep places open. Laris might go for you, he might go for me, and he might go for my businesses. I'm betting on all three. Any other questions?"

There were none.

"Okay," I said. "One last thing: as of this moment, I am offering five thousand gold for Laris's head. I think you could all use that. I don't expect it'll be easy to collect, and I don't want anybody doing anything stupid and getting himself killed trying for it, but if you see a chance, there's no need to hesitate.

"Wyrn and Miraf'n, stick around the office. The rest of you, that's all. Beat it."

They shuffled out, leaving me alone with Kragar.

"Say, boss—"

"What is it, Kragar?"

"Does that business about doubling salaries apply—"

"No."

He sighed. "I didn't think so. Anyway, what's the plan?"

"First, find four more enforcers. You have until this time tomorrow. Second, we'll see what we learn about what kind of income Laris has and figure out how we can hurt him."

"Okay. Can we afford the extra enforcers?"

"We can afford it—for a while. If things go on too long, we'll have to figure out something else."

"Do you think he'll give us the two days?"

"I don't know. He might—"

Melestav was standing at the door. "I just got a report, boss. Trouble. Nielar's place."

"What kind of trouble?"

"I don't know exactly. I got part of a message, asking for help, and then the guy got hit."

I stood up and headed out of the office, picking up Wyrn and Miraf'n on the way.

"Boss," said Kragar, "are you sure you ought to go out? That sounds like a—"

"I know. Come along behind me and keep your eyes open."

"Okay."

"*Loiosh, stay alert.*"

"*I'm always alert, boss.*"

4

"You expect to be unavailable?"

THE CITY OF ADRILANKHA lies along the southern coast of the Dragaeran Empire. It spent most of its existence as a middle-sized port city and became the Imperial capital when Dragaera City became a bubbling sea of chaos, on that day four hundred some years ago when Adron almost usurped the throne.

Adrilankha is as old as the Empire. It had its real beginnings in a spot that recently (in Dragaeran terms) became a cornerstone of the new Imperial Palace. It was there that, thousands of generations ago, Kieron the Conqueror met with the Shamans and told them that they could run wherever they wanted to, but that he and his Army of All Tribes would stand and wait for the "Eastern Devils." From there, he walked alone down a long trail that ended in a high cliff overlooking the sea. It is said by those who make it their business to say things that he stood there, unmoving, for five days (hence the five-day Dragaeran week) awaiting the arrival of the Tribe of the Orca, who had promised reinforcements, as the Eastern army closed in.

The spot was known as "Kieron's Watch" until the Interregnum, when the spells that had kept that part of the cliff from falling into the sea collapsed. I've always thought that amusing.

By the way, for those of you with an interest in history, the Orcas finally arrived, in time. They proved utterly useless as fighters on land, but Kieron won the battle anyway, thus securing the foundations of an Empire of Dragaerans.

Shame about that.

The path he walked is still known as Kieron Road, and leads from the new Imperial Palace down through the heart of the city, past the docks, and finally peters out with no ceremony somewhere in the foothills west of town. At some unspecified point, Kieron Road becomes Lower Kieron Road, and passes through a few not-very-nice neighborhoods. Along one of these stretches is the restaurant my father used to own, where he'd built up the small fortune that he later squandered buying a title in the Jhereg. The result of this is that I'm a citizen of the Empire, so now I can find out what time it is.

When I reached the age of deciding to get paid for what I was doing anyway (beating up Dragaerans), my first boss, Nielar, worked out of a small store on Lower Kieron Road. Supposedly, the store sold narcotics, hallucinogens, and other sorcery supplies. His real business was an almost continuous game of shareba, which he somehow kept forgetting to notify the Empire's tax collectors of. Nielar taught me the system of payoffs to the Phoenix Guards (since most of them are actually Dragons, you can't bribe one about anything important, but they like to gamble as much as anyone, and don't like taxes any more than most), how to make arrangements with the organization, how to hide your income from the Imperial tax collectors, and a hundred other little details.

When I took this area over from Tagichatn, Nielar was suddenly working for me. He was the only one who showed up to pay me the first week I was running the area. Later, he tore out the narcotics business and expanded to running s'yang stones. Then he put in a brothel upstairs. All in all, the place was my biggest single earner. So far as I know, the idea of holding out part of my cut never even occurred to him.

I stood next to Kragar in the burnt-out ruins of the building. Nielar's body lay before me. The fire hadn't killed him; his skull was caved in. Loiosh nuzzled my left ear.

After a long time, I said, "Arrange for ten thousand gold for his widow."

"Should I send someone over to tell her?" Kragar asked.

"No," I sighed, "I'll do it myself."

Some time later, at my office, Kragar said, "Both of his enforcers were in there, too. One may be revivifiable."

"Do it," I said. "And find the other one's family. See that they're well paid."

"Okay. What now?"

"Shit. What now? That cash just about exhausted me. My biggest source of income is gone. If someone delivered Laris's head to me right now, I couldn't pay him. If the revivification fails, and we have to pay that guy's family, that'll do it."

"We'll have more in a couple of days."

"Great. How long will that last?"

He shrugged. I spun my chair and threw a dagger into the target on the wall. "Laris is too Verra-be-damned good, Kragar. He took one shot, before I could move, and crippled me with it. And you know how he could do it? I'll bet he knows every copper I make, where I make it, and how I spend it. I'll bet he has a list of everyone who works for me, strengths and weaknesses. If we get out of this thing, I'm going to build me the best spy network this organization has ever seen. I don't care if I have to keep myself a Verra-be-damned pauper to do it."

Kragar shrugged. "That's *if* we get out of this."

"Yeah."

"Do you think you could get to him yourself, boss?"

"Maybe," I admitted. "Given time. For that, though, I'd have to wait until some of the reports came back. And it'd take me at least a week, more like three, to set it up."

Kragar nodded. "We need to be earning in the meantime."

I thought over a few things. "Well, okay. There's one thing that might work to get some cash. I wanted to hold it in reserve, but it doesn't look like I'm going to be able to."

"What is it, boss?"

I shook my head. "Take charge here. If there's any emergency, get hold of me."

"Okay."

I opened my bottom-left desk drawer and rummaged around until I found a fairly serviceable enchanted dagger. I scratched a rough circle on the floor and made a few marks in it. Then I stepped into the middle.

"Why do you do all that drawing, boss? You don't need to—"

"It helps, Kragar. See you later."

I drew on my link to the Orb and was in the courtyard of Morrolan's Castle, feeling sick. I avoided looking down because the sight of the ground, a mile below, would not have helped at all. I stared straight at the great double doors, some forty yards in front of me, until I no longer felt like throwing up.

I walked up to them. Walking in Morrolan's courtyard feels exactly like walking on flagstone, except your boots don't make any noise, which is disconcerting until you get used to it. The doors swung open when I was about five paces away, and Lady Teldra stood facing me, a warm smile on her face.

"Lord Taltos," she said, "we're delighted to see you, as always. I hope you'll be able to stay with us for at least a few days this time. We see you so seldom."

I bowed to her. "Thank you, Lady. A short mission only, I'm afraid. Where can I find Morrolan?"

"The Lord Morrolan is in his library, my lord. I'm certain he'd be as delighted to see you as the rest of us."

"Thanks," I said. "I can find my own way."

"As you wish, my lord."

It was always like that, with her. And she made you believe all that stuff, too.

As she'd said, I found Morrolan in the library. When I walked in, he was sitting with a book open on the table before him, holding a small glass tube suspended by a piece of thread over a black candle. He looked up as I came in, and set the tube aside.

"That's witchcraft," I told him. "Cut it out. *Easterners* do witchcraft; Dragaerans do sorcery." I sniffed the air. "Besides, you're using basil. You should be using rosemary."

"I was an accomplished witch three hundred years before you were born, Vlad."

I snorted. "You *still* should be using rosemary."

"The text failed to specify," he said. "It's been rather badly burned."

I nodded. "Where were you trying to see?"

"Around the corner," he said. "It was merely an experiment. But please, sit down. What may I help you with?"

I sat in a large, overstuffed chair done in black leather. I found a piece of paper on a table next to it, and a pen. I picked these up and began writing. As I did so, Loiosh flew over to Morrolan's shoulder. Morrolan dutifully scratched his head. Loiosh accepted graciously, and flew back. I handed Morrolan the paper, and he looked at it.

"Three names," he said. "I fail to recognize any of them."

"They're all Jhereg," I said. "Kragar should be able to put you in touch with any of them."

"Why?"

"They're all good at security."

"You wish me to hire an assistant for you?"

"Not exactly. You may want to consider one of these after I'm unavailable."

"You expect to be unavailable?"

"In a manner of speaking. I expect to be dead."

His eyes narrowed. "What?"

"I don't know of any other way to put it. I expect that I'll be dead soon."

"Why?"

"I'm overmatched. Someone's after my territory and I don't intend to let him have it. I think he'll be able to take me, and that means I'll be dead."

Morrolan studied me. "Why will he be able to 'take' you?"

"He has more resources than I do."

" 'Resources'?"

"Money."

"Oh. Please enlighten me, Vlad. How much money does something like this take?"

"Eh? Hmmm. I'd say about five thousand gold . . . every week for as long as it lasts."

"I see. And how long is it liable to last?"

"Oh, three or four months is usual. Sometimes six. Nine is a long time, a year is a very long time."

"I see. I presume that this visit is not an underhanded way of soliciting funds."

I pretended surprise. "Morrolan! Of course not! Ask a Dragon to support a Jhereg war? I wouldn't even consider it."

"Good," he said.

"Well, that's all I came by for. I guess I'll be heading back now."

"Yes," he said. "Well, good luck. Perhaps I'll see you again."

"Perhaps," I agreed. I bowed and took my leave. I wandered down the stairs, down the hall, and to the front doors. Lady Teldra smiled as I walked past her, and said, "Excuse me, Lord Taltos."

I stopped and turned. "Yes?"

"I believe you are forgetting something."

She was holding out a large purse. I smiled. "Why, yes, thank you. I wouldn't want to have forgotten that."

"I hope we see you again soon, my lord."

"I almost think you will, Lady Teldra," I said. I bowed to her, and returned to the courtyard to teleport.

I arrived on the street outside of the office and hurried in. When I got into the office itself I yelled for Kragar. Then I dumped the gold onto my desk and quickly counted it.

"Sacred shit, Vlad! What did you do, lighten the Dragon treasury?"

"Only a part of it, my friend," I said as I finished the counting. "Say about twenty thousand worth."

He shook his head. "I don't know how you did it, boss, but I like it. Believe me, I like it."

"Good. Help me figure out how to spend it."

That evening, Kragar made contact with seven free-lance enforcers and persuaded five of them to come to work for me for the duration. While he was doing that, I reached Temek.

"*What is it, boss? We're just getting start—*"

"*I don't care. What do you have, so far?*"

"*Huh? Not much of anything.*"

"*Forget the 'not much.' Do you have even one place? Or one name?*"

"*Well, there's a real popular brothel on Silversmith and Pier.*"

"*Where exactly?*"

"*Northwest corner, above the Jungle Hawk Inn.*"

"*Does he own the inn, too?*"

"*Don't know.*"

"*Okay. Thanks. Keep at it.*"

When Kragar checked in, to report procuring number two, I said, "*Take a break for a while. Get hold of Narvane. Have him stop what he's doing—he's helping Temek—long enough to wipe out the second floor of the Jungle Hawk Inn on Silversmith and Pier. Just the second floor. Got it?*"

"*Got it boss! Looks like we're off!*"

"*You bet your bonus we're off. Get busy.*"

I took a piece of paper and began scratching out some notes. Let me see, to protect each of my businesses against direct sorcerous attack for two months would cost . . . hmm. Make it one month then. Yes. That would leave me enough to work with. Good. Now, I'd want to—

"*Cut it out, boss.*"

"*Huh? Cut what out, Loiosh?*"

"*You're whistling.*"

"*Sorry.*"

Burning down an enemy's business is not a normal thing for a Jhereg war. It's expensive and it gets noticed, neither of which is good. But Laris had hoped to take me out with one good shot. My response was to let him see that I was not only not down, but I wasn't even hurting. This was a lie, but it should discourage any more of the heavy-handed nonsense.

Narvane reported in the next morning to say that the job had gone fine. He got a nice bonus for his trouble, and orders to lie low for a while. I met with the new enforcers and assigned them to their tasks, all of which involved defensive work—protecting this or that place. I still didn't have enough information on Laris's operation to know how I could hurt him, so I had to protect myself.

The morning went by quietly enough. I imagine Laris was assessing his position based on the events of last night. He might even be regretting the whole thing—but of course, he was now in too deep to back out.

I wondered how he'd hit me next.

A sorceress arrived promptly an hour after noon. I put five hundred gold into her hand. She walked out onto the street, raised her hands, concentrated for a moment, nodded, and left. Five hundred gold for five seconds' work. It was enough to make me regret my profession. Almost.

An hour or so later, I went out, with Wyrn and Miraf'n as bodyguards, and visited each of my businesses. No one even seemed to notice me. Good. I hoped the quiet would last long enough for Temek to collect a reasonable amount of information. It was frustrating, operating blind like that.

The rest of the day passed nervously, but with nothing happening. Ditto for the next day, except that various sorcerers from the Bitch Patrol came by each of my places and protected them from sorcery. Direct sorcery, I mean. There's no way to protect them from, say, someone levitating a fifty-gallon canister of kerosene over a building, lighting it, and then dropping it. But the enforcers I'd hired should be able to spot something like that, maybe even in time to do something about it.

To that end, I threw down more gold to keep a sorceress on full-time call. Actually using her would cost extra, but this way I was ready.

Reports from Temek indicated that Laris had taken similar measures. Other than that, Temek seemed to be having little luck. Everyone was being very close-mouthed. I had Miraf'n bring him a bag with a thousand Imperials to help open a few of those mouths.

The next day, Endweek, was much like the last, until shortly after noon. I was just hearing the news that the enforcer who'd been killed trying to protect Nielar had been revivified successfully when—

"Boss!"

"What is it, Temek?"

"Boss, you know the moneylender who works out of North Garshos?"

"Yeah."

"They got him, while he was on his way over to you. Dead. It looks like an axe job; half of his head is missing. I'm bringing the money in."

"Shit."

"Right, boss."

I told Kragar, while cursing myself for six kinds of a fool. It had just never occurred to me that Laris would go after the people making deliveries. Of course he knew when they were made, and from where, but it's one of the great unwritten laws of the Jhereg that we don't steal from each other. I mean, it has never happened, and I'll bet you all kinds of things that it never will.

But that didn't mean that those managers were safe. There wasn't any reason in the world why they couldn't be nailed, and the gold simply left on them.

I was just getting up a good round of cursing when I realized that there were more productive things to do. I didn't know any of these managers well enough to make contact with them psionically, but—

"Kragar! Melestav! Wyrn! Miraf'n! In here, quick! I'm going to lock the doors and sit tight. Divide up the businesses, teleport over to them *right now*, and don't let anyone leave who hasn't yet. Later, I'll arrange protection for them. Now, go!"

"Uh, boss—"

"What is it, Melestav?"

"I can't teleport."

"Damn. Okay. Kragar, cover for him, too."

"Check, boss."

There was a rush of displaced air that made my ears pop, and Melestav and I were alone. We looked at each other.

"I guess I still have a lot to learn about this business, eh?"

He gave me a faint smile. "I guess so, boss."

They reached all but one in time. He, too, was left for dead, but was revivifiable. The gold he was carrying almost paid for his revivification.

I wasted no more time. I got in touch with Wyrn and Miraf'n and told them to return at once. They did so.

"Sit down. Okay. This bag contains three thousand gold Imperials. I want you two to figure out where they're planning to take out H'noc—he runs the brothel that's just up the street. Find out where the assassin is, and get him. I don't know if you two have ever 'worked' before, and I don't care. I think you're up to this; if you don't, tell me. There's probably only one of them. If there's more, just get one. You can use H'noc as a decoy if you want, but you only have about another hour until we're past our usual delivery time. After that, they'll probably be suspicious. Do you want the job?"

They looked at each other, and, I imagine, spoke about it psionically. Wyrn turned back to me and nodded. I passed the bag over.

"Go do it, then."

They stood up and teleported out. About then I noticed that Kragar had come in. "Well?" I asked.

"I went ahead and arranged for them to bring in the gold over the next two days, except for Tarn, who can teleport. He should be in any time."

"Okay. We're broke again."

"*What?*"

I explained what I'd done. He looked doubtful, then nodded. "I guess you're right, it's the best thing to do. But we're hurting, Vlad. Are you going to be able to get more where we got that?"

"I don't know."

He shook his head. "We're learning too slow. He's staying ahead of us. We can't keep this up."

"By Barlen's scales, I know it! But what should we do?"

He looked away. He didn't have any better idea than I did.

"Don't sweat it, boss," said Loiosh. *"You'll think of something."*

I was pleased someone was feeling optimistic.

"For an assassin, you're a real sweetheart."

Here's A DISMAL THOUGHT for you: it seems that every friend I have almost killed me once. Morrolan, for example. I'd hardly been running my area for three weeks when he decided to hire me for a job. Now, I don't work for people outside of the organization. I mean, why should I? Are they going to back me up if I get caught? Can I count on them to pay my legal fees, bribe or threaten witnesses, and, above all, keep their mouths shut? Not a chance.

But Morrolan wanted me for something, and he found such a unique way of hiring me that I was filled with admiration. I expressed my admiration in such glowing terms that he nearly took my head off with Blackwand, the infantry battalion disguised as a Morganti sword.

But these things pass. Eventually, Morrolan and I became good friends. Good enough, in fact, that he, a Dragonlord, had given me a loan to carry on a Jhereg war. But were we good enough friends that he'd do so twice in three days?

Probably not.

It's been my experience that, just when things look bleakest, they continue to look bleak.

"*I guess this is my day for dismal thoughts, Loiosh.*"

"*Check, boss.*"

I teleported from my apartment to a spot just outside of the office building, and went inside without waiting for my stomach to settle. Wyrn was already standing in the street waiting for me, and Miraf'n was by the door.

"How did it go?" I asked.

"Done," said Wyrn.

"Okay. After this, you two might want to make yourselves scarce for a couple of days."

Miraf'n nodded; Wyrn shrugged. The three of us went into the shop, and past it into the suite of offices.

"Good morning, Melestav. Is Kragar in yet?"

"I didn't see him. But you know Kragar."

"Yeah. Kragar!"

I went into my office and found that there were no messages waiting for me. That meant no new disasters, anyway.

"Uh, boss?"

"Wha—? Good morning, Kragar. Nothing new, I see."

"Right."

"Anything from Temek?"

"Narvane is back working with him. That's all."

"Okay. I—"

"*Boss!*"

"*Temek! We were just discussing you. You have something?*"

"*Not exactly. But listen: I was doing some snooping around Potter's Market and Stipple Road, and stopped in this little klava hole to listen to the gossip, and this old Teckla comes up to me, some guy I'd never seen before, right? And he says, 'Tell your boss that Kiera has something for him. She'll meet him in the back room of the Blue Flame in one hour. Tell him that.'*

"*He got up and walked out. I followed him, not ten steps behind, but he was gone when I stepped outside. Anyway that's it. I think it may be a setup, boss, but—*"

"*When did it happen?*"

"*About two minutes ago. I looked for the guy, then got in touch with you.*"

"*Okay. Thanks. Get back to work.*"

I folded my hands and thought about it.

"What was it, Vlad?"

I related the conversation to him. He said, "Kiera? Do you think he meant Kiera the Thief?"

I nodded.

"It must be a setup, Vlad. Why would—"

"Kiera and I have been friends for a long time, Kragar."

He looked startled. "I didn't know that."

"Good. Then chances are, Laris doesn't. And that means this is probably straight."

"I'd be careful, Vlad."

"I intend to be. Can you get some people over there, right now, to look it over? And have a teleport block set to keep everyone out?"

"Sure. Where did you say?"

"The Blue Flame. It's on—"

"I know. Hmmm. You 'worked' there about a year and a half ago, didn't you?"

"How the hell did you hear about that?"

He gave me an inscrutable smile. "There's something else," he said.

"Yeah?"

"The owner is into us for a hundred and fifty. I'll bet he's going to be real cooperative, if we approach him right."

"I wonder if Kiera knew that?"

"Could be, boss. She, as they say, gets around."

"Yeah. Okay. We've got about fifty minutes. Get to work."

He left. I chewed on my thumb for a moment.

"Well, Loiosh, what do you think?"
"I think it's straight, boss."
"Why?"
"Just a feeling."
"Hmmm. Well, since it's your job to have feelings, I guess I'll go with it. But if you're wrong, and they kill me, I'm going to be very disappointed in you."
"I'll bear that in mind."

Miraf'n stepped outside first, followed by Loiosh, then by Wyrn. I came next, with Varg and Glowbug after me. Loiosh flew in high circles, gradually moving ahead of us.
"All clear, boss."
"Good."
All of this to walk one short block.
When we reached the Blue Flame, which was stuck between a pair of warehouses as if it were trying to hide, Glowbug went in first. He came back, nodded, and Loiosh and Varg went in, with me following. The lighting in the Flame was too dim for my taste, but I could still see well enough. There were four booths against the walls on either side, two tables of four in the middle, and three deuces in between. At a far booth, facing me, was a Jhereg named Shoen, whom Kragar had hired.

Shoen was one of those free-lance types who can do just about anything, and do it well. He was small, maybe six feet six inches, and compact. His hair was slicked back, like Varg's. He ran muscle, hustled a little loan business, did some "cleaning," sometimes ran shareba games—at one time or another he'd done damn near everything. For a while, he even worked as an organization contact in the Imperial Palace. He certainly did "work"—in fact, he was one of the more dependable assassins I knew of. If he weren't so addicted to gambling, or if he were a better gambler, he'd have made enough to retire on years ago. I was very pleased that we had him on our side.

Sitting alone at a deuce on the other side was a young kid (maybe three hundred) named Chimov. He had been in the organization for less than ten years, but had already "worked" at least twice. This is considered good. (I did better, but I'm an Easterner.) His hair was black, straight, and cut neatly at ear level. His face had a sharpness reminiscent of the House of the Hawk. He didn't talk much, which the Jhereg considers very good for someone his age.

All in all, I felt quite well protected as I sauntered into the back room. Wyrn, Miraf'n, and Loiosh checked it out in front of me. The room had one large, long table, ten chairs, and was empty.
I said, "Okay, you two, take off."
Wyrn nodded.
Miraf'n looked doubtful. "You sure, boss?"
"Yes."
They left. I sat down in one of the chairs and waited. The only door into the

room was closed, there were no windows, and there was a teleport block around the building. I wondered how Kiera would get in.

Two minutes later I was still wondering, but it was academic.

"Good morning, Vlad."

"Damn," I said. "I would have seen you coming in, but I blinked."

She chuckled, gave me a courtesy, and kissed me warmly. She sat down at my right. Loiosh landed on her shoulder and licked her ear. Kiera scratched under his chin.

"So, what did you want to see me about?"

She reached into her cloak and removed a small pouch. She deftly opened it and gestured. I held out my hand, and a single blue-white crystal fell into it. It was perhaps a third of an inch in diameter. I turned and held it up to a lamp.

"Very nice," I said. "Topaz?"

"Diamond," she said.

I spun back to see if she were joking. She wasn't. I studied it again.

"Natural?"

"Yes."

"Including the color?"

"Yes."

"And the size?"

"Yes."

"Guaranteed?"

"Yes."

"I see." I spent another five minutes or so studying the thing. I'm not a lapidary, but I know something about gems. I could detect no flaws.

"I assume you've appraised her. What's she worth?"

"Open market? Maybe thirty-five thousand if you look around for a buyer. Twenty-eight or thirty on quick sale. A cleaner would give at least fifteen—if he'd touch the deal at all."

I nodded. "I'll give you twenty-six."

She shook her head. I was startled. Kiera and I never bargained. If she offered me something, I gave her the best price I could, and that was that.

But she said, "I'm not selling it. It's yours." Then, "Close your mouth, Vlad; you're creating a draft."

"Kiera, I . . ."

"You're welcome."

"But *why?*"

"What a question! I've just handed you a fortune, and you want to know why?"

"Yeah. Shut up, boss." Loiosh licked her ear.

"You're welcome, too," she said.

It suddenly occurred to me, looking at the stone, that I'd seen either her, or her cousins, before. I looked at Kiera. "Where did you get this?" I asked.

"Why in the world would you want to know that?"

"Tell me, please."

She shrugged. "I had occasion to visit Dzur Mountain recently."

I sighed. That's what I'd thought. I shook my head and held the stone out to her. "I can't. Sethra's a friend of mine."

Then Kiera sighed. "Vlad, I swear by the Demon Goddess that you are harder to help than Mario is to sneak up on." I started to speak, but she held up her hand. "Your loyalty to your friend does you credit, but give me—and her—some credit, too. She can't help support a Jhereg war any more than Morrolan can. That didn't stop Morrolan, did it?"

"How did you—?"

She cut me off. "Sethra knows what became of this stone, though she'd never admit it. All right?"

I was struck speechless once more. Before I could talk, Kiera handed me the pouch. I mechanically put the stone into the pouch, the pouch into my cloak. Kiera leaned over and kissed me. "For an assassin," she said, "you're a real sweetheart." Then she was gone.

Later that day, Temek reported in with a list of five establishments owned by Laris. I arranged for some wizards to appear in two of them as customers to begin infiltration. *Wizard*, by the way, can mean either a particular kind of very powerful sorcerer, or, in the Jhereg, someone who does any one specific job very well. If you wonder how to tell which is meant—well, so do I.

Anyway, four of the wizards started penetrating two of Laris's businesses, while Kragar made arrangements for the other places. We hit the first one that evening. Nine toughs, mostly from the House of the Orca and hired for two gold per, descended on the place. Laris had two enforcers there, each of whom got one of our people before he was overpowered. The invaders used knives and clubs on the customers. There were no fatalities, but no one would be wanting to visit that place for a while.

Meanwhile, I hired more of these types to protect my own businesses from similar treatment.

Two days later we hit another one, with excellent results. That evening, Temek reported that Laris had dropped out of sight and was apparently running things from some hidden location.

The next morning Narvane, following up a rumor, found Temek's body in an alley behind the first place we'd hit. He was unrevivifiable.

Three days after that, Varg reported that he'd been approached by one of Laris's people to cooperate in an attempt to get me. Two days later, Shoen found the individual who'd approached Varg, alone. The guy was coming back from his mistress's flat. Shoen finalized him. A week after that, two of the wizards who were infiltrating one of Laris's establishments were blown to pieces in the middle of dinner in a small klava hole, by a spell thrown from the next table.

A week later we pulled another raid on one of Laris's places. This time we hired twenty-five toughs to help us. Laris had built up his defenses, so six of my people took the trip, but they did the job.

Sometime in there, Laris must have lost his temper. He had to have paid through the nose, but he found a sorcerer who could break through my sorcery protection spells. A week after my raid, my cleaner's shop went up in flames, along with the cleaner and most of his merchandise. I doubled the protection everywhere else. Two days later, Narvane and Chimov were caught on their way to escort H'noc in to me with his payment. Chimov was quick and lucky, so he was revivifiable; Narvane was not so quick but much luckier, and managed to teleport to a healer. The assassins escaped.

Eight days later, two things happened on the same evening, at nearly the same moment.

First, a wizard sneaked into a building housing a brothel run by Laris, carefully spread more than forty gallons of kerosene, and lit it. The place burned to the ground. The fires were set in front on the second story and in back on the first; no one was even scorched.

Second, Varg came to see me about something important. Melestav informed me; I told him to send Varg in. As Varg opened the door, Melestav noticed something—he still doesn't know what—and yelled for him to stop. He didn't, so Melestav put a dagger into his back and Varg fell at my feet. We checked, and found that it wasn't Varg at all. I gave Melestav a bonus, then went into my office, shut the door, and shook.

Two days later, Laris's people staged a full-scale raid on my office, complete with burning out the shop. We held them off without losing anyone permanently, but the cost was heavy.

Narvane, who'd taken over from Temek, found one more source of Laris's income. Four days after the raid on me, we hit it—beat up some customers, hurt some of his protection people, and set fire to the place.

By which time certain parties had had enough of the whole thing.

That day, I was standing in the rubble in front of my office, trying to decide if I needed a new place. Wyrn, Miraf'n, Glowbug, and Chimov surrounded me. Kragar and Melestav were there, too. Glowbug said, "Trouble, boss."

Miraf'n immediately stepped in front of me, but I had time to catch sight of four Jhereg walking toward the ruined building. It appeared that there was someone in the middle, but I couldn't be sure.

They reached the place and the four of them stood facing my bodyguards. Then a voice I recognized called out from among them, "Taltos!"

I swallowed, and stepped forward. I bowed. "Greetings, Lord Toronnan."

"They stay. You come."

"Come, Lord Toronnan? Where—"

"Shut up."

"Yes, my lord." *One of these days, bastard, I'm going to do you.*

He turned and I began following. He looked back and said, "No. That thing stays, too." It took me a moment to figure out what he was saying, then: "*Get ready, Kragar.*"

"*Ready, boss.*"

Out loud, I said, "No. The jhereg stays with me."

His eyes narrowed and we matched stares. Then he said, "All right."

I relaxed. We went north to Malak Circle, then headed east on Pier Street. Eventually we came to what had once been an inn, but was now empty, and went inside. Two of his people stopped by the door. Another was waiting inside. He carried a sorcery staff. We stood before him, and Toronnan said, "Do it."

There was a twisting in my bowels, and I found myself with Toronnan and two of his bodyguards in an area I recognized as Northwest Adrilankha. We were in the hills, where the houses were damn near castles. About twenty yards in front of us was the entrance to a pure white one, the great double doors inlaid with gold. A real pretty place.

"Inside," said Toronnan.

We walked up the steps. A manservant opened the door. Two Jhereg were just inside, their gray cloaks looking new and well cut. One of them nodded at Toronnan's enforcers and said, "They can wait here."

My boss nodded. We proceeded inward. The hall was bigger than the apartment I'd lived in after selling the restaurant. The room it emptied into, like a sewer into a cesspool, was bigger than the apartment I was living in. I saw more gold invested in knickknacks around the place than I'd earned in the last year. None of this went very far to improve my mood. In fact, by the time we were ushered into a small sitting room, I was beginning to feel more belligerent than frightened. Sitting there with Toronnan for more than ten minutes, waiting, didn't help either.

Then this guy walked in, dressed in the usual black and gray, with bits of gold lacing around the edges. His hair was graying. He looked old, maybe two thousand, but hale. He wasn't fat—Dragaerans don't get fat—but he seemed well-fed. His nose was small and flat; his eyes, deep and pale blue. He addressed Toronnan in a low, full, harsh voice: "Is this him?"

Who did he think I was? Mario Greymist? Toronnan only nodded.

"Okay," he said. "Get out."

Toronnan did so. The big shot stood there staring at me. I was supposed to get nervous, I guess. After a while I yawned. He glared.

"You bored?" he asked.

I shrugged. This guy, whoever he was, could snap his fingers and have me killed. But I wasn't about to kiss his ass; my life isn't worth that much.

He pulled a chair out with a foot, sat in it. "So you're a hardcase," he said. "I'm convinced. You've impressed me. Now, you wanna live, or not?"

"I wouldn't mind," I admitted.

"Good. I'm Terion."

I stood and bowed, then sat. I'd heard of him. He was one of the big, big bosses, one of the five who ran the organization in the city of Adrilankha (and Adrilankha had about ninety percent of the business). So I was impressed.

"How may I serve you, lord?"

"Aw, c'mon, boss. Tell him to jump in chaos, stick out your tongue, and spit in his soup. Go ahead."

"You can lay off your attempts to burn down Adrilankha."

"Lord?"

"Can't you hear?"

"I assure you, lord, I have no desire to burn down Adrilankha. Just a small part of it."

He smiled and nodded. Then, with no warning, the smile vanished and his eyes narrowed to slits. He leaned toward me and I felt my blood turn to ice water.

"Don't play around with me, Easterner. If you're going to fight it out with this other teckla—Laris—do it in a way that doesn't bring the whole Empire down on us. I've told him, now I'm telling you. If you don't, I'll settle it myself. Got that?"

I nodded. "Yes, my lord."

"Good. Now get the fuck outta here."

"Yes, lord."

He got up, turned his back on me, and left. I swallowed a couple of times, stood, and walked out of the room. Toronnan was gone, with all of his people. Terion's servant showed me the door. I did my own teleport back to my office. I told Kragar that we were going to have to change our methods.

We didn't have time to do so, however. Terion had been right, but he had acted too late. The Empress had already had enough.

6

"I'm going to take a walk."

W HEN I SAY "EMPRESS" you probably get an image of this old, stern-looking matron, with iron-gray hair, dressed in gold robes, with the Orb circling her head as she issues edicts and orders affecting the lives of millions of subjects with a casual wave of the sceptre.

Well, the orb *did* circle her head; that part is right. She wore gold, too—but nothing as simple as robes. She would often wear . . . but, never mind.

Zerika was a young three or four hundred, which is like mid-twenties to a human. Her hair was golden—and if I'd meant "blond" I would have said "blond." Her eyes were the same color, rather like a lyorn's, and deeply set. Her forehead was high, her brows light and almost invisible against very pale skin. (Notwithstanding the rumors, however, she was *not* undead.)

The House of the Phoenix is always the smallest, because they won't consider you a Phoenix unless an actual phoenix is seen to pass overhead at the time of your birth. The Interregnum had eliminated every Phoenix except Zerika's mother—who died in childbirth.

Zerika was born during the Interregnum. The last Emperor had been a decadent Phoenix, and since this was the seventeenth Cycle, the next Emperor had to be a Phoenix too, since a reborn Phoenix is supposed to follow a decadent Phoenix every seventeen Cycles. So far as I can tell, by the way, a reborn Phoenix is an Emperor of the House of the Phoenix who doesn't become decadent by the end of his reign. Anyway, since Zerika was the only Phoenix living at the time, this meant it had to be Zerika. (All of this business about "what makes a Phoenix" is very strange when combined with aspects of the relationships among Houses—such as genetics. I mean, it seems absurd to have the opinion that most Dragaerans seem to have about cross-breeds, when there is, at the moment, no other way to produce a Phoenix heir except through cross-breeding. I may go into this at some point.)

In any case, at the tender age of one hundred or thereabouts she came to Deathsgate Falls and passed, living, through the Paths of the Dead and so came to the Halls of Judgment. There she took the Orb from the shade of the last Emperor and returned to declare the Interregnum at an end. This was about the time my great-great-great-great-great-great-great-great grandfather was being born.

That business about descending Deathsgate Falls, by the way, is quite impressive. I know, because I've done it myself.

But the point is that this background gave Zerika a certain understanding of the human condition—or at least the Dragaeran condition. She was wise and she was intelligent. She knew that there was nothing to be gained by interfering in a duel between Jhereg. On the other hand, I guess what Laris and I had been doing to each other was too much to ignore.

We woke up the morning after the meeting with Terion to find the streets patrolled by guards in Phoenix livery. Notices were posted explaining that no one was allowed in the streets after nightfall, that no groups of more than four could assemble, that all use of sorcery would be carefully observed and regulated, that all taverns and inns were shut down until further notice. There was also the unspoken statement that no illegal activity of any kind would be tolerated.

It was enough to make me want to move to a better neighborhood.

"Where do we stand, Kragar?"

"We can keep up like this—supporting everything and not earning—for about seven weeks."

"Do you think this will last seven weeks?"

"I don't know. I hope not."

"Yeah. We can't reduce our forces unless Laris does, and we don't have any way of knowing if Laris will. That's the worst part of it—this would be the perfect time to start infiltrating his organization, but we can't because he doesn't have anything running, either."

Kragar shrugged. "We'll just have to sit tight."

"Hmmmm. Maybe. Tell you what: why don't we find a few places he's connected to that are legitimate—you know, like restaurants—and make friends with some of the management types."

"Make friends?"

"Sure. Give them presents."

"Presents?"

"Gold."

"Just give it to them?"

"Yeah. Not ask for anything. Have people hand them money, and say it comes from me."

He looked more puzzled than ever. "What will that do?"

"Well, it works with court advisors, doesn't it? I mean, isn't that the kind of thing the connections do? Just maintain good relationships so that if they need something, people will be well-disposed toward them? Why not try it here? It can't do any harm."

"It costs."

"Screw that. It might work. If they like us, that makes it more likely they'll tell us something. And maybe they can tell us something useful. If not right away, then someday."

"It's worth a try," he admitted.

"Start out with five hundred, and spread it around a bit."

"You're the boss."

"Next: we really should get some idea of when we can open something up. Do you have any guesses at all? Days? Weeks? Months? Years?"

"At least days, maybe weeks. Remember—those guards don't like this any more than we do. They'll be fighting it from their end, and all the merchants who aren't involved are going to be fighting it from *their* end. Also, it goes without saying that all the organization contacts in the Palace will be working on it. I don't think it can last more than a month."

"Will it stop all at once, or gradually disappear?"

"Could be either way, Vlad."

"Hmmph. Well, could we open, say, one game, in a week?"

"They might let us get away with it. But once you open up a game, what happens the first time a customer runs short of cash? We need to have someone to lend him money. And then maybe he gets behind on his payments, so he starts stealing. We need a cleaner. Or—"

"We don't have a cleaner in any case."

"I'm working on that."

"Oh. All right. But yes, I see your point. It's all tied in."

"And there's another thing: whoever opens up is going to be pretty nervous. That means that you should really make personal visits—and that's dangerous."

"Yeah."

"One thing we could do is find a new office. I can still smell the smoke in here."

"We could, but . . . do you know where Laris's office is?"

"I know, but he doesn't go there anymore. We don't know where he is."

"But we know where his office is. Fine. That's where my next office will be."

He looked startled, then shook his head. "Nothing like confidence," he said.

Narvane was in touch with me pretty constantly that week, and was slowly getting a feel for the work. After what had happened to Temek, he was being careful, but we were accumulating a list of places and a few names.

I tried doing a small witchcraft spell on Laris, just to see if there was any point in attacking him that way, but I got nothing. That meant that he was protected against witchcraft—and indicated that he really did know me, since most Dragaerans don't think of the art as anything to bother with.

I had enforcers following those people we knew, trying to get their movements down so we could use this information later. We approached a couple of them with large sums, hoping to find out where Laris was hiding, but we didn't get any takers.

The project to make friends with Laris's people went better, although just as slowly. We got nothing useful, but there were indications that we might in the future. I had some people speak to the Phoenix Guards. We learned from them that they weren't happy about the duty, didn't expect it to last long, and that they were as impatient to start earning their gambling money again as we were to start needing to pay them. I considered the matter.

Six days after Zerika put her foot down, I met with Kragar and Smiley Gilizar. Smiley had been protecting Nielar, and was pretty much recovered from being revivified. He got his name because he smiled almost as much as Varg—that is, not at all.

Varg, however, rarely had any expression. Smiley had a permanent sneer. When he looked like he wanted to bite you in the leg, he was happy. When he got angry, his face became contorted. He had picked up an Eastern weapon called a lepip, which was a heavy metal bar with leather wrapped around it to prevent cuts. When he wasn't doing protection, he did muscle work. He'd started on the docks, collecting for a short-tempered lender called Cerill. When Cerill was fed up with being reasonable, he'd send Smiley, and then send someone else the next day to reason with whatever was left.

So Smiley sat there, scowling at Kragar and me, and I said, "Smiley, our friend H'noc is going to open up his brothel tomorrow evening. He's being protected by Abror and Nephital. I want you to go over to help them out."

He sneered even more, as if it were beneath him.

I knew him well enough to ignore this, however. I continued: "Stay out of the way of our customers, so you don't scare them. And if the guards try to shut the place down, just let them. Can you handle that?"

He snorted, which I took for a yes.

"Okay, be there at the eighth hour. That's all."

He left without a word. Kragar shook his head. "I'm amazed that you can get rid of him that easy, Vlad. You'd think you'd have to do a demon banishment or something."

I shrugged. "He's never 'worked,' as far as I know."

Kragar grunted. "Anyway, we ought to know something by tomorrow. Any word from Narvane?"

"Not much. He's been going slow."

"I suppose. But he should at least be checking to see if Laris is opening something."

I agreed. I got hold of Narvane and gave the necessary orders. Then I sighed. "I hate being in the dark like this. We have a good groundwork for the future, but we still know hardly anything about him."

Kragar nodded, then brightened. "Vlad!"

"Yes?"

"Morrolan!"

"Huh?"

"Aren't you his security consultant? Doesn't he have a spy network?"

"Sure, Kragar. And if you want to find out how many sorcerers Lord Whointheheck of the House of the Dragon has, I could tell you in three minutes, along with their specialities, ages, and tastes in wine. But that doesn't help us."

He got a vacant look, and said, "There ought to be a way to use that . . ."

"If you think of one, let me know."

"I will."

H'noc reached me late in the evening of the next day.

"*Yes?*"

"*Just wanted to tell you that we haven't been bothered by any guards yet.*"

"*Good. Customers?*"

"*Maybe two.*"

"*Okay. It's a start. Have you seen anyone who looks like he might be working for Laris?*"

"*How would I know?*"

"*All right. Stay in touch.*"

I looked up at Kragar, who was spending more time in my office than in his own these days. "I just talked to H'noc. No problems; no customers."

He nodded. "If we make it through the night, maybe we should open up a cleaner tomorrow."

"Sure," I said. "Who?"

"I know a few thieves who've been talking about getting into that end."

"In the middle of a war?"

"Maybe."

"All right. Check into it."

"Will do."

Kragar found a cleaner, and we opened up a couple of nights later. At the same time, Narvane found out that Laris wasn't doing much of anything. We began to breathe easier. Soon, we decided, the Phoenix Guards would just disappear, and things would be back to normal.

Normal? Exactly what *was* "normal" at this point?

"Kragar, what happens when the Phoenix Guards disappear?"

"Things go back to . . . oh. I see what you mean. Well, in the first place, we're back on the defensive. He starts moving in on us, we start trying to find out all we can about him—and by the way, we should have more than just Narvane working on that."

"I know. We will, but—it seems to me that this is our big chance to get ahead."

"Uh . . . *what* is?"

"This. Now. When neither of us can attack the other, but we can get our businesses going again. We should push it as far as we can. Get as much going as possible, to build up some cash, and make as many friends among Laris's people as we can, get Narvane and whoever else we can digging into him—the whole bit."

Kragar thought that over, then nodded. "You're right. We've got the cleaner working, that means we can open up a lender. Three days? Two?"

"Two. We're going to be paying extra bribes, but that shouldn't go on too long."

"Right. And once that's going, we could start one of the small shareba clubs. A week from today, say? If everything goes well?"

"That sounds right."

"Good. And we won't need too much protection at first. Let's put Wyrn and Miraf'n helping Narvane. And maybe Chimov and Glowbug, too. But keep them all on the rotation for bodyguards."

"Not Chimov. I don't want any free-lancer knowing too much about what I know. Make it N'aal. He isn't good at it, but he can learn."

"Okay. I'll talk to them, and let Narvane in on it."

"Good. Are we leaving anything out?"

"Probably, but nothing I can think of."

"Then let's get at it."

"It's going to be nice seeing you do some work again, boss."

"Shut up, Loiosh."

It took Narvane only a couple of days to work the extra help into his organization. The day the lender started, I began to get reports from them, and was impressed. While they still didn't know many of his people—and those they did were right at the bottom—they found out seven establishments that Laris was running. To our surprise, none of them had reopened. Laris was lying low. I didn't know whether to be overjoyed or nervous. But there were still Phoenix Guards all over the place, so we felt safe.

A few days later, I opened up a small shareba game, and the next day a game of s'yang stones and a game of three-copper mud. Our list on Laris grew, but he *still* wasn't doing anything. I wondered what it meant.

"Hey, Kragar."

"Yeah?"

"How many Dzur does it take to sharpen a sword?"

"I dunno."

"Four. One to sharpen it, three to put up enough of a fight to make it worthwhile."

"Oh. Is there some point to that?"

"I think so. I think it has something to do with needing to have opposition in order to act."

"Hmmmm. Is this leading somewhere, or are you just being obscure?"

"I'm going to take a walk. Who's protecting me today?"

"A walk? Are you sure it's safe?"

"Of course not. Who's on duty?"

"Wym, Miraf'n, Varg, and Glowbug. What do you mean, a walk?"

"I'm going to visit my businesses. Word will get around that I did so, and that I'm not worried about either Laris or the Empire, customers will relax, and business will pick up. True or not true?"

"You're going to show that you aren't worried by walking around with four bodyguards?"

"True or not true?"

He sighed. "True, I guess."

"Call them in."

He did so.

"Stay here," I told him, "and keep things running."

We walked out of the office, past the ruins of the front of the shop (I didn't dare let anyone close enough to me to let them do repairs), and into the street. There were a pair of Phoenix Guards at the northwest corner of Garshos and Copper Lane. We went that way, Loiosh flying ahead, and I could feel their eyes on me. We went east on Garshos to Dayland, and I was surprised that I didn't see any others. We went to the cleaner's, which was set up in the basement of an inn called The Six Chreotha, which looked like it had been slowly falling to ruin for a few thousand years.

I went in to see the cleaner. He was a cheery-looking guy named Renorr: short, dark, with the curly brown hair and flat features that claimed he had Jhegaala somewhere in his background. His eyes were clear, which proved that he hadn't been in the business long. Cleaning stolen goods is not something one can bribe Imperial guards about, so one must be careful not to let them find out one is doing it. Fences always end up with shifty, frightened eyes.

Renorr bowed and said, "I'm honored to meet you at last, lord."

I nodded.

He gestured outside. "They seem to have left."

"Who? The guards?"

"Yes. There were several near here this morning."

"Hmmm. Well, that's all to the good, then. Maybe they're reducing their forces."

"Yes."

"How's business?"

"Slow, lord. But picking up a bit. I'm just getting started."

"Okay." I smiled at him. "Keep it going."

"Yes, lord."

We walked back out, continued to Glendon, followed it to Copper Lane, and headed back north. As we walked past the Blue Flame I stopped.

"*What is it, boss?*"

"*Those guards, Loiosh. There were two of them on that corner fifteen minutes ago; now they're gone.*"

"*I don't like this. . . .*"

Glowbug said, "Notice the guards are missing, boss? That's a demon of a coincidence. I don't like it."

"Bide," I told him.

"*I think we should get back to the office, boss.*"

"*I don't think—*"

"*Remember what you said about my 'feelings'? Well, this one is strong. I think we should get back right away.*"

"*Okay, you've talked me into it.*"

"Back to the office," I told Glowbug. He seemed relieved. Varg made no response whatsoever. Wyrn nodded, his eyes dreamy, and his half-smile didn't change. Miraf'n nodded his great, shaggy head.

We went past the Blue Flame and I started to relax. We reached the corner of Garshos and Copper, and Wyrn and Miraf'n looked down both ways carefully, then nodded. We went past the corner and came into sight of my office. I heard a strange, shuffling sound behind me, a false step, and spun in time to see Varg falling to his knees, a look of shock on his face. With the corner of my eye I saw Glowbug falling.

"*Look out, boss!*"

For the briefest instant, I couldn't believe it was really happening. I had known all along that my life was in danger, but I hadn't really believed that I, Vlad Taltos, assassin, could be taken out as easily as any Teckla on the street. But Glowbug was down, and I saw the hilt of a dagger protruding from Varg's back. He was still conscious, trying to crawl toward me, his mouth working silently.

Then my reflexes took over, as I realized that I was still alive, and that Wyrn and Miraf'n would be covering me from behind. I reached for my rapier as I tried to spot the knife-thrower, and—

"*Behind you, boss!*"

I spun, and got a glimpse of Wyrn and Miraf'n backing away as a tall Dragaeran with—wait a minute. *Backing away?* They were. They were watching me closely as they carefully stepped backwards, away from the scene. Meanwhile, a tall Dragaeran was coming at me, slowly and steadily, with a greatsword in her hands.

I changed my mind about the rapier and drew a throwing knife with each hand. I wanted to get at least those two bastards who had sold me out. Loiosh left my shoulder, flying into the face of the assassin before me. That gave me the time I needed to take aim and—

Something told me to dodge, so I did, to my right, as something sharp scraped along the right side of my back. I spun, both daggers flashing, and—

Loiosh screamed psionically as there was a ripping in my left side, from behind. I realized that the assassin with the greatsword had gotten past Loiosh. I felt a coldness, and I became aware that there was a piece of steel actually *inside* of me, among my bones and muscles and organs, and I felt sick. I ignored my desire to turn that way, and found the one who had attacked from behind. She was very short and held a pair of large fighting knives. She was staring straight at me, dispassionately. The sword was taken from my side with a sudden wrenching, and I found myself on my knees. The assassin in front of me struck full forward, one knife cutting across for my throat, the other thrusting for my chest. I tried to force my arms up to parry—

And there was blood flowing from her mouth, and she was falling at my feet. The knife she was slashing with scored a gash across my chest. As she hit the ground, the other blade found a home in my stomach. I heard flapping wings behind me and was pleased that Loiosh was alive, as I waited for the sword-stroke from behind that would finish me.

Instead, I heard a voice that sounded remarkably like Aliera's, crying, "You—you're a Dragon!" And the ringing sound of clashing steel. Somehow, I twisted around as I fell, and saw that it was, indeed, Aliera, wielding a greatsword that was taller than she was, and dueling with the assassin. Watching them was Morrolan himself, fury on his face, Blackwand in his hand. Aliera's blade swung high as the assassin's cut low and Loiosh said, *"Twist!"*

I did, but not in time to prevent the other one, who was still alive, from planting her dagger, to the hilt, in my kidney. There was pain such as I had never felt before, and I screamed. A muscle spasm jerked me to my knees and around and down, flat on my stomach, on the blade that was already there, and I only wanted to die quickly and have it over.

For an instant before I got my wish, my face was a few inches from the other assassin's, blood still streaming from her mouth, her eyes set in a look of grim determination. I suddenly realized that she was an Easterner. That almost hurt more than the rest of it, but then the pain went away, and me with it.

7

"I guess there's just a time for doing dumb things."

LINGERING TRACE OF A fading green light, but no eyes to see it with. Memory like a well, awareness like a bucket—but who pulls the rope? It occurred to me that "me" had occurred. Existence without sensation, and the bucket hadn't yet reached the water.

I knew what "sight" was when it came, and I found myself staring into a pair of bright round things that I eventually realized were "eyes." They floated in gray fog and seemed to see me. That must be significant. "Brown" occurred to me, looking at the eyes, at about the same moment that I saw a face fitting around them. Looking at the face, other terms came to mind. "Little girl" was one. "Cute" was another. And "somber."

I wondered if she were human or Dragaeran, and realized that more of me had returned.

She studied me. I wondered what she was seeing. Her mouth opened and sound issued forth. I realized that I'd been hearing the sounds for quite some "time" and had not been aware of it. The sounds were utterly dead, as if in a room that was completely without echo.

"Uncle Vlad?" she said again, but it registered this time.

Two words. "Uncle" and "Vlad." Both had meaning. "Vlad" meant me, and I was delighted with the discovery. "Uncle" had something to do with family, but I wasn't sure exactly what. I thought about the words more, deeming them important. As I did so, a wave of green light seemed to come from all around me, bathing me for a moment, then stopping.

I realized that this, too, had been going on for some time.

Sensations multiplied, and I felt that I had a body again. I blinked, and found it delightful. I licked my lips, and that was nice, too. I turned my attention back to the little girl, who was still watching me closely. She seemed relieved now.

"Uncle Vlad?" she said, like a litany.

Oh, that's right. "Vlad." Me. I was dead. The Easterner, the pain, *Loiosh.* But he'd been alive, so maybe . . .

"Uncle Vlad?"

I shook my head, and tried speaking. "I don't know you," I said, and heard that my voice was strong. She nodded enthusiastically.

"I know," she said. "But Mommy's awful worried about you. Won't you please come back?"

"Come back?" I said. "I don't understand."

"Mommy's been trying to find you."

"She sent you to look for me?"

She shook her head. "She doesn't know I'm here. But she's *really* worried, Uncle Vlad. And so's Uncle 'Rollan. Won't you *please* come back?"

Who could refuse a request like that? "Where am I, then?"

She cocked her head to the side, looking puzzled. Her mouth opened and closed a few times. Then she shook her head again. "I don't know, but just come back, okay?"

"Sure, honey, but how?"

"Follow me," she said.

"Okay." She moved away a few feet, stopped, and looked back. I found myself moving toward her, but I didn't seem to be walking. I had no sense of how fast we were traveling, or from where to where, but the grayness gradually darkened.

"Who are you?" I asked her as we moved.

"Devera," she said.

"I'm pleased to meet you, Devera."

She turned back to me and giggled, lighting up her face. "We've met before, Uncle Vlad." That triggered some more memories that I couldn't quite place, but—

"Oh, Uncle Vlad?"

"Yes, Devera?"

"When we get back, don't mention to Mommy that you saw me, okay?"

"Okay. Why not? Aren't you supposed to be here?"

"Well, not exactly. You see, I haven't really been born yet. . . ."

Wherever we were became completely black, and I felt suddenly isolated. Then, once more, I was bathed in green light, and I remember no more.

. . . the dzur had scored a long scratch in the jhereg's wing. The jhereg's jaws were going for the dzur's neck, but the dzur nearly had its mouth around the long, snakelike neck of the jhereg. The jhereg was of the normal breed, not one of the nonpoisonous giant ones that dwelt above Deathsgate Falls, yet it was one of the largest I had ever seen, and should be able to give a good fight to. . . . I blinked. The scene hadn't changed. The orange-red sky was right, but I realized that I was inside, on a bed, in fact. I was looking at a painting that filled the ceiling above me. Someone's idea of a joke, no doubt, to have me wake up to that sight. Could I view the painting so that it appeared the jhereg was winning? I could and did. It was a nice painting. I took a deep breath and—*I was alive!*

I turned my head and looked around the room. It was spacious, as far as I was concerned—twenty-two and a half feet in the direction of the bed, maybe fourteen the other way. No windows, but a nice circulation of air. There was

a fireplace centered in the wall my feet pointed to, with a cozy little fire crack-
ling away in it and sending occasional sparks into the room. I twisted and saw
that a door was centered in the other wall. Black candles were scattered
throughout, providing most of the light. Yet there were enough of them to give
the room a bright appearance despite the black walls.

Black, black, black. The color of sorcery. Lord Morrolan, Castle Black. Yet,
he wouldn't have used black candles unless he were doing witchcraft, and I felt
no traces of a spell. Nor would he have a painting like that. So—Dzur Mountain, of course.

I leaned back against the pillow (goose feathers, a luxury!) and slowly set
about moving my limbs. I made each one move, and each finger and toe. They
responded normally, but it took some effort. I saw my cloak and clothing neatly
folded on a stand three feet from my head. I noticed with amusement that
whoever had undressed me had left Spellbreaker wrapped around my wrist,
which was why I hadn't immediately felt undressed.

I heaved myself to a sitting position. I became aware of a general sense of
weakness and pains throughout my body. I welcomed them, as more signs of
life, and swung my feet over the edge of the bed.

"Going to say hello, boss?"

I spun, and spotted Loiosh high on top of a tall dresser in the far corner of
the room. *"Good morning, or whatever it is. I'm glad you're all right."*

He flew down and landed on my shoulder; licked my ear. *"That goes double
for me, boss."*

There was a chamber pot in one corner of the room, which I made a much-
needed use of. I dressed slowly, finding several of my more obvious weapons
neatly laid out beneath the cloak. Most of the contents of the cloak itself hadn't
been disturbed. Dressing was painful. Enough said.

There was a soft clap at the door about the time I finished. "Come in."

Aliera entered. "Good morning, Vlad. How are you feeling?"

"Well enough, all things considered." Morrolan was standing in the doorway
behind her. We exchanged nods.

"We would have been here sooner," he said, "but we had to visit another of
our patients."

"Oh? Who?"

"The 'lady' who attacked you," said Aliera.

"She's alive?" I swallowed involuntarily. Being killed attempting to do a job
is one of the very few things that terminates the agreement between assassin
and employer; I'd been hoping that they'd both taken the trip.

"Both of them are," she said. "We revivified them."

"I see." That was different. They had the option of resuming the agreement
now, or not. I hoped they chose not to.

"Which reminds me," said Morrolan. "Vlad, I apologize to you. The Easterner should not have been able to attack you. I caused ruptures in several of
her internal organs, which should have sent her into shock at once. It did not
occur to me to continue watching her."

I nodded. "She's probably a witch," I said. "Witchcraft is good for that." He knew that, of course; I was just needling him. "But it ended up all right. How did things go with the other one?"

"She is a very good fighter," said Aliera. "Remarkably good. We fought for more than a minute, and she wounded me twice."

It was nicely ironic that Aliera, who specialized in sorcery, had dueled blade to blade with the one, while Morrolan, one of the finest blades in the Empire, had used sorcery. But both were far, far above the norm at either, so it really didn't matter.

I nodded. "When was it?"

Aliera said, "We performed the revivification as soon as we had you back. You've slept for two days."

"I don't know how to thank you—or was it Sethra?—for revivifying me."

"It was I," said Aliera, "and no thanks are necessary."

"How hard was it?"

She shook her head. "The most difficult I've ever tried. I thought we'd lost you. It was quite a task to repair your body, even before the revivification. Then I made four tries before it worked. I slept for half a day afterwards."

It was only then that I remembered the dream I'd had. I started to mention it, but Aliera was continuing.

"I think you should be resting now. Try to stay on your back for at least a day. Also, don't—"

This reminded me of something else, so I interrupted. "Excuse me, Aliera, but—how did you and Morrolan happen to be there?"

". . . Morrolan dragged me along. Ask him."

I turned and let my eyebrows do so.

"Kragar," he said. "He explained that you required immediate assistance, but he didn't know the form. I happened to be with Aliera at the time. It seems we were nearly too late. And, to repeat, I apologize for my sloppiness with the Easterner."

I brushed it aside. "All right. I'll take your advice now, Aliera. I think I'd like to sleep."

"Are you hungry?" she asked.

I checked the relevant part of me, then nodded. "A bit. Perhaps when I wake up."

"All right. I'll speak to Sethra about it. Do you feel any nausea, or would you be up to a full meal?"

"I feel fine," I told her. "Just tired."

"Good."

I bowed to each of them and sat back on the bed as they left.

"You're no more tired than I am, boss."

"True. But I am sore. Quiet for a minute."

I reached out for contact with Kragar. It took a while, but eventually he responded.

"Vlad! Welcome back!"

"Thanks. It's nice to be alive again."

"I imagine. Aliera told me you'd taken the trip, but they'd brought you back. I was beginning to worry, though. It's been three days."

"I know. How are Varg and Glowbug?"

"Glowbug is okay; the dagger caught his kidney, but we got to him in time." He paused. "Varg didn't make it. The revivification failed."

I cursed, then asked, "How's our income?"

"A trickle."

"Hmph. How about standing funds?"

"Around nine thousand left."

"Okay. Thirty-five hundred each for anyone who brings me Wyrn and Miraf'n."

"Boss, they're going to be protected, you'll never—"

"Fine. Then I won't have to pay anything. But put the word out."

Mental shrug. "Okay," he said. "Anything else?"

"Yes. Tighten up. I mean, everybody. No action until I'm back, but I don't *want* anybody out alone, ever. Got that?"

"Got it."

"And blow another thousand on bumping up the protection on every place we have. I don't want any more surprises."

"Check. Anything else?"

"Yeah. Thanks."

"You're welcome."

"What tipped you off?"

"I got a message from one of those people we've been trying to cultivate as friends. It seems that the thing was arranged in an upstairs room of his tavern, and he decided to help us out."

"Well I'll be. . . . Give him two hundred."

"I gave him one-fifty already."

"Good. Kragar . . . all the Phoenix Guards disappeared, went away, just about the time I left the office. I can't believe that's a coincidence, and I can't believe they have the Empress helping them out—or the commander of the Phoenix Guards, for that matter. Do you know anything about it?"

"Our contact said he heard it would be 'taken care of.' "

"Hmmmm. I see. Check up on it, all right?"

"I'll try."

"Good. And do you know who those two were? The ones who got me? They were damn good. They did half the job anyway, even after Morrolan and Aliera showed up."

There was a pause. "Boss? You don't know?"

"What are you talking about? How could I know?"

"Think about it, boss. Two assassins. Female. One Dragaeran, one Easterner. One with a greatsword, one with daggers. How many teams like that are there?"

"Oh . . . I—uh, I'll be talking to you later, Kragar."

"Sure, Vlad."
And the contact was broken.

When you talk about assassins, good ones, the name Mario Greymist has a place by itself. He is the best there is, ever has been, or, as far as I'm concerned, ever could be. But after Mario, there are several names that come to mind, among those few who know such things: the ones who are good, dependable, command high rates, and are feared by anyone thinking of making a powerful enemy within the organization.

Most assassins work alone. I mean, murder is a very private thing. But there are a few teams. One of these teams is on the list I mentioned above. I'd heard of them, and their names have been linked to a score of jobs in the last five years. None of these tales is certain, and most are probably wrong, but still. . . . This team involved a Dragaeran, using a greatsword with all the skill of a Dragonlord, and an Easterner using a dagger. Both were women—and the Right Hand of the Jhereg has very few women. (There's Kiera the Thief, and maybe a few others, but they are a rarity.) This pair of assassins called themselves "The Sword of the Jhereg" and "The Dagger of the Jhereg," and no one knew anything about where they'd come from. It was very hard to get hold of them—usually, if you wanted them, you just put the word out on the streets and hoped they'd hear and be interested.

It should be pointed out that the most I've ever been offered for an assassination is six thousand gold, and these two won't even talk to you for less than eight or nine. It had never occurred to me to send them after Laris, because they'd have wanted at least twenty thousand, and there was no way I could raise that kind of cash without committing everything to the one shot—a stupid thing to do since anyone can fail. (I haven't yet, but I've been lucky.)

I wondered how much I was worth, and where Laris had found the funds. I discovered that I was shaking, which was stupid, since the threat was over. Unless they decided to complete the job. I continued shaking.

"You okay, boss?"

"Not really. Let's take a walk."

I stepped out of the room into the cold, black stone halls of Dzur Mountain. I knew where I was at once. To my right would be the sitting room, where I'd first met Sethra. To my left would be more bedrooms. On impulse, I turned to the left. There were doors on either side of the hall. The hall continued past them. I stopped. Could the assassins be in one of these? Or one in each? I decided to keep walking; there was nothing to be gained by seeing them. I mean, as an assassin, I never had anything to say to my targets; as a target, what was I going to say to my assassins? Plead for my life? Sure. No, there was no point in . . . I discovered that I hadn't moved. I sighed.

"I guess there's just a time for doing dumb things, Loiosh."

I opened the door as quietly as I could and looked inside.

She was awake and looking at me. Her face was calm, her eyes expressionless. No question about it, she was as human as I was. Her eyes moved down to my right hand, which I discovered was gripping a dagger at my belt. She didn't seem to be frightened.

She was sitting up, a blue nightgown showing her pale skin in the dim light of a single set of candles. Her hair was dark brown, almost black. Her eyes were darker yet, a vibrant contrast with the shade of her skin. The nightgown was intended to be modest, but it was also intended for a Dragaeran, so it fell rather low on her. She showed no embarrassment.

Her eyes traveled from the dagger to my face. We studied each other for a time; then I forced my hand to relax, and release its grip on the weapon.

Dammit! *I* was the one who was armed, *she* was the one who was helpless. There was no reason for *me* to be afraid of *her*. I managed to speak.

"Have you a name?" My voice sounded dry, almost cracked.

"Yes," she said, in a soft contralto.

I waited for her to continue. When she showed no signs of doing so, I said, "Will you tell me what it is?"

"No."

I nodded. The Dagger of the Jhereg wished to be called the Dagger of the Jhereg. So be it.

"How did your partner evade Loiosh?" I asked.

"She didn't. I gave her some herbs so she wouldn't be affected by the poison, and she just ignored him."

I waited for Loiosh to make some remark about that; when he didn't, I said, "How much was my head worth to you?"

"You'd be flattered."

She continued looking at me. The candles flickered and did things to her hair, and face, and neck, and the shadows of her breasts against the back wall. I swallowed.

Then she said, "We've returned the payment."

I felt a sense of relief, as if the Imperial Executioner had been handed a stay just as he raised his staff. I felt it show on my face and cursed my weakness.

Her eyes came to rest on Loiosh, then she held out her hand. He hesitated and twitched nervously on my shoulders.

"*Boss . . .*"

"*Up to you, chum.*"

He flew over to her and wrapped his talons around her wrist. She scratched under his chin, going with the scales.

"The jhereg is beautiful," she said.

"His name is Loiosh."

"I know."

"Oh, of course. You must have found out quite a bit about me."

"Not enough, apparently. How did Morrolan and Aliera find out, by the way?"

"Sorry."

She nodded. "You . . . have a talent for making people underestimate you."

"Thank you very much." I walked into the room and let the door swing shut behind me. With a careful effort to appear casual, I sat at the edge of the bed. "So, what now?"

She shrugged, which was worth coming in just to see. "I don't know. Morrolan and Aliera tried to mind-probe me before. It didn't work, so I don't know what they'll try next. Do you?"

I was startled. "What were they trying to find out?"

"Who hired us."

I laughed. "They could have just asked me. Don't worry. They aren't bad types, for Dragonlords."

She smiled back at me, ironically. "And you'll protect me, right?"

"Sure. Why not? You've given the money back, even though you didn't have to, which is proof that you aren't coming after me again. And we Easterners ought to stick together, don't you think?"

She caught the point of that, and dropped her eyes. "I've never 'worked' on a human before, Vlad. I almost didn't take it, but . . ." She shrugged again. I wondered how I could make her keep doing that.

"I'm glad Aliera is good at revivification," I said.

"I suppose so."

"For both our sakes," I added, because I meant it. She looked at me carefully. There was a moment when time did strange things. If I had thrown my stones right, I could have kissed her then. So I did. Loiosh flew off her arm as our lips met, lightly. It was hardly an intense kiss, but I discovered that I'd closed my eyes. Odd.

She continued looking at me, as if she could read something in my face. Then she said, very deliberately, "My name is Cawti."

I nodded, and our mouths met again. Her arms went around my neck. When we came up for air, I reached up and slid the nightgown over her shoulders and down to her hips. She pulled her arms free and began working at the clasp of my cloak. I decided that this was insane. She would never have a better chance of getting one of my daggers and finishing me. *Verra!* I thought to myself, *I think I've lost it.*

My cloak dropped to the floor, and she helped me take off my jerkin. I paused to remove my boots and stockings, then we fell back together, and the sensation of her small, strong body against mine, her breasts against my chest and her breathing in my ear, my hand on the small of her back, her hand behind my neck—I'd never felt anything like it before, and I wanted to just stay like that, forever, and not take it any further.

My body, however, had its own set of rules, and let me know of them. I began stroking her lower spine. She pulled my head away and kissed me; this time we both meant business. I tasted her tongue, and that was nice too. I heard myself making small moaning sounds as my lips traveled down to her throat, then to the valley between her breasts. I kissed each one, carefully, and went back to her lips. She started fumbling for the catch to my breeches, but I interfered by finding her buttocks with my right hand and crushing her to me again.

We drew back and looked at each other once more. Then we paused long enough to send Loiosh out of the room, because love, like murder, shouldn't have witnesses.

8

"I'll stay here and clean up the blood."

IT IS SAD BUT true that there are a strictly limited number of times when waking up with the thought, "Hey, I'm alive!" is really astonishing. I hadn't quite hit the limit yet, so I had the obligatory reaction, followed by, "Dear Verra, I hurt."

My side, where the broadsword had taken me, felt hot and feverish, and the area around my kidney, where my lover had put her dagger into me, itched, burned, and ached. I moaned. Then I became aware of the sound of voices, outside the room and perhaps a bit down the hall.

My arm was around Cawti's shoulder, her head on my chest. I enjoyed the sensation, but I was curious about the voices. Moving as carefully as I could, I succeeded in not waking her up. I dressed carefully, making sure nothing clinked.

Meanwhile, the voices had been growing gradually louder. As soon as I felt dangerous again I opened the door, and identified Aliera's voice, although I still couldn't distinguish the words. The dark stone walls of the hallway greeted me; the air was cold and dank, the hallway high and wide. I thought back to my first visit to Dzur Mountain and shuddered. I turned toward the voices. I identified the other voice as Morrolan's. As I approached, he was speaking.

"... you say may be true, but that hardly makes it any of our affair."

"Any of our affair? Whose is it then? I—there! You see? You've woken up one of my patients."

"It is just as well," countered Morrolan, nodding to me. "You have *exhausted* all of *my* patience."

I was in a long room, dimly lit and filled with books. There were several chairs nearby, all done in black leather, but they were empty. Morrolan and Aliera stood facing each other. Morrolan's arms were crossed on his chest; Aliera's hands were on her hips. As she turned to me, I saw that her eyes, normally green, had turned blue. This is as much of a danger sign as the stiffening of a dragon's neck tentacles. I found a chair and sat down, to ease the pain a bit. This looked like it was going to be a good one.

Aliera snorted at his comment and turned back. "Ha! It's your own fault if you can't see the obvious. What's the matter, isn't it subtle enough for you?"

"If there was anything to see," he parried, "I would doubtless have seen it long before you."

Aliera pressed the attack. "If you had the sense of honor of a teckla, you'd see it as clearly as I do."

"And had you the eyesight of a teckla, you would be able to see what does and does not concern us."

This forced Aliera into a parry. "How could it not concern us? A dragon is a Dragon is a Dragon. Only this one happens to be a Jhereg. I want to find out why, and so should you."

Morrolan gestured toward me with his head. "Have you met Vlad's assistant, Kragar? He's as much of a Dragon—"

She snorted again. "That snake? He was thrown out of the House, as you well know."

"Perhaps so was—"

"If so," she stopthrust, "we'll find out, and then why."

"Why don't you simply ask her?"

"She'd never tell me, you know that. She won't even admit that she is a Dragon, much less—"

Morrolan snorted and tried a fancy maneuver, saying, "You know quite well that your only interest in this is to find someone else to be heir."

"So what? What have my motives to do with—"

"Aliera!" said Morrolan suddenly. "Perhaps we should ask Sethra."

She stopped and cocked her head to the side. "Ye-e-ess. An excellent idea. Why don't we? Perhaps *she* can talk some sense into your head."

He sidestepped that. "Let's go see her, then." He turned to me. "We'll be back shortly."

"Fine," I said. "I'll stay here and clean up the blood."

"What?"

"Never mind."

They vanished. I stood up painfully and made my way back to the Dag—to Cawti's room. Cawti. I let the name roll around in my head. CAW-ti. Cawwww-tiii. Cawti. A good, Eastern name. I started to open the door, stopped, and clapped softly.

"Who is it?" came from inside.

"Your victim," I said.

"Which one?"

"Funny, funny."

"Come in," she said. "At your own risk."

I slipped inside. "Good morning."

"Mmmmmm."

"It occurs to me that you didn't kill me last night."

"Oh, but I did," she said. "Six times. But I lost count and revivified you seven times."

I sat down on the bed next to her. She still hadn't dressed. I ignored the dryness in my mouth. "Oh. I must have forgotten."

"You could have killed me, too, you know." Her voice was suddenly serious.

"Yes," I said slowly. "But you knew I wouldn't. I had no such knowledge of you."

"I'll take your word for that." She laughed lightly. I put her laugh, with her shrug, on the list of things I wanted to make her do more often. The candle sputtered, so I rummaged around until I found a few more, and lit them all with the remaining stub. I returned to the bed and tapped her side lightly. She moved closer to the wall and I lay down. She rested her head on my arm.

There were a few pleasant minutes of silence, then I said, "I overheard an interesting conversation just now."

"Oh?"

"Concerning your partner."

She tensed. "What about her?"

I described the conversation. She pulled away from me, leaning on her arm to watch me as I spoke. Her brows were drawn together as she listened. She looked very beautiful that way, too.

I finished the tale, and said, "*Is* she a Dragonlord?"

Cawti shook her head. "That isn't my secret to tell."

"Okay. You look worried."

She smiled a little and put her head back on my chest. "For an assassin, you're quite sensitive, Lord Taltos."

"In the first place, I'm not an assassin—you've been listening to too many rumors about me. In the second, the same goes for you, doubled. And in the third, isn't 'Lord Taltos' a bit out of place, all things considered?"

She chuckled. "As you wish, Vlad. Vladimir." She repeated it, slowly. "Vladimir. VLA-di-meer. Vlaaaadimeer. Vladimir. I like it. A good Eastern name."

"Shit," I said. "Help me off with this damned jerkin, will you? And careful not to stab yourself. . . ."

Some time later, while engaged in serious snuggling, I said, "Morrolan and Aliera are liable to check up on your partner, you know."

"Mmmmm. They won't find anything."

"Don't be too sure, Cawti. They've surprised me before."

She tsked. "Shouldn't let yourself be surprised, Vladimir."

I snorted, and withheld a few remarks. "I'm serious. They're bound to find out something. You don't have to tell me what it is, but you ought to think about it. Have you been in touch with her?"

"Of course."

"Then warn her—"

"Why do you care?"

"Huh? I don't know. Jhereg are Jhereg, I guess. You aren't a threat to me anymore, and I don't see why they should be meddling. Or Aliera, rather. Morrolan doesn't see why, either."

"Mmmmmm."

I shrugged, causing her head to bounce on my chest. She giggled, which amazed and delighted me no end. Have you ever met an assassin who giggled? The absurdity of the whole situation was—

I decided that I had to get out of there. I sat up, dislodging her. "I'm going to check on our hosts and see what they're doing now."

"Like hell you are, my love. What's really bothering you?"

"What did you call me?"

She sat up too, the bedclothes falling to her waist. She glared. "Don't start getting mushy with me, you murdering Easterner."

"What did you call me?"

"A murdering Easterner."

"Yes, dear, and so are you. I meant before that."

"Vladimir . . ."

"Oh, Deathsgate. I'm getting out of here." I dressed quickly and stepped into the hall, using all of my willpower to avoid looking back at her. I returned to my room, favoring my injured side, and collapsed on the bed. Loiosh gave me a good chewing out (literally) for deserting him, after which I got in touch with Kragar.

"What's new?" I asked him.

"I have some information about the Phoenix Guards—they weren't just withdrawn in the area around where the job was done, they were taken out of the whole area. They're gone."

"Great. Well, I'm pleased they aren't around, but I wonder what it means. Any ideas?"

"No."

"Okay. I want you to try to find out something for me."

"Sure. What?"

"Everything you can on the Sword of Jhereg."

"Is this a joke?"

"Do you think it's likely to be?"

"Fine. I'll get back to you in a hundred years or so. Vlad, how am I—"

"She was once a Dragonlord; that should help. She was probably expelled."

"Wonderful. Should I try to bribe a Lyorn or a Dragon?"

"The Lyorn would be safer, but the Dragon is more likely to help."

"I was being sarcastic."

"I know. I wasn't."

He sighed telepathically. *"I'll see what I can do. Would you mind telling me what we're doing this for?"*

That was a tricky one. I didn't feel like telling him that his boss had become infatuated with his own executioner.

"Oh," I told him. *"I'm sure you can figure it out if you really work at it."*

Silence, then: *"You want to find out if there was anything shady in her expulsion, so you can clear her and have her owe you a favor, and then turn her back on Laris. Right? Not bad."*

Hmmmm. Not bad at all. *"Clever,"* I told him. It *was* clever. I'd have to give him a bonus, if it worked out. *"Now, get on it."* I broke the contact. I stretched out on the bed. After all of this, I really *did* need to sleep. I also needed to get my emotions under control.

The first thing I noticed when I woke up was that my side and back didn't hurt so much. Also, I actually felt refreshed. I lay there for a few minutes, just breathing and enjoying it, then forced myself to get up. In addition to feeling refreshed, I also felt filthy from sleeping in my clothes. I stripped and found a tub of water in the corner, did a quick spell to heat it, and washed. As I did this, I managed to put Cawti out of my mind, at least for a little while, and concentrate on my real problem—Laris.

The idea Kragar had had wasn't bad at all, but it depended on too many things that were outside of my control. Still, it was worth checking into. Also worth checking into was the question of why the Phoenix Guards had chosen that moment to leave. How could he have arranged that? Where had the orders come from?

I snapped my fingers, getting soapy water in my eye. *That* question, at least, I could get answered. I concentrated on a certain Tsalmoth, who worked for Morrolan and reported directly to me. . . .

"Who is it?" said Fentor.

"Vlad."

"Oh! Yes, milord?"

"We need some information. . . ." I explained what I was after, and he agreed to check into it. I broke the contact and chatted with Loiosh while I finished up my bath. I looked disgustedly at my filthy clothes, shrugged, and started to put them on again.

"Check the dressing table, boss."

"Eh?"

But I did, then smiled. Aliera had been thorough. I donned the change of clothes happily, then stepped out into the hall with Loiosh riding on my right shoulder. It seemed as if I were beginning to get things done. Good. I wandered down to the library, found it empty, and took the stairs up to where the dining room and various sitting rooms were.

The next thing, I decided, was to see if I could get more information from whoever it was that had tipped Kragar off about the assassination. The fact that we'd actually learned something from him was a very good sign. My biggest problem was still lack of information, and this could mean we were starting to solve it. I thought about getting in touch with Kragar again to ask him to work on that more, but decided against it. As they say: if you have someone stand for you, don't jog his sword arm while he does.

I found Morrolan and Aliera in the first sitting room I came to, along with Sethra. Sethra Lavode: tall, pale, undead, and faintly vampiric. I'd heard her age placed at anything from ten to twenty thousand years, which is a significant portion of the age of the Empire itself. She dressed in and surrounded herself with black, the color of sorcery. She lived in Dzur Mountain; maybe she *was* Dzur Mountain, for there are no records of a time when she, or someone of her family, didn't live there. Dzur Mountain was its own mystery, and not subject to being understood by one such as me. The same may be said of Sethra.

Physically, though, she had the high, thin features of the House of the Dragon. The upward slant of her eyes and the unusually extreme point to her ears made one think of Dzurlords. There had been rumors that she was half Dzur herself, but I doubted them.

To Sethra, even more than to most Dragaerans, an Easterner's lifetime was a blink of an eye. Maybe that's why she was so tolerant of me. (Morrolan's tolerance was due to having lived among Easterners for many years of his youth, during the Interregnum. Aliera's tolerance I've never understood; I suspect she was just being polite to Morrolan.) Most Dragaerans had heard of Sethra Lavode, but few had met her. She was periodically considered a hero, and had been Warlord of the Empire (while she was still living) and Captain of the Lavodes (when there were still Lavodes). At other times, such as the present, she was considered an evil enchantress and Dzurlord bait. Periodically, some fledgling hero would go up the Mountain to destroy her. She turned them into jhegaala or yendi and sent them back. I'd told her that this wasn't going to help, but she just smiled.

At her side was the dagger called Iceflame, which was sort of Dzur Mountain in hand, or something. I don't know enough about it to say more, and thinking about it makes me nervous.

I bowed to each of them, and said, "Thank you for the sanctuary, Sethra."

"It's no trouble, Vlad," she responded. "I enjoy your company. I'm pleased to see that you're recovering."

"So am I." I sat down, then asked, "What can you fine specimens of Dragonhood tell me about the Phoenix Guard?"

Morrolan arched an eyebrow. "What did you wish to know? Is it your desire to join?"

"Could I?"

"I'm afraid," he said, "that your species is against you there."

"But not my House?"

He looked startled and glanced at Aliera.

She said, "A Jhereg could join if he wanted to. There have been some, I think—none who are actually a part of the business end, I suppose, but some who've bought Jherge titles instead of being Houseless."

I nodded. "So it isn't all Dragons, eh? That's what I was wondering about."

"Oh, no," said Aliera. "It's mostly Dragons, because all Dragons must serve periodically, but there are others from every House in the guards—except Athyra, who are never interested, and Phoenix, because there aren't enough of them."

"Suppose some colonel of some army of Dragonlords is serving. Would he be a colonel in the guards?"

"No," said Sethra. "Rank among the guards has nothing to do with any other rank. Officers in private armies often serve under their own blademen."

"I see. Does this ever cause problems?"

"No," said Aliera.

"Why the interest?" asked Sethra.

"I'm bothered by the fact that the guards who were enforcing the Imperial Edict left just at the right time for our friends to nail me. I can't believe it was coincidence."

They looked at each other. "I can't think of any way," said Sethra.

"Whose decision would it have been? The Empress's? Or whoever leads the guards?"

"The Empress sent them; she would have had to order their withdrawal," said Aliera. Morrolan nodded.

"All right," I said, "I don't think she would have been involved in this on purpose, would she?" Three heads shook. "Then is there anyone who could have made the suggestion to her that 'now would be a good time,' and be confident that she'd act on it at once?"

Sethra and Aliera looked at Morrolan, who was at court more often than they. He drummed his fingers on the arm of his chair. "Her lover," he said, "is said to be an Easterner. I've never met him, but he might have such influence. Then there are her advisors, but, to be candid, she hardly listens to most of them. I believe that she listens seriously to me, but I could be deluding myself. And, in any case, I made no such request of her. She pays attention to Sethra the Younger, but Sethra has no interest in anything save invasion plans for the East."

Sethra Lavode nodded. "It's good to have an ambition," she said. "Sethra the Younger is the only apprentice I've ever had who's never tried to kill me."

I turned back to Morrolan. "You can't think of anyone else?"

"Not at present."

"All right then, what else? A faked message, maybe? Do this right now, signed so-and-so?"

"Who," said Morrolan, "would write a message rather than reach her psionically?"

"Well, someone she doesn't speak with often. It must be hard to reach her directly, so—"

"No, it isn't," said Aliera, looking at me as if puzzled.

"It isn't?"

"Of course not. Any citizen can reach Zerika through his link. Didn't you know that?"

"No . . . but she must get thousands of people—"

"Not really," she said. "If she doesn't consider it worth her time, she destroys the person. This keeps the amount of contact down quite a bit."

"Oh . . . My father never saw fit to mention that. I guess he was afraid I might do it. In any case, I still don't see who could and would have convinced her to withdraw the troops. Morrolan, you're well respected around court. Will you try to find out for me?"

"No," said Morrolan. "As I have explained to you, I will have nothing to do with any Jhereg war, directly or indirectly."

"Yeah, okay." I was pleased to see Aliera shoot him a brief look of disgust. It occurred to me then that the easiest thing to do would be to create something real that would make the Empress want to pull the troops out. What could it be? Civil disturbance? Threat of an invasion of some sort?

"Kragar."

"Yes, Vlad?"

"*See if there was anything going on in the city that would have called for Phoenix Guards to handle.*"

"*Good idea, boss.*"

"*That's what I pay myself for.*"

Then I reached Fentor and had him check into any possible external threats. With any luck, I'd know within a day or two. I turned my attention back to the others. Aliera and Sethra were deep into another discussion.

"Certainly," Sethra was saying. "And as far as I'm concerned, let her."

Aliera frowned. "We're just getting on our feet, Sethra. We can't afford to go off East with tens of thousands of troops until we're sure the Empire is stable."

"What's this about?" I asked.

"You set off another argument, Vlad," Morrolan explained. "Aliera is opposed to Sethra the Younger's conquering the East until the Empire is stable. Sethra the Younger thinks that will make it stable, and our own Sethra," he indicated her with his head, "feels, as I do, that since Sethra—the other one— wants to do it, why not? What harm is there? They'll throw us out again in a few hundred or a thousand years. That was why Kieron the Conqueror left them there in the first place—so we'd have someone to fight and wouldn't tear ourselves apart."

I could have said many things about this, but I let it go.

"That isn't the point," said Aliera. "If we drain off enough resources, what happens if a *real* enemy shows up? The Easterners are no threat to us now—"

"*What* real enemy?" said Sethra. "There isn't—"

I stood and left them to their argument. It couldn't have anything to do with me, in any case.

9

"I guess they wanted to see you."

I RETURNED TO MY room and decided that I wanted to see Cawti again; also, that I was looking forward to dinner that evening with Sethra, Morrolan, and Aliera. I realized that I could become very comfortable at Dzur mountain, while Kragar kept things going at the office. In other words, while everything I'd built up went over Deathsgate Falls. Not that Kragar was incompetent, but there are certain things one must do oneself, and I'd been gone four days already.

"Aliera?"

After a pause, a response came. *"Yes, Vlad?"*

"Something has come up. I'm going to have to return to the office right away. Please convey my apologies to Sethra and Morrolan."

"As you wish. But don't exert yourself."

"I wouldn't think of it."

"Would you like help with the teleport?"

"Yes, please. That would be very nice."

"All right, I'll be right down," she concluded vocally, standing in front of me. Damn show-off. I gave her an image of the alley behind a row of buildings facing Malak Circle, and pulled back to show where it was relative to parts of Adrilankha that she knew. She nodded.

"Ready?" she asked.

"Ready."

There was a twist, and a burbling in my stomach, and I was there. I could have teleported to just outside the office building, but I wanted to look around and get a feel for the area, as well as give my stomach a chance to recover.

Walking through the streets wasn't as risky as it may sound. Though I didn't have any bodyguards, no one even knew that I was around. The only way Laris could really get me was to have an assassin standing around next to my office, hoping I'd walk back in. I'd never taken "work" like that, but I have an idea of the risks associated with it. The longer you stand around a place, the more chance there is that someone will be able to identify you as the one doing the job. Paying someone to do that would cost more than paying the Sword and the Dagger to just finalize the individual. So I wasn't very worried.

The neighborhood looked a bit subdued. It was early afternoon, and this area didn't really get going until nightfall, but it was still too quiet. Have you ever known a part of a city so well that you could tell what kind of mood it was in? So well that the scent of barbecuing lyorn legs told you that all was not normal? So you could hear that the street-hawkers were just a little bit more quiet than usual? That tradesmen and Teckla were wearing clothes with, perhaps, just a bit less color than they normally did? Where the scented fires of a hundred passersby making offerings to a dozen gods at a score of small altars brought a sense of weariness to the heart, instead of renewal?

I knew this part of Adrilankha that well, and that was the kind of mood it was in. I didn't need to talk to Kragar to know that business hadn't recovered. I thought about this, and, as I approached the office itself, I discovered something very important: Laris wasn't worried about money.

"Look out, boss!"

Not again, by the teeth of Dzur Mountain! I hit the ground, rolled to my right, came up to my knees, and spotted two Jhereg that I didn't recognize moving at me from either side. *Two* of them, for the love of Verra! They both held daggers. Loiosh was in front of one, buffeting his face and trying to sink his teeth into him. The other one suddenly stumbled and fell to his knees a few feet away from me, with three shuriken sticking out of him. I realized then that I'd thrown them. Not bad, Vlad.

I scrambled to my feet and spun, looking for more. I didn't spot them, so I turned back in time to see the other assassin fall to the ground. As he fell, I saw N'aal behind him, holding a large fighting knife with fresh blood on it. Next to him was Chimov, also holding a knife, looking around anxiously.

"Boss!" said N'aal.

"No," I snapped. "I'm Kieron the Conqueror. What's going on around here? Why do we have Verra-be-damned assassins standing outside the Verra-be-damned office in the middle of the Verra-be-damned afternoon?"

Chimov just shrugged. N'aal said, "I guess they were looking for you, boss."

Some days everyone and his sibling is a Verra-be-damned jongleur. I brushed past them and stormed into the office. Melestav jumped when I came in, but relaxed when he saw it was me. Kragar was in my office, sitting in my Verra-be-damned chair. He greeted me warmly.

"Oh, it's you," he said.

One . . . two . . . three . . . four. . . .

"Kragar, may I please have my chair back?"

"Oh, sure, boss. Sorry. Whatsamatter, hard day dodging assassins? I assumed you wanted some excitement, or why did you go walking into the middle of them without letting anyone know you were coming? I mean, it would have been easy—"

"You're pushing it."

He got up. "Whatever you say, Vlad."

"Kragar, just what is going on around here?"

"Going on?"

I gestured toward the outside.

"Oh. Nothing."

"Nothing? You mean 'no business'?"

"Almost none."

"But what about those assassins?"

"I didn't know they were there, Vlad. D'you think I'd have just left them there?"

"But they must be costing Laris a fortune."

He nodded. I was interrupted by contact with Melestav.

"Yeah?"

"N'aal is here."

"Send him in."

He came in. "Boss, I—"

"Just a minute. Three things. First, good work taking out the one. Second, next time I'll expect you to spot them before they spot me. Three, next time I'm almost nailed like that, if you're around, keep your bleeding wiseass remarks to yourself or I'll cut your bleeding throat for you. Got it?"

"Yeah, boss. Sorry."

"Okay. What d'you want?"

"I thought you'd want these." He tossed my shuriken, complete with bloodstains, on my desk. "I remember hearing that you don't like them left around, and—"

I stood up, walked around my desk, and slipped a dagger out from my cloak. Before N'aal could react, I put it in him, between the forth and fifth ribs, angled up. A look of shock came into his face as I stepped out of the way. Then he fell.

I turned to Kragar, still gripped by fear and icy rage. Also, my back and side hurt like the Great Sea of Chaos. "Kragar, you are a very fine administrative assistant. But if you ever want to run an area, make it as far from me as possible, or else learn how to keep discipline. That guy's no fool; he should know better than to walk in here with a murder weapon, with the corpse's blood still on it. In the four days I've been gone, you've managed to convince everyone around here that they don't have to think anymore, and as a result I almost got butchered out there. You son-of-a-bitch, this is my *life* we're talking about!"

"Take it easy, boss. Don't—"

"Shut up, Loiosh."

"Now," I continued, "see if you can get him revivified. Out of your pocket. If not, *you* may have the honor of giving his next of kin the bonus. Understand?"

Kragar nodded, looking genuinely crestfallen. "I'm sorry, Vlad," he said, and seemed to be looking for something else to say.

I went back to my desk, sat down, leaned back and shook my head. Kragar wasn't incompetent, at most things. I really *didn't* want to lose him. After this, I should probably do something to show I trusted him. I sighed. "Okay, let's forget it. I'm back now. There's something I want you to do."

"Yeah?"

"N'aal was not completely wrong. I should not have left the shuriken in the body; but he should not have brought them back to me. I don't know that the Empire ever employs witches, but if it does, a witch could trace that weapon back to its wielder."

Kragar listened silently. He knew nothing about witchcraft.

"It has to do with body aura," I explained. "Anything that's been around me for any length of time is going to pick up a sort of psychic 'scent' that a witch can identify."

"So, what do you do about it? You can't count on always taking the weapon with you."

"I know. So what I'm going to do is to start changing weapons every couple of days or so, so that nothing is on me long enough to pick up my aura. I'm going to make a list of all my weapons. I want you to go around and get ones to match. I'll put the ones I'm done with in a box, and you can use them for trade next time, which should cut down on the cost a bit. Okay?"

He looked startled. Well, I wasn't surprised. I was putting a lot of trust in him to tell him what weapons I had concealed about me, even if, as he would suspect, I were keeping a few back. But he nodded.

"Good," I said. "Come back in an hour and I'll have the list made up. Memorize and destroy it."

"Check, boss."

"Good. Now go away."

"Boss . . ."

"Sorry I snapped at you, Loiosh. And good work with that assassin."

"Thanks, boss. And don't worry about it. I understand."

Loiosh had always been understanding, I decided. It was only then, as I began writing, that it really hit me just how close I'd come once again. I reached the trash bucket just before my stomach emptied itself. I got a glass of water and rinsed out my mouth, then had Melestav empty and clean the bucket. I sat there shaking for some time before I got to work on the list for Kragar.

I gave Kragar the list, and he took off to fill it. Shortly after that I got a message from Melestav.

"Boss . . . there are some people here to see you."

"Who?"

"People in uniform."

"Oh shit. Well, I shouldn't be surprised." I made sure there was nothing incriminating on my desk. *"Okay, send them in."*

"How bad do you suppose this is going to be, Loiosh?"

"You can always claim self-defense, boss."

The door opened and two Dragaerans dressed in the golden uniforms of the House of Phoenix came marching in. One looked around the office contemptuously, as if to say, "So this is how the scum live." The other looked at me with a similar expression, as if to say, "So this is the scum."

"Greetings, my lords," I said. "How may I serve the Empire?"

The one who was looking at me said, "You are Baronet Vlad of Taltos?" He pronounced it "Taltoss," instead of "Taltosh," so he must have had written orders, for whatever that was worth.

"Baronet Taltos will do," I said. "I am at your service, lords."

The other one turned his glance to me, snorted, and said, "I'll bet."

The first one asked me, "What do you know about it?"

"About what, my lord?"

He shot a glance at the other, who closed the door of my office. I took a deep breath, and exhaled slowly, knowing what was coming. Well, it happens sometimes. When the door was shut, the one who'd been doing most of the talking pulled a dagger from his belt.

I swallowed and said, "My lord, I'd like to help—" which was as far as I got before the hilt of the dagger, held in his palm, smashed into the side of my head. I went flying out of the chair and landed in the corner.

"Loiosh, don't do anything."

There was a pause then, *"I know, boss, but—"*

"Nothing!"

"Okay, boss. Hang in there."

The one who'd just hit me was standing over me now. He said, "Two men were murdered just outside of the door of this place, Jhereg." He made it sound like a curse. "What do you know about it?"

"Lord," I said, "I don't know *oomph!*" as his foot took me in the stomach. I'd seen it just in time to move forward, so he missed my solar plexus.

The other one came up then. "Did you hear him, Menthar? He don't know oomph. How about that?" He spat on me. "I think we should take him to the barracks. What do you think?"

Menthar muttered something and kept looking at me. "I've heard you're a tough one, Whiskers. Is that true?"

"No, lord," I told him.

He nodded and said to the other one, "This isn't a Jhereg; this is a Teckla. Look at him squirm. Doesn't it make you sick?"

His partner said, "What about those two murders, Teckla? You sure you don't know anything about them?" He reached down and hauled me up, so that I was against the back wall. "You *real* sure?"

I said, "I don't know what—" and he caught me under the chin with the pommel of his dagger, which had been hidden in his hand. My head cracked against the wall and I felt my jaw break. I must have lost consciousness for an instant, because I don't remember sliding to the floor.

Then Menthar said, "You hold him for me."

The other guard agreed. "But be careful. Easterners are fragile. Remember the last one."

"I'll be careful." He looked at me and smiled. "Last chance," he said. "What do you know about those two dead men outside?"

I shook my head, which hurt like blazes, but I knew trying to talk would hurt more. He hefted his dagger, hilt up, and swung his arm back for a good windup. . . .

I don't know how long the whole thing lasted. It was certainly one of the worst I'd been through, but if they'd chosen to take me back to their barracks it would have been worse. Phoenix Guards are never *ordered* to beat up Jhereg, or Easterners, or anyone else, but some of them don't like us.

This beating was peculiar. I'd been bashed around before; it was one of the prices I paid for living according to my own rules instead of the Empire's. But why this time? The two dead men were Jhereg, and the usual attitude of Imperial Guards to such things is: let 'em kill each other off, for all we care. It could have been just another excuse to beat up an Easterner or a Jhereg, but they'd seemed genuinely angry about something.

These thoughts came to me through a thick haze of pain as I was lying on my office floor. I was concentrating as hard as I could on figuring out the reason behind the beating so that I could avoid thinking about how every inch of me hurt. I could tell there were people around me, but I couldn't open my eyes to see who they were, and they were talking in whispers.

After a time, I heard Melestav say, "Here she is, move back," followed by the sound of a long garment dragging across the floor. This was followed by a gasp. I decided I must be quite a sight.

The newcomer said, "Get away from him." I recognized, with surprise and some relief, Aliera's voice. I tried to force my eyes to open, but they wouldn't.

I heard Kragar say, "How bad is he, Aliera?" but she chose not to answer him. That didn't necessarily mean that I was in bad shape; Aliera so utterly despised Kragar that she preferred not to speak to him whenever possible.

"*Kragar . . .*"

"*Are you all right, Vlad?*"

"*No, but never mind that. They seemed mad about something in particular. Any idea what?*"

"*Yeah. While they were . . . while they were here, I got Daymar to do a mind-probe.*"

"*Kragar, you know I don't like Daymar to know—never mind. What did he find out?*"

We were interrupted by Aliera saying, "Sleep, Vlad." I was going to argue, but I discovered that she wasn't just making a suggestion. I saw a pale green light, and I slept.

Aliera was there when I woke up again, as was the picture of the dzur and the jhereg. This led to the realization that I could see again. I took stock of my various body parts, and found that, while I still hurt, it was mostly dull aches instead of flaming agony. Aliera is a very good healer.

"I might as well move in here," I said.

"I heard what happened, Vlad," said Aliera. "On behalf of the House of the Dragon, I apologize."

I grunted.

"The one who beat you—his name is Menthar? He is off duty in four months."

I felt my eyes trying to widen. I studied her. Her lips were pressed tightly together, and her eyes were gray. Her hands were in fists, at her sides. "Four months," she repeated, "and then he's fair game."

"Thank you," I said. "I appreciate the information."

She nodded. Dragonlords were Dragonlords, and usually hated Jhereg and Easterners both—but they didn't approve of attacking people who couldn't defend themselves, and Aliera knew enough about how the Jhereg operated to know that if a representative of the Empire wanted to knock around a Jhereg, the Jhereg would just have to take it. But, I suppose, there's something about being in the guard, and watching us get away with everything we get away with, that frustrates them. For my part, I didn't feel any moral outrage at what had happened to me. I just wanted to tear that guy's arms off. . . . Four months.

"Thank you," I said again. "I think I want to sleep now."

"Good," she said. "I'll be back in a while."

She left and I got in touch with Kragar. *"You were saying?"*

"Vlad! How are you?"

"About how you'd expect. Now, what did Daymar find out?"

"The guards were pulled out the other day because they were needed somewhere else. There was a riot in the Easterners' Quarter. That may explain why those two took it out on you. I suppose they aren't happy with any Easterners now. There have been other beatings of Easterners in the last few days. A few have been beaten to death."

"I see. It can't have been very big or we'd have heard about it."

"No. It was small, short, and pretty bloody, from what Daymar could tell. I'm checking into it, just on general principles."

"Okay, so that mystery is solved. Now: who set off the riot? Laris, I suppose. We need to find out how he has influence around there. That's quite a bit farther south than anything else he has."

"Okay. I'll see if we can find out. Don't expect much, though."

"I won't. Anything yet on that other business?"

"A bit, but not enough to help, I don't think. Her name is Norathar, and she's of the e'Lanya line. I've found references to her being expelled from the House, but no details—yet."

"Good. Keep working on it. Next point: how can Laris afford to keep assassins sitting outside the office?"

"Well, didn't you say the Sword and the Dagger had returned their payment?"

"Yeah. But that begs the question. How could he afford to hire them? Plus pay whatever it must have cost to start trouble in the Easterners' Quarter?"

"Uh . . . I don't know. I guess he has more cash than we thought."

"Right. But how did he get it?"

"*Maybe the same way you did?*"

"*That's just what I was thinking. Maybe he's being supported by someone who's rich.*"

"*It could be, Vlad.*"

"*So, let's look into it.*"

"*Sure. How do we do that?*"

"*I don't know. Think about it.*"

"*Check. And, Vlad . . .*"

"*Yeah?*"

"*Next time you come back here, warn us first, okay?*"

"*Yeah.*"

After breaking that contact, I got hold of Fentor at Castle Black, gave him the information about the riot, and asked him to find out what he could about it. Then I really did sleep.

"*Wake up, boss!*"

It was like the drumbeat that sends a squadron into alert status. I was sitting up, holding a dagger under the blanket, looking at—

"Good afternoon, Vladimir. Is that a knife in your hand, or are you happy to see me?"

"Both," I said, sheathing the blade. She tapped my side and I moved over to let her sit down. We exchanged a light kiss. She drew back and studied me.

"What happened?"

"It's a long story."

"I've got nothing but time."

I told her what had happened. She shook her head and, when I was finished, held me.

Wow.

"What now?" she asked.

I said, "Do you and your partner ever give friends a bargain?"

"Do you?"

"I didn't think so."

She held me a little tighter.

"*Would you two rather I left, boss?*"

"Maybe in a bit."

"*Hmmph. I was being snide, if you didn't notice.*"

"I noticed. Shut up."

"By the way, Vladimir, Sethra is giving a banquet."

"Really? In honor of what?"

"In honor of all of us being alive."

"Hmmmm. They'll probably be trying to pump you and Norathar for information."

"I expect they—how did you find out her name?"

I did a smug chuckle.

"I guess," she said, "I'll just have to torture the information out of you."

"I guess so," I said. *"Okay, Loiosh, you can leave now."*

"Jerk."

"Yeah."

10

"I dislike killing my guests."

IT IS POSSIBLE TO break meals down into types. There is the formal dinner, with elegant settings, carefully selected wines, and orchestrated conversation. Then there are Jhereg business meetings, where you ignore the food half the time, because to miss a remark, or even a glance, can be deadly. There is the quiet, informal get-together with a Certain Person, where neither food nor conversation is as important as being there. We also have the grab-something-and-run, where the idea is to get food inside of you, without taking time for either conversation or enjoyment. Next, we have the "good dinner," where the food is the whole reason for being there, and conversation is merely to help wash it down.

And there is one other type of dinner: sitting around a fine, elegant table, deep under Dzur Mountain, with an undead hostess, a pair of Dragonlords, and a team of Jhereg assassins, one of whom was once a Dragon herself, the other of whom is an Easterner.

The conversation at a dinner of this type is unpredictable.

For most of the meal, Morrolan entertained us with a few notes on sorcery that aren't usually included in tomes, and probably shouldn't be. I enjoyed this—mostly because I was sitting next to Cawti (by chance? With Aliera around? Ha!) and we generally concentrated on rubbing our legs together under the table. Loiosh made a few remarks about this that I won't dignify by repeating.

Then, while I was distracted, the conversation changed. Suddenly, Aliera was engaging the lady known as the Sword of the Jhereg in a bantering exchange comparing Dragon customs to Jhereg customs, and I was instantly alert. Aliera didn't do *anything* by accident.

"You see," Aliera was saying, "we only kill people who deserve it. You kill anyone you're paid to kill."

Norathar pretended surprise. "But you're paid too, aren't you? It's merely a different coin. A Jhereg assassin would be paid in gold, or so I assume—I've never actually met one. A Dragon, on the other hand, is paid by satisfying his bloodlust."

I chuckled a little. Score one for our team. Aliera also smiled and raised her glass. I looked at her closely. Yes, I decided, she wasn't doing any idle Jhereg-baiting. She was searching for something.

"So tell me," Aliera asked, "which do you consider the better coin to be paid in?"

"Well, I've never bought anything with bloodlust, but—"

"It can be done."

"Indeed? What can you buy, pray tell?"

"Empires," said Aliera e'Kieron. "Empires."

Norathar e'Lanya raised her eyebrow. "Empires, my lady? What would I do with one?"

Aliera shrugged. "I'm sure you could think of something."

I glanced around the room. Sethra, at the head of the table and to my right, was watching Aliera intently. Morrolan, to her right, was doing the same. Norathar was next to him, and she was also studying Aliera, who was at the other end of the table. Cawti, next to her and to my left, was looking at Norathar. I wondered what was going on behind her mask. I always wonder what's going on behind people's masks. I sometimes wonder what's going on behind *my* mask.

"What would you do with one?" asked Norathar.

"Ask me when the Cycle changes."

"Eh?"

"I," she said, "am currently the Dragon Heir to the Throne. Morrolan used to be, before I arrived."

I remembered being told about Aliera's "arrival"—hurled out of Adron's Disaster, the explosion that brought down the Empire over four hundred years ago, through time, to land in the middle of some Teckla's wheat field. I was later told that Sethra had had a hand in the thing, which made it more believable than it would be otherwise.

Norathar seemed faintly curious. Her eyes went to the Dragonhead pendant around Aliera's neck. All Dragonlords wear a Dragonhead somewhere visible. The one Aliera wore had a blue gem for one eye, a green gem for the other. "E'Kieron, I see," said Norathar.

Aliera nodded, as if something had been explained.

I asked, "What am I missing?"

"The lady," said Aliera, "was no doubt curious about my lineage, and why I am now the heir. I would guess that she has remembered that Adron had a daughter."

I said, "Oh."

It had never occurred to me to wonder how Aliera came to be the heir so quickly, although I'd known she was since I was introduced to her. But sitting at the same table with the daughter of the man who had turned an entire city into a seething pool of raw chaos was a bit disconcerting. I decided it was going to take me a while to get used to.

Aliera continued her explanations to Norathar. "The Dragon Council informed me of the decision when they checked my bloodlines. That is how I became interested in genetics. I am hoping that I can prove there is a flaw in me, somewhere, so I won't have to be Empress when the Cycle changes."

"You mean you don't *want* to be Empress?" I asked.

"Dear Barlen, no! I can't imagine anything more dull. I've been looking for a way out of it since I've been back."

"Oh."

"Your conversation is really gifted today, boss."

"Shut up, Loiosh."

I worked all of this over in my mind. "Aliera," I said at last, "I have a question."

"Hm?"

"If you're the Dragon Heir, does that mean your father was the heir before you? And if he *was* the heir, why did he try the coup in the first place?"

"Two reasons," she said. "First, because it was the reign of a decadent Phoenix, and the Emperor refused to step down when the Cycle changed. Second, Daddy wasn't really the heir."

"Oh. The heir died during the Interregnum?"

"Around then, yes. There was a war, and he was killed. There was talk of his child not being a Dragon. But that was actually before the Disaster and the Interregnum."

"He was killed," I echoed. "I see. And the child? No, don't tell me. She was expelled from the House, right?"

Aliera nodded.

"And the line? E'Lanya, right?"

"Very good, Vlad. How did you know?"

I looked at Norathar, who was staring at Aliera with eyes like mushrooms.

"And," I continued, "you have been able to scan her genes, and you've found out that, lo and behold, she really *is* a Dragonlord."

"Yes," said Aliera.

"And if her father was really the Heir to the Throne, then . . ."

"That's right, Vlad," said Aliera. "The correct Heir to the Throne is Norathar e'Lanya—the Sword of the Jhereg."

The funniest thing about time is when it doesn't. I'll leave that hanging there for the moment, and let you age while the shadows don't lengthen, if you see what I mean.

I looked first at Cawti, who was looking at Norathar, who was looking at Aliera. Sethra and Morrolan were also looking at Aliera, who wasn't focusing on anything we could see. Her eyes, bright green now, glittered with reflected candlelight, and looked upon something we weren't entitled to see.

Now, while the Cycle doesn't turn, and the year doesn't fail, and the day gets neither brighter nor darker, and even the candles don't flicker, we begin to see things with a new perspective. I looked first at my lover, who had recently killed me, who was looking at her partner, who should be the Dragon Heir to the Orb—next in the Cycle. This Dragonlord-assassin-princess-whatever matched stares with Aliera e'Kieron, wielder of Kieron's Sword, traveler from the past, daughter of Adron, and current Heir to the Orb. And so on.

The funniest thing about time is when it doesn't. In those moments when it loses itself, and becomes (as, perhaps, all things must) its opposite, it becomes a thing of even greater power than when it is in its old standard tear-down-the-mountains mood.

It even has the power to break down the masks behind which hide Dragons turned Jhereg.

For an instant, then, I looked at Norathar and saw her clearly, she who had once been a Dragonlord. I saw pride, hate, grim resignation, dashed hopes, loyalty, and courage. I turned away, though, because, odd as it may seem to you who have listened to me so patiently and so well, I really don't like pain.

"What do you mean?" she whispered, and the world went back to its business again.

Aliera didn't answer, so Sethra spoke. "The Dragon Council met, early in the Reign of the Phoenix this Cycle, before the Interregnum, to choose the heir. It was decided that the e'Lanya line should take it when the time comes. The highest family of that line were the Lady Miera, the Lord K'laiyer, and their daughter, Norathar."

Norathar shook her head and whispered again. "I have no memories of any of this. I was only a child."

"There was an accusation made," said Sethra, "and Lord K'laiyer, your father, challenged his accuser. There was war, and your parents were killed. You were judged by sorcerers and your bloodlines were found to be impure."

"But then—"

"Aliera scanned you, and the sorcerers who made the first judgment were wrong."

I broke in, saying, "How hard is it to make a mistake of that kind?"

Aliera snapped back to the present and said, "Impossible."

"I see," I said.

"I see," said Norathar.

We sat there, each of us looking down, or around the room, waiting for someone to ask the obvious questions. Finally, Norathar did. "Who did the scan, and who made the challenge?"

"The first scan," said Sethra, "was done by my apprentice, Sethra the Younger."

"Who's she?" I asked.

"As I said, my apprentice—one of many. She served her apprenticeship—let me see—about twelve hundred years ago now. When I'd taught her all I could, she did me the honor of taking my name."

"Dragonlord?"

"Of course."

"Okay. Sorry to interrupt. You were talking about the scan."

"Yes. She brought the results to me, and I brought them to the Dragon Council. The council had a committee of three do another one. Lord Baritt was one—" Morrolan, Aliera and I exchanged glances here. We'd met his shade in the Paths of the Dead, and had three completely different impressions of the old bas- . . . gentleman. Sethra continued. "Another was of the House of the Athyra, as the expert, and someone from the House of the Lyorn, to make sure everything was right and proper. The committee confirmed it and the council acted as it had to."

Norathar asked, "Who made the accusation?"

"I did," said Sethra Lavode.

Norathar rose to her feet, her eyes burning into Sethra's. I could almost feel the energy flowing between them. Norathar said, between clenched teeth, "May I have my sword back, milady?"

Sethra hadn't moved. "If you wish," she said. "However, there are two things I want to say."

"Say them."

"First, I made the accusation because that was my duty to the House of the Dragon as I saw it. Second, while I'm not as fanatical about it as Lord Morrolan, I dislike killing my guests. Remember who I am, lady!"

As she said this, she stood and drew Iceflame—a long, straight dagger, perhaps twelve inches of blade. The metal was a light blue, and it emitted a faint glow of that color. Anyone with the psionic sensitivity of a caterpillar would have recognized it as a Morganti weapon, one which kills without chance of revivification. Anyone with any acquaintance with the legends surrounding Sethra Lavode would have recognized it as Iceflame, a Great Weapon, one of the Seventeen. Whatever power it was that hid in, under, and around Dzur Mountain, Iceflame was tied to it. The only other known artifacts with power to match it were the sword Godslayer and the Imperial Orb. Loiosh dived under my cloak. I held my breath.

At that moment, I felt, rather than saw, a knife fall into Cawti's hand. I felt a tear in loyalties that was almost physically painful. What should I do if there was a fight? Could I bring myself to stop Cawti, or even warn Sethra? Could I bring myself to allow Sethra to be knifed in the back? Demon Goddess, get me out of this!

Norathar stared back at Sethra and said, "Cawti, don't." Cawti sighed quietly, and I breathed a prayer of thanks to Verra. Then Norathar said to Sethra, "I'd like my sword, if you please."

"You won't hear my reasons, then?" asked Sethra, her voice even.

"All right," said Norathar. "Speak."

"Thank you." Sethra put Iceflame away. I exhaled. Sethra sat down and, after a moment, so did Norathar, but her eyes never left Sethra's.

"I was told," said the Dark Lady of Dzur Mountain, "that your ancestry was questionable. To be blunt, I received word that you were a bastard. I'm sorry, but that's what I was told."

I listened intently. Bastardy among Dragaerans is far more rare than among Easterners, because a Dragaeran can't conceive accidentally—or so I've been told. In general, the only illegitimate children are those who have one sterile parent (sterility is nearly impossible to cure, and not uncommon among Dragaerans). *Bastard*, as an insult, is far more deadly to a Dragaeran than to an Easterner.

"I was further told," she continued, "that your true father was not a Dragon." Norathar still didn't move, but she was gripping the table with her right hand. "You were the oldest child of the Dragon Heir. It was necessary to bring this to the attention of the council, if it was true.

"I could," she went on, "have sneaked into your parents' home with my apprentice, who is skilled in genetic scanning." Aliera gave a barely audible sniff here. I imagine she had her own opinion of Sethra the Younger's abilities. "I chose not to, however. I confronted Lord K'laiyer. He held himself insulted and refused to allow the scan. He declared war and sent an army after me."

She sighed. "I've lost count of how many armies have tried to take Dzur Mountain. If it's any consolation, he was a masterful tactician, certainly worthy of the e'Lanya line. But I had the assistance of several friends, a hired army, and Dzur Mountain itself. He gave me a bit of trouble, but the issue was never in doubt. By the end of the engagement, both of your parents were dead."

"How?" asked Norathar through clenched teeth. A good question, too. Why weren't they revivified?

"I don't know. They were in the battle, but I didn't kill them personally. They both had massive head injuries, due to sorcery. Beyond that, I can't tell you."

Norathar nodded, almost imperceptibly. Sethra continued. "I formally took possession of their castle, of course. We found you there. You were about four years old, I think. I had my apprentice do the scan, and you know the rest. I turned your castle over to the House. I don't know what became of it, or your parents' possessions. Perhaps there are relatives. . . ."

Norathar nodded again. "Thank you," she said. "But this hardly changes—"

"There's another thing. If my apprentice made a mistake, it reflects on me. Further, it is obvious that my actions were the immediate cause of all this. I trust Aliera's abilities with genetics more than anyone else's—and she says you are the product of Dragonlords on both sides, with e'Lanya dominant. I want to know what happened. I intend to investigate. If I kill you, that will make it more difficult. If you destroy me, of course, that will make it impossible. I would appreciate it if you would withhold any challenge until I've made this investigation. Then, if you wish, I will entertain a challenge on any terms you name."

"Any terms?" asked Norathar. "Including plain steel?"

Sethra snorted. "Including a Jhereg duel, if you wish."

The least shadow of a smile crossed Norathar's lips as she seated herself. "I accept your terms," she said. Cawti and I relaxed. Morrolan and Aliera, as far as I could tell, had been interested but unworried.

Morrolan cleared his throat and said, "Well then, perhaps we should discuss just how we're going to proceed."

Sethra said, "Tell me this: if there was a plot of some kind, could Baritt have been involved?"

Aliera said "No" at the same instant that Morrolan said "Yes." I chuckled. Aliera shrugged and said, "Well, maybe."

Morrolan snorted. "In any case," he said, "is it likely that they could fool an Athyra? And would an Athyra be involved in a plot of this type? Not to mention a Lyorn? If this was a plot, as you say, they would have had to convince the Athyra to help, and I have trouble believing they could do that. And there is no Lyorn in the world who would go along with it—that is why they're included in things like that."

Sethra nodded to herself.

I said, "Excuse me, but what is the procedure for getting a Lyorn and an Athyra to help with something like this? I mean, do you just walk over to the House of the Lyorn and yell, 'We're doing a genetic investigation, anyone want to help?' What do you do?"

Sethra said, "With the House of the Lyorn, it is an official request, through the Empire, for the assistance of the House. With the Athyra, someone will propose a wizard he knows or has heard of, and the council approves it."

"And the House of the Lyorn is likely to choose someone who's familiar with this kind of thing," I added.

Sethra nodded.

"Okay," I said. "But—Aliera, how hard would it be to fool a genetic scan?"

"A complicated illusion spell would do it," she said slowly. "*If* whoever did the scan was incompetent."

"What if he wasn't?"

"He wouldn't be fooled."

"Could Sethra the Younger be fooled?"

"Easily." She snorted.

I shot a glance at Sethra Lavode; she didn't seem convinced. I set it aside for the moment. "What about Baritt?"

"No," said Aliera.

Morrolan agreed. "Whatever he is—was—he was most assuredly *not* incompetent."

"So," I continued, "if someone did a spell to make it look like she wasn't a full Dragon, Baritt must have been in on it. The Lyorn could have been fooled."

"Vlad," said Morrolan, "the Athyra would have to have been in on it, too—and you'll have to convince me of that."

"I haven't figured that out yet," I admitted. "But one thing at a time. Sethra, how did Sethra the Younger first hear about this?"

"I don't know, Vlad. It was more than four hundred years ago."

"At your age, Sethra, that's almost yesterday."

She raised an eyebrow. Then her eyes moved up and to the left as she tried to remember. "She said that she heard through a friend who'd been drinking with Lady Miera. She said that Lady Miera had told her friend about it, and her friend told her."

"And the friend's name?"

She sighed and leaned back in her chair. She rested her hands on top of her head, leaned her head back, and rolled her eyes straight up. We sat there, hardly daring to breathe. Suddenly she straightened up. "Vlad, it was Baritt!"

Why, I wondered, doesn't this surprise me?

I shook my head. "If you people want to find out what Baritt knows about this, I can tell you where to find him, but don't expect me to go along with you. I've been to Deathsgate once; that will last a lifetime—at least. I've got my own problems. There's a guy who's trying to send me there. Figuratively speaking," I added. "I understand they don't allow Easterners in.

"Anyway," I continued, "Sethra, do you remember who the Lyorn was?"

"I never knew," she said. "My part of it was over, and I wanted nothing more to do with it. I wasn't along when they did the second scan."

"Oh. So I suppose you don't know who the Athyra was, either."

"Right."

"It'll all be in the records," Aliera put in. "We can find out."

I nodded. "Then I don't think there's anything more to do about this at the moment, right?"

There were nods from Sethra, Aliera, and Morrolan. Norathar and Cawti had been watching us the entire time without any expression. It occurred to me that it was odd for me to have taken the lead in this investigation into the history of the House of the Dragon. But then, in a certain sense, investigation is one of the things I'm good at. Cawti could have done it as well, but she had even less interest than I did.

"The next question," said Morrolan, "is how we're going to present this to the Dragon Council. I would suggest that Aliera and I appear before them and—"

Aliera interrupted. "Perhaps later would be better for this. It's really a matter to be discussed among Dragons."

There was a brief, uncomfortable silence; then Cawti stood up. "Excuse me," she said. "I believe that I'd like to retire now."

Sethra stood and bowed an acknowledgment as Cawti left. Then Sethra sat down again, and Morrolan said, "I wonder what troubles her?"

Typical.

"The end of a partnership," Norathar said, and it seemed that there were new lines of pain around her eyes and jaw. But then, she was a Dragonlord now, so she could show her feelings. She stood, bowed, and followed Cawti out of the room.

I followed them with my eyes, then glanced at the table. The food was cold and the wine was warm. If there had been an onion, it would have been rotten clear through.

11

"A quick game, boss?"

THEY LEFT ME ALONE at the table, so I thought about onions for a while. I was still thinking about them when I felt someone reaching for me psionically.

"Who is it?"

"Fentor, at Castle Black, milord. I have the information you wanted."

"On the riot? Good, let's have it."

"It was confined to three blocks, near—"

"I know where it was. Go on."

"Yes, milord. It was a row of flats, all owned by the same person. He'd started raising rents about four weeks before, and letting things deteriorate, and then began beating Easterners who were slow in paying."

"I see. Who owned the flats?"

"A Jhereg, lord. His name is—"

"Laris."

"Yes, milord."

I sighed. *"Had he owned the property for long?"*

There was a pause. *"It didn't occur to me to check, lord."*

"Do so. And find out who he bought it from."

"Yes, milord."

"Is there anything more?"

"Not yet, milord, but we're still working on it."

"Good. Another thing, too: I suspect someone triggered the riot deliberately. Try to find out."

"Yes, milord."

We broke the contact. The conversation made me realize, among other things, that I'd been neglecting my own affairs again. I got in touch with Kragar and told him to expect me in two minutes. Then I made contact with Sethra, explained that I had to leave, and would she be good enough to teleport me back to my office? She would and did.

I didn't have to tell her where it was, either. Sometimes I wonder about her.

Kragar was waiting for me, along with Glowbug and someone I didn't recognize. We went into the still-unrepaired building, and I told Kragar to come into the office with me. I shut the door, looked around, and didn't see him. I opened up the door again and said, "Kragar, I said to—"

"Boss?"

I turned, and saw him this time.

"Damn it, Kragar, stop *doing* that."

"Doing what, Vlad?"

"Never mind. *Cut it out, Loiosh.*"

"*I didn't say a thing, boss.*"

"*You were laughing up your wing.*"

I sat down and put my feet up on the desk. "Who's the new guy?"

"An enforcer. We need another one, and we can almost afford it. He knows he's staying on subject to your approval."

"What's his name?"

"Stadol."

"Never heard of him."

"He's called 'Sticks.' "

"Oh. So *that's* Sticks." I yelled, "Melestav, send Sticks in."

The door opened and he walked in.

"Sit," I told him.

He did.

Sticks might have gotten his name because he looked like one, but that can be said of almost all Dragaerans. Still, he was taller and thinner than most, and carried himself as if every bone in his body were jelly. His arms swung easily when he walked, and his knees sagged a bit. He had sandy hair, straight, and worn to his ears. One lock dangled over his forehead and looked like it would get in his eyes. He periodically threw his head to the side to clear it, but it flopped down almost right away.

In fact, the nickname came from his preference for using two three-foot clubs. He beat people up with them.

I said, "I'm Vlad Taltos." He nodded. "You want to work for me?"

"Sure," he said. "The money's good."

"That's because things are hot right now. You know about that?"

He nodded again.

"You ever 'work'?"

"No. No future in it."

"That's debatable. I've heard of you doing some muscle a few years back. What have you been doing since?"

He shrugged. "I have some connections with a few minstrels, and with some taverns. I help introduce them, and they give me a percentage. It's a living."

"Then why leave it?"

"No future in it."

". . . Okay. You're in."

"Thanks."

"That's it for now."

He made a slow climb to his feet and ambled out. I turned back to Kragar. It took me a moment to find him, then I asked him: "Anything new?"

"No. I'm working on the patron angle, but I haven't come up with anything."

"Keep on it."

"Right."

"Get Narvane and Shoen here."

"Right."

He got hold of them and we sat back to wait. While we were waiting . . .

"*Milord?*"

"*Yes, Fentor?*"

"*You were right. There was someone who provoked the riot. It looks deliberate.*"

"*Pick him up and hold him. I'm going to want to—*"

"*We can't, milord.*"

"*Dead?*"

"*Yes, milord. In the riot.*"

"*I see. Chance, or was someone after him?*"

"*I can't tell, milord.*"

"*All right. What about the previous landlord?*"

"*The Jhereg Laris has owned those flats for about nine weeks, milord. We don't know who he bought them from. The records are confused, and there seems to have been some false names used.*"

"*Untangle it.*"

"*Yes, milord.*"

"What was that?" asked Kragar when I broke the contact.

I shook my head and didn't answer. He stood, went to my closet, and came back with a box. "You asked for these."

The box contained a rather large selection of cutlery, of various sorts. Seeing them gathered together like that, I was a little amazed that I could fit it all around my person. I mean, there were—no, I don't think I want to give the specifics.

I thought about sending Kragar out while I changed weapons, then decided against it. I picked up the first thing I came to, a small throwing knife, tested its edge and balance, and put it into my cloak in place of the one like it that I had there.

It was surprising how long it took to go through all the weapons I carried and replace them. When I'd finally finished the chore, Narvane and Shoen were waiting. As I stepped out of the office, I ran a hand through my hair and adjusted my cloak with the other hand, thus allowing me to brush my arms along my chest, making sure various things were in place. A very useful nervous gesture.

Narvane acknowledged me with a flicker of the eyes. Shoen nodded brusquely. Sticks, flopped all over a chair, lifted a hand, and Glowbug said, "Good to see you, boss. I was beginning to think you were a myth."

"If you're beginning to think, Glowbug, it's an improvement already. Let's go, gentlemen."

This time, Loiosh was the first one out of the door, followed by Glowbug and Narvane. The other two followed me, leaving Kragar behind. We turned left and headed up to Malak Circle. I said hello to a few customers I knew personally, and to some people who worked for me. I got the impression that, in the last day, business had picked up. This was a considerable relief. There was still a feeling of tension in the air, but it was more in the background.

We reached the Fountain Tavern, then the first door to the left. "Sticks," I said.

"Hm?"

"This is where the trouble started. Laris opened up a small business upstairs, without even dropping me a polite note about it."

"Mm."

"For all I know, it's still going on. Glowbug and Shoen will wait out here with me."

"Okay."

He turned and went up the stairs. Narvane followed wordlessly. As they went in, I saw Sticks pulling a pair of clubs out from his cloak. I leaned against the building to wait. Glowbug and Shoen stood in front of me, to either side, casually alert.

"*Watch above, Loiosh.*"

"*I'm already doing it, boss.*"

It wasn't long before we heard a crash from up and to the right. We looked, and a body came flying out the window, landing in a heap about ten feet from me. A minute or so later, Narvane and Sticks reappeared. Sticks was holding something in his left fist. With the club in the other hand, he drew a series of squares in the dirt in front of me.

I looked at him questioningly, but before he could say anything, I noticed a crowd had begun to gather around the body. I gave them all a smile.

Sticks opened his left hand then, and dropped several stones, some white, some black, onto the squares he'd drawn in the street.

"A quick game, boss?"

"No thanks," I told him. "I don't gamble."

He nodded sagaciously. "No future in it," he said. We continued on around the circle.

Eventually, I returned to my office; I was pleased to be able to tell Kragar to expect an increase in our take this week. He grunted.

"Do something for me, Kragar."

"What?"

"Go visit that guy who told us about the setup. Find out if he knows anything more."

"Visit him? Personally?"

"Yeah. Face to face and all that."

"Why?"

"I don't know. Maybe to find out if he's unusual, so we can guess if we're going to get any other takers."

He shrugged. "All right. But won't that be putting him in danger?"

"Not if no one notices you."

He grunted again. "All right. When?"

"Now will be fine."

He sighed, which was a welcome relief from the grunts, and left.

"Now what, Loiosh?"

"Got me, boss. Find Laris?"

"I'd love to. How? If he weren't protected against witchcraft, I'd just try to nail him where he is."

"It works out even, boss. If we weren't protected against sorcery, he'd nail us where we are."

"I suppose. Hey, Loiosh."

"Yeah, boss?"

"I feel like I've been, I don't know, brushing you off lately, when I've been around Cawti. I'm sorry."

His tongue flicked against the inside of my ear. *"It's okay, boss. I understand. Besides, one of these days, I'll probably find someone myself."*

"I hope so. I think. Tell me something: have I been off *recently? I mean, this business with Cawti, do you think it's been getting in my way? I feel like I've been distracted or something."*

"A little, maybe. Don't worry about it. You've been doing all right when things get rough, and I don't think there's anything you can do about it anyway."

"Yeah. You know, Loiosh, I'm glad you're around."

"Aw, shucks, boss."

Kragar returned about two hours later.

"Well?"

"I'm not sure if I learned anything useful or not, Vlad. He doesn't have any idea where Laris is, but he's willing to tell us if he finds out. He was pretty nervous about meeting me, but that's understandable. Well, not *nervous*, exactly. Surprised, maybe, and caught off guard. Anyway, he hadn't heard anything that struck me as useful."

"Hmmmm. Did you get any feel for whether there might be others like him?"

Kragar shook his head.

"Okay," I admitted, "I guess that didn't get us anywhere. How about our other sources? Have we found anyone else who works for Laris?"

"A couple. But we can't do anything about them until we have more funds. Paying for 'work' would break us right now."

"Just two days until Endweek. Maybe we'll be able to do something then. Leave me alone for a while now. I want to think."

He made an exit. I leaned back, closed my eyes, and was interrupted again.

"Milord?"

"*What is it, Fentor?*"

"*We found out part of it. The flats had belonged to a Dragonlord who died, and they've been sort of kicking around since then.*"

"*How long ago did he die?*"

"*About two years ago, milord.*"

"*I see. And you can't find out who got possession after that?*"

"*Not yet, milord.*"

"*Keep working on it. Who was the Dragon, by the way?*"

"*A powerful sorcerer, lord. He was called Baritt.*"

Well now. . . . By all the Lords of Judgment, how was I going to fit *this* into my thinking? Coincidence came to mind, was thrown away, and kept coming back. How could it be coincidence? How could it *not* be coincidence?

"*Milord?*"

"*Fentor, find out everything you can about that, right away. Put more people on it. Break into Imperial records, bribe recordsmiths, whatever you have to, but find out.*"

"*Yes, milord.*"

Baritt . . . Baritt. . . .

A powerful sorcerer, a wizard, a Dragonlord. He was old when he died, and had made such a name for himself that he was no longer referred to by his lineage. Rather, his descendants referred to themselves as "e'Baritt." He had died only two years ago, and his monument, near Deathsgate Falls, had been the site of the bloodiest battle since the Interregnum.

Baritt.

It was easy enough to imagine him involved in some sort of conspiracy within the House of the Dragon, but what could he have to do with the Jhereg? Could *he* be Laris's patron? Or could one of his descendants be? If so, why?

What's more, if there was a relationship between my problem with Laris and Norathar's problem with Baritt, that meant a deep intrigue of some kind, and Dragonlords simply *aren't* intriguers—with the possible exception of Aliera, and then only within a limited sphere.

Was I really going to have to visit Deathsgate Falls and the Paths of the Dead again? I shuddered. Remembering my last visit, I knew that those who dwell there would not take my coming again at all kindly. Would it do any good if I did? Probably not; Baritt had certainly not been well disposed toward me last time.

But it *couldn't* be coincidence. His name turning up like that, owning the very flats that had been used by Laris. Why hadn't they merely passed to his heirs? Because someone had played with the records? Maybe, which would explain why Fentor was having so much trouble tracking down the ownership. But then, who? Why?

I reached out for contact with Morrolan.

"*Yes, Vlad?*"

"*Tell me about Baritt.*"

"*Hmmph.*"

"*I already knew that.*"

"*Precisely what do you wish to know, Vlad?*"

"*How did he die?*"

"*Eh? You don't know?*"

"*If I knew—no, I don't know.*"

"*He was assassinated.*"

Oh. That at least explained some of the remarks he'd made to me.

"*I see. How was it done? I'm surprised a sorcerer as skilled as Baritt would allow himself to be cut down.*"

"*Hmmm. As I recall, Vlad, there is a saying among you Jhereg . . .*"

"*Ah. Yes. 'No matter how subtle the wizard, a knife between the shoulder blades will seriously cramp his style.'*"

"*Yes.*"

"*So it was a Jhereg?*"

"*What other assassins do you know of?*"

"*There are plenty of amateurs who'll knife anyone for five gold. A Jhereg will hardly ever 'work' on anyone who isn't in the House; there usually isn't any need to, unless someone is threatening to go to the Empire about something, or—*"

I stopped dead.

Morrolan said, "*Yes, Vlad? Or . . . ?*"

I let him hang there. Or, I had been about to say, unless it's done as a special favor, set up by a Jhereg, for a friend from another House. Which meant that maybe, *maybe* it hadn't been Baritt behind the whole thing, after all. Maybe he'd been working with whoever it was, and this other person then needed Baritt taken out. And this other person was Laris's patron. And, since Laris had helped out with Baritt, his patron was ready to help Laris get rid of me. A simple exchange of favors.

"*Vlad?*"

"*Sorry, Morrolan, I'm trying to figure something out. Bide a moment, please.*"

"*Very well.*"

So Laris's patron was someone who had been working with Baritt about two years ago. Yes. Who would know?

"*Morrolan, who would be likely to know someone who was working with Baritt shortly before his death?*"

"*I'm not sure, Vlad. I don't know, myself. We never had much to do with each other while he was alive. Perhaps you should show up at Castle Black and ask around.*"

"*Yes . . . perhaps I'll do that. Well, thank you. I'll talk to you later.*"

"*Certainly, Vlad.*"

Well, well, and well.

At the very least, Laris was in it with someone else, and this someone else, presumably a Dragonlord, was helping him against me. If I could find out who he was, I might be able to nullify him simply by threatening to expose him; Dragons don't think highly of their own kind helping out Jhereg.

Finding him involved discovering who had owned those flats. Hmmm. I reached out for—

"Fentor."

"Yes, milord?"

"Make a list of every currently living descendant of Baritt. Have it ready in an hour."

"An hour, milord?"

"Yes."

"But—yes, milord."

I broke the link, and opened another one.

"Who is it?"

"Hello, Sethra."

"Oh, Vlad. Good evening. What can I do for you?"

"Is it still necessary to hold Norathar and Cawti prisoner?"

"I was just discussing that with Aliera. Why?"

"It would be helpful if Cawti were free this evening."

"I see." There was a pause, then: "Very well, Vlad. Neither Aliera nor Morrolan objects."

"You'll release both of them?"

"The Easterner was the only one in doubt. Norathar, as far as we're concerned, is a Dragon."

"I see. Well, thank you."

"You're welcome. I'll tell them at once."

"Make it five minutes from now, all right?"

"If you wish."

"Thank you."

Then I took a deep breath and began concentrating on Cawti, whom I didn't really know all that well. But I thought about her face, her voice, her—

"Vladimir!"

"Got it on the first guess. What are you doing tonight?"

"What am I—? What do you suppose I'm doing? Your friends still haven't allowed us to leave."

"I think that can be arranged. If so, would the lady be so kind as to allow me to escort her to a small gathering this evening?"

"I should be honored, most gracious lord."

"Excellent. Then I'll see you in an hour."

"I'll be looking forward to it."

I broke the contact and yelled for my bodyguards to escort me home, so I could get properly dressed for the occasion. It doesn't do to underdress for Castle Black.

12

"Friendly, isn't she?"

TWO TELEPORTS AFTER LEAVING home I was at Castle Black with Cawti and an unsteady stomach. Cawti was dressed to kill in long trousers of light gray, a blouse of the same color, and a gray cloak with black trim. I wore my good trousers, my good jerkin, and my cloak. We looked like a matched set.

Lady Teldra admitted us, greeted Cawti by name, and bade us visit the banquet hall. We must have been quite a sight: a pair of Easterners, both in Jhereg colors, with Loiosh on my left shoulder, putting him between us.

No one particularly noticed us.

I reached Fentor and told him where I was. He showed up, found me, and surreptitiously handed me a slip of paper. After he left, Cawti and I wandered around for a bit, seeing people and studying Morrolan's "dining room," and being casually insulted by passersby. After a while, I introduced her to the Necromancer.

Cawti bowed from the neck, which is subtly different than bowing the head. The Necromancer seemed uninterested, but returned the bow. The Necromancer didn't care whether you were a Dragaeran or an Easterner, a Jhereg or a Dragon. To her, you were either living or dead, and she got along better with you if you were dead.

I asked her, "Did you know Baritt?"

She nodded absently.

"Do you know if he was working with anyone shortly before his death?"

She shook her head, just as absently.

"Well, uh, thanks," I said, and moved on.

"Vladimir," said Cawti, "what's this business with Baritt all about?"

"I think someone is backing up Laris—someone big, probably in the House of the Dragon. I think whoever it is was working with Baritt at some point. I'm trying to find out who."

I took her to a corner and pulled out the list Fentor had handed me. There were seven names on it. None of them meant anything to me.

"Recognize any of the names?"

"No. Should I?"

"Descendants of Baritt. I'm going to have to check them out, I think."

"Why?"

I gave her a rundown on the story of the riot. Her beautiful face drew up into an ugly sneer. She said, "If I'd known what he had in mind—"

"Laris?"

She didn't answer.

"Why take it so hard?" I asked her.

She stared at me. "Why take it so hard? He's using our people. That's us, Easterners, being set up to be beaten and killed just to manipulate a few guards. What do you mean, why take it so hard?"

"How long have you lived in the Empire, Cawti?"

"All my life."

I shrugged. "I don't know. I guess I'm used to it, that's all. I expect things like that."

She looked at me coldly. "It doesn't bother you anymore, eh?"

I opened and shut my mouth a couple of times. "It still bothers me, I guess, but . . . Deathsgate, Cawti. You know what kind of people live in those areas. I got out of it, and you got out of it. Any of them—"

"Crap. Don't start on that. You sound like a pimp. 'I don't use 'em any more than they want to be used. They can do something else if they want. They like working for me.' Crap. I suppose you feel the same way about slaves, right? They must like it or they'd run away."

To be honest, it had never occurred to me to think about it. But Cawti was looking at me with rage in her lovely brown eyes. I felt a sudden flash of anger and said, "Look, damn it, *I've* never 'worked' on an Easterner, remember, so don't give me any—"

"Don't throw that up at me," she snapped. "We've been over it once. I'm sorry. But it was a job, all right? That has nothing to do with your caring about what happens to our own people." She kept glaring at me. I've been glared at by experts, but this was different. I opened my mouth to say something about what it had to do with, but I couldn't. It suddenly hit me that I could *lose* her, right now. It was like walking into a tavern where you're going to finalize someone, and realizing that the guy's bodyguards might be better than you. Except then, all you're liable to lose is your life. As I stood there, I realized what I was on the verge of losing.

"Cawti," I started to say, but my voice cracked. She turned away. We stood like that, in a corner of Morrolan's dining room, with multitudes of Dragaerans around us, but we might as well have been in our own universe.

How long we stood there I don't know. Finally, she turned back to me and said, "Forget it, Vlad. Let's just enjoy the party."

I shook my head. "Wait."

"Yes?"

I took both of her hands, turned her around, and led her into a small alcove off to the side of the main room. Then I took both of her hands again and said, "Cawti, my father ran a restaurant. The only people who came in were Teckla and Jhereg, because no one else would associate with us. My father, may the Lords of Judgment damn his soul for a thousand years, wouldn't let me associate with Easterners because he wanted to be accepted as Dragaeran. You, maybe, got a title after you'd made some money, so you could get a link to the Orb. I was given a title through my father, who spent our life savings on it, because he wanted to be accepted as Dragaeran.

"My father tried to make me learn Dragaeran swordsmanship, because he wanted to be accepted as Dragaeran. He tried to prevent me from studying witchcraft, because he wanted to be accepted as Dragaeran. I could go on for an hour. Do you think we were ever accepted as Dragaeran? Crap. They treated us like teckla droppings. The ones that didn't despise us because we were Easterners hated us because we were Jhereg. They used to catch me, when I went on errands, and bash me around until—never mind."

She started to say something, but I cut her off. "I don't doubt that you could tell me stories just as bad; that isn't the point." My voice dropped to a whisper. "I hate them," I said, squeezing her hands until she winced. "I joined the organization as muscle so I could get paid for beating them up, and I started 'working' so I could get paid for killing them. Now I'm working my way up the organization so I can have the power to do what I want, by my own rules, and maybe show a few of them what happens when they underrate Easterners.

"There are exceptions—Morrolan, Aliera, Sethra, a few others. For you, maybe Norathar. But they don't matter. Even when I work with my own employees, I have to ignore how much I despise them. I have to make myself pretend I don't want to see every one of them torn apart. Those friends I mentioned—the other day, they were discussing conquering the East, right in front of me, as if I wouldn't care."

I paused and took a deep breath.

"So I have to not care. I have to *convince* myself that I don't care. That's the only way I can stay sane; I do what I have to do. And there's precious little pleasure in this life, except the satisfaction of setting a goal, worthwhile or not, and meeting it.

"How many people can you trust, Cawti? I don't mean trust not to stab you in the back, I mean *trust*—trust with your soul? How many? Up until now, Loiosh has been the only one I could share things with. Without him, I'd have gone out of my head, but we can't really talk as equals. Finding you has . . . I don't know, Cawti. I don't want to lose you, that's all. And not for something as stupid as this."

I took another deep breath.

"I talk too much," I said. "That's all I wanted to say."

While I'd been speaking, her face had relaxed, the rage draining out of it. When I finished, she came into my arms and held me, rocking me gently.

"I love you, Vladimir," she said softly.

I buried my face in her neck and let the tears come.

Loiosh nuzzled my neck. I felt Cawti scratching his head.

A bit later, after I'd recovered, Cawti brushed my face with her hands and Loiosh licked my ear. We walked back to face the multitude. Cawti placed her hand on my left arm as we walked; I covered it with my right hand and squeezed.

I noticed the Sorceress in Green, but avoided her, not feeling like a confrontation just then. I looked for Morrolan, but didn't see him. I noticed the Necromancer talking to a tall, dark-haired Dragaeran woman. The latter turned for a moment, and I was suddenly struck by her resemblance to Sethra Lavode. I wondered. . . .

"Excuse me," I said, approaching them. They broke off and looked at me. I bowed to the stranger. "I am Vladimir Taltos, House Jhereg. This is the Dagger of the Jhereg. May I ask whom I have the honor of addressing?"

"You may," she said.

I waited. Then I smiled and said, "Whom do I have the honor of addressing?"

"I am Sethra," she said. Bingo!

"I have heard much of you from your namesake," I told her.

"No doubt. If that is all you wish to say, I am engaged just at the moment."

"I see," I said politely. "As a matter of fact, if you can spare a few moments—"

"My dear Easterner," she said, "I am aware that Sethra Lavode, for reasons best known to herself, chooses to tolerate your presence, but I am no longer apprenticed to her, so I see no reason why I should. I have no time for Easterners, and no time for Jhereg. Is all of this clear to you?"

"Quite." I bowed once more; Cawti did the same. Loiosh hissed at her as we turned away.

"Friendly, isn't she?"

"Quite," said Cawti.

At that moment Morrolan came in, escorting Norathar. She was dressed in black and silver, the colors of the House of the Dragon. I looked at Cawti; her face was expressionless. We approached them, fighting our way through the crowd.

Norathar and Cawti locked eyes, and I couldn't see what was passing between them. But then they smiled, and Cawti said, aloud, "The colors are most fetching. You wear them well."

"Thank you," said Norathar softly. I noticed that there was a ring on the little finger of her right hand. On its face was a dragon, with two red eyes.

I turned to Morrolan. "Is it official?"

"Not yet," he said. "Aliera is speaking to the Dragon Council about setting up an inquiry. It may take a few more days."

I looked back at Norathar and Cawti, who were talking a few paces away from us. Morrolan was silent. It is a very rare skill in a man, and far more rare in an aristocrat, to know when to be still, but Morrolan had it. I shook my head as I watched Cawti. First, I'd become angry with her, then I had poured out my problems at her feet; when all the time her partner of—how long?—at least five years, was on the verge of becoming a Dragonlord.

By the Demon Goddess! What Cawti must have gone through as a child would have been very much like what I went through, or worse. Her friendship with Norathar must have been like my relationship with Loiosh, and she was watching it end. Gods, but I can be an insensitive ass when I try!

I looked at Cawti then, from behind and to the side. I'd never really *looked* at her before. As any man with the least amount of experience can tell you, looks mean absolutely nothing as far as bedding is concerned. But Cawti would have been attractive by the standards of any human. Her ears were round, not the least bit pointed, and she had no trace of facial hair. (Contrary to some Dragaerans' belief, only male Easterners have whiskers—I don't know why.) She was smaller than I, but she had long legs that made her seem taller than she was. A thin face, almost hawklike, and piercing brown eyes. Hair was black, perfectly straight, falling below her shoulders. She obviously paid a fair amount of attention to it, because it glistened in the light and was cut off exactly even.

Her breasts were small, but firm. Her waist, slender. Her buttocks were also small, and her legs slim but well muscled. Most of this, you understand, I was remembering rather than seeing, but as I looked, I decided that, even on this level, I'd done rather well for myself. A crude way of putting it, I suppose, but—

She turned away from Norathar and caught me looking at her. For some reason, this pleased me. I held out my left arm as she came up; she pressed it. I reached for contact with her and it came more easily than last time.

"*Cawti . . .*"

"*It's all right, Vladimir.*"

Norathar came up to us then, and said, "I'd like a word with you, Lord Taltos."

"Call me 'Vlad.' "

"As you wish. Excuse us," she said to the others, and we walked a bit away.

Before she could say anything I started in. "If you're going to give me any of the don't-you-dare-hurt-her dung, you can forget it."

She gave me a thin smile. "You seem to know me," she said. "But why should I forget it? I mean it, you know. If you hurt her needlessly, I'll kill you. I just feel I should tell you that."

"The wise falcon hides his claws," I said, "and it's the poor assassin who warns his target."

"Are you trying to make me angry with you, Vlad? I care about Cawti. I care enough to destroy anyone who causes her pain. I feel I should let you know, so you can avoid doing it."

"How kind of you. What about you? Haven't you hurt her more than I ever could?"

To my surprise, she didn't even start to get angry. She said, "It may look that way, and I know I've hurt her, but not as badly as you could. I've seen the way she looks at you."

I shrugged. "I don't see that it matters," I said. "The way things are looking, I'm liable to be dead in a week or two anyway."

She nodded, but didn't say anything. She was, let us say, not overwhelmed with sympathy.

"If you really don't want her hurt, you might try helping me to stay alive."

She chuckled a bit. "Nice try, Vlad. But you know I have standards."

I shrugged, and mentioned something that had been bothering me for a while. "If I'd heard he was looking for you, I would have put everything on the line and hired you myself, and then I wouldn't be in this mess."

"The one who employed us didn't need to look for us; he knew where to find us, so there was no chance of your hearing."

"Oh. I wish I'd been so privileged."

"I have no idea how he found out—it isn't common knowledge. But it doesn't matter. I've said what I wanted to, and I think you under—"

She broke off, looking over my shoulder. I didn't turn around, just from habit.

"*What is it, Loiosh?*"

"*The bitch you met last time. The Sorceress in Chartreuse, or whatever.*"

"*Great.*"

"May I interrupt?" came the voice from behind me.

I looked at Norathar and raised my eyebrows. She nodded. I turned then, and said, "Lady Norathar e'Lanya, of the House of the Dragon, this is—"

"I am the Sorceress in Green," said the Sorceress in Green. "And I am quite capable of introducing myself, Easterner."

I sighed. "Why do I get the feeling that I'm not wanted here? Never mind." I bowed to Norathar and Loiosh hissed at the Sorceress.

As I walked away, the Sorceress was saying, "Easterners! I'll be just as pleased when Sethra the Younger goes after them. Won't you?"

I heard Norathar say, "Hardly," in a cold tone of voice, and then I was thankfully out of earshot. Then it hit me: I was looking for an Athyra who had been involved in the plot against Norathar. The Sorceress in Green was an Athyra. Just maybe, I decided, I'd have to think about how to verify or disprove this.

I returned to Cawti and said, "Is there anything keeping you here?"

She looked startled, but shook her head.

"Should we leave?" I asked.

"Weren't you going to be checking on that list?"

"This party runs thirty hours a day, five days a week. It'll wait."

She nodded. I gave Morrolan a bow, then we went out the door and down to the entryway without taking our leaves of anyone else. One of Morrolan's sorcerers was standing near the door. I had him teleport us back to my apartment. The sick feeling in my stomach when we arrived was not, I think, due only to the teleport.

My flat, at that time, was above a wheelwright's shop on Garshos Street near the corner of Copper Lane. It was roomy for the money because it was an attic, and the sloping ceiling would have annoyed a Dragaeran. My income, just before the business with Laris had started, had me thinking about getting a larger place, but it was just as well I hadn't.

We sat down on the couch. I put my arm around her shoulder, and said, "Tell me about yourself." She did, but it isn't any of your business. I'll just say that I was right in my earlier guesses about her experiences.

We got to talking about other things, and at one point I showed her my target in the back room, set so I could throw through the hall and give myself a thirty-foot range. The target, by the way, was in the shape of a Dragon's head. She thought that was a nice touch.

I took out a brace of six knives and put four of them into the left eye of the target.

She said, "Good throwing, Vladimir. May I try?"

"Sure."

She put five into the right eye, and the sixth less than half an inch off.

"I see," I said, "that I'm going to have to practice."

She grinned. I hugged her.

"Vlad," said someone.

"What the bleeding deviltries of Deathsgate Falls do you—Oh, Morrolan."

"Bad time, Vlad?"

"Could be worse. What is it?"

"I've just spoken to Aliera. She has found the names of the Lyorn and the Athyra who were involved in the test on the Lady Norathar. Also, you may wish to inform your friend Cawti that the Dragon Council has authorized an official scan for tomorrow, at the sixth hour past noon."

"All right. I'll tell her. What are the names?"

"The Lyorn was Countess Neorenti, the Athyra was Baroness Tierella."

"Baroness Tierella, eh? Morrolan, could Baroness Tierella be the real name of the Sorceress in Green?"

"What? Don't be absurd, Vlad. She—"

"Are you sure?"

"Quite sure. Why?"

"Never mind; I just lost a theory I liked. Okay, thank you."

"You are most welcome. A good evening to you, and I'm sorry you couldn't stay at my party longer."

"Another time, Morrolan."

I gave Cawti the news about Norathar, which broke the mood, but what was I supposed to do? I went into the kitchen and got us some wine, then got in touch with Fentor.

"Yes, milord?"

"House of the Lyorn, Countess Neorenti. House of the Athyra, Baroness Tierella. Are they alive? If so, find out where they live. If not, find out how they died. Get right on it."

"Yes, milord."

Cawti sighed.

"I'm done," I said quickly. "It was just—"

"No, it isn't that," she said. "I only wish there were some way I could help you with Laris. But all the information I have came from him, and I couldn't tell you that, even if it was useful."

"I understand," I said. "You have to live with yourself."

She nodded. "Things were so easy, just a week ago. I mean, I was happy . . . I guess. We were secure. My reasons for wanting to kill Dragaerans are the same as yours, and Norathar, well, she just hated everything. Except me, I suppose." I put my arm back around her shoulder. "Now, well, I'm happy that she has what she wants, even if she'd managed to convince herself she didn't want it anymore, but me—" She shrugged.

"I know," I said. Now, would you like to hear something crazy? I wanted, badly, to say something like, "I hope I can take her place for you," or maybe, "I'll be here," or even, "I love you, Cawti." But I couldn't. Why? Because, as far as I could tell, I was going to be dead in a little while. Laris was still after me, still had more resources than I did, and, most important, he knew where to find me, and I didn't know where to find him. So, under the circumstances, how could I do anything that would tie her to me? It was crazy. I shook my head and kept my mouth shut.

I looked up at her and noticed that she was staring over my shoulder and nodding slightly.

"*Loiosh!*"

"*Yeah, boss?*"

"*What are you telling her, damn you?*"

"*What you'd tell her yourself, boss, if you weren't a dzur-brained fool.*"

I made a grab for him, but he fluttered over to the windowsill. I stood up, growling, and felt a touch on my arm.

"Vladimir," she said calmly, "let's go to bed."

Well, between wringing the neck of a wiseass, know-it-all jhereg, and making love to the most wonderful woman in the world—I mean, the choice wasn't hard to make.

13

"Well, what did you think I'd do? Kiss him?"

"M̲ILORD?"

"*Yes, Fentor?*" I came more fully awake and pulled Cawti closer to me.

"*I've located Countess Neorenti.*"

"*Good work, Fentor. I'm pleased. What about the Athyra?*"

"*Milord, are you certain about her name? Baroness Tierella?*"

"*I think so. I could check on it a little more, I suppose. Why? Can't find her?*"

"*I've checked the records as thoroughly as I can, Milord. There has never been anyone named 'Tierella' in the House of the Athyra, 'Baroness' or anything else.*"

I sighed. Why does life have to be so Verra-be-damned complicated?

"*Okay, Fentor. I'll worry about it tomorrow. Get some sleep.*"

"*Thank you, milord.*"

The contact was broken. Cawti was awake, and snuggled closer to me.

"What is it, Vladimir?"

"More trouble," I said. "Let's forget it for now."

"Mmmmmmm," she said.

"*Loiosh.*"

"*Yeah, boss?*"

"*You are provisionally forgiven.*"

"*Yeah, I know.*"

A few brief, happy hours later we were up and functional. Cawti offered to buy me breakfast and I accepted. Before we left, she wandered around the rooms, looking into nooks and crannies. She commented on a cheap print of an expensive Katana sketch of Dzur Mountain, sneered good-naturedly at some imitation Eastern cut glass, and would have continued all day if I hadn't finally said, "Let me know when you're through with the inspection. I'm getting hungry."

"Hm? Oh. Sorry." She gave the flat another look. "It's just that I suddenly feel as if this were home."

I felt a lump in my throat as she took my arm and guided me to the door.

"Where shall we eat? Vladimir?"

"What? Oh. Uh, anywhere's fine. There's a place just a couple of doors up that has clean silver and klava that you don't need a spoon for."

"Sounds good."

Loiosh settled on my shoulder and we went down to the street. It was about four hours after dawn, and a few things were just beginning to get going, but there was little street traffic. We went into Tsedik's and Cawti bought me two greasy sausages, a pair of burned chicken eggs, warmed bread, and adequate klava to wash it down with. She had the same.

I said, "I just realized that I haven't cooked a meal for you yet."

"I was wondering when you'd get around to it." She smiled.

"You know I cook? Oh. Yeah." She continued eating. I said, "I really ought to do a job on your background, just to make us even, you know."

"I told you most of it last night, Vladimir."

"Doesn't count," I sniffed. "Not the same thing."

Midway through the meal, I noted the time and decided to do some business. "Excuse me," I said to Cawti.

"Morrolan . . ."

"Yes, Vlad?"

"The Athyra you gave me isn't."

"I beg your pardon?"

"She isn't an Athyra."

"What is she, pray?"

"As far as I know, she doesn't exist."

There was a pause. *"I shall look into this and inform you of the results."*

"Okay."

I sighed, and the rest of the meal passed in silence. We kept it short, because being in a public restaurant without bodyguards can be dangerous. All it would take would be a waiter who knew what was going on to get a message to Laris's people, and they could send someone in to nail me. Cawti understood this, so she didn't make any comment when I rushed a bit.

She understood it so well, in fact, that she stepped out of the place ahead of me, just to make sure there was no one around. Loiosh did the same thing.

"Boss, stay back!" And, *"Vladimir!"*

And, for the first time in my life, I froze in a crisis. Why? Because all of my instincts and training told me to dive and get away from the door, but my reason told me that Cawti was facing an assassin.

I stood there like an idiot while Cawti rushed out, and then there was someone in front of me, holding a wizard's staff. He gestured, and then Spellbreaker was in my hand and swinging toward him before I knew what I was doing. I felt a tingling in my arm and knew that I'd intercepted something. I saw the guy in front of me curse, but before he could do anything else there was a dagger sticking out of the side of his neck. Whatever Cawti was doing, she apparently had time to keep an eye on the door. As I scrambled through, drawing a stiletto, I managed a psionic *"Help!"* to Kragar. Then I saw three more of them. Sheesh!

One was yelling and trying to fight off Loiosh. Another was dueling, sword to sword, with Cawti. The third spotted me as I emerged and his hand flicked out. I dived toward him, rolling (this is not easy with a sword at your hip), and whatever he threw missed. I lashed out with both feet, but he danced back out of the way. There was a knife in his left hand, set for throwing. I hoped he'd miss any vital spots.

Then the knife fell from his hand as a dagger blossomed from his wrist. I took the opportunity to roll up and do unto him what he'd been about to do unto me. I considered his heart an adequate vital spot; I didn't miss it.

A quick glance at Cawti showed me that she was doing all right against her man, who apparently wasn't used to a swordsman who presented only the side. I drew my rapier and took two steps toward the one Loiosh was engaging. He gave Loiosh a last swipe, turned to face me, raised his blade, and took the point of my rapier in his left eye. I turned back to Cawti. She was cleaning her weapon.

"Let's move, troops," I said, as Loiosh returned to my shoulder.

"Good idea. Can you teleport?"

"Not when I'm this excited. You?"

"No."

"How about walking, then. Back to my office."

Cawti cleaned her blade, while I dropped mine where it was. Then I led us back into Tsedik's and out the back door, and we began a leisurely stroll back to the office. If we walked fast, we'd attract even more attention than we already had, but I don't know if there is anything in the world more difficult than trying to stroll while your heart is racing and the adrenaline is pumping through your system. I was trembling like a teckla, and the knowledge that this made me an even easier target didn't help.

We had gone less than a block toward the office when four more Jhereg showed up: Glowbug, N'aal, Shoen, and Sticks.

"Good morning, gentlemen," I managed. They all greeted me. I refrained from telling N'aal that he looked well, because he might have thought I was mocking him. He didn't seem resentful, though.

We made it back to the office without incident. I contrived to be alone when I finally lost my breakfast. It hadn't been that good, anyway.

I've known Dragaerans, and I mean known, not just heard of, who can eat a meal, go out and have an incredibly close brush with death, then come home and eat another meal. You might run into one of these jokers an hour later and ask if anything interesting has been happening, and he'll shrug and say, "Not really."

I don't know if I admire these types or just feel sorry for them, but I'm sure not like that. I have a variety of reactions to almost dying and none of them involves being plussed. It's especially bad when it comes as the result of an assassination attempt, because such attempts are, by nature, unexpected.

But my reactions, as I said, vary. Sometimes I become paranoid for a few hours or days, sometimes I become aggressive and belligerent. This time, I sat very still at my desk for a long time. I was shaken and I was scared. The sight of those four—*four*—kept running through my mind.

I was definitely going to have to do something about this Laris fellow.

"*Time to get moving, boss.*"

"Eh?"

"*You've been sitting there for about two hours now. That's enough.*"

"*It can't have been that long.*"

"*Humph.*"

I noticed Cawti was in the room, waiting for me. "How long have you been there?"

"About two hours."

"It can't—have you been talking to Loiosh? Never mind." I took a couple of deep breaths. "Sorry," I said. "I'm not used to this."

"You should be by now," she remarked dryly.

"Yeah. I've got that to console me. How many people do you know who have survived . . ."

"Yes, Vlad? What is it?"

I sat there thinking for a very long time indeed. Then I asked the question again, in a less rhetorical tone of voice. "How many people do you know who have survived even two assassination attempts, let alone three?"

She shook her head. "There are damn few who survive the first one. I don't think I've ever heard of anyone surviving two. As for three—it's quite an accomplishment, Vladimir."

"Is it?"

"What do you mean?"

"Look Cawti, I'm good, I know that. I'm also lucky. But I'm not *that* good, and I'm not *that* lucky. What does that leave?"

"That the assassins were incompetent?" she said, raising an eyebrow.

I saw it and raised one. "Are you?"

"No."

"So what else does it leave?"

"I give up. What?"

"That the attempts weren't real."

"What?"

"What if Laris hasn't been trying to kill me?"

"That's absurd."

"I agree. But so is surviving three assassination attempts."

"Well, yes, but—"

"Let's think about it, all right?"

"How can I think about it? Damn it, I did one of them myself."

"I know. All right, we'll start with you, then. Were you actually hired to assassinate me, or were you hired to make it look like you were trying to assassinate me?"

"Why on Dragaera—?"

"Don't evade the issue, please. Which was it?"

"We were hired to assassinate you, damn it!"

"That's admissible at Court, you know. Never mind," I said quickly as she started flushing. "Okay, you say you were hired to assassinate me. Suppose you were given the job of making it look good. How—"

"I wouldn't take it. And get myself killed?"

"Skip that for the moment. Just suppose. How would you deal with the questions I've been asking, if your job was to make me think Laris wanted to kill me?"

"I—" she stopped and looked puzzled.

"Right. You'd answer just as you've been answering."

"Vladimir," she said slowly, "do you actually think that's the case?"

"Uh . . . not really. But I have to allow for the possibility. Don't I?"

"I guess," she said. "But where does that leave you?"

"It means that, for the moment, we can forget about you and Norathar."

"You still haven't said *why* he'd want to do this."

"I know. Skip that, too. Let's take the attempt outside the office. I've told you about it, right?"

"Yes."

"Okay. I got out of that because I'm quick and accurate and, mostly, because Loiosh warned me in time, and took care of one of them so that I was free to deal with the other."

"I was wondering if you'd remember that, boss."

"Shut up, Loiosh."

"Now," I continued, "how could Laris, and therefore anyone he hired, *not* have known about Loiosh?"

"Well, of course he knew about him—that's why he sent two assassins."

"But they underestimated him?"

"Well—forgive me, Loiosh—but he didn't do all that well against Norathar and me. Also, you reacted better and more quickly than Laris could have expected. As I told you before, Vladimir, you have a talent for making people underestimate you."

"Maybe. Or maybe he gave the job to a pair of incompetents, hoping they'd bungle it."

"That's absurd. He couldn't *tell* them to bungle it, that would be suicide. And he couldn't *know* they'd fail. As I understand it, they almost got you."

"And, maybe, even if they had, they wouldn't have made it permanent. We can't question them. Which reminds me, you could also have been told not to make it permanent. Were you?"

"No."

"Okay, skip that. Maybe he figured I'd survive, and, if I didn't, that I'd be revivified."

"But you still haven't said why."

"Wait for it. Now, about today—"

"I was wondering when you were going to get to that. Did you see what the one threw at you?"

"The sorcerer?"

"No, the other one."

"No. What was it?"

"A pair of large throwing knives, with thin blades. And they were perfectly placed for your head."

"But I ducked."

"Oh, come on, Vlad. How could he know that you'd react that quickly?"

"Because he knows me—he's studied me. Deathsgate, Cawti. That's what I'd do—what I've been trying to do as best I can."

"I have trouble—"

"Okay, just a minute then." I yelled past her. "Melestav! Get Kragar in here."

"Okay, boss."

Cawti looked an inquiry at me, but I held up a finger as a signal to wait. Kragar came into the room. He stopped, glanced at Cawti, and looked at me.

"This lady," I informed him, "is the Dagger of the Jhereg." As I said it, I looked a question at her.

"Might as well," she said. "It doesn't much matter anymore."

"Okay," I said. "She is also known as Cawti. Cawti, this is Kragar, my lieutenant."

"Is that what I am?" he mused. "I've wondered."

"Sit down." He sat. "Okay, Kragar. You're Laris."

"I'm Laris. I'm Laris? You just said I was your lieutenant."

"Shut up. You're Laris. You get word that I'm sitting in a restaurant. What do you do?"

"Uh . . . I send an assassin over."

" 'An' assassin? Not four?"

"Four? Why would I send four? Laris wants to kill you, not give you Imperial Honors. With four assassins, you have three eyewitnesses to the thing. He'd get one good guy. There are plenty of 'workers' who wouldn't have any trouble finalizing you if they knew you were sitting in a restaurant. If he couldn't find someone good, he might go with two. But not *four*."

I nodded and looked at Cawti. "The way you and Norathar work keeps you out of contact with a large part of the Jhereg. But Kragar's right."

"Is that what happened, boss?" Kragar asked, looking puzzled.

"Later," I told him. "Now, let's suppose that you didn't have anyone around who could do it, or any two. For some reason, anyway, you want to use four of them. What do you tell them to do?"

He thought for a moment.

"Do I know where you're sitting, and what the layout of the place is?"

"Whoever told you I was there told you that stuff, too, or else you get back in touch with him and ask."

"Okay. Then I tell them that stuff, and say, 'go in there and do him.' What more is there to say?"

"You wouldn't have them wait outside?"

He shook his head, looking more puzzled than ever. "Why give you a chance to be up and moving? If you're sitting down—"

"Yes," said Cawti suddenly. "When I stepped outside, they were just standing there, waiting. That's been bothering me, but I didn't realize it until now. You're right."

I nodded. "Which means that either Laris, or his button-man, is a complete incompetent, or—that's all for now, Kragar."

"Uh . . . good. Well, I hope I helped." He shook his head and left.

"Or," I continued to Cawti, "he wasn't really trying to kill me after all."

"If he was trying to fool you," she said, "couldn't he have done a better job of it? After all, you figured it out. If you're going to use success or failure to prove intention—"

"If we follow that reasoning, then I'm *supposed* to figure out that he's only bluffing, right? Come on, lover. We aren't Yendi."

"Okay," she said. "But you still haven't said *why* he'd only want to bluff you."

"That," I admitted, "is a tricky one."

She snorted.

I held my hand up. "I only said it's tricky—not that I'm not trickier. The obvious reason for him not to kill me is that he wants me alive."

"Right," she said. "Brilliant."

"Now, what reason could he have for wanting me alive?"

"Well, I know of at least one good reason, but I don't think you're his type."

I blew her a kiss and hacked my way onward. "Now, there are several possible reasons why he might want me alive. If any—"

"Name one."

"I'll come back to that. If any of them is true, then he might be hoping to scare me into making a deal. We might be hearing from him any time, asking me if I'll accept terms. If I do hear from him, what I say will depend on if I can figure out what he's after, so I know how *badly* he wants to keep me alive. Got it?"

She shook her head. "Are you *sure* you aren't part Yendi? Never mind. Go on."

"Okay. Now, as for reasons why he might want me alive, the first thing that comes to mind is: he might not like something that will happen when I die. Okay, now, what happens when I die?"

"I kill him," said Cawti.

"One possib—What did you say?"

"I kill him."

I swallowed.

"Well," she said angrily, her nostrils flaring, "what did you think I'd do? Kiss him?"

"I . . . Thank you. I didn't realize . . ."

"Go on."

"Could he know that?"

She looked puzzled. "I don't think so."

Which suddenly made me wonder about something. *"Loiosh, could someone have—?"*

"No, boss. Don't worry about it."

"Are you sure? Love spells—"

"I'm sure, boss."

"Okay. Thanks."

I shook my head. "Okay, what I was *going* to say is, some of my friends—that is, my other friends—might come down on him. Not Aliera—she's the Dragon Heir, and the Dragon Council would have a lyorn if she started battling Jhereg—but Morrolan might go after Laris, and maybe Sethra would. Laris might be worried about that. But if so, why did he start the war? Maybe he only found out about my friends after it was too late to back out."

"That's quite a chain of supposition, Vladimir."

"I know, but this whole thing is a big chain of supposition. Anyway, another possibility is that he started the war knowing all this, but had some other reason for starting the war anyway, and hopes to get something without having to kill me."

"What reason?"

"What's the war about?"

"Territory."

"Right. Suppose that there is some particular area he wants. Maybe there's something buried around here, something important." She didn't look convinced. I continued. "You saw the front of this place? They staged a raid on it. I didn't think anything of it at the time, but maybe my office is sitting right on top of something they want."

"Oh, come on. This is so farfetched I can't believe it."

"All right," I said, backing up a bit. "I'm not saying that I've hit dead center, I'm just trying to show you that there are possibilities."

She grimaced. "You aren't going to convince me," she said. "This whole thing is based on assuming that Norathar and I are part of the hoax. Maybe I can't prove to you that we aren't, but *I* know we're not, so I'm not going to be convinced."

I sighed. "I don't really believe you are, either."

"Well, then, where does that leave your theory?"

I thought about it for a while. Then, *"Kragar."*

"Yeah, Vlad?"

"Remember that tavernkeeper who tipped us off?"

"Sure."

"You said that he heard it being arranged—do you know if he heard someone actually talking to the assassins?"

"Yes, he did. He said the button-man addressed them by name. That's how I knew who we were up against."

"I see. When you went to see him, you said he was, how did you put it?

'Surprised and caught off guard.' Now, can you take a guess about whether he was more afraid of you, or afraid of being seen with you?"

"That's pretty subtle, Vlad."

"So are you, Kragar. Try."

There was a pause. *"My first reaction was that he was afraid of me personally, but I don't see—"*

"Thanks."

I turned back to Cawti. "Would you mind telling me where this thing was set up?"

"Huh?"

"You've admitted that you were hired to assassinate me. All I want to know is where it was arranged."

She looked at me for a long moment. "Why? What does this have to do with—"

"If my suspicions are confirmed, I'll tell you. If not, I'll tell you anyway. Now, where was it arranged?"

"A restaurant in Laris's area. You know I can't be more specific—"

"Which floor?"

"Huh?"

"Which floor?"

This earned me a quizzical look. "The main floor."

"Right," I said. "And a restaurant, not a tavern. Okay. And you didn't discuss it with him personally, did you?"

"Certainly not."

"So you don't even know who the job came from?"

"Well . . . not technically, I suppose. But I assumed—" She stopped, and her eyes grew wide. "Then who—?"

"Later," I said. "We'll get to that. It isn't what you think—I think. Give me a moment."

She nodded.

"Kragar."

"Yes, Vlad?"

"Our friend the tavernkeeper—I would like him to become dead."

"But boss, he—"

"Shut up. Finalize him."

"Whatever you say, Vlad."

"That's right. Whatever I say." I thought for a moment. "Have Shoen do it—he's reliable."

"Okay."

That's the trouble with not having any button-men: you have to do all the dirty work yourself.

14

"Lord Morrolan, I must insist."

I LEANED BACK IN my chair. "The next question," I said, "is why they—Cawti? What is it?"

She was staring at me through slitted eyes.

"He set us up," she said. "Or someone did."

"Hmmm. You're right. I was so involved in my problem that I didn't see it from your end."

"You said I was wrong before, when it occurred to me that someone else had done it. Why?"

"We got the information from one of Laris's people. That means that he must have had a hand in it."

"You're right. So it was him."

"But *why*, Cawti? Why does he want me to think he's after me?"

"I'll ask you another one," she said. "Why use *us*?"

"Well," I said, "it was certainly convincing."

"I suppose. When I tell Norathar about this—" she stopped, and a strange look came over her face.

"What is it?"

"I can't tell Norathar about this, Vladimir. She's the Dragon Heir now, or soon will be. If she gets involved in Jhereg activities at this point, she'll lose her position. I can't do that to her. I wish I hadn't told her about the earlier attempt on you."

"Mmmm," I said.

"So it's you and me. We'll find that bastard, and—"

"How? He's vanished. He's protected against sorcery traces and even blocked against witchcraft. I know; I've tested."

"We'll find a way, Vladimir. Somehow."

"But why? What is he after?"

She shrugged, took out a dagger, and started flipping it. My breath caught for a moment, watching her. It was as if she were a female version of me. . . .

"Okay," I continued, "what are the anomalies? First, hiring a team of assassins with the kind of reputation you and Norathar have, just to pull off a bluff. Second, doing it in such a way that you two find out and are still alive. He must have known that you wouldn't be pleased about this, and—"

"No," said Cawti. "The only reason I'm alive is that Norathar refused to speak to Aliera unless she revivified me. And the only reason Norathar is alive is that Aliera was convinced she was a Dragonlord and wanted to hear her story." She chuckled. "Norathar wouldn't talk to her anyway."

"I see," I said softly. "I hadn't known that. Well then, if this *was* his plan, he could have pretty much counted on you two being . . . That's it, then."

"What?"

"Just a minute. Is it? No, that doesn't make sense, either. Why . . . ?"

"What is it, Vladimir?"

"Well, what if the *point* was to kill you and Norathar? But that doesn't make sense."

She thought about it for a minute. "I agree; it doesn't. There are other ways to have killed us. And why continue the bluff after it failed?"

"I agree, but . . . could Laris know about Norathar's background?"

"I don't see how. I suppose it's possible, but why would he care?"

"I don't know. But look: the part of this that could most reasonably be a slip is that you and Norathar are still alive. So the only thing that *should* have been accomplished, so far, is the deaths of you two. Now of the two of you, it makes the most sense that someone would want Norathar killed, and it probably has to do with her background. What if we assume that's the case and go from there. What does that get us?"

"It still doesn't explain the war on you. Why not just kill her? Or, if he wants to be devious, give us the job of killing you and hire someone else to finalize us there?"

I nodded. "There's more to this than I can see," I admitted. "I know just the person we're going to want to talk to about it."

"Who?"

"What Dragonlord do you know of with the most interest right now in who the heir is? Who could have set this whole thing up, just to have Norathar dead, then revivified, then made the Dragon Heir? And maybe make attempts on my life just to make things look good? Who is it who most wants to find a new heir to the throne?"

She nodded. "Aliera."

"I'm going to arrange a teleport," I said.

Cawti and I leaned on each other for support. We stood in the courtyard of Castle Black, which floated above a small village about 175 miles northeast of Adrilankha. The tip of Dzur Mountain could be seen to the east, which was a more pleasant view than looking down provided.

"I'm sick," I remarked conversationally.

Cawti nodded.

"The couple that heaves together, cleaves together."

"Shut up, Loiosh."

Cawti chuckled. I glanced at her sharply.

"Loiosh, did you say that to her, too?"

"Shouldn't I have?"

"You shouldn't have said it at all. But that isn't what I meant. It's just . . . interesting."

By then our stomachs had settled down a bit; we approached the doors. They opened, displaying a wide hallway and Lady Teldra. She bestowed compliments upon us, during which we learned that Aliera was with Morrolan in the library. I told her we could find our own way. We went up the stairs, not stopping, as I usually did, to look at the artwork, and clapped at the door to the library.

"Enter," said Morrolan.

We did, and I could tell by looking at their faces that a remarkable thing was occurring: they weren't arguing about anything.

"Is one of you sick?" I asked.

"No," said Morrolan. "What leads you to ask?"

"Never mind. I have to talk to you, Aliera. Morrolan, this probably concerns you, too, so you may as well hear it."

"Sit down, then," he said. "Wine?"

"Please." I looked over at Cawti. She nodded. "Two," I said. "Where is Norathar?"

"She is being examined," said Aliera.

"Oh. Probably just as well."

One of Aliera's fine eyebrows climbed. "She shouldn't hear this?"

"Not yet, anyway."

As we pulled up chairs, a servant appeared with wine. Morrolan favors sparkling wines, whereas I think such things are an abomination. But, since he knows that, he brought a dry white, nicely chilled. I raised my glass in salute, sipped, and let my tongue enjoy itself while I tried to figure out how to tell Aliera what I had to tell her, and how to find out from her what I wanted to know.

When she'd had enough of waiting, she said, "Yes, Vlad?"

I sighed and blurted out the story of the assassination attempts as best I could, not going into any more detail than necessary about my own affairs, and never actually *saying* that Cawti had admitted trying to kill me. I mean, Aliera knew it, but habits are hard to break.

As I spoke, she and Morrolan became more and more alert. They occasionally exchanged glances. I finished up by saying that I could see no reason why Laris would have wanted Norathar dead, but I couldn't explain things any other way. Did they have any ideas?

"No," said Aliera. "But it doesn't matter. And, as soon as I can track him down, it will matter even less."

Morrolan coughed gently. "I would suggest, my dear cousin, that you at least wait until the Lady Norathar's position is confirmed. You are currently the heir, and the council hardly approves of Dragons involving themselves with Jhereg."

"So what?" she snapped. "What will they do to me? Find me unfit to be Empress? Let them! Besides, Norathar is certain to be confirmed."

"Hardly," said Morrolan. "She has a long history of associating with the Jhereg."

"Completely justified, under the circumstances."

"Nevertheless—"

"Nevertheless, I don't care. I'm going to find this Jhereg, and I'm going to show him Kieron's Sword. You are welcome to assist me. Hindering me would be an error."

She stood up and glared at Morrolan. "Well?"

I turned to Cawti and said in a normal tone of voice, "Don't worry about it; they do this all the time." She giggled. Neither Aliera nor Morrolan appeared to hear me.

Morrolan sighed. "Sit down, Aliera. This is nonsense. All I am asking you to do is wait a day or two, until we know the results of the council's decision on Lady Norathar. If she fails to become the heir, we will discuss it then. There is nothing to be gained by rushing out there like this. You have no way of finding him."

She glared at him for a moment longer, then seated herself. "Two days, then," she said. "At the most. Then I kill him."

"I'll help," said Cawti.

Aliera started to object, but Cawti interrupted. "It's all right," she said. "You forget: I've worked with Dragaerans before. I really don't mind at all."

Cawti and I happily accepted Morrolan's hospitality in the form of a good lunch. Then I excused myself and went back into the now deserted library to think.

All of this business with Norathar, I decided, was fine, but it wasn't helping me find Laris, or at least get him off my back. Cawti and Aliera could talk about killing him, but they couldn't find him any more than I could, even if Aliera was telling the truth. And I couldn't afford to wait. If this kept up, I'd be out of business in a matter of weeks, at best.

It occurred to me that I might be able to get a message to him, proposing a truce. But he wouldn't go for it. And when I remembered Nielar's body, lying in the rubble of his shop, and the years I'd worked with Temek, and with Varg, I knew that I wouldn't go for it either.

Which brought me back to finding Laris, which brought me back to the big questions: Who has been working with Baritt shortly before his death? Was this person Laris's patron? How did this fit in with the business with Norathar? Was it Aliera? If not, who? And how to find out for sure?

I had reached that point when Cawti, Morrolan, and Aliera walked in. Before they could even sit down, I said, "Morrolan, did you find out anything yet about that Athyra?" I tried to keep an eye on Aliera as I asked the question, but her face betrayed nothing.

"No. Sethra is looking into the matter. Is there something in particular you wish to know?"

"Yes. You said that an Athyra is likely to be recommended by someone: can you find out who recommended the one used in Norathar's earlier examination?"

He nodded. "I see why you are asking. We must assume that the Athyra was, as you would say, 'a ringer,' and whoever recommended her may have known this. Very well, I'll see if I can find out. But I doubt that it was recorded, and it is unlikely that anyone remembers."

"Except the one who did it, of course. Hmmm. Is there any way of putting together a list of everyone who *could* have made the suggestion?"

Morrolan looked startled. "Why—yes, that should be possible. I shall look into it immediately."

"Thank you," I said.

"It is nothing."

"How much will that help, Vlad?" asked Aliera after Morrolan had left.

"I don't know," I said carefully. "It's impossible in something like this to tell who's a willing dupe, who's an unwilling dupe, and who might be behind it. But if we can find out who made the recommendation, it'll at least be a start."

She nodded. "What about the Lyorn?"

"I haven't spoken to her yet. But look: I was told that the Lyorn was only there to make sure all the forms were followed. Say they were. There isn't any reason why the Lyorn couldn't have been taken in by whoever fooled Sethra the Younger about the first examination."

"True."

"So, of the people involved, we have: Sethra the Younger, who was duped or involved; the Lyorn, who was duped or involved; Baritt, who was duped or involved and then assassinated; and someone posing as an Athyra, or an Athyra using a false name."

"In other words, we have nothing."

"Right. We have to find out who that 'Athyra' was; she's our only clue to whoever is behind it—if, in fact, she isn't behind it herself."

"Well, Vlad, don't you have the name of the Lyorn noble? Why don't you ask her? She's liable to remember, or at least have written it down—Lyorns write everything down."

"Now there," I said, "is an idea." I considered for a moment. What would Aliera do if . . . "But Lyorns don't like to talk to Jhereg," I said suddenly. "Is there any chance that you can find out for me?"

"What is her name, and where does she live?"

I told her.

"I'll find out for you," she said.

"Thank you."

She bowed to Cawti and me, and left.

"Why did you do that, Vladimir?"

"To find out what Aliera will do about it. If the Lyorn shows up recently dead, we have our answer. If not, we'll see what Aliera says the Lyorn told her." I sighed, and settled back to think. Cawti came up behind me and began rubbing my shoulders. I reached up with both hands and touched hers. She leaned over my head and kissed me upside down, dislodging Loiosh.

"*You two are disgusting.*"

"*Quiet. I'm busy.*"

There was a clap at the door. We sighed and Cawti straightened up.

"Come in," I called.

Norathar came in, death written all over her face. I stood up and glanced at Cawti, whose eyes were locked with Norathar's.

"The examination showed you aren't a Dragon," I suggested.

"Wrong," she said.

"Then what happened?"

"I am now confirmed as a Dragonlord—but not as the heir."

"Oh," I said. "I'm sorry. If you two would rather—"

"It isn't that," she snapped. "They wish to 'observe' me for a while before making me the heir. I have to serve a stint in the Phoenix Guard, to 'prove' myself. As if I have any desire to be Emperor, anyway!"

I shook my head. "Doesn't *any* Dragonlord ever want to be Emperor?"

"No," said Norathar.

"Okay. You're upset that they don't trust you enough to make it immediate?"

"Some. But I found out something else. I'm afraid that it isn't something I can discuss with you, Lord Taltos. But my sister and I—" She stopped, and I guessed that she and Cawti were conversing psionically. After a moment, Norathar turned to me and said, "So you know."

"About why your attack on me failed? And what it means?"

"Yes."

"Yes."

"Then you'll understand why my sister and I must leave for the moment. We have to attend—"

"How did you find out?"

"I was told."

"By whom?"

"I swore not to say."

"Oh."

"Farewell for the—"

"Wait a minute, please. I have to think. There's something, before you go. . . ."

"Make it quick."

I ignored the looks of inquiry Cawti was giving me, and reached out—"*Morrolan! Come back here, quick!*"

"*Why?*"

"*No time. Hurry!*"

And then, "*Aliera, there's trouble. Morrolan's on his way, you should be here, too.*" Whether Aliera was innocent or not, she would want to stop Norathar—I hoped.

Morrolan came bursting into the room, Aliera following by a second or two.

Morrolan's blade was at his side, but Aliera was holding eight feet of glistening black steel. They looked at me.

"What is it, Vlad?" asked Morrolan.

"The Lady Norathar wants to go out Jhereg-hunting."

"So?"

"So the Dragon Council has—"

"This isn't any of your business, Lord Taltos," said Norathar coldly, her hand on the hilt of her blade.

"—accepted her as a Dragon, but—"

Norathar drew her blade. Loiosh hissed and gathered himself on my shoulder. I had a brief glimpse of Cawti, a look of anguish on her face, but then Morrolan's longsword, Blackwand, was in his hand. He gestured with it toward Norathar, and her blade swung and buried itself deeply into a wooden beam against the wall of the library. She looked at Morrolan, wonderment in her eyes.

"My lady," he said, "at Castle Black, I do not allow the killing of my guests except under conditions where they can be revivified. Further, you, as a Dragonlord, should not have to be reminded of treatment of guests."

After a moment, Norathar bowed. "Very well," she said. She wrenched her sword out of the beam and sheathed it with the plain efficiency of a Jhereg, instead of the flash of a Dragonlord. "I'll be leaving then. Let's go, sister."

"Aliera, stop them!"

As I finished "speaking," Morrolan turned to Aliera. "What did you just do?"

"I put a teleport block around Castle Black," she said. "I hope you don't mind."

Norathar's eyes widened, then narrowed to slits. "Lord Morrolan," she said slowly, "I must insist—"

"Oh, for the love of Verra," I said. "Can you at least give me thirty seconds to finish my sentence?"

"Why?"

"Why not?"

She stared at me, but Dragonlords have been trying to stare me down since I was nineteen.

I said, "The Dragon Council wants to observe her for a while, before officially making her the heir. If she goes running off after Jhereg, that'll do it. I felt you two should know, and at least have the chance to talk her out of it before she does something that commits her. That's all. Now, the rest of you argue about it. I'm leaving before someone takes my head off."

I didn't quite run out of the library. I went down to the entryway and found a small sitting room. I helped myself to a glass of cheap wine and quaffed it, thinking dark thoughts.

The bottle was half empty when someone clapped at the door. I ignored it. It was repeated, and I ignored it again. Then the door opened. My scowl died when I saw that it was Cawti. She sat down.

"How did you find me?"

"Loiosh."

"Oh. What happened?"

"Norathar has agreed to wait two days before doing anything, same as Aliera."

"Great."

"Vladimir?"

"Yes?"

"Why did you do it?"

"Do what? Stop her?"

"Yes. Don't you want someone to take Laris out?"

"She isn't going to have any better luck finding him than I will. The same goes for you and for Aliera."

"But, still, with more of us looking . . ." She let the sentence die, and I didn't pick it up again. After a minute or so, I remembered my manners and poured her some cheap wine, too. She sipped it, delicately, thumb and forefinger around the stem, little finger off in space somewhere, just like at Court. And she kept her eyes fixed on me the whole time.

"Why, Vladimir?" she repeated.

"I don't know. Why ruin her chances for nothing?"

"Who is she to you?"

"Your partner."

"Oh."

She set the glass down and stood up. She walked over to my chair and looked down at me for a moment. Then she dropped to one knee, took my right hand in hers, kissed it, and rubbed her cheek against it. I opened my mouth to make some smart remark about was I supposed to pat her head, or what, but Loiosh brought his head around and smacked me in the larynx so I couldn't speak.

Then, still holding my hand, Cawti looked up at me and said, "Vladimir, it would make me the happiest of women if you would consent to be my husband."

About three hundred years later I said, "What?"

"I want to marry you," she said.

I stared at her. Finally I burst out with "Why?"

She stared back at me. "Because I love you."

I shook my head. "I love you, too, Cawti. You know that. But you can't want to marry me."

"Why?"

"Because, damn it, I'm going to be dead in a few days!"

"You said Laris was bluffing."

"Maybe he is, but he won't be if I keep coming after him. And whatever game he's playing, he *has* to make it real sooner or later."

"He won't get you," she said calmly, and I almost believed her.

I kept staring at her. Finally I said, "All right, I'll tell you what. When this business with Laris is over, if I'm alive, and you still want to, I mean, well, um, of course I will. I, oh, Deathsgate, Cawti. I don't know what to say."

"Thank you, lord."

"By the Lords of Judgment, get off the floor! You're making me feel like—I don't know what."

She calmly got up off her knees and stood before me. Then she broke into a grin, jumped, and landed on my lap. The chair went over backwards and we ended up on the floor in a tangle of limbs and clothes. Loiosh barely escaped in time.

Two hours and three bottles of wine later, we staggered back up to the library. Morrolan was alone there. I was just sober enough not to want him to know how drunk we were, so, somewhat regretfully, I did a quick sobering spell.

He looked us over, raised an eyebrow, and said, "Come in."

"Thank you," I said. I turned to Cawti, and noticed that she'd given herself the same treatment. A shame.

"Will you two be staying this evening?"

Cawti looked at me. I nodded. "I still need to check over that list of Baritt's descendants. Which reminds me, did you find out who might have recommended the Athyra?"

"One of my people is compiling the list. It should be ready by this evening some time."

"Good. I asked Aliera to find out about the Lyorn. Do you know if she did?"

"She is speaking to Norathar at the moment; I think they're attempting to determine how to locate this Laris person."

"Oh. Well, tomorrow, maybe."

"Yes. I'm having my dinner brought to me in the small dining room. I believe Aliera, Sethra, and Lady Norathar will be joining me. Would the two of you care to also?"

I looked at Cawti. "We'd be delighted," she said.

"Excellent. And, afterwards, you can join the party in the main dining room and continue your investigation."

"Yes," I agreed. "Maybe I can even avoid having any words with your Athyra friend."

"Athyra friend? I don't believe there have been any Athyra nobles present for some time."

"You know who I mean: the Sorceress in Chartreuse, or whatever."

Morrolan smiled. "The Sorceress in Green. I'll admit she looks like one, though."

Something went off in the back of my head. "She isn't?" I asked. "What is she then?"

"House of the Yendi," said Morrolan.

15

"I imagine he's being well paid."

"WHAT IS IT, VLAD? Why are you staring at me?"

"I can't believe what I just heard. A Yendi? Are you sure?"

"Of course I'm sure. What is it?"

"Morrolan, how many Yendi does it take to sharpen a sword?"

He looked at me through slitted eyes. "Tell me," he said.

"Three. One to sharpen the sword, and one to confuse the issue."

"I see." He chuckled a bit. "Not bad. What has that to do with our situation?"

"I don't know exactly, but—wherever you find a Yendi, you find a plot. A devious plot. Twisted, confusing, just the kind of thing we're facing. I don't know what it's about, but she—the Sorceress in Green—has been hanging around all of us since things started. She's been near you, near me, near Aliera, and indirectly near Norathar and Cawti and Sethra. All of us. This can't be an accident.

"And if that weren't enough, she looks like an Athyra. We're sitting here trying to find an Athyra who doesn't exist, and now we find a Yendi who resembles one and who's been around the whole time. And you don't think she has something to do with all this?"

"I see what you mean," he said. "I think I shall speak to her, and—"

"No!"

"I beg your pardon?"

"Don't speak to her. Don't let her know, yet. The only advantage we have is that she doesn't know we're suspicious. We don't dare lose that until we know what she's after."

"Hmmm. It is axiomatic that no one but a Yendi can unravel a Yendi's scheme."

"Maybe. But to paraphrase Lord Lairon e'N'vaar, maybe I use different axioms."

He thought about it for a while, then said, "All right, Vlad. What's your plan?"

"I don't have one yet. First, I want to think over what we know and see if I can make some sense of it."

"All right."

"Cawti, why don't you find Norathar and Aliera?"

She nodded. Morrolan said, "You might need help," and the two of them went off.

I sat pondering for about half an hour, until the four of them returned, along with Sethra.

"Well," said Aliera, "what have you figured out?"

"Nothing," I said. "On the other hand, I haven't given up, either."

"Great," said Norathar.

"Sit down," I suggested. They all pulled up chairs around me. I felt like I was back in the office, with my enforcers sitting around waiting for orders.

"Vladimir?"

"Yes, Cawti?"

"Morrolan told Aliera about the Sorceress in Green. I didn't think to warn him not to."

"Damn. All right. So either the Sorceress is warned, or Aliera isn't involved. I'm beginning to doubt that Aliera is behind this in any case. We'll see."

I said, "First of all, Lady Norathar, can—"

"You can drop the 'Lady,' Vlad."

I was startled. "Thank you," I said. I saw Cawti flash her a smile, and I understood. "All right, Norathar, are you sure you can't tell us how you found out what Laris did?"

"Yes," she said.

"All right. But think about it. If it was the Sorceress in Green—"

"It wasn't."

"Whoever it is, that person might be working with the Sorceress in Green, or perhaps is being used by her. I wish you could tell us who it is."

"Sorry. But I don't think it would help."

Cawti said, "Do you really think the Sorceress in Green is behind it?"

"Let's just say it's a real good guess. We won't know for sure who's behind it until we know what they're after."

Cawti nodded.

I continued. "Let's try to put the events in order. First, just before the Interregnum, someone decides that he doesn't want Lord K'laiyer to take the Orb. Maybe this someone is the Sorceress in Green, or the Sorceress in Green is working for him, okay?"

There were nods from around the room.

"Okay, the first thing he—or she—does is make it look like Norathar is a bastard. Of course, when confronted with this, K'laiyer fights, and, naturally, when fighting Sethra, loses. During the battle, they make sure K'laiyer ends up dead. This makes Adron the heir. So far, so good. Either that is what they wanted, or they didn't have time to deal with him. Because then we have Adron's Disaster, and two-hundred-some years of Interregnum. Still, nothing happens. Afterwards, Morrolan is the heir. *Still* nothing happens."

I looked at them again. They were watching me closely. I continued. "For over two hundred and forty years after the Interregnum, nothing. So whoever is behind it, if he is still around, doesn't object to Morrolan. But then, three years or so ago, Aliera shows up. Within a year Baritt, who is probably one of the conspirators, is assassinated. Two years after that, Norathar is set up, killed, revivified, and is suddenly going to be the heir. That's where we are as I see it."

Either Aliera hadn't caught any implication against her, or she was a fine actress. She seemed deep in thought, but not otherwise affected by what I'd been saying. Norathar said, "Vlad, is there any chance that the Sorceress in Green could have known Aliera well enough to know that we'd be brought back?"

I said, "Uh . . . you mean, then, that even *that* was part of her plan? I don't know." I turned to Aliera.

She chewed her lip for a moment, then shrugged. "Anything is possible with a Yendi," she said.

"Not that," said Morrolan. We turned to him. "You are forgetting that I was there, too. If you are supposing that she set it up so that Aliera would kill, then revivify, Norathar, then she must have known that I would be with Aliera. I will not believe that she could predict exactly where we would have been standing when we teleported, and if I had happened to be closer to Norathar than Aliera was, I'd have attacked, and I'd have used Blackwand."

Norathar paled as he said this. I swallowed and felt a little queasy myself. If Norathar had been killed by Blackwand, nothing and no one could have re-vivified her, nor would she have been reborn, as Dragaerans believe happens to anyone who isn't brought to the Paths of the Dead, and some who are. I wondered if Aliera could have arranged that. Or was Morrolan in on it too?

"You're getting paranoid, boss."

"Occupational hazard, Loiosh."

I cleared my throat and said, "I think we can safely assume that Norathar was expected to die permanently."

The others agreed.

"Now," I said, "let us turn to Laris. He may be well hidden, and well pro-tected, but he is certainly losing money and taking big chances by not killing me. Why?"

"I imagine," said Cawti, "that he's being well paid."

"He'd have to be paid a lot to take that big a risk."

Cawti shrugged. "Perhaps he owes her a favor, or something."

"A big favor. Besides, I'm guessing that he killed Baritt as repayment of . . . wait a minute."

They all looked at me. Finally, Morrolan said, "Yes, Vlad?"

I turned to Cawti. "What do you know of Laris's history?"

"A fair bit. When I was studying you, I came across references to him from time to time, back when you both worked for Welok the Blade. And of course, I hear things now and then."

"Did you hear that he ran the war for Welok against the Hook?"

She and Norathar nodded.

"I was involved," said Norathar.

"Why did Welok let him run the war? And how did he win? He didn't have any experience at the time."

Cawti and Norathar studied me. "The Sorceress in Green?" asked Norathar.

I said, "It sure looks like he had something on Welok, or else knew how to get around him. What if our friend the sorceress maneuvered for him, and helped him with the war?"

Cawti said, "You think she's running the war against you, too?"

"Maybe. I met Laris, and he impressed me. I don't think he's a dupe, but I could be wrong. On the other hand, it's possible that the sorceress has something on him and can make him do what she wants. Especially if she can arrange for him to win in the end anyway, or tells him she can."

"If she has something on him," said Norathar, "why doesn't he just kill her?"

As a Jhereg, she was still a Dragon.

"Any of a number of reasons," I replied. "He might not know who she is. The hold might not disappear with her death. Maybe he can't reach her. I don't know."

"Any idea what that hold might be?" asked Cawti.

I frowned. "Could be anything. My first guess is that he's the one who finalized Baritt, and the sorceress has proof—easy enough if she had him do it, say as a favor in exchange for her help against the Hook."

"I can see it," said Cawti. Norathar concurred.

"This speculation is quite entertaining," said Morrolan, "but I fail to see where it helps."

"We're trying to understand what they're doing," I said. "Every detail we get helps put it together."

"Maybe," he said. "But I should like to hear your opinion on why the Sorceress in Green would do all this."

"Do what?" I asked.

"I'm not certain precisely what she's doing—"

"Exactly."

He nodded, slowly. "All right. I see."

I turned to Sethra, who hadn't said a word the entire time. "Have you any ideas, or guesses?"

"Not exactly," she said slowly. "But I'm beginning to suspect that the answer lies mostly before the Interregnum, the first time this conspiracy acted. What were they after, exactly?"

"Yes," I said slowly. "We should at least look into it." I glanced at Norathar; she looked like her teeth hurt. Well, I could hardly blame her.

"The motive for that one," said Cawti, "seems clear at least: it was an attempt to gain the Orb."

I shook my head. "I've been told that no Dragon wants the Orb."

"What about Adron?" she asked, looking at Aliera.

Aliera smiled. "A point," she said. "But my father didn't really want the Orb, he was forced to make a try for it out of a sense of duty."

I stared at her. "Wait a minute. Did your father know the Sorceress in Green?"

Aliera looked startled. "I . . . believe they were acquainted, yes. But if you're thinking that my father was the one behind the whole thing—"

"I wouldn't say I *think* so; I'm just checking into it."

She glared at me, and her eyes turned to steely gray. "If you feel you must."

"I feel I must. How well acquainted were they?"

"They often saw each other, and Sethra, at Dzur Mountain. Ask Sethra. She knows better than I."

I turned to Sethra. "Well?"

"I doubt," she said, "that Adron was behind a conspiracy of this type. It isn't his style. Besides, he and Baritt got along quite well."

"That proves nothing," I said. "Or, if anything, it makes the case stronger against him. How well did he get along with the Sorceress in Green?"

Sethra closed her eyes, as if having trouble remembering. Then she said, "We all got along in those days. Adron was never especially close to the sorceress, though."

"So," I said, "if Adron felt it his duty to take the Orb, he might have felt it was his duty to make sure *he* was the next Dragon Emperor."

"I don't believe it," snapped Aliera, becoming more angry by the minute. I started laughing. She stood up, glaring. "Mind letting me in on the joke, Vlad?"

"I just can't help but see how funny it is. We're talking about a guy who, trying to take the Orb, blew up half the Dragaeran Empire, created a Sea of Amorphia where the biggest city in the Empire used to be, killed I don't know how many millions of people, and you're upset because I'm wondering if he faked a bit of evidence to make his path a little easier."

Cawti started laughing, too. None of the others seemed to think it was funny. That made it even funnier, and, for a moment, I almost had hysterics. Aliera said, "That's different. This involved tricking Sethra, who was a friend. There is such a thing as honor in the House of the Dragon."

Strangely, that sobered me up. It wasn't any less funny, but, in a way, it was sad, too. Presently Cawti got the better of her mirth. I said, "All right, Aliera. Maybe he didn't do it himself, but the Sorceress in Green could have done it without his knowledge, couldn't she?"

Aliera sat down again and sniffed. "I doubt it."

"All right, then, how did Adron and Norathar's father, K'laiyer, get along?"

Aliera shrugged and looked away haughtily. I turned to Sethra. She looked uncomfortable, but said, "They had disagreements, I remember. They weren't bitter enemies, by any means, but they did disagree."

"Of course they disagreed!" said Aliera. "My father felt the Dragons had to take the throne, K'laiyer didn't."

Sethra nodded. "That was pretty much it," she said. "They didn't agree on how immediate the problem was."

"What problem?"

"The decadence of the Emperor. Phoenix Emperors always become decadent at the end of their reign, except every seventeenth Cycle, when we have a reborn Phoenix, such as Zerika. Since that was at the end of the Great Cycle—seventeen Cycles—it was especially bad. The Empire appeared to be falling apart, there were Easterners making encroachments on the eastern border, and Adron felt the Emperor should either step down or be removed."

"And K'laiyer didn't?"

"No. I remember him pointing out to me that the 'encroachments' were into territories where most of the population was made up of Easterners anyway. He said that it was basically their land, and he saw no reason why they shouldn't have it back."

"I think I would've liked the guy," I said.

"Maybe," said Sethra. "He was likeable enough. And he would have made a good Emperor, I think."

"It sounds to me," I said, looking at Aliera, "as if Adron was—"

"I believe it is time to dine," said Morrolan. "Perhaps we should continue this after the meal?"

I smiled a bit, nodded, stood, and offered Cawti my arm. She took it, and we headed toward the small dining room. I hoped this meal would be easier to digest than the last one with this crowd.

Which set me to remembering that meal. Which set me to remembering the days I had spent in Dzur Mountain. Most of the memories were quite pleasant.

But I remembered one conversation. . . . *That* couldn't have anything to do with this. Could it? The whole thing, just to accomplish *that*? But then, Dragaerans are Dragaerans.

"Wait a minute."

Morrolan sighed and turned around. "Yes, Vlad?"

"I just—"

"Can it wait?"

"Uh . . . let's go in and sit down while I think about it." My mind was racing like a cat-centaur. I think I bumped into a few people and walls as I found my place.

I noticed that we were sitting in exactly the same positions that we'd been in before. A servant brought wine. I drank some without tasting it.

"All right, Vlad," said Morrolan, in a resigned tone of voice. "What is it?"

"I think I might have just figured out who's behind this, and why."

I suddenly had everyone's attention.

"Go on," said Morrolan.

"Verra, but this is convoluted. But, with the Sorceress in Green doing the planning, how could it not be?"

"Well, who is it?"

"Let me put it this way: I'm going to guess that, between two and three years ago, the Sorceress in Green had a falling out with a certain individual she'd been friendly with up until then."

I turned to Sethra. "Am I right?"

She looked puzzled. Then, suddenly, her nostrils flared and her eyes widened. After a moment, she nodded.

"That's it, then."

"What, Vlad?" said Morrolan, still calm.

"You're enjoying keeping everyone in suspense, aren't you, boss?"

"Shut up, Loiosh."

"Okay, I'll put it this way: Suppose Norathar has just been killed. By Morrolan and Aliera. End of problem. So, the correct heir to the throne is out of the way, right? Who's next?"

"Aliera," said Morrolan.

"Right. But information comes out that she was involved in a Jhereg war. Then what?"

"Mmmmm," said Morrolan. "The council might—"

"Assume further that the council is being manipulated. Maybe just a bit, maybe a lot, but there are strings being pulled."

"All right, so Aliera is out as heir, if that's what you want."

"Right. And, by the same logic, Morrolan, so are you. Who's next?"

They looked at each other. "I don't know," said Aliera at last.

"Neither do I. But, in a sense, it doesn't matter. I'm sure the Sorceress in Green knows. Whoever it is probably isn't even involved—it's merely someone whose politics are known. No Dragon wants to be heir, you said. What does every Dragon want to be?"

"Warlord," said Aliera, with no hesitation.

"Right. Morrolan, why don't you send for that list, if it's ready now."

"But . . . all right." He concentrated for a moment. "It's on the way."

"What list?" asked Sethra.

"I asked Morrolan to collect the names of everyone who might have suggested the Athyra wizard who helped on Norathar's scan.

"Now," I continued, "if Morrolan or Aliera were Emperor, each would have appointed the other Warlord, so you both had to go. Norathar had been harmless before, but with things moving as they were, it was safest to eliminate her, too.

"Before the Interregnum, there was an obvious choice for Warlord if Adron were Emperor, so—"

"Who?" said Cawti.

"I'll get to it. Anyway, without his knowledge, it was arranged for him to become the heir. When he failed, the Phoenix remained in power, so there was no immediate problem. Then Morrolan became the heir, which was fine—"

"It was?" said Morrolan.

"Yes—until Aliera suddenly arrived. Then, the person who *would* have been Warlord under you was out. And, worse than that, Aliera's politics were wrong. You both had to go. Baritt, who had been willing to help until then, drew the line at this. He had to go, too.

"So, the Warlord-to-be and the Sorceress in Green, who was a good friend as well as being a Yendi, laid new plans. The first thing they did was pretend to quarrel, so they wouldn't be linked in anyone's mind.

"The plan took two years to mature, which is quick work for a Yendi. The fact that you two became friendly with me, and that I moved up in the Jhereg so quickly, must have helped quite a bit.

"First, they were going to kill Norathar."

"Why?" said Morrolan.

"Because Aliera was looking everywhere for someone to be Dragon Heir instead of her. She wouldn't deliberately do something to get herself disqualified by the council; she wouldn't consider it honorable. But she was trying to find someone with 'purer genes,' or whatever it is the Dragons look for. That would have led her, eventually, to the e'Lanyas."

"It did," said Aliera. "I was trying to find out what had happened to Norathar already, just on the chance that she could lead me to another relative."

I nodded. "So they had to kill her, because, as soon as Aliera found her, she'd realize that she was, in fact, pure."

"All right," said Morrolan. "Go on."

"The idea," I said, "was to kill Norathar and discredit the two of you for helping me. I suspect that someone slipped somewhere, and you two were supposed to have been alerted sooner. I don't think they wanted to cut it as close as they did. But it worked anyway—until you, Aliera, spoiled everything by revivifying Norathar. Then they had to improvise. The first thing they did was to test Norathar, just to see if she could, in fact, be of use to them as Emperor."

"How?" asked Norathar.

"Don't you remember the Sorceress in Green asking you how you felt about invasion plans for the East? I didn't think anything of it at the time, but—"

"You're right!"

"Yes. And if you had said you were in favor, they would have stopped right there, finished me off, and found a way to convince you to make the right person Warlord. Since your politics were wrong, they tipped you off about Laris so you'd go rushing off to kill him—he's expendable—and disqualify yourself as heir."

Cawti shook her head. "But why continue the fake assassination attempts, Vladimir?"

In answer, I turned to Norathar. "If there hadn't been two failed attempts on my life, would you have believed that you'd been set up, even after you were told?"

Her eyes narrowed, then she shook her head. Cawti nodded.

At that point, right on cue, a servant arrived, holding a piece of paper. He gave it to Morrolan.

Morrolan glanced at it. "Find," I said, "the name of the person whom you would have named Warlord if Aliera had not shown up."

He did, and his mouth dropped open. Sethra leaned past Aliera and took the list from Morrolan's limp hand. She glanced at it, nodded, and threw it down onto the middle of the table, her eyes cold as the blade of Iceflame.

"I would rather," she said, "that she had tried to kill me."

There were nine names on the list. The third one down was Sethra the Younger.

16

"Vladimir and I will just watch."

W E ALL SAT THERE looking at each other; then Morrolan cleared his throat.
"Shall we eat?" he said.

"Why don't we?" said Sethra.

Morrolan gave the necessary orders. I have no idea what appeared, but I must have eaten it, because I have no memory of being hungry later.

"Will they be here tonight?" asked Norathar at one point.

Morrolan said, "I would expect them to be." There was no need to ask who "they" were.

"Then perhaps we should plan to meet with them. Do you agree, sister?" Norathar asked Cawti.

"Not here," I said. "Morrolan forbids the mistreatment of his guests."

"Thank you, Vlad," said Morrolan.

"You're welcome."

"But surely," said Aliera, "under the circumstances—"

"No," said Morrolan.

Before another storm could erupt, I said, "We should still verify all of our guesses before we do anything else."

Norathar looked at me. "You mean you aren't sure?"

"I'm sure. But it should still be verified."

"How?"

"I've a way. It may take a little time. But then, we're eating anyway."

"Fentor."

"Yes, milord?"

"Have you tracked down the ownership of those flats, yet?"

"No, milord."

"Maybe it'll help if I give you a couple of names that might tie into them. Sethra the Younger, and the Sorceress in Green."

"I'll check into it, milord."

"Very good. Get hold of me as soon as you have something."

"Yes, milord."

"With luck," I said aloud, "we'll know something soon."

"Vladimir," said Cawti, "how should we approach them?"

"Yes," said Morrolan dryly. "You wouldn't want her to turn you into a newt."

"I'll get better," I said. "In any case we can't attack them here if we want to do anything permanent to them. Does anyone know where the sorceress lives?"

"One never knows where a Yendi lives," said Sethra.

"Yeah. One possibility is Laris. If I can arrange to meet with him, I might be able to show him that his partners are stabbing him in the back. Maybe he'll help us set them up."

"But aren't you still going to try to kill him?" asked Aliera. "If you aren't, I am."

"And I," said Norathar.

"Sure I am, but *he* doesn't have to know that."

Aliera's eyes narrowed. "I will have nothing to do with such a plan."

"Nor will I," said Morrolan.

"Nor I," said Sethra.

"Nor I," said Norathar.

I sighed. "Yeah, I know. You insist that everything be honorable, upright, and in the open. It isn't fair to take advantage of someone, just because he's been trying to assassinate you and conspiring against your friends, right?"

"Right," said Aliera, with a perfectly straight face.

"You Dragons amaze me," I said. "You claim it's unfair to attack someone from behind, but somehow it's a fair fight even when it's against someone both of you know is weaker, less experienced, and less skilled than you. That's not taking advantage? What rubbish."

"Vlad," said Morrolan, "it's a matter of—"

"Never mind. I'll think of something—wait a minute, I think I'm getting that verification now."

I had a brief conversation with Fentor, then turned back to them. "It's confirmed," I said. "Sethra the Younger, through intermediaries, owns a row of flats that were used as part of the setup for the attempt on me by Cawti and her friend the Dragonlord."

"Very well," said Morrolan. "How do we proceed?"

"It is vain to use subtlety against a Yendi," said Sethra. "Make it something simple."

"Another axiom?"

She smiled coldly. "And I'll deal with Sethra the Younger myself."

"It's simple enough," I said a while later, "but Cawti and I aren't at our best right after a teleport."

"Cawti and you," said Aliera, "will have no need to do anything."

I looked at Cawti.

"I don't mind," she said. "Vladimir and I will just watch."

I nodded. I intended to do more than that, but there was no need to tell them about it. Except—

"Excuse me, Morrolan, but just to be safe, may I borrow a Morganti knife?"

His brows furrowed. "If you wish."

He concentrated for a moment. Soon a servant appeared with a wooden box. I opened it, and saw a small, silver-hilted dagger in a leather-covered sheath. I took it partway out and at once recognized the feel of a Morganti weapon. I replaced it in the sheath and slipped it into my cloak.

"Thank you," I said.

"It is nothing."

We stood up and looked at each other. No one seemed able to find anything suitable to say, so we just stepped out of the small dining room and walked over to the central part of the castle, where the main dining room was.

We walked in and spotted Sethra the Younger almost right away. Loiosh left my shoulder and began flying around the room, staying high enough to be unobtrusive. (Morrolan's banquet hall had ceilings that were forty feet high.) Morrolan approached Sethra the Younger and spoke quietly with her.

"Found her, boss. Northeast corner."

"Good work."

I gave this information to Morrolan, who began guiding Sethra the Younger that way. The rest of us converged on the Sorceress in Green; we reached her at about the same time Morrolan did. She looked at him, looked at Sethra, then looked at us. There was, perhaps, the smallest widening of her eyes.

Morrolan said, "Sethra the Younger, Sorceress, for the next seventeen hours you are not welcome in my home. After that time, you may return." He bowed.

They looked at each other, then at the rest of us. Others in the hall began to watch, sensing that something unusual was occurring.

Sethra the Younger started to say something, but stopped—the sorceress had probably told her psionically that it was pointless to argue. The two of them bowed.

Sethra Lavode stepped up behind her namesake and put a hand on her arm, above the elbow. They looked at each other, but their expressions were unreadable.

Then, abruptly, the Sorceress in Green was gone. Loiosh returned to my shoulder, and I looked at Aliera. Her eyes were closed in concentration. Then Sethra the Younger disappeared. Sethra Lavode left with her.

"What will she do to her?" I asked Morrolan.

He shrugged and didn't answer.

Presently Aliera spoke, her eyes still closed. "She knows I'm tracing her. If she stops to break the trace, we'll have time to catch up with her."

"She'll find the most advantageous place she can," I said.

"Yes," said Aliera.

"Let her," said Norathar.

Cawti swept her hair back with both hands just as I was adjusting my cloak. We smiled at each other, as we realized what the gestures meant. Then—

"Now!" said Aliera.

There was a wrenching in my bowels, and Castle Black vanished.

*   *   *

The first thing that hit me was the heat—an agony of flames. I started to scream, but the pain went away before I had the chance. We seemed to be standing in the heart of a fire. From somewhere off to my left I heard a dry voice say, "Quick work, Aliera."

I recognized the voice as belonging to the Sorceress in Green. She continued: "You may as well dispense with your teleport block; I'm not going anywhere."

It occurred to me that she must have prepared herself while teleporting, then brought us into a furnace. Apparently, Aliera had figured it out and put a protection spell around us before we had time to be incinerated.

"You all right, Loiosh?"

"Fine, boss."

Then the flames surged around us and went out. We were in a room, about twenty feet on a side, with blackened walls. We were standing in ash that came above our ankles. The Sorceress in Green stood before us, her eyes as cold as the fires had been hot. In her hand was a plain wooden staff.

"You had best leave," she said coolly. "I am surrounded by my own people, and you can hardly do anything to me before they get here."

I glanced at Aliera.

The Sorceress in Green gestured with her staff, and the wall behind her collapsed upon itself. On the other side of it, I could see about thirty Dragaerans, all armed.

"Last chance," said the sorceress, smiling.

I coughed. "Are all Yendi so melodramatic?" I inquired.

The sorceress gave a signal, and they stepped onto the ash.

Aliera gestured, and we were surrounded by flames again for a moment; then they died.

"Nice try, my dear," said the sorceress. "But I'd thought of that already."

"So I see," said Aliera. She turned to Morrolan. "Do you want her, or the troops?"

"It is your choice."

"I'll take her, then."

"Very well," said Morrolan, and drew Blackflame. I saw the faces of the men and women facing us as they realized that he was holding a Morganti blade, and one of power that, beyond doubt, none of them had encountered before. Morrolan calmly walked up to them.

"Remember," I told Cawti, "we're just here to watch."

She flashed me a nervous smile.

Then there was a flicker of motion to my side, and I saw Norathar charge for the sorceress, blade swinging. Aliera hissed and leapt after her. A spell of some kind must have gone off behind me, because I heard a dull boom and smoke came billowing past.

The sorceress slipped past the front line of her troops and raised her staff. Fires leapt from it toward Norathar and Aliera, but Aliera held her hand up and they fizzled out.

Morrolan, Norathar, and Aliera hit the front line at the same instant. Blackwand cut a throat, swept across the chest of the next guard, and, with the same motion, buried itself high in the side of a third. Morrolan slipped to his right like a cat before anyone even struck at him, withdrawing Blackwand, then sliced open two bellies. He parried a cut and impaled the attacker's throat, then stepped back, facing full forward, slightly on his toes, blade held at head height and pointing toward his enemies. In his left hand was a long dagger. The room was filled with the sound of screams, and those who'd been watching Morrolan turned pale.

I saw three more guards at Norathar's feet. Aliera, meanwhile, was wielding her eight-foot greatsword like a toy, flipping it back and forth amid their ranks. She had accounted for five so far.

Then, incredibly, the dead guards began to stand up—even the ones slain by Blackwand. I looked at the sorceress, and saw a look of profound concentration on her face.

"Hold them!" cried Aliera. She stepped back a pace, held her blade with her right hand, and stabbed the air with her left. The corpses who'd been trying to rise stopped. The sorceress gestured with her staff. They continued. Aliera stabbed the air. They stopped. They started again.

Then Aliera did something else, and the sorceress cried out as a blue glow began in front of her. After a moment it went away, but I could see perspiration rolling down her face.

Morrolan and Norathar had ignored all of this, and by now more than half of the enemy had fallen.

I spoke to Cawti out of the corner of my mouth. "Should we do something?"

"Why? They're Dragonlords; they enjoy this kind of thing. Let them do it."

"There is one thing I'm going to have to do, though. And pretty soon, it looks like."

"What?"

About then Norathar broke through the line. The sorceress cried out and swung her staff, and Norathar fell over, clutching the air.

Cawti moved before I could do anything. She got through to her friend, somehow, and knelt by her side.

The ones who'd been fighting Norathar turned to Aliera, and she had to defend herself again. I took out a pair of throwing knives and, just to test, threw them at the sorceress. Naturally, they veered away from her when they got close.

I heard Morrolan curse and saw that his left arm hung uselessly at his side, and that there was red over the black of his cloak.

Aliera was still locked in some kind of struggle with the sorceress while holding off three guards. There was a sudden flurry near her as two more of them came at her. There was an impossible tangle of metal, and three of the guards were down. Aliera was still up, but there was a knife sticking out of her low on her back, and a broadsword actually through her body, just to the right of the spine, front to back, above the waist. She seemed to be ignoring it; I guess sorcery is also good for overcoming shock. But no matter how skilled a sorceress she was, her gown was ruined.

Norathar seemed to be alive, but dazed. This, it appeared, would be the best chance I had. I drew two fighting knives, then ran forward as fast as I could through ash up to my calves. When I reached the fighters, I watched Aliera closely, then ducked under a swing. I left the knives in the stomachs of two fighters who had no ability to deal with an Easterner rolling past them; then I was beyond the line, about four feet from the sorceress. Spellbreaker was in my hand before I stood up, and I swung it in front of me.

She had seen me, of course, and greeted me with a gesture of her staff. I felt a tingling in my arm. I screamed, and fell over backward.

"Vladimir!"

"Stay there!"

I opened my eyes and saw that the sorceress had turned away. I smoothly got to my feet, drew the Morganti dagger Morrolan had lent me, came up behind her, and brought Spellbreaker crashing down on the back of her head.

The effect on her was minimal, since she'd had some sort of shield around her; she jerked a bit and turned around. But, while the shield had prevented the chain from hitting her, the chain had brought the shield down. Before she could do anything there was the point of a Morganti dagger against her throat.

Morrolan and Aliera were dealing with the last of her defenders, but Morrolan seemed unsteady on his feet and Aliera's lips were clamped tight with the concentration of holding herself together. Cawti was helping Norathar to her feet. I didn't have much time, so I spoke quickly.

"This fight isn't any of my business, and I'll get out of the way if you give me what I want. But if you don't tell me where Laris is, I'll cut your throat— with this. And if you warn him, I'll be after you as long as I live."

She didn't even hesitate.

"He's on the top floor of a warehouse on Pier Street. Two buildings east of the corner of Pier and One-Claw, on the south side of the street."

Shows you how much loyalty you can expect from the House of the Yendi. "Thank you," I said, and backed away, still holding the dagger and Spellbreaker.

She turned away from me, apparently taking me at my word. She did something that was probably putting her defenses back up. At that moment, however, Kieron's greatsword, in the hands of Aliera e'Kieron, swept the head from the last of the defenders.

Morrolan stepped forward, and a black streak came from the point of Blackwand and struck the sorceress. This, I was told later, took her defenses down again. And before she could do anything else, there was a sweep from Norathar's blade and the sorceress's staff went flying—and her right hand with it.

She cried out and dropped to her knees, and it was in that position that Norathar impaled her, directly through the chest.

There was dead silence in the room. The Sorceress in Green stared up at

Norathar with a look of complete disbelief on her face. Then blood came from her mouth and she fell in a heap at the feet of the Sword of the Jhereg.

Cawti came up next to me. I nodded toward the three of them, standing around the body.

"Honor," I muttered, "in the House of the Dragon."

Aliera collapsed. Cawti squeezed my arm.

We returned to Castle Black, leaving the body of the Sorceress in Green where it was. I helped myself to a large glass of brandy, which I despise, but it's stronger than wine and I didn't want to suggest Piarran Mist; somehow this didn't feel like a time to celebrate.

"She was quite an accomplished sorceress," said Aliera weakly, from the couch where the Necromancer was working on her. There were nods from around the room.

"Vlad," said Morrolan, whose arm was in a sling, "what was it that you did to her, and why?"

"She had some information I wanted," I explained. "I got it."

"And then you let her go?"

I shrugged. "You said you didn't need my help."

"I see." I noticed Cawti holding a grin behind her hand. I slipped her a wink. Morrolan asked, "What was the information?"

"Do you remember that I'm in the middle of a war? Laris was backed by her, but he still has the resources to hurt me. He's going to find out that she's dead very soon. When he does, he'll start coming after me for real—I have to make sure the war is over before he does. I figured that she knew where Laris is hiding. I hope she wasn't lying."

"I see."

Cawti turned to me. "Shall we finish it up, then?"

I snorted. "Do you think it'll be that easy?"

"Yes."

I thought about it. "You're right. It will be." I closed my eyes for a moment, just to make sure there wasn't anything I'd forgotten.

"*Kragar.*"

"*Hello, Vlad.*"

"*How's business?*"

"*A little better.*"

"*Good. Get hold of the Bitch Patrol. In exactly two and a half hours, I want a teleport block to prevent anyone from leaving a certain warehouse.*" I told him where it was.

"*Got it, boss.*"

"*Good. In exactly one-half hour, I want the following people in the office: Shoen, Sticks, Glowing, Narvane, N'aal, Smiley, and Chimov.*"

"*Uh . . . that's all?*"

"*Don't be funny.*"

"*Have we got something, Vlad?*"

"Yeah. We've got something. And I don't want any mistakes. This ought to be quick, painless, and easy. So get everyone there, and make sure the sorceress you find is competent."

"Gotcha, boss."

The contact was broken.

Cawti and I stood up. "Well, thank you for the entertainment," I said, "but I'm afraid we have to be on our way."

Norathar bit her lip. "If there's anything I can do . . ."

I looked at her for a moment, then I bowed low. "Thank you, Norathar, and I mean that sincerely. But no. I think, for the first time in months, everything is under control."

We left them and went down to the entryway, where one of Morrolan's people teleported us back to my office. This time I made sure to warn them we were coming.

17

"You what?"

NOW, I SUPPOSE, YOU expect me to tell you how I caught up with Laris after a long chase through the streets of Adrilankha, cornered him at last, how he fought like a dzur and I barely managed to kill him before he did me in. Right? Crap.

There were only two things that could have gone wrong. One, the Sorceress in Green might have lied about where Laris was, and two, she might have had time to warn him. But, in both cases, why? To the sorceress, he was merely a tool. And, since we'd discovered what they were up to, he was no longer a useful tool.

I didn't really think the Sorceress in Green had had time to warn Laris before Norathar finished her. And, if she had lied about where he was, there was no harm done. So I explained my plan to everyone in my office, which took about half an hour. I did make one point worth mentioning: "If anyone here has the idea that he can do well for himself by telling Laris about this, he can forget it. Laris had a backer; the backer is dead. Right now, we're holding nothing but flat stones, and he has nothing but round ones. So don't try to be clever."

I rummaged around my bottom-left drawer until I found a suitable weapon— a stiletto with a thin handle and a seven-inch blade. I put it into my belt on the right side. We sat around waiting for another half-hour, then Shoen and Chimov got up and slipped out the door. The rest of us waited ten minutes more, then stood.

"Luck, boss," said Kragar.

"Thanks."

Loiosh flew high above us as we set out toward Malak Circle. Cawti was leading. Sticks and Glowbug were to my right and left, and the others were walking in front and back.

We reached the circle and jogged over to Pier. We had almost reached Silversmith when I received a message from Shoen.

"He has four outside, boss. Two at the door, two making rounds."

"Okay. I'll send help."

"Thanks."

"Narvane and Smiley, run up ahead. Shoen is in charge of the operation. You have five minutes to get set up."

They ran off while the rest of us slowed to a casual stroll, hardly moving at all.

"*Still clear, boss.*"

"*Okay.*"

Cawti looked back at me and nodded. Six minutes later, Shoen reported in. "*All set, boss. It'll take between five and ninety seconds, depending on where the patrollers are.*"

"*Okay. Hold for now.*"

We reached the place on Pier where it curves, just before you get to One-Claw.

"*How are they placed, Shoen?*"

"*If you give the word now, about thirty seconds.*"

"*Do it.*"

"*Check.*"

I held up my hand, and we stopped. I mentally counted off ten seconds, then we started walking again, quickly. We came around the curve and the building was in sight. The only people we could see were Shoen and Chimov. Presently, Narvane appeared next to them, then Smiley. We reached them a few seconds later.

I checked the Imperial Clock.

"The teleport block should be up now. Check it, Narvane."

He closed his eyes for a moment, then nodded.

I said, "The door."

N'aal said, "Maybe we should clap first."

Shoen and Glowbug stood by the door. They looked at each other, nodded, and Glowbug brought his mace down on the door mechanism just as Shoen set his shoulder into the middle. The door fell in.

N'aal said, "Won't you feel stupid if it was unlocked?"

I said, "Shut up."

Cawti slipped between them before we could move and stepped inside. There was a flurry of movement, and I heard the sound of falling bodies as Glowbug, N'aal, and Shoen went in. Loiosh landed on my shoulder as Chimov and Smiley stepped past the threshold. I followed, with Sticks and Narvane bringing up the rear.

It was a big, empty warehouse, with two bodies in it. Both had knives sticking out of them. We saw the stairs right away and took them. We didn't meet anyone on the way up. I left N'aal and Smiley to hold the bottom of the stairs to the third floor while the rest of us went up.

We emerged into a large, empty room. About five feet ahead of us were three smaller rooms; to the right, ahead, and to the left. Offices, I supposed.

Just as we got there, three Jhereg appeared from a room to the right. They stood there with their mouths hanging open. Sticks leapt at them, with Glowbug a little behind. Glowbug still had his mace, and he was grinning like an idiot. Sticks had his sticks. It took them about three seconds.

Then I sent Glowbug and Shoen to the right. I was about to send Chimov and Narvane to open the door ahead of us when I heard, "What's the ruckus about, gentlemen?" from the room to the left. I recognized Laris's voice.

I caught Narvane's eye. He stood in front of the door; the rest of us positioned ourselves behind it. Narvane raised his hand and the door flew in.

It was a small room, with about eight or nine padded chairs and two desks. One of the desks was empty; Laris was behind the other one. There were four other Jhereg in the room.

For an instant, no one moved. Then Laris turned to one and said, "Teleport."

We just waited.

The Jhereg he'd spoken to said, "There's a block up."

Cawti entered the office. Still none of them did anything. Sticks came in with his two clubs, then Glowbug with his mace. Then the rest of us.

Laris and I looked at each other, but neither of us spoke. What was there to say? I looked at his enforcers, most of them with half-drawn weapons. I told my people to stand aside. We cleared a path to the door. Sticks hefted his weapons, looked at Laris's enforcers, and cleared his throat.

He said, "No future in it, gentlemen."

They looked at the horde of us. Then, one by one, they stood up. They held their hands out, clear of their bodies. One by one, without a glance at Laris, they filed out.

I said, "All of you except Cawti, escort them out of the building." I drew the blade I'd selected.

When we were alone with Laris, I shut the door with my foot. Cawti said, "He's yours, Vladimir."

I made it quick. Laris never said a word.

An hour later I was staring at Aliera, my mouth hanging open. "You *what?*"

"I revivified her," she said, looking at me quizzically, as if to say, "Why should you find this unusual?" I was sitting in the library of Castle Black, with Morrolan, Cawti, Norathar, and Sethra. Aliera was on her back, looking pale but healthy.

I sputtered like a klava-boiler, then managed, "Why?"

"Why not?" she said. "We'd killed her, hadn't we? That was enough humiliation. Besides, the Empress is a friend of hers."

"Oh, great," I said. "So now, she—"

"She won't do anything, Vlad. There isn't anything she *can* do. When we revivified her we did a mind-probe and wrote down the details of every plot of any kind she's ever been involved in, and we gave her a copy so that she knows we know." She smiled. "Some of them were rather interesting, too."

I sighed. "Well, have it your way, but if I wake up dead one morning, I'll come to you and complain about it."

"That's telling her, boss."

"Shut up, Loiosh."

Norathar, to my amazement, said, "I think you did the right thing, Aliera."

"So do I," said Sethra.

I turned to the latter. "Indeed? Tell us what you did to Sethra the Younger."

"The House of the Dragon," she said, "has decided that Sethra the Younger can never be Emperor or Warlord, nor can any of her heirs."

"Huh," I said. "But what did *you* do to her?"

She gave me a dreamy kind of half-smile. "I believe I found a suitable punishment for her. I made her explain the entire affair to me, then—"

"Oh? What did she say?"

"Nothing surprising. She wished to conquer the East, and complained to the Sorceress in Green, who was her friend, that when Lord K'laiyer became Emperor, he wouldn't authorize an invasion of the East. The sorceress came up with a scheme to make sure Adron became the Dragon Heir because they knew Adron would appoint Baritt to be Warlord, and Baritt was sympathetic to the invasion idea. Baritt agreed, mostly because he thought Adron would be a better Emperor than K'laiyer—sorry, Norathar."

Norathar shrugged. Sethra continued.

"After Adron's Disaster, they just let things lie. When Zerika took the throne and things got going again, Morrolan proved to be the heir. They arranged for Sethra the Younger to become friendly with Morrolan and found that he wouldn't object to an invasion, so they relaxed. When Aliera showed up out of nowhere and became the heir, they went back to work again. They came up with the idea of discrediting Aliera and Morrolan, using your friendship with Vlad. They already knew Laris, because he'd done some of the dirty work in arranging the fake genetic scan. When Baritt refused to cooperate, they had Laris kill him. Then they used that as a threat to make Laris attack you. Apparently he was perfectly willing to take over your territory, Vlad, but had to be convinced not to kill you right away. They told him he could have you after their plans were complete. You know the rest, I think."

I nodded. "Okay. Now, about Sethra the Younger . . ."

"Oh yes. I had the Necromancer gate her to another Plane. Similar to Dragaera, but time runs at a different rate there."

"And she's stuck?" It seemed rather harsh to me—better to kill her. Besides, I wasn't nearly as upset with her as I was with the Sorceress in Green.

But, "No," said Sethra. "She can come back when her task is finished. It shouldn't take more than a week of our time."

"Task?"

"Yes." Once more, Sethra gave us her dreamy little smile. "I put her in the desert, with plenty of food, water, shelter, and a stick. And I set her to writing, 'I will not interfere with the Dragon Council,' in the sand, eighty-three thousand, five hundred and twenty-one times."

Picture an old man—an Easterner, almost seventy years old, which is a *very* impressive age for our race. But he's in good condition for his age. He is poor, but not destitute. He has raised a family in the midst of the Dragaeran Empire and done it well. He has buried (an Eastern term for "out-lived"; I'm not sure why) a wife, a sister, a daughter, and two sons. The only surviving descendant is one grandson, who nearly gets himself killed every few weeks or so.

He is almost completely bald, with only a fringe of white hair. He is a large, portly man, yet his fingers are still nimble enough with the rapier to give a good battle to a younger man, and to shock the sorcery out of any Dragaeran who doesn't understand Eastern-style fencing.

He lives in the Eastern ghetto, on the south side of Adrilankha. He ekes out a living as a witch, because he refuses to let his grandson support him. He worries about his grandson, but doesn't let it show. He'll help, but he won't live through his children, and he won't live their lives for them. When one of his sons tried to make himself into an imitation Dragaeran, he was saddened and felt his son was doomed to disappointment, but he never offered a word of criticism.

I went to see this old gentleman the day after Laris's death. Walking through the filth in the streets made me want to retch, but I hid it. Anyway, we all know Easterners are filthy, right? Look at how they live. Never mind that they can't use sorcery to keep their neighborhoods clean the way Dragaerans do. If they want to use sorcery, they can become citizens of the Empire by moving into the country and becoming Teckla, or buying titles in the Jhereg. Don't want to be serfs? They're stubborn, too, aren't they? Don't have the money to buy titles? Of course not! Who'd give them a good job, seeing how filthy they are?

I tried not to let it bother me. Cawti tried too, but I could see the strain around the corners of her eyes and feel it in the purposeful way she walked. I should have felt good about coming back here—successful Easterner boy walks through the old neighborhood. I should have, but I didn't. I only felt sick.

There was no sign above my grandfather's shop, and nothing on display. Everyone in the neighborhood knew who he was and what he did, and he didn't care about anyone outside it. Dragaerans had stopped using witchcraft when the Interregnum ended and sorcery worked again.

As I walked under the doorway (no door), my head brushed a set of chimes and set them ringing. His back was to me, but I could see that he was making candles. He turned around and his face lit up in an almost toothless grin.

"Vladimir!" he said. He looked at me, smiled at Cawti, and stood looking at me again. He and I could communicate psionically (he had taught me how), but he refused to do so unless it was necessary. He considered psionic communication something too precious to use casually—though, as was his custom, he never criticized me for using psionics as I do. So we traveled when we wanted to speak with each other. And, since we had to pass through areas where Easterners walking alone are in danger, and since he refused to be teleported, he seldom left the area.

"Vladimir," he said again. "And who is this?"

Loiosh flew over, as if the question had been about him, and happily accepted some neck scratching.

"Noish-pa," I said, "I'd like you to meet Cawti."

She gave him a curtsy, and he positively beamed.

"Cawti," he repeated. "Do you have a patronymic?"

"Not anymore," she said. I bit my lip. Someday I'd ask her what that meant, but not now.

He gave her a kindly smile, then looked at me, his eyes twinkling and a thin, white eyebrow climbing a broad forehead.

"We'd like to get married," I said. "We want your blessing."

He came forward and hugged her, and kissed both cheeks. Then he hugged me. When he pulled back, I saw tears at the corners of his eyes.

"I'm happy for you," he said. Then his brows furrowed, for just a moment, but I knew what he was asking.

"She knows," I said. "She's in the same line of work herself."

He sighed. "Oh, Vladimir, Vladimir. Be careful."

"I will, Noish-pa. Things are looking better for me. I almost lost everything a while ago, but I'm all right now."

"Good," he said. "But how did you come to almost lose everything? That isn't good."

"I know, Noish-pa. For a while, the shadows were distracting me so I couldn't see the target."

He nodded. "But come in, have something to eat."

"Thank you, Noish-pa."

Cawti said, timidly (I think it was the only time in her life she's been timid about anything), "Thank you . . . Noish-pa."

And his grin became even wider as he led us inside.

The next day I moved into Laris's old office and set up business. I met with Toronnan, and set about trying to take control of the area Laris had been running—but that really belongs to a different tale. Besides, as I speak these words, I don't know how it's going to turn out, so I may not be telling you about it after all. I've still got word out for Wyrn and Miraf'n, and money to pay for their heads, so I expect that very soon I'll be seeing them—after a fashion.

The same day I moved into Laris's old office I finally got a chance to cook Cawti a meal. I have to say I outdid myself, too—goose with Eastern red pepper, Valabar-style kethna dumplings, anise-jelled . . . but you don't want to hear about that.

I will say, though, that while I was cooking, I came across an onion that had a small bad spot on the side. I cut the spot out, and the rest of the onion was perfectly fine.

Life is like that, sometimes.

TECKLA

This is the city: Adrilankha, Whitecrest.

The capital and largest city of the Dragaeran Empire contains all that makes up the domain, but in greater concentration. All of the petty squabbles within the seventeen Great Houses, and sometimes among them, become both more petty and more vicious here. Dragonlords fight for honor, Iorich nobles fight for justice, Jhereg nobles fight for money, and Dzurlords fight for fun.

If, in the course of this squabbling, a law is broken, the injured party may appeal to the Empire, which oversees the interplay of Houses with an impartiality that does credit to a Lyorn judging a duel. But the organization that exists at the core of House Jhereg operates illegally. The Empire is both unwilling and unable to enforce the laws and customs governing this inner society. Yet, sometimes, these unwritten laws are broken.

That's when I go to work. I'm an assassin.

Prologue

I FOUND AN ORACLE about three blocks down on Undauntra, a little out of my area. He wore the blue and white of the House of the Tiassa, and worked out of a hole-in-the-wall above a bakery, reached by climbing a long, knotted wooden stairway between crumbling walls to a rotting door. The inside of the place was about right. Leave it at that.

He wasn't busy, so I threw a couple of gold Imperials onto the table in front of him and sat opposite him on a shoddy octagonal stool that matched his. He looked to be a bit old, probably pushing fifteen hundred.

He glanced at the pair of jhereg riding my shoulders, but chose to pretend to be unexcited. "An Easterner," he said. Brilliant. "And a Jhereg." The man was a genius. "How may I serve you?"

"I have," I told him, "suddenly acquired more cash than I've ever dreamed of having. My wife wants me to build a castle. I could buy a higher title in the Jhereg—I'm now a baronet. Or I could use the money to expand my business. If I choose the latter, I risk, um, competition problems. How serious will these be? That's my question."

He put his right arm on the table and rested his chin on it, drumming the tabletop with the fingers of his left hand while staring up at me. He must have recognized me; how many Easterners are there who are high up in the organization and wander around with jhereg on their shoulders?

When he'd looked at me long enough to be impressive, he said, "If you try to expand your business, a mighty organization will fall."

Well, la-dee-da. I leaned over the table and slapped him.

"Rocza wants to eat him, boss. Can she?"

"Maybe later, Loiosh. Don't bother me."

To the Tiassa, I said, "I have a vision of you with two broken legs. I wonder if it's a true one?"

He mumbled something about sense of humor, and closed his eyes. After thirty seconds or so, I saw sweat on his forehead. Then he shook his head and brought out a deck of cards wrapped in blue velvet with his House insignia on them. I groaned. I hate Card readers.

"Maybe he wants to play shereba," said Loiosh. I caught the faint psionic echo of Rocza laughing.

The oracle looked apologetic. "I wasn't getting anything," he explained.

"All right, all right," I said. "Let's get on with it."

After we went through the ritual, he tried to explain all the oracular meanings the Cards revealed to him. When I said, "Just the answers please," he looked hurt.

He studied the Mountain of Changes for a while, then said, "As far as I can see, m'lord, it doesn't matter. What's going to happen doesn't depend on any action you're going to take."

He gave me the apologetic look again. He must have practiced it. "That's the best I can do."

Splendid. "All right," I said. "Keep the change." That was supposed to be a joke, but I don't think he got it, so he probably still thinks I have no sense of humor.

I went back down the stairs and out onto Undauntra, a wide street packed full of craft shops on the east side and sparsely settled with small homes on the west, making it look oddly lopsided. About halfway back to my office, Loiosh said, *"Someone's coming, boss. Looks like muscle."*

I brushed my hair back from my eyes with one hand and adjusted my cloak with the other, allowing me to check a few concealed goodies. I felt tension in Rocza's grip on my shoulder, but left it to Loiosh to calm her down. She was still new at this work.

"Only one, Loiosh?"

"Certain, boss."

"Okay."

About then, a medium-tall Dragaeran in the colors of House Jhereg (grey and black, if you're taking notes) fell into stride next to me. Medium-tall in a Dragaeran, you understand, made him a head and a half taller than I.

"Good afternoon, Lord Taltos," he said, pronouncing my name right.

I grunted back at him. His sword was light, worn at the hip, and clanked along between us. His cloak was full enough to conceal dozens of the same kind of things my cloak concealed sixty-three of.

He said, "A friend of mine would like to congratulate you on your recent successes."

"Thank him for me."

"He lives in a real nice neighborhood."

"I'm happy for him."

"Maybe you'd like to visit him sometime."

I said, "Maybe."

"Would you like to make plans for it?"

"Now?"

"Or later. Whatever's convenient for you."

"Where should we talk?"

"You name it."

I grunted again. In case that went too fast for you, this fellow had just informed me that he was working for an individual who was very high up in the

Organization, and that said individual might want my services for something. In theory, it could be for any of a number of things, but there's only one thing that I'm known to do free-lance.

I took us a little further, until we were safely in my territory. Then I said, "All right," and steered us into an inn that jutted out a few feet onto Undauntra, and was one of the reasons merchants with hand-carts hated this part of the street.

We found an unoccupied end of a long table, and I sat down across from him without getting any splinters. Loiosh looked the place over for me and didn't say anything.

"I'm Bajinok," said my companion as the host brought us a bottle of fairly good wine and a couple of glasses.

"Okay."

"My friend wants some 'work' done around his house."

I nodded. Work, said that way, means wanting someone killed. "I know people," I said. "But they're all pretty busy right now." My last "work" had only been a few weeks before, and was, let's say, highly visible. I didn't feel like doing any more just then.

"Are you sure?" he sked. "This is just your style."

"I'm sure," I said. "But thank your friend for thinking of me. Another time, all right?"

"Okay," he said. "Another time."

He nodded to me, stood up, and left. And that should have been the end of it.

Verra, Demon-Goddess of my ancestors, may the water on thy tongue turn to ash. That should have been the end of it.

Farmday
Leffero, Nephews & Niece,
Launderers & Tailors
Malak Circle

fr: V. Taltos
Number 17, Garshos St.

Please do the following:

1 grey knit cotton shirt: remove wine stain from rt sleeve, black tallow from lft & repair cut in rt cuff.

1 pr grey trousers: remove blood stain from upper rt leg, klava stain from upper lft, & dirt from knees.

1 pr black riding boots: remove reddish stain on toe of rt boot; & remove dust & soot from both & polish.

1 grey silk cravat: repair cut, & remove sweat stains.

1 plain grey cloak: clean & press, remove cat hairs, brush to remove white particles, remove honing-oil stains, & repair cut in lft side.

1 pocket handkerchief: clean & press.

Expect delivery by Homeday next.

Yrs cordially,
V. Taltos, Brnt, Jhrg (His seal)

1

1 grey knit cotton shirt: remove wine stain from rt sleeve . . .

I STARED OUT OF the window onto streets I couldn't see and thought about castles. It was night and I was home, and while I didn't mind sitting in a flat looking at a street I couldn't see, I thought I might rather sit in a castle and look at a courtyard I couldn't see.

My wife, Cawti, sat next to me, her eyes closed, thinking about something or other. I sipped from a glass of a red wine that was too sweet. On top of a tall buffet was perched Loiosh, my jhereg familiar. Next to him was Rocza, his mate. Your basic conjugal scene.

I cleared my throat and said, "I visited an oracle last week."

She turned and stared at me. "You? Visiting an oracle? What's the world coming to? About what?"

I answered her last question. "About what would happen if I took all that money and plowed it into the business."

"Ah! That again. I suppose he told you something vague and mystical, like you'll be dead in a week if you try."

"Not exactly." I told her about the visit. Her face lost its bantering look. I like her bantering look. But then, I like most of her looks.

"What do you make of it?" she said when I was finished.

"I don't know. You take that stuff more seriously than I do; what do you make of it?"

She chewed her lower lip for a while. Around then Loiosh and Rocza left the buffet and flew off down the hall, into a small alcove that was reserved for their privacy. It gave me ideas which I suppressed, because I dislike having my actions suggested to me by a flying reptile.

Finally, Cawti said, "I don't know, Vladimir. We'll have to wait and see, I guess."

"Yeah. Just something more to worry about. It's not as if we don't have enough—"

There was a thumping sound, as if someone were hitting the door with a blunt object. Cawti and I were up at almost the same instant, myself with a dagger, she with a pair of them. The wine glass I'd been holding dropped to the floor and I shook droplets off my hand. We looked at each other and waited. The thumping sound was repeated. Loiosh came tearing out of the alcove and came to rest on my shoulder, Rocza behind him, complaining loudly. I started to tell him to shut her up, but Loiosh must have because she became quiet. I knew this couldn't be a Jhereg attack, because the Organization doesn't bother you at home, but I had made more than one enemy outside of the Jhereg.

We moved toward the door. I stood on the side that would open, Cawti stood directly in front of it. I took a deep breath, let it out, and put my hand on the handle. Loiosh tensed. Cawti nodded. A voice from the other side said, "Hello? Is anyone there?"

I stopped.

Cawti's brows came together. She called out tentatively, "Gregory?"

The voice came back. "Yeah. Is that you, Cawti?"

She said, "Yes."

I said, "What the—?"

"It's all right," she said, but her voice lacked certainty and she didn't sheath her daggers.

I blinked a couple of times. Then it occurred to me that Gregory was an Eastern name. It was the Eastern custom to strike someone's door with your fist if you wanted to announce yourself. "Oh," I said. I relaxed a bit. I called out, "Come in."

A man, as human as I, started to enter, saw us, and stopped. He was small, middle-aged, about half bald, and startled. I suppose walking through a doorway to find three weapons pointing at you would be enough to startle anyone who wasn't used to it.

I smiled. "Come on in, Gregory," I said, still holding my dagger at his chest. "Drink?"

"Vladimir," said Cawti, I suppose hearing the edge in my voice. Gregory didn't move and didn't say anything.

"It's all right, Vladimir," Cawti told me directly.

"With whom?" I asked her, but I made my blade vanish and stood aside. Gregory stepped past me a bit gingerly, but not handling himself too badly, all things considered.

"I don't like him, boss," said Loiosh.

"Why not?"

"He's an Easterner; he ought to have a beard."

I didn't answer because I sort of agreed; facial hair is one of the things that sets us apart from Dragaerans, which was why I grew a mustache. I tried to grow a beard once, but Cawti threatened to shave it off with a rusty dagger after her second set of whisker burns.

Gregory was shown to a cushion, sitting down in a way that made me realize that he was prematurely balding rather than middle-aged. Cawti, weapons also gone, sat on the couch. I brought out some wine, did a little cooling spell, and poured us each a glass. Gregory nodded his thanks and sipped. I sat down next to Cawti.

"All right," I said. "Who are you?"

Cawti said, "Vlad . . ." Then she sighed. "Vladimir, this is Gregory. Gregory: my husband, the Baronet of Taltos."

I saw perhaps the faintest of curl to his lip when she recited my title, and took an even stronger dislike to him. *I* can sneer at Jhereg titles; that doesn't mean anyone else can sneer at mine.

I said, "Okay. We all know each other. Now, who are you, and what are you doing trying to knock down my door?"

His eyes flicked from Loiosh, perched on my right shoulder, to my face, to the cut of my clothes. I felt like I was being examined. This did nothing to improve my temper. I glanced over at Cawti. She bit her lip. She could tell I was becoming unhappy.

"Vladimir," she said.

"Hmmm?"

"Gregory is a friend of mine. I met him while visiting your grandfather a few weeks ago."

"Go on."

She shifted uncomfortably. "There's a lot more to tell. I'd like to find out what he wants first, if I may."

There was just the least bit of an edge to her voice, so I backed off.

"Should I take a walk?"

"Dunno. But thanks for asking. Kiss."

I looked at him and waited. He said, "Which question do you want me to answer first?"

"Why don't you have a beard?"

"What?"

Loiosh hissed a laugh. "Never mind," I said. "What do you want here?"

He looked back and forth between Cawti and me, then fixed his glance on her and said, "Franz was killed yesterday evening."

I glanced at my wife to see what effect this was having on her. Her eyes had widened slightly. I held my tongue.

After a pair of breaths, Cawti said, "Tell me about it."

Gregory had the nerve to glance significantly in my direction. It almost got him hurt. He must have decided that I was all right, though, because he said, "He was standing at the door of the hall we'd rented, checking people, when someone just walked up to him and cut his throat. I heard the commotion and ran down, but whoever it was had vanished by the time I got there."

"Did anyone see him?"

"Not well. It was a Dragaeran though. They all—you—never mind. He was wearing black and grey."

"Sounds professional," I remarked, and Gregory looked at me in a way that you ought never to look at someone unless you are holding a blade at his throat. It was becoming difficult to let these things pass.

Cawti glanced at me quickly, then stood up. "All right, Gregory," she said. "I'll speak to you later."

He looked startled, and opened his mouth to say something, but Cawti gave

him one of those looks she gives me when I carry a joke too far. She saw him
to the door. I didn't stand up.

"All right," I said when she came back. "Tell me about it."

She studied me for a moment, as if looking at me for the first time. I knew
enough not to say anything. Presently she said, "Let's take a walk."

There was no time in my life up to that point when I was as filled with so
many strong, conflicting emotions as when we returned from that walk. No
one, including Loiosh, had spoken during the last ten minutes, when I had run
out of sarcastic questions and removed Cawti's need for terse, biting answers.
Loiosh rhythmically squeezed alternate talons on my right shoulder, and I was
subliminally aware of this and comforted by it. Rocza, who sometimes flies
over our heads, sometimes rests on my other shoulder, and sometimes rests on
Cawti's, was doing the last. The Adrilankhan air was cutting, and the endless
lights of the city cast battling shadows before our feet as I found and opened
the door to the flat.

We undressed and went to bed speaking only as necessary and answering in
monosyllables. I lay awake for a long time, moving as little as possible so Cawti
wouldn't think I was lying awake. I don't know about her, but she didn't move
much.

She arose before me the next morning and roasted, ground, and brewed the
klava. I helped myself to a cup, drank it, and walked over to the office. Loiosh
was with me; Rocza stayed behind. There was a cold, heavy fog in from the
sea and almost no breeze—giving what is called "assassin's weather," which is
nonsense. I said hello to Kragar and Melestav and sat down to brood and be
miserable.

"*Snap out of it, boss.*"

"*Why?*"

"*Because you've got things to do.*"

"*Like what?*"

"*Like finding out who shined the Easterner.*"

I thought that over for a moment. If you are going to have a familiar, it
doesn't do to ignore him. "*All right, why?*"

He didn't say anything, but presently memories began to present themselves
for my consideration. Cawti, as I'd seen her at Dzur Mountain after she had
killed me (there's a story there, but never mind); Cawti holding me after someone else tried to kill me; Cawti holding a knife at Morrolan's throat and explaining how it was going to be, while I sat paralyzed and helpless; Cawti's
face the first time I had made love with her. Strange memories, too—my emotions at the time, filtered through a reptilian mind that was linked to my own.

"*Stop it, Loiosh!*"

"*You asked.*"

I sighed. "*I suppose I did. But why did she have to get involved in something
like that? Why—?*"

"*Why don't you ask her?*"

"I did. She didn't answer."

"She would have if you hadn't been so—"

"I don't need advice on my marriage from a Verra-be-damned . . . no, I suppose I do, don't I? All right. What would you do?"

"Ummm . . . I'd tell her that if I had two dead teckla I'd give her one."

"You're a lot of help."

"Melestav!" I yelled. "Send Kragar in here."

"Right away, boss."

Kragar is one of those people who are just naturally unnoticeable. You could be sitting in a chair looking for him and not realize that you were sitting in his lap. So I concentrated hard on the door, and managed to see him come in.

"What is it, Vlad?"

"Open your mind, my man. I have a face to give to you."

"Okay."

He did, and I concentrated on Bajinok—the fellow I'd spoken with a few days before, who had offered me "work" that would be "just my style." Could he have meant an Easterner? Yeah, maybe. He had no way of knowing that to finalize an Easterner would defeat the whole purpose of my having become an assassin in the first place.

Or would it? Something nasty in my mind bade me remember a certain conversation I'd recently had with Aliera, but I chose not to think about it.

"Do you know him?" I asked Kragar. "Who does he work for?"

"Yeah. He works for Herth."

"Ah ha."

"Ah ha?"

"Herth," I said, "runs the whole South Side."

"Where the Easterners live."

"Right. An Easterner was just killed. By one of us."

"*Us?*" said Loiosh. "*Who is us?*"

"*A point. I'll think about it.*"

"What does that have to do with us?" asked Kragar, introducing another meaning of us, just to confuse us. Excuse me.

I said, "I don't know yet, but—Deathsgate, I do know. I'm not ready to talk about it yet. Could you set me up a meeting with Herth?"

He tapped his fingers on the arm of his chair and looked at me quizzically. It wasn't usual for me to leave him in the dark about things like that, but he finally said, "Okay," and left.

I took out a dagger and started flipping it. After a moment I said to Loiosh, "*She still could have told me about it.*"

"*She tried. You weren't interested in discussing it.*"

"*She could have tried harder.*"

"*It wouldn't have come up if this hadn't happened. And it is her own life. If she wants to spend half of it in the Easterners' ghetto, rabble-rousing, that's her—*"

"*It hardly sounds like rabble-rousing to me.*"

"*Ah,*" said Loiosh.

Which shows how much good it is to try to get the better of your familiar.

I'd rather skip over the next couple of days, but as I had to live them, you can at least put up with a sketch. For two solid days Cawti and I hardly exchanged a word. I was mad that she hadn't told me about this group of Easterners, and she was mad because I was mad. Once or twice I'd say something like, "If you'd—", then bite it back. I'd notice that she was looking at me hopefully, but I'd only notice too late, and then I'd stalk out of the room. Once or twice she'd say something like, "Don't you even care—", and then stop. Loiosh, bless his heart, didn't say anything. There are some things that even a familiar can't help you work out.

But it's a hell of a thing to go through days like that. It leaves scars.

Herth agreed to meet me at a place I own called The Terrace. He was a quiet little Dragaeran, only half a head taller than I, with an almost bashful way of dropping his eyes. He came in with two enforcers. I also had two, a fellow who was called Sticks because he liked to beat people with them, and one named Glowbug, whose eyes would light up at the oddest times. The enforcers found good positions for doing what they were paid for. Herth took my suggestion and ordered the pepper-sausage, which is better tasted than described.

As we were finishing up our Eastern-style desert pancakes (which, really, no one should make except Valabar's, but these were all right), Herth said, "So what can I do for you?"

I said, "I have a problem."

He nodded, dropping his eyes again as if to say, "Oh, how could little me help someone like you?"

I went on, "There was an Easterner finalized a few days ago, by a professional. It happened in your area, so I was wondering if, maybe, you could tell me a bit about what happened, and why."

Now, there were several possible answers he could have given me. He could have explained as much as he knew about it, he could have smiled and claimed ignorance, he could have asked me what my interest was. Instead, he looked at me, stood up, and said, "Thanks for the dinner; I'll see you again, maybe." Then he left.

I sat there for a while, finishing my klava. "*What do you make of that, Loiosh?*"

"*I don't know, boss. It's funny that he didn't ask why you wanted to find out. And if he knows, why did he agree to the meeting in the first place?*"

"*Right,*" I said.

I signed the bill and left, Sticks and Glowbug preceding me out of the place. When we reached the office I told them to take off. It was evening, and I was usually done by that time, but I didn't feel like going back home just then. I changed weapons, just to kill time. Changing weapons is something I do every two or three days so that no weapon is around my person enough to pick up my aura. Dragaeran sorcery can't identify auras, but Eastern witchcraft can, and should the Empire ever decide to employ a witch—

"*I'm an idiot, Loiosh.*"

"*Yeah, boss. Me, too.*"

I finished changing weapons and made it home quickly.

"Cawti!" I yelled.

She was in the dining room, scratching Rocza's chin. Rocza leapt up and began flying around the room with Loiosh, probably telling him about her day. Cawti stood up, looking at me quizzically. She was wearing trousers of Jhereg grey that fit low on her hips, and a grey jerkin with black embroidery. She glanced at me with an expression of remote inquiry, her head tilted to the side, her brows raised in that perfect face, surrounded by sorcery-black hair. I felt my pulse quicken in a way that I had been afraid it wouldn't any more.

"Yes?" she said.

"I love you."

She closed her eyes then opened them again, not saying anything. I said, "Do you have the weapon?"

"Weapon?"

"The Easterner who was killed. Was the weapon left there?"

"Why, yes, I suppose someone has it."

"Get it."

"Why?"

"I doubt whoever it was knows about witchcraft. I'll bet I can pick up an aura."

Her eyes grew wide, then she nodded. "I'll get it," she said, and reached for her cloak.

"Shall I go with you?"

"No, I don't . . ." Then, "Sure, why not?"

Loiosh landed on my shoulder and Rocza landed on Cawti's and we went down the stairs into the Adrilankha night. In some ways things were better, but she didn't take my arm.

Is this starting to depress you? Heh. Good. It depressed me. It's much easier to deal with someone you only have to kill. As we left my area and began to cross over into some of the rougher neighborhoods, I hoped someone would jump me so I could work out some of what I was feeling.

Our feet went *clack clack* to slightly differing rhythms, occasionally synchronizing, then falling apart. Sometimes I'd try to change my step to keep them together, but it didn't do much. Our paces were our usual compromise, worked out long ago, between the shorter steps she was most comfortable with and my longer ones. We didn't speak.

You identify the Eastern section first by its smell. During the day the whole neighborhood is lousy with open-air cafes, and the cooking smells are different from anything the Dragaerans have. In the very early morning the bakeries begin to work; the aroma of fresh Eastern bread reaches out like tendrils to gradually take over the night smells. But the night smells, when the cafes are

closed and the bakeries haven't started, are the smells of rotting food and human and animal waste. At night the wind blows across the area, toward the
sea, and the prevailing winds are from the slaughterhouses northwest of town.
It's as if only at night can the area's true colors, to mix a metaphor, come to
the surface.

The buildings are almost invisible at night. Lamps or candles glowing in a
few windows provide the only light, so the nature of the structures around you
is hidden, yet the streets are so narrow that sometimes there is hardly room to
walk between the buildings. There are places where doors in buildings opposite
each other cannot be opened at the same time. At times you feel as if you were
walking through a cave or in a jungle, and your boots tramp through garbage
more often than on the hard-packed rutted dirt of the street.

It's funny to go back there. On the one hand, I hate it. It is everything that
I've worked to get away from. But on the other, surrounded by Easterners, I
feel a tension drain out of me that I don't notice except when it is gone; and
it hits me again that, to a Dragaeran, I am an *other*.

We reached the Eastern section of town past midnight. The only people
awake at that hour were derelicts and those who preyed on derelicts. Both
groups avoided us, according us the respect given to anyone who walks as if
he was above any dangers in a dangerous area. I would be lying if I said that
I wasn't pleased to notice this.

We reached a place where Cawti knew to enter. The "door" was a doorway
covered by a curtain. I couldn't see a thing inside, but I had the feeling I was
in a narrow hallway. The place stank. Cawti called out, "Hello."

There were faint rustling sounds, then, "Is someone there?"

"It's Cawti."

Heavy breathing, rustling, a few other voices mumbling, then flint was struck,
there was a flash of light, and a candle was lit. It hurt my eyes for a moment.
We were standing in front of a doorway without even a curtain. The inside of
the room held a few bodies that were stirring. To my surprise, the room was,
as far as I could tell in the light of the single candle, clean and uncluttered
except for the blanketed forms. There was a table and a few chairs. A pair of
beady eyes was staring at us from a round face behind the candle. The face
belonged to a short, very fat male Easterner in a pale dressing gown. The eyes
rested on me, flicked to Loiosh, Cawti, Rocza, and came back to me.

"Come in," he said. "Sit down." We did, as he went around the room to
light a few more candles. As I sat in a soft, cushioned chair, I counted a total
of four persons on the floor. As they sat up, I saw that one was a slightly plump
woman with greying hair, another was a younger woman, the third was my
old friend Gregory, and the fourth was a male Dragaeran, which startled me.
I studied his features until I could place his House, and when I identified him
as a Teckla I didn't know whether to be less surprised or more.

Cawti seated herself next to me. She nodded to all present and said, "This is
my husband, Vladimir." Then she indicated the fat man who had been up first
and said, "This is Kelly." We exchanged nods. The older woman was called

Natalia, the younger one was Sheryl, and the Teckla was Paresh. She didn't supply patronymics for the humans and I didn't push it. We all mumbled hellos.

Cawti said, "Kelly, do you have the knife that was found by Franz?"

Kelly nodded. Gregory said, "Wait a minute. I never mentioned a knife being left by his body."

I said, "You didn't have to. You said it was a Jhereg who did it."

He grimaced at me, screwing his face up.

"Can I eat him, boss?"

"Shut up, Loiosh. Maybe later."

Kelly looked at me, which means he fixed me with his squinty eyes and tried to see through me. That's what it felt like, anyway. He turned to Cawti and said, "Why do you want it?"

"Vladimir thinks we might be able to find the assassin from the blade."

"And then?" said Kelly, turning to me.

I shrugged. "Then we find out who he worked for."

Natalia, from the other side of the room, said, "Does it matter for whom he worked?"

I just shrugged. "It doesn't matter to me. I thought it might to you."

Kelly went back to staring at me through his little pig eyes; I was amazed to discover that he was actually making me uncomfortable. He nodded a little, as if to himself, then left the room for a moment, returning with a knife wrapped in a piece of cloth that had probably once been part of a sheet. He handed cloth and weapon to Cawti. I nodded and said, "We'll be in touch."

We walked out the door. The Teckla, Paresh, had been standing in front of it. He moved aside as we headed toward the door, but not as quickly as I would have expected. Somehow that struck me as significant.

It was still several hours until sunrise as we made our way back toward our part of town. I said, "So, these are the people who are going to take over the Empire, huh?"

Cawti gestured with the bundle she held in her left hand. "Someone thinks so," she said.

I blinked. "Yeah. I guess someone does."

The stench of the Eastern area seemed to linger much further on the way back to our flat.

2

. . . black tallow from lft . . .

Down in the basement under my office is a little room that I call "the lab," an Eastern term that I picked up from my grandfather. The floor is hard-packed dirt, the walls are bare, mortared rock. There is a small table in the center and a chest in the corner. The table holds a brazier and a couple of candles. The chest holds all sorts of things.

Early in the afternoon of the day after we procured the knife, the four of us—Cawti, Loiosh, Rocza and me—trooped down to this room. I unlocked it and led the way in. The air was stale and smelled faintly of some of the things in the chest.

Loiosh sat on my left shoulder. He said, *"Are you sure you want to do this, boss?"*

I said, "What's that supposed to mean?"

"Are you sure you're in the right frame of mind to cast spells?"

I thought about that. A caution from one's familiar is something that no witch in his right mind dismisses without consideration. I glanced at Cawti, who was waiting patiently, and maybe guessing some of what I was thinking about. There was a lot of emotional mayhem hammering around my insides. This can be good, as long as it can be put into the spell. But I was also in something of a funk, and when I get that way I mostly feel like sleeping. If I didn't have energy to direct the spell, it could get out of control.

"It'll be all right," I told him.

"Okay, boss."

I dumped the old ashes out of the brazier into a corner of the room and made a mental note to myself to clean that corner one of these days. I opened the chest and Cawti helped me put new coals into the brazier. I tossed away the old black candles and replaced them. Cawti positioned herself to my left, holding the knife. I called upon my link to the Orb and caused the wick of one of the candles to become hot enough to ignite. I used it to light the other candle, and, with some work, the coals in the brazier. I put this and that into the fire and set the dagger in question before it.

It's all symbolic, you know.

I mean, I sometimes wonder if it would work with water that I only *thought* had been purified (whatever "purified" means). And what if I used incense that smelled right, but was just ordinary incense? What if I used thyme that someone just picked up at the market on the corner, and told me was off a ship from the East? I don't know, and I don't think I'll ever find out, but I suspect it wouldn't matter. Every once in a while, you find something that really *is* all in the mind.

But these thoughts form the before and after of the spell. The during is all sensation. Rhythms pulse through you in time to the flickering of candles. You take yourself and plunge or are plunged into the heart of the flames until you are *elsewhere*, and you blend with the coals and Cawti is there beside you and inside you weaving in and out of the bonds of shadow you build that ensnare you like a small insect in a blue earth derivative and you find you have touched the knife and now you *know* it for a murder weapon, and you begin to feel the person who held it, and your hand goes through the delicate slicing motion he used and you drop it, as he did, his work done, as is yours.

I pushed it a little, trying to glean all I could from the moment of the casting. His name occurred to me, as something I'd known all along which chose to creep into my consciousness just at this moment, and about then that part of me that was really Loiosh became aware that we were on the down side of the enchantment and began to relax the threads that guarded the part of Loiosh that was me.

It was about there that I realized something was wrong. There is a thing that happens when witches work together. You don't know the other witch's thought; it is more that you are thinking his thoughts for him. And so, for a moment, I was thinking about me, and I became aware that there was a core of bitterness in me, directed at me, and it shook me.

There was never the danger Loiosh had feared, largely because he was there. The spell was drifting apart by then anyway, and we were all carefully letting go and drifting with it, but a big lump formed itself in my throat, and I twitched, knocking over a candle. Cawti reached forward to steady me and we locked eyes for a moment as the last of the spell flickered and collapsed and our minds became our own again.

She dropped her eyes, knowing that we had felt what we had felt.

I opened the door to let the smoke out into the rest of the building. I was a bit tired, but it hadn't been all that difficult a spell. Cawti and I went back up the stairway next to each other but not touching. We were going to have to talk, but I didn't know what to say. No, that wasn't it; I just couldn't make myself.

We went into my office and I yelled for Kragar. Cawti sat in his chair. Then she yelped and stood up upon discovering that he was in it. I smiled a bit at Kragar's innocent look. It was probably funnier than that, but we were feeling the tension.

I said, "His name is Yerekim. I've never heard of him. Have you?"

Kragar nodded. "He's an enforcer for Herth."

"Exclusively?"

"I think so. I'm pretty certain. Should I check?"

"Yes."

He simply nodded, rather than making a comment about being overworked. I think Kragar picks up on more than he admits. After he had slithered out of the room, Cawti and I sat in silence for a moment. Then she said, "I love you, too."

Cawti went home, and I spent part of the day getting in the way of people who worked for me and trying to act as if I ran my business. The third time Melestav, my secretary, mentioned what a nice day it was I took the hint as well as the rest of the day off.

I wandered through the streets, feeling powerful, as a force behind so much of what happened in the area, and insignificant, because it mattered so little. But I did get my thoughts in order, and made some decisions about what I would do. Loiosh asked me if I knew why I was doing it and I admitted that I didn't.

The breeze came from the north for a change, instead of in from the sea. Sometimes the north wind can be brisk and refreshing. I don't know, maybe it was my state of mind, but then it just felt chilly.

It was a lousy day. I resolved not to listen to Melestav's opinion on the weather anymore.

By the next morning Kragar had confirmed that, yes, Yerekim worked only for Herth. Okay. So Herth wanted this Easterner dead. That meant that it was either something personal about this Easterner—and I couldn't conceive of a Jhereg having a personal grudge against an Easterner—or this group was, in some way, a threat or an annoyance.

That was most likely, and certainly a puzzle.

"Ideas, Loiosh?"

"Just questions, boss. Like, who would you say is leader of that group?"

"Kelly. Why?"

"The Easterner they shined—Franz—why him instead of Kelly?"

In the next room, Melestav was riffling through a stack of papers. Above me, someone was tapping his foot. Sounds of a muted conversation came through the fireplace from somewhere unknown. The building was still, yet seemed to breathe.

"Right," I said.

It was around the middle of the afternoon when Loiosh and I found ourselves back in the Easterners' quarter. I couldn't have found the place no matter how hard I looked, but Loiosh was able to pick it out at once. In the daylight, it was another low, squat, brown building, with a pair of tiny windows flanking the door. Both windows were covered by boards, which went a long way toward explaining how stuffy it had been.

I stood outside the curtained doorway, started to clap, stopped, and banged on the wall. After a moment the Teckla, Paresh, appeared. He positioned himself in the middle of the doorway, as if to block it, and said, "Yes?"

"I'd like to see Kelly."

"He is not here." His voice was low, and he spoke slowly, pausing before each sentence as if he were organizing it in his head before committing it to the air. He had the rustic accent of the duchies to the immediate north of Adrilankha, but his phrasings were more those of a Chreotha or Vallista craftsman, or perhaps a Jhegaala merchant. Odd.

"Do you believe him, Loiosh?"

"I'm not sure."

So I said, "Are you quite certain?"

Something flickered then—a twitching at the corners of his eyes—but he only said, "Yes."

"There's something weird about this guy, boss."

"I noticed."

"There's something weird about you," I told him.

"Why? Because I'm not trembling in fear at the mere sight of your colors?"

"Yeah."

"I'm sorry to disappoint you."

"Oh, I'm not disappointed," I said. "Intrigued, maybe."

He studied me for a moment, then stepped back from the doorway. "Come in, if you want," he said.

I didn't have anything better to do just then, so I followed him in. The room didn't smell much better during the day, with its windows boarded shut. It was lit by two small oil lamps. He indicated a cushion on the floor. I sat down. He brought in an Eastern wine that was mostly water and slopped some into chipped porcelain cups, then sat facing me. He said, "I intrigue you, you say. Because I don't seem to fear you."

"You have an unusual disposition."

"For a Teckla."

I nodded.

We sipped our wine for a while, the Teckla looking off into space while I studied him. Then he started talking. I listened to what he said, becoming more and more intrigued as he spoke. I don't know that I understand all of it, but I'll give it to you as I remember it and you can decide for yourself.

You're titled, aren't you? Baron, isn't it? Baronet, then. All right. It doesn't really matter to you, I know. We both know what Jhereg titles are worth; I daresay you know to the nearest copper penny. The Orca *do* care; they make certain that orders of nobility are given or withdrawn whenever it's proper, so the quartermaster is of a higher rank than the bosun, yet lower than the mate. You didn't know that, did you? But I've heard of a case where an Orca was stripped of her county, granted a barony, stripped of that, given a duchy, then another county, then stripped of both and given her original county back, all within the same forenoon. A bookkeeping error, I was told.

But, do you know, none of those counties or duchies really existed. There are other Houses like that, too.

In the House of the Chreotha, titles are strictly hereditary, and lifelong unless something unusual happens, but there, too, they are not associated with any land. But you have a baronetcy, and it is real. Have you ever been there? I can see by the look on your face that it never occurred to you to visit it. How many families live in your dominion, Baronet Taltos? That's all? Four? Yet it has never occurred to you to visit them.

I'm not surprised. Jhereg think that way. Your domain is within some name-less barony, possibly empty, and that within a county, maybe also empty, and that within a duchy. Of what House is your Duke, Baronet? Is he a Jhereg, also? You don't know? That doesn't surprise me, either.

What am I getting at? Just this: Of all the "Noble Houses"—which means every House except my own—there are only a few which contain any of the aristocracy, and then only a few of that House. Most of those in the House of the Lyorn are Knights, because only the Lyorns continue to treat titles as they were when first created, and Knight is a title that has no land associated with it. Have you thought of that, most noble Jhereg? These titles were associated with holdings. Military holdings, at first, which is why most of the domains around here are those of Dragonlords; this was once the Eastern edge of the Empire, and Dragons have always been the best military leaders.

My master was a Dzurlord. Her great-grandfather had earned the title of Baron during the Elde Island wars. My master had distinguished herself before the Interregnum during some war with the East. She was old, but still healthy enough to go charging off to do one thing or another. She was rarely at home, yet she was not unkind. She did not forbid her Teckla to read, as many do, and I was fortunate enough to be taught at an early age, though there was little enough reading matter to be found.

I had an older sister and two younger brothers. Our fee, for our thirty acres, was one hundred bushels of wheat or sixty bushels of corn, our choice. It was steep, but rarely above our means, and our master was understanding during lean years. Our closet neighbor to the west paid one hundred and fifty bushels of wheat for twenty-eight acres, so we counted ourselves lucky and helped him when he needed it. Our neighbor to the north had thirty-five acres, and he owed two gold Imperials, but we saw little of him so I don't know how hard or easy his lot was.

When I reached my sixtieth year I was granted twenty acres a few miles south of where my family lived. All of the neighbors came and helped me clear the land and put up my home, which I made large enough for the family I hoped to have someday. In exchange, I had to send to my master four young kethna every year, so by necessity I raised corn to feed them.

After twenty years I had paid back, in kind, the loans of kethna and seedlings that had gotten me started, and I thought myself well off—especially as I'd gotten used to the stench of a kethna farm. More, there was a woman I'd met in Blackwater who still lived at home, and there was, I think, something between us.

It was on an evening late in the spring of my twenty-first year on my own that I heard sounds far to the south. Cracking sounds, as a tree will make when it begins to topple, but far, far louder. That night, I saw red flames to the south. I stood outside of my house to watch, and I wondered.

After an hour, the flames filled the sky, and the sounds were louder. Then came the greatest yet. I was, for a moment, blinded by a sudden glare. When the spots cleared from my eyes I saw what seemed to be a sheet of red and yellow fire hanging over my head, as if it were about to descend on me. I think I screamed in terror and ran for my house. By the time I was inside the sheet had descended, and all of my lands were burning, and my house as well, and that was when I looked fully upon death. It seemed to me then, Lord Taltos, that I had not had enough of a life for it to end that way. I called upon Barlan, he of the Green Scales, but he had, I guess, other calls to make. I called upon Trout, but he brought me no water to dampen the flames. I even asked Kelchor, Goddess of the cat-centaurs, to carry me from that place, and my answer was smoke that choked me and sparks that singed my hair and eyebrows and a creaking, splintering groan as part of the house fell in.

Then I thought of my springhouse. I made it out the door and somehow lived through the flames that, my memory tells me, reached taller than I, and made it there. It was built of stone, of course, for the dampness would have rotted timber, so it still stood. I was badly burned, but I made it into the stream.

I lay there trembling for what must have been the whole night and into the day. The water was warm, even hot, but still cooler than the air around it. I fell asleep in that stream, and when I awoke—well, I will not try to describe the desolation around me. It was only then, I am ashamed to say, that I thought of my livestock, who had died during the night as I nearly had. But there was nothing to be done for them now.

And what did I do then, Baronet? Laugh if you will, but my first thought was that I could not pay my master for the year, and must go throw myself on her mercy. Surely, I thought, she would understand. So I began to walk toward her keep—southward.

Ah! I see that you have thought it out. So did I, as I began to take my first steps. Southward was where her castle stood, and southward was the origin of the flames. I stopped and considered for some time, but eventually I continued, for I had nowhere else to go.

It was many miles, and all I saw around me as I walked were burnt-out homes and charred ground, and blackened woods that had never been cleared, until now. Not another soul did I see during the entire journey. I came to the place where I had been born and had lived most of my life, and I saw what was left.

I performed the rites as best I could for them, and I think I was too numb to realize what it meant. When I had finished I continued my journey, sleeping in an empty field, warmed by the ground itself, which still felt the heat from the scorching it had endured.

I came to the keep and, to my surprise, it seemed unharmed. Yet the gate was closed, and no one answered my calls. I waited outside for minutes, hours, finally the whole day and that night. I was ravenously hungry and called out from time to time, but no one answered.

At last it was, I think, hunger more than anything else that led me to climb over the walls. It wasn't difficult, since none opposed me. I found a burnt log that was long enough, dragged it to the wall, and used it as a ladder.

There was no living being in the courtyard. I saw half a dozen bodies dressed in Dzur livery. I stood there and trembled, cursing my stupidity for not having brought food from the springhouse.

I think I stood there for an hour before I dared to enter, but eventually I did. I found the larder and ate. Slowly, over the course of weeks, I gathered the courage to search the keep. During this time I slept in the stables, not daring to make use of even the servant's quarters. I found a few more bodies in my search, and burned them as best I could, though, as I said, I knew few of the rites. Most of them were Teckla—some I recognized, a few I had once called friends—gone to serve the master, and now gone forever. What became of my master I never found out, for I think none of the bodies was hers.

I ruled that castle then, Baronet. I fed the livestock with the grain that had been hoarded there, and butchered them as I needed. I slept in the lord's bed-chamber, ate her food, and most of all, I read her books. She had tomes on sorcery, Baronet. A library full of them. And history, and geography, and stories. I learned much. I practiced sorcery, which opened before me a whole world, and the spells I'd known before seemed only games.

Most of a year passed in this way. It was late in the winter when I heard the sounds of someone pulling on the bell rope. The old fear that is my heritage as a Teckla, and at which you, my Lord Jhereg, must take such delight in sneering, came back then. I trembled and looked for a place to hide.

But then something came over me. Perhaps it was the magic I had learned; perhaps it was that all I had read had made me feel insignificant, and fear therefore seemed foolish; perhaps it was simply that, having survived the fire, I had learned the full measure of terror. But I didn't hide. Instead I went down the great winding stairway of what I now thought of as my home and threw open the doors.

Before me stood a noble of the House of the Lyorn. He was very tall and about my age, and wore a golden-brown, ankle-length skirt, a bright red shirt and a short fur cape. He wore a sword at his belt and a pair of vambraces. He didn't wait for me to speak, simply saying, "Inform your master that the Duke of Arylle will see him."

What I felt then is, I suppose, something you have felt often, but I never had before. That amazing, delicious rush of anger that a boar must feel when it charges the hunter, not really aware that it is overmatched in every way except ferocity, and is why the boar sometimes wins, and the hunter is always afraid. But there he stood, in *my* castle, and asked to see my master.

I stepped back a pace, drew myself up, and said, "I am master here."

He barely glanced at me. "Don't be absurd," he said. "Fetch your master at once or I'll have you beaten."

I had read quite a bit by then, and what I had read put the words into mouth that my heart wanted to speak. "My Lord," I said, "I have told you that I am master here. You are in my home, and you are lacking in courtesy. I must ask you to leave."

Then he did look at me, with such contempt that, had I been in any other frame of mind, it alone would have crushed me. He reached for his sword, I think now only to beat me with the flat, but he never drew it. I called upon my new skills and threw a blast at him that, I thought, would have burnt him down on the spot.

He gestured with his hands, and looked startled, but he seemed to take me seriously for the first time. That, my good Baronet, was a victory that I shall always treasure. The look of respect that came over him was as delicious to me as a cool drink to a man dying of thirst.

He hurled a spell at me. I knew I could not stop it, but I ducked out of the way. It exploded against the far wall behind me in a mass of flame and smoke. I threw something at him, then ran back up the stairs.

For the next hour I led him on a merry chase throughout the keep, stinging him with my spells and hiding before he could destroy me with his. I think that I laughed and mocked him, too, although I cannot say for certain.

At length, though, as I stopped to rest, I realized that he would surely kill me eventually. I managed to teleport myself back to the springhouse I knew so well.

I never saw him again. Perhaps he had come to ask about tribute he was due, I don't know. But I was changed. I made my way to Adrilankha using my new sorcerous skills for money among the Teckla households I passed. A skilled sorcerer willing to work for the pittance a Teckla can pay is rare, so, with time, I accumulated a goodly sum. When I came to the city, I found a poor, drunken Issola who was willing to teach Court manners and speech for what I could afford to pay. No doubt he taught me poorly by Court standards, yet I learned enough so that I could work with my equals in the city and compete fairly, I thought, as a sorcerer.

I was wrong, of course. I was still a Teckla. A Teckla who fancied himself a sorcerer was, perhaps, amusing, but those who need spells to prevent burglary, or to cure addictions, or secure the foundations of buildings, will not take a Teckla seriously.

I was destitute when I found my way to the Easterners' quarter. I will not pretend that life has been easy here, for Easterners have no more love for humans than most humans do for Easterners, yet my skills were, at least sometimes, useful.

As for the rest, Lord Taltos, suffice it to say that I chanced to meet Franz, and I spoke of life as a Teckla, and he spoke of the common thread that connects the Teckla and the Easterner, and of bare survival for our peoples, and of hope that it needn't always be this way. He introduced me to Kelly, who taught me to see the world around me as something I could change—something I *had* to change.

Then I began to work with Franz. Together we found more Teckla, both here and those who slaved under masters far more vicious than my own. And when I would speak of the terror of the Empire under which we all suffered, Franz would speak of hope that, together, we could make a world free from terror. Hope was always half of his message, Baronet Taltos. And action was the other half—building hope through our own actions. And if, from time to time, we didn't know how, Kelly would lead us to discover it ourselves.

They were a team, my good Jhereg. Kelly and Franz. When someone fails at a task, Kelly can verbally tear him to pieces; but Franz was always there to help him try again, in the streets. Nothing frightened him. Threats pleased him, because they showed he was scaring someone, and proved we were on a good path. That was Franz, Lord Taltos. That was why they killed him.

I hadn't asked why they had killed him.

But all right. I chewed over his story for a few minutes. "Paresh," I said, "what was that about threats?"

He stared at me for a moment, as if I'd just seen a mountain collapse and asked of what kind of stone it was made. Then he turned his face away. I sighed. "All right," I said. "When will Kelly be back?"

He faced me again, and his expression was like a closed door. "Why do you want to know?"

Loiosh squeezed my shoulder with his talons. *"Take it easy,"* I told him. To Paresh I said, "I want to speak with him."

"Try tomorrow."

I thought about trying to explain myself to him so he would, perhaps, answer me. But he was a Teckla. Whatever else he was, he was still a Teckla.

I stood up and let myself out and walked back to my side of town.

3

. . . & repair cut in rt cuff.

WHEN I ARRIVED ON familiar ground again it was early evening. I saw no reason to return to the office so I made my way toward home.

One was lounging against a wall on Garshos, near Copper Lane. Loiosh started to warn me just about the time I noticed the guy, which was just as he noticed me. Then Loiosh said, *"There's another one behind you."*

I said, *"Okay."* I wasn't too worried, because if they'd wanted to kill me I would never have seen them. When I reached the one in front of me he was blocking my path, and I recognized him as Bajinok, which meant Herth—the guy who ran South Adrilankha. My shoulders went limp and my hands twitched. I stopped a few paces away from him. Loiosh watched the one behind me. Bajinok looked down at me and said, "I've got a message."

I nodded, guessing at what it was.

He continued, "Stay away. Keep out of it."

I nodded again.

He said, "Do you agree?"

I said, "Can't do it, I'm afraid."

His hand went to his sword hilt, just as an idle, threatening gesture. He said, "Are you sure?"

"I'm sure."

"I could make the message more explicit," he said.

Since I didn't feel like having my leg broken just then I threw a knife at him, underhanded. This was something I'd spent a lot of time practicing, because it is so fast. I don't know of anyone who has ever been seriously injured by a knife thrown that way except by me, and even with me it takes a lot of luck. On the other hand, *anyone* will flinch.

While he was busy flinching, and the knife was hitting him hilt first in the stomach, Loiosh was flying into the face of the other one. I had my rapier out before Bajinok had recovered, and I used the time to step out into the street to make sure neither of them could get behind me.

Bajinok's sword was in his hand by then and he had a dagger in the other. He was just coming into a guard position when my point took him in the right leg, above the knee. He cursed and stepped back. I followed and put a cut across the left side of his face, and, with the same motion, a good, deep one on his right wrist. He took another step back and I skewered him in the left shoulder. He went over backward.

I looked at the other one, who was big and strong-looking. He showed signs of having been bit in the face by Loiosh. He was swinging his sword wildly over his head while my familiar stayed out of his reach and laughed at him. I spared a quick glance for Bajinok, then, with my left hand, found a knife, aimed, and carefully threw it into the middle of the other guy's stomach. He grunted and cried out and swung in my direction, coming close enough to my wrist to take some hair off my arm. But that was all he had in him. He dropped his sword and knelt on the street, bent over, holding his stomach.

I said, "Okay, get going." I did my best to sound as if I weren't breathing hard.

They looked at each other, then the one with my knife in his stomach teleported out. When he was completely gone, Bajinok stood up and began limping away, holding his injured shoulder. I changed my mind about going straight home. Loiosh continued watching Bajinok as I turned up the street.

"I'd just take it as a warning," said Kragar.

"I don't need you for the obvious stuff."

"I could argue that," he said. "But never mind. The question is, how hard is he going to push it?"

"That," I said, "*is* the kind of stuff I need you for."

"I don't know," he said, "but I assume we're going to get ready for the worst."

I nodded.

"*Hey, boss.*"

"*Yeah?*"

"*Are you going to tell Cawti about this?*"

"*Huh? Of course I'm going to . . . oh. I see what you mean. When things start to get complicated, they don't go halfway, do they?*"

Kragar seemed to have left the room by then, so I took out a dagger and threw it as hard as I could into the wall—the one without a target on it. The gash it left there wasn't the first, but it may have been the deepest.

When I went home a few hours later I still hadn't decided, but Cawti wasn't there. I sat down to wait for her. I was careful not to drink too much. I relaxed in my favorite chair, a big, overstuffed grey thing with a prickly surface that makes me avoid it when I'm unclothed. I spent quite a while relaxing before I began to wonder where Cawti was.

I closed my eyes and concentrated for a moment.

"*Yes?*"

"*Hi. Where are you?*"

She paused, and I was suddenly alert. "*Why?*" she said finally.

"*Why? Because I want to know. What do you mean, why?*"

"*I'm in South Adrilankha.*"

"Are you in any danger?"

"No more than an Easterner is always in danger living in this society."

I bit back a response of *spare me* and said, *"All right. When will you be home?"*

"Why?" she asked and all sorts of prickly things started buzzing around inside of me. I almost said, "I was almost killed today," but it would have been neither true nor fair. So I said *"Never mind"* and severed the link.

I stood up and went into the kitchen. I drew a pot of water and set it on the stove, threw a couple of logs into the stove itself. I stacked up the dishes, which Loiosh and Rocza had already licked clean, and wiped off the table, throwing the crumbs into the stove. I got the broom out and swept the kitchen, threw the refuse from the floor after the crumbs from the table. Then I took the water off the stove and washed the dishes. I used sorcery to dry them because I've always hated drying. When I opened the cupboard to put them away I noticed that it was getting a bit dusty so I took everything out and went over all the shelves with a cloth. I felt the faint stirrings of psionic contact then, but it wasn't Cawti so I ignored it and presently it went away.

I cleaned up the floor below the sink, then mopped the whole floor. I went into the living room, decided I didn't feel like dusting and sat down on the couch. After a couple of minutes I got up, found the brush, and dusted off the shelves next to the door, under the polished wooden dog and the stand with the miniature portrait of Cawti on it, and the carved lyorn that looked like jade but wasn't, and the slightly larger stand with the portrait of my grandfather. I didn't stop and talk to Cawti's portrait.

Then I got a rag from the kitchen and wiped down the tea table that she'd given me last year. I sat down on the couch again.

I noticed that the lyorn's horn was pointing toward Cawti. When she's upset, she can pick the strangest things to think are deliberate, so I got up and turned it, then sat down again. Then I got up and dusted off the *lant* I'd given her last year that she hadn't even turned in twelve weeks. I walked over to the bookshelf and picked out a book of poems by Wint. I looked at it for a while, then put it back because I didn't feel like fighting with obscurity. I picked up one of Bingia, then decided that she was too depressing. I didn't bother with Torturi or Lartol. I can be shallow and clever on my own; I don't need them for it. I consulted the Orb, then my internal clock, and both told me that I wouldn't be able to sleep yet.

"Hey, Loiosh."

"Yeah, boss?"

"Want to see a show?"

"What kind?"

"I don't care."

"Sure."

I walked over to Kieron Circle instead of teleporting because I didn't care to arrive with my stomach upset. It was a bit of a hike, but walking felt good. I picked a theater without looking at the title, as soon as I found a show that was starting right away. I think it was an historical, taking place during the reign of a decadent Phoenix so they could use all the costumes they had lying around from the last fifty years of productions. After about fifteen minutes I started hoping someone would try to cut my purse. I took a quick glance behind me, and saw an elderly Teckla couple, probably blowing a year's savings. I gave up on that idea.

I left at the end of the first act. Loiosh didn't mind. He didn't think the actor playing the Warlord should have been allowed out of North Hill. He's a real snob when it comes to theater. He said, *"The Warlord is supposed to be a Dragon, boss. Dragons stomp, they don't skulk. And he almost tripped over his sword three times. And when he was supposed to be demanding that more troops be conscripted, it sounded as if he was asking for—"*

"Which one was the Warlord?"

He said, *"Oh. Never mind."*

I walked home slowly, hoping someone would do something to me so I could do something back, but all was quiet in Adrilankha. At one point someone approached me as if he were going to pull on my cloak and I started to get ready for action, but he turned out to be an old, old man, probably an Orca, who was under the influence of something. Before he could open his mouth I asked him if he had any spare copper. He looked confused so I patted his shoulder and walked on.

When we got back, I hung up my cloak, took off my boots and checked the bedroom. Cawti was home and asleep. Rocza was resting in her alcove.

I stood over Cawti, hoping she'd wake up and see me looking at her and ask what was wrong so I could storm at her and she'd apologize and everything would be fine. I stood there for what must have been ten minutes. I might still be standing there, but Loiosh was around. He wasn't saying anything, but he makes me self-conscious about wallowing in self-pity for more than ten minutes at a time, so I undressed and crawled into bed next to Cawti. She didn't wake up. A long, long time later I fell asleep.

I wake up slowly.

Oh, not always. I remember a couple of times when I've woken to Loiosh screaming in my mind and found myself in the middle of a fight. Once or twice I was woken up badly and unfortunate things almost happened, but those are rare. Usually there is a time between awake and asleep that, in retrospect, feels like it lasts for hours. That's when I clutch at my pillow and wonder if I really feel like getting up. Then I roll over, look at the ceiling and the thoughts of what I'm going to do that day trickle into my head. That's what really wakes me up. I've tried to organize my life so that there is something to get up for on any given day. Today we're going to the Eastern section for the spice markets. Today I'm going to close that deal on a new brothel. Today I'm going to visit Castle Black and check on Morrolan's security setup and chat with Aliera.

Today I'm going to follow this guy and confirm that he does visit his mistress every other day. That kind of thing.

When I woke up the next morning, I learned that I was made of better stuff than I had thought, because I got out of bed without having a single reason to. Not one damned reason. Cawti was up, but I didn't know if she was home or not; neither thought gave me any impulse to see the world outside of my room. My business was running itself; I had no obligations to fulfill. The only thing interesting in my life was finding out the story behind who had killed the Easterner, and that was for Cawti, who seemed not to care.

But I made it into the kitchen to start heating water. Cawti was in the living room reading a tabloid. I felt a tightening in my throat. I started the water, then went into the bathroom. I used the chamber pot and cleaned it with sorcery. Neat. Efficient. Just like a Dragaeran. I shaved in cold water. My grandfather shaved in cold water (before he grew his beard) because he says it makes you better able to stand the winters. That sounds like nonsense to me, but I do it out of respect for him. I chewed on a tooth stick, rubbed down my gums, and rinsed my mouth out. By then the water was hot enough for my bath. I took it, dried myself, cleaned up the bathroom, dressed, and dumped the water out the back. Splash. I stood and watched the puddles and rivers it made running down the alley. I've often wondered why no one claims to read the future in dumped bath water. I looked to the left and saw the ground was dry beneath my neighbor's back porch. Ha! I was up earlier than she again. So there, world. One small victory.

I walked into the living room and sat down in my chair, facing the couch. I caught a glimpse of a headline on Cawti's tabloid that read, "Call for the investigation—" on about four lines of big black print, and that wasn't the whole thing. She put the thing down and looked at me.

I said, "I'm mad at you."

She said, "I know. Should we go out and eat?"

I nodded. For some reason, we can't seem to discuss things at home. We went to our favorite klava hole with Loiosh and Rocza on my shoulders and I ignored the tension and twisting in my stomach long enough to order a few eggs and drink some klava with very little honey. Cawti ordered tea.

She said, "Okay. Why are you mad?" which is like getting in the first cut to put the other guy on the defensive.

So I said, "Why didn't you tell me where you were?"

She said, "Why did you want to know?" with a bit of a smile as we realized what we were doing.

I said, "Why shouldn't I?" and we both grinned, and I felt just a little better for just a little while.

Then she shook her head and said, "When you asked where I was and when I'd be back, it sounded as if you wanted to approve or disapprove of it."

I felt my head snap back. "That's absurd," I said. "I just wanted to know where you were."

She glared at me. "All right, so I'm absurd. That still doesn't give you the right—"

"Dammit, I didn't say *you* were absurd and you know it. You're accusing me—"

"I didn't accuse you of anything. I said how I felt."

"Well, by saying that you felt that way, you were implying that—"

"This is ridiculous."

Which was the perfect chance to say, "All right, so I'm ridiculous," but I know better. Instead, I said, "Look, I was not then trying, nor have I ever tried, to dictate your actions. I came home, you weren't there—"

"Oh, and this is the first time that's happened?"

"Yes," I said, which we both knew wasn't true, but the word came out before I could stop it. The corner of her mouth twitched up and the eyebrow lowered, which is one of my favorite things that she does. "All right," I said. "But I was worried about you."

"About me?" she said. "Or afraid that I was involved in something you don't approve of?"

"I already know you're involved in something I don't approve of."

"Why don't you approve of it?"

I said, "Because it's *stupid*, first of all. How are five Easterners and a Teckla going to 'destroy the despotism' of an Empire? And—"

"There are more. That's only the tip of the iceberg."

I stopped. "What's an iceberg?"

"Ummm . . . I don't know. You know what I mean."

"Yeah. The thing is, it's not even nearing a Teckla reign. I could see something like this if the Teckla were near the top of the Cycle, but they're not. It's the Phoenix, and then the Dragons if we're still alive when the Cycle changes; the Teckla aren't even in the running.

"And in the second place, what's wrong with what we have now? Of course it isn't perfect, but we live well enough and we got it on our own. You're talking about giving up our careers, our life-style, and everything else. And for what? So a bunch of nobodies can pretend they're important—"

"Careful," she said.

I stopped in mid-diatribe. "All right," I said. "Sorry. But have I answered your question?"

She was quiet for a long time, then. Our food showed up and we ate it without saying anything at all. When we'd turned the scraps over to Loiosh and Rocza, Cawti said, "Vladimir, we've always agreed never to hit each other's weak spots, right?"

I felt a sinking sensation when she said that, but I nodded.

She continued, "All right, this is going to sound like that's what I'm doing, but I don't mean it that way, okay?"

"Go on," I said.

She shook her head. "Is it okay? I want to say it, because I think it's important, but I don't want you to just shut me out, the way you do whenever I try to get you to look at yourself. So will you listen?"

I drained my klava, signaled the waiter for more and doctored it appropriately when it came. "All right," I said.

"Until just recently," she began, "you thought that you had found your line of work because you hated Dragaerans. Killing them was your way of getting back at them for what they'd put you through while you were growing up. Right?"

I nodded.

"Okay," she continued. "A few weeks ago, you had a talk with Aliera."

I winced. "Yeah," I said.

"She told you about a previous life in which—"

"Yeah, I know. I was a Dragaeran."

"And you said you felt as if your whole life had been a lie."

"Yes."

"Why?"

"Hm?"

"Why did it shake you so much?"

"I don't—"

"Could it be because you've felt all along as if you had to justify yourself? Could it be that somewhere, deep down, you think it is *evil* to kill people for money?"

"Not people," I said by reflex. "Dragaerans."

"People," she said. "And I think you've just proved my point. You were forced into this line of work, just the way I was. You had to justify it to yourself. You've justified it so thoroughly that you kept on doing 'work' even after you no longer had to, when you were making enough money from running your area that the 'work' was pointless. And then your justification fell apart. So now you don't know where you stand, and you have to wonder whether you are, really, deep down, a bad person."

"I don't—"

"Let me finish. What I'm getting at is this: No, you *aren't* a bad person. You have done what you had to do to live and to help provide us both with a home and a comfortable life. But tell me this, now that you can't hide behind hating Dragaerans any more: What kind of Empire do we have that forces someone like you to do what you do, just to live, and to be able to walk down the streets without flinching? What kind of Empire not only produces the Jhereg, but allows it to thrive? Can you justify *that*?"

I let her comments percolate through me for a while. I got more klava. Then I said, "That's the way things are. Even if these people you're running around with *aren't* just nut cases, nothing they do is going to change that. Put in a different Emperor and things will just go back to being the way they are in a few years. Sooner than that, if it's an Easterner."

"That," she said, "is a whole 'nother subject. The point I'm making is that you're going to have to come to terms with what you do, at whose expense you live, and why. I'll help as much as I can, but it is your own life you have to deal with."

I stared into my klava cup. Nothing in it made anything any clearer.

After another cup or two I said, "All right, but you still haven't told me where you were."

She said, "I was conducting a class."

"A class? On what?"

"Reading. For a group of Easterners and Teckla."

I stared at her. "My wife, the teacher."

"Don't."

"Sorry."

Then I said, "How long have you been doing this?"

"I just started."

"Oh. Well." I cleared my throat. "How did it go?"

"Fine."

"Oh." Then another, nastier thought occurred to me. "Why is it only now that you've started doing this?"

"Someone had to take over for Franz," she said, confirming exactly what I was afraid of.

"I see. Has it occurred to you that this may be what he'd been doing that someone didn't like? That this was why he was killed?"

She looked straight at me. "Yes."

A chill spread along my backbone. "So you're asking—"

"I'm not Franz."

"Anyone can be killed, Cawti. As long as someone is willing to pay a professional—and it's clear that someone is—*anyone* can be killed. You know that."

"Yes," she said.

"No," I said.

"No what?"

"Don't. Don't make me choose—"

"*I* am choosing."

"I can't let you walk into a situation where you're a helpless target."

"You can't stop me."

"I can. I don't know how yet, but I can."

"If you do, I'll leave you."

"You won't have that choice if you're dead."

She paused to wipe up the klava that had spilled from my cup. "We are not helpless, you know. We have support."

"Of Easterners. Of Teckla."

"It is the Teckla who feed everyone else."

"I know. And I know what happens to them when they try to do anything about it. There have been revolts, you know. There has never been a successful one except during the reign of the Orca, right before the Teckla. As I said, we aren't there now."

"We're not discussing a Teckla revolt. We're not talking about a Teckla reign; we're talking about breaking the Cycle itself."

"Adron tried that once; remember? He destroyed a city and caused an interregnum that lasted more than two hundred years, and it still didn't work."

"We aren't doing it with pre-Empire sorcery, or magic of any kind. We're doing it with the strength of the masses—the ones who have the *real* power."

I withheld my opinion of what real power is and who has it. I said, "I can't allow you to be killed, Cawti. I just can't."

"The best way to protect me would be to join us. We could use—"

"Words," I said. "Nothing but words."

"Yes," said Cawti. "Words from the minds and hearts of thinking human beings. There is no more powerful force in the world, nor a better weapon, once they are applied."

"Pretty," I said. "But I can't accept it."

"You'll have to. Or, at least, you'll have to confront it."

I didn't answer. I was thinking. We didn't say any more, but before we left the klava hole I knew what I was going to have to do. Cawti wasn't going to like it.

But then, neither was I.

4

1 pr grey trousers: remove blood stain from upper rt leg . . .

JUST IN CASE I haven't made it clear yet, the walk over to the Easterners' section takes a good two hours. I was getting sick of it. Or maybe not. Now that I think back on it, I could have teleported in three seconds, then spent fifteen or twenty minutes throwing up or wishing I could. So I guess maybe I wanted the time to walk and think. But I remember thinking that I was spending altogether too much time just walking back and forth between the Malak Circle district and South Adrilankha.

But I made it there. I entered the building and stood outside the doorway, which now had a curtain. I remembered not to clap, and I didn't feel like pounding on the wall, so I called out, "Is anyone in there?"

There was a sound of footsteps, the curtain moved and I was looking at my friend Gregory. Sheryl was behind him, watching me. I couldn't tell if anyone else was in the room. Since it was Gregory who was standing there, I brushed past him and said, "Is Kelly around?"

"Come right in," said Sheryl. I felt a little embarrassed. No one else was in the room. In one corner was a tall stack of tabloids, the same one Cawti had been reading.

Gregory said, "Why do you want to see him?"

"I plan to leave all my worldly wealth to the biggest idiot I can find and I wanted to interview him to see if he qualified. But now that I've met you, I can see there's no point in looking any further."

He glared at me. Sheryl laughed a little and Gregory flushed.

Kelly appeared through the curtain then. I looked at him more closely than I had before. He really was quite overweight, as well as short, but I somehow wanted to call him extremely chubby instead of fat. Cute, sort of. His forehead was flat, giving the impression that his head was large. His hair was cut very short, like half an inch, and he had no sideburns at all. His eyes had two positions, narrowed and squinting, and he had a very expressive mouth, probably because of the amount of fat surrounding it. He struck me as one of those people who can turn from cheerful to vicious in an instant; like Glowbug, say.

He said, "Right. Come on." Then he turned and walked toward the rear of the flat, leaving me to follow him. I wondered if that was a deliberate ploy.

The back room was narrow and stuffy and smelled of pipe smoke, although

Kelly didn't have the teeth of a smoker. Come to think of it, he probably didn't have any vices at all. Except overeating, anyway. Shame he was an Easterner. Dragaerans can use sorcery to remove excess fat; Easterners tend to kill themselves trying. There were rows of leather-bound books and all around the room, with black or sometimes brown bindings. I couldn't read any of the titles, but the author of one of them was Padraic Kelly.

He nodded me into a stiff wooden chair and sat in another one behind a rickety-looking desk. I pointed to the book and said, "You wrote that?"

He followed my pointing finger. "Yes."

"What is it?"

"It's a history of the uprising of two twenty-one."

"Where was that?"

He looked at me closely, as if to see if I were joking, then said, "Right here, in South Adrilankha."

I said, "Oh." I cleared my throat. "Do you read poetry as well?"

"Yes," he said.

I sighed to myself. I didn't really want to walk in and start haranguing him, but there didn't seem to be a whole lot else to talk about. What's the use? I said, "Cawti's been telling me something about what you do." He nodded, waiting. "I don't like it," I said, and his eyes narrowed. "I'm not happy that Cawti's involved." He kept staring at me, not saying anything.

I sat back in the chair, crossed my legs. "But all right. I don't run her life. If she wants to waste her time this way, there's nothing I can do about it." I paused, waiting for him to make some sort of interjection. When he didn't, I said, "What bothers me is this business of teaching reading classes—that's what Franz was doing, wasn't it?"

"That, and other things," he said, tight-lipped.

"Well then, I'm offering you a deal. I'll find out who killed Franz and why, if you drop these classes, or get someone else to teach them."

He never took his eyes off me. "And if not?"

I started to get irritated, probably because he was making me feel uncomfortable and I don't like that. I clenched my teeth together, stifling the urge to say what I thought of him. I finally said, "Don't make me threaten you. I dislike threatening people."

He leaned over the desk, and his eyes were narrowed more than usual, his lips were pressed tightly together. He said, "You come in here, on the heels of the death of a man who was martyred to—"

"Spare me."

"Quiet! I said martyred and I meant it. He was fighting for what he believed in, and he was killed for it."

He stared hard at me for a moment, then he continued in a tone of voice that was softer but cutting. "I know what you do for a living," he said. "You don't even realize the depths to which you've sunk."

I touched the hilt of a dagger but didn't draw it. "You're right," I said. "I don't realize the depths to which I've sunk. It would be really stupid of you to tell me about it."

"Don't tell me what is and is not stupid. You're incapable of judging that, or anything else that falls outside the experience of your tiny world. It doesn't even occur to you that there could be anything *wrong* with selling death as if it were any commodity on the market."

"No," I said. "It doesn't. And if you're quite finished—"

"But it isn't just you. Think of this, Lord Killer: How much of what anyone does is something he'd do willingly, if he didn't have to? You accept that without thinking about it or questioning it, don't you? While Easterners and Teckla are forced to sell half their children to feed the rest. You think it doesn't happen, or do you just refuse to look at it?"

He shook his head, and I could see his teeth were clenched in his jowls and his eyes were so narrow I'm surprised he could see out of them. "What you do—mankind doesn't get any lower. I don't know if you do it because you have no choice, or because you've been so twisted that you like it, but it doesn't matter. In this building you will find men and women who can be proud of what they do, because they know there will be a better future for it. And you, with your snide, cynical wit, not only refuse to look at it, but try to tell us how to go about it. We have no time for you or for your deals. And your threats don't impress us either."

He paused, maybe to see if I had anything to say. I didn't.

He said, "Get out of here."

I stood up and left.

"The difference between winning and losing is whether you feel like going home afterwards."

"Not bad, boss. So where are we going?"

"I don't know."

"We could go back to Herth's place, spit in his soup and see what he says about that."

I didn't think this was at all a good idea.

It was still afternoon, and the Easterners' section was in full swing. There were markets every few blocks, and each was different. This one was yellow, orange, red, and green with vegetables and smelled like fresh things and the sound was a low hum. That one was pale and pink and smelled of meat, most of it still good, and it was quieter, so you could even hear the wind rattling around inside your ear. The next one was mostly fabrics and the loudest, because no one bargains like a fabric merchant, with screams and yells and pleading. They don't ever seem to tire of it, either. I get tired of things. I get tired of lots of things. I get tired of walking around Morrolan's castle to check up on his guards, traps, and alarms. I get tired of talking to my associates in codes that even I don't understand half the time. I get tired of breaking out in a sweat every time I see the uniform of the Phoenix Guards. I get tired of being treated with contempt for being a Jhereg by other Houses, and for being an Easterner by Jhereg. And I was getting tired, every time I thought of Cawti, of a tightening in my middle instead of that warm, dropping, glowing feeling I used to have.

"You have to find an answer, boss."

"I know. I just tried."

"So try something else."

"Yeah."

I found that I had wandered over to the area near where my grandfather lived, which couldn't have been an accident although it felt like one. I walked through his doorway and set the chimes ringing. They were cheerful. I actually started feeling better as I stepped over the threshold. Chimes. Now, there's a witch for you.

He was sitting at his table, writing or drawing with a quill pen on a big piece of parchment. He was old, but very healthy. A big man. If Kelly was chubby, my grandfather was portly. His head was almost completely bald, so it reflected the little lamps of the shop. He looked up when he heard the chimes and gave me a big grin with his remaining teeth.

"Vladimir!"

"Hello, Noish-pa."

We hugged and he kissed my cheek. Loiosh flew off my shoulder onto a shelf until we were done, then flew to Noish-pa's arm for some chin-scratching. His familiar, a large furry cat named Ambrus, jumped into my lap when I sat down and poked his nose at me. We got reacquainted. Noish-pa hooked a small card onto the string that held the chimes and motioned me into his back room. I smelled herb tea and started feeling even better.

He served us, *tsk*ing when I put honey in mine. I sipped it. Rose hip.

"So, how is my grandson?"

"So-so, I guess, Noish-pa."

"Only so-so?"

I nodded.

"You have a problem," he said.

"Yeah. It's complicated."

"Simple things are never problems, Vladimir. Some simple things are sad, but never problems."

"Yeah."

"So, how did this problem start?"

"How did it start? Someone named Franz was killed."

"Ah! Yes. A terrible thing."

I stared at him. "You know about it?"

"It is on everyone's tongue."

"It is?"

"Well, these people, his . . . what is the word? *Elvtarsok?*"

"Friends? Associates?"

"Well, these people are everywhere, and they talk about it."

"I see."

"But you, Vladimir. You are not one of these people, are you?"

I shook my head. "Cawti is."

He sighed. "Vlad, Vlad, Vlad. It is silliness. If a revolution comes along, of course you support it. But to go out of your way like this is to put your head on the block."

"When has revolution come along?"

"Eh? In two twenty-one."

"Oh. Yes. Of course."

"Yes. We fought then, because it was what we did, but some can't forget that and think we should be always fighting."

I said, "What do you know about these people?"

"Oh, I hear things. Their leader, this Kelly, he is a fighter they say."

"A fighter? A brawler?"

"No, no. I mean he never quits, that is what I hear. And they are getting bigger, you know. I remember I heard of them a few years ago when they had a parade of twenty people, and now they have thousands."

"Why do people go there?"

"Oh, there are always those who aren't happy. And there has been violence here; beatings and robbing of people, and they say the Phoenix Guards of the Empire don't stop it. And some landlords raise their rent because some of their houses burn down, and people are unhappy about that, too."

"But none of that has anything to do with Cawti. We don't even live around here."

He shook his head and *tsked*. "It is silliness," he repeated.

I said, "What can I do?"

He shrugged. "Your grandmother did things I didn't like, Vladimir. There is nothing to be done. Perhaps she will lose interest." He frowned. "No, that is unlikely. Cawti does not lose interest when she becomes interested. But there, it is her life, not yours."

"But Noish-pa, that's just it. It's her *life*. Someone killed this Franz, and now Cawti is doing just what he was doing. If she wants to run around with these people and stir up trouble, or whatever they're doing, that's fine, but if she were killed, I couldn't stand it. But I can't stop her, or she'll leave me."

He frowned again and nodded. "Have you tried things?"

"Yes. I tried talking to Kelly, but that didn't do anything."

"Do you know who it was who killed this Franz fellow?"

"Yeah, I know who."

"And why?"

I paused. "No, I don't really know that."

"Then you must find out. Perhaps you will find that there is nothing to worry about, after all. If there is, perhaps you will find a way to solve it without risk to your wife."

Your wife he said. Not *Cawti* this time, it was *your wife*. That was how he thought. Family. Everything was family, and we were all the family he had. It suddenly occurred to me that he was probably disappointed in me; I don't think he approved of assassins, but I was family so that was that.

"What do you think of my work, Noish-pa?"

He shook his head. "It is terrible, what you do. It is not good for a man to live by killing. It hurts you."

"Okay." I was sorry I had asked. I said, "Thank you, Noish-pa. I have to go now."

"It was good to see you again, Vladimir."

I hugged him, collected Loiosh, and walked out of his shop. The way back to my side of town was long, and I still didn't feel like teleporting.

When Cawti came home that evening, I was soaking my feet.

"What's the matter?" she asked.

"My feet hurt."

She gave me a half-smile. "Somehow this doesn't surprise me. I mean, *why* do your feet hurt?"

"I've been walking a lot the last few days."

She sat down across from me and stretched out. She was wearing high-waisted grey slacks with a wide black belt, a grey jerkin and a black vest. She'd hung up her half-cloak. "Anywhere in particular?"

"The Easterners' section, mostly."

She turned her head to the side a bit, which was one of my favorite things to see her do. It made her eyes seem huge in that beautiful, thin face with her perfectly sculpted cheekbones. "Doing what?"

"I went in to see Kelly."

Her eyes widened. "Why?"

"I explained that he should make sure you weren't doing anything that might put you in danger. I implied that I'd kill him if he did."

The look of curiosity changed to disbelief, then anger. "Did you really," she said.

"Yeah."

"You don't seem nervous about telling me about it."

"Thank you."

"And what did Kelly say?"

"He said that, as a human being, I rated somewhere between worthless scum and wretched garbage."

She looked startled. Not upset, startled. "He said that?"

"Not in so many words. Quite."

"Hmmm," she said.

"I'm glad to see that this outrage against your husband fills you with such a righteous indignation."

"Hmmm," she said.

"Trying to decide if he was right?"

"Oh, no," she said. "I know he's right. I was wondering how he could tell."

"Cawti—" I said, and stopped because my voice broke.

She came over, sat beside me, and put her hand on my leg. "I'm sorry," she said. "I didn't mean that and I shouldn't have joked about it. I know he's wrong. But you shouldn't have done what you did."

"I know," I said, almost whispering.

We were silent for a time. She said, "What are you going to do now?"

"I think," I said, "that I'm going to wait until my feet feel better. Then I'm going to go out and kill someone."

She stared at me. "Are you serious?"

"Yes. No. I'm not sure. Half, I guess."

"This is hard for you. I'm sorry."

I nodded.

She said, "It's going to get harder."

"Yeah."

"I wish I could help you."

"You have. You'd do more if you could."

She nodded. After that there wasn't any more to say, so she just sat next to me for a while. Presently, we went into the bedroom and slept.

I was in the office early the next morning, with Loiosh and Rocza. I let them out my window so Loiosh could continue showing Rocza around. He had gradually been teaching her the ins and outs of the city. He enjoyed it, too. I wondered what that would do to a marriage—one having to train the other. With those two it could become strained, too—Loiosh did the teaching, but the jhereg female is dominant.

"Hey, Loiosh—"

"None of your Verra-be-damned business, boss."

That was hardly fair; he'd been butting into *my* marriage. Besides, I had a right to know if I was going to be subjected to more cheap North Hill theater than what I was generating. But I didn't push it.

By the time they returned, a couple of hours later, I knew what I was going to do. I got an address from Kragar, along with a dirty look for not telling him why I wanted it. Loiosh and Rocza attached themselves to my shoulders and I went down the stairs and out of the office.

Lower Kieron Road, near Malak Circle, is the widest street in this part of town and is filled with inns set back from it and markets jutting out into it and hotels, some with small business inside of them. I owned all the small businesses. Lower Kieron took me south and west. It got gradually narrower, and more and more tenements appeared. Most of them had once been green but were now painted dirty. I abandoned Lower Kieron to follow a narrow little street called Ulor.

Ulor widened after a bit, and about there I turned onto Copper Street, which was different from the Copper Lane near my place, or the Copper Street to the east or the Copper Street even further east or the others that I don't remember. After a few paces, I turned left into a fairly nice looking inn with long tables of polished wood and long benches. I found the host and said, "Do you have a private room?"

He allowed as to how he did, although his look implied it wasn't normally polluted by the presence of Easterners. I said, "My name is Vlad. Tell Bajinok that I'm here."

He nodded and called for a serving man to carry the message. I spotted where the back room must be and entered it. It was empty. I was pleased that it had a real door. I closed it and sat, back to the door (Loiosh was watching), on one of the benches at a table that was a shorter version of the ones in the main room. I wondered how many people Bajinok would bring along. If it was more than one, this probably wouldn't work. But then, he might not bring anyone. I decided I had pretty good odds.

Presently, the door opened and Bajinok came in along with another Jhereg I hadn't seen before. I stood up before they could sit down.

"Good morning," I said. "I hope I didn't disturb you."

Bajinok scowled a little. "What?" he said.

"A man of few words," I told him. "I like that." Loiosh hissed, which he might have thought was agreement.

"What do you want?"

"I thought we might continue our discussion of the other day."

The Jhereg who was with Bajinok rolled his shoulders and scratched his stomach. Bajinok wiped his hands on his cloak. I checked the clasp of my cloak with one hand and brushed my hair back with the other. I didn't know about them, but all of *my* weapons were ready.

He said, "If you have something to say, say it."

"I want to know why Herth wanted that Easterner killed."

Bajinok said, "Drop dead, Whiskers."

I gestured with my right hand as if I were about to say something important. I suppose in a way I was. The gesture produced a dagger that went straight up under the unknown's chin and into his head. He crumbled, fell against me and slid to the floor. By the time he hit, I had taken another dagger from my cloak and was holding the point of it directly in front of Bajinok's left eye.

I said, "The instant anyone appears in this room, or opens the door, or you even look like you're in psionic communication with someone, I'm going to kill you."

He said, "Okay."

"I thought you might want to tell me a few things about Herth and why he wanted that Easterner killed."

Without moving his head, he glanced down at the corpse. Then he looked back up the blade of the dagger. "You know," he said, "I just might at that."

"Good," I said cheerfully.

"Mind if I sit down?"

"No. Go ahead."

He did, and I moved behind him and held my blade against the back of his neck. He said, "This is going to get you killed, you know."

"We all have to die sometime. And we Easterners don't live that long anyway. Of course, that's a good reason not to rush things, I suppose. Which brings us back to Franz." I increased the pressure against the back of his neck. I felt him flinch. I stayed alert for any attempt to teleport out. I could kill him before he was gone if I was quick.

He said, "Yes. Franz. He was a member of some kind of group—"

"I know about it."

"Okay. Then there isn't much more I can tell you."

I pressed the knife against his neck again. "Try. Were you told to kill him in particular, or just some member of the group?"

"I was given his name."

"Have you been keeping tabs on what these people have been doing?"

"Herth has."

"I know that, idiot. I mean, are you the one who's been watching them?"

"No."

"Who is?"

"A fellow named Nath."

"Where can I find him?"

"Are you going to kill me?"

"Not if you keep talking."

"He lives above a carpetmaker way to the west, just north of the Easterners' area. Number four Shade Tree Street."

I said, "Okay. Do you plan to tell Herth about this talk?"

"Yes."

"You'll have to tell him what you told me."

"He's very understanding that way."

"In that case, I need a good reason for leaving you alive."

"You said you would."

"Yes, that is a good reason. I need another one."

"You're a dead man, you know."

"I know."

"A dishonest dead man."

"I'm just in a bad mood. I'm usually a very honest dead man. Ask anyone."

"Okay. I'll keep my mouth shut for an hour."

"Would you keep your word to someone who lied to you?"

He considered that for a moment, then said, "Yes."

"Herth must be a very understanding fellow."

"Yes. Except when his people are killed. He doesn't understand that at all."

I said, "Okay. You can leave."

He stood up without another word and walked out. I replaced my dagger, left the one in the body and walked back out into the main room. The host didn't give me a second glance. I made it onto the street and headed back toward my office. I could feel Loiosh's tension as he strained to look into every corner of every alley we passed.

"You shouldn't have killed that guy, boss."

"If I hadn't, Bajinok wouldn't have taken me seriously. And I'm not certain I could have controlled two of them."

"Herth will be after your head now."

"Yes."

"You can't help Cawti if you're dead."

"I know."

"Then why—"

"Shut up."

Even I didn't think that was much of an answer.

5

I TELEPORTED TO A place I knew in Nath's neighborhood, so I wouldn't have to waste any of Bajinok's hour. Then I wasted a good fifteen minutes while my stomach recovered from the teleport.

Shade Tree Street must have been an old name. There were a few stumps in the ground to the sides, and the hotels and houses were set back quite a ways from the crude stonework curbing on either edge of the street itself, which was as wide as Lower Kieron. The width indicated that the area had once had a lot of shops and markets, and that later it had been one of the better sections of town. That was probably before the Interregnum, however. Now it was a little on the low side.

Number four was right in the middle, between number fifteen and number six. It was of brown stonework, two stories tall, with two flats in it. The one on the bottom had a chreotha crudely drawn on the door. I went up the wooden steps and they didn't creak at all. I was impressed.

The door at the top had a stylized jhereg on it, etched on a metal plate above the symbol for Baron. *"Was I quiet enough, Loiosh?"*

"I think so, boss."

"Okay."

I checked the spells on the door, then checked them a second time. I'm a lot sloppier when I'm not actually about to kill someone, but there's no reason to be *too* sloppy. The door held no surprises. The wood itself was thin enough that I could handle it. I let Spellbreaker fall into my left hand, took a couple of careful breaths, then smacked the door with Spellbreaker and, at the same time, kicked with my right leg. The door flew open and I stepped into the room.

He was alone. That meant it was likely that Bajinok had actually kept his word. He was sitting on a low couch, reading the same tabloid that Cawti had been reading. I kicked the door shut behind me and crossed to him in three steps, drawing my rapier as I did so. He stood up and stared at me, wide-eyed. He made no effort to reach for a weapon. It was possible he wasn't a fighter, but it would be stupid to count on it. I held the point of my weapon up to his left eye and said, "Good afternoon. You must be Nath."

He stared at me, his eyes wide, holding his breath.

I said, "Well?"

He nodded.

I gave him the same speech I'd given Bajinok about not leaving or trying to reach help. He seemed to find it convincing. I said, "Let's sit down and chat."

He nodded again. He was either very frightened or a good actor. I said, "An Easterner named Franz was killed a few days ago."

He nodded.

I said, "Herth had it done."

He nodded again.

I said, "You pointed him out to Herth."

His eyes widened and he half-shook his head.

I said, "Yes. Why?"

"I didn't—"

"I don't care if you suggested the killing or not. I want to know what it was about Franz that you told Herth. Tell me quickly, without thinking about it. If I get the idea that you're lying, I'll kill you."

His mouth worked for a bit, and his voice, when he spoke, was a squeak. "I don't know. I just—" he stopped long enough to clear his throat. "I just told him about them. All of them. I said what they were doing."

"Herth wanted to know names?"

"Not at first. But a few weeks ago he told me to give him reports on all of the Easterners—their names, what they did, everything."

"You had all that?"

He nodded.

I asked, "Why?"

"I've been here for most of the year. Herth heard rumors about this group and sent me to check on them. I've been keeping track."

"I see. And then he tells you to give him the names, and two weeks later Franz is killed."

He nodded.

I said, "Well, why did he want someone killed, and why Franz?"

He said, "I don't know."

"Guess."

"They were troublemakers. They interfered with business. They were always around, you know? And they were giving reading lessons. When Easterners—" He stopped, looking at me.

"Go on."

He swallowed. "When Easterners get too smart, well, I guess it doesn't help business any. But it might have been something that happened before I came. Herth is careful, you know? He wouldn't tell me more than he had to."

"And Franz?"

"He was just one of them."

"What about Kelly?"

"What about him? He never did much that I could see."

I refrained from commenting on his eyesight.

"Boss."

"*Yeah, Loiosh?*"

"*Your hour is about gone.*"

"*Thanks.*"

I said, "Okay. You get to live."

He seemed relieved. I turned, walked out the door and down to the street and made my way through some alleys as quickly as I could. There was no sign of pursuit.

"*Well, what do you think, Loiosh?*"

"*He wanted to kill one of them, and Franz was as good a choice as any.*"

"*Yeah. I think so, too. Why did he want to kill one of them?*"

"*I don't know.*"

"*Well, what now?*"

"*Boss, do you have an idea how much trouble you've gotten yourself into?*"

"*Yeah.*"

"*I was just wondering. I don't know what to do now, boss. We're close to the Easterners' area, if there's anything you want there.*"

I started heading that way as I thought about it. What was the next step? I had to find out if Herth was going to keep after them now, or if he had accomplished whatever it was he hoped to accomplish. If Herth wasn't going to do anything to these people, I could relax and only worry about how I was going to keep him from killing me.

The street I was on dead-ended unexpectedly, so I backtracked a ways until I found one I knew. Tall, windowless houses loomed over me like gloating green and yellow giants, with balconies sometimes almost meeting above me, cutting off my view of the orange-red sky.

Then, at a cross street named Twovine, the houses became older, paler, and smaller and the street widened and I was in the Easterners' section. It smelled like the countryside, with hay and cows and manure where they were selling cow's milk on the street. The breeze became sharper with the widening of the avenue, in swirls that kicked dust up in my eyes and stung my face.

The street curved and twisted and others joined it and left it, and then I saw Sheryl and Paresh standing on a street corner, holding that same damned tabloid and accosting passers-by. I walked up to them. Paresh nodded coolly and turned his back to me. Sheryl's smile was a little friendlier, but she also turned away when two young Easterners came by, holding hands. I heard her saying something about breaking the Imperium, but they just shook their heads and walked on.

I said, "Am I off limits?"

Sheryl shook her head. Paresh turned and said, "Not at all. Do you want to buy a copy?"

I said I didn't. He didn't seem surprised. He turned away again. I stood there for a few more seconds before realizing that I was making a fool of myself by standing, and I'd look stupid leaving. I addressed Sheryl. "Will you talk to me if I buy you a cup of klava?"

"I can't," she said. "Since Franz was murdered we don't work alone."

I bit my tongue when a few remarks about "working" came to mind, then got an idea.

"Well, Loiosh?"

"Oh, sure boss. Why not?"

I said to Sheryl, "Loiosh can stick around."

She looked startled and glanced at Paresh. Paresh looked at Loiosh for a moment, then said, "Why not?"

So Loiosh hung around and got his revolutionary indoctrination while I led Sheryl into an Easterner klava hole located right across the street. It was long, narrow, darker than I like except when I want to kill someone; everything was of wood in surprisingly good condition, considering. I led us all the way to the far end and put my back to the wall. That isn't really a useful way of protecting yourself, but on that occasion it made me feel better.

I had promised to buy her a cup of klava, but actually it came in a glass. I burned my hand on the side when I first picked it up, then, setting it down, slopped some onto the table and burned my leg. I put cream in to cool it down, which didn't help much because they warmed the cream. Tasted good though.

Sheryl's eyes were wide and bright blue, with just a hint of freckles around them. I said, "You know what I'm doing?"

"Not exactly," she said. There was the hint of a smile about her lips. It suddenly occurred to me that she might think I was making a pass at her. Then it occurred to me that maybe I wanted to. She was certainly attractive, and had a bit of the innocent wanton about her that I found stimulating. But no, not now.

I said, "I'm trying to find out why Franz was killed, and then I'm going to do whatever I have to to make sure that Cawti isn't."

The almost-smile didn't waver, but she shook her head. "Franz was killed because they're scared of us."

There were a lot of snappy answers that I didn't make. Instead I said, "Who is scared?"

"The Imperium."

"He wasn't killed by the Imperium."

"Perhaps not directly, but—"

"He was killed by a Jhereg named Herth. Herth doesn't kill people for the Imperium. He's too busy trying to keep the Imperium from finding out that he kills people."

"It may look like that—"

"All right, all right. This isn't helping."

She shrugged, and by now the smile was gone. On the other hand, she wasn't looking angry, so it was worth continuing. I said, "What was he doing, in particular, that would threaten a Jhereg trying to make money, in particular?"

She was quiet for a while, and at last said, "I don't know. He sold papers, just as I was doing, and he spoke at meetings, just as I do, and he gave lessons on reading, and on revolution, just as I do—"

"Wait. You also give reading lessons?"

"We all do."

"I see. All right."

"I guess what it was is that he did more of everything. He was tireless, and enthusiastic, and everyone responded to that—both we, and people we'd run across. When we'd travel through the neighborhoods, he always remembered people better than the rest of us, and they always remembered him. When he spoke, he was better. When he gave reading lessons, it was like it was vital to him that everyone learned to read. Whenever some group that I was in was doing something, he was always there, and whenever some group that I *wasn't* in was doing something, he was always there, too. Do you see what I mean?"

I nodded and didn't say anything. The waiter came and poured more klava. I added cream and honey and used the napkin to hold the glass. Glass. Why not a cup? Stupid Easterners; can't do anything right.

I said, "Do you know any of the Jhereg who operate around here?"

She shook her head. "I know there are some, but I wouldn't recognize them. There are a good number of Dragaerans, and a lot of them are Jhereg, but I couldn't tell you 'that guy works for the organization,' or something."

"Do you know what kind of things they have going on?"

"No, not really."

"Are there places to gamble?"

"Huh? Oh, sure. But they're run by Easterners."

"No, they're not."

"How do you know?"

"I know Herth."

"Oh."

"Are there prostitutes?"

"Yes."

"Brothels?"

"Yes."

"Pimps?"

She suddenly looked, perhaps, the least bit smug. "Not any more," she said.

"Ah ha."

"What?"

"What happened to them?"

"We drove them off. They're the most vicious—"

"I know pimps. How did you drive them off?"

"Most of the pimps around here were really young kids."

"Yes. The older ones run brothels."

"They were part of the gangs."

"Gangs?"

"Yes. Around here there isn't much of anything for kids to do, so—"

"How old kids?"

"Oh, you know, eleven to sixteen."

"Okay."

"So they formed gangs, just to have something to do. And they'd wander around and make trouble, break up stores, that kind of thing. Your Phoenix Guards couldn't care less about what they do, as long as they stay in our area."

"They aren't *my* Phoenix Guards."

"Whatever. There have been gangs around here for longer than I've been alive. A lot of them get involved in pimping because it's about the only way to make money when you don't have any money to start with. They also terrorize a lot of the small shopkeepers into paying them, and steal a little, but there just isn't that much to steal and no one to sell it to."

I suddenly thought about Noish-pa, but no, they wouldn't mess around with a witch. I said, "Okay, so some of them got into pimping."

"Yes."

"How did you get rid of them?"

"Kelly says that most of the kids in the gangs are in because they don't have any hope of things being better for them. He says that their only real hope is revolution, so—"

"Fine," I said. "How did you get rid of them?"

"We broke up most of the gangs."

"How?"

"We taught them to read, for one thing. Once you can read it's harder to remain ignorant. And when they saw we were serious about destroying the despots, many of them joined us."

"Just like that?"

For the first time she glared at me. "It's taken us ten years of work to get this far, and we still have a long way to go. Ten years. It wasn't 'just like that.' And not all of them stayed in the movement, either. But, so far, most of the gangs are gone and haven't come back."

"And when the gangs broke up, the pimps left?"

"They needed the gangs to back them up."

"This all fits."

She asked, "Why?"

I said, "The pimps worked for Herth."

"How do you know that?"

"I know Herth."

"Oh."

"Have you been involved for ten years?"

She nodded.

"How did you—"

She shook her head. We sipped our klava for a while. Then she sighed and said, "I got involved when I was looking for something to do after my pimp was run out of the neighborhood."

I said, "Oh."

"Couldn't you tell I used to be a whore?" She was looking hard at me, and trying to make her voice sound tough and streetwise.

I shook my head and answered the thought behind the words. "It's different among Dragaerans. Prostitution isn't thought of as something to be ashamed of."

She stared at me, but I couldn't tell if she was showing disbelief or contempt. I realized that if I kept this up, I'd start to question the Dragaeran attitude too, and I didn't need any more things to question.

I cleared my throat. "When did the pimps leave?"

"We've been chasing them out gradually over the last few years. We haven't seen any around this neighborhood for months."

"Ah ha."

"You said that already."

"Things are starting to make sense."

"You think that was why Franz was murdered?"

"All the pimps gave some portion of their income to Herth. That's how these things work."

"I see."

"Was Franz involved in breaking up the gangs?"

"He was involved in everything."

"Was he *especially* involved in that?"

"He was involved in everything."

"I see."

I drank some more klava. Now I could hold the glass, but the klava was cold. Stupid Easterners. The waiter came over, replaced the glass, filled it.

I said, "Herth is going to try to put the pimps back in business."

"You think so?"

"Yes. He'll think that he's warned you now, so you should know better."

"We'll drive them out again. They are agents of repression."

"Agents of repression?"

"Yes."

"Okay. If you drive them out again, he'll get even nastier."

I saw something flicker behind her eyes, but her voice didn't change. "We'll fight him," she said. I guess she saw some look on my face at that, because she started looking angry again. "Do you think we don't know how to fight? What do you think was involved in breaking up the gangs in the first place? Polite conversation? Do you think they just let us? Those at the top had power and lived well. They didn't just take it, you know. We can fight. We win when we fight. As Kelly says, that's because all the real fighters are on our side."

That sounded like Kelly. I was quiet for a while, then, "I don't suppose you people would consider leaving the pimps alone."

"What do you think?"

"Yeah. What happened to the tags?"

"The what?"

"The girls who worked for the pimps."

"I don't know. I joined the movement, but that was a long time ago when things were just starting. I don't know about the rest of them."

"Don't they have a right to live, too?"

"We all have a right to live. We have a right to live without having to sell our bodies."

I looked at her. When I'd spoken to Paresh, I had somehow gotten past his rote answers to the person underneath. With Sheryl, I couldn't. It was frustrating.

I said, "Okay. I've found out what I wanted to, and you have some information to take back to Kelly."

She nodded. "Thanks for the klava," she said.

I paid for it and we walked back out to the corner. Paresh was there, arguing loudly with a short male Easterner about something incomprehensible. Loiosh flew back to my shoulder.

"Learn anything, boss?"

"Yeah. You?"

"Nothing I wanted to know."

Paresh nodded to me. I nodded back. Sheryl smiled at me then took up a stance on the corner. I could almost see her planting her feet.

Just to be flashy, I teleported back to my office. What's a little nausea compared to flash? Heh. Vlad the Sorcerer.

I wandered around outside of the office until my stomach settled down, then went in. As I went down the hall toward the stairs, I heard Sticks talking in one of the sitting rooms. I stuck my head in. He was seated on a couch next to Chimov, a rather young guy who I'd recruited during a Jhereg war some time before. Chimov was holding one of Sticks's clubs. It was about two feet long and had a uniform diameter of maybe an inch. Sticks was holding another one, saying, "These are hickory. Oak is fine, too. It's just what you're used to, really."

"Okay," said Chimov, "but I don't see how it's any different from a lepip."

"If you hold that way, it isn't. Look. See? Hold it here, about a third of the way from the back. It's different with different clubs, depending on length and weight, but you want to get the balance right. Here. Your thumb and forefinger act like a hinge, and if you catch the guy in the stomach, or somewhere soft, you use the heel of your hand to bounce it off. This way." He demonstrated, bouncing the club off thin air, as far as I could tell.

Chimov shook his head. "Bounce? Why are you bouncing it, anyway? Can't you get more power into it holding it all the way back?"

"Sure. And if I'm trying to break a guy's knees, or his head, that's what I do. But most of the time I'm just trying to get a message across. So I bounce this off his head ten or twelve times, then mess up his face a little and tap his ribs once or twice, and he understands things that, maybe, he didn't understand before. The idea isn't to prove how tough you are, the idea is to convince him that he wants to do what you're being paid to make him do."

Chimov tried a few swings.

"Not like that," said Sticks. "Use your fingers and your wrist. If you go flailing around like that you'll just wear yourself out. There's no future in it. Here, watch...."

I left them to their conversation. I knew that kind of conversation because I'd had plenty of them myself. Now it was starting to bother me.

Maybe what everyone had been saying to me was starting to affect my thinking. Worse, maybe they were right.

6

... & dirt from knees.

I NODDED TO MELESTAV as I walked past him, and plopped into my chair. Someday I'll have to describe how you go about plopping into a chair while wearing a rapier at your hip. It takes practice.

All right, Vlad. You've just made a hash of things, going in and killing that bastard, getting Herth on your tail when you didn't need to. That's done. Let's not make it worse. This is a problem just like any other problem. Find a bite-size piece of it and solve that, then go on to the next one.

I closed my eyes and took two deep breaths.

"Boss," said Melestav. "Your wife's here."

I opened my eyes. "Send her in." Cawti entered the room like an angry dzur, and looked at me as if I were the cause of her anger. Rocza was on her shoulder. Cawti shut the door behind her and sat down across from me; we looked at each other for a while. She said, "I spoke with Sheryl."

"Yeah."

"Well?"

"I'm glad to see you, too, Cawti. How's your day been?"

"Stop it, Vlad."

Loiosh shifted uncomfortably. I decided he didn't really have to hear this, so I got up, opened the window and let him and Rocza out. *"In a while, chum."*

"Yeah boss." I left the window open and faced Cawti again.

"Well?" she said again.

I sat down and leaned back. "You're angry," I said.

"My, but you're perceptive."

"Don't get sarcastic with me, Cawti, I'm not in the mood for it."

"I don't really care what you're in the mood for. I want to know why you felt the need to interrogate Sheryl."

"I'm still trying to learn exactly what happened to Franz and why it happened. Talking to Sheryl was part of that."

"Why?"

"Why am I trying to find out about Franz?" I paused and considered telling her that I wanted to save her life, but decided that would be both unfair and ineffective. I said, "Partly because I said I would, I guess."

"According to her you spent the entire time mocking everything we believe in."

"According to her, perhaps I did."

"Why was it necessary?"

I shook my head.

"What," she said, biting out each word, "is that gesture supposed to mean?"

"It indicates the negative."

"I want to know what you're doing."

I stood up and took half a step toward her then sat down again. My hands opened and closed. "No," I said. "I won't tell you what I'm doing."

"You won't."

"That is correct. You saw no need to tell me when you got involved with these people, and you didn't see any need to tell me what you were doing yesterday; I see no need to give you an account of my actions."

"You seem to be doing everything you can to hurt our movement. If that isn't the case, you should—"

"No. Everything I could do to hurt your movement would be a lot simpler and be over much more quickly and leave no room for doubt. I am doing something else. You aren't with me on it because you've said you weren't. I've been trying to investigate Franz's killing on my own, and you've done everything to keep me out of it except put a knife in me, and maybe that's next. You have no right to do that and then try to interrogate me like the Imperial Prosecutor. I won't put up with it."

She glared. "That's quite a speech. It's quite a lot of crap."

"Cawti, I've made my position clear. I need not, and will not, put up with any more of this."

"If you're going to stick your nose into—"

"Get out of my office."

Her eyes widened. Then narrowed. Her nostrils flared. She stood motionless for a moment, then turned and walked out of my office. She didn't slam the door.

I sat there, trembling, until Loiosh came back. Rocza wasn't with him. I decided Rocza must be with Cawti. I was glad because I knew Cawti would need someone.

After letting Loiosh in, I walked out of the office and let my feet carry me where they would, as long as it wasn't to the Easterners' section. I felt a ridiculous urge to find the oracle I'd spoken to a couple of weeks before and kill him; even now I can't think why I wanted to do that. I actually had to talk myself out of it.

I didn't notice where I was going. I paid no attention to direction, or people around me, or anything else. A couple of Jhereg toughs saw me, took two steps toward me, then went away again. It was only much later that I realized that they had been two enforcers for an old enemy, and probably felt they had something to settle with me. I guess they changed their minds. By then Spellbreaker was in my left hand and I was swinging it as I walked, sometimes smacking it at buildings and watching parts of the walls crumble away, or just flailing wildly, hoping someone would get close enough. I don't know how much time went by, and I've never asked Loiosh, but I think I walked for over an hour.

Think about that for a minute. You've just made an enemy who has the resources to keep a tail on you wherever you go, and you've made him mad enough to kill you. So what do you do? Walk around without any protection for an hour making as big a spectacle of yourself as you can.

This is not what I call intelligent.

One cry of, *"Boss!"* was all Loiosh had time for. As far as I was concerned, it was like waking up from sleep to find yourself surrounded by hostile faces. Several of them. I saw at least one wizard's staff. A voice came from somewhere inside of me. It sounded absurdly calm, and it said, "You're dead now, Vlad." I don't know what that triggered, but it enabled me to think clearly. It was as if I had only an instant to do something, but the instant stretched out forever. Options came and went. Spellbreaker could probably break the teleport block they must have put around me, but there was no way I could teleport out before they had me. I might be able to take a few of them with me, which is a good thing for a Dzur hero to do if he wants to be remembered, but it felt quite futile just then. On the other hand, you don't send a group of eight or nine if you want to kill someone; maybe they had something else in mind. No way to guess what, though. I put all of the force of command I could muster into a psionic message: *"Loiosh. Go away."*

I felt him leave my shoulder and was ridiculously pleased. Something tingled in the back of my neck. I felt the ground against my cheek.

The first thing I heard, just before I opened my eyes, was, "You will note that you are still alive."

Then I did open them and found that I was looking at Bajinok. Before becoming aware of anything else, I remarked to myself what a perfect thing that had been for him to say. The timing, I guess, is what really got to me. I mean, *just* as I was becoming conscious, before I even noticed the chains holding me onto the hard iron chair or the feeling of being caught in a net of sorcery. Before, in fact, I noticed that I was naked. The chair was cold.

I looked back at him, feeling the need to say something, but not able to come up with anything. He waited, though. Just naturally polite, I guess. The room was well lighted and not too small—about twelve paces on the sides I could see (I didn't turn around). There were five enforcer types behind Bajinok, and from the way they stared at me, their hands on various pieces of hardware, they took me seriously. I felt flattered. In a corner of the room were my clothing and assorted junk. I said, "As long as you have all of my clothes in a pile, could you be a pal and have them cleaned? I'll repay you, of course."

He smiled and nodded. We were both going to be cool professionals about this. Oh, goody. I stared at him. I became aware that I wanted, almost desperately, to break the chains that were around my arms and legs and get up and kill him. Strangle him. Visions filled my brain of the enforcers battering me with their swords and spells which bounced off me or fell harmless as I squeezed the life out of him. I fought to keep this wish off my face and out of my actions. I wished Loiosh were there with me while I was glad he wasn't. I have strong opinions about ambivalence.

He pulled up a chair and sat facing me, crossed his legs, leaned back. He could have chosen to be in that position when I regained consciousness, but I guess he liked dramatic gestures as much as I do. "You are alive," he said, "because we need some answers from you."

"Ask away," I said. "I'm feeling awfully cooperative."

He nodded. "If I told you that we'll let you live if you give us the answers, you wouldn't believe me. Besides, I don't like to lie. So instead I will tell you, quite truthfully, that if you don't give us the answers, you will very badly want to die. Do you understand this?"

I nodded because my mouth was suddenly very dry. I felt queasy. I was aware of all sorts of spells in the room; probably spells that would prevent any sorcery I might try. I still had my link to the Orb, of course (which told me I'd only been unconscious for ten minutes or so), but I doubted I could do anything with it. Still . . .

He said, "What is your connection to this group of Easterners?"

I blinked. He didn't know? Maybe I could use that. Perhaps if I stalled, I could try witchcraft. I'd used it before in situations where I shouldn't have been able to. I said, "Well, they're Easterners, and I'm an Easterner, so we just sort of naturally—" Then I screamed. I can't, now, recall what hurt. I think everything. I have no memory of some particular part of me hurting, but I knew that he was right; this would do it. I wanted to die. It lasted for such a brief time that it was over before I screamed, but I knew I couldn't take more of it, whatever it was. I was drenched with sweat, and my head drooped and I heard myself making small whimpering sounds like a puppy.

No one said anything. After a long time I looked up. I felt like I had aged twenty years. Bajinok had no expression on his face. He said, "What is your connection to the group of Easterners?"

I said, "My wife is one of them."

He nodded. So. He had known. He was going to play that kind of game with me—asking some questions he knew the answers to and some that he didn't. Wonderful. But that was all right, because I knew I wasn't going to lie any more.

"Why is she with them?"

"I think she believes in what they're doing."

"What about you?"

I paused, my heart pounding with fear, but I had to ask. "I . . . don't understand your question."

"What are you doing with those Easterners?"

A sense of relief flooded me. Yes. I could answer that. "Cawti. I don't want her killed. Like Franz was killed."

"What makes you think she will be?"

"I'm not sure. I don't yet—that is, I don't know why Franz was killed."

"Do you have any theories?"

I paused again, trying to understand the question, and I guess I waited too long because they hit me with it. Longer this time. Eternity. Maybe two seconds. Dear Verra, *please* let me die.

When it stopped, I couldn't speak for a moment, but I knew I had to had to had to or they'd do it again again again, so, "I'm trying. I—." I had to swallow and was afraid to, but I did, and shuddered with relief when it didn't happen. I tried to speak again. "Water," I said. A glass was tipped into my mouth. I swallowed some and spilled more down my chest. Then I spoke quickly so they wouldn't think I was trying to stall. "They were cutting into your—Herth's—business. I'm guessing it was a warning."

"Do they think so?"

"I don't know. Kelly—their leader—is smart. Also I told one of them I thought so."

"If it is a warning, will they heed it?"

"I don't think so."

"How many of them are there?"

"I've only seen about half a dozen, but I've been told that—"

I was staring right at the door when it burst open and several shiny things came flying through it past Bajinok and past my head. Their were grunts from behind me. Someone had probed the room and found the position of everyone in it. Good work. Probably Kragar.

Bajinok was fast. He didn't waste any time with me, or with the intruders, he just stepped over to one of the sorcerers and they began a teleport. Sticks, who was standing in the doorway, didn't spare more than a glance at him, before moving into the room. Something else shiny flashed by me and I heard another grunt behind my right shoulder, then noticed that Kragar was also in the doorway, throwing knives. Loiosh flew into the room then, and Glowbug was right behind him. Glowbug's eyes were shining like the lamps at the Dragon Gate of the Imperial Palace. The thought, "You're being rescued," flashed into my head, but I couldn't drum up more than a passing interest in whether the attempt would be successful.

Watching Sticks was interesting, though. He was dealing with four of them at once. He had a club in each hand and a look of concentration on his face. The clubs became a blur, but never invisible. He was very graceful. He would bounce a club off a head, then hit a side while the other club crossed over to the top of the first head, and like that. When they tried to hit him he would work the attack into his actions as if he'd planned it all along. He started moving faster, and soon their weapons flew from their hands and they started to stumble. Then Sticks, as if culminating a dance, finished them. One at a time, both clubs to the top of the head, not quite at the same time. Ker-thump. Ker-thump. Ker-thump. Ker-thump. The first hit the ground as he nailed the third.

The second hit the ground as he got the fourth. As the third fell, Sticks stepped back and looked around, and as the last one fell he put his clubs away.

Glowbug's voice came from over my shoulder. "Got 'em all, Kragar."

"Good." His voice came from right next to me, and I saw that he was working on the chains.

"You all right, boss?"

The chains fell off my arms, and I felt the ones around my legs being worked on. A lady in grey and black came into the room. Kragar said, "We'll be ready in a moment, milady." I thought, Left Hand. Sorceress. Hired to teleport us home.

"Boss?"

The chains were gone from my legs now. "Vlad?" said Kragar. "Can you stand up?"

It would be nice to collapse into bed, I decided. I noticed Glowbug collecting my clothing.

"Boss? Say something."

Sticks looked at me, then looked away. I think I saw him mouthing an obscenity.

"Damn it, boss! What's wrong?"

"All right," said Kragar. "Glowbug, help me get him standing. Gather round." I felt Loiosh clutching my shoulder. I was dragged to my feet. "Go," said Kragar.

"Boss? Can't you—"

A twist in my gut, a massive disorientation and head-spinning, and the world went around and around inside of my skull.

"—answer?"

I threw up on the ground outside of my home. They held me, and Sticks, now holding the bundle of my belongings, stood close by. "Get him inside," said Kragar. They tried to help me walk but I collapsed and almost fell.

"Boss?"

They tried again with no better results. Kragar said, "We'll never get him up the stairs this way."

"I'll dump these things inside the house, and—no, wait." Sticks vanished from sight for a moment and I heard him speaking to someone in low tones. I heard the words, "drunk" and "brothel," and what seemed to be a child's voice answering him. Then he came back without the bundle and took my legs and they carried me into the house.

Sticks dropped my legs at the top of the stairs and clapped. I heard a child say, "I'll leave these here." There was a rustling sound, and the child said, "No, that's all right," and there were soft footsteps descending. After waiting for someone to answer the clap, Sticks opened the door and I was dragged inside.

"Now what?" said Glowbug.

I could hear barely concealed distaste in Kragar's voice as he said, "We need to get him cleaned up, I think, and—Cawti!"

"Loiosh told me to come home right away. What—Vlad?"

"He needs to be cleaned up and put to bed, I think."

"Are you all right, Vlad?"

Loiosh flew off my shoulder. Probably to Cawti, but I was staring in the other direction just then so I couldn't tell. Cawti was silent for a moment, then she said, "Put him in the bath. Through here." It sounded as if she was having trouble keeping her voice steady.

After a while there was hot water on me, and Cawti's hands were gentle. I learned that I'd soiled myself somewhere in there, as well as throwing up all over my chest and stomach. Kragar came into the room and he and Cawti got me standing and dried me off, then got me into the bed and left me there. Loiosh, silent now, sat next to me, his head on my cheek. Rocza made scratching sounds on the bedpost to my left.

From the next room, I could hear Cawti saying, "Thank you, Kragar."

Kragar said, "Thank Loiosh." Then their voices dropped and I could only hear mutterings for a while.

Later, the door to the flat closed and I heard Cawti make her way into the bathroom, and the sound of the pump. After a while she came back into the bedroom and put a damp cloth over my forehead. She put Spellbreaker around my left wrist and covered me with blankets. I settled back into the bedding and waited to die.

It was funny. I'd always wondered what my last thoughts would be, if I had time to think them. It turned out that my last thoughts were of how I was thinking my last thoughts. That was funny. I chuckled somewhere, deep down inside of me where I can't be hurt. If Aliera was right about reincarnation, perhaps my next life would be better. No. I *knew* Aliera was right. My next life probably wouldn't be any better than this one. Well, I don't know. Maybe you learn something each life. What had I learned in this lifetime? That it's always the good guys against the bad guys, and you can never tell who the good guys are, so you settle for killing the bad guys. We're all bad guys. No. Loiosh isn't a bad guy. Cawti isn't—well—oh, what's the use? I should just—

—I realized with some surprise that I was still alive. It occurred to me then that I might *not* die. I felt my heart speed up. Was it possible? A certain sense of what I could only call reality began to seep in then, and I knew I was going to live. I still couldn't accept it emotionally—I didn't really believe it—but I somehow knew it. I reached for my right sleeve dagger but it was gone. Then I remembered that I was naked. I lifted my head and saw the bundle of my clothing and weapons, with the rapier jutting out, over in the corner, and I knew I couldn't reach it. I felt Spellbreaker around my left wrist. Would that do? How? I could hardly strangle myself. Maybe I could bash myself over the head.

I worked my left arm free and stared at the thin gold chain. When I first found it, Sethra Lavode had suggested I find a name for it. She was evasive when I asked why. Now I looked at it closely, wrapped tightly about my wrist, clinging, but never squeezing. I let my arm fall off the side of the bed and it uncoiled and fell into my hand. I lifted it, and it worked itself into a pose, hanging in midair like a coiled yendi. As I moved my hand, the rest of it didn't move, as if the other end was fixed in space, twelve inches above me.

What are you? I asked it. *You have saved my life more than once, but I don't really know what you are. Are you a weapon? Can you kill me now?*

It coiled and uncoiled then, as if it were considering the matter. I had never seen it do that before. The trick of hanging in midair it had been doing when I had first found it, but that had been under Dzur Mountain, where strange things are normal. Or was it in the Paths of the Dead? I couldn't remember any more. Did it mean to take me back there now? Easterners aren't allowed into the Paths of the Dead, but was I really an Easterner? What *was* an Easterner, really? Were they different from Dragaerans? Who cared? That was easy, Easterners cared and Dragaerans cared. Who *didn't* care? Kelly didn't care. Did the Lords of Judgment care?

Spellbreaker formed shapes in the air before me, twisting and coiling like a dancer. I barely noticed when Loiosh flew out of the room. It was still dancing for me a few minutes later when Cawti returned, holding a steaming cup of tea.

"Drink this, Vlad," she said, her voice trembling. Spellbreaker dipped low, then climbed high. I wondered what would happen if I let go of the end I was holding, but didn't want to take the chance that it would stop. I felt a cup pressed against my lip and hot tea dribbled into my mouth and onto my chest. I swallowed by reflex and noticed an odd taste. It occurred to me that perhaps Cawti was poisoning me. When the cup came again, I drank greedily, still watching Spellbreaker's dance.

When the cup was empty, I lay back, waiting for oblivion. There was some part of me that was mildly surprised when it came.

7

1 pr black riding boots:
remove reddish stain on toe of rt boot...

I DON'T REMEMBER ACTUALLY waking up. I stared at the ceiling for a long time without focusing on it. Awareness of sensations increased slowly—the smooth linen of finely woven sheets, the scent of Cawti's hair next to my face, her warm, dry hand in mine. With my other hand I touched myself, face and body, and I blinked. Loiosh's tail was draped across my neck—feather-light and scaly.

"*Boss?*" Tentative.

"*Yes, Loiosh. I'm here.*"

He rested his head against my cheek. I smelled Adrilankha's morning in the breeze through the window. I licked my lips, squeezed my eyes tightly shut, and opened them. Memory returned, piercing as a needle. I winced, then trembled. After a moment I turned toward Cawti. She was awake and looking at me. Her eyes were red. I said, "Some of us will do anything for sympathy." My voice cracked as I said it. She squeezed my hand.

After a moment, she chuckled softly. "I'm trying to find a way to say, 'Are you all right?' that doesn't sound like you ought to be put away somewhere." I squeezed her hand. Loiosh stirred and flapped around the room once. Rocza stirred from somewhere and hissed.

"If you mean am I about to kill myself, the answer is no." Then I said, "You didn't sleep, did you?" She made a gesture that I took as, "No, I didn't." I said, "Maybe you should." She looked at me with swimming red eyes. I said, "You know, this doesn't really solve anything."

"I know," she said, and this time it was her voice that broke. "Do you want to talk about it?"

"About—what happened yesterday? No. It's too close. What did you give me? It *was* a poison, wasn't it?"

"In the tea? Yes. Tsiolin, but just a mild dose so you'd sleep."

I nodded. She moved over next to me and I held her. I stared at the ceiling a while longer. It was made of beaded ceiling board, and Cawti had painted it a very pale green. "Green?" I had said at the time. "It represents growth and fertility," she had explained. "Ah ha," I had said and we went on to other things. Now it just looked green. But she was holding me. Make of this what you will.

I got up and took care of morning things. When I looked back in, Cawti was sleeping. I went out with Loiosh and sat in Kigg's for a while and drank klava. I was very careful to watch all around as I left home. I've never been attacked when I was ready for it; it's always come unexpectedly. That's odd only because of the amount of time I seem to spend expecting to be attacked. I wondered what it would be like not to have to worry about that. If these Easterners had their way, and their daydreams turned out real, that might happen. But it wouldn't matter to me, anyway. I couldn't remember a time when I wasn't careful to watch around me as much as possible. Even when I was young there were too many kids who didn't like Easterners. I was stuck as I was, whatever happened. But still—

"*I think you have too much on your mind, boss.*"

I nodded. "*All right, chum. Tell me what to ignore.*"

"*Heh.*"

"*Right.*"

"*About these Easterners—Kelly's group . . .*"

"*Yeah?*"

"*What if you didn't have to worry about Cawti's life, or about Herth, or any of it. How would you feel about them?*"

"*How can I know that?*"

"*How would you feel about Cawti being one of them?*"

Now that was a good question. I chewed it over. "*I guess I just don't think much of a group that's so wrapped up in its ideals that it doesn't care about people.*"

"*But about Cawti—*"

"*Yeah. I don't know, Loiosh. There was never really the chance to find out what's involved. How much time will it take? Am I going to see her at all? Is she going to want to give them money? How much? There are too many things I don't know. She ought to have told me about it.*"

I drank some more klava and thought about things. I was very careful walking out of the place.

When I got into the office I didn't stop long enough to say hello to Kragar and Melestav; I went straight into the basement. Next to the lab is a large, empty room with many lanterns. I lit them. I drew my rapier, saluted my shadow, and attacked it.

Parry head. What had happened to me last night?

Step in, step out. It was worse than being told I was a reincarnated Dragaeran. Or different, at least.

Step in, cut flank, step out. Maybe I should just forget that I'd tried to kill myself. Except that I might try again, and maybe I'd succeed. But then, maybe it would have been best if I had.

Step in, cut cheek, cut neck, step out. That was nonsense. On the other hand, there was no denying that I had actually wanted to kill myself last night; had tried to do so. It was hard to believe.

Parry flank, parry head, step in, cut leg, thrust chest. The pain, though—that incredible pain. But it was over. I was going to have to get to Herth before he got to me, and it might not change how Cawti felt toward me anyway, and I wouldn't even get paid for it. But no matter; I would have to make sure he couldn't do that to me again. Ever.

Step back, parry a thrust, disengage, stop-cut, step in, cut neck. I'm not the suicidal type. There are many assassins who don't care if they live or die, but I've never been one. Or I never was one before. Forget it. I could spend the rest of my life trying to decide what it meant that I'd wanted to end it. There were things that I had to do and this was getting nowhere. I was going to have to kill Herth, and that was that.

Salute. I just wished I didn't have to.

I also wished I'd installed a bath down here.

"Kragar."

"Yeah?"

"I'm done mucking about."

"Good. It's about time."

"Shut up. I want full details on Herth. I mean, everything. I want to know his mistress's favorite color and how often she washes her hair. I want to know how much pepper he puts in his soup. I want to know how often he takes a—"

"Right, boss. I'll get on it."

"Can you get him before anything happens to Cawti?"

"I don't know. I don't know for sure that anything will happen to Cawti. But we can't take chances. I'll have to—" I paused as a thought hit me. I threw it away and it came back. There was one thing I could do that might help.

"She isn't going to like it if she finds out, boss."

"By Verra's fingers, Loiosh! She hasn't liked anything I've done since this mess started. So what? Do you have any other ideas?"

"I guess not."

"Neither do I. I should have done this days ago. I haven't been thinking. Is Rocza with her now?"

He paused. *"Yes."*

"Then let's go."

"What about protection for you?"

I felt suddenly queasy as I remembered the day before. *"I'm not going to be charging around like a blind man this time."*

"Aren't you?"

That sounded rhetorical so I didn't answer.

I teleported directly from my office, just in case someone was waiting outside. The Easterners' section was starting to look more and more familiar as I spent more and more time there. I had mixed feelings about this.

I asked, *"Is she moving?"*

"She was, boss. She stopped a while ago."

"How far are we?"

"I could fly there in five minutes."

"Great. How far are we?"

"Half an hour."

Streets curved and twisted like Verra's sense of humor, and it was, in fact, a good half-hour before we found ourselves near a large park. A crowded park. There were thousands there, mostly human. I gawked. The last time I had seen that many people gathered in one place there was a battle being fought. I hadn't liked it.

I took a deep breath and began to make my way into and through the crowd, Loiosh steering. (*"This way. Okay, now back to the right. Over there, somewhere."*) Loiosh was being careful not to let Rocza know he was in the area. He could have been unhappy about it, but I guess he chose to look at it as a game. I was being careful not to let Cawti know I was in the area, and there was nothing gamelike about it.

I spotted her, standing on a platform that seemed to be the center of the crowd's attention. She was scanning the crowd, although most people looking at her wouldn't have known it. At first I thought she was looking for me, but then I understood and chuckled. Kelly was standing at the front of the platform, declaiming in a thundering voice about "their" fear of "us," and Cawti was acting as his bodyguard. Great. I moved up toward the platform, shaking my head. I wanted to act as *her* bodyguard, without her seeing me. She was looking for someone trying to sneak up to the platform—in other words, she was looking for someone doing just what I was trying to do.

When I realized that, I stopped where I was—about forty feet away—and watched. I really can't tell you what the speech was about; I wasn't listening. He didn't turn the crowd into a raging mob, but they seemed interested, and there were occasional cheers. I felt lost. I'd never before been in a large group of people while trying to decide if one member of the group was going to kill another member. I assume there are ways of doing it, but I don't know them. I checked back on the platform from time to time, but nothing was happening. I occasionally caught phrases from Kelly's speech, things like, "historical necessity," and "we aren't going to them on our knees." In addition to Kelly, Gregory was up there, and Natalia, and several Easterners and a few Teckla I didn't recognize. They also seemed to be interested in whatever Kelly was talking about.

Eventually the gathering broke up with much cheering. I tried to stay as close behind Cawti as I could without being spotted. It wasn't very close. Groups formed, one around each of those who had been on the platform, except for Cawti. She was hanging around Kelly. As things thinned out I kept expecting to see someone else who, like me, was just sort of lagging behind, but I didn't.

After half an hour, Kelly, Gregory and Natalia left the area. Things were pretty quiet by then. I followed them. They returned to Kelly's house and disappeared inside. I waited. The weather was good, for which I was grateful; I hate standing around waiting in the cold and rain.

The trouble was, it left me with too much time to think, and I had too much to think about.

I had actually tried to kill myself. Why? That had been the first time I'd been tortured, certainly, but I'd had information beaten out of me before; was it really all that different? I thought of the pain and heard myself screaming and a shudder ran through my body.

Other times, when I'd been forced to give up information, I had been in control. I had been able to play with them—giving them this or that tidbit and holding back what I could. This time I had just spilled my guts. Okay, but that still didn't account for it. I'm just not the suicidal type. Am I? Verra, what's wrong with me?

After a while I said, "*Loiosh, keep watching the house. I'm going to visit Noish-pa.*"

"*No, boss. Not without me.*"

"*What? Why not?*"

"*Herth is still looking for you.*"

"*Oh. Yeah.*"

Cawti came out of the house after a few hours. It was getting on toward evening. She headed toward home. I followed. A few times Rocza, on her shoulder, began looking around nervously and Loiosh suggested we drop back for a while, so we did. That was pretty much the excitement. I wandered around for an hour or so then went home myself. Cawti and I didn't say a lot, but I caught her looking at me a few times with a worried expression on her face.

You can repeat a lot of that for the next day. She left the house and I followed her while she stood around selling tabloids (a new one, I saw; the banner said something about landlords) and talking to strangers. I watched the strangers closely, especially the occasional Dragaeran. I checked with Kragar to see how he was doing, and he said he was working on it. I left him alone after that. I had only bothered him at all because of a growing sense of frustration.

Frustration? Sure. I was following Cawti around desperately trying to keep her alive and knowing that it was pointless. I couldn't be sure they were about to kill one of the Easterners, and there was no reason to think it would be Cawti and, frankly, there wasn't much I could do anyway. Assassins work by surprise. But if the assassin can surprise the target, chances are he can also surprise one bodyguard who is twenty or thirty feet away. Trying to protect Cawti was almost an exercise in futility. But then, there wasn't anything else I could do except think, and I was tired of thinking.

"*Boss.*"

I glanced in the direction that had Loiosh's attention. It was the corner of a large, brown building—the kind that has flats for several families. "*What is it?*"

"*I saw someone there, tall enough to be a Dragaeran.*"

I watched for a while but there was no further movement. Cawti still stood next to a vegetable stall, along with Sheryl, exchanging comments with the vendor from time to time. For half an hour I alternated between watching Cawti and watching the corner, then I gave up and went back to watching my wife while Loiosh kept an eye on the spot where he'd seen someone. Eventually Cawti and Sheryl left and walked back to the building I thought of as their headquarters, though Cawti referred to it only as Kelly's place. I tried to see if they were being followed, but I couldn't be certain.

Cawti went inside and Sheryl kept going. I stationed myself out of sight down the street where I could watch the door. I was getting to know that door better than I'd ever wanted to know a door. I was glad, at least, that Cawti couldn't teleport.

It was getting on toward evening when a Dragaeran in Jhereg colors walked boldly up to the door and inside. I checked my weapons and started after him quickly, but he was out again before I was halfway across the street. I turned the other way and seemed uninterested and he didn't notice me. When I looked back he was walking hurriedly away. I thought about following him, but the most I could do was confirm that Herth had sent him. So what?

He was, I decided, probably a messenger. Or he could have been a sorcerer and he'd just killed everyone in the house. Or—at that moment Cawti, Paresh and Natalia left as if they were in a hurry. I followed. They headed northeast, which is toward the center of the city. (The Easterners' section is South Adrilankha, which is mostly west of central Adrilankha. Make sense of that if you care to.)

Before crossing the unmarked border into Dragaeran terrain (a street called Carpenter), they turned and followed a couple of side streets. Eventually they stopped and gathered around something on the ground. Cawti knelt down while the others stood over. Paresh began looking around. I walked toward them and he saw me. He straightened quickly and his hand went up as if he were about to do something sorcerous and Spellbreaker came into my hand. But he did nothing, and presently I was close enough to be recognized in the fading orange-red light, as well as to see that Cawti was kneeling next to a body. She looked up.

Paresh was tense, the muscles on his neck standing out. Natalia seemed only mildly interested and a bit fatalistic. Cawti stared at me hard.

Paresh said, "What have you to do with this?"

"Nothing," I said, figuring I'd allow him exactly one such question. He nodded rather than pushing it, which half disappointed me.

Cawti said, "What are you doing here, Vlad?"

Instead of answering, I approached the body. I looked, then looked away, then looked again, longer. It had once been Sheryl. She had been beaten to death. She was not revivifiable. Each leg was broken at the knee, above it, and below. Each arm was broken at the elbow. The bruises on each side of her face—what was left of it—matched. The top of her head had been staved in. And so on. It was my professional judgment that it had been done over the course of several hours. And if you can't make professional judgments, what's the point of being a professional? I looked away again.

"What are you doing here, Vlad?" asked Cawti.

"I was following you."

She looked at me, then nodded, as if to herself. "Did you see anything?"

"Loiosh maybe caught a glimpse of someone watching while you were at the market, but then you went into Kelly's place and I just watched the door."

"You didn't see fit to tell anyone?"

I blinked. Tell someone? One of them? Well, I suppose that made sense. "It didn't occur to me."

She stared, then turned her back. Paresh was almost glaring at me. Natalia was looking away, but when I looked closer, I could see that she was almost trembling with anger. Cawti's hands were closed into fists, and she was tightening and loosening them rhythmically. I felt myself start to get angry, too. They didn't want me around at all; they certainly hadn't asked me to watch Sheryl. Now they were all at the boiling point because I hadn't. It was enough to—

"They aren't mad at you, boss."

"Eh?"

"They're mad at Herth for doing it, and maybe at themselves for having allowed him to."

"How could they have prevented it?"

"Don't ask me."

I turned to Paresh, who was closest. "How could you have prevented it?"

He just shook his head. Natalia answered, though, in a strained voice, as if she could barely speak. "We could have built the movement faster and stronger, so they wouldn't have dared to do this. They should be scared of us by now."

This wasn't the time to explain what I thought of that. Instead, I helped them carry Sheryl's body back to Kelly's place. We didn't get more than a few glances as we made our way through the darkening streets. I suppose that says something. The three of them acted as if I should feel honored that they were allowing me to help. I didn't comment on that, either. We left the body in the hallway while they went in and I left without saying anything.

On the way over to Noish-pa's I was taken with the irrational fear that I would find him murdered. I'll save you the suspense and tell you that he was fine, but it's interesting that I felt that way.

As I walked past the chimes he called out, "Who is there?"

"Vlad," I said.

We hugged and I sat down next to Ambrus. Noish-pa puttered around putting on tea and talking about the new spice dealer he'd found who still soaked absinthe in mint-water for a fortnight, the way it was supposed to be done. (A fortnight, if you're interested, is one day less than three weeks. If you think that's a peculiar period of time for which to have a special term, I can't blame you.)

When the tea was done and appreciated and I had made a respectful hello to Ambrus while Noish-pa did the same to Loiosh, he said, "What troubles you, Vladimir?"

"Everything, Noish-pa."

He looked at me closely. "You haven't been sleeping well."

"No."

"For our family, that is a bad sign."

"Yes."

"What has happened?"

"Do you remember that fellow, Franz, who was killed?"

He nodded.

"Well," I said, "there's another one. I was there when they found her body just now."

He shook his head. "And Cawti is still with these people?"

I nodded. "It's more than that, Noish-pa. They're like children who've found a Morganti dagger. They don't know what they're doing. They just keep going about their business as if they could stand up to the whole Jhereg, not to mention the Empire itself. That wouldn't bother me if Cawti weren't one of them, but I just can't protect her; not forever. I was standing outside their meeting place when the messenger showed up to tell them where to find the body—or so I assume. But he could just as easily have been a sorcerer and destroyed the entire house and everyone in it. I know the guy behind it—he'd do it. They don't seem to understand that and I can't convince them."

After I'd run down, Noish-pa shifted in his chair, looking thoughtful. Then he said, "You say you know this man, who is doing these things?"

"Not well, but I know of him."

"If he can do this, why hasn't he?"

"It hasn't been worth his effort, yet. It costs money and he won't spend more than he has to."

He nodded. "I'm told they had a gathering yesterday."

"What? Oh, yeah. In a park near here."

"Yes. They had a parade, too. It went by. There were a lot of people."

"Yes." I thought back to the park. "A few thousand, anyway. But so what? What can they do?"

"Perhaps you should speak to this Kelly again, try to convince him."

I said, "Maybe."

After a while he said, "I have never seen you so unhappy, Vladimir."

I said, "It's my work, I suppose, one way or another. We play by rules, you know? If you leave us alone, we'll leave you alone. If somebody gets hurt who isn't part of the organization, it means he was sticking his nose where it didn't belong. That isn't our fault, that's just how it is. Kelly's people did that—they butted in where they shouldn't have. Only they didn't, really. They—I don't know. Damn them to Verra's dungeons, anyway. Sometimes I wish I could just complete Herth's job for him, and sometimes I'd like to—I don't know what. And you know, I can't even get a good enough feel for Herth to send him for a walk. I'm too tied up in this. I ought to hire someone to do it for me, but I just *can't*. Don't you see that? I have to—" I blinked. I'd been rambling. I'd lost Noish-pa some time before. I wondered what he thought of all that.

He looked at me with a somber expression on his face. Loiosh flew over onto my shoulder and squeezed. I drank some more tea. Noish-pa said, "And Cawti?"

"I don't know. Maybe she feels the same way, and that's why she found these people. She killed me, you know."

His eyes widened. I said, "That's how we met. She was hired to kill me and she did. I've never killed an East—a human. She has. And now she's acting as if—never mind."

He studied me, and I suppose he remembered our last conversation, because he asked, "How long have you been doing this, Vladimir? This killing of people."

He sounded genuinely interested in the answer, so I said, "Years."

He nodded. "It is perhaps time that you thought about it."

I said, "Suppose I'd joined the Phoenix Guard, if they'd have me. One way or another, that's killing people for money. Or enlisted in some Dragonlord's private army, for that matter. What's the difference?"

"Perhaps there is none. I have no answer for you, Vladimir. I only say that perhaps it is time you thought about it."

"Yeah," I said. "I'm thinking about it."

He poured more tea and I drank it and after a while I went home.

8

... & remove dust & soot from both ...

I REMEMBER THE WALL of Baritt's Tomb.

It wasn't really a tomb, you understand; there was no body inside. The Serioli go in for tombs. They build them either underground or in the middle of mountains, and they put dead people in them. It seems weird to me. The Dragaerans sometimes build monuments to dead big shots like Baritt, and when they build one they call it a tomb because it looks like what the Serioli use and because Dragaerans aren't too bright.

Baritt's Tomb was huge in every dimension, a grey slate monstrosity, with pictures and symbols carved into it. It was stuck way out in the east, high up in the Eastern Mountains near a place where Dragaerans trade with Easterners for eastern red pepper and other things. I got stuck in the middle of a battle there once. I've never forgotten how it felt. One army was made up of Easterners who died, the other was made up of Teckla who died. On the Dragaerans' side were a couple of Dragonlords who were never really in any danger. That's one memory that stays with me. No one was going to hurt Morrolan or Aliera, and they laid about themselves like pip-squeak deities. The other thing I remember was watching all of this happen and almost chewing my lip off from helplessness.

The venture wasn't useless, you understand. I mean, Morrolan got a good fight, Sethra the Younger got Kieron's greatsword while Aliera got one more her size, and I got to learn that you can never go home. But in the battle itself there was nothing I could do unless I wanted to be one of the Teckla or one of the Easterners who were falling like ash from Mount Zerika. I didn't, so I just watched.

That's what came back to me now. Every time I feel helpless, in fact, that memory returns to haunt me. Each scream from each wounded Easterner, or even Teckla, remains with me. I know that Dragons consider assassination to be less "honorable" than butchering Easterners, but I've never quite understood why. That battle showed me what futility was, though. So many deaths for such a small result.

Of course, I finally did ... something—but that's another tale. What I remember is the helplessness.

Cawti wasn't speaking to me.

It wasn't that she refused to say anything, it was more that she didn't have anything to say. I walked around the house in bare feet all morning, swatting halfheartedly at jhereg who got in my way and staring out various windows hoping one of them would show something interesting. I threw a couple of knives at our hall target and missed. Eventually I collected Loiosh and walked over to my office, being very careful all the way.

Kragar was waiting for me. He looked unhappy. That was all right; why should he be any different?

"What is it?" I asked him.

"Herth."

"What about him?"

"He doesn't have a mistress, he doesn't eat soup, and he never takes a—"

"What do you mean? You can't find out anything about him?"

"No, I tracked him pretty well. The good news is that he isn't a sorcerer. But other than that, he's like you; he doesn't have any regular schedule. And he doesn't have an office; he works right out of his home. He never visits the same inn twice in a row, and I haven't found any pattern at all to his movements."

I sighed. "I half expected that. Well, keep on it. Eventually something will show up. No one lives a completely random life."

He nodded and walked out.

I put my feet up on the desk, then took them down again. I got up and paced. It hit me once more that Herth was planning to send me for a walk. There was probably someone out there, right now, trying to pin down my movements so he could get me. I looked out my office window but I didn't see anyone standing in the street opposite my door holding a dagger. I sat down again. Even if I managed to get Herth first, whoever it was had still taken the money, was still committed to getting me. I shivered.

There was one thing, at least: I could relax about Cawti for a while. Herth had given them another subtle warning. He wouldn't do anything else until he saw what effect that had. This meant that I could work on keeping myself alive. How? Well, I could gain some time by killing whoever was after me, which would force Herth to go to the bother of finding another assassin.

Good idea, Vlad. Now, how you gonna do it?

I thought of a way. Loiosh didn't like it. I asked him if he had any other suggestions and he didn't. I decided to do it at once, before I could consider how stupid it was. I got up and walked out of the office without speaking to anyone.

Loiosh tried to spot him as I wandered around the neighborhood, checking on my businesses, but didn't manage. Either I wasn't being followed, or the guy was skilled. I spent the late morning and early afternoon at this. My own effort wasn't so much directed at spotting my assassin as at looking as if I felt safe. Trying to appear calm under such circumstances is not easy.

Finally, as the afternoon wore on, I headed back for the Easterners' section.

There, at the same time as I had on the previous two days, I stationed myself near Kelly's headquarters and I waited. I had no more than passing interest in who went in and out of there, but I noticed that it was quite active. Cawti showed up with my friend Gregory, each of them carrying large boxes. Easterners and Teckla I didn't recognize ran in and out of the place all day. As I said, though, I didn't watch too closely. I was waiting for the assassin to make his move.

This was not the perfect place to get me, you understand; I was mostly hidden by the corner of a building and could see nearly everywhere around me. Loiosh watched over my head. But it was the only place I'd been going to at a regular time over the past few days. If I could keep this up, he'd realize that it was his best shot at me. He'd take it, and maybe I could kill him, which would give me a rest while Herth found someone else.

The unfortunate part was that I had no idea when he'd move. Staying alert for an attack for several hours is not easy, especially when what you want is to go charging out and hurt someone just for the sake of doing so.

Easterners and Teckla continued to come and go from Kelly's place. As the afternoon wore on, they would leave carrying large stacks of paper. One of them, a Teckla I didn't recognize, had a pot and brushes as well as the sheets of paper, and he started gluing them up on the walls of buildings. Passers-by stopped to read them, then went on their way.

I spent several hours there and the presumed assassin never showed. That was all right; he probably wasn't in a hurry. It was also possible he had a better idea for where to shine me. I was especially careful as I began to walk home. I arrived without incident.

Cawti still wasn't home when I dropped off to sleep.

The next day I got up without waking her. I cleaned up the place a bit, made some klava, and sat around drinking it and shadow-fencing. Loiosh was involved in some sort of deep conversation with Rocza until Cawti got up a bit later and took her out. Cawti left without saying a word. I stayed around the house until late in the afternoon, when I went back to that same spot.

The previous day I'd noticed that Kelly's people had seemed busy. Today the place was empty. There was no activity of any kind. After a while, I carefully left my little niche and looked at one of the posters they'd been gluing up the day before. It announced a rally, to be held today, and said something about ending oppression and murder.

I thought about finding the rally but decided I didn't want to deal with one of those again. I went back to my spot and waited. It was just about then that they began to show up. Kelly came back first, along with Paresh. Then several I didn't recognize, then Cawti, then more I didn't recognize. Most of them were Easterners, but there were a few Teckla.

They kept coming, too. There was a constant stream of traffic through that little place, and still more milling around outside. It made me so curious that a couple of times I caught myself paying more attention to them than to the probable assassin who was probably watching me. This would be—what?—the fourth day I'd stationed myself there. If the assassin were reckless, he'd have taken me on the third. If he were exceptionally careful, he'd wait another couple of days, or for a place more to his liking. What would I have done? Interesting question. I would either have waited for a better place, or made my move today. I almost smiled, thinking of it that way. Today is the day I would have killed myself if I'd been paid to.

I shook my head. My mind was wandering again. Loiosh took off from my shoulder, flew around a bit, then resumed his place.

"He's either not here or he's well hidden, boss."

"Yeah. What do you make of the goings-on across the street?"

"Don't know. They're stirred up like a bees' nest, though."

It didn't die down, either. As the afternoon wore on, more and more Easterners, and a few Teckla, would go into Kelly's flat for a while and come out, often carrying stacks of paper. I noticed one group of about six emerging with black headbands that they hadn't been wearing when they went in. A bit later another group went in, and they also wore the headbands when they came out. Cawti, as well as the others I knew, were popping in and out every hour or so. Once when she emerged she had on one of the headbands, too. I could only see it across her forehead because it matched her hair so well, but I thought it looked pretty good.

It was getting on toward evening when I noticed that one group loitering around the place had sticks. I looked closer and saw that one of them had a knife. I licked my lips, reminded myself to stay alert for my man, and kept watching.

I still didn't know what was going on, but I wasn't surprised, as another hour or so came and went, to see more and more groups of Easterners carrying sticks, knives, cleavers, and even an occasional sword or spear.

Something, it seemed, was Happening.

My feelings were mixed. In an odd way I was pleased. I had had no idea that these people could get together anything on the kind of scale—there were now maybe a hundred or so armed Easterners hanging around the street—that they were managing. I took a sort of vicarious pride in it. But I also knew that, if this continued, they would attract the kind of attention that could get them all hurt. My palms were sweaty, and it wasn't just from worrying about the assassin I assumed must be nearby.

In fact, I realized, I could almost relax about him. If he were the gutsy type, now would be a perfect time to get me. But if he'd been the gutsy type, he would have moved yesterday or the day before. I had the feeling he was more my kind. I wouldn't have gone near a situation like this. I like to stick to a plan, and a hundred armed, angry Easterners were unlikely to have been part of this guy's plan.

The street continued to fill up. In fact, it was becoming out and out crowded. Easterners with weapons were walking directly in front of me. It was all I could do to remain unnoticed; part of the street and not really there. I couldn't for the life of me figure out what they were doing other than milling around, but they all seemed to think it important. I considered leaving, since I was pretty certain that the presumed assassin would have left long ago.

About then the door to Kelly's place opened and Kelly came out flanked by Paresh and Cawti, with a couple of Easterners I didn't recognize in front of him. I don't know what that guy has, but I couldn't believe how quiet everything got. All of a sudden the entire street was silent. It was eerie. Everybody gathered around Kelly and waited, and they must have been practically holding their breaths to make so little noise.

He didn't get up on any kind of platform or anything, and he was pretty short, so he was completely hidden from me. I only gradually became aware that he was speaking, as if he'd started in a whisper and was talking louder and louder as he went. Since I couldn't hear him, I tried to judge the reaction he was getting. It was hard to tell, but it was quite certain that everyone was listening.

As his voice rose, I began to catch occasional phrases, then larger portions of his speech as he shouted it. "They are asking us," he declaimed, "to pay for their excesses, and we are saying we won't do it. They have forfeited any rights they may once have had to rule our destinies. We have now the right—and the obligation—to rule our own." Then his voice suddenly dropped again, but a little later it rose once more. "You, gathered here now, are only the vanguard, and this battle is only the first." And, still later, "We are not blind to their strengths, as they are blind to ours, but we're not blind to their weaknesses, either."

There was more like that, but I was too far away to get a good idea of what was going on. Still, they were waving weapons in the air, and I saw that the street was even more full than it had been when he'd started speaking. Those in back could no more hear than I could, but they pressed forward, eagerly. The atmosphere was almost carnivallike, especially far back in the crowd. They would hold up their sticks or knives or kitchen cleavers and wave them about, yelling. They would clasp each other's shoulders, or hug each other, and I saw an Easterner nearly cut the throat of a Teckla he was trying to hug.

They had no understanding of or respect for their weapons. I decided I was scared and had better leave. I stepped out of my corner and headed home. I made it with no trouble.

When Cawti arrived, close to midnight, her eyes were glowing. More than her eyes, in fact. It was as if there were a light shining inside of her head, and some of the luminescence was coming out of the pores of her skin. She had a smile on her face, and her smallest movements, as she took off her cloak and got a wine glass from the buffet, had an enthusiasm and verve that couldn't be missed. She was still wearing the black headband.

She had looked at me that way, once upon a time.

She poured herself a glass of wine and came into the living room, sat down.

"What is it?" I asked her.

"We're finally doing something," she said. "We're moving. This is the most exciting thing I can remember."

I kept my reaction off my face as best I could. "And what is this thing?"

She smiled and the light from the candles made her eyes dance. "We're shutting it down."

"Shutting what down?"

"The entire Easterners' quarter—all of South Adrilankha."

I blinked. "What do you mean, shutting it down?"

"No traffic into or out of South Adrilankha. All the merchants and peasants who pass through from the west will have to go around. There are barricades being set up all along Carpenter and Twovine. They'll be manned in the morning."

I struggled with that for a moment. Finally, "What will that do?" won out over "How are you doing it?"

She said, "Do you mean short-term, or what are we trying to achieve?"

"Both," I said. I struggled with how to put the question, then came up with, "Aren't you trying to get the peasants on your side? It sound like this will just make them mad if they have to travel all the way around South Adrilankha."

"First of all, most of them won't want to go around, so they'll sell to Easterners or go back."

"And that will get them on your side?"

She said, "They were born on our side." I had some trouble with that, but I let her continue. "It isn't as if we're trying to recruit them, or convince them to join something, or show what great people we are. We're fighting a war."

"And you don't care about civilian casualties?"

"Oh, stop it. Of course we do."

"Then why are you taking food out of the mouths of these peasants who are just trying to—"

"You're twisting things. Look, Vlad, it's time we struck back. We have to. We can't let them think they can cut us down with impunity, and the only defense we have is to bring together the masses in their own defense. And yes, some will be hurt. But the big merchants—the Orcas and the Tsalmoth and the Jhegaala—will run out of meat for their slaughterhouses. They'll be hurt more. And the nobility, who are used to eating meat once or twice every day, will be very unhappy about it after a while."

"If they're really hurt, they'll just ask the Empire to move in."

"Let them ask. And let the Empire try. We have the entire quarter, and that's only the beginning. There aren't enough Dragons in the Guard to reopen it."

"Why can't they just teleport past your barricades?"

"They can. Let them. Watch what happens when they try."

"What will happen? The Phoenix Guard are trained warriors, and one of them can—"

"Do nothing when he's outnumbered ten or twenty or thirty to one. We have all of South Adrilankha already, and that's only the beginning. We are finding support in the rest of the city and among the larger estates surrounding it. That, in fact, is what I'm going to be working on starting tomorrow. I'm going to visit some of those slaughterhouses and—"

"I see. All right, then: why?"

"Our demands to the Empress—"

"Demands? To the Empress? Are you serious?"

"Yes."

"Uh . . . all right. What are they?"

"We have asked for a full investigation into the murders of Sheryl and Franz."

I stared at her. I swallowed, then stared some more. Finally I said, "You can't mean it."

"Of course we mean it."

"You went to the Empire?"

"Yes."

"Do you mean to tell me that, not only have you gone to the Empire over a Jhereg killing, but you are now *demanding* that it be investigated?"

"That's right."

"That's crazy! Cawti, I can see Kelly or Gregory coming up with a notion like that, but you *know* how we operate."

"We?"

"Cut it out. You were in the organization for years. You know what happens when someone goes to the Empire. Herth will kill every one of you."

"Every one of us? Each of the thousands of Easterners—and Dragaerans— in South Adrilankha?"

I shook my head. She knew better. She *had* to know better. You never, never, *never* talk to the Empire. That is one of the few things that can make a Jhereg mad enough to hire someone to use a Morganti blade. Cawti *knew* that. And yet here she was, positively glowing about how they had just put all of their heads on the executioner's block.

"Cawti, don't you realize what you're doing?"

She looked at me hard. "Yes. I realize exactly what we're doing. I don't think you do. You seem to think Herth is some sort of god. He isn't. He certainly isn't strong enough to defeat an entire city."

"But—"

"And that isn't the point, anyway. We aren't counting on the Empire to give us justice. We know better, and so does everyone who lives in South Adrilankha. The thousands who are following us in this aren't doing it because they love us, but because of their *need*. There will be a revolution because they need it bad enough to die for it. They follow us because we know that, and because we don't lie to them. This is only the first battle, but it's starting, and we're winning. That's what's important—not Herth."

I stared at her. At last I said, "How long did it take you to memorize that?"

Fires burned behind her eyes and I was struck by a wave of anger and I badly wished I'd kept my mouth shut.

I said, "Cawti—"

She stood up, put on her cloak and walked out.

If Loiosh had said anything I'd probably have killed him.

9

. . . & polish.

I STAYED UP ALL night, walking around the neighborhood. I wasn't completely nuts, the way I'd been before, but I suppose I wasn't quite rational, either. I did try to be careful and I wasn't attacked. Morrolan reached me psionically at some point in there, but claimed it wasn't important when I asked why, so I didn't find out what he wanted. After a few hours I had calmed down a bit. I thought about going home, but realized that I didn't want to go home to an empty house. Then I realized that I didn't want to go home to find Cawti waiting up for me, either.

I sat down in an all-night klava hole and drank klava until my kidneys cried for mercy. When daylight began to filter down through the orange-red haze that Dragaerans think is a sky, I still wasn't feeling sleepy. I ate a couple of hen's eggs at a place I didn't know, then wandered over to the office. That earned me a raised eyebrow from Melestav.

I sniffed around the place and made sure that everything was running smoothly. It was. Once, some time ago, I'd left the office in Kragar's hands for a few days and he'd made an organizational disaster of the place, but he seemed to have learned since then. There were a couple of notes indicating people wanted to see me about business-type things, but they weren't urgent so I decided to let them sit. Then I reconsidered and gave them to Melestav with instructions to have Kragar check into them a little more. When someone wants to see you—and someone is after your head—it might be a set up. Just to satisfy your curiosity, they were both legitimate.

I would have dozed then but I was still too worked up. I went down to the lab and took off my cloak and my jerkin and cleaned up the place, which had needed it for some time. I threw all the old coals away, swept and even polished a bit. Then I coughed for a while from the dust in the air.

I went back upstairs, cleaned myself up and left the building. Loiosh preceded me, and we were very careful. I slowly walked over toward South Adrilankha, staying as alert as I could. It was just before noon.

I stopped and had a leisurely meal at a place that didn't like Easterners or didn't like Jhereg or both. They overcooked the kethna, didn't chill the wine, and the service was slow and just on the edge of rude. There wasn't a lot I could do about it since I was out of my area, but I did get even with them; I overtipped the waiter and overpaid for the meal. Let them wonder.

As I approached South Adrilankha on Wheelwright, I began to notice a certain amount of tension and excitement on the faces I passed. Yeah. Whatever these Easterners were doing, they were certainly doing it. I saw a pair of Phoenix Guards walking briskly the same way I was, and I became unobtrusive until they passed.

I stopped a couple of blocks from Carpenter to study things. The street here was quite wide, as this was a main road for goods from South Adrilankha. There were crowds of Dragaerans—Teckla and an occasional Orca or Jhegaala—milling around and either looking west or heading that way. I thought about sending Loiosh to take a look, but I didn't want to be separated from him for that long; there was still my presumed assassin to worry about. I moved west another block, but the street curved and I couldn't see Carpenter.

Have you ever seen a fight break out in an inn? Sometimes you know what's going on before you actually see the fight, because the guy next to you snaps his head around, half stands up, and stares, and then you see two or three people backing away from something that's hidden by someone else standing right in front of you. So you're suddenly all nerve endings, and you stand up and move back a bit, and that's when you see the brawlers.

Well, this was kind of like that. At the far end of the block, where it curved a little to the north, everyone was staring off toward Carpenter and having the kind of conversation where you keep looking at the object of interest instead of the person to whom you're talking. I noticed about five Dragaerans in Phoenix livery looking officious but not doing anything. I decided they were waiting for orders.

I walked that last block very slowly. I began to hear occasional shouts. When I got around the corner, all I could see was a wall of Dragaerans, lined up along Carpenter between the Grain Exchange and Molly's general store. There were a few more uniforms present. I did another check for possible assassins and began to move into the crowd.

"Boss?"

"Yeah?"

"*What if he's in the crowd waiting for you?*"

"*You'll spot him before he gets to me.*"

"*Oh. Well, that's all right then.*"

He had a point, but there was nothing I could do about it. Getting through a tightly packed group of people without being noticed is not one of the easiest things to do unless you happen to be Kragar. It took all of my concentration, which means I didn't have any to spare for someone trying to kill me. It's hard to describe how you go about it, yet it is something that can be learned. It involves a lot of little things, like keeping your attention focused in the same direction as everyone around you; it's amazing how much this helps. Sometimes you dig an elbow into someone's ribs because he'd notice you if you didn't. You have to catch the rhythm of the crowd and be part of it. I know that sounds funny, but it's the best I can do. Kiera the Thief taught me, and even she can't really explain it. But explanations don't matter. I got up to the front of the crowd without calling attention to myself; leave it at that. And once I was there I saw what the commotion was about.

I guess when I'd first heard Cawti speaking of putting up barricades, I'd sort of pictured it as finding a bunch of logs and laying them across the street high enough to keep people out. But it wasn't like that at all. The barricade seemed to have been built from anything someone didn't want. Oh, sure, there was a bit of lumber here and there, but that was only the start of it. There were several broken chairs, part of a large table, damaged garden tools, mattresses, the remains of a sofa, even a large porcelain washbasin with its drainpipe sticking up into the air.

It completely filled the intersection, and I saw a bit of smoke drifting up from behind it as if someone had a small fire going. There were maybe fifty on the other side watching the Dragaerans and listening to insults without responding. The Easterners and Teckla who manned the barricade had sticks, knives and a few more swords than I'd seen the day before. Those on my side were unarmed. The Phoenix Guard—I saw about twenty—had their weapons sheathed. Once or twice a Dragaeran would look like he was about to climb the barricade and ten or fifteen Easterners would just go over there, opposite him, and stand close together, and he'd climb down again. When that happened, the uniforms would kind of watch closely, as if they were ready to move, but they'd relax again when the Dragaeran climbed down.

A cart, drawn by an ox, came down the street from the other side. It got about halfway down the block and three Easterners went over and talked to the driver, who was Dragaeran. They talked for a while, and I could hear that the driver was cursing, but eventually she turned around in the street and went back the way she came.

It was exactly as Cawti said: They weren't letting anyone either in or out of South Adrilankha. They had built a makeshift wall and, if that wasn't enough, the Easterners behind it were ready to deal with anyone who climbed over. No one was getting past them.

When I'd seen all I wanted to, I got past them and headed down the street toward Kelly's flat on the assumption that things must be popping there. I took my time though, and made a couple of detours to other streets that intersected Carpenter to see if things were the same. They were. Carpenter and Wheelwright had the biggest crowd, because that was the biggest and busiest intersection, but the others I checked were also locked up tight. I watched a few repetitions of scenes I'd already witnessed. This became boring so I left.

I made my twisting, winding way to my spot across from Kelly's flat, checked my weapons and began waiting. I'd been coming here every day for quite a while now, and following no other pattern. Unless I was completely wrong about Herth wanting to kill me (which I couldn't believe), the assassin would have to realize that this was his best shot. Unless he suspected a trap. Would I have suspected a trap? I didn't know.

There wasn't much activity at Kelly's. Paresh was standing outside, and so were a couple of Easterners I didn't recognize. People would enter and leave every so often, but there was no sign of the frenzied activities of the last few days. An hour and a little more slipped by this way, while I struggled to stay alert and ready. I was starting to feel fatigued from lack of sleep, which worried me; fatigued is not the best way to feel when you are expecting an attempt on your life. I also felt grimy and generally unclean, but that didn't bother me as it fit my mood.

The first sign that something was going on occurred when Cawti and Gregory showed up, hurrying, and disappeared into the headquarters. A few minutes later Gregory went running out again. I checked my weapons because it felt like the thing to do. Ten minutes later a group of about forty, led by Gregory, showed up and began hanging around the place.

Within a minute after that, four Phoenix Guards arrived and stationed themselves directly in front of Kelly's door. My mouth was suddenly very dry. Four Phoenix Guards and forty Easterners and Teckla, yet I was scared for the Easterners and Teckla.

I wondered if their presence meant that the barricades were down, or whether they'd broken the barricades, but then I realized that there were bound to be a large number of Guards stationed in South Adrilankha all the time. I guessed we'd be seeing more soon. Then I noticed something: of the four Guards, three of them wore clothing that was green, brown and yellow. I looked closer. Yes, these four Phoenix Guards consisted of three Teckla and a Dragon. This meant that the Empress was worried enough about this situation to use conscripted Teckla. I licked my lips.

Cawti appeared from within and began speaking to the Dragonlord. She still wore Jhereg colors and Rocza was riding on her left shoulder. I couldn't tell what effect she was having on him, but I assumed he wasn't going to be overflowing with good will.

They spoke for a while and his hand strayed to his sword hilt. I caught my breath. Another unbreakable Jhereg rule is, you *don't* kill Imperial Guards. On the other hand, it wasn't at all clear to me that I was going to have a choice. I am not so completely in control of myself as I would sometimes like to believe. Perhaps that is what I've learned from all of this.

The Guard didn't draw, however, he merely gripped his weapon. And Cawti could take care of herself, and the Guards were outnumbered ten to one. I reminded myself to stay alert for the presumed assassin.

Eight more Phoenix Guards showed up. Then another four. The ratio continued to be three Teckla for each Dragon. One from this last group had a brief conference with the fellow who'd been speaking to Cawti, then she—the new Guard—resumed negotiations. I guess she out-ranked the other one or something. About thirty more of Kelly's people appeared then, and you could almost feel the temperature in the area rise. I saw Cawti shake her head. They talked some more and Cawti shook her head again. I wanted to make contact with her—to say, hey, I'm here; is there something I can do? But I knew the answer already, and asking would only distract her.

Stay alert, Vlad, I told myself.

The Guard abruptly turned away from Cawti and I heard her issue her orders in a clear, crisp voice: "Back off thirty feet. Weapons sheathed, stay alert." The Guards followed her orders at once, the Dragons looking efficient and smart in their black uniforms, trimmed with silver, with the Phoenix breast insignia and gold half-cloak of the Phoenix. The Teckla who were Guards looked just a bit silly in their peasant outfits with Phoenix insignia and gold half-cloaks. They seemed to be trying to look calm. Cawti went back inside. Natalia and Paresh emerged and circulated among the Easterners, speaking to small groups of them. Pep talks, probably.

Twenty minutes later about forty or fifty more citizens arrived. All of these had knives that were long enough to be almost swords. They were well-muscled men and carried their knives like they knew how to use them. It occurred to me that they probably came from one of the slaughterhouses. Ten minutes after that, about twenty more Phoenix Guards showed up. This continued for most of another hour, with the street gradually filling up until I could no longer see the door to Kelly's flat. I could, however, see the Captain (or whatever; I didn't know what rank she was) of the Phoenix Guards. I had her face in half profile, about thirty feet away to my right. She reminded me just a bit of Morrolan— Dragon features—but she wasn't nearly as tall. I got the impression that she wasn't at all happy about this situation—there were only Teckla and Easterners to be fought, but there were a lot of them, on their home territory, and three-fourths of her forces were Teckla. I wondered what Kelly was up to. My guess (I was right, too) was that the Empress had learned who was behind all of this trouble and had sent her Guards to arrest him, and he had no intention of going.

Okay, but was he going to let a couple of hundred of his "people" die to prevent it? Sure, that made sense. He was following a principle; what did he care if people were killed? What puzzled me was that this wouldn't save him unless he won. Teckla or not, there were also Dragons among those Guards (and one Dzur, I noticed). Some of them were probably sorcerers. This could be a real bloodbath. Of course, Paresh was a sorcerer, and so was Cawti, but I didn't like the odds.

I was trying to puzzle this out when another group arrived. There were six of them surrounding a seventh and they were Dragaerans. They did not, however, represent the Empire. The six were obviously Jhereg bodyguard or muscle types. The seventh was Herth.

My palms became simultaneously itchy and sweaty. I knew I couldn't make a move right then and hope to live through it, but Verra! how I wanted to! I hadn't known that I had that much capacity for hate left in me until I saw this man who had had me tortured to the point where I had broken, and given them information to destroy a group my wife was willing to give her life for.

It was as if he epitomized all of the bile I'd swallowed in my lifetime, and I stood there shaking and staring and hating.

Loiosh squeezed my shoulder. I tried to relax and stay alert for the assassin.

Herth spotted the captain and walked right up to her. A couple of Guards got in between them and Herth's bodyguards stepped in to face them and I wondered if I was going to see a different fight than the one I'd expected. But the captain pushed the other Guards aside and faced Herth. Herth stopped about twenty feet away from her and his bodyguards moved back. I had a perfect view of them both. I had a perfect shot at Herth. I could have dropped two of those bodyguards with a pair of throwing knives, scattered the others with a handful of shuriken, and shined Herth before the Dragons could stop me. I couldn't have made it out alive, but I could have had him. Instead I squeezed into the corner of the building and watched and listened and cursed under my breath.

"Good afternoon, Lieutenant," said Herth. So I was wrong about her rank. So big deal.

"What do you want, Jhereg?" The Dragonlord's voice was clipped and harsh. I would almost guess she didn't like Jhereg.

"You seem to have a problem."

She spat. "In five minutes I won't anymore. Now clear out of here."

"I think I can arrange to have this problem solved peaceably, Lieutenant."

"I can arrange for you to be—"

"Unless you enjoy killing civilians. Maybe you do. I wouldn't know."

She stared at him for a while. Then she walked up and stood nose to nose with him. One of his bodyguards started forward. Herth gestured to him and he stopped. The lieutenant slowly and carefully drew a long fighting knife from a hip sheath next to her sword. Without removing her eyes from Herth's she tested it with her thumb. Then she showed it to him. Then she drew it along his cheek. First across one side, then the other. I could see lines of red where she'd cut him. He didn't flinch. When she was done, she wiped the blade on his cloak, put it away, and walked slowly away from him.

He said, "Lieutenant."

She turned. "Yes?"

"My offer still stands."

She considered him for a moment. "What's the offer?"

"Let me speak to this person, the one inside, and allow me to convince him to end this silly inland blockade."

She nodded slowly. "Very well, Jhereg. Their time is about up. I'll give you an additional ten minutes. Starting now."

Herth turned toward the door to Kelly's flat, but even as he did so I heard it swing open. (It was only then that I realized how quiet the street had become.) At first I couldn't see the door, but then the Easterners in front of it moved aside and I saw fat, little Kelly, with Paresh on one side of him and Cawti on the other. Paresh's attention was fixed on Herth, and his eyes were like daggers. Cawti was looking over the situation like a pro, and her black headband suddenly seemed incongruous. What really caught my attention, though, was that Herth's back was to me and there was only one bodyguard between us. It hurt to do nothing.

Kelly spoke first. "So," he said, "You are Herth." He was squinting so hard I couldn't see his eyes. His voice was clear and strong.

Herth nodded. "You must be Kelly. Shall we go inside and talk?"

"No," said Kelly flatly. "Anything you have to say to me, the whole world can hear, and the whole world can hear my answer, as well."

Herth shrugged. "All right. You can see the kind of situation you're in, I think."

"I can see it more clearly than either you or that friend of yours who cuts your face before granting your wishes."

That stopped him for a moment, then he said, "Well, I'm giving you a chance to live. If you remove—"

"The Phoenix Guard will not attack us."

Herth paused, then chuckled. The lieutenant, hearing this, looked amused.

Then I noticed Natalia, Paresh and two Easterners I didn't know. They were walking along the line of Phoenix Guards, handing each of them, even the Dragons, a piece of paper. The Dragons glanced at it and threw it away, the Teckla started talking to each other, and reading it aloud for those who couldn't read.

Herth paused to watch this drama, looking vaguely troubled. The lieutenant matched his expression, except she seemed a bit angry. Then she said, "All right, that will be enough—"

"What's the problem, then?" asked Kelly in a loud voice. "What are you afraid they'll do if they read that?"

The lieutenant swung and stared at him, and they held that way for a moment. I caught a glimpse of the paper that someone had dropped and the breeze brought near me. It began, "BROTHERS—CONSCRIPTS" in large print. Underneath, before the breeze carried it away again, I read, "You, conscripted Teckla, are being incited against us, Easterners and Teckla. This plan is being put into operation by our common enemies, the oppressors, the privileged few—generals, bankers, landlords—"

The lieutenant turned away from Herth and grabbed one of the leaflets and read it. It was fairly long, so it took her awhile. As she read, she turned pale and I saw her jaw clench. She glanced over at her command, many of whom had broken formation and were clearly discussing the leaflet, some waving it about as if agitated.

At this moment Kelly began speaking, over Herth's head, as it were. He said, "Brothers! Conscripted Teckla! Your masters—the generals, the captains, the aristocrats—are preparing to throw you against us, who are organizing to fight them, to defend our right to a decent life—to walk the streets without fear. We say join us, for our cause is just. But if you don't, we warn you, don't let them send you against us, for the steel of our weapons is as cold as the steel of yours."

As he began to speak, Herth frowned and backed away. The whole time he was speaking, the lieutenant kept making motions toward him, as if she'd shut him up, then back toward her troops, as if to order them forward. When he stopped speaking at last, there was silence in the street.

I nodded. Whatever else I thought about Kelly, he'd handled this situation in a way I hadn't expected him to, and it seemed to be working. At least, the lieutenant didn't seem to quite know what to do.

Herth finally spoke. "Do you expect that to accomplish anything?" he asked. It seemed rather weak to me. To Kelly too, I guess, because he didn't answer. Herth said, "If you're done with your public speaking, and hope to avoid arrest or slaughter, I suggest that you and I try to make arrangements for—"

"You and I have nothing whatever to arrange. We want you and yours out of our neighborhoods entirely, and we won't rest until that is done. There is no basis for discussion between us."

Herth looked down at Kelly and I could imagine, although I couldn't see it, the cold smile on Herth's face. "Have it as you will then, Whiskers," he said. "No one can say I didn't try."

He turned and walked back toward the lieutenant.

Then I was distracted because someone else showed up. I didn't notice him at first because I was watching Kelly and Herth, but he must have been making his way along the street the entire time, past the Phoenix Guards and the Easterners, and right up to the door to Kelly's flat.

"Cawti!" came the voice as from nowhere. It was a voice I knew, though I can hardly think of one I less expected to hear at that moment.

I looked at Cawti. She, as amazed as I, was staring at the old, bald, frail Easterner who stood next to her. "We must speak," said my grandfather. I couldn't believe it. His voice, in the continuing silence that followed the confrontation between Herth and Kelly, carried all the way over to my side of the street. But was he going to start throwing our family business around? Now? In public? What was he up to?

"Noish-pa," she said. "Not now. Can't you see—?"

"I see much," he said. "Yes, now." He was leaning on a cane. I knew that cane. The top could be unscrewed to reveal—a sword? Heavens, no. He carried a rapier at his hip. The cane held four vials of Fenarian peach brandy. Ambrus was curled up on his shoulder and seemed no more upset by any of this than he was. Herth didn't know what to make of him, and a quick glance told me that the lieutenant was as puzzled as I was. She was biting her lip.

"We must go off the street so we can talk," said my grandfather.

Cawti didn't know what to say.

I began cursing anew under my breath. Now there was no question: I was going to have to do something. I couldn't let my grandfather be caught in the middle of this.

Then my attention was drawn back to the lieutenant, who shook herself and stood up straighter. Her troops seemed to still be in a state of some confusion, talking in animated tones about the flyer and Kelly's speech. The lieutenant turned toward the mob of Easterners and said in a loud voice, "Clear away, all of you." No one moved. She drew her blade, a strange one that curved the wrong way, like a scythe. Kelly locked eyes with Herth. Cawti's gaze shifted among the lieutenant, my grandfather, Kelly and Herth. I let a dagger fall into my hand, wondering what I could do with it.

The lieutenant hesitated, studied her troops, then called out, "Weapons at ready." There was some sound of steel being drawn as the Dragons did so, and a few of the Teckla. The Easterners gripped their weapons and moved forward, forming a solid wall. A few more of the Guard drew weapons. I spared Kelly a glance and he was looking at my grandfather, who was looking at him. They exchanged nods, as of old acquaintances. Interesting.

My grandfather drew his rapier. He said to Cawti, "This is no place for you."

"Padraic Kelly," called the lieutenant in a piercing voice, "I arrest you in the name of the Empress. Come with me at once."

"No," said Kelly. "Tell the Empress that unless she agrees to a full investigation into the murders of our comrades, by tomorrow there will be no clear road into or out of the city, and by the following day the docks will be closed. And if she attacks us now, the Empire will fall by morning."

The lieutenant called, "Forward!" and the Phoenix Guard took a step toward the Easterners and I knew what I could use the dagger for. This was because in a single instant Kelly, my grandfather, and even Cawti were swept out of my mind. Everyone's attention was focused on the advancing Guards and the Easterners. Everyone's, that is, except mine. My attention was focused on Herth's back, about forty feet away from me.

Now he was mine. Even his bodyguards were all but ignoring him. Now I could take him and be away, cleanly. It was as if my entire life were about to be fulfilled in one thrust of an eight-inch stiletto.

Out of habit from the last four days, I gave myself a last caution before I moved away from the wall. Then I took a step toward Herth, holding the knife low against my body.

Then Loiosh screamed in my mind and there was suddenly a knife coming at my throat. It was attached to a Dragaeran who wore the colors of House Jhereg.

The assassin had finally made his move.

10

1 grey silk cravat: repair cut . . .

THE FACT THAT I was ready for him did nothing to prevent the cold sweat that broke out all over me when I saw him. For one thing, he was ready for me, too, and he had the jump. All thought of Herth was instantly gone, replaced by thoughts of survival.

Sometimes, in this kind of situation, time slows down. Other times it speeds up, and I'm only aware of what I'm doing after I've done it. This was one of the former. I had time to see the knife come toward my throat, and to decide on a countering move, make it, and sit back wondering if it would work. While disarming myself is never my favorite thing to do in a fight, it was my only option. I flipped my knife at him, jumped the other way, and hit the ground rolling. I kept moving as I came up in case he decided to throw some pointy things at me, too. As it happened, he did, and one of them—a knife, I think— came close enough to make the hair on my neck stand up. But I avoided everything else long enough to draw my rapier. As I did so, I told Loiosh, *"I can handle this; take care of Cawti."*

"Right, boss." And I heard him flap-flap away.

That was actually one of the biggest lies I've ever told, but I was very much aware that mayhem was going to be breaking out around me when the Easterners clashed with the Phoenix Guards, and I didn't want to be distracted by worrying about Cawti.

Around then, as I came to a guard position, I realized that Herth's bodyguards had shots at my back, and that there were more than seventy Phoenix Guards there, any of whom might look over this way in between cutting down Easterners. I licked my lips, felt scared, and concentrated on the man before me—a professional killer who had accepted money to kill me.

I took my first good look at the assassin. A nondescript sort of guy with maybe a trace of the Dzur in the slant of his eyes and the point of chin. He had long straight hair with a neat widow's peak. *Points all over the bastard,* I thought. His eyes were clear and light brown and his glance strayed over me, studying. If things weren't going as he planned (which, I guarantee, they weren't) it didn't show in his expression.

He'd drawn a sword by this time. He was standing full forward with a heavy rapier in his right hand and a long fighting knife in his left. I presented only my side, as my grandfather had taught me. I closed with him before he could throw anything else at me, stopping when we were point-to-point—that is, just at the distance from each other where the points of our blades could barely touch. From here, the concentration he'd need for a good windup with that knife would give me time to get in at least one good cut or thrust, which would settle the issue if I was lucky.

I wondered if he were a sorcerer. I glanced at his knife but didn't see anything to indicate that it was a magical weapon. Not that there had to be anything to see. My hands were sweaty. I remembered that my grandfather had recommended light gloves for fencing, for just that reason. I resolved to get some if I lived through this.

He made a tentative pass, either recognizing or knowing that I fought strangely and trying to get a feel for my style. He wasn't as fast as I'd feared, so I placed a light cut on his right hand to teach him to keep his distance.

It was frightening to be having this kind of fight with Phoenix Guards in the area, but they were all involved in the slaughter of Easterners and were thus too busy to notice us—

No, they weren't.

I realized quite suddenly that five or six seconds had passed and there were no sounds of battle.

He didn't realize it yet and tried rushing me then. He did a fine job of it, too. There was no warning that he was about to go, and the timing of his slash, at an angle from my right to left, was very good. I avoided the attack, letting his blade slide up mine, screeching, until I could deflect it. I noted his speed. He had a certain grace, too; the kind that came with long training. And he was utterly passionless. From looking at his face, I couldn't tell if he was confident, worried, gleeful, or what.

I made a halfhearted riposte, trying to figure out how to get out of this situation. I mean, I would have loved to finalize him, but not with the Phoenix Guard looking on, and it wasn't at all clear that I could manage to in any case. He blocked my riposte with his dagger. I decided that he probably wasn't a sorcerer, since sorcerers like to use enchanted daggers for spell-casting, and no one likes to parry with enchanted cutlery.

He kept coming up on the ball of his right foot and tensing his left leg. I resolved not to let it distract me. I kept my attention on his eyes. No matter how you're fighting, sword, spell, or empty-handed, your opponent's eyes are your first indication of when he'll move.

There was a second or two of inaction, during which I would have loved to have launched an attack but didn't dare. Then, I guess, he realized that there were no sounds of battle from around us. Without warning he bounded back a couple of steps, a couple more, then turned and walked briskly away, disappearing around the corner of a building.

I stood there breathing heavily for just a moment, then I suddenly thought of Herth again. If he'd been in sight I probably would have shined him, Phoenix

Guard or no. But when I turned around I didn't see him. Loiosh landed on my shoulder.

The two lines, Kelly's group and the Phoenix Guards, faced each other about ten feet apart. Most of the Guards seemed very unhappy about the situation. Kelly's people seemed solid and determined; a human wall with knives and sticks bristling from it like thorns from a vine.

I was alone in the middle of the street, about sixty feet to the side of the Phoenix Guards, some of whom were looking at me. Most of them, however, watched their lieutenant. She was holding her peculiar blade over her head, parallel to the ground in a gesture that suggested "hold," or perhaps, "sit," "stay," or "heel."

Cawti stood next to my grandfather and they were staring at me. I sheathed my sword so I wouldn't be as interesting. The Easterners were still watching the Guards, most of whom were watching their lieutenant. She, at least, hadn't seen me. I moved to a slightly more open part of the street so the assassin couldn't come back at me without giving me time to react. Then the lieutenant spoke in a voice that carried quite well, although it seemed that she wasn't shouting. She said, "I have received communication from the Empress. All troops back off to the other side of the street and stand ready."

The Phoenix Guard did so, the Teckla happily, the Dragons less so. I'll say this for Kelly: He didn't gloat. He just stood watching everything with his jowl set. I mean, it didn't surprise me that much that he didn't look relieved; I might have been able to manage that. But keeping the gloat off my face when the troops pulled back would have been beyond me.

I made my way over to where my family stood. I couldn't read Cawti's expression. My grandfather said, "He was pressing you, Vladimir. If he had continued, he would have had the initiative and your balance would have been not right."

"Pressing me?"

"Each time he shifted his feet, he would end with his weight more forward. It is a trick some of these elfs use. I think they don't know they are doing it."

I said, "I'll remember, Noish-pa."

"But you were careful, which is good, and your wrist was supple but firm, as it should be, and you didn't linger after the stop-cut, as you used once to do."

"Noish-pa—," said Cawti.

"Thank you," I said.

"You shouldn't be here," said Cawti.

"And why should I not?" he said. "What is there to this life that is so worth saving?"

Cawti glanced around as if to see who was listening to us. I did, too. No one seemed to be.

"But why?"

"Why am I here? Cawti, I don't know. I know that I cannot change how you are, or what you will do. I know that girls aren't the same in Faerie as back home, and do what they want to, and that is not always a bad thing. But I came to tell you that you can come to see me if you want, and if you want to talk about things, yes? Vladimir, he comes now and then when he is troubled, but you don't. That is all I have to say. Yes?"

She looked at him for a moment, and I saw there were tears in her eyes. She leaned forward and kissed him. "Yes, Noish-pa," she said. Ambrus meowed. My grandfather smiled with what was left of his teeth, turned, walked away, leaning on his cane. I stood next to Cawti watching him. I tried to think of something to say but couldn't.

Cawti said, "Now we know why he was here; why were you here?"

"I was trying to convince that assassin to do just what he did. The idea was for me to shine him."

She nodded. "You've marked him?"

"Yeah. I'll set Kragar to work on it."

"So you know he has your name, and you'll have his, and you'll be trying to kill each other. What do you think he'll do now?"

I shrugged.

Cawti said, "What would you do?"

I shrugged again. "Dunno. Either return the money and run as far and as fast as I can, or move right away. Within the day, maybe within the hour. Try to catch the guy before he could set things up."

She nodded. "Me, too. Do you want to drop out of sight?"

"Not especially. There are—"

The lieutenant began speaking again. "All citizens harken. The following words are from the Empress: You are hereby informed that a full investigation, as you . . . requested, is and has been taking place in accordance with Imperial procedure. You are ordered to disband at once and remove all obstructions from the street. No arrests will take place if these things are done."

Then she turned and faced her troops. "Return to duty. That is all." The Guards resheathed their weapons. The reactions from the Guards were interestingly diverse. Some of the Dragons gave us looks that read, "You're lucky this time, scum," and others were mildly regretful, as if they had been looking forward to the exercise. The Teckla seemed relieved. The lieutenant didn't spare us another look or gesture, she simply rejoined her unit and walked away.

I turned back to Cawti, but as I did Paresh touched her on the shoulder and gestured to the headquarters. Cawti reached out and squeezed my arm once before following him. As she was disappearing, Rocza left her shoulder and landed on mine.

"*Someone thinks I need help, boss.*"

"Yeah. Or I do. Do you mind?"

"*Naw. I can use the company. You've been too quiet lately. I've been getting lonely.*"

I didn't have an answer for that.

I didn't take any chances going back to the office; I teleported, then went inside to be sick rather than waiting in the street.

"Any luck with Herth, Kragar?"

"I'm working on it, boss."

"Okay. I've got another face. Ready?"

"What do you mean—Oh. Okay. Go ahead."

I gave him the image of the assassin. I said, "Know him?"

"No. Do you have a name?"

"No. I want one."

"Okay. I'll have a picture made and see what I can find."

"And when you find him, don't waste time asking me. Have him sent for a walk." Kragar raised an eyebrow at me. I said, "He's the one who's got my name. He almost had my head today, too."

Kragar whistled. "How'd you get out of it?"

"I was ready for it. I guessed someone was after me, so I gave him a pattern to my movements to sucker him out."

"And then you didn't manage to shine him?"

"A little matter of seventy or eighty Phoenix Guards in the area. Also, he wasn't as surprised as I'd hoped, and he was pretty good with a blade."

Kragar said, "Oh."

"So now I know what he looks like, but not his name."

"And so you give me the fun part, huh? All right. Do you have anyone in mind?"

"Yeah. Mario. If you can't find him, use someone else."

Kragar rolled his eyes. "Nothing like specific instructions. All right."

"And bring me a new set of weapons. Might as well do something with my hands while I wait for you to solve all my problems for me."

"Not all of them, Vlad. I can't do anything about your height."

"Go."

He went out and left me with Loiosh, Rocza, and my thoughts. I realized I was hungry and thought about having someone bring me some food. Then it occurred to me that I was going to be teleporting everywhere for a while now, so maybe that wasn't a good idea. Loiosh and Rocza hissed back and forth, then started chasing each other around the room until I opened the window and told them to do it outside. I was very careful to stand to the side when I opened it. I don't know of an assassin who would choose to try to get someone from across a street, but the guy was probably pretty desperate by now. At least, I would have been. I shut the window and drew the drapes.

I could at least accomplish a few things that I'd been too busy for.

"Melestav!"

"Yeah?"

"Is Sticks in the office today?"

"Yes."

"Send him up here."

"Right."

A few minutes later Sticks sauntered in and I handed him a purse with fifty Imperials in it. He weighed it without counting it and looked at me. "What's this for?"

I said, "Shut up."

He said, "Oh. That. Well, thanks." He sauntered out again.

Kragar came back in with a new set of toys for me. I shut the door after him and set up about changing weapons. I took off my cloak and began removing things from it and replacing them as I went. When the cloak was done I started digging things out of the ribbing of my jerkin and other places. While I was removing the dagger from my left sleeve, I noticed Spellbreaker. I guess I'd been avoiding thinking about it since that night, but now I let it fall into my hand.

It hung there, just like an ordinary chain. I studied it. It was about eighteen inches long, golden, made of thin links. The gold didn't seem to be plating; it had never scratched or anything. But the chain didn't seem heavy enough for solid gold, and it certainly wasn't soft. I tried digging a fingernail into one of the links and it felt like a fine steel.

I decided that I really ought to try to find out what I could about the thing, if I lived through this. I continued changing weapons while I thought about that. What would it take to live through this?

Well, I'd have to kill the assassin, that was certain. And Herth. No, correct that: I was going to have to kill Herth *before* I killed the assassin, or Herth would just hire another one. I thought about hiring someone to kill Herth. That would be the intelligent thing to do. For one thing, then I'd know that he'd go down even if I did. And I still had all of that cash lying around; more than I'd ever dreamed of having. If Mario decided to show up and walk into my office, I could even meet his figure.

The trouble was, not many assassins besides Mario would agree to take on the job. Herth was a boss—a much bigger one than I. He was the kind who doesn't take a pee without four or five bodyguards there in case his pecker decides to attack him. Shining someone like that requires getting to at least one or two of his bodyguards, or Mario, or finding someone who doesn't mind dying, or a great deal of luck.

I could forget Mario; no one even knew where he was. Maybe Kelly knew someone who wanted to make a suicide attack on a Jhereg boss, but I don't hang around with that sort of individual. Getting to his bodyguards might be possible, but it takes time. You have to find the ones who will take, check them out afterwards to make sure they've taken, and set up a time when both you and they can do it with a minimum of risk. I didn't have that kind of time before the assassin made another attack.

That left luck. Did I feel lucky? No, I didn't.

So where did that leave me?

Dead.

I finished changing weapons while I thought about it. I looked at it from a few other angles. Could I somehow convince Herth to cease hostilities? Laughable. Especially since I *still* had to make sure he wouldn't kill Cawti. I mean, that's what had gotten me into this mess, I might as well—

Was it? Is that why I'd gotten involved in all of this nonsense? Well, no, not at first; at first I had wanted to find the murderer of this Franz fellow whom I'd never met. I'd wanted to do that to help patch things up with Cawti. Shit. Why was *I* trying to patch things up with *her*? She was the one who'd gotten involved in all this without mentioning it to me. Why did I have to go sticking my nose into a place where I wasn't wanted and I didn't want to be? Duty? A pretty word, that. Duty. Doo-tee. Easterners—some of them—made it sound like doo-dee; the kind of thing you hum to yourself while changing weapons. Doo-dee-da-dee-dee-do. What did it mean?

Maybe "duty" can't just hang there in a void; maybe it has to be attached to something. A lot of Easterners attached it to Barlan, or Verra, or Crow, or one of the other gods. I couldn't do that; I'd been around Dragaerans too long and I'd picked up their attitudes toward gods. What else was there? The Jhereg? Don't make me laugh. My duty toward the Jhereg is to follow its rules so I don't get shined. The Empire? My duty toward the Empire is to make sure it doesn't notice me.

That left it pretty small. Family, I guess. Cawti, my grandfather, Loiosh, and Rocza. Sure. That was a duty, and one I could be proud to do. I thought about how empty I'd felt before Cawti came into my life, and even the memory was painful. Why wasn't that enough?

I wondered if Cawti had felt this way. She didn't have the organization; she just had me. She used to have a partner and they'd needed each other, but her partner had become a Dragonlord and heir to the Orb. Now what did she have? Was that why she'd gotten involved with Kelly's people? To give her something to do, so she'd feel useful? Wasn't I enough?

No. Of course not. No one can live his life through someone else, I knew that. So what did Cawti have to live for? She had her "people." This group of Easterners and an occasional Teckla who got together to talk about overthrowing the Empire. Cawti hung around with them, helped build barricades in the streets, stood up to Phoenix Guards, and came home convinced that she'd done her "duty." Maybe that's what duty was—something you do to make yourself feel useful.

Fine. That was Cawti. Where was *my* duty? Doo-deedle-deedle-dee. My duty was to die, because I was going to anyway, so I might as well call it a duty. You're getting cynical, Vlad, stop it.

I had about finished changing my weapons so I just sat there, holding a dagger that was destined for my right boot. I leaned back and closed my eyes. All of this was really beside the point if I was going to be killed soon. Or was it? Was there something I ought to be doing, even if I were dying? Now that would be a good test of "duty," whatever I meant by it.

And I realized there was. I had gotten myself involved in this thing up to my neck mostly with the idea of keeping Cawti alive. If it was really as clear as all that that I was going to die, I'd have to make sure that Cawti was safe before I let anyone kill me.

Now there was a pretty little problem.

Doo-dee-deedee-dee-dum. I started flipping the dagger.

11

. . . & remove sweat stains.

A LITTLE LATER, WITH the seeds of an idea taking shape in my head, I called for Kragar, but Melestav said he was out. I gnashed mental teeth and kept thinking. What, I wondered, would happen if I was killed and Cawti wasn't? My cynical half said it wouldn't be my problem. But beyond that, I guessed that my grandfather and Cawti would be able to look out for each other. There had been some sort of communication going on between them on the street there, something that had left me out. Were they going to get together and talk about how terrible I was? Was I going to die of paranoia?

Ignoring all of that, however, Cawti would be faced with an interesting problem if Herth killed me: She'd want to kill Herth herself, but she didn't want to be an assassin any more. Or at least, after the way she'd spoken to me I assumed she didn't want to be an assassin any more. On the other hand, it couldn't hurt Kelly any to have his biggest enemy taken off the stage. Too bad I'd have to die to pull it off. Hmmm.

I idly wondered whether there would be a way to convince Cawti I was dead long enough for her to kill Herth. My reappearance afterward would certainly be fun. On the other hand, it could get very embarrassing if she chose not to go after him, and even more embarrassing if Herth found out I was alive.

Still, no need to dismiss it out of hand. It was better—

"You're looking morbid again, Vlad."

I didn't jump. "How kind of you to say so, Kragar. Anything on Herth?" He shook his head. I continued, "All right, a couple of thoughts have been buzzing around my head. I want to let one of them keep buzzing. The other one is to set things up to do it the long way."

"Buy off his protection?"

I nodded.

"Okay," he said. "I'll get started on it."

"Good. What about the assassin?"

"The artist should be just about finished. He said I have a very good mind for detail. Since I got the image from you, I think you ought to be flattered."

"Okay, I'm flattered. You know what to do with the picture."

He nodded and left and I went back to planning my death—or at least thinking about it. It seemed completely impractical, but tempting anyway. The triumphant return was what sounded best, I suppose. Of course, that wouldn't work too well if by the time I returned Cawti was shacking up with Gregory or someone.

I held that thought, just to see how much it bothered me. It more or less didn't, which somehow bothered me.

Loiosh and Rocza scratched on the window. I put the dagger I'd been flipping in its sheath and let them in. I stayed to the side, just in case. They seemed a bit exhausted.

"Sightseeing?"

"Yeah."

"Who won the race?"

"What makes you think we were racing, boss?"

"I didn't say you were; I just asked who won."

"Oh. She did. Wingspan."

"Yeah, that'll do it. I don't suppose you went anywhere near South Adrilankha, did you?"

"As a matter of fact we did."

"Ah. And the barricades?"

"Gone."

Loiosh settled on my shoulder. I sat down and said, "A while ago you asked me what I'd think of Kelly's group if Cawti weren't involved."

"Yeah."

"I've been thinking about it. I decided it doesn't matter. She is involved, and I have to work with things on that basis."

"Okay."

"And I think I know what I have to do about it."

He didn't say anything. I could feel him picking moods and random thoughts out of my brain. After a moment he said, "Do you really think you're going to die?"

"Yes and no. I guess I don't really believe it. I mean, we've been in situations before that have seemed this bad or worse. Mellar was tougher and smarter than Herth and the situation was worse. But I don't see how to get out of this one. I haven't been operating very well lately; maybe that's part of it."

"I know. So what is it you're going to do?"

"Save Cawti. I don't know about the rest, but I have to do that much."

"Okay. How?"

"I can only think of two ways: One is to wipe out Herth, and probably his whole organization, so no one else can pick up the pieces and carry on."

"That doesn't seem too likely."

"No. The other way is arrange things so that Herth has no reason to go after Cawti."

"That sounds better. How do you plan to do it?"

"By wiping out Kelly and his little band myself."

Loiosh didn't say anything. From what I could pick up of his thoughts, he was too amazed to speak. I thought it a rather clever idea myself. After a while Loiosh said, *"But Cawti—"*

"I know. If you can think of a way for me to convince both Cawti and Herth that I've died, that might work too."

"Nothing comes to mind, boss. But—"

"Then let's get to work."

"I don't like this."

"Protest noted. Let's get busy. I want to have it over with tonight."

"Tonight."

"Yeah."

"Okay, boss. Whatever you say."

I took out a piece of paper and started making a diagram of everything I remembered in Kelly's place, making notes where I wasn't sure of something, and trying to make guesses about back windows and so on. Then I stared at it and tried to decide how to handle things.

This could not, by any stretch of the imagination, be called as assassination. It would be more like a slaughter. I was going to have to kill Kelly for certain, because if he survived I wouldn't have accomplished anything. Then Paresh, because he was a sorcerer; then as many of the others as possible. There was no point in even trying to plan this out in the kind of detail I usually use; not when trying to shine five or more at once.

The thought of a fire or explosion crossed my mind, but I rejected the idea; buildings were too closely packed there. I didn't want to burn down all of South Adrilankha.

I picked up the diagram and studied it. There was certainly going to be a back entrance to the building, and probably a back entrance to the flat. I'd been quite a ways into it and hadn't seen a kitchen, and Kelly's private office had two doorways, so I could probably start in back and work my way forward, to make sure no one was awake in that part of the house. Since everyone seemed to sleep in that front area, I would end there, cut Kelly's throat, then Paresh's. If everyone else was still sleeping by then, I would take them one at a time. I woudn't have to worry about revivifications, since these were Easterners with no money, but if I could I'd go back and make sure anyway. Then I'd leave.

South Adrilankha would wake up tomorrow and these people would be gone. Cawti would be very upset, but she couldn't put the organization back together just by herself. At least, I hoped she couldn't. There were several other Easterners and Teckla involved in this, but the core would be gone and I didn't think those who remained would be able to do anything that could threaten Herth.

I studied the diagram then destroyed it. I leaned back in my chair, closed my eyes, went over the details, making sure I hadn't left anything out.

I got to Kelly's building halfway between midnight and dawn. The front door was only a curtain. I went around to the back. There was something of a door there, but it had no lock. I carefully and thoroughly oiled the hinges, and entered. This put me at the back of the building in a narrow hallway outside of Kelly's flat. Rocza was nervous on my right shoulder. I asked Loiosh to keep her quiet and soon she settled down.

I looked down the hall but couldn't see the front door—or anything else, for that matter. I have pretty fair night vision, but there are those who see better than I do. *"Is there anyone in the hall, Loiosh?"*

"No one, boss."

"Okay. Where's the back entrance to the flat?"

"Right here. If you put your hand out to the right you'll touch it."

"Oh."

I slipped past the curtain and was inside. I smelled food, some of it probably edible. There was certainly the stink of rotting vegetables.

After waiting a moment to check for the sounds of breathing, I risked a small sorcerous light from the tip of my forefinger. Yes, I was in a kitchen, and a bigger one than I'd expected. There were a few cupboards, an ice-chest, a pump. I lowered the light just a bit, held my forefinger in front of me and headed toward the front room.

I passed through the room where I'd spoken with Kelly. It was pretty much as I remembered it, except for a few more boxes. On one of them I caught the glitter of steel. I looked closer and saw a long dagger, which I recognized as the murder weapon—or else one very much like it. I checked it closer. Yeah, that was it.

I was starting to go past it into the next room, the library, when I sensed someone behind me. Trying to remember this now, it seems to me that Rocza tightened her grip on my shoulder just at that moment, but Loiosh didn't notice anything. In any case, my reaction to such things is foreordained: I spun, twisting a bit to the side, and drew a dagger from the inside my cloak.

At first I didn't see anything, yet I continued to feel that there was someone in the room with me. I let the light from my forefinger fail and moved to the side, thinking that if I couldn't see him, there was no reason to let him see me. Then I became aware of a faint outline, as if there were a transparent figure in front of me. I didn't know what this meant, but I knew it wasn't normal. I let Spellbreaker fall into my left hand.

The figure didn't move, but it gradually grew more substantial, and it occurred to me that the room was dark as Verra's hair and I shouldn't be able to see anything.

"Loiosh, what do you see?"

"I'm not sure, boss."

"But you do see something."

"I think so."

"Yeah. Me, too." Rocza stirred uneasily. Well, I didn't blame her. Then I realized what I must be seeing and I blamed her even less.

*   *   *

It had been made pretty clear to me that I wasn't welcome, the time I walked the Paths of the Dead with Aliera and visited the Halls of Judgment. It was a place for the souls of Dragaerans, not the living bodies of Easterners. In order to arrive there, a body had to be sent over Deathgate Falls (which would certainly insure it was a corpse even it hadn't been before). Then it floated down the river, fetching up somewhere along a stretch of bank, from which the soul could travel—but never mind that now. If the soul handled things right, it would reach the Halls of Judgment, and unless some god especially liked or disliked the guy, he'd take his place as part of a thriving community of dead persons.

All right, fine.

What might happen to him if he isn't brought to Deathgate Falls? Well, if he was killed with a Morganti dagger, the issue was settled. Or, if he'd worked out some arrangement with his favorite god, then the god had the pleasure of doing anything he wanted with the soul. Other than that, he'd be reincarnated. You don't have to believe me, of course, but some recent experiences have convinced me that this is fact.

Now, most of what I know about reincarnation I learned from Aliera before I believed in it, so I've forgotten a great deal of what she said. But I remember that an unborn child exerts a kind of mystical pull and will draw in the soul most suited to it. If no soul is appropriate, there will be no birth. If there is no child appropriate to a soul, the soul waits in a place that the necromancers call "The Plane of Waiting Souls" because they aren't very imaginative. Why does it wait there? Because it can't help it. There is something about the place that pulls at the Dragaeran soul.

But what about Easterners? Well, it's pretty much the same, as far as I can tell. When it comes down to a soul, there just isn't that much difference between a Dragaeran and an Easterner. We aren't allowed into the Paths of the Dead, but Morganti weapons have the same effect on us, and we can make deals with any god who feels like it, and we're probably reincarnated if there's nothing else going on, or at least that's what the Eastern poet-seer, Yain Cho Lin, is reported to have said. In fact, according to the *Book of the Seven Wizards*, the Plane of Waiting Souls pulls at us while we're waiting, just like it does Dragaerans.

The book says, however, that it doesn't pull quite as hard. Why? Population. There are more Easterners in the world, so there are fewer souls waiting for places to go, so there are fewer souls to help call the others. Does this make sense? Not to me, either, but there it is.

One result of this weaker pull is that, sometimes, the soul of an Easterner will be neither reincarnated nor will it go to the Plane of Waiting Souls. Instead it will, well, just sort of hang around.

At least, that's the story. Believe it or not, as you choose.

I believe it, myself.

I was seeing a ghost.

*   *   *

I stared at it. Staring seems to be the first thing one does when seeing a ghost. I wasn't quite sure what the second thing ought to be. According to the stories my grandfather had told me when I was young, screaming was highly thought of. But if I screamed I'd wake up everyone in the place, and I needed them to be sleeping if I was going to kill them. Also, I didn't feel the urge. I knew I was supposed to be frightened, but when it came down to it, I was much more fascinated than scared.

The ghost continued to solidify. It was a bit luminescent, which was how I could see it. It was emitting a very faint blue glow. As I watched, I began to see the lines of its face. Soon I could tell that it was an Easterner, then that it was male. It seemed to be looking at me—that is, actually seeing me. Since I didn't want to wake everyone up, I moved out of the room, back into Kelly's study. I made a light again and navigated the floor to his desk and sat down. I don't know how I knew the ghost would follow me, but I did and he did.

I cleared my throat. "Well," I said. "You must be Franz."

"Yes," said the ghost. Can I say his voice was sepulchral? I don't care. It was.

"I'm Vladimir Taltos—Cawti's husband."

The ghost—no, let me just call him Franz. Franz nodded. "What are you doing here?" As he spoke he continued to solidify, and his voice became more normal.

"Well," I said. "That's a bit hard to explain. What are *you* doing here?"

His brow (which I could now see) came together. "I'm not sure," he said. I studied him. His hair was light, straight, and neatly combed. How does a ghost comb his hair? His face was pleasant but undistinctive, his demeanor had that honest and sincere look that I associate with spice salesmen and dead lyorn. He had a peculiar way of standing, as if he were leaning ever so slightly forward, and when I spoke he turned his head just a bit to the side. I wondered if he was hard of hearing, or just very intent on catching everything that was said. He seemed to be a very intense listener. In fact, he seemed intense just in general. He said, "I was standing outside the meeting hall—"

"Yes. You were assassinated."

"Assassinated!"

I nodded.

He stared at me, then looked at himself, then closed his eyes for a moment. Finally he said, "I'm dead now? A ghost?"

"Something like that. You should be waiting for reincarnation, if I understand how these things work. I guess there aren't any pregnant Easterners around here who quite fit the bill. Be patient."

He studied me, sizing me up.

"You're Cawti's husband."

"Yes."

"You say I was assassinated. We know what you do. Could it have been—"

"No. Or rather, it could have but it wasn't. A fellow named Yerekim did it. You people were getting in the way of a guy named Herth."

"And he had me killed?" Franz suddenly smiled. "To try to scare us off?"

"Yeah."

He laughed. "I can guess how well it worked for him. We organized the whole district, didn't we? Using my murder as a rallying point?"

I stared. "Good guess. It doesn't bother you?"

"Bother me? We've been trying to unite Easterners and Teckla against the Empire all along. Why would it bother me?"

I said, "Oh. Well, it seems to be working."

"Good." His expression changed. "I wonder why I'm back."

I said, "What do you remember?"

"Not much. I was just standing there and my throat started itching. Then I felt someone touch my shoulder from behind. I turned around and my knees felt weak and then . . . I don't know. I remember waking up, sort of, and feeling . . . worried, I guess. How long ago did it happen?"

I told him. His eyes widened. "I wonder what brought me back?"

"You say you felt worried?"

I nodded.

I sighed inaudibly. I had a good guess what had brought him back, but I chose not to share it with him.

"Hey, boss."

"Yeah."

"This is really weird."

"No it isn't. It's normal. Everything is normal. It's just that some normal things are weirder than other normal things."

"Oh. That explains it then."

Franz said, "Tell me what's happened since I died."

I complied, being as honest as I could. When I told him about Sheryl his face grew hard and cold and I remembered that I was dealing with a fanatic. I tightened my grip on Spellbreaker but continued the recitation. When I told him about the barricades a gleam came into his eye, and I wondered just how effective Spellbreaker would be.

"Good," he said when I'd finished. "We have them running now."

"Um, yeah," I said.

"Then it was worth it."

"Dying?"

"Yes."

"Oh."

"I should talk to Pat if I can. Where is everyone else?"

I almost told him they were asleep, but I caught myself. "I'm not sure," I said.

His eyes narrowed. "You're here alone?"

"Not at all," I said. Loiosh hissed to emphasize the point. He glanced at the two jhereg, but didn't smile. He seemed to have as big a sense of humor as the others. I added, "I'm sort of watching the place."

His eyes widened. "You've joined us?"

"Yes."

He smiled at me, and there was so much warmth in his expression that I would have kicked him, only he was incorporeal. "Cawti didn't think you would."

"Yeah, well."

"Exciting, isn't it?"

"Exciting. Yes, it certainly is that."

"Where's the latest issue?"

"Issue?"

"Of the paper."

"Oh. Um . . . it's around here somewhere."

He looked around the office, which I was still lighting up with my finger, and finally found one. He tried to pick it up, couldn't, kept trying, and finally managed. Then he set it down. "It's hard to hold things," he said. "Do you suppose you could turn the pages for me?"

"Uh, sure."

So I turned pages for him, and grunted agreement when he said things like, "No, he's missing the point," and, "Those bastards! How can they do that?" After a while he stopped and looked at me. "It was worth dying, but I wish I could be back in it again. There's so much to be done."

He went back to reading. I noticed that he seemed to be fading. I watched for a while, and the effect continued slowly but detectably. I said, "Look, I want to find people and let them know you're around, all right? Can you sort of keep an eye on things? I'm sure if anyone comes in you can scare him to death."

He smiled. "All right. Go ahead."

I nodded and went back out the way I'd come, through the kitchen and out the door.

"*I thought we were going to kill them all, boss.*"

"*So did I.*"

"*Couldn't you have gotten rid of the ghost with Spellbreaker?*"

"*Probably.*"

"*Well then, why—*"

"*He's already been killed once too often.*"

"*But what about the rest of them?*"

"*I changed my mind.*"

"*Oh. Well, I didn't like the idea anyway.*"

"*Good.*"

I teleported to a point a block from my house. There were lamps in the street that provided enough light to tell me I was alone. I made my way home very carefully, checking for the assassin.

"*Why did you change your mind, boss?*"

"*I don't know. I have to think about it some more. Something about Franz, I guess.*"

I made my way up the stairs and into the house. The sounds of Cawti's gentle breathing came from the bedroom. I removed my boots and cloak, then went in, undressed, and climbed into bed carefully so I wouldn't wake her.

As I closed my eyes I saw Franz's face before me. It took longer than it should have to fall asleep.

12

1 plain grey cloak: clean & press . . .

I SLEPT LATE AND woke up slowly. I sat up in bed and tried to organize my thoughts and decide how to spend the day. My latest great scheme hadn't worked at all, so I went back to an earlier one. Was there any way, really, to convince both Cawti and Herth that I'd been killed? Herth so he'd leave me alone, Cawti so she'd kill Herth for me. I couldn't think of anything.

"You know what your problem is, boss?"

"Huh? Yeah. Everyone wants to tell me what my problem is."

"Sorry I brought it up."

"Oh, go ahead."

"You're trying to find a good trick to use, and you can't solve this with tricks."

That stopped me. I said, *"What you do mean?"*

"Well, look, boss: What's been bothering you is that you're running into all these people who think you shouldn't be what you are, and you have to decide whether to change or not."

"Loiosh, what's bothering me is that there's an assassin out there who has my name and—"

"Didn't you say yesterday that we'd been in worse places before?"

"Yeah. And I've come up with some trick to get out of them."

"So why haven't you this time?"

"I'm too busy answering questions from jhereg who think that the only problem is great sorrow with my lot in life."

Loiosh giggled psionically and didn't say anything else. That's one trait Loiosh has that I've never found in anyone else: He knows when to stop pushing and let me just think about things. I suppose it comes from sharing my thoughts. I can't think of any other way to get it.

I teleported to the office. I wondered if my stomach would ever get used to the abuse. Cawti once told me that when she was working with Norathar they teleported almost everywhere, and her stomach never adjusted. They almost blew a job once, she said, because she threw up on the victim. I won't give you the details; she tells it better than I do.

I called Kragar into my office. "Well?"

"We've identified the assassin. His name is Quaysh."

"Quaysh? Unusual."

"It's Serioli. Means, 'He Who Designs Interesting Clasps For Ladies' Jewelry.' "

"I see. Do we have someone on him?"

"Yeah. A guy named Ishtvan. We used him once before."

"I remember. He was quick."

"That's the guy."

"Good. Who recognized Quaysh?"

"Sticks. They used to hang around together."

"Hmmm. Problem?"

"Not as far as I know. Business."

"Yeah. Okay, but tell Sticks to stay alert; if he knows that he knows who he is, and he doesn't know he knows—"

"What?"

"Just tell Sticks to be careful. Anything else important?"

"No. I'm putting together information on Herth's bodyguards, but it's going to be a while before we know enough to approach one."

I nodded and sent him about his business. I scratched under Loiosh's chin. I teleported—again—to South Adrilankha. I made my way to Kelly's place to see what was happening there. I stayed away from the corner I'd occupied before and took up a looser position down the street. Now the object was not to be noticed.

People who don't know this business seem to overrate the importance of looks in general and clothing in particular. This is because that's what one notices. You don't usually notice the way someone is walking, or the direction he's looking, or his movement through the crowd; you notice his appearance and his clothing. Nevertheless, that isn't what attracted your attention. You see people every day who look funny but don't attract attention. I mean, you certainly can't expect someone to say, "I didn't see this guy who looked funny," or, "There was someone wearing really weird clothes but I didn't notice him." An oddly shaped nose or unusual hair or a strange way of dressing are what you *remember* about someone you notice, but they aren't usually what calls him to your attention.

I was dressed oddly, for that area, but I was just being me, in the middle of the street where everyone else was, doing what everyone else was doing. No one noticed me, and I kept an eye on Kelly's flat to see if there was anything unusual going on. That is, I wanted to know if they'd discovered Franz.

After an hour or so I couldn't tell, so I made my way a little closer to the building, then a little closer, then I slipped around to the side, up against another one just like it. I pressed my ear against the wall. It was even thinner than I'd thought, so I had no trouble hearing what was going on inside.

They weren't talking about Franz at all.

Kelly was speaking, something about, "It's as if you're saying, 'I know you aren't interested, but—' under your breath." His voice was biting, sarcastic.

Cawti said something, but it was too low for me to hear. Too low for Kelly, too, because he said, "Speak up," in a tone that made me wince. Cawti spoke again, and I still couldn't hear her, and then Paresh said, "That's absurd. It's twice as important now. You may not have noticed, but we're in the middle of an uprising. Every mistake we make now is twice as deadly. We can't afford *any* errors."

Then Cawti muttered something else and I heard several exclamations, and Gregory said, "If you feel that way, why did you join us in the first place?" Natalia said, "You're looking at it from *their* view. You've been trying to be an aristocrat all your life, and even now you're trying. But we aren't here to change places with them, and we aren't going to destroy them by accepting their lies as facts." And then Kelly said something, and others did as well, but I'm not going to relate any more of it. It isn't any of your business, and it isn't any of mine even though I heard it.

I listened, though, to quite a bit of it, getting redder and redder. Loiosh kept squeezing his talons on my shoulder and at one point said, *"Rocza's pretty upset."* I didn't answer because I didn't trust myself to speak, even to Loiosh. There was a door right around the corner from me, and I could have gone in there and Kelly would have died before he knew what hit him.

It was hard not to do it.

The only thing that distracted me was that I kept thinking things like, "How can she put up with that?" And, "Why does she *want* to put up with that?" It also occurred to me that all of the others were either very brave or very trusting. They knew as well as I did that Cawti could have killed the lot of them in seconds.

The woman I married would have done so, too.

I finally stole away from the building and had some klava.

She'd changed sometime in the last year, and I hadn't noticed. Maybe that was what bothered me the most. I mean, if I really loved her, wouldn't I have seen that she was turning from a walking death-machine into a . . . a whatever she was? But then, turn it around. I *did* love her; I could tell because it hurt so much, and I hadn't noticed, so there I was.

There was no point in wondering *why* she'd changed. No future in it, as Sticks would say. The question was, were we going to change together? No, let's be honest. The question was, was I going to pretend to be something I wasn't, or even try to *become* something I wasn't, in order to keep her? And when I put it that way I knew that I couldn't. I wasn't going to become another person on the chance that she'd come to love me again. She had married me, just as I was, and I had married her the same way. If she was going to turn away from me, I'd just have to live with it as best I could.

Or not. There was still Quaysh, who'd agreed to kill me, and Herth, who would try again if Quaysh failed. So maybe I wouldn't have to live with it at all. That would be convenient, but not really ideal. I ordered more klava, which came in a glass, which reminded me of Sheryl, which didn't cheer me up.

I was still in this gloomy frame of mind an hour later when Natalia came in accompanied by an Easterner I didn't know and a Teckla who wasn't Paresh. She saw me and nodded, then thought about it and joined me, after saying something to her companions. I invited her to sit and she did. I bought her a cup of tea because I was feeling expansive and because she didn't like klava. We just looked at each other until the tea arrived. It smelled better than the klava, and it came in a mug. I resolved to remember that.

Natalia's life was crudely sketched on her face. I mean, I couldn't see the details, but the outline was there. Her hair was dark but greying; the thin grey streaks that don't seem dignified but merely old. Her brow was wide and the furrows in it seemed permanent. There were deep lines next to her nose, which I'm sure had been a cute button when she was younger. Her face was thin and marked with tension, as if she went around with her jaw clenched. And yet, deep down behind it all, there was a sparkle in her eyes. She seemed to be in her early forties.

As she sipped on her tea and formed opinions of me that were as valid as mine of her, I said, "So, how did you get involved in all of this?"

She started to answer and I sensed that I was about to get a tract, so I said, "No, never mind. I'm not sure I want to hear."

She favored me with a sort of half-smile, which was the most cheerful thing I'd run into from her yet. She said, "You don't want to hear about my life as a harem girl for an Eastern king?"

I said, "Why yes, I would. I don't suppose you really were one though, were you?"

"I'm afraid not."

"Just as well," I said.

"I was a thief for a while, though."

"Yeah? Not a bad occupation. The hours are good, anyway."

"It's like anything else," she said. "It depends on your stature in the field."

I thought about Orcas who will knife anyone for twenty Imperials, and said, "I suppose. I take it you weren't at the top."

She nodded. "We lived on the other side of town." She meant the other side of South Adrilankha. To most Easterners, South Adrilankha was all of town there was. "That was," she continued, "after my mother died. My father would bring me into an inn and I would steal the coins the drinkers left on the bar, or sometimes cut their purses."

I said, "No, that isn't really the top of the profession, is it? But I suppose it's a living."

"After a fashion."

"Did you get caught?"

"Yes. Once. We'd agreed that if I was caught he'd go through the motions of beating me, as if it were my own idea. Then when I was finally caught, he did more than go through the motions."

"I see. Did you tell what really happened?"

"No. I was only about ten, and I was too busy crying and screaming that I'd never steal again, and I'm sorry, and anything else I could think of to say."

The waiter returned with more klava. I didn't touch it, having learned from experience.

I said, "Then what happened?"

She shrugged. "I never did steal again. We went into another inn, and I wouldn't steal anything, so my father took me out and beat me again. I ran away and I've never seen him since."

"You were how old, did you say?"

"Ten."

"Hmmm. How did you live, if you don't mind my asking?"

"Since all I knew about were inns, I went into one and asked to sweep the floor in exchange for a meal. The owner said yes, so that's what I did for a while. At first I was too scrawny to have any trouble with the customers, but later I had to hide during the evenings. I was charged for oil, so I'd sit in my room in the dark, covered with blankets. I didn't really mind, though. Having a room all to myself was so nice that I didn't miss the light or the heat.

"When the owner died I was twelve, and his widow sort of latched on to me. She stopped charging me for the oil, which was nice. But I guess the biggest thing she did for me was to teach me to read. From then on I spent all my time reading, mostly the same eight or nine books over and over again. I remember there was one that I couldn't understand no matter how many times I read it, and another one of fairy stories, and one was a play, something about a ship-wreck. And one was all about where to grow what field crops for best results, or something. I even read that, which shows how desperate I was. I still didn't go down to the common room in the evening, and there wasn't anything else to do."

I said, "So there you were when Kelly came along, and he changed your life, and made you see this and that and the other, right?"

She smiled. "Something like that. I used to see him selling papers on the corner every day when I ran my errands. But one day, just out of nowhere, I realized that I could buy one and it would be something *new* to read. I had never heard of bookstores. I think Kelly was around twenty then.

"For the next year I'd buy a paper every week, then run off before he could talk to me. I had no idea what the paper was about, but I liked it. After a year or so, it finally began to sink in and I started thinking about what it was saying, and what it had to do with me. I remember it coming as a shock to me when I realized that there was something, somehow, *wrong* when a ten-year-old child had to go into inns to steal."

"That's true," I said. "A ten-year-old child should be able to steal in the streets."

"Stop it," she snapped, and I decided she probably had a point so I mumbled an apology and said, "So, anyway, that's when you decided to save the world."

I guess her years had taught her a certain kind of patience, because she didn't glare at me cynically as Paresh would have, or close up as Cawti would have. She shook her head and said, "It's never that simple. I started talking to Kelly, of course, and we started arguing. I didn't realize until later that the only reason I kept returning to him was that he was the only person I knew who listened to me and seemed to take me seriously. I don't think I ever would have done anything about it, but that was the year the tavern tax came down."

I nodded. That had been before my time, but I could still remember my father talking about it in that peculiar, hushed tone he always used when talking about something the Empire did that he didn't like. I said, "What happened then?"

She laughed. "A lot of things. The first thing was that the inn closed, almost right away. The owner sold it, probably for just enough to live on. The new owner closed it until the tax fuss settled, so I was out on the street without a job. That same day I saw Kelly, and his paper had a big article about it. I said something to him about his silly old paper, and this was *real*, and he tore into me like a dzur after lyorn. He said that was what the paper was about, and the only way to save the jobs was this and that and the other. I don't remember most of it, but I was pretty mad myself and not thinking too clearly. I told him the problem was the Empress was greedy, and he said that no, the Empress was desperate, because of this and that, and the next thing I knew he was sounding like he was on her side. I stormed off and didn't see him again for years."

"What did you do?"

"I found another inn, this one on the Dragaeran side of town. Since Dragaerans can't tell how old we are anyway, and the owner thought I was 'cute,' they let me serve customers. It turned out that the last waiter had been killed in a knife fight the week before. I guess that should have told me what kind of place it was, and it was that kind of place, but I did all right. I found a flat just on this side of Twovine, and walked the two miles to work every day. The nice thing was that the walk took me past a little bookstore. I spent a lot of money there, but it was worth it. I especially loved history—Dragaeran, not human. And the stories, too. I guess I couldn't tell them apart very well. I used to pretend I was a Dzurlord, and I'd fight the battle of the Seven Pines then go charging up Dzur Mountain to fight the Enchantress all in one breath. What is it?"

I suppose I must have jumped a bit when she mentioned Dzur Mountain. I said, "Nothing. When did you meet Kelly again?"

My klava was cool enough to pick up and just barely warm enough to be worth drinking. I drank some. Natalia said, "It was after the head tax was instituted in the Eastern section. A couple who lived downstairs from me also knew how to read, and they ran into a group of people who were trying to get up a petition to the Empress against the tax."

I nodded. Someone had come to my father's restaurant with a similar petition years later, even though we lived in the Dragaeran part of the city. My father had thrown him out. I said, "I've never understood why the head tax was even instituted. Was the Empire trying to keep Easterners out of the city?"

"It had to do largely with the uprisings in the eastern and northern duchies that ended forced labor. I've written a book on it. Would you like to buy a copy?"

"Never mind."

"Anyway," she continued, "my neighbors and I got involved with these people. We worked with them for a while, but I didn't like the idea of going to the Empire on our hands and knees. It seemed wrong. I guess my head was just filled with those histories and stories I'd read, and I was only fourteen, but it seemed to me that the only ones who ever got anything from the Empress had to ask boldly and prove themselves worthy." She said "boldly" and "worthy" with a bit of emphasis. "I thought we ought to do something wonderful for the Empire, then ask that the tax be lifted as our reward."

I smiled. "What did they say to that?"

"Oh, I never actually proposed it. I wanted to, but I was afraid they'd laugh at me." Her lips turned up briefly. "And of course they would have. But we had a few public meetings to talk about it, and Kelly started showing up at them, with, I think, four or five others. I don't remember what they said, but they made a big impression on me. They were younger than a lot of those there, but they seemed to know exactly what they were talking about, and they came in and left together, like a unit. They reminded me of the Dragon armies, I guess. So after one of the meetings I went up to Kelly and said, 'Remember me?' And he did, and we started talking, and we were arguing again inside of a minute, only this time I didn't walk away. I gave him my address and we agreed to stay in touch.

"I didn't join him for another year or so, after the riots, and the killings. It was just about the time the Empress finally lifted the head tax."

I nodded as if I knew the history she was speaking of. I said, "Was Kelly involved in that?"

"We were all involved. He wasn't behind the riots or anything, but he was there all the time. He was incarcerated for a while, at one of the camps they set up when they broke us up. I managed to avoid the Guards that time, even though I'd been around, too, when the Lumber Exchange was torched. That was what finally brought the troops in, you know. The Lumber Exchange was owned by a Dragaeran; an Iorich, I think."

"I hadn't known that," I said truthfully. "You've been with Kelly ever since?"

She nodded.

I thought about Cawti. "It must be difficult," I said. "I mean, he must be a hard man to work with."

"It's exciting. We're building the future."

I said, "Everyone builds the future. Everything we do every day builds the future."

"All right, I mean we're building it *consciously*. We know what we're doing."

"Yeah. Okay. You're building the future. To get it, you're sacrificing the present."

"What do you mean?" Her tone was genuinely inquisitive rather than snappy, which gave me some hope for her.

"I mean that you're so wrapped up in what you're doing that you're blind to the people around you. You're so involved in creating this vision of yours that you don't care how many innocent people are hurt." She started to speak but I kept going. "Look," I said, "we both know who I am and what I do, so there's no point pretending otherwise, and if you think it's inherently evil, then there isn't anything more to say. But I can tell you that I have never, *never* intentionally hurt an innocent person. And I'm including Dragaerans as people, so don't think I'm pulling one on you that way because I'm not."

She caught my eye and held it. "I didn't think you were. And I won't even discuss what you mean by innocent. All I can say is that if you really believe what you've just said, nothing I can say will change your mind, so there isn't any point in discussing it."

I relaxed, not realizing that I'd been tense. I guess I'd expected her to lambaste me or something. I suddenly wondered why I cared, and decided that Natalia seemed to be the most reasonable of these people that I'd yet met, and I somehow wanted to like, and be liked by, at least one of them. That was stupid. I'd given up trying to make people "like" me when I was twelve years old, and had the results of that attitude beaten into me in ways I'll never forget.

And with that thought a certain anger came, and with the anger a certain strength. I kept it off my face, but it came back to me then, as a chilly, refreshing wave. I had started down the path that led me to this point many, many years before, and I had taken those first steps because I hated Dragaerans. That was my reason then, it was my reason now, it was enough.

Kelly's people did everything for ideals I could never understand. To them, people were "the masses," individuals only mattered by what they did for the movement. Such people could never love. Not purely, unselfishly, with no thought for why and how and what it would do. And, similarly, they could never hate; they were too wrapped up in *why* someone did something to be able to hate him for doing it.

But I hated. I could feel my hatred inside of me, spinning like a ball of ice. Most of all, right now, I hated Herth. No, I didn't really *want* to hire someone to send him for a walk, I wanted to do it myself. I wanted to feel that tug of a body as it jerks and kicks while I hold the handle and the life erupts from it like water from the cold springs of the Eastern Mountains. That's what I wanted, and what you want makes you who you are.

I put down a few coins to pay for the klava and the tea. I don't know how much Natalia knew of what was going on in my head, but she knew I was done talking. She thanked me and we stood up at the same time. I bowed and thanked her for her company.

As I walked out, she picked up her two companions by sight and they left the place just ahead of me, turned, and waited for her by the door. As I left, the Easterner looked at my grey cloak with the stylized jhereg on it and sneered. If the Teckla had done it I'd have killed him, but it was the Easterner so I just kept walking.

13

...remove cat hairs...

THE CHIMES SOUNDED, LIGHT and tinkling, as I stepped into the shop. My grandfather was writing in a bound tablet with an old-fashioned pencil. As I came in he looked up and smiled.

"Vladimir!"

"Hello, Noish-pa." I hugged him. We sat down and he said hello to Loiosh. Ambrus jumped into my lap and I greeted him properly. Ambrus never purred when stroked, but he somehow let you know when he liked what you were doing anyway. My grandfather told me once that Ambrus only purred when they were working magic together; the purr was a sign that everything was all right.

I studied my grandfather. Was he looking a bit older, a little more worn than he used to? I wasn't sure. It's hard to look at a familiar face as if it were that of a stranger. For some reason my eyes were drawn to his ankles, and I noticed how thin and frail they looked, even for his size. Yet, again for his size, his chest seemed large and well-muscled beneath a faded tunic of red and green. His head, bald save for the thinnest fringe of white hair, gleamed in the candlelight.

"So," he said after a while.

"How are you feeling?"

"I am fine, Vladimir. And you?"

"About the same, Noish-pa."

"Yes. There is something on your mind?"

I sighed. "Were you around in two twenty-one?"

He raised his eyebrows. "The riots? Yes. That was a bad time." He shook his head as he spoke and the corners of his mouth fell. But it was funny; it seemed, at the same time, that his eyes lit up just a bit, way down deep.

I said, "You were involved?"

"Involved? How could I not be involved? It was everyone; we were part of it or we hid from it, but we were all involved."

"Was my father involved?"

He gave me a look that I couldn't read. Then he said, "Yes, your father, he was there. He and I, and your grandmother too, and my brother Jani. We were at Twovine and Hilltop when the Empire tried to break us." His voice hardened a bit as he said that. "Your father killed a Guard, too. With a butcher knife."

"He did?"

He nodded.

I didn't say anything for a while, trying to see how I felt about this. It seemed odd, and I wished I'd known it while my father was still alive. There was a brief pang from knowing that I'd never see him again. I finally said, "And you?"

"Oh, they gave me a post after the fight, so I guess I was there too."

"A post?"

"I was a block delegate, for M'Gary Street north of Elm. So when we met, I had to go there for everyone from our neighborhood and say what we wanted."

"I hadn't known about that. Dad never talked about it."

"Well, he was unhappy. That was when I lost your grandmother—when they came back in."

"The Empire?"

"Yes. They came back with more troops—Dragons who had fought in the East."

"Would you like to tell me about it?"

He sighed and looked away for a moment. I guess he was thinking about my grandmother. I wished I'd met her. "Perhaps another time, Vladimir."

"Sure. All right. I noticed that Kelly looked at you as if he recognized you. Was it from then?"

"Yes. I knew him. He was young then. When we spoke of him before I didn't know it was the same Kelly."

"Is he a good man, Noish-pa?"

He glanced at me quickly. "Why this question?"

"Because of Cawti, I suppose."

"Hmmph. Well, yes, he is good, perhaps, if what he does you call good."

I tried to decipher that, then came at it from another angle. "You didn't seem to think much of Cawti being involved with these people. Why is that, if you were involved in it yourself?"

He spread his hands. "Vladimir, if there is an uprising against the landlords, then of course you want to help. What else can you do? But this is different. She is looking to make trouble where there is none. And it was never something that came between Ibronka—your grandmother—and me."

"It didn't?"

"Of course not. That happened, and we were all a part of it. We had to be part of it or we would be with the counts and the landlords and the bankers. It was one or the other then, it was not a thing for which I abandoned my family."

"I see. Is that what you want to tell Cawti, if she comes to see you?"

"If she asks I will tell her."

I nodded. I wondered how Cawti would react, and decided that I no longer knew her well enough to guess. I changed the topic then, but I kept noticing that he gave me funny looks from time to time. Well, I could hardly blame him.

I let things churn around in my head. Franz's ghost or no Franz's ghost, it would be most convenient for me if Kelly and his whole band were to fall off the edge of the world, but there was no good way to arrange that.

It also seemed that the biggest problem with getting to Herth was that he could take as much time as he wanted in getting me, and it wasn't hurting him at all. The Easterners had cut back on his business in some neighborhoods, but not all, and he still had his contacts and hired muscle and legmen all set to go back to business as usual as soon as the time was right. And he was a Dragaeran; he would live another thousand years or so, so what was his hurry?

If I could make him move at all, I might be able to force him out into the open, where I could get another shot at him. Furthermore . . . hmmm. My grandfather was silent, watching me as if he knew how fast my brain was working. I started putting together a new plan. Loiosh had no comment on it. I looked at it from a couple of different directions as I sipped herb tea. I held the plan in my head and bounced it off several different possible problems, and it rebounded just fine. I decided to go ahead with it.

"You have an idea, Vladimir?"

"Yes, Noish-pa."

"Well, you should be about it then."

I stood up. "You're right."

He nodded and said nothing more. I bade him good-bye while Loiosh flew out of the door in front of me. Loiosh said everything was all right. I was still feeling worried about Quaysh. It would be much harder to implement my plan if I were dead.

I had only walked a couple of blocks when I was approached. I was passing an outdoor market, and she was leaning against a building, her hands behind her back. She seemed to be about fifteen years old and wore a peasant skirt of yellow and blue. The skirt was slit, which meant nothing, but her legs were shaved, which meant a great deal.

She moved away from the wall as I walked by and she said hello. I stopped and wished her a pleasant day. It suddenly occurred to me that this could be a set-up; I ran a hand through my hair and adjusted my cloak. She seemed to think I was trying to impress her and showed me a pair of dimples. I wondered how much extra the dimples were worth.

"Anything, Loiosh?"

"Too crowded to tell for sure, boss, but I don't see Quaysh."

I decided it was probably just what it seemed to be.

She asked if I cared to take her somewhere for a drink. I said maybe. She asked if I cared to take her somewhere for a screw. I asked her how much, she said ten and seven, which worked out to an Imperial, which was a third of what my tags were charging.

I said, "Sure." She nodded without bothering with the dimples and led me around the corner. I let a knife fall into my hand, just in case. We entered an inn that displayed a sign with several bees buzzing about a hive. She spoke to the innkeeper and I put my knife away. I handed him seven silver coins. He gestured with his head toward the stairs and said, "Room three." The inn was pretty full for the afternoon, and there was a haze of blue smoke. It smelled old and foul and stale. I would have guessed that everyone in the place was a drunk.

She led me up to room three. I insisted she go in first and watched her for signs that someone else was in there. I didn't see any. When she turned back to me, Loiosh flew in.

"Okay, boss. It's safe."

She said, "Do you want *that* in here, too?"

I said, "Yeah."

She shrugged and said, "Okay."

I entered the room. The curtain fell shut behind me. There was a mattress on the floor and a table next to it. I gave her an Imperial. "Keep it," I said.

"Thanks."

She took off her blouse. Her body was young. I didn't move. She looked at me and said, "Well?"

As I came toward her, she put on a fake dreamy smile, turned her face up to me, and held her arms out. I slapped her. She stepped back and said, "Hey!" I moved in and slapped her again. She said, "None of that!" I drew a knife from my cloak and held it up. She screamed.

As the sound echoed and bounced around the room, I grabbed her arm and dragged her into a corner next to the doorway and held her there. There was fear in her eyes now. I said, "That's enough. Open your mouth again and I'll kill you." She nodded, watching my face. I heard footsteps outside and I let go of her. The curtain swung aside and a big bludgeon entered, followed by a large Easterner with a black beard.

He charged in, stopped when he saw the empty room, and started to look around. Before he had a chance to do so I had grabbed hold of his hair and was pulling his head into my knife, which was pressed against the back of his neck. I said, "Drop the club." He tensed as if he were about to spring and I pressed harder. He relaxed and the club fell to the floor. I turned to the whore. The look on her face told me that this was her pimp, rather than just a bouncer for the inn or some interested citizen. "Okay," I told her. "Get out of here."

She ran around us to pick up her blouse and left without looking at either of us, or stopping to dress. The pimp said, "You a bird?"

I blinked. "Bird? Phoenix. Phoenix Guard. I like that. Lord Khaavren will like that. No, I'm not. Don't be stupid. Who do you work for?"

He said, "Huh?"

I kicked the back of his knee and he sat down. I knelt on his chest and put the point of my knife in front of his left eye. I repeated my question. He said, "I don't work for anyone. I'm on my own."

I said, "So I can do whatever I want to you, and no one will protect you, is that right?"

This put a different light on things. He said, "No, I got protection."

I said, "Good. Who?"

Then his eyes fell on the jhereg emblazoned on my cloak. He licked his lips and said, "I don't want to get involved."

I couldn't help smiling at that. "How much more involved can you get?"

"Yeah, but—"

I created some pain for him. He yelped. I said, "Who protects you?"

He gave me an Eastern name that I didn't recognize. I moved the knife a bit away from his face, relaxed my hold on him a little and said, "Okay. I'm working for Kelly. Know who I mean?" He nodded. I said, "Good. I want you off the streets. For good. You're out of business as of now, okay?" He nodded again. I grabbed a lock of his hair then, sliced it off with my knife, held it in front of him and put it away inside my cloak. His eyes widened. I said, "I can find you now any time I want to. Understand?" He understood. "All right. I'm going to be back here in a few days. I'll want to see that fine young lady I just spoke to. And I want to see that she hasn't been hurt. If she has been I'll take pieces of you home with me. If I can't find her, I won't bother with the pieces. Can you understand that?" Apparently we were still communicating; he nodded. I said, "Good," and left him there. I saw no sign of the tag.

I left the inn and walked west about half a mile and went into a little cellar place. I asked the host, an ugly, squinty guy, if he knew where I could find some action.

"Action?"

"Action. You know, shereba, s'yang-stones, whatever."

He looked at me blankly until I passed an Imperial across the counter. Then he gave me an address a few doors down. I followed his directions and, sure enough, there were three shereba tables in use. I spotted the guy who was running it, sitting with the back of his chair against a wall, dozing. I said, "Hi. Sorry to bother you."

He opened one eye. "Yeah?"

I said, "Know who Kelly is?"

"Huh?"

"Kelly. You know, the guy who shut down the whole—"

"Yeah, yeah. What about him?"

"I work for him."

"Huh?"

"You're out of business. Game over. Closed. Get everyone out of here."

The room was small, and I'd been making no effort to keep my voice down. The card playing had stopped and everyone was watching me. Just as the pimp had, this guy noticed the stylized jhereg on my cloak. He seemed puzzled. "Look," he said. "I don't know who you are, or what kind of game you're playing—"

I stole a trick from the Phoenix Guards: I smacked him across the side of his head with the hilt of a dagger, then brandished the dagger. I said, "Does this straighten things out for you?" I heard movement behind me.

"Trouble, Loiosh?"

"No, boss. They're leaving."

"Good."

When the room was empty, I let the guy up. I said, "I'll be checking on you. If this place does any more business, I'll have your ass. Now get out."

He left in a hurry. I left more slowly. I allowed myself one evil chuckle, just because I felt like it. By the time I was done it was early evening and I'd terrorized three whores, as many pimps, two game operators, a bookie and a cleaner.

A good day's work, I decided. I headed back to the office to talk to Kragar, to put the second part of the plan into operation.

Kragar thought I was crazy.

"You're crazy, Vlad."

"Probably."

"They'll all just desert you."

"I'm going to keep paying them."

"How?"

"I'm rich, remember?"

"How long can that last?"

"A few weeks, of which I'll only need one."

"One?"

"Yeah. I spent today stirring up Herth and Kelly and pointing them at each other." I gave him a quick summary of the day's activities. "It'll take them maybe a day, each, to figure out who really did it. Herth will come after me with everything he has, and Kelly . . ."

"Yeah?"

"Wait and see."

He sighed. "All right. You want every business you own shut down by to-morrow morning. Fine. Everyone in hiding for a week. Fine. You say you can afford it, okay. But this other business, in South Adrilankha, I just can't see it."

"What's to see? We're just continuing what I started today."

"But fires? Explosions? That's no way to—"

"We have people who can do that sort of thing properly, Kragar. We were trained by Laris, remember?"

"Sure, but the Empire—"

"Exactly."

"I don't get it."

"You don't have to. Just handle the details."

"Okay, Vlad. It's your show. What about our own places? Like this one, for instance."

"Yeah. Get hold of the Bitch Patrol and protect them. Full sorcerous protection, including teleport blocks, and increase what we have here. I can—"

"—Afford it. Yeah, I know. I still think you're crazy."

"So will Herth. But he's going to have to deal with it anyway."

"He'll come after you, if that's what you want."

"Yep."

He sighed, shook his head and left. I leaned back in my chair, feet up on my desk, and made sure I hadn't missed anything.

Cawti was home when I got there. We said hello and how was your day and like that. We settled down in the living room, next to each other on the couch so we could feel nothing had changed, but a foot or so apart so we didn't have to take chances. I got up first, stretching, and announcing that I was going to go to sleep. She hoped I'd sleep well. I suggested that she probably needed some sleep herself, and she allowed that she did and would be in soon. I retired. Loiosh and Rocza were a bit subdued. I can't imagine why. I feel asleep quickly, as I always do when I have a plan working. It's one of the things that keeps me sane.

I teleported to the office early the next morning and waited for reports. Herth was about as quick on the uptake as I'd thought he'd be. I heard that attempts had been made to penetrate the spells around my office building and one or two other places.

"Glad you suggested we protect them, Kragar," I said.

He mumbled.

"Something bothering you, Kragar?"

He said, "Heh. I hope you know what you're doing."

I started to say, "I always know what I'm doing," but that would have rung a bit hollow, so I said, "I think so." That seemed to satisfy him.

"Okay, then, what's next?"

I mentioned someone important in the organization, and what my next step was. Kragar looked startled, then nodded. "Sure," he said, "He owes you one, doesn't he?"

"Or two or three. Set it up for today if possible."

"Right."

He was back in an hour. "The Blue Flame," he said. We shared a smile of common memories. "The eighth hour. He said he'd take care of all protection, which means he knows something of what's going on."

I nodded. "He would."

"Do you trust him?"

"Yeah," I said. "I'll have to trust him eventually, so I might as well trust him for this."

Kragar nodded.

Later in the day I received word that we'd torched a couple of buildings in

South Adrilankha. By now Herth must be biting his nails, wishing he could get his hands on me. I chuckled. *Soon,* I told him, *soon.*

I felt a funny sort of mental itch, and knew what it meant.

"*Who is it?*"

"*Chimov. I'm near Kelly's headquarters.*"

"*What's up?*"

"*They're moving out of the place.*"

"*Ah ha. Find out where they're going.*"

"*Will do. They have a whole crowd. It looks like they expect trouble. They're also posting handbills, and passing out leaflets all over the place.*"

"*Have you read one?*"

"*Yeah. It's about a mass meeting for tomorrow afternoon in Naymat Park. The big print at the top says 'A Call To Arms.'*"

"Well," I said. "*Excellent. Stay with it, and keep out of trouble.*"

"*Right, boss.*"

"Kragar!"

"Yeah?"

"Oh. Get someone over to Kelly's headquarters. Make it four or five. As soon as it's empty, go in and trash the place. Break up any furniture that's left, smash up walls, wreck the kitchen, that kind of thing."

"Okay."

I spent the rest of the day like that. Messages would come in, about this or that work of destruction completed, or some attack by Herth foiled, and I'd sit there and snap out the response to it. I was operating efficiently again, and it felt so good I kept going far into the evening, tightening this or that piece of surveillance, adding this or that nudge to Kelly or Herth. Of course, the office was just about the safest place for me to be just then, which was another good reason for working late.

As evening wore on, I exchanged messages with an Organization contact inside the Imperial Palace, and learned that, yes, the powers-that-be had noted what was going on in South Adrilankha. Herth's name had come up, but so far mine had not. Perfect.

When it got near to the eighth hour after noon I collected Sticks, Glowbug, Smiley and Chimov and we made our way to the Blue Flame. I left them near the door, because my guest had already arrived and he had promised to handle protection. And, in fact, I noticed a pair of customers and three waiters who looked like enforcers. I bowed as I approached the table.

He said, "Good evening, Vlad."

I said, "Good evening, Demon. Thanks for coming." He nodded and I sat. The Demon, for those of you who don't know, was a big man on the Jhereg council—the group that makes decisions affecting the whole business end of House Jhereg. He was generally considered the number-two man in the Organization; not someone to mess around with. However, as Kragar had mentioned, he owed me a favor for some "work" I'd done for him recently.

We exchanged amenities for a while, then, as the food showed up, he said, "So, you've gotten yourself into trouble, I hear."

"A bit," I said. "Nothing I can't handle, though."

"Indeed? Well, that's nice to hear." He gave me a kind of puzzled look. "Then why did you want to meet with me?"

"I'd like to arrange for nothing to happen."

He blinked. "Go on," he said.

"The Empire may start to take notice of the game that Herth and I are playing, and when the Empire notices, the Council notices."

"I see. And you want us not to interfere."

"Right. Can you give me a week to settle things?"

"Can you keep the trouble confined to South Adrilankha?"

"Pretty much," I said. "I won't be touching him anywhere else, and I've shut down and protected everything I own, so it will be hard for him to hit me. There may be one or two bodies turning up, but nothing to cause great excitement."

"The Empire isn't too keen on bodies turning up, Vlad."

"There shouldn't be too many. None, in fact, if my people are careful. And, as I say, it ought to be settled in a week."

He studied me. "You have something going, don't you?"

I said, "Yeah."

He smiled and shook his head. "No one can say you aren't resourceful, Vlad. All right, you have a week. I'll take care of it."

I said, "Thanks."

He offered to pay for the meal, but I insisted. It was my pleasure.

14

. . . brush to remove white particles . . .

I GOT THE FULL escort home from my bodyguards. They left me just outside the door, and as I stepped past the threshold I felt the draining of a tension that I hadn't known had been building up. You see, while my office is very well protected, one's home is strictly inviolate by Jhereg custom. Why? I don't know. Perhaps for the same reason temples are; just a matter of you ought to be safe somewhere no matter what, and everyone is too open to attacks this way. Maybe there's another reason for it. I'm not sure. But I've never heard of this custom being violated.

Of course, I'd never heard of anyone stealing from the Jhereg before it happened, either, but you have to depend on something.

Don't you?

Anyway, I was home and safe and Cawti was in the living room, reading her tabloid. My heart skipped, but I recovered and smiled. "Home early," I remarked.

She didn't smile when she looked up at me. "You bastard," she said, and there was real feeling behind the words. I felt my face flushing, and a sick feeling started in the pit of my stomach and spread out to all salient points. It wasn't as if I hadn't known she'd find out what I was doing, or hadn't known what her reaction was going to be, so why should it come as such a shock when she did just what I'd expected her to?

I swallowed and said, "Cawti—"

"Didn't you think I'd find out what you were up to, beating up Herth's people and blaming it on us?"

"No, I knew you would."

"Well?"

"I'm working a plan."

"A plan," she said, her voice dripping contempt.

"I'm doing what I have to."

She managed an expression that was half-sneer and half-scowl. "What you have to," she said, as if she were discussing the mating habits of teckla.

"Yeah," I said.

"You have to do everything you can to destroy the only people who—"

"The only people who are going to cost you your life? Yes. And for what?"

"A better life for—"

"Oh, stop it. Those people are so full of great ideals that they can't manage to understand that there are *people* in the world, people who shouldn't get tromped over without reason. *Individuals.* Starting with you and me. Here we are, on the verge of—I don't know what—on account of these great saviors of humanity, and all you can see is what's happening to *them.* You're blind to what's happening to us. Or else you don't care anymore. And this doesn't tell you that there's something wrong with them?"

She laughed, and it was a hateful laugh. "Something wrong with *them?* That's your conclusion? Something wrong with the movement?"

"Yeah," I said. "That's my conclusion."

Her mouth twisted, she said, "Do you expect me to buy that?"

I said, "What do you mean, buy?"

"I mean, you can't sell that product."

"What am I supposed to be selling?"

"You can sell anything you want, as far as I'm concerned."

"Cawti, you aren't making sense. What—"

"Just shut up," she said. "Bastard."

She'd never called me names before. It's still funny, how that stung.

For the first time in quite a while I felt anger toward her. I stood there looking at her, feeling my feet seem to attach to the floor and my face harden, and I welcomed the cold rush of it, at first. She stood there, glaring at me (I hadn't even noticed her standing up) and that just fed into it. There was a ringing in my ears, and it came to me, as from a distance, that I was out of control again.

I took a step toward her, and her eyes grew wide and she backed up half a step. I don't know what would have happened if she hadn't, but that was sufficient to give me enough control to turn and leave the house.

"Boss, no! Not outside!"

I didn't answer him. In fact, his words didn't even penetrate until the cool evening breeze hit my face. Then I understood that I was in some sort of danger. I thought of teleporting to Castle Black, but I also knew that I was in no state of mind to teleport. On the other hand, if I were attacked, that would suit my mood perfectly.

I started walking, keeping as tight a control on myself as I could, which wasn't very. Then I remembered the last time I'd gone charging around the city with no regard for who saw me, and that sent chills through me, which cooled me down a bit and I became more careful.

A little more careful.

But I have to think that Verra, my Demon-Goddess, watched over me that night. Herth had to have had Quaysh and everyone else looking for me, yet I wasn't attacked. I stormed through my area, looking at all the closed shops, at my office with yet a few lights burning, at the dead fountain in Malak Circle, and I wasn't even threatened. While I was in Malak Circle I stopped for a while, sitting at the edge of the crumbling fountain. Loiosh looked around anxiously, anticipating an attack, yet it felt as if what he was doing had nothing to do with me.

As I sat there, faces began to appear before me. Cawti looked at me with pity on her face, as if I had caught the plague and wouldn't recover. My grandfather looked stern but loving. An old friend named Nielar stared at me, calmly. And Franz appeared, oddly enough. He gave me a look of accusation. That was funny. Why should I care about *him* of all people? I mean, I hadn't known him at all while he was alive, and the little bit I'd known of him after his death told me that we had nothing in common. Except for the unique circumstances of our meeting, he would have had nothing whatever to do with me.

Why did my subconscious decide to bring him up?

I knew plenty of Dragaerans who seemed to feel that the Teckla were Teckla because that was how things were, and whatever happened to them was fine, and if they wanted to better themselves, let them. These were the lords of the land, and they enjoyed being what they were, and they deserved it and no one else did, and that was that. Okay. I could understand that attitude. It had nothing to do with the way things really were for the Teckla, but it made a lot of sense for the way things were for the Dragons.

I knew a few Dragaerans who cried aloud over the plight of the Teckla, and the Easterners for that matter, and gave money to charities for the poor and the homeless. Most of them were fairly well-off, and sometimes I wondered at my own contempt for them. But I always had the feeling that they secretly despised those they helped, and were so guilt-ridden that they blinded themselves to the way things were in order to convince themselves that they were doing some good, that they actually made a difference.

And then there were Kelly and his people; so wrapped up in how they would save a world that they didn't care about anyone or anything except the little ideas they had floating around their little heads. Completely, utterly ruthless, all in the name of humanity.

Those were the three groups I saw around me, and it came to me then, as I imagined Franz looking at me with an expression that oozed sincerity as a festering wound oozes pus, that I had to decide where I fit.

Well, I certainly wasn't with the third group. I could only kill individuals, not whole societies. I have a high opinion of my own abilities, but it isn't so high that I'm willing to destroy an entire society on the strength of an opinion, nor would I be willing to set up thousands of people to be slaughtered if I was wrong. When someone messed up my life—as had happened before and would happen again—I took it personally. I wasn't ready to blame it on something as nebulous as a society and try to arouse the population to destroy it for me. I took it as it was; someone messing up my life, to be dealt with using a clean, simple dagger. No, I wasn't about to find myself with Kelly's people.

The second group? No; I had earned what I had, and no one was going to make me feel guilty about having it, not even the Franz that my subconscious dredged up in a futile effort to torment me. Those who wallowed in guilt they hadn't earned deserve no better than they gave themselves.

I had once been part of the first group, and perhaps I still was, but now I didn't like the idea. *They* were the people I had hated so long. Not Dragaerans, but those who lorded it over the rest of us, and displayed their wealth, culture and education like a club they could beat us with. *They* were my enemies, even if I'd spent most of my life unaware of it. *They* were the ones I wanted to show that I could come up out of nowhere and make something of myself. And how surprised they had been when I did so!

Yet I couldn't, even now, consider myself one of them. Maybe I was, but I couldn't make myself believe it. Only once in my life have I truly hated myself, and that was when Herth broke me and made me face the fact that there was more to life than the will to succeed; that sometimes, no matter how hard he tries, there are things a man *can't* succeed at, because the forces around him are stronger than he is. That was the only time I'd hated myself. To put myself into the first group would be to hate myself again, and I couldn't do that.

So, where did that leave me? Everywhere and nowhere. On the outside, looking in. Unable to help, unable to hinder; a commentator on the theatrics of life.

Did I believe that? I wondered, but no answer came forth. On the other hand, I was certainly having an effect on Kelly. Herth, too, for that matter. That might have to be enough for me. I noticed that the air had become chilly, and I realized that I was calmer now and that I should go somewhere safe.

Since I was already at Malak Circle, I stopped in at the office and said hello to a few people who were still working. Melestav was in. I said, "Don't you ever go home?"

"Yeah, well, things are popping right now, and if I don't keep things organized these bozos will screw everything up."

"Herth is still trying to get us?"

"Here and there. The big news is that the Empire has moved into South Adrilankha."

"*What?*"

"About an hour ago, a whole Company of Phoenix Guards came in and just occupied the place as if it were an Eastern city."

I stared at him. "Was anyone hurt?"

"A few score of Easterners were killed or injured, I guess."

"Kelly?"

"No, none of his people were hurt. They moved, remember."

"That's right. What reason did the Empire give?"

"Disturbances, that kind of thing. Isn't this what you were expecting?"

"Not this quickly, or in that much force, or with anyone killed."

"Yeah, well you know Phoenix Guards. They hate dealing with Easterners anyway."

"Yeah. Do you have Kelly's new address?"

He nodded and scribbled it out on a piece of paper. I glanced at it and saw that I could find the place; it was only a few blocks from the old one.

"Oh, by the way," said Melestav, "Sticks wants to see you. He was thinking tomorrow, but he's still hanging around in case you came in this evening. Should I get him?"

"Oh, all right. Send him in."

I wandered into my office and sat down. A few minutes later Sticks showed up. He said, "Can I talk to you for a minute?"

I said, "Sure."

He said, "You know Bajinok?"

I said, "Yeah."

"He wanted me to help set you up. You said you like to know about these things."

I nodded. "I do. Okay, you got a bonus coming."

"Thanks."

"When did he talk to you?"

"About an hour ago."

"Where?"

"The Flame."

"Who was with you?"

"No one."

"Okay. Be careful."

Sticks mumbled something and walked out. I blinked. Was I beyond being shocked or frightened? Or was I too far gone to care? No, I cared. I hoped nothing would happen to him. He'd also been the one to identify Quaysh, and between the two things that could make him a real juicy target.

In fact, an irresistible target.

And why would they wait? An hour ago, he said? This wasn't an especially difficult piece of work, and Herth had people on his payroll who did the simple cutthroat things because it was part of their jobs.

I stood up. "Melestav!"

"Yeah, boss?"

"Has Sticks left?"

"I think so."

I cursed and sprinted through the building after him. A little voice in my head said, "Set-up," and I wondered. I opened the door and Loiosh flew out ahead of me. I stepped out onto the street, and looked around.

Well, yes and no.

I mean, it *was* a set-up, but I wasn't the one being set up. I saw Sticks, and I saw the form coming quickly up behind him. I yelled, "Sticks!" and he turned and stepped to the side as a shadowy figure lurched toward him and stumbled. There was a dull thud as Sticks nailed the assassin with a club, and the latter fell to the ground. It was only then that I realized I'd thrown a knife. I came up to them.

Sticks retrieved my knife from the back of the individual on the ground before us, wiped it on the fellow's cloak, and handed it to me. I caused it to vanish. "Did you shine him?"

Sticks shook his head. "He'll be all right, I think, if he wakes up before he bleeds to death. Should we get him off the street?"

"No. Leave him here. I'll have Melestav let Bajinok know he's here, and they can do their own clean-up."

"Okay. Thanks."

"Don't mention it. Be careful, all right?"

"All right." He shook his head. "I sometimes wonder why I'm in this business."

"Yeah," I said. "Me, too."

I went back inside and gave Melestav the necessary orders. He didn't seem surprised, but then I haven't surprised him since the time I brought Kiera the Thief into the office.

I sat down at my desk again and pushed aside all thoughts of what the Phoenix Guards were doing in South Adrilankha, and my responsibility for it. It wasn't that I didn't care, but I was involved in a war right now, and if I kept letting myself be distracted I was going to make a mistake, and after that I wouldn't be able to save Cawti, Sticks, myself or anyone else.

I had a war to win.

Sometime before, I'd been involved in a war where I was one of the contestants, as opposed to a mere participant. I learned the importance of information, of striking first, of keeping your enemy off balance and of thoroughly protecting your own area and people.

Herth had a bigger organization than I, but since I was the one who made it a full-scale war, I'd gotten in some good strikes at him. Furthermore, I had pretty much made sure that he couldn't hurt my organization. Of course, doing this resulted in a drastic loss of income, but I was quite well off at the moment, and I didn't think this would take long. I didn't really intend or expect to win this war in the usual way, I just wanted to force Herth out into the open so I could kill him. I thought to do it by making such a mess in his area that he'd have to take a hand in keeping it together.

That was half the plan, at any rate. The half involving Kelly was harder, but I had hopes for it. Damn Phoenix Guards, I thought. Damn the Empress. Damn Lord Khaavren. But Kelly was still in the same mess. I mean, what other choice did he have, if everyone else behaved as expected? And he probably realized that, judging from Cawti's reaction—

I thought about Cawti, and my plans and schemes fell away from my fingertips, where they'd been dancing for me. I saw only her for a moment and I cursed under my breath.

"So talk to her, boss."

"I just tried that, remember?"

"No, you argued with her. What if you tell her your whole plan?"

"She won't like it."

"But she might not be as upset with you as she is now."

"I doubt it will matter."

"Boss, you remember that what first got you upset was that she hadn't told you that she was involved with Kelly and those people?"

"Yeah . . . okay."

I sat for a bit longer, then went over to the front door, waving away body-guards. I took a deep breath, made sure my mind was clear, drew on the Orb, shaped the threads of power, twisted them around myself and pulled them tight. There was the awful lurch, and I stood in the entry way outside the door to my flat. I leaned against the wall until the nausea was under control.

The instant I walked into the flat I knew something was wrong. So did Loiosh. I stood just inside the door, not closing it, and let a knife fall into my right hand. I looked carefully around the living room, trying to determine what was funny. And you know, we didn't get it? After fully ten minutes, we just gave up and went inside, still being careful, Loiosh going in ahead of me.

No, no one was waiting to kill me.

No one waiting for me at all. I went into the bedroom, and saw that Cawti's clothing had been cleared out of the closet. I went back into the living room and saw that, of all things, the *lant* was missing, which is what Loiosh and I had noticed when we first came in. Funny how things like that work.

I tried to reach Cawti psionically but I couldn't. She wasn't interested in receiving my communication, or else I wasn't concentrating well enough to reach her. Yes, I decided, that must be it, I just couldn't think clearly enough right now to communicate psionically.

"Kragar?"

"Yes, Vlad?"

"Any word from Ishtvan?"

"Not yet."

"Okay. That's all."

Yeah, that must be the problem.

I went into the bedroom and shut the door before Loiosh could enter. I lay down on the bed—on Cawti's side—and tried to bring tears. I couldn't. At last, fully dressed, I slept.

15

...remove honing-oil stains...

I WOKE UP VERY early in the morning feeling tired and still dirty. I undressed, bathed, and climbed back into bed and slept a bit longer.

It was only when I woke up the second time, just before noon, that I remembered that Cawti had left. I allowed myself to stare at the ceiling for two minutes, then forced myself to get up. I kept stopping as I shaved, looking to see if there was any outward change in the face that stared back at me. I didn't see anything.

"Well, boss?"

"I'm glad you're around, chum."

"Know what you're going to do?"

"You mean about Cawti?"

"Yeah."

"Not really. I didn't know she'd leave. Or I didn't believe it. Or I didn't know how hard it would hit me. I feel like I'm dead inside, you know what I mean?"

"I can feel it, boss. That's why I asked."

"I don't know if I'm up to handling what's going to happen now."

"You need to have things settled with Cawti."

"I know. Maybe I should try to find her."

"You'll have to be careful. Herth—"

"Yeah."

I made myself ready, checked my hardware and teleported to South Adrilankha. I rested a while in a small park, with a good view all around me—a very bad place for Quaysh—then I headed for an eating place. On the way I spotted and avoided two groups of Phoenix Guards. I found a table and ordered klava. As the waiter was leaving I said, "Excuse me."

"Yes, my lord?"

"Would you please bring that in a cup?"

He didn't even look startled. "Yes, my lord," he said. Just like that. And he did it. All this time, and the solution was as easy as asking for it. Wasn't that profound?

"I doubt it, boss."

"Me, too, Loiosh. But it starts the day right. And speaking of starting the day, can you find Rocza?"

A moment later Loiosh said in a hurt tone, "No. She's blocking me."

"I didn't know she could do that."

"Neither did I. Why would she?"

"Because Cawti figured out that I could trace her that way. Damn. Well, okay, so we go to Kelly's place and either wait for her or make them tell us where she is. Any other ideas?"

"Sounds good to me, boss. And when I get hold of that slimy reptile—"

I was pleased by the klava, which I had with honey and warmed cream. I forced myself not to think about anything that mattered. I left a few extra coins on the table to show them how much I appreciated their cup. Loiosh preceded me out the door. He said everything looked all right and I left the place, heading toward Kelly's new headquarters. I avoided another contingent of Phoenix Guards on the way. They really were all over the place. None of the citizens seemed too happy with them, and it seemed mutual.

The first thing I decided upon seeing Kelly's new place was that it looked like Kelly's old place. The brown was a different shade, and his flat was on the right side instead of the left, and it was set a little farther back from the road, and there was just a little more space between buildings, but it had obviously been cast in the same mold.

I walked through the doorway. The flat itself had a real door. A heavy door, with a lock on it. I looked closer, just from curiosity. A *good* lock, and a *very* heavy door. It would take a great deal of work to break into this place, and it would be almost impossible to do silently. I wondered about windows and other doors. In any case, I decided I was impressed. Cawti had probably advised them. I started to clap, remembered, and, after a moment's hesitation, pounded on the door with my fist.

It was opened by my dear friend Gregory. His eyes widened as he saw me, but I didn't let him start in on me. I just pushed past him. It was rude, I know, and that still bothers me to this day, but I'll just have to learn to live with it.

One look told me that this flat was laid out the same as the other; I was almost certain I could walk into the next room and be in a library, through that to Kelly's office, and through that to a kitchen. But this room was cleaner; the cots were collapsed and pushed against the wall. The windows, I noticed, were heavily boarded.

Kelly was sitting in the room, talking to Natalia and a Teckla I didn't recognize. Cawti wasn't there. The talking stopped when I walked in, and they all stared at me. I smiled a big smile and said, "Is Cawti around?" Then they all looked at Kelly, except for Natalia, who kept looking at me. She said, "Not at the moment."

I said, "I'll wait, then," and watched them. Natalia kept watching me, the others watched Kelly, who squinted at me, his lips in a bit of a pout. Then, quite suddenly, he stood up and said, "Right. Come on back and I'll talk to you." He turned and headed toward the rear of the flat, assuming I would follow obediently. I cursed under my breath, smiling, and did so.

This office was as neat and well-organized as the other had been. I sat down on the other side of the desk. Kelly folded his hands over his stomach and looked at me, his eyes performing their usual squint.

"So," he said. "You've decided to call in the Empire and force us to respond."

"Actually," I said, "I just came to see Cawti. Where is she?"

His expression didn't change, he just continued watching me. "You have a Plan," he said at last, pronouncing the capital letter, "and the rest of the world is filled with details that may or may not have something to do with it. You weren't out to get us, we're just a convenient tool."

He didn't put it as a question, which is partly why I felt stung; he was accusing me of something like what I had been thinking was wrong with him. I said, "My primary interest is actually saving Cawti's life."

"Not your own?" he shot back, his eyes squinting just a bit more.

"It's too late for that," I said. That startled him a little; he actually seemed surprised. I felt inordinately pleased about this. "So, as I said, I'd like to see Cawti. Will she be around later?"

He didn't answer. He just kept looking at me, his head back and his chin down, hands wrapped over his belly. I started to get mad. "Look," I told him, "you can play all the games you want to, just don't include me in them. I don't know what you're really after and I don't much care, all right? But, now or later, you're going to be carved up between the Empire and the Jhereg, and if I have any say in it my wife isn't going to be carved up with you. So you can drop the superior act; it doesn't impress me."

I was ready for him to blow up, but he didn't. His eyes hadn't even narrowed any more. He just kept watching me, as if he were studying me. He said, "You don't know what we're after? After all you've been through, you really don't know what we're after?"

I said, "I've heard the rhetoric."

"Have you listened to it?"

I snorted. "If what everybody around here parrots originates with you, then I've heard what you have to say. That isn't what I came here for."

He leaned back a little more in his chair. "That's all you've heard, eh? The parroting of phrases?"

"Yeah. But as I said, that isn't—"

"Did you listen to the phrases being parroted?"

"I told you—"

"Have you never understood more than you could put into words? Many people only respond to the slogans—but they respond because the slogans are true and touch a spark in their hearts and their lives. And as for the ones who don't want to think for themselves, we teach them to anyway." Teach? I suddenly thought of what I'd overheard of them berating Cawti and wondered if that was what they called teaching. But Kelly continued, "Did you talk to Paresh? Or Natalia? Did you ever, once, *listen* to what they said?"

"Look—"

He shifted forward in his chair, just a bit. "But none of that matters. We aren't here to justify ourselves to you. We're Teckla and Easterners. In particular, we are that portion of that group that understands what it's doing."

"Yeah? What *are* you doing?"

"We are defending ourselves the only way we can, the only way there is— by uniting and using the power that we have due to our own role in society. With this, we can defend ourselves against the Empire, we can defend ourselves against the Jhereg, and we can defend ourselves against you."

La dee da. I said, "Can you?"

He said, "Yes."

"What's to stop me from killing you, say, now?"

He didn't bat an eyelash, which I call bravado, which a Dzur would consider brave and a Jhereg would consider stupid. He said, "Right. Go ahead, then."

"I could, you know."

"Then do it."

I cursed. I didn't kill him, of course. That was something I knew Cawti would never forgive me for, and it wouldn't accomplish anything anyway. I needed Kelly there to push his organization into the path of Herth and the Phoenix Guards so they could be neatly cleaned up. But I needed Cawti out of the way first.

I noticed that Kelly was still watching me. I said, "So, you exist only to defend yourselves, and the Easterners?"

"And the Teckla, yes. And the only defense is—but I forget; you aren't interested. You're so busy chasing fortune up over a mountain of corpses that you have no time to listen to anyone else, have you then?"

"Poetic, aren't you?" I said. "Have you ever read Torturi?"

"Yes," said Kelly. "I prefer Wint. Torturi is clever, but shallow."

"Um, yeah."

"Similar to Lartol."

"Yeah."

"They came out of the same school of poetry, and the same epoch, historically. It was after the reconstruction at the end of the ninth Vallista reign, and the aristocracy was feeling bitter toward—"

"All right, all right. You're quite well-read for a . . . whatever it is you are."

"I am a revolutionist."

"Yeah. Maybe you're a Vallista yourself. Creation and destruction, all wrapped up in one. Only you don't seem too effective at either."

"No," he said. "If I were of one of the Dragaeran Houses, it would be the Teckla."

I snorted. "You said it; I didn't."

"Yes. And it is another thing you don't understand."

"No doubt."

"But what I said is true for you as well—"

"Careful."

"And all human beings. The Teckla are known as a House of cowards. Is Paresh a coward?"

I licked my lips. "No."

"No. He has something worth fighting for. They are known as stupid and lazy as well. Does this match your experience?"

I started to say, "Yes," but then decided that, no, I couldn't say they were lazy. Stupid? Well, the Jhereg had been hoodwinking Teckla for years now, but that only meant we were clever. And, furthermore, there were so many of them it could be that I only ran across the stupid ones. It was hard to conceive of the total number of Teckla even within Adrilankha. Most of them were not customers of the Jhereg. "No," I said, "I guess not completely."

"The House of the Teckla," he said, "embodies all the traits of all the Dragaeran Houses. As does the Jhereg, by the way, and for much the same reason: Those Houses will allow others into their ranks with no questions asked. The aristocracy—the Dzur, the Dragons, the Lyorn, occasionally others—see this as a weakness. The Lyorn allow no one in; some of the others require the passing of a test. They think this strengthens their House, because it reinforces those things they desire—usually strength, quickness and cunning. These are thought to be the greatest virtues by the dominant culture—the culture of the aristocracy. If so, the mixing of blood without these traits must be a weakness. Because they think it's a weakness, you see it as a weakness, too. It is not; it is a strength.

"By requiring those traits, or whichever ones they do require, what are they leaving out that might occur on its own? All of these traits exist in some measure in the Teckla, the Jhereg and some Easterners—along with other things that we aren't even aware of, but that make us human. Think about what it means to be human. It's far more important than species or House." He stopped and studied me again.

I said, "I see. Well, now I've learned something about biology, history, and Teckla politics all in one sitting. That, and what is required to be a revolutionist. Thank you, it's been very instructive. Except I'm not interested in biology, I don't believe your history and I already knew what it takes to be a revolutionist. Right now I want to know what it takes to find Cawti."

He said, "Just what is it that you've found it takes to be a revolutionist?"

I knew he was trying to change the subject, but I couldn't resist. I said, "The worship of ideas to such an extent that you become totally ruthless toward people—friends, enemies and neutrals alike."

"The worship of ideas?" he said. "That's how you see it?"

"Yeah."

"And where do you suppose these ideas came from?"

"I can't see that it matters a whole lot."

"They come from people."

"Mostly dead people, I imagine."

He shook his head, slowly, but it seemed his eyes were twinkling, just a bit. "So," he said, "you have no ethics at all?"

"Don't bait me."

"Then you do?"

"Yeah."

"But you'll abandon them for anyone who matters to you?"

"I told you not to bait me. I won't tell you again."

"But what are professional ethics other than ideas that are more important than people?"

"Professional ethics guarantee that I always treat people as they ought to be treated."

"They guarantee that you do what's right, even if it isn't convenient at the moment?"

"Yes."

"Yes."

I said, "You're a smug bastard, aren't you?"

"No, but I can tell that you're speaking nonsense. You talk about our ideas as if they fell from the sky. They didn't. They grew out of our needs, out of our thoughts and out of our fight. Ideas aren't just thought up one day, and then people come along and decide to adopt them. Ideas are as much a product of their times as a particular summoning spell is the result of a particular Athyra reign. Ideas always express something real, even when they're wrong. People have been dying for ideas—sometimes incorrect ideas—since before history. Would that happen if those ideas weren't based on, and a product of, their lives and the world around them?

"As for us, no, we're not smug. Our strength is that we see ourselves as part of history, as part of society, instead of just individuals who happen to have the same problem. This means we can at least look for the right answers, even if we aren't completely right all the time. It certainly puts us a step ahead of the individualists. It's all well and good to recognize that you have a problem and try to solve it, but for the Easterners and Teckla in this world, these aren't problems that an individual can solve."

I guess when you get in the habit of making speeches it's hard to stop. When he'd run down, I said, "I'm an individual. I solved them. I got out of there and made something of myself."

"How many bodies did you climb over to do it?"

"Forty-three."

"Well?"

"What of it?"

"What of it yourself?"

I stared at him. He was squinting hard again. Some of the things he was saying were uncomfortably close to things I'd been thinking about myself; but I didn't go around building elaborate political positions around my insecurities, nor inciting rebellion as if I knew better than the rest of the world how everything ought to be.

I said, "If I'm so worthless, why are you wasting your time talking to me?"

"Because Cawti is valuable to us. She's still new, but she could turn into an excellent revolutionist. She's having trouble with you, and it's hurting her work. I want it settled."

I controlled myself with an effort. "That fits," I said. "Okay, then, I'll even let you manipulate me into helping you manipulate Cawti so she can help you manipulate the entire population of South Adrilankha. That's how it works, isn't it? All right, I'll go along. Tell me where she is."

"No, that isn't how it works. I'm not making any deals with you. You called in the Phoenix Guards to manipulate us into an adventure that would destroy us. Whatever reasons you had for this, it didn't work. We aren't getting involved in any adventures now. We held a mass meeting yesterday at which we urged everyone to stay calm and not to allow the Guards to provoke an incident. We're ready to defend ourselves against any attacks, but we won't allow ourselves to be endangered by—"

"Oh, stop it. You're doomed anyway. Do you really think you can stand up to Herth? He has more hired killers working for him than Verra has hairs on her . . . head. If I hadn't forced him into action, he would have destroyed you as soon as he realized you weren't going to back down."

Kelly asked, "Does he have more hired killers than there are Easterners and Teckla in Adrilankha?"

"Heh. I don't know of *any* professionals who are Teckla, and I'm just about the only Easterner I know."

"Professional killers? No. But professional revolutionists, yes. This Jhereg killed Franz, and we mobilized half of South Adrilankha. He killed Sheryl and we mobilized the other half. You've brought the Phoenix Guards in, probably thinking you were working on some big plan to solve all your problems, when in fact you did exactly what the Empire required of you—you gave them a pretext to move in. All right, here they are, and they can't do anything. The instant they overstep themselves, we'll take the whole city."

"If you're that close, why don't you do it?"

"We don't want it yet. The time isn't right for it. Oh, we could hold the city for a while, but the rest of the country isn't ready, and we can't stand against the rest of the country. But if we have to, we will, because it will serve as an example and we'll grow because of it. The Empire can't crush us because the rest of the country would rise; they see us as representing them."

"So they're just going to give you what you want?"

He shook his head. "They can't fully investigate the murders because it would expose how closely the Jhereg is tied to the Empire, and the Jhereg itself would have to fight back and total chaos would ensure. They know what we *can* do, but they don't know what we're *going* to do, so all they can do is move their troops in, and hope that we make a mistake and lose the confidence of the masses so they can crush us—our movement and the citizens alike."

I stared at him. "Do you really believe all that? You still haven't told me what's going to stop Herth from bringing six or seven assassins in here and just cleaning you out."

"Weren't you, yourself, trying to play Herth off against the Empire?"

"Yeah."

"Well, you didn't have to. We almost took the city the last time the Jhereg killed one of our people, and the Jhereg know very well that if it happens again the Empire will have to move against them. How is that going to affect this Herth fellow?"

"Hard to say. He's getting desperate."

Kelly shook his head again and leaned back in his chair. I studied him. Who did he remind me of? Aliera, perhaps, with that cocksure attitude. Maybe Morrolan, with his feeling that, well, of course he could destroy anyone who got in his way, because that's just how things are. I don't know. There was no question that the man was brilliant, but—I didn't know then, and I still don't.

I was trying to figure out my next riposte when Kelly's head shot up, and at the same time Loiosh spun around. Kelly said, "Hello, Cawti."

I didn't turn. Loiosh started hissing and I heard Rocza hiss back. Loiosh flew off and I heard wings flapping and much hissing. Cawti said, "Hello, Vlad. Do those two remind you of anything?"

I did turn around then, and there were circles under her eyes. She looked haggard and worn. I wanted to hold her and tell her it was all right, except I didn't dare, and it wasn't. Kelly stood up and left. I suppose he expected me to be grateful.

When he was gone, I said, "Cawti, I want you out of this. This little group is going to be crushed and I want you somewhere safe."

She said, "Yeah, I figured that out last night, after I left."

Her voice was quiet as she spoke, and I heard no harshness or hate in it. I said, "Does it change anything?"

"I'm not sure. You're asking me to choose between my beliefs and my love."

I swallowed. "Yeah, I guess that's what I'm doing."

"Are you sure you have to?"

"I have to make sure you're safe."

"What about you?"

"That's another question. It doesn't apply to this."

"The only reason you did all that was—"

"To save your life, dammit!"

"Stop it, Vlad. Please."

"Sorry."

"You did it because you're so full of how powerful Herth is that you can't see how weak he is compared to the armed might of the masses."

I started to tell her to stop that noise about the "armed might of the masses," but I didn't. I thought about it for a minute. Well, yeah, if the masses were armed, and had leaders they trusted and all that, yeah, they could be powerful. If, if, if. I said, "What if you're wrong?"

She actually stopped and thought about that for a moment, which surprised me. Then she said, "Remember outside the old place, when the Phoenix Guards showed up? Herth just stood there while that Dragonlord cut his face. Herth hated her and wanted to kill her, but he just stood there and took it. Who was more powerful?"

"Okay, the Dragonlord. Go on."

"The Dragonlord just stood there, troops and all, while Kelly laid down our demands. Can you really think that Kelly is more powerful than a Dragon warrior?"

"No."

"Neither can I. The power was the armed might of the masses. You *saw* it. You think you, by yourself, are stronger than it is?"

"I don't know."

"You admit you might be wrong?"

I sighed, "Yeah."

"Then why don't you stop trying to protect me? It's insulting, in addition to everything else."

I said, "I *can't*, Cawti. Don't you see that? I just can't. You don't have the right to throw your life away. No one does."

"Are you sure I'm throwing my life away?"

I closed my eyes, and felt the start of tears that I hadn't been able to shed the night before. I stopped them. I said, "Let me think about it, all right?"

"All right."

"Are you coming back home?"

"Let's wait until this is over, then we'll see where we are."

"Over? When will it be over?"

"When the Empress withdraws her troops."

"Oh."

Loiosh came back in and landed on my shoulder. I said, *"Everything settled, chum?"*

"Pretty much, boss. I'm not going to be flying too well for a few days. She got in a good one on my right wing."

"I see."

"Nothing to worry about."

"Yeah."

I stood up and walked past Cawti without touching her. Kelly was in the other room, deep in conversation with Gregory and a few others. None of them looked up as I left. I stepped outside, carefully, but saw no one suspicious. I teleported back home, deciding that Kragar could handle things at the office better than I could right now.

The stairs up to my flat seemed long and steep, and my legs felt leaden. Once inside, I collapsed on the couch again and stared off into space for a while. I thought about cleaning the place up, but it didn't really need it and I didn't have the energy.

Loiosh asked if I'd like to see a show and I didn't.

I spent a couple of hours sharpening my rapier because it seemed likely I'd be needing it soon. Then I stared off into space for a while, but no ideas fell from the sky and landed on me.

After a while I got up and selected a book of poems by Wint. I opened the book at random, and was at a poem called "Smothered."

"*. . . Was it for naught I bled for thee,
Defying omnipotent powers?*

*The blood was mine; the battle, thine,
To smother in bright-blooming flowers. . . .*"

I read it to the end, and wondered. Maybe I was wrong. It didn't seem obscure at all, just then.

16

. . . & repair cut in lft side.

I WOKE UP IN the chair, the book on my lap. I felt stiff and uncomfortable, which is natural after sleeping in a chair. I stretched out to loosen my muscles, then bathed. It was pretty early. I put some wood in the stove and kicked it up with sorcery, then cooked a few eggs and warmed up some herb bread that Cawti had made before she left. It was especially good with garlic butter. The klava helped, and it helped to do the dishes and clean up the place. By the time that was done I felt almost ready for the day.

I wrote a few letters of instruction to various people, in case of my demise. I kept them terse. I sat down and thought for a while. I hate, I mean *hate*, changing a plan at the last minute, but there was no way around it. Cawti wasn't going to be safe. Furthermore, there was the chance that Kelly was right. No, there just wasn't any way to arrange for all of my enemies to neatly destroy each other; I had to do something else. I ran down the events of the past few days and my options for dealing with the situation I had created, and eventually hit on the idea of bringing my grandfather into things.

Yeah, that might work, as long as he didn't show up while there was still fighting going on. I put what passed for the finishing touches on the idea.

I concentrated on Kragar, and soon he said, *"Who is it?"*

"It's me."

"What is it?"

"Can you reach Ishtvan?"

"Yeah."

"Give him Kelly's new address in South Adrilankha, and have him wait there, out of sight, this afternoon."

"Okay. Anything else?"

"Yeah." I gave him the rest of his instructions.

"Do you really think he'll go for it, Vlad?"

"I don't know. Right now it's our best shot, though."

"Okay."

Then I drew my rapier and made a few passes in the air, loosening up my wrist. Supple but firm, my grandfather always said.

I checked all of my weapons as carefully as I ever have, then I organized my thoughts and teleported. Unless I was very much mistaken, today would be it.

*   *   *

There was a nasty wind whipping through the streets of South Adrilankha. It wasn't terribly chilly, but it had something of a sting from the dust it kicked up. It played havoc with my cloak as I leaned against a wall near Kelly's headquarters. I moved to a place out of the wind that also provided better concealment, although not quite as good a view. I watched the Phoenix Guards march by in neat groups of four. They were trying to maintain order where there was no disorder, and some of them, mostly the Dragons, were either bored or grumbling. The Teckla seemed to be enjoying it; they could strut around the street and be important. They were the ones who were constantly gripping the hilts of their weapons.

The interesting thing was how easy it was to tell the political affiliations of the passers-by. There were no headbands, but they weren't necessary. Some people would walk the streets furtively, or go quickly to their destinations as if they were afraid of being out on the streets. Others seemed to savor the tension in the air; they would walk with their heads up, glancing about themselves as if something might *happen* at any moment, and they didn't want to miss it.

By early afternoon Ishtvan was probably around somewhere, though I didn't see him. Quaysh was, too, I assumed. Quaysh knew that I knew he was there, but I felt hopeful that Quaysh didn't know Ishtvan was there.

I reached Kragar again. *"Anything exciting happen?"*

"No. Ishtvan is there."

"Good. So am I. All right, send the message."

"You're sure?"

"Yeah. Now or never. I won't have the nerve again."

"Okay. And the sorceress?"

"Yes. Send her to the apothecary across from Kelly's. And have her wait. Does she know me by sight?"

"I doubt it. But you're pretty easy to describe. I'll make sure she recognizes you."

"Okay. Have at it."

"Right, Vlad."

And we were committed.

The note that Herth would be receiving was quite simple. It said: "I'm prepared to compromise, if you'll arrange for the removal of the Phoenix Guards. Because of the Guards, I can't leave my flat. You may arrive at your convenience.—Kelly."

Its strength was its weakness: It was too obvious to be the fake that it was. But Kelly and Herth couldn't know each other well enough to communicate psionically, so messages were required. Herth was bound to have a very low opinion of Kelly, which was also important. In order for this to work, Herth had to believe that Kelly was scared of the Phoenix Guards, and Herth had to think that Kelly was ignorant of how much of a threat these guards were to a

Jhereg. *I* knew that Kelly was really aware of all that, but presumably Herth didn't.

So, the questions were: Would Herth show up in person? How many body-guards would he bring? And, what other precautions would he take?

The sorceress arrived before anything else happened. I didn't recognize her. She was a tall Jhereg with black hair in tight curls. Her mouth was harsh and she showed some signs of Athyra in her ancestry. She wore the Jhereg grey. She entered the shop. I followed carefully. She saw me as I entered and said, "Lord Taltos?" I nodded. She gestured at Kelly's building. "You want a block to prevent anyone from teleporting out. Is that all?"

"Yes."

"When?"

I pulled out a coin, studied it with eye and fingers for a moment, and handed it to her. "When this heats up."

"All right," she said.

I left the shop, still being very careful. I didn't want to be attacked just yet. I resumed my old position and waited. A few minutes later a Dragaeran in the colors of House Jhereg showed up.

I said, *"All right, Loiosh. Take off."*

"Are you sure?"

"Yeah."

"Okay, boss. Good luck."

He flew away. That put a time limit on things. The bloody part of the day had to be over within, I guessed, about thirty minutes. I drew a dagger and held it low, and pushed myself deeper into the shadows cast by the tall old house I was standing against. Then I put the dagger away and fingered my rapier, but didn't draw it. I touched Spellbreaker, but left it wrapped around my wrist. I squeezed my hands into and out of fists.

What was going on inside Kelly's flat, I could only guess at. But I had no doubt that the Jhereg had been a messenger from Herth. He would have walked in and said, "Herth is on his way." Neither Kelly nor the messenger would know why, so—

Natalia and Paresh left the building, walking in opposite directions.

—Kelly would send for help. From whom? From the "people," of course. My earlier plan had required this, and I could have then informed the Phoenix Guards of it and incited mutual destruction. I wasn't going to do that now, however, because Cawti was still part of it.

Four Jhereg showed up. Enforcers, hired muscle, leg-men. Two of them went inside to check the place over, while the others studied the area, looking for people like me. I stayed hidden. If Ishtvan was there, he did too. Likewise Quaysh. I was getting a lesson in how easy it is to hide on a city street, and how hard it is to find someone who is hiding.

About seven minutes later Herth showed up, along with Bajinok and another three bodyguards. They entered the flat. I concentrated for a moment and performed a very simple spell. A coin heated up. A teleport block occurred around Kelly's flat.

Just about that time, Easterners and an occasional Teckla began to congregate on the street. One of the legmen outside went in, presumably to report on this development. He came out again. Then Phoenix Guards began to collect on the opposite side of the street. In a surprisingly short time—like five minutes, maybe—there was a repeat of the scene before: about two hundred armed Easterners on one side, eighty or so Phoenix Guards on the other. That to you, Kelly. Instant confrontation, courtesy of Baronet Taltos.

Trouble was, I no longer wanted a confrontation. That plan had involved having Cawti out of the way, so I could kill Herth while Ishtvan killed Quaysh and the Guards killed Kelly and his band. But I hadn't sent the messages informing the Phoenix Guards of this occurrence; they had found out on their own. Damn them anyway.

Well, there was no way of pulling out at this stage. By now Herth would be inside, he would have realized that the message didn't come from Kelly, and he would have realized that there was a teleport block around the building. He would deduce that I was out here somewhere, waiting to kill him. What would he do? Well, he might just try to come out, hoping that I wouldn't try anything with the Phoenix Guards all around. Or he might call for more bodyguards, surround himself completely and walk out of the place; far enough away to be able to teleport. He was probably pretty unhappy now.

The lieutenant who'd been there last time was not in sight. Instead, the commander of the Phoenix Guard was an old Dragaeran who wore the blue and white of the House of the Tiassa beneath the gold cloak of the Phoenix. He had that peculiar, stiff-yet-relaxed pose of the longtime soldier. Had he been an Easterner, he would have had a long mustache to pull. As it was, he scratched the side of his nose from time to time. Other than that, he hardly moved. I noticed that his blade was very long but lightweight, and I decided that I didn't want to fight him. Then it occurred to me that this was an old Tiassa in command of Phoenix Guards, and I realized that it was probably the Lord Khaavren himself, the Brigadier of the Guards. I was impressed.

Easterners and Guards continued to gather, and now Kelly stepped outside and looked around, along with Natalia and a couple of others. Soon they went back in. I was able to tell nothing from watching Kelly. A bit later Gregory and Paresh went out and began speaking to the Easterners, quietly. I assumed they were telling them to remain calm.

I flexed my fingers. I closed my eyes and concentrated on the building across the street. I remembered the hallway. I saw the broken porcelain below next to my right foot, but ignored it; it could have been cleaned up. I called up a picture of the reddish stain that was probably liquor on the floor and against the wall. Then I remembered the stairs in the middle of the hall, probably leading down to a cellar, with a curtain at the top. The ceiling above it was pitted with broken paint and chipped woodwork. A frayed rope dangled from it. The rope had probably once held a candelabrum. I remembered the thickness of the rope and the way the frayed end had hung and the shape of the frays. I recalled the layer of dust just inside the curtain. And the curtain itself, woven in zigzags of dark brown and an ugly, dirty blue, both against a background that might once have been green. The smell of the hallway, compressed, dust-choked and stuffy, so thick I could almost taste it; I *could* taste the dust in my mouth.

I decided I had it. I held it there, fixed, and called upon my link to the Orb, and the power rushed through me to the forms I created and shaped and spun, until they matched, in a deep yet inexplicable way, the picture and scent and taste I held in my mind.

I drew them in, my eyes tightly closed, and I knew I had caught *somewhere*, because the sickening movement began in my bowels. I gave the last twist and opened my eyes, and, yes, I was there. It didn't look or smell quite the way I remembered it, but close enough. In any case, it hid me quite effectively.

I was assuming that there were bodyguards in the hallway, so I tried to keep silent. Have you ever felt you were about to throw up, and yet had to keep silent? But let's not dwell on that; I managed. After a while I risked a look past the curtain. I saw a bodyguard standing in the hall. He was about as alert as it is possible to be when nothing is immediately happening, which isn't all that alert. I ducked my head back without being seen. I looked the other way, toward the back door, but didn't see anyone. There may have been one or two outside the back door, or just inside the back entrance to the flat itself, but I could ignore them for now either way.

I listened closely and I could make out Herth's voice, speaking peremptorily. So he was inside. He was well-protected, of course. My options seemed rather limited. I could try to pick off his protection one by one. That is, find a way to quiet these two without alerting those inside, remove the bodies and wait until someone investigated, repeated as needed. It was attractive in a way, but I had real doubts about my ability to handle that many without a noise; and, in any case, Herth might duck out at any moment if he decided that was his best chance.

On the other hand, there was only one other option, and that was stupid. I mean, *really* stupid. The only time for doing something that stupid is when you're so mad you can't think clearly, you expect to die anyway, you have weeks of frustration built up to the point where you want to explode and you figure maybe you can take a few of them with you, and, generally, you just don't care any more.

I decided this was the perfect time.

I checked all my weapons, then drew two thin and extremely sharp throwing knives. I kept my arms at my sides so the knives, if not hidden, at least wouldn't be obvious. I stepped out into the hall.

He saw me at once, and stared. I was walking toward him, and I seem to recall that I had a smile on my lips. Yes, in fact I'm sure of it. Maybe that's what stopped him, but he just stared at me. My pulse was racing by then. I kept walking, waiting until either I was close enough or he moved. My guess,

looking back on those ten steps down the hall, was that I would have been cut
down at once if I'd tried to rush him, but by walking toward him, smiling, I
threw him out of his reckoning. He stared at me as if hypnotized, making no
motion until I was right up to him.

Then I nailed him, one knife in his stomach, which is one of the most disa-
bling of non-fatal wounds. He crumbled to the floor right at my feet.

I took a knife from my boot; one I could throw as well as cut or stab with.
I entered the room.

Two bodyguards were just looking up toward the doorway and tentatively
reaching for weapons. The messenger was sitting on a couch with his eyes
closed, looking bored. Bajinok stood next to Herth, who was talking to Kelly.
I could see Kelly's face, but not Herth's. Kelly wasn't pleased. Cawti stood next
to Kelly and she spotted me at once. Paresh and Gregory were in the room,
along with three Easterners and a Teckla who I didn't recognize.

Also next to Herth was a bodyguard who was staring right at me. Whose
eyes were widening. Who had a knife in his hand. Who was ready to throw it
at me. Who fell with my knife high on the right side of his chest.

As he fell, he managed to release his weapon, but I slipped to the side and it
only grazed my waist. As I avoided it, I turned to kill Herth, but Bajinok had
stepped in front of him. I cursed to myself and moved farther into the room,
looking for my next set of enemies.

The other two bodyguards drew weapons, but I was faster than I thought
I'd be. I sent each of them a small dart coated with a poison that would make
their muscles constrict, and I put a couple of other things into their bodies as
well. They went down, got up, and went down again.

Meanwhile, my rapier was out and I had a dagger in my left hand. Bajinok
pulled a lepip from somewhere, which was nasty because it could break my
blade if it hit. Herth was staring at me over Bajinok's shoulder; he hadn't yet
drawn a weapon. I don't know, maybe he didn't have one. I avoided a strike
from Bajinok and riposted—taking him cleanly through the chest. He gave one
spasm and fell. I looked over at the guy who'd acted as a messenger. He had
a dagger in his hand and was half standing up. He dropped the dagger and sat
down again, his hands well clear of his body.

It had been less than ten seconds since I'd stepped into the room. Now three
bodyguards were down in various stages of discomfort and uselessness (not to
mention two more in the hall), Bajinok was probably dying, and the remaining
Jhereg on Herth's side had declared himself out of the action.

I couldn't believe it had worked.

Neither could Herth.

He said, "What are you, anyway?"

I sheathed my rapier and drew my belt dagger. I didn't answer him because
I don't talk to my targets; it puts the relationship on entirely the wrong basis.
I heard something behind me and saw Cawti's eyes widen. I threw myself to
the side of the room, rolled, and came to a kneeling position.

A body—one that I hadn't put there—was lying on the floor. I noticed that

Cawti had a dagger out, held down to her side. Herth still hadn't moved. I checked the body to make sure it wasn't anything more than that. It wasn't. It was Quaysh. There was a short iron spike protruding from his back. Thank you, Ishtvan, wherever you are.

I stood up again and turned to the messenger. "Get out," I said. "If those two bodyguards outside start to come in here, my people outside will kill you." He might well have wondered why, if I had people outside, they hadn't killed the bodyguards. But he didn't say anything; he just left.

I took a step toward Herth and raised my dagger. At this point I didn't care who saw me, or if I was going to be turned over to the Empire. I wanted this finished.

Kelly said, "Wait."

I stopped, mostly from sheer disbelief. I said, "What?"

"Don't kill him."

"Are you nuts?" I took another step. Herth had absolutely no expression on his face.

"I mean it," said Kelly.

"I'm glad."

"Don't kill him."

I stopped and stepped back a pace. "Okay," I said. "Why?"

"He's *our* enemy. We've been fighting him for years. We don't need you to step in and settle it for us, and we don't need an Imperial, or even a Jhereg, investigation into his death."

I said, "This may be hard for you to believe, but I don't really give a teckla's squeal what you want. If I don't kill him now, I'm dead. I thought I was anyway, but things seem to have worked out so that I might live. I'm not going to—"

"I think you can arrange for him not to come after you, without killing him yourself."

I blinked. Finally I said, "All right, how?"

"I don't know," said Kelly. "But look at his situation: You've battered his organization almost out of existence. It's going to take everything he has just to put it together. He is in a position of weakness. You can manage something."

I looked at Herth. He still showed no expression. I said, "At best, that just means he's going to wait."

Kelly said, "Maybe."

I turned back to Kelly. "How do you know so much about how we operate and what kind of situation he's in?"

"It's our business to know everything that affects us and those we represent. We've been fighting him for years, one way or another. We have to know him and how he operates."

"Okay. Maybe. But you still haven't told me why I should let him live."

Kelly squinted at me. "Do you know," he said, "that you are a walking contradiction? Your background is from South Adrilankha, you are an East-

erner, yet you have been working all your life to deny this, to adopt the attitudes of the Dragaerans, to almost *be* a Dragaeran, and more, an aristocrat—"

"That's a lot of—"

"At times, you affect the speech patterns of the aristocracy. You are working
to become, not rich, but *powerful*, because that is what the aristocracy values
above all things. And yet, at the same time, you wear a mustache to assert your
Eastern origins, and you identify with Easterners so much that, I'm told, you
have never plied your trade on one, and, in fact, turned down an offer to
murder Franz."

"So, what does this—?"

"Now you have to choose. I'm not asking you to give up your profession,
despicable as it is. I'm not asking you for *anything*, in fact. I'm telling you that
it is in the interest of our people that you not murder this person. Do what
you want." He turned away.

I chewed on my lip, amazed at first that I was even thinking about it. I shook
my head. I thought about Franz, who was actually pleased to have his name
used for propaganda after he died, and Sheryl, who would probably have felt
the same, and I thought about all that Kelly had said to me over the last few
times we spoke, and about Natalia, and I remembered the talk with Paresh, so
long ago it seemed, and the look he'd given me at the end. Now I understood
it.

Most people never have the chance to choose what side they're on, but I did.
That's what Paresh was telling me, and Sheryl and Natalia. Franz had thought
I had chosen. Cawti and I had reached a point where we could choose our
sides. Cawti had chosen, and now I had to. I wondered if I could choose to
stay in the middle.

It suddenly didn't matter that I was standing in a crowd of strangers. I turned
to Cawti and said, "I should join you. I know that. But I can't. Or I won't. I
guess that's what it comes down to." She didn't say anything. Neither did
anyone else. In the awful silence of that ugly little room, I just kept talking.

"Whatever this thing is that I've become is incapable of looking beyond itself.
Yes, I'd like to do something for the greater good of humanity, if you want to
call it that. But I can't, and we're both stuck with that. I can cry and wail as
much as I want and it doesn't change what I am or what you are or anything
else."

Still, no one said anything. I turned to Kelly and said, "You will probably
never know how much I hate you. I respect you, and I respect what you're
doing, but you've diminished me in my own eyes, and in Cawti's. I can't forgive
you for that."

For just an instant then he was human. "Have I done that? We're doing what
we have to do. Every decision we make is based on what is necessary. Is it
really I who has done this to you?"

I shrugged and turned toward Herth. Might as well make it complete. "I hate
you most of all," I said. "Much more than I hate him. I mean, this goes beyond

business. I want to kill you, Herth. And I'd love to do it slow; torture you the way you tortured me. That's what I want."

He was still showing no expression, damn his eyes. I wanted to see him cringe, at least, but he wouldn't. Maybe it would have been better for him if he had. Maybe not, too. But staring at him, I almost lost it again. I was holding a stiletto, my favorite kind of weapon for a simple assassination; I longed to make him feel it, and having him just stare at me like that was too much. I just couldn't take it. I grabbed him by the throat and flung him against a wall, held the point of my blade against his left eye. I said some things to him that I don't remember but were never above the level of curses. Then I said, "They want me to let you live. Okay, bastard, you can live. For a while. But I'm watching you, all right? You send anyone after me and you've had it. Got that?"

He said, "I won't send anyone after you."

I shook my head. I didn't believe him, but I figured I'd at least bought some time. I said to Cawti, "I'm going home. Coming with me?"

She looked at me, her forehead creased and sorrow in her eyes. I turned away.

As Herth started to move toward the door, I heard the sound of steel on steel from behind me, and a heavy sword came flying into the room. Then a Jhereg came in, backing up. At his throat was a rapier, and attached to the rapier was my grandfather. Ambrus was on his shoulder. Loiosh flew into the room.

"Noish-pa!"

"Yes, Vladimir. You wished to see me?"

"Sort of," I said. I had some mad in me that hadn't washed away yet, but it was going. I decided I had to get outside of there before I exploded.

Kelly said, "Hello, Taltos," to my grandfather.

They exchanged nods.

"Wait here," I said to no one in particular. I walked out into the hall, and the bodyguard I had wounded was still moaning and holding his stomach, although he had removed the knife. There was another one next to him who was holding his right leg. I could see wounds on both legs and both arms and a shoulder. They were small wounds, but probably deep. I was pleased that my grandfather was still as good as I remembered. I walked past them carefully and out into the street. There was now a solid line of armed Easterners and an equally solid line of Phoenix Guards. There were no Jhereg bodyguards there anymore, however.

I walked through the Guards until I found their commander. "Lord Khaavren?" I said.

He looked at me and his face tightened. He nodded once.

I said, "There will be no trouble. It was a mistake. These Easterners are going to leave now. I just want to tell you that."

He stared at me for a moment, then looked away as if I were so much carrion. I turned and went into the apothecary. I found the sorceress and said, "Okay, you can lift it. And if you want to earn some more, Herth will be coming out onto the street soon, and I think he'd appreciate a teleport back home."

"Thanks," she said. "It's been a pleasure."

I nodded and walked back toward Kelly's flat. As I did so, Herth emerged with several wounded bodyguards, including one who had to be helped along. Herth didn't even look at me. I went past him, and I saw the sorceress approach and speak to him.

When I went back inside, my grandfather was nowhere to be seen and neither was Cawti. Loiosh said, *"They've gone back into Kelly's study."*

"Good."

"Why did you send me instead of reaching him psionically?"

"My grandfather doesn't approve of it, except for emergencies."

"Wasn't this an emergency?"

"Yeah. Well, I also wanted you out of the way so I could go ahead and do something stupid."

"I see. Well, did you?"

"Yeah. I even got away with it."

"Oh. Does that mean everything's all right now?"

I looked back toward the study where my grandfather was talking with Cawti. *"Probably not,"* I said. *"But it's out of my hands. I thought I'd probably be dead after this, and I wanted someone here who could take care of Cawti."*

"But what about Herth?"

"He promised to leave me alone in front of witnesses. That will keep him honest for a few weeks, anyway."

"And after that?"

"We'll just have to see."

17

1 pocket handkerchief: clean & press.

THE NEXT DAY I received word that the troops had been withdrawn from South Adrilankha. Cawti didn't show up. But I hadn't really expected her to.

To take my mind off things, I took a walk around my neighborhood. I was beginning to enjoy the feeling that I was in no more danger than I'd been before this nonsense started. It might not last, but I'd enjoy it while I could. I even walked a bit outside of my area, just because walking felt so good. I hit a couple of inns that I don't usually visit and that was fine. I was careful not to get drunk, even though it probably wouldn't have mattered.

I passed by the oracle I'd been to so long before and thought about going in, but I didn't. It did make me wonder, though, what I ought to do with all of that money. It was clear that I wasn't going to be building Cawti a castle. Even if she came back to me, I doubted she'd want one. And the idea of buying a higher title in the Jhereg seemed ludicrous. That left—

Which is when the solution hit me.

My first reaction was to laugh, but I couldn't afford to laugh at any idea just then, and besides, I'd look foolish standing in the middle of the street laughing. The more I thought about it, though, the more sense it made. From Herth's perspective, that is. I mean, as Kelly had said, the man was almost washed up; this let him get out alive and removed any need on his part to kill me.

From my end it was even easier than that. It would entail many administrative problems, of course, but I could use a few administrative problems. Hmmm. I finished the walk without incident.

Two days later I was sitting in my office, taking care of the details of getting things operating again and a few other matters. Melestav came in.

"Yeah?"

"A messenger just arrived from Herth, boss."

"Oh, yeah? What did he have to say?"

"He said, 'Yes.' He said you'd know what it was about. He's waiting for a reply."

"Well I'll be damned," I said. "Yeah. I know what it's about."

"Any instructions?"

"Yeah. Go into the treasury and pull out fifty thousand Imperials."

"Fifty *thousand*?"

"That's right."

"But—all right. Then what?"

"Give it to the messenger. Arrange for an escort. Make sure it gets to Herth."

"All right, boss. Whatever you say."

"Then come back in here; we have a lot of work to do. And send Kragar in."

"Okay."

"I'm already here."

"Huh? Oh."

"What just happened?"

"What we wanted to. We have the prostitution, which we'll have to close down or clean up, the strongarm stuff, which we'll kill, and the gambling, cleaners, and small stuff, which we can leave alone."

"You mean it worked?"

"Yeah. We just bought South Adrilankha."

I got home late that night and found Cawti asleep on the couch. I looked down at her. Her dark, dark, hair was in disarray over her thin, proud face. Her cheekbones stood out in the light of the single lamp, and her fine brows were drawn together as she slept, as if she was puzzled by something a dream was telling her.

She was still beautiful, inside and out. It hurt to look at her. I shook her gently. She opened her eyes, smiled wanly and sat up.

"Hello, Vlad."

I sat down next to her, but not too close. "Hello," I said.

She blinked sleep out of her eyes. After a moment she said, "I had a long talk with Noish-pa. I guess that was what you wanted, wasn't it?"

"I knew I couldn't talk to you. I hoped he could find the way to say things I couldn't."

She nodded.

I said, "Do you want to tell me about it?"

"I'm not sure. What I said to you, a long time ago now, about how unhappy you are and why, that's all true, I think."

"Yeah."

"And I think what I'm doing, working with Kelly, is right, and I'm going to keep doing it."

"Yeah."

"But it isn't the whole answer to every question, either. Once I decided that I'd do this, I thought it would solve everything, and I treated you unfairly. I'm sorry. The rest of life doesn't stop because of my activities. I'm working with Kelly because that's my duty, but it doesn't end there. I also have a duty toward you."

I looked down. When she didn't go on, I said, "I don't want you coming back to me because you feel it's your duty."

She sighed. "I see what you mean. No, that isn't how I meant it. The problem is that you were right, I *should* have spoken to you about it. But I couldn't bring myself to risk—to risk what we have. Do you see what I mean?"

I stared at her. Do you know, that had never occurred to me? I mean, I knew I felt frightened and insecure; but I never thought that *she* could feel that way, too. I said, "I love you."

She made a gesture with her arm and I moved over to her and put my arm around and held her. After a while I said, "Are you moving back in?"

She said, "Should I? We still have a lot to work out."

I thought about my latest purchase and chuckled. "You don't know the half of it."

She said, "Hmm?"

I said, "I've just bought South Adrilankha."

She stared. "You *bought* South Adrilankha? From Herth?"

"Yeah."

She shook her head. "Yes, I guess we do have things to talk about."

"Cawti, it saved my life. Doesn't that—?"

"Not now."

I didn't say anything. A moment later she said, "I'm committed now; to Kelly, to the Easterners, to the Teckla. I still don't know how you feel about that."

"Neither do I," I said. "I don't know if it would be easier or harder to work it out with you living here again. All I know is that I miss you, that it hurts to go to sleep without you."

She nodded. Then she said, "I'll come back then, if you want me to, and we'll try to work it out."

I said, "I want you to."

We didn't celebrate then, or anything, but we held each other, and for me that was a celebration, and the tears I shed onto her shoulder felt as clean and good as the laugh of a condemned man, unexpectedly freed.

Which, in a way, described me quite well, just then.